I0661489

The Devil's Memoirs
(Vol. 2)

OTHER TITLES TRANSLATED
BY STUART GELZER

Paul Féval - *The Hunchback*
Paul d'Ivoi - *Miss Musketeer*
Paul d'Ivoi - *Queen of Illusions*
Anonymous - *Harry Dickson vs. Mysteras*
Anonymous - *Harry Dickson vs. Krik-Krok, The Walking Dead*

The Devil's Memoirs (Volume 2)

by
Frédéric Soulié

Translated from the French by
Stuart Gelzer

A Black Coat Press Book

Translation Copyright © 2025 by Stuart Gelzer.
Introduction Copyright © 2025 by Nina Cooper & Jean-Marc Lofficier.
Cover illustration Copyright © 2025 by Aurelien Maccarelli.

ISBN 978-1-64932-347-7. First Printing. February 2025. Published by Black
Coat Press, an imprint of Hollywood Comics.com, LLC, 18321 Ventura Blvd.
Suite 915, Tarzana, CA 91356. All rights reserved. Except for review purposes,
no part of this book may be reproduced or transmitted in any form or by any
means, electronic or mechanical, including photocopying, recording, or by any
information storage and retrieval system, without permission in writing from the
publisher. The stories and characters depicted in this novel are entirely fictional.
Printed in the United States of America.

TABLE OF CONTENTS

THE DAUGHTER OF A PEER OF FRANCE

Chapter XLII: Background

Luizzi threw himself onto his bed and began to read. This is what he read:

I'm the daughter of the Marquis de Vaucloix, who like so many others was ruined by exile. In 1809 he married my mother in Munich; she too was French, and of a distinguished family. My birth cost her her life, and I was barely four when my father returned to France in 1814. Wishing to reward him for his loyalty, King Louis XVIII made him a peer of France and gave him an appointment in the royal household. The emoluments for that position weren't enough to cover my father's expenses, and when the "exiles' billion" indemnity was passed,[1] the portion that came to him did no more than settle the many debts he'd contracted since his return to France. As for me, I was brought up in a boarding school, where I was given the kind of education considered suitable for a young lady of high rank and great fortune. I drew well, I sang tastefully, I danced wonderfully, and I dressed marvelously. I had opinions on contemporary literature, I was a partisan of Italian music, I could hold a conversation with ease that passed for wit. Otherwise I was perfectly ignorant of my father's situation, and he took pleasure in indulging my taste for luxuries.

When I was eighteen, and beginning to grow bored of my girls' school, my father visited one day and surprised me by announcing that I was finally going to enter the world I'd only seen in fleeting glimpses and that I imagined to be so delightful. I won't describe my girlish joy when I found myself mistress of my own time, which I could dispose of at will, dreaming of the sweetest triumphs, planning a life of pleasure, anticipating close friendships, and occasionally allowing myself to indulge in distant thoughts of love. You can see I'm proceeding methodically, and telling you what I was like at eighteen and how defenseless I was against any kind of misfortune. It took only a few months to rob me of that self-confidence.

---

[1] As noted previously, in 1825 nobles who'd fled the Revolution were partly compensated for property they'd lost. That act of indemnity was commonly referred to as the *loi du milliard aux émigrés* (the "exiles' billion law").

My father chose one day a week to receive guests, but those who attended his salon were almost entirely men; some spent the evening playing cards, others talked politics. Half a dozen elderly women accompanied their husbands, and burdened me so with expressions of their protective interest in me that I loathed them. But what surprised me most about my father's salon wasn't the absence of young men and women my own age, it was the presence of certain individuals whose names and manners marked them as coarsely bourgeois.

The first few evenings he hosted his salon, my father made me sing to show off what he called my talent. The first time I was listened to politely. The second time, in the middle of the most virtuosic passage in my aria, I heard one of the whist players cry in a tremendous voice, "Six of clubs and four honors—we win threefold!" The third time the people around the piano barely suspended their conversations. I gave up on pleasing the company, as two or three of the less philistine among them put it, and the chore of receiving my father's guests became almost unbearable to me.

Winter finally came, and I heard less talk about parties and balls than I had even in my boarding school. I tried to make sense of my solitude; because my youth, my ideas, my hopes, cut me off completely from everyone around me. Gradually I gave way to profound boredom, without my father either noticing or wishing to notice. One evening, when the gathering at our salon was larger than usual, I'd withdrawn into a corner. Resting one elbow on the arm of a sofa, I thought back with regret to our happy evenings at the boarding school and the girlish confessions we'd shared about our dreams for the future. And yet I wasn't one of those girls with romantic illusions about life. I didn't count on obsessed lovers and towering wealth. A heart that loved me, a temperament in sync with mine, affluence matching my own: those were my wishes. They weren't particularly extravagant—unless in this world hoping for a tranquil, respectable, happy life is the worst of extravagances. In any case, I'd already reached the point of lamenting my shattered illusions; and I was only nineteen, I was beautiful, and I knew I had in my mind and my heart all a woman needs to love and be loved.

No doubt my thoughts had carried me far away, because suddenly I heard a voice behind me saying, "A heart that sighs hasn't found its prize."

That commonplace saw wouldn't have seemed so ill-mannered to me if it hadn't been made vulgar by the person who said it. He was an ugly man with a beaming face, wearing a tiny cravat and an enormous shirt collar; his monstrously fat body was barely contained in vast brightly colored patterned waistcoats, and he always wore a light brown coat over very short black trousers, with white cotton stockings and laced shoes. The presence of that man in the Marquis de Vaucloix's salon had always been a surprise to me; and though he'd never talked to me more than anyone else had, I disliked him the most of all of them. His blunt experience of men and things made him assume motives of self-interest in almost any story he heard, and he exposed those motives with a cynical contempt for humanity that wounded all of my youthful ideals.

If anyone besides him had noticed my sadness, I probably would've made some excuse and attributed it to not feeling well; but I was shocked such a coarse onlooker had understood my thoughts, and I replied curtly, "I want for nothing, sir, and there's nothing I want."

"Hmm! Hmm!" said the fat man, sitting down unceremoniously next to me and blowing his nose loudly into a blue cotton handkerchief. "Any girl who isn't married wants something."

"Well! And who told you I wanted to be married, sir?"

He stared at me and laughed in my face with uncommon impudence. "I don't need to be told; it's obvious."

"How clever you are!" I said scornfully, for the man annoyed me.

"Cleverer than you think," he replied, undeterred by my having turned my back to him. "Because I've done you the favor of finding you what you're looking for: a husband."

"A husband!" I cried, turning around.

"Oh, ho, ho!" he chuckled with a wink. "That word made you prick up your ears!"

"Sir," I replied, stung by the way he'd interpreted my surprise, "allow me to put an end to a conversation my father wouldn't approve of."

"I beg your pardon—a thousand times. But it's exactly because I have your father's permission that I dare speak to you as I have."

In my astonishment I looked around for my father, and saw him watching me from a corner of the parlor. A slight nod of his head informed me that he wished me to listen to Monsieur Carin. Now that I've written down his name, it must be clear who it was who was talking to me.

He went on, "As you can see, I'm not so unbecoming as my big shoes make me look. And since the word husband has been uttered, it's pointless for me to tread water any longer. I'm talking about my son."

"Your son!" I cried in astonishment, eyeing him from head to toe as if to deduce what the son of such a creature could be like.

The man didn't miss a single thought of mine, and he replied in a bitter, joking tone, "Don't be afraid. My son dresses well; he's a pompous show-off who cleans his nails with Windsor soap and puts old-fashioned oil in his hair. He's a very proper fellow; he purses his lips when he talks, and he uses a pince-nez. He's a baron. I bought him a baronetcy, and I'll buy him a marquisate if you'd like to be a marquise."

I lacked the power to reply to that uncouth proposition, but I was so humiliated I turned away to hide my tears.

Monsieur Carin noticed; rising abruptly, he said, "Listen, miss. Now you've been informed. Think it over all night. Tomorrow I'll present the young man, and you can decide tomorrow night. The business has to be settled; I have no time to lose."

He walked away, leaving me stunned by his manner of proceeding and by a marriage proposal as alarming as a warning of doom. I tried to approach my father, but he avoided me so carefully that he made it clear he wanted no explanations. Contrary to my usual practice, I stayed in the parlor till no one was left but a few tireless card players; I hoped to force my father to hear me out.

But just before he sat down at a card table he said to me in passing, "Be ready first thing tomorrow. You'll have the honor of being presented to the royal family."

That second piece of news astonished me as much as the first, but also reassured me. I naturally connected the thought of my presentation to that of my marriage, and somehow in my heart I felt confident I wouldn't be sacrificed in any marriage made under such honorable auspices. Monsieur Carin had told me to spend all night thinking over his proposition. He'd been right: I didn't sleep at all, and did nothing but weep—so distant was what was happening to me from the ideas I'd had about marriage. A word girls never speak aloud, but that they whisper constantly in their hearts, the word "love," had as yet no meaning for me. But, Édouard, if you only knew how often my young friends and I ended an account of our plans by saying, "Oh, I'll never marry anyone except the man I love," you'd understand my fears when I found myself threatened with being given to a man I didn't know, you'd understand the sorrow that remains when youthful hopes vanish.

I'd never imagined I'd be driven to wish for something contrary to my father's wishes; and when I probed my own feelings about that I sensed an unconquerable weakness. I'd certainly heard of girls who put up a vigorous resistance to their family's plans; but to me that was like an entertaining romantic story with no connection to my life. Sometimes, late at night, just between us with our ignorant young hearts, a story had slipped in about some girl who'd preferred death to a repugnant marriage, and we'd sighed heavily over her misfortune and wept with admiration at such great courage; but when that thought occurred to me about myself I felt incapable of carrying it out, either because I rejected it or because it frightened me.

I was like a poor wretch who hears about some great lord's feast, and who turns away to eat his bread soaked in tears, without feeling either hope or envy, so distant is he from such good fortune. My heart lacked courage, and to hope to die was a fate too far above me. I therefore saw nothing that could rescue me from the misery that loomed—though I'd even thought of throwing myself at the feet of the king and putting myself under his protection; but that was nonsense, because I wouldn't even have known how to tell him what misfortune had made me unhappy. Besides, to speak to the king, to throw myself at his feet, would've been a violent act of will; and how would I have found the strength for that, if I didn't even have enough to stand up to my father, whose authority over me had always been benevolent?

I'm telling you all this, Édouard, to show you I'm a very weak woman, who can do nothing for others or for herself.

The next day came. My father sent me word to be ready for the hour of Mass. I sent back asking to see him immediately; I was told we'd have time to talk on our way to the Tuileries Palace. So I went down to the parlor, where I overheard Monsieur Carin's voice coming from my father's study. I was about to withdraw, when he opened the door and said peremptorily, "Make the king see reason. As for me, I have only one thing to say to you, as the Spanish put it: *Si no, no.*"[2]

I turned away so as not to look at that man, who seemed to be disposing of me even more freely than my father.

He paused, then went on, "And after the king, make the young lady see reason. Because I don't intend to give away my money for a girl who looks like she's being led to the scaffold. Thanks all the same!"

He left, and I looked up at my father: he was blushing with shame. I could tell it wasn't from indignation or anger, because he avoided my eyes. "Come, come," he said. "It's time."

He went out ahead of me. I followed, reflecting that another girl would've dared not to follow him, and would've forced an explanation. When I reached the courtyard he was already in the carriage and was angrily crumpling some papers he'd been handed. He was so irritated I thought I wouldn't need to speak to him; he barely looked at me, instead reading those papers angrily and muttering, "This has to stop. Enough, enough…"

When he'd calmed down a little he folded the papers and put them in his pocket, then drew out other papers that he read carefully and with a certain complacency. "He can't refuse me," he repeated in a low voice after every line. "That would be too ungrateful. And yet they're such ingrates!"

My father's sorrow had almost made me forget my own pain, and I said softly, "You've had bad news, haven't you?"

"How do you know?"

"I sensed it."

"No, Louise," he said, pulling himself together. "On the contrary, I'm on the verge of getting everything I've wished for: a splendid settlement for you, with a distinguished man, one who's destined for a political fortune as great as his financial fortune."

"Are you referring to Monsieur Carin's son?"

"Yes. A man who's risen far above his birth, a man of great ideas and great vision, a man whose position and future I'm proud to be able to guarantee."

---

[2] "If it's no, then it's no."

I didn't fully understand him, but it seemed to me he had some difficulty uttering those praises. I gathered my resolve in both hands, meaning to strike a firm blow, and in a shaking voice I spoke the words that felt to me like the very limit of audacity. "I haven't yet seen this…"

"Oh, you'll see him!" said my father with mocking cruelty. "You won't be led to the altar like a sacrificial victim. The time has passed for those barbaric marriages in which noble families sacrificed the happiness of their children. Don't be afraid of all that nonsense, which was used so skillfully by the Philosophes and the Jacobins, and which was embraced so idiotically by the liberal bourgeoisie."

His tone of voice was more than enough to keep me from making any further comment. Soon we reached the palace. Only then did my father look at me. Noticing my pallor and my sadness, he said abruptly, "What's the matter? What's wrong with you? What do you expect people to think when they see you looking like that? They'll think you're being sacrificed… that I'm…"

He stopped before speaking the next word; but, as ignorant as I was, I could guess it. The awful thing Monsieur Carin had said—"I don't intend to give away my money for a girl who looks like she's being led to the scaffold"—came back to me. I realized people would say my father was selling me. I burst into tears.

My father stamped his foot angrily, then composed himself and said, "Come now, Louise, be reasonable. Nothing's settled. If you don't like the young man we'll look elsewhere. But stay calm in front of all these people who'll be watching us. I have enough enemies at court who'd like nothing better than an excuse to badmouth me."

As he spoke, he dried my eyes with his handkerchief. I stopped crying.

"That's better, Louise. You're a good girl. Keep up your hopes: soon we'll be happy."

We got out of the carriage, and he led me toward the chapel.

I've recorded that scene in its smallest details, Édouard, to make you understand how, in the midst of my carefree life, I was suddenly seized by the fear of some threatened calamity I couldn't define, how I felt like I was walking down a road full of pitfalls, though I couldn't see them clearly all around me, how I dreaded the place I was being led to, without knowing where it was or what it was. That was what my whole life consisted of then: fear without material foundation but that I couldn't dismiss as folly; sorrow that had no corporeal presence but that always stayed near me, like the shadow of my life; fear of some invisible phantom; pain without any visible wound! But all these ruminations will tell you less of what I've suffered than will the tale that still remains unfinished.

We reached the chapel. The king hadn't yet arrived. I could tell people were watching me curiously; but the sanctity of the place limited that kind of attention to a few furtive glances that quickly returned to the open pages of the missal. The few words that were murmured could've been those of a prayer. I sat in the spot reserved for me, and soon the king appeared. I'd been brought up with religious behavior rather than with sincere thoughts about religion. I carried out my Christian duty with respect rather than with zeal. Never before that day had I turned to God to ask him from the bottom of my heart for mercy and aid: I'd never yet felt the need for his aid and his mercy. But that day my terror gave meaning to the mute prayers I addressed to the Eternal. Unlike most of the women around me—unlike what I myself would've done in other circumstances—I didn't follow the divine liturgy like some solemn spectacle toward which reverence is a duty; no, I prayed fervently, desperately, and I barely noticed that the last words of the service had been spoken.

My father had told me to come join him as soon as Mass was over. I left the chapel, and he drew me quickly into a long gallery. Then he stopped, saying, "The king will pass by. Make sure you answer him properly if he speaks to you."

Charles X soon appeared, followed by the Dauphin and the Dauphine.[3] With benevolent grace, the king accepted several petitions that were handed to him. He spoke with satisfaction to the people who accompanied him—but when he caught sight of my father a slight shadow of displeasure crossed his face. "Is that you, Vaucloix?"

My father bowed and took my hand to present me. The king, who hadn't seen him do that, moved on, saying, "Follow me."

My father obeyed, and I stood there in confusion, not knowing what to do, thinking the king had avoided seeing me. I looked all around, almost distraught. My eyes met those of the Dauphine; she approached me, and said with a gesture of great kindness, "Go with your father, miss."

I curtsied and obeyed, without the presence of mind to say a word to her. The king walked fairly quickly; I had trouble threading my way past the people in his entourage, and we'd crossed several rooms without my managing to get close to him, when he entered another parlor, into which only my father followed him. I caught up just then; expecting to be left there alone, I couldn't help calling out, "Father!"

The king turned and looked at me with a severity that gradually gave way to an expression of interest. "Are you Mademoiselle de Vaucloix?"

"Yes, Your Majesty."

"Well then, come with us."

I entered the room with my father, who seemed put out by my presence. The door to Charles X's study closed behind us. I stayed by the entrance, while my father followed the king to the far corner of the room. My father was speaking quietly, and I couldn't hear what he said, but he seemed to be asking urgently for a favor the king didn't want to grant. The conversation grew heated, and

---

[3] The heir to the throne, and his wife.

they forgot I was there, because I heard the king reply with some intensity, "Yes, yes, I know it's the expression you all use: as ungrateful as a Bourbon."

My father seemed to be apologizing, but Charles X went on energetically, "And that's the expression you use to make us do the very things that are held so bitterly against us."

My father replied, and I thought I heard him refer to services rendered.

"I haven't forgotten," said the king.

"And yet, Your Majesty, you still refuse me what you've granted to several other men: to Count C—, to the Marquis de B—. They didn't lose their fortunes in exile; on the contrary, they made their fortunes serving the Republic and the Empire!"

The king turned away angrily; then finally he answered, "Who is this man anyway?"

He listened carefully to my father's reply. Presumably wishing to round out his case with some powerful argument, my father drew the papers out of his pocket and handed them to the king. But no sooner did Charles X have them in his hands than my father cried, "I beg your pardon, Your Majesty! I made a mistake. Those aren't the right ones."

The king held onto the papers and looked at my father with a severity that made him lower his eyes. "Never mind, marquis, never mind. These papers will enlighten me more than anything you could tell me."

Then he began to look over the papers. From a distance I could tell, by the page size and the red ribbon with which they were bound, they were the papers that had made my father so angry. The king's face grew darker and darker the more he read, and finally he cried, "This is a frightful mess! So much money!"

My father gestured, and the king glanced over at me. I understood the gesture as a reminder not to say anything in front of the daughter that might compromise the father. For just a moment they looked at me, and I knew I'd become the subject of their discussion, because their gestures and their glances kept turning unconsciously toward me. That new conversation, held in low voices, came to an end, and I heard the king say severely, "If I do it, sir, it'll be for her sake, so she doesn't die in poverty. It'll be for the sake of the dignity of the name you bear."

Though the king had spoken quietly, I'd overheard those words; and now he came quickly toward me. My fathered followed him, looking shaken. He gave me a glance of despair and clasped his hands as if in supplication—a gesture that caused me great pain.

"Your father wishes to marry you off, miss?" the king asked me abruptly.

"Yes, Your Majesty."

"And are you happy with the marriage?"

I glanced at my father, who motioned to me.

"Let her speak, sir," said the king, who'd seen the gesture. Then he repeated, "Do you happily agree to this marriage?"

14

"Yes, Your Majesty, happily," I replied with such enthusiasm that the king was surprised.

He studied me sadly and with a look of great pity. Then he said softly, "Very well, miss. I have no right to oppose such honorable devotion. Very well!"

He pulled on a bell rope.

"Not now, Your Majesty," said my father.

"No, no, I don't want to hear any more about it."

A page appeared, and Charles X sent for a secretary, who soon arrived, carrying a briefcase. The king, who'd been pacing around his study, said immediately, "The order concerning the Marquis de Vaucloix's son-in-law!"

The secretary handed it to him. The king signed it and gave it to my father, saying, "There it is, sir." Then he turned to me and said with a bow, "Be happy, miss."

We withdrew, and quickly crossed all the anterooms. We went downstairs, and our carriage was brought forward to meet us.

"Home!" said my father. "And make it snappy."

As soon as we set off, the agitation that seemed to possess him burst out with a violence that astonished me. "We have it!" he cried. "We have it!... It wasn't easy... Without you, I'd have failed... But you were wonderful... And even those papers I gave the king by mistake... I couldn't have done better if I'd tried... That's the first time a bailiff's orders have ever been good for something!... But there are some lucky days on which everything helps... Ah, poor Louise, you'll be happy too: it's a colossal fortune, and you'll teach them how to make decent use of it... It was a master stroke... I had to pull it off today—because otherwise, tomorrow... But I have it! And here it is, here it is!..." With great self-satisfaction he looked over the order the king had given him.

As for me, I was as concerned about my father's elation as I'd been about his despair. Can you understand the uncertainty and anxiety that filled me, after the scene I'd just witnessed? It seemed as if I'd performed a great sacrifice—but I didn't know what that sacrifice was. The king and my father seemed to pity me, but I didn't know why. I was hesitant to question my father, because I was afraid it was too late now. I watched him sadly in his transports of joy, hoping for and dreading the explanation that couldn't be long in coming.

Chapter XLIII: The First Interview; the Meeting with the Creditors

We arrived at our mansion. As we got out of the carriage, the concierge said to my father, "Monsieur Carin is in the parlor..."

"Very good, very good!" interrupted my father. "Come, my girl. We'll go tell him the good news."

He led me along, and we entered the parlor.

"Here it is! Here it is!" cried my father, holding up the king's order.

"Signed?" asked Monsieur Carin as he hurried toward my father.

"Signed! Come with me so I can tell you about it."

The two of them went out together, leaving me alone in the parlor with a young man whom my father had presumably not noticed standing in a window alcove when we came in. He'd bowed silently to me, and I'd barely had time to return his bow before my father and Monsieur Carin left. I felt embarrassed at first, because as I'd walked past the young man I'd noticed his gaze—or rather his pince-nez—aimed at me. I found him so impertinent that I stopped lowering my eyes and looked straight at him. I have to tell you the truth, Édouard: he was uncommonly handsome.

Seeing I was angry, he lowered his pince-nez with such remarkable grace that he resembled a vanquished knight surrendering his sword. I was about to withdraw, when he stepped forward and said without the least awkwardness, "Will Mademoiselle de Vaucloix permit me to introduce myself?"

I didn't know what to say; I knew I was blushing, and I could do no more than bow slightly. I was all the more vexed by my embarrassment because I could tell it had been noticed, and by a man with a natural interest in it—because I'd heard the whole of the announcement my father had interrupted before the concierge was done: "Monsieur Carin is in the parlor with the baron, his son." So the man before me was my future husband.

Remember all the emotions I'd just been put through, the mystery that surrounded me, the pity I'd inspired, the strangeness of everything that was happening—and to top all of that strangeness, that sudden interview, with no go-between, no preparation. It would've been enough to upset a bolder girl than I was.

And I have to tell you everything, Édouard. The image of the husband I was destined to marry had featured prominently in my nighttime fears: not knowing him, I'd based his appearance on his father's description of him, and Monsieur Carin's boast of "Windsor soap and old-fashioned hair oil" had terrified me. So imagine my surprise when, instead of the caricature I'd expected, I found a man of polished elegance and—I'll say it again—perfect beauty. The sight of him filled me with a quite novel surprise: he outdid by far all the handsome lovers women dream of when they've never yet been in love. And that was happening at the very moment I thought I was being handed over to a monster! Allow me to use that word, because I was experiencing a little of the joyful astonishment of the maiden given to the River Scamander to be devoured, who finds instead a handsome young man kneeling before her.[4]

Nevertheless I said nothing, and my future husband must've been as embarrassed as I was, for he too said nothing. I allowed myself to glance at him, to be reassured by his own discomfiture. He stood motionless before me, looking at me with a smile whose meaning I don't dare explain to you, now that I think I understand it: then it frightened me without my realizing it, to the point that my distress and the shame it caused me brought me almost to tears. His self-assurance bothered me, and I resented him for not making use of it to come to my rescue. At that moment I'd have given a great deal to have, I won't say the presence of mind, but the boldness of some women. I was ashamed at being so completely overwhelmed.

I wanted to get out of that foolish position at any price, and I got out of it clumsily. "Did you wish to speak to my father, sir?" I asked as coldly as I could.

"No, miss, the truth is you're the one I wish to speak to."

"I'm not sure I ought to…"

"Given the way my father and yours are managing things, there's a risk it may be quite a while before they remember it's necessary for us to be introduced. So let's act as if they hadn't forgotten, since after all it has to happen sooner or later; and allow me to have a conversation with you that I've been yearning for."

All of that was delivered in a firm, clear tone that showed how free the speaker was in his thoughts and words. I felt like a little girl before that man, and if I hadn't seen he was young I would've thought I was listening to a solemn old rhetorician entering a debate he counts on winning.

He offered me his hand and led me to a seat, and sat down near me. "They want to marry us," he said with a simper. "But that'll require permission from on high. Do you think they'll get it?"

"You saw my father's delight, sir. As far as I can tell, the king has given his permission to…"

"I beg your pardon, miss. The king may permit what you might wish to forbid."

I blushed and looked away.

"The king may say yes," he went on, "where you might say no… What do you say?"

---

[4] In Greek mythology, Trojan maidens went to the nearby River Scamander (who was also a malformed river god) to bathe and to pray, "Scamander, take my virginity!"

Such a direct question wounded me more than it embarrassed me. The man was so sure of what he was saying, compared to me in my ever-growing confusion! I fell back on one those ready-made expressions you learn from mediocre books, and replied with a stammer, "I'll obey my father, sir..."

Monsieur de Carin gracefully drew back from me, and I barely had to look at him to know he was considering me in a most impertinent manner. He was silent for a moment, then he took my hand and kissed it in a very marked way, saying with slight mockery, "No one could be more beautiful, or more... good."

His tone of voice, and the way he said the word "good," felt like an insult to me. A flash of anger went through me—only a flash, in truth, because it didn't last long enough either to inspire me with an equally insulting comeback or to give me the strength to withdraw.

Our two fathers returned.

"He, he!" said Monsieur Carin. "The introductions are all taken care of! Well, Guillaume, I told you I'd give you a beautiful wife... One who's a little awkward, a little shy..."

"Are you trying to say a little stupid, sir?" I replied, stung by Monsieur Carin's tone.

"The lady's right," chuckled Monsieur Guillaume.

I looked at my father. He was blushing with embarrassment; but I was still stunned that he'd let pass without protest the insult that had been directed at me. And I felt an inexpressible pity—for him and for me—when I saw him trying to soften what Monsieur Guillaume had said by adding, "Indeed, Monsieur Carin, my daughter's right; you seem to be paying her a backhanded compliment."

"All right, all right," said Monsieur Carin. "The young fellow will teach her how girls get smart."

Even before I had time to be amazed at that second boorishness, he went on, "Come now, there's no time to waste! Guillaume, you go to the church and City Hall and the notary. You, marquis, you go to your... you know what... and offer them twenty-five percent if they'll give you forty, and that'll make them happy. I've kept the most recalcitrant ones for myself, and I promise I'll bring them around. General gathering here tonight! Everything has to be finished today. You understand we can't publish the banns till the contract is signed: if there were any doubt about the business, we wouldn't get a discount of a single sou, and that's not our game. Guillaume, make sure it isn't published till three days from now."

"I understand, father," said Guillaume impatiently. "Do you take me for a fool?"

"Monsieur Guillaume is right," I added immediately, carried away by wanting to pay my future father-in-law back, and not noticing the expression I was repeating didn't apply directly to what he'd just said.

Guillaume made a slight face, which showed me I'd only reinforced the low opinion he had of me. I stamped my foot angrily.

My father, though he must've guessed what I was going through, was annoyed by that sign of impatience. "Come now, Louise," he scolded. "Don't be childish. Think carefully, and try to obey me."

"The lady has given me reason to expect that happiness," said Guillaume; then he bowed and withdrew, along with his father and mine.

I was left alone: such was my first meeting with my future husband. By placing me unexpectedly face to face with him, and provoking in me an awkwardness perfectly natural in a girl, chance had made Guillaume see me in a light he thought was accurate, and that he didn't try to correct. You'll see later that he was one of those men for whom first impressions are all-important, due to the faith they have in the infallibility of their own judgment. You who know me, Édouard, you know whether or not I'm vain! And yet you should understand the humiliation of a girl who isn't young enough to be treated like a child, who knows she's been dismissed as a fool—enough of a fool that she can be called one to her face without her even suspecting it.

Listen to me carefully, Édouard, and don't get annoyed at all these details from my life. They're necessary to make you see that misery doesn't always arise from what can be called a misfortune. Yes, I was miserable that day, without my being able to tell anyone that anything unfortunate had happened to me. I had to settle for weeping while I steeled myself with absolute resolve to resist my father. That resolve added to my anguish, because I feared I'd retreat at the first order or word from my father, and that I'd accomplish nothing besides forging weapons to be used against me. And yet I was so ashamed at the thought of surrendering weakly that I had no choice but to make the effort to resist, however futile I knew it to be. It was a duty I had to myself.

Filled with that anxiety, I waited all day for my father, but I waited in vain. Before he came home, a dozen or so people of fairly low appearance had arrived at our residence and had occupied the parlor. From time to time the servants came to tell me all those people were calling for my father with astonishing insolence, making outrageous comments about him, saying he was cheating them, threatening to leave and to teach him to make appointments he skipped, the way he always skipped his appointments. Given what I've told you about my father's habits and what I'd overheard being said around me, you can guess it was a gathering of his creditors. But you can also guess how completely ignorant I was about what was going on. The only thing that stood out for me in all I'd heard and all that was being reported to me was the contempt being shown toward my father.

Meanwhile the uproar in the parlor had grown so loud, according to the servants, that I couldn't believe them, and I went to find out for myself, determined to make an appearance, if necessary, to put an end to it. Just as I paused at a glass door to peek around a curtain and see what kind of men they were and listen to their remarks, I saw my father enter, and heard a general cry, followed by sarcastic cheers: "Ah, there you are!... How kind of you!... So, what do you want with us?... Are you going to make more promises?... If that's all you've got, no thanks—they're worth nothing anymore..." and a thousand other things shouted from all sides of the parlor by voices that seemed to be trying to outdo each other in their insolence.

"It's not a question of promises," replied my father in a tone and with a manner that seemed awfully obsequious to me. "It's a question of money—hard cash."

"To be paid in three months?" said someone.

"To be paid tomorrow, or tonight, if you like."

"Then it's simple," said another. "Pay up, and we'll treat you well. You owe me ten thousand nine hundred and twenty-three francs, and the receipt will be ready as soon as the cash is."

There was a moment of silence. Then my father went on, "You can assume, gentlemen, that I only found enough money to satisfy you by imposing terrible sacrifices on myself. So I should tell you, those sacrifices will have been pointless if you don't help me, if you don't grant me a discount on what I owe you."

It was as if twenty voices all cried as one, "Not one sou!"

And one of them added, "You owe me or you don't owe me; I want all or nothing."

Another said, "For twelve thousand francs I've certainly bought the right to say a marquis, a peer of France, swindled me."

And yet another said, "Come on, come on, it's always the same story. There's not a single sou at the end of it."

My father drew a billfold from his pocket, set it on the table, opened it, and showed them a great number of banknotes. I have no words for the revolting impulse that made all those men hurry to the table; my father disappeared from view in a circle of vultures, as the last to arrive stood on tiptoe to see what he was offering them. Two of them moved away from the circle, motioning to each other, and came quickly toward the door behind which I was hidden.

"Where the devil did he get all that money?" asked one of them, and I recognized him as the decorator who'd furnished our mansion.

"Considering he has nothing left to sell."

"Not even his vote in the Chamber of Deputies."

"Unless it's his daughter."

"He's certainly capable of that!"

"Maybe the king paid his debts again; Charles X is fond of the marquis."

"Say, that's an idea! How much money is he showing off over there?"

"Maybe twelve, maybe fifteen bundles of ten thousand francs."

"So, roughly fifty thousand écus. That's not even a quarter of what he owes."

"If he's offering a quarter, that means he can pay half; and if he can pay half, that means he's got all of it in hand. I'm not signing anything."

"Certainly not!"

"No, let's let the others fall for it. You know he'll pay the holdouts in full."

"He's about to make his offer—let's listen."

Indeed my father was speaking again, as if in answer to a question. "What am I offering, gentlemen? I'm offering twenty-five percent."

The two men who'd been talking nudged each other.

"Twenty-five percent!" cried a fat man. "I provided all four wheels for your berline—and you've let them spatter me with too much mud for me to be satisfied with being paid for just one of them! I'll give you a five percent discount, which is my entire profit from the sale. I'll consent to having done the work for nothing, but I'm not going to take a loss of even one percent beyond that."

With that, the carriage-maker came and sat down next to the decorator, saying, "What do you think of all this?"

"I'll accept the twenty-five percent. I'd rather have that than nothing, assuming we can get it. We'll be paid ten, and promised the rest in three years."

"You think?" asked the carriage-maker.

"Well, the Marquis de Vaucloix owes one million two hundred thousand francs. Because he showed you seventy or eighty thousand francs, you think you've seen Peru.[5] As for me, he owes me more than fifty thousand francs; if he were willing to give me ten thousand in cash, I'd take it on the spot."

"Damn! Damn!" said the carriage-maker. "That's what you're thinking?"

"Certainly. It's one more postponement. If he didn't have the immunity of the peerage, he'd long since have been rotting away in Sainte Pélagie. But since he has it, he can thumb his nose at us. So, whatever he's offering, I'll take it."

"Listen, he's saying something again."

My father had in fact begun speaking; and since the men near me fell silent to listen, I was able to hear him. "I've asked you all here so you can all be clear about what I'm going to do. I'm offering twenty-five percent—but I'm telling you that if there's even one holdout, I'm paying nothing."

A collective shout went up.

"Nothing," repeated my father. "I'm not going to make such a huge sacrifice if it doesn't buy me some peace, if I'm still going to be pursued by a thousand whiners. So take a look and decide. I'll give you half an hour to think it over."

"It's robbery!" came the cry from all sides. "You can't treat honest men with that kind of impudence!"

"Ha, ha!" replied my father. "You gentlemen in trade treat your creditors differently when you go bankrupt: you give them ten percent and consider them lucky to get it."

---

[5] "Peru" was a byword for the fabulously rich silver mines of the Spanish colony of Peru.

At those words a thousand cries and insults, each angrier than the next, rang out all over the parlor. My father seemed to want to escape, and he moved toward the door where I was. The decorator stopped him, and while the others were all arguing loudly he said to him in a low voice, "Offer forty percent, and I'll arrange it for you."

"I'm offering twenty-five."

"In that case you'll get nothing."

"And neither will they."

"Your furniture is valuable. I could sell it."

"Since you're the one who sold it to me, you think it's worth a hundred and fifty thousand francs?"

The decorator gestured impatiently and went on, "That's not the point. Come on, make an effort, go to thirty-five."

My father hesitated, and finally said in a low voice, "Thirty."

"No, thirty-five."

"Thirty, and that'll leave me without a single sou."

"Word of honor?"

"Sir!"

"Fine, thirty, it's a deal, and let me handle it."

My father slipped out the door, and caught sight of me. "What are you doing here?" he asked in annoyance.

I lowered my eyes.

"Did you hear me?" he asked.

Silence was still my only response. But then he seemed to forget about me; he returned to the door and began listening to the conversations going on in the parlor. I'd expected him to be angry with me, I even wanted him to be. I needed him to recover a little dignity, even if only toward me. But he said nothing, and began to watch through the door just as I had. He muttered quietly, "Ah, good!... They're signing!... Very good! Very good!"

The wait lasted a long time, but my father never left the door even for a moment, sometimes smiling, sometimes anxious. Finally the noise abated a little, and suddenly my father stepped back as if to make room for someone who was coming out. The decorator appeared.

"Well?" asked my father.

"Everybody signed."

"At twenty-five percent?"

"No, at thirty, as you agreed. Here's the contract you drew up. The only thing left is for you to hand me the money. You promised them cash tonight, so you can't keep them waiting. It was quite a struggle, and I hope you won't forget me. But, hell, when you've been a plain-dealing man all your life, it pays off. You couldn't have done it yourself."

What terrible things I was hearing! But my father wasn't listening: he was going through the receipts and checking them against his debts. "And here's yours," he said to the decorator.

"Mine? It seems to me I've done enough for you, marquis, and I don't deserve to take a loss like the rest of them."

"I can't do anything more for you."

"Well, then!" said the decorator, taking all the receipts back again. "No deal."

"Wait. I'll give you thirty-five percent."

"You know, I'm a fair man. And I make enough at what I do. Give me sixty and we're done."

"No, thirty-five."

The decorator turned to the door, receipts in hand. "Fifty, and not another word."

My father hesitated, and the decorator opened the door.

"Forty," said my father.

"Fifty," said the decorator.

"All right, fifty," replied my father.

The decorator closed the door again. "That's a loss of twenty-five thousand francs," he said with a sigh. "All right, let's tally it up. Six hundred and twenty-five thousand francs of debt paid at thirty percent comes to a hundred and eighty-six thousand francs. Plus twenty percent on top of that for my share, which is fifty-two thousand francs, comes to ten thousand four hundred francs, for a grand total of one hundred and ninety-six thousand four hundred francs."

My father checked his math and said, "Here's a hundred and ninety-seven thousand francs. You owe me six hundred francs."

"That'll cover my fee," said the decorator.

"Absolutely not!"

"Come on, don't be petty. If I'd let you handle it you'd have gotten nothing."

"Oh, fine. And now get rid of all those vampires."

"Give me time to settle each one's account, and you'll never see them again. But don't go back in there—you'd find yourself greeted with some fairly peculiar compliments!"

The decorator went back into the parlor, carrying the sheaf of papers, and settled himself at the table, where everyone surrounded him.

"Did you get it?" they asked.

"I got it."

There was a general cheer. Someone added, "If we hadn't been in such a hurry, we could've gotten thirty or forty percent."

But just then my father motioned for me to follow him.

You must find it surprising that I'm telling you all this in such minute detail, Édouard. It's not that I understood in the least at the time; but later I grew used to hearing talk of business, and I could finally make sense of that jargon. The best comparison would be to someone who hears words spoken in a foreign language; those words remain in his memory; and later, when he learns that language, he understands what was said to him earlier. Besides, I soon heard those particulars repeated, and they became the subject of conversation in my presence often enough for me to retain them fully now.

Meanwhile I'd followed my father into my own small parlor, and the first thing he said was, "I'm delighted you overheard everything. That'll make clearer to you than I could why you have to marry Baron de Carin. It's only thanks to that marriage I was able to clear all my debts, as you've just seen."

I've already told you how weak I was. I've also told you I was determined nevertheless to speak my mind to my father. But as soon as I found an excuse to abandon my resistance, I seized on it happily. I realized that the sacrifice being made of me, and that I hadn't been willing to accept blindly, could be interpreted honorably. I told myself I was saving my father; and, all too happy not to have to stand up to his will, I gave way out of weakness, calling my cowardice an act of courage. I'm being frank, Édouard, I'm telling you the truth about myself: my first reaction was to feel happy for having a reason to give in.

"Father," I replied, "your wish is my command, and I'm proud to think that by obeying you I can repay you even part of all you've done for me."

"Well said, Louise!" said my father, moved just a little. "Your intended is coming here. Be more gracious to him: he's a distinguished man."

"What he's doing for you, father, already guarantees him my gratitude."

My father's only response was a bitter sigh.

Soon after that, Monsieur Carin came in, followed by his son. From the doorway Monsieur Carin cried, "All hail to you, my dear sir! I couldn't have done it better myself! They accepted twenty-five percent."

"You mean thirty," said my father.

"Twenty-five. I ran into the carriage-maker, and he told me it was twenty-five. He showed me what he'd just been paid."

"I'm telling you, I gave them thirty. Here's how it happened—my daughter witnessed it all…" And then my father told them the whole story involving the decorator.

"Well!" said Monsieur Carin. "The good man pocketed five percent on the whole business, which is to say thirty-one thousand francs, plus twenty-six thousand francs on his own debt, at fifty percent, which comes to fifty-seven thousand francs. That settles quite nicely his bill of fifty-two thousand francs!"

"That crook!" cried my father.

"Isn't there a way to make him cough it back up?" asked Guillaume.

"I'll think it over," answered Monsieur Carin. "But we'll see about all that in good time."

24

In fact, I found out later the decorator had only been acting as agent for Monsieur Carin himself, who thereby recovered part of the loan he'd made to my father.

Monsieur Carin added, "I went to the justice ministry to settle about the king's order, but nothing can be done till after the wedding. So, Guillaume, you won't really be the heir to the Marquis de Vaucloix's peerage for another two weeks."

Those words came as a flash of light to me: they explained the meaning of the scene that had taken place at the palace. And at that moment I understood that in all that had happened I'd counted for nothing. They'd bought my father's peerage, and no doubt they were just taking me as one of the costs of the deal. The realization came to me so suddenly and so completely that I couldn't help giving a cry of surprise.

"Didn't she know about it?" asked Monsieur Carin.

"I was about to explain everything just as you arrived," replied my father angrily.

"Hell!" said Monsieur Carin with alarm, and he turned to me. "You consent, don't you? Because I trusted to that when I released my money."

My father gestured impatiently.

"No new tricks, I hope, marquis!" said Monsieur Carin, growing animated. "This time it would be a scam: I have neither a letter of credit nor a receipt for the two hundred and fifty thousand francs I gave you as the payoff. We need to talk this over."

How can I tell you, Édouard? My father, whose humiliation had already given me so much pain, suddenly revealed himself in an even sadder light. Taking advantage of the lack of a written contract, which Monsieur Carin was objecting to, he replied haughtily, "Well, sir, if my daughter doesn't consent, I can't exactly drag her to the altar by force."

"What's that supposed to mean?" asked Monsieur Carin, who'd gone pale with fury.

"It means," answered Guillaume coldly and curtly, "the marquis has swindled us!"

"Sir!" cried my father, advancing threateningly.

I threw myself between them, and said to Guillaume, "Don't worry, sir, you won't lose your money."

"How about that!" said the boy's father. "You're a good girl. That's worth more than having brains."

Guillaume came close to me and said, with his usual precise elegance of gesture and expression, "My happiness is what I would've lost."

Forgive me, Édouard, for what I'm going to say, but those words filled me with pity: I thought my future husband was a fool. So that you don't protest at that word, I should explain his personality right away—a personality whose unspeakable tyranny few people could guess at. I'm no longer talking about a mere girl's feelings; I've tried in vain in this account to report strictly the emotions I felt at the time, but that's like what I was saying before about business jargon. Now that I understand those emotions, they've lost the meaning they had at first, and I can't retrieve it. I don't know if I can make myself clear... but imagine someone shows you white shapes on the horizon; at first glance you think they're clouds; then someone comes along and tells you they're mountains, and points them out to you in detail, and tells you their height and how far away they are. Well, once you've heard that explanation, you can try as hard as you like to recover your first impression, but you can no longer see clouds on the horizon, because the real mountains always stand in the way of your perceptions.

So I can remember very well that what Guillaume had said wounded me. At the time, however, I didn't think to describe him with the word I used earlier, "a fool." But experience came, and experience taught me to see clearly, and gave meaning to the displeasure I'd felt, and erased my initial reaction forever. And yet that reaction hadn't mislead me: it foretold unhappiness.

Chapter XLIV: The Wife of a Fool

Yes, Édouard, there are flaws that produce more sorrow than the worst vices. As I told you, Guillaume was handsome; his education, though superficial, had been broad; he had a vast fortune; he'd known every kind of success. I won't speak of his mistresses, though he spared me nothing in his descriptions of his triumphs. I'm too poor a student of the human heart to know whether he'd ever been loved; but I think I know the world well enough to be sure he'd had many women.

Guillaume had a compulsion for writing verse, and an even more fatal compulsion for reading it aloud. In our salon we had a few men of distinction who were sometimes willing to share their poetry with us, but I never saw any of them achieve a success anywhere close to my husband's. He was a mediocre musician, and prided himself on composing, and on singing his own compositions; they were met with cries of enthusiasm in which only I could discern the mocking praise of men of wit. As for Guillaume, the applause made him swoon with joy, and left him in no doubt that, if he'd wanted to, he could've rivaled the greatest poets and the greatest composers. I sometimes ventured a timid remark about that frenzied admiration—which only led to my being called envious. Early in our marriage, since I was the first person with whom Guillaume shared his compositions, I tried to point out a few weaknesses and even some basic musical errors; he couldn't find words to describe his scorn for my presumption.

For it has to be said, in my husband's eyes I was just a pretty doll, and a stupid one, who had to be shushed the moment she began to speak to save her from uttering nonsense. I swear, I never met anyone more self-assured than Guillaume. He settled every question with a conviction that often embarrassed better-informed men. Even his father had surrendered his own robustly independent mind to the domination of his son's opinions. There was one area in which Guillaume's abilities did in fact equal his father's: in the handling of money matters, especially in skillful speculative investment. Monsieur Carin, seeing his son's grasp of a subject in which he himself was a past master, assumed he had the same gift for anything outside his own understanding.

From time to time I tried, by means of some slight witticism, to suggest I wasn't completely without intelligence and judgment; but that subtle touch just slid off the triple armor of vanity that protected my husband. Finally, offended by his condescension toward me, I lobbed a few pointedly sarcastic remarks at him; but I didn't even get the reward of angering him, because he just laughed, the way you would at a child's rude comment.

We kept a loge at the Opéra and at the Théâtre des Italiens, and I tried to take refuge in that treat for the eyes and ears: but in vain. Guillaume's presence, and his comments, spoiled it for me every time. Priding himself on the originality of his opinions, he admired everything other people considered bad, and praised everything they found mediocre. I tried to push back, but he was surrounded by a fawning entourage of men who contradicted what I knew to be their own opinions so as to support his, and I was always defeated. You can't imagine the servile wretches there are in society, Édouard; and for you to understand what I had to suffer from them I need to tell you about the kind of company I saw.

We were married two weeks after the scene I described to you earlier. The wedding stunned me by its luxury. The mansion to which I was taken, and which had been kept from me as a surprise, was of uncommon magnificence. We didn't throw parties, but sometime after our wedding we held a splendid assembly. I'd gone out a few days earlier to pay my newlywed calls, and I'd given out the invitations in person. If I'd had some knowledge of the world, those visits would've served as my first lesson. We called indiscriminately at the homes of the high nobility, where my father's rank obligated me to present myself, and at the lavish homes of the men in high finance who constituted my husband's circle. In the former I was personally made welcome; in the latter all the graciousness was directed at my husband. I didn't pay much attention to that, and it was only a couple of weeks later I learned a woman can find respect elsewhere that she's denied in her own home, in places where that respect is withheld from the master of the house.

As a result, not one person from the social world I'd belonged to came to our assembly, and our parlors were filled with nothing but my husband's personal acquaintances. His vanity was injured; but his vanity didn't want to believe that a man born a commoner, with a wife acquired through a sordid speculation, could alienate such a proud world—and he blamed their cold shoulder on me. I tell you, Édouard, it was a cruel day when a hundred letters arrived, minute after minute, bringing our guests' poorly disguised refusals. I would've kept them from my husband, but—with a care I think was a well-planned insult—they were all addresses to him personally. They pursued him right up to the time the assembly began, and bit by bit they led to a quarrel between us, heated enough and prolonged enough that the servants had to come warn us the guests were already arriving in the parlors. Neither of us had even thought about dressing for company. Don't forget, Édouard, a woman is writing this; be tolerant of what you'd call frivolities, little things that can still have painful consequences. A mere nothing is enough, and a shared life begun badly can drift away from happiness for the slightest reason, like a pencil line that at the start deviates from perfect straightness by only a hair's breadth but by the end has wandered far from the goal.

After that social insult, which Guillaume was able to hold against me—if not personally, then at least as a member of the "insolent class" that had rebuffed him—there followed one of those misfortunes of life that seem like nothing but are sometimes much. I'd waited too late; I didn't have a hairdresser; so as not to be too tardy in appearing at our assembly, I entrusted myself to a chambermaid who didn't have the skill to dress me in the magnificent diamonds my husband had given me. I also forgot a fan, decorated by R—, that Guillaume had mentioned. I committed every blunder possible.

I hurried to reach the parlor; I entered. Appalled by the angry glare Guillaume threw me when I showed up holding flowers, I came in awkwardly, I didn't know how to repair the error of arriving late at my own party, I was clumsy and tongue-tied, and the guests came to my rescue with such insistent pity that I felt tears approaching. I was ridiculous. Édouard, do you understand the full import of that word to a man like my husband? From that moment on my cause was doomed. I can't describe the idiotic scene that followed that assembly; it was harsh enough to make me doubt myself, to the point that in smaller gatherings I no longer had the courage to play the piano and sing, though past success would've taught me I could do it without needing to summon courage.

Now imagine the life of a woman who's weak and whose head is constantly under her husband's foot! I was bound to fail in my struggle—because in spite of my weakness I did struggle. That's when I learned a sad fact about humankind: vanity is a stronger driving force than happiness. I'd surrendered my happiness at the first crisis; long after that I still fought for my vanity. But in doing so, in the end I used up the little strength I had, because the attacks came from such mundane directions that I often found myself defenseless. My instructions to the servants were always poorly worded; I was wrong to receive company at such and such an hour, and wrong not to receive company at the same hour. My husband was so completely convinced I was stupid that he criticized everything I did and everything I said without even thinking about it. And he criticized me in that sneering, contemptuous, bludgeoning manner against which nothing works except silence.

Here I should explain how I came to be defending my cause all by myself. You've already seen how my "class," as my husband called it, had abandoned me; so I found myself relegated to a social world that saw me only in relation to him. I've referred to the servility of humankind; now I understood it. Most of them needed Guillaume and the vast financial capital he controlled, and they flattered him by joining him to mock me. My birth—what they referred to as my "gentility"—made enemies for me of all the wives in that commercial world; and, though a few of them weren't afraid to rebuke Guillaume for his pretensions, it was never done for my benefit, because I'd robbed them of the richest and best-looking match in their circle.

Are you surprised, Édouard, that in my cruel position I found no one to support me? Only one man, Count Cerny, defied the aristocracy's anathema against our household. He came several times, and made himself my champion. I was grateful to him for his courage, and I showed it by the warmth of my welcome. Within a month the whole of the Chaussée d'Antin neighborhood was outraged by my scandalous behavior. The dandies on the stock exchange, who'd never wasted a thought on me, found themselves humiliated by what they called the triumph of the emissary from the "faubourg Germain."[6] I had to ask Count Cerny to spare me his well-meant attention.

I can imagine you reading my letter, Édouard, and flipping through the pages to see if, in the midst of my description of all that isolation, I'll finally name the man I turned to for help. Alas! Haven't I already said enough bad things about my father, and must I be reduced to making more accusations against him? My father didn't live with us, and rarely visited. And when he did visit, can you think why? He needed money, he needed a loan from my husband. If you knew the humiliations Guillaume imposed on my father as the price of the assistance he gave him, Édouard, you'd see why I wouldn't want to add to that awful torture the report of the pain it gave me.

I'm poor now, Édouard, and sometimes you're surprised at my courage in putting up with certain privations: it's because I learned, better than anyone, the cost of having desires beyond one's means. Besides, my father was led astray by a terrible passion: he was a gambler. Whereas I, as you know, have never been strong enough to sustain any passion. I lived in luxury without enjoying it; I live in poverty without suffering from it.

As you can see, Édouard, I was rejected on all sides: bullied by Guillaume in his blind stupidity, mocked by his entourage in their servility, made a target of ridicule by their wives out of hatred. I resigned myself to it, I kept my mouth shut, I forbore judgment; and after I'd been married a year it was said I was an imbecile who meant to be spiteful but didn't know how. I failed at everything. I got pregnant and fell ill. In his vanity my husband forced me to go to the races to show me his magnificent new horses—which bolted, and frightened me terribly, and made me miscarry. Guillaume was coarse enough to remark that I was "not even good for making babies."

Can you comprehend that life, Édouard? Can you imagine how vile, insulting, and awful it was? And remember, I lacked even the opportunity for solitude and reflection: every day I was dragged to balls and parties and performances. It was my unwitting duty to satisfy one of my husband's vanities. After a while I realized the new jewelry he constantly lavished on me wasn't the loving attention on his part I'd assumed it to be: it was a provocation aimed at the luxuries of richer men. I think if he could've dressed his horse in lamé robes and costly necklaces, he'd have left me at home.

I lived that way for two years, by the end of which I'd reached a level of self-neglect that almost justified everything that was said about me. And then an event of enormous importance in itself, since it brought about a national revolution, changed my life and produced the catastrophe that left me in the condition

---

[6] A malapropism for the faubourg Saint Germain, a neighborhood that was home to many aristocrats.

I'm in now. I'd gotten married in July 1828; two years later the revolution that sent the Bourbons into exile broke out.[7]

We were staying in the country, near Blois, when the *Moniteur* brought us word of the July Ordinances.[8] You can't conceive my husband's wild delight at the news. "Finally!" he cried. "That yapping, insolent Chamber of Deputies will be brought to heel. A gaggle of lawyers and shopkeepers with empty pockets who'll be all too happy to lick the boots of the king when he dares to stand up to them! It's time the reins of power came back into their rightful hands—the great names and the great fortunes! Now's the time for the Chamber of Peers to take its true and rightful place as the upper Chamber! Oh, if only I was already... By the way, have you heard any news from your father?"

"Yes, he wrote to me from the Pyrenees. The waters at Aix have done him a lot of good."

My husband let slip a look of disappointment whose awful meaning I didn't grasp at the time. "Well," he went on after a short pause, "it'll have to come eventually. Meantime, this doesn't hurt matters. The aristocracy can now hope for a solid constitution: it'll lead the country, instead of being towed along behind like some tired old machine. An aristocracy that's young, strong, rich, that understands the brand-new necessities of our time and has the skill to re-build the past!" As he spoke, my husband was pacing around vigorously, reading and rereading the *Moniteur*. From time to time he cried out with angry impatience, "And not to be there right now!"

"Couldn't we start for Paris?" I asked.

"Is that what I'm talking about?" he replied with a look of scorn and a shrug.

You can see I was a fool, and I didn't understand what it was about my father's life that provoked my husband to such intense regret. Alas, I didn't remain in error for long. Though I'd never paid attention to politics, I was naturally on my father's side, and on my husband's side, so I found nothing surprising about his excitement. But I soon learned how little rational basis there was for his ideas.

Monsieur Carin senior, who'd come to the country with us, had been away from the estate when the important news arrived. He returned in the midst of his son's loudest exclamations. At first the father just listened anxiously; then he

---

[7] The July Revolution of 1830 deposed Charles X and brought his cousin Louis Philippe, Duke of Orléans, to the throne as a constitutional monarch; the principle of the hereditary right of kings gave way to that of popular sovereignty.

[8] In the July Ordinances, Charles X, under pressure from the ongoing political upheavals, issued decrees dissolving the Chamber of Deputies, abolishing freedom of the press, barring the middle class from future elections, and calling for new elections.

stood up, shaking his head, and said, "That's all well and good, but I say the whole thing is a huge mistake."

"Sure," replied my husband. "You've just been with Monsieur D—, a fanatical liberal, and he got you all turned around."

"Actually, I've just been with Count M—, a fanatical ultra-royalist, who told me the news, and I knew he was crazy, and so are you."

"Oh, come on, father!" laughed my husband scornfully. "You can't possibly believe what you're saying!"

"I believe what I say, and I say what I believe. This decree is a huge mistake. I said it before, and I'm saying it again."

"Fine," said my husband with the utter scorn he had for any opinion that wasn't his own. "A mistake from your point of view."

"And my point of view is at least as good as yours, mister Baron de Carin!" replied his father angrily. "I forgave Count M—'s foolish enthusiasm: he's a petty nobleman who thinks he'll become a great lord because the taxpayers can't vote. But as for you: you think France is going suffer this slap without returning it?"

"Oh, France! France!" said my husband in the same scornful tone. "Where is France, anyway? What is France, really? Is it made up of fifty thousand imbecile voters and two hundred insolent Deputies? France will do the right thing and shut up."

"It will not shut up, mister baron!" cried Monsieur Carin, more worked up against his son than I'd ever seen him. "The fifty thousand imbecile voters and the two hundred insolent Deputies are the elite of this nation, you hear me, mister baron? And they won't let themselves be insulted for the benefit of a class that showed you the door—you, my son, Guillaume Carin!"

"I don't hold the king's party responsible for the insults of a few men."

"Well, good for you! You've got greatness of soul! But it's not going to be like that everywhere, I promise you that. I'm a royalist; I've proven it. I haven't forgotten that the tyrant Bonaparte wanted to convict me in the provisioning scandal of 1813, and if the allies hadn't shown up I'd have danced at the end of a rope, along with all my millions.[9] I'm a royalist, heart and soul, but I'm a royalist for the king, not for the gang of exiles he brought back with him and who are eating us alive."

"And who had all of their assets confiscated," said my husband.

"And some of those assets have come to you," said Monsieur Carin. "Anyway, listen, I hate the nobility. It's just who I am, the way worshiping them is just who you are. I'd like to believe you're my son, but you sure wouldn't know it from that."

---

[9] In 1813 Napoleon demanded that wealthy businessmen fund the provisioning of his armies. Corrupt dealing involving Empress Josephine diverted some of funds, and the financiers were held responsible.

"And I'm proud of it."

"You're proud of it! Where'd you come from, then?"

"Careful, father, someone might hear you."

"What do I care? Does my birth make me blush? My father was a carpenter and my mother was a fishwife. They made their fortune, it's true, and I built on that. But that doesn't make me better than them, and I'm not going to let a bunch of petty nobles and bandits step on my toes."

"It's not about that, father," said my husband, alarmed at Monsieur Carin's agitation. "It's about measures dictated by necessity, and which the king had both the right and the duty to carry out."

"Don't make me laugh with your rights and duties! Unbelievable! You really think just because some government minister gave a big hypocritical speech when the decrees were announced, that's going to persuade the voters to let themselves be fleeced of their rights without saying a word? That freedom of the press can be taken away with one stroke of the pen without people getting upset?"

"Do the people even care about that kind of thing? What do elections matter to them? They don't vote. What do they care about freedom of the press? They don't even know how to read!"

"My poor boy, I pity you! I know the common people don't take part in elections, but the elections are in the hands of the middle class, and the people trust them."

"They're even more insolent than the nobles."

"Sure, but they're not nobles, and the working class and the middle class are kindred by being commoners. They were allies in '89, and you'll make them allies again by giving them the same enemies: the nobility and the clergy. You're great political thinkers on paper, you modern experts, but you don't know the people. You don't take into account the people's hatreds or memories or fears."

"But this isn't about the nobility and the clergy. It's about the monarchy."

"And what does the monarchy want?"

"It wants respect. A monarchy that's lasted fourteen centuries doesn't want to be the slave of an upstart Chamber that was born yesterday."

"You're nuts! Can there be a Chamber on condition that there be no Chamber? And you, first of all, if you were where you'd like to be, would you let them kick you out because you happened to disagree with the government?"

"Oh, now, the Chamber of Peers, that's a different matter. That's the true elite of the nation."

"A splendid elite, that it so happens you'll be part of."

"But, father…"

"Leave me alone! The Bourbons are going to get thrown out again, and they'll have earned it."

"We'll see about that."

"You can see already. There'll be an uprising in Paris by tomorrow."

"My poor father, you think it's still '93."

"I think what I feel! When I read that issue of the *Moniteur*, my heart pounded as if I'd been slapped. I didn't reason my way to that feeling; I was just furious. And I'm built like everybody else, and everybody else is built like me, and you'll see what happens."

The argument went on and on; and though it didn't shed much light from any direction on that important issue, I was silently in agreement with Monsieur Carin. I took seriously the instinctive popular anger he'd felt, and I could imagine how strongly it might affect the masses—who wouldn't be held back from their first impulsive reaction by the motives he had of wealth and alliance by marriage.

As always happens to men rich in self-satisfaction, contradiction only amplified my husband's zeal. He responded to news of the first mass demonstrations with his usual disdain, saying, "One company of Guardsmen with their riding crops in hand, and it'll all be over." Then, when he saw it took only three days to overthrow that fourteen-hundred-year-old monarchy, he didn't abandon his unreasoning self-assurance: unable to admit that the decrees he'd approved of could've been mistaken, he put the blame on those who'd carried them out. He said everything that had gone wrong had been their fault, and that stationing a few more regiments in Paris would've guaranteed success. He didn't give up that peremptory tone till the newspapers brought word of Louis Philippe's election to the throne and the approval of the new Charter.[10]

That was when another string of sorrows began for me, which I'm not afraid to entrust to your discretion, Édouard. But doesn't it strike you as odd that a woman's life could be made miserable by a clause in her country's political constitution? The new Charter, voted on by both Chambers and upheld by the king, stated that within a year a law would be introduced to settle the question of the hereditary peerage. The storm that broke out in Guillaume's heart at that news was truly a kind of madness. His father enjoyed making him angry by mocking his shattered ambitions; and you have to understand that in the whole business it was I who felt the backlash from both the son's fury and the father's jokes. I won't describe the first scene it provoked; but it was followed by others so bitter that the first one no longer remains even a painful memory.

A few days later several letters from my father arrived for my husband, which he didn't share with me. Monsieur Carin had gone to Paris and come back. Meanwhile my father had left the spa at Aix and come to our estate. He was extremely upset: his political opinions were his faith, loyalty to the Bourbons his religion, and from the moment he arrived he announced his intention to follow the Bourbons once more into exile.

---

[10] The Charter of 1830 established a constitutional monarchy and introduced many other liberal reforms.

"We'll talk about it more tomorrow," said my husband, more affectionately than usual. "First you should rest."

That night, after I'd gone upstairs to bed, Guillaume came my room. Carefully closing the door, he said he had something important to discuss with me. Seeing my considerable surprise, he thought he should impress on me, in his usual manner, the significance of what he was going to ask me to do. "Don't be alarmed!" he said. "It's nothing too out of the way. I just want you to take on the job of persuading your father not to leave France. I assume the marquis's departure would make you unhappy enough for you to be able to find arguments that would change his mind."

"My sorrow is the only argument I could use, and I trust enough in my father's love for him to spare me that separation."

"Well put. Persuade him you'd be left in despair, and me too."

"I'm grateful for the sentiment. Since you're counting on me to succeed at this, I assume there are other reasons I could bring up."

"And what reasons would those be?" asked Guillaume, sitting down and examining me.

Dare I admit it to you, Édouard? I believed I saw a way to improve Guillaume's opinion of me on a few points; and I applied myself to listing reasons I thought would matter to him. "My father's old, and to leave France at his age would mean wishing to die abroad."

"Quite right, quite right."

"He has no need to give the Bourbons this final proof of his devotion; his entire life speaks for him."

"Very good, very good."

"In fact he can show them his loyalty by one final action on his own behalf. As a few others have done, he can refuse to take the oath the new government is requiring of peers of France, and protest by withdrawing."

"I beg you, don't say a word to him about that."

"Why not?"

"Why not! Because I didn't marry you for that."

"What do you mean?"

"Listen, Louise. For once in your life, try to understand me. That's not too much to ask, is it?"

"I'll do my best, sir."

"Oh, don't put on your martyred look, please. What I'm about to tell you is serious. Listen carefully. The law concerning the hereditary peerage won't be introduced for another year. They didn't put off a question like that without good reason: they wanted to allow time for tempers to cool. I believe it's more than likely the heredity peerage won't be abolished. If that's the case, then my rights will survive—if your father takes the oath. Now, you can understand why I don't intend to sacrifice those rights to some fit of old-fashioned loyalty: they certainly cost me plenty."

I couldn't deny that Guillaume's point of view was reasonable; but he had a gift for coating everything he said with vileness. That coarse reminder of the price he'd paid for his ambitions disgusted me, and I replied, "There are questions of honor every man must judge entirely for himself, and I have no right to give such advice to my father."

"Well, well! Where'd you learn a pretty phrase like that? It rings nicely, but I have to warn you it's not appropriate here. I want you—you hear me?—I want you to persuade the Marquis de Vaucloix to take the oath."

"I can't take on a task like that. I won't do it."

"Listen," said Guillaume angrily, "your father will take the oath when I want and how I want. But it doesn't suit me to drive him to that decision myself. It has to be you who leads him to it. I'm reluctant to use force, but your refusal would leave me no choice."

"Force, toward my father!" I cried. "And you dare threaten me with that!"

"Let's not get melodramatic, please. Will you, yes or no, spare me the unpleasantness of provoking a scene with your father? Go to him tonight. I let him know you wanted to talk to him in private; he's waiting up for you. And since you're so big on pretty phrases, here's one I'd like you to use on him: the only dowry he bestowed on you was the inheritance of his peerage, and his duty as a man of honor is to preserve it by any means in his power."

"By any means, except perjury."

"Enough of your foolish stubbornness!" said Guillaume furiously. "Are you refusing? I warn you, I loathe scandal and uproar, but if it has to come that, I'll do it, and then... But you won't refuse."

Guillaume's earlier threat against my father hadn't particularly alarmed me; but the tone in which he'd spoken just now truly terrified me. I contained myself and said, "My refusal shouldn't matter much to you, because you can assume that even if I carry out your errand it'll be pointless."

"That's what we'll soon find out."

"You really want me to do it? All right, I'll try tomorrow."

"Tonight, I told you."

"All right, tonight. I'll go in a little while."

"No, right now... Good God! I have my reasons. Follow me. I'll go with you as far as your father's rooms. And don't forget, you have to succeed."

Though I was convinced the effort was pointless, I agreed to follow my husband, to spare my father the scene my husband threatened. I thought my giving in would be enough to satisfy Guillaume. He led me to the door of my father's rooms, and motioned for me to go inside.

Chapter XLV: A Political Oath

Trembling, I obeyed my husband and entered my father's bedroom. But I came out again immediately. "He's lying on his bed, fully dressed!" I told Guillaume.

"Oh, I know that."

"But he's asleep!"

"Well," he said savagely, "wake him up!"

"Who's there?" asked my father as he got up.

My husband pushed me into the room, and I answered, "It's me."

"You're late, Louise, and I was afraid I'd have to leave without saying goodbye."

"What!" I cried. "You're leaving us already?"

"I can't remain on French soil after the king has left it. I'm going to join him."

"Oh, father! Have you thought carefully about exile like that at your age?"

"The king is older than I am."

"Have you considered you'd be leaving me alone in France?"

"Alone, Louise? Alone with your husband. You're speaking without thinking."

"But does he know about your plans to leave?"

"It doesn't matter. He has to approve them."

"Still, father, you could consult him."

"Why? I don't need anyone's advice to do my duty."

"This unexpected parting might upset him."

"Upset him! Why?"

I gathered all my courage. Lowering my eyes, I said, "His marriage gave him certain hopes, which your leaving would ruin."

"I don't understand."

"By going into exile, you'll be renouncing your peerage."

"And if I stay, does he think I can keep it?"

"Perhaps he has reason to hope so."

My father lifted my head, which I'd kept bowed. Looking me in the eye, he said, "Louise, are you talking to me like this on your own behalf?"

"I don't wish to be parted from you, and I want to persuade you to..."

"To perjure myself!"

"No, father, but..."

"He forced you to come here, Louise. There's neither ambition nor baseness in your heart. I forgive you, but let's speak no more about it."

"With her, perhaps," said my husband as he came in and slammed the door behind him. "But with me it's a different matter."

"So I wasn't mistaken, and those insinuations in your last letter..."

"I see you understood those insinuations. And when you left your carriage at the relay stop I too understood—that you planned to escape me."

"Well, who could keep me from leaving?"

"I could."

"You're raving."

"Not as much as you think. Listen carefully, marquis! The letter you gave me an hour ago, which conveys your resignation to the Chamber of Peers, is in the hands of a courier who's waiting downstairs on horseback. If you want, he'll set off. Tomorrow morning he'll be in Paris, tomorrow by noon you'll no longer be a peer of France, and all the privileges of the peerage will cease to apply to you. The day after tomorrow a consular ruling will authorize your physical detention, effective immediately. With money you can buy anything you want; and before you reach any port, no matter which, to set sail, you'll be arrested and taken to Sainte Pélagie, where you can exercise your fealty to His Majesty Charles X."

"That's a despicable crime!" I cried in despair.

"Oh, spare us your interruptions. Your father understands me much better than you do."

Indeed, the first look of anger on my father's face had given way to an expression of genuine serenity. "I understand you, Baron de Carin. You're right. Let it be as you wish. Give me back my letter of resignation; I won't send it."

I didn't even have time to be astonished at my father's concession, because my husband cried, "Really! And if your resignation isn't sent, you'll remain a peer of France, and at liberty long enough to get to Paris and then to Le Havre? And from there, when you're safe aboard an English ship, you'll send that resignation at your leisure? No, marquis, no. I'm not such a fool as all that."

"Then what do you want me to do?"

"What I want is for the courier to leave for Paris within the next hour; I want him to be carrying either your resignation—in which case you know what awaits you—or your oath of fealty to the new regime; and then..."

"That's a treachery I'll never commit."

"Come now, marquis, let's not give words more importance than they have. Think of your oath to the king as a promissory note you're signing. You know better than anyone nobody ever redeems that at face value."

"And you know as well as I do what happens to those who don't pay at all."

"You make arrangements with them as the need arises, and that's what I'm proposing to you. Take the oath, and I'll negotiate a clear discharge of all your new debts."

"No. No. Let the courier take my resignation!"

38

"Have you considered that you're sacrificing your annuity as a peer of France?"

"Yes."

"You realize that's the only income you have left?"

"Yes."

"You remember that your choice leads straight to Sainte Pélagie?"

"Yes."

"Sir," I cried, "you wouldn't dare!"

My husband shot me a glance that made me tremble.

My father continued, "Yes, Louise, he'd dare. You don't know him yet. For quite a while I've known he was capable of anything."

"He knew that even before we were married," snickered Guillaume, "and you have him to thank for the speed with which it was arranged."

I bowed my head to avoid looking at those two men—one of them my father and the other my husband. And yet I recoiled from the calamity that threatened the one and the crime planned by the other, and I raised my voice again. "In heaven's name! Take a day to think it over, both of you. And when you're calmer..."

"This decision must be made within the hour," interrupted Guillaume. "Tomorrow it'll be too late."

"Well then," said my father as he rose, "let the courier go!"

My husband knocked over a chair in his anger, showing how little he'd expected that decision.

"Yes," went on my father, his resolve only strengthened by Guillaume's reaction, "yes, let him go. I'll finish a life of loyalty and honor with one last act of honor and loyalty."

"Honor!" cried Guillaume furiously. "You speak of honor—you who've treated as a joke the most commonplace pledges of integrity, you who staked your own daughter on a speculation, you who..."

"Send away your courier, sir," replied my father. "I prefer poverty, I prefer prison, to the treachery of taking an oath like that. Yes," he continued, growing animated, "my honor and my loyalty are intact, and I count on them above all in my hope to be forgiven for having been poor and not having been able to bear it. But now that the time has come to sacrifice honor and loyalty for the fortune that has always eluded me, I reject that fortune. Yes, I'll be poor; yes, I'll die in prison. But the peerage, the object of your ambitions, will escape you. That's how I'll atone for the wrong I did in making you the heir to it."

"Then so be it!" cried my husband in his fury. He opened the window and called out.

"Sir!" I cried. "Wait!"

He turned. My father, still not recovered from his illness and now overwhelmed by the discussion, had dropped into a chair.

My husband closed the window and suddenly grew calmer. "One more thing," he said. "This conversation took a turn, such that I wasn't able to make you listen to reason. Compose yourself, and listen carefully. Don't assume that when I advise you to take the oath, marquis, I'm proposing treason. No. Don't you know as well as I do that a political oath never bound anyone?"

"Except men of honor."

"But there exist men of honor who'll take an oath so as not to quit the battlefield entirely. What happens to the cause of the Bourbons if everyone deserts it this way? Isn't it better to remain in a position to defend it, inch by inch, and to undermine the new regime by active opposition?"

"The opposition of a single man, the opposition of a man who has nothing to contribute except his loyalty!"

"The opposition of a man who'll become the rallying hope of his cause. Listen, sign this oath and I'll free you of all your debts; I'll open my house to you, and make you the master there; it can become the headquarters for all gatherings of the legitimate royalists."

"Your house, where I'll be on your payroll, right? Where I'll be the servant of your ambitions?"

"No. I'll give you an independent income, beyond anything you could hope for. You like luxury, gambling, expensive living; I'll pay for that."

"You'll give me ten thousand francs a year, like what you'd pay a clerk."

"Neither ten thousand nor twenty thousand. It'll be forty thousand francs a year."

My father shook his head.

"Fifty... sixty thousand."

He shook his head again, with a glance in my direction.

"Leave us!" said my husband.

I rose and went out. I was no longer afraid Guillaume would turn violent. I'd just watched the remnants of old honor bend beneath the temptation of money, and I withdrew to spare my father the shame of having a witness to the sad bargain.

I left; but instead of going back to my own rooms I stopped in the small unlit parlor just outside my father's bedroom. I took a seat in a corner, devastated by what I'd just seen and heard, and I stayed there, not daring to think about what was happening.

Only a few minutes had gone by when my husband came out and crossed the parlor without seeing me. When he reached the antechamber he met Monsieur Carin, his father, who'd probably been waiting for him there.

"Is it done?" asked Monsieur Carin.

"Yes."

"How much?"

"A hundred thousand."

"A hundred thousand francs a year! You're mad—that's ruinous."

"Yes… if we had to pay it."

"So you found a way out?"

"The law abolishing the hereditary peerage won't be introduced for a year. Between now and then we'll see what happens: he's awfully worn down!"

"There's a lot of strength left in that body."

I couldn't hear anything further, because they both lowered their voices. Finally I heard my husband say, "Meanwhile, we have to send off that courier."

"Come."

They both went out.

Those words might not have meant anything to me if I'd heard them in other circumstances. But after the scene I'd just witnessed, a ghastly daylight illuminated them. They were counting on my father dying soon. But what would they do if his death didn't come soon enough? Recoiling from the thought of an awful crime, I tried to convince myself that my own fears lent those words a meaning they didn't have. Still, I wanted to go back to my father to tell him everything.

As I entered his bedroom I stopped—for I was about to accuse my husband of planning a terrible crime, with no proof beyond a few words that, in my distress, I might've misunderstood. I needed time to think, so I returned to my own rooms in that awful uncertainty, taking my father's side because he was the more unfortunate of the two, but unable to decide definitely in his favor over my husband.

Being exposed to such upsetting emotions took its toll on me: I fell victim to a high fever, and for several days I didn't see my father, and I was told he too was unwell and was confined to his bedroom. My suspicions hadn't abated, and every morning I asked anxiously for news of him. The servants who came to me answered in some embarrassment. I believed they were concealing his death from me; in desperation I got up to go to him. The servants tried to stop me from leaving my bedroom, but my anxiety and my fever gave me such uncommon strength that they fell back before me.

Only half dressed, I hurried along the corridors of the chateau. Just before I reached my father's rooms I heard loud voices coming from the ground floor. As I listened I recognized the loudest voice of all as my father's. The uproar was so violent I took it for a quarrel. Suddenly a door opened, and I understood the cause of the noise. They were all seated around a table, laughing and arguing and talking over each other. It was a drunken feast.

A chambermaid had followed me. I turned to her and asked, "What's going on?"

"Oh, my God, ma'am, it's been like this the whole week you've been sick."

"Is my husband there?"

"Yes, ma'am."

"And my father too?"

"The marquis is the worst-behaved of all of them," said the girl, lowering her eyes.

You know, Édouard, if a woman told you she'd had to throw herself between her husband and her father, against whose chest he'd raised his dagger, you'd say she'd suffered the most awful calamity. And yet her misfortune would've been nothing compared to what I was going through. I felt horribly sure what Guillaume's plan was, and I could neither prevent it nor denounce it. How could I, a wife, have put a stop to the carousing that amounted to premeditated murder? How could I, a daughter, have said to my father, "They're taking advantage of your unruly habits, the ease with which you can be led into every kind of excess, to end a life that's standing in their way and has gone on too long"?

Perhaps a woman stronger than I am—a woman capable of seeing her position in its full horror—would've been driven mad. And perhaps a woman stronger than I am could've said to her husband's face, "I know your plans," or to her father, "I know they're using your vices to kill you." But I couldn't do it.

I returned to my rooms, sicker than before, but with a will to be healed that served me better than all the care I was getting. I have to tell you, Édouard, in my lonely nights I'd considered every possible way of saving my father, and I'd realized the surest was to tell him the truth; but even knowing that, I'd always shrunk from the challenge of delivering such a difficult message. You can't conceive the weakness that overcomes some spirits in the face of any action that calls for decisiveness. You may have met cowards in your life, men whom not even the worst insult can push to confront danger; who, in real peril, can't even summon the courage to save their own lives. The way those men are when facing a sword or a pistol is the way I was when facing a determined act of my own will.

I wanted to get well, and I got well, not to confront my husband, nor to warn my father, but to place myself between them and forestall the crime. Yes, Édouard, I gave myself the sad task of joining them at all those banquets, hoping to moderate them by my presence. Using the excuse of my father's health, I made a few timid remarks I feared he'd find disrespectful and my husband would understand too clearly. I was afraid when they rode away from the estate and afraid when they stayed home. If my father got into a carriage I watched him anxiously; if he chose a horse to go for a ride I was anxious about the horse. I accompanied him everywhere I could: I followed him when he went hunting, I placed him next to me at the dinner table, I wore him out with questions, I took away his glass.

What more can I tell you? I spent six months in terrible anxiety, guarding the victim without daring to look the murderer in the eye, watching my father's health suffer, and no longer in any doubt about my husband's plot—because the care he took to tempt the poor old man told me enough. You can't imagine the way my husband—always so vain, so cold, so imperious—made himself into the slave of my father's least desires! And my father was delighted by his courtesy, his companionship, his attention. For a long time I kept up the sad chore I'd imposed on myself, happy every time I gained a few days' quiet respite for my father, despairing every time my husband found some new trick for dragging him into fatal excess.

And yet I was prepared to yield to necessity: the time had come, either to speak up or to abandon a supervision that had become pointless and that my father resisted as a foolish, wrongheaded nuisance. I was on the point of being forced to choose between denunciation of the crime and mute complicity in it, when my father, his strength exhausted, fell gravely ill. By a terrible coincidence, just then the law abolishing the hereditary peerage was brought before the Chambers. The first newspaper reports we saw left us in no doubt that it would pass.

It's easy to describe material facts, Édouard; it's much harder to make clear those facts that are only revealed to us by a kind of intuition. The day the *Moniteur* brought word of the new law, my husband was sitting by my father's bed. God alone knows the secrets of men's thoughts: may he break my pen in my hand if I'm lying! But I swear Guillaume, with his finger on the date printed in the *Moniteur* and his eye on the sick man, carefully calculated that the time required for debating and passing the law would be long enough for my father to die before the law dispossessed him. A sinister smile followed Guillaume's silent contemplation, and I felt myself grow cold when he said to my father, "It's nothing. A couple of days of rest, and then the day after tomorrow a carriage ride and a good dinner, and you'll be fine."

Once again I was about to call out to my father, "He's killing you, he wants to kill you!" But one of those vague hopes onto which my cowardice always sought to fasten itself came to me and led me into the pitiful recourse of expecting time and luck to bring about a rescue I could perhaps have secured by acting on the spot. I thought I could safeguard my father's life till the fatal law went into effect, after which Guillaume would give up a plot that could no longer benefit him.

I moved in with my father; I had a bed set up in a small room adjoining his bedroom, and there, never shutting my eyes, I watched over the care he was given. I myself prepared the soothing drinks the doctors ordered; I turned away strangers who came to visit him; I became an intolerable jailer. And yet I couldn't keep my husband out; and though I felt sure he wouldn't dare undermine the physical life I was protecting around the clock, still I could see he was undermining the feeble remains of the spirit.

Guillaume read to my father regularly and assiduously from the newspaper. Knowing he'd anger him by dwelling on a subject that concerned him so directly, he chose the most upsetting speeches and the harshest articles to spark conversation. And then he provoked him, goading him into a violent rage, and didn't stop till the old man was drained of strength. In vain I begged them both to avoid discussing such matters. Since Guillaume didn't irritate my father by disagreeing with him, since on the contrary it was by pandering to his hatreds and cheering at his tirades that he drove him into a dangerous fury, my father waited impatiently every day for the news; and Guillaume had managed things so cleverly it would've been as dangerous to hide the papers from my father as it was to bring them to him.

I lived like that, caught between the victim and his torturer, feeling the pain from every blow without being able to parry a single one, but sustained by the hope that had kept me silent; for the end of the Parliamentary debate was drawing near, and with it would come the end of the murderous effect it was having in our house. The law had now been introduced in the Chamber of Peers, and— out of a prudence whose motive I didn't suspect—Guillaume had allowed my father to believe it would be rejected by the Chamber whose greatest privilege that law was intended to abolish. On the strength of that belief I'd secured a few days of respite, and the slight improvement it brought in my father's condition had given me hope that a calm life, free from violent emotions, would soon restore him to health.

Guillaume even seemed to have given up his terrible plan. He no longer brought the newspapers, saying they had nothing important in them and the debate over the law wouldn't last long. With my usual weakness, and gauging the persistence of other people by my own, I thought my husband had grown tired of the awful role he'd been playing; and my only fear was that he might start in again when debate over the law resumed. I began to feel some optimism about the future, and I put off preparing for new dangers, because I found it a great burden.

A day came that set all of my fears at ease. In a long conversation among the three of us, politics was set aside and we spoke only of trips we looked forward to, of a happy future, of our only care being the enjoyment of our fortune safe from all revolutionary upheavals. That night I went to bed with a light heart, and after resisting sleep for so many weeks I let myself drift off. In any case I wasn't concerned, because I'd carefully locked my father's door and no one could get in.

Suddenly I awoke to a terrible racket. I jumped up, and saw my husband coming in with a few servants, who'd broken down the door. "What's going on?" I cried, hurrying to my father.

"What!" cried my husband savagely. "Your father's been ringing desperately for help for half an hour, and you've been right here, and you ask what's going on? And we've been hammering on the door for ten minutes and you refused to open it!"

"Me?" I cried. "I was asleep!"

"And yet we find you up."

At that I thought I grasped both the crime that had been committed and the intention to blame me for it, and I turned toward my father. He was sitting up in bed, and he said with a laugh, "Well! You're all mad. I rang quietly because I didn't want to wake this poor child. I rang louder when no one came. And I must say you were rather impatient, because I was about to get up to let you in when you broke down the door with a crash."

"And what is it you want, father?"

"Just a little herbal tea. The cup on the table by my bed had such a foul smell I didn't even taste it."

I tried to take the cup. My husband grabbed it and tossed the contents into the fireplace, saying, "So this is how you take care of your father! There's no need to lock the door against us."

I'd swear to it even now: the agitated look on my husband's face, and the care he'd taken to get rid of the tea whose smell had displeased my father, convinced me a crime had been intended, and I was appalled at the thought of the web of circumstantial evidence that would've made me responsible if it had succeeded. My father drank the cup of herbal tea my husband brought him now, while I was still devastated by the idea of the danger both he and I had just escaped.

"Now that the crisis is over," said my father with a smile, "everybody go back to bed, because I feel like I could sleep again."

Everyone left, and I alone remained there.

"Well? Aren't you going back to bed?" asked my father.

"Oh my God! My God!" I cried, bursting into tears.

"What's wrong, Louise? Why don't you answer? What's wrong?"

"Oh, father, don't ask me any questions. But I beg you, I implore you, don't eat or drink anything unless I bring it to you."

"Louise! Louise! You're mad. Do you realize the seriousness of what you're saying?"

"Listen, father, listen! Do you remember the terrible night Guillaume forced you to sign the oath and send it off?"

"Yes."

"Well, this is what I heard him say when he left you..." I repeated what Guillaume and Monsieur Carin had said to each other. I explained how troubled I'd been by all the reckless behavior he'd been led into. I told him why I'd arranged to be with him night and day. In short, I told him everything.

My father's exasperation knew no bounds. He could speak of nothing but revenge, and he ordered me to say nothing to Guillaume. "He won't give up," he said. "He'll try again, and once I have proof of his crimes in my hands, it'll be my turn to make him obey me."

I use the word "exasperation" to describe my father's anger to you, because in fact he was neither surprised nor outraged. His only thought was to return wrong for wrong, and to take advantage of what he'd just learned. I'd saved my father—but only to see him constantly laying a trap for my husband. He meant to doom him. How else can I put it?

45

The morning after that scene, my father greeted Guillaume with good-natured thanks for his concern for him the night before. He scolded me for locking the door, which should remain open night and day to such a fine son-in-law. But Guillaume guessed it was a trap; and maybe it wasn't out of cleverness—maybe while I was denouncing him to my father he'd been hidden behind that door, a door that was now open to him but that he no longer wanted to pass through.

To give Guillaume a chance to try again, my father insisted I move out of his rooms. I obeyed. I was exhausted by so many horrors; my head and my heart could no longer cope with the fears that haunted me. Every morning I expected either to learn my father was dead or to find the house filled with magistrates summoned against my husband. Nothing happened, and a week later my father, no longer concerned about Guillaume, told me I was a madwoman whose imagination had built up dismal conspiracies.

You might think my sufferings could get no worse than that, Édouard. You'd be wrong! The word "madwoman," which my father applied to me with a smile, my husband used seriously. I was handed over to doctors, to whom he reported everything I'd said against him, as proof of that madness. Everyone pitied the poor husband for having a wife like that, and I was put under round-the-clock observation.

Two months later, when the law abolishing the hereditary peerage had passed, my father died. Guillaume came to bring me the news; in my outrage I couldn't help crying, "It came too late, didn't it?"

The doctor who was there said quietly, "It's an obsession."

A week later I was put in a mental asylum. That's where I'm writing to you from, Édouard; that's where I've lived for a year now; that's where I'll die soon, if you don't find a way to get me out.

The manuscript came to an end. The Devil stood before Luizzi.

"So where exactly are we?" cried Luizzi.

"In a madhouse."

"And that woman who was asleep?"

"That's Madame de Carin."

"But is she really mad?"

"Ask the doctors."

"Did her husband really attempt all those crimes?"

"Ask the police."

"How would the police know?"

"By asking the one who knows everything."

"You mean you, Satan? Well then, tell me the truth."

"Sure!" said the Devil, whistling a tune. "You'll say I'm slandering society. But didn't you deduce anything from that story?"

"I deduced that I probably slept through the twenty months I gave you."

"Some days you're actually pretty smart."

"Meanwhile, there's been a revolution?"

"You mean a farcical comedy."

"I assume you're going to tell me about it, since I can't go back out into the world without knowing the particulars of such an important event."

"You're asking for a lot: upstarts more impudent than the ones they replaced, servile groveling more shameful than the groveling people felt justified in despising before, incoherent opposition to the government by men who used to condemn all opposition to the government, the same mistakes, the same crimes, the same stupidity, just dressed in different clothes! That's all."

"I want to hear the details."

"Well, I might tell you—if the job you still have to finish leaves you time to hear it."

"What job is that?"

"Henriette Buré is here. And your sister, the little girl you saw at Madame Dilois's, is wasting away in poverty."

"We have to save them."

"All right. First we have to get out of here. Follow me…"

And the Devil led the way.

THE SISTER OF CHARITY

Chapter XLVI: A Scene from the Peasant Revolt

They had to get out of that madhouse, and Luizzi followed the Devil. As long as they were walking through that enormous building, all went well: doors and walls opened before Satan to give him free passage, and Luizzi quickly slipped through behind him. But as soon as they got outside he had great trouble keeping up with his infernal guide. The night was utterly black, and a harsh wind drove a steady icy rain into Luizzi's face. The dirt on the road, soaked by the rain, stuck to his shoes so it was as if he were walking in mud overshoes— till the mud sucked off his shoes and left our friend holding one foot in the air while he felt around in the dark with his toes for the other shoe. As for Satan, he strode over that muddy ground as easily as if he's been walking on glowing coals—the usual road-paving material in his empire. He stopped in silence every time the baron stopped and swore like the damned, and he waited patiently till Luizzi had put his shoes back on.

At that point they were on a narrow lane bordered on both sides by high earthen banks topped by impenetrable hedges. Great oaks and ancient elms grew intermittently along those hedges and spread their vast branches out across the narrow lane far enough to span its width and rest against the hedge on the opposite side. Like some aerial cavalry corps riding at a gallop, the wind passed straight through those trees and those hedges, shouting and howling and carrying away clouds of leaves that looked in the night like flocks of birds racing away as fast as their wings would beat. Then suddenly, as if those invisible squadrons had run up against more powerful troops, the wind stopped and broke. They could hear it pulling back and charging again in irregular whining gusts. The torn leaves passed over again in a whirlwind and fell here and there on the damp ground, like a flock of songbirds dispersed and decimated by the scattered pellets of a shotgun blast. Then the loud noises fell silent for a moment, and they could hear the murmur of the rain falling on the trees, and the mournful call of an owl, and the distant crowing of a rooster.

The storm picked up again, crossing and recrossing and battling, striking heavy muffled blows and uttering a piercing whistle: not one of those splendid roiling storms, crisscrossed by brilliant flashes of lightning and speaking majestically out of great claps of thunder, that strike your soul with a holy terror filled with admiration, in which you stand with your head bare to soak in their warm aroma and breathe their electric air; but one of those black storms that grip the body with cold and the heart with sadness, against which you carefully shut your doors and windows so you can huddle next to the glowing hearth or curl up under your bedcovers.

Meanwhile Luizzi was still following the Devil, and he had enough to do to keep up with him not to be able to question him. The further they went, the harder the walking became, and finally in a fit of impatience the baron cried, "We're on the road to hell!"

"The road to hell, master," replied Satan, "is smooth and easy. There's a fine paved way down the middle for people in carriages, and asphalt sidewalks for the pedestrians. It's shaded by flowering green trees. Along the sides of the road there are tall linden trees and lovely inns, with cheerful dance halls and big restaurants and gaming rooms fit for a prince and prostitutes dressed like honest women. You can eat there, drink there, sleep there; you can gamble away your health, your life, your fortune anytime and anywhere. The road to hell is almost as beautiful as the boulevard des Italiens will be someday."

"So then this must be the path of righteousness?" laughed the baron.

"Could be."

"If so, it's hard and disagreeable."

"Are you tired already? And yet you're not one of those badly dressed, badly nourished children who live in this region; you're not an old blind man hunched over his cane; you're not a pale sickly girl; and you're not walking down this road to go to the rescue of some unfortunate stranger. You're a man in the prime of life, and you're doing it to save yourself and regain your fortune and your freedom."

"Fine! But I highly doubt any human beings besides me are out on the road at this hour and in this weather, unless they're bandits, and those gentlemen aren't usually weak children or old blind men or pale sickly girls."

"At the end of this lane, where it intersects several other paths, you'll meet the child, the old man, and the girl. Ask them for shelter for the night."

"On what pretext?"

"You'll tell them you're a traveler who's lost."

"They won't believe me, because it isn't normal for a respectable man to be out on foot in the middle of the night on some remote lane. They'll take me for a bandit."

"So there's nothing in the world between the rich man who rides down the road in his berline with post-horses and the bandit who sneaks through the night on dark paths? Frugality, poverty, misery all face other kinds of stormy weather."

"But if they ask me my name, how will they believe a Baron de Luizzi could come to be out with no carriage in a place like this?"

"If you tell them you're Baron de Luizzi, they'll take you for the madman who's escaped from the place we've just left, because your name must be known in the area around it. Think up a name and a profession, and figure out how to get out of this fix."

"So you're planning to abandon me there?"

"What did I promise you? That I'd give you your freedom, and you're free. Your fortune? In Paris you'll recover your income of two hundred thousand livres: unlike lots of others, your banker took advantage of the July Revolution to recover his footing in business, and Rigot's claim against your assets has been dismissed."

"You also promised you'd restore my good reputation."

"You were acquitted at the court of assize. Everyone testified in your favor, saying you'd been insane for a long time. And since Rigot's lawyer recovered and he's perfectly healthy, they didn't look too closely at the whole thing."

"In other words I'm reentering society as some kind of paroled convict?"

"You're mistaken, master: the crime you committed is one of those society forgives easily."

"Why's that?"

"Because there was no apparent motive. If you'd tried to kill a man to take his money or his wife or his name, you'd be a villain. If you'd attempted murder out of revenge or hatred, you'd be a vile scoundrel. But you wanted to kill him just to kill him; you're a monomaniac, a man suffering from vertigo, for whom science has a stack of incontestible explanations that make you very interesting. The idea is a modern invention, which I owe to the young men's bar association, and which I expect to turn to my advantage. Besides, in the middle of the giant upheaval that's just roiled France, your case went completely unnoticed. Most of the people who know you never heard about it, and by finding a different set of friends you'll be a brand-new man in the circle you join."

"How far away am I from Paris?"

"Eighty leagues."[11]

"What is this place?"

"It's the municipality of Vitré."[12]

"How am I supposed to get to Paris without money?"

"That's not my problem."

"But there must be a way of getting some!"

"There are three: borrowing it, stealing it, or earning it. Your choice. As for me, I've kept my promise. Farewell."

---

[11] About 320 kilometers, or 200 miles.

[12] Vitré is in the Vendée region, which was the center of a bloody pro-royalist counterrevolutionary insurgency in western France between 1793 and 1796. That quasi-guerrilla war is often referred to simply as "the Vendée," but it's also known as the "Peasant Revolt," which gives this chapter its title.

And just as they reached the place where the lane divided into several paths, the Devil vanished, and Luizzi found himself a few steps away from a small group of people who were about to pass by in front of him.

"Who goes there?" cried a loud voice.

"Alas," answered Luizzi, "I'm an unlucky traveler who was waylaid by a gang of bandits. After dragging me into the woods they took my money and my papers, and I got lost trying to find my way back to the main road from Laval to Vitré."

No sooner had Luizzi finished speaking than a boy of about twelve, who'd been circling him and examining him carefully, cried out a little scornfully, "It's a gentleman, grandpa!"

"Watch him closely, Matthieu," replied the old man.

A woman's voice said gently, "And what is it you want, my good man?"

"Shelter for the night, if it's no trouble."

"It's no trouble, sir," said the old man. "We won't get much sleep at our house tonight, and one more or less around the fireplace won't make anyone colder. Come along, sir, and follow us. You must need to get warmed up."

"Grandpa Bruno," said the boy, "we're just two pistol shots from the house. I'll run ahead and tell them it's us, with Sister Angélique and a gentleman. You can't miss it from here—just keep going straight in this direction."

"All right," said the old man, starting down the path to which his grandson had led him. "Let's hurry."

Luizzi was surprised at how easily the blind man had swallowed his story; but he was even more surprised when the old man, asking him questions, spoke of his fictitious adventure as something completely natural. "Was it a big gang that attacked you?"

"A dozen men," said Luizzi, whose vanity wouldn't let him stint on the number of his attackers.

"Did you notice among them a tall thin man with a goatskin on his back and a red bonnet under his hat?"

"That's right. I thought I spotted a tall fellow, dressed more or less the way you describe."

"I knew it. That's Bertrand's gang. Oh, if I hadn't lost my sight, that old scoundrel wouldn't dare hang around these parts like that. He knows I shoot straight—or rather I used to shoot straight."

"But didn't that Bertrand used to be a friend of yours?" asked Sister Angélique, who was walking next to the old man.

"Yes, yes, in the days of the Republic we cried, 'Long live the king!' together. And I'm sure if I hadn't picked him up half dead off the field at Croix Bataille he'd long since have been buried with all the holy priests who died that famous day.[13] But we fought a fair war in those days: we didn't attack remote houses to loot them and guzzle all their wine; we didn't stop travelers out late on the roads to strip them and rob them—because those bandits took everything, didn't they, sir?"

"Everything! Absolutely everything!" answered Luizzi.

"Oh, those cowardly wretches!" said old Bruno.

"But didn't you say they'd fought valiantly just a few hours ago?" asked the nun.[14]

"That's true. And if—instead of making it easy for the Red Pants to retreat by opening the gates to the grounds—we'd wanted to attack their rear, not one of them would've been left alive."

"Is that when the wounded officer took shelter at your house?" she asked.

"He didn't take shelter. He was wounded by the hedge in the courtyard, and just as he'd led the attack he was the last to retreat. That's why his soldiers were already long gone and didn't see him fall, and when the Chouans who were chasing them passed him they must've thought he was dead. More than two hours later, when we went out to inspect around the house, we found him sprawled on the ground, and we took him inside. My son Jacques went to fetch the doctor, and since none of our plowboys had the guts to go find you, I took charge of it. But, since unfortunately I lost my sight six months ago and I couldn't find my way, Matthieu came along."

As they were speaking, old Bruno, Sister Angélique, and Luizzi arrived at a small courtyard enclosed by a wall, whose entrance was blocked by gates like on the private roads in the royal forests. There was a narrow gap on either side of the gates; and when our travelers had passed through, the baron—bothered by two dogs who came up to him to sniff him curiously—could see a long irregular group of single-story buildings. One door was open; the brightly lit interior they would've glimpsed through it was masked by a group of people standing in the doorway.

"Is that you, father?" cried a powerful voice over the intensifying wind and rain.

"It's me, Jacques," said the old man.

---

[13] Croix-Bataille was the site of a battle during the first War in the Vendée. The Catholic clergy were strongly represented on the side fighting against the atheistic Revolution.

[14] In 1832 supporters of the recently deposed Charles X and his heir, the so-called Henri V, tried unsuccessfully to rally a short-lived second War in the Vendée to reverse the July Revolution. The "Red Pants" (*Culottes Rouges*) were the troops of the new king, Louis Philippe. The peasant rebels were known as the Chouans, just as they'd been in the 1790s. The shared counterrevolutionary Legitimist cause created a sense of continuity between 1793 and 1832, as if it were a single ongoing guerrilla insurgency, the Chouannerie.

The people in the doorway withdrew and left it open for them. The old man led the way in, taking off the goatskin coat he wore, and his grandson hung it from a nail inside the chimney, where several others were already drying. The man who'd spoken was sitting by the fire with his feet up on the grate, his elbow on his knee, and his chin resting on his hand. He watched carefully while little Matthieu led his grandfather to a seat by the fire. Then he turned slightly toward the Sister of Charity, whose long black mantle a servant had taken; pointing toward a door, he said, "The wife is in there with the sick man. Step in there for a little bit. You'll see the prescription the doctor left and that he said to show you. If there's nothing urgent, come back and dry off a little, for it's sad weather out."

The nun went into the room he'd pointed out. The master of the house, turning to the baron, went on, "Have a seat, sir, and warm yourself. So they didn't even leave you a coat to cover you?" he added, seeing the water running off Luizzi's clothes. "You can't stay like that, it's enough to make a frog catch cold. Wife!" he cried. "Bring the clothes and the suits from the wounded man's room, and we'll give the gentleman a little time to undress and dress... I apologize, sir! We only have these two rooms, and we do the best we can."

Luizzi was about to thank him, when the peasant cried out angrily, "Who left that door open? You want someone to shoot us right here by the fire? Close it and lock it."

"That was me, father," said little Matthieu. "But Lion and Beauty are in the yard, and they won't let any strangers get near the house."

"All right," said Jacques, softening. Then he added in a mutter, "It's not the ones the dogs don't recognize I'm worried about, it's the ones who come here all the time as friends."

"You're right," said the old blind man, who'd set his feet on top of his wooden clogs as if they were a stool, the better to expose them to the warmth of the fire. "You're right. Given what the gentleman told me, it was Bertrand's gang that attacked him."

"You know this Bertrand?" asked Jacques.

"No," replied Luizzi, "but based on the description your father gave me: a tall man..."

"There's more than one Chouan as tall as Bertrand, and if you didn't get a good look at him..."

"It was already night when they stopped my carriage."

"Your carriage!" said Jacques in surprise. "Whereabouts was that?"

"Well, on the main road from Vitré to Laval," said Luizzi, already sorry he'd mentioned the word carriage.

"And you were coming from?"

"From Vitré," said Luizzi, more and more embarrassed.

"What happened to the horses and the postilion who was driving you?"

"I must admit, I have no idea."

"Bonfils," said the master of the house to a plowboy who was fixing a pitchfork in a corner of the large room, "go to the relay stop and find out what happened to the carriage that got waylaid. How long ago was that?"

"Two hours," said Luizzi impulsively.

"Two hours!" echoed Jacques. "That's odd." He gave Luizzi a suspicious look.

But just then Jacques's wife, Marianne, appeared, saying, "Everything's ready for the gentleman in the other room."

Jacques motioned to the baron to go ahead, and followed him closely with his eyes.

As Luizzi was about to go through the door he met the nun coming out, and saw her face for the first time. The woman's features struck him as if they were those of someone he'd met before; and it seemed to him that his face had the same effect on her, because she stopped suddenly and gave a quiet exclamation. But they passed each other in the doorway without anyone else noticing what had happened.

Luizzi found himself in a much smaller room than the first one. One corner was filled by a large four-poster bed with curtains of green serge that were completely closed, so the light from a small standing lamp wouldn't bother the sick man. On a chair Luizzi saw the clothes meant for him. As he dressed he tried to recall where and when he'd met Sister Angélique before; but the memory, which at first had been so vivid, blurred in his mind, and he decided he'd been struck by her resemblance to someone else he knew.

Meanwhile he took advantage of this first moment alone to think over his situation. He realized that, thanks to his recklessness, his position had become quite suspect, and his usual habit of referring to his servants and his carriage had made his alleged adventure fairly hard to explain. Certainly a carriage wouldn't vanish without a trace; and he was pondering how to get out of that fix when it occurred to him that maybe he could confide his name to the wounded officer and put himself under his protection.

"If he's a young man," thought Luizzi, "it'll be easy to persuade him I was locked up in a madhouse for no reason, and he'll help me get back to Paris." To confirm his hopes, he opened the bed curtains a little; but he couldn't make out the face of the man hidden in the shadows cast by the curtains, and he was about to pick up the lamp to see him better—when he noticed Jacques standing in the open doorway.

"You're rather inquisitive, sir!" said the peasant.

Taken by surprise, Luizzi tried to play it off with a witticism; and with ill-considered facetiousness he replied, "Some friends of mine are serving in the regiment that's garrisoned in this region. I was afraid it might be one of them who was wounded, and I wanted to check."

"All you had to do was ask us his name."

"You know it?"

"Yes."

"So what's his name?"

"First tell me your friends' names."

The baron threw out a few names at random, and the peasant said curtly, "That's not him." Then he added roughly, "Supper's waiting for you."

Luizzi accepted the invitation and went back to the larger room. In his absence the long table in the middle of the room had been laid: a chair for the master of the house stood at one end, and the rest of the company sat along the sides on wooden benches. Besides the people already mentioned, there were two women servants and three farm hands. The entire meal, consisting of a plate of cabbage and buckwheat biscuits, had already been served out. When Luizzi reached the place assigned to him, between old Bruno and his daughter-in-law and across from the nun, they all murmured a *Benedicite* to themselves and sat down. Luizzi alone hadn't taken part in the moment of blessing, and they all noticed it with displeasure. Small jugs of cider stood here and there along the table, from which they all took as much as they wanted. Only Jacques had a bottle of wine next to him; but he took none, and merely poured glasses for his father and for Sister Angélique, who declined.

"Drink, drink," he said to her, "it'll strengthen you for a sleepless night."

"I'm used to keeping vigil, and I'm not used to wine," the nun replied. "But I think you'd do better to offer some to the gentleman, who probably doesn't like cider."

Her advice seemed to displease Jacques; but he didn't show it openly, and he passed the bottle to Luizzi, who also declined, saying he was neither thirsty nor hungry. Then he added, "I asked you for shelter for a few hours, and as soon as it's daylight I'll rid you of an unwanted guest."

"As you wish. But I should warn you, we have no bed to offer you."

"I didn't expect one. And while I'm waiting for morning I'll talk with Sister Angélique, if she'll permit me."

She nodded her agreement and lowered her eyes, which since the beginning of supper had been fixed on Luizzi. He'd been examining her no less carefully; and though he couldn't say where he'd seen her fresh lovely face before, he was forced to acknowledge that it awoke faint memories in him.

Meanwhile supper had come to an end. The complete silence that reigned around the table allowed them all to hear the power of the storm rattling the doors and shutters. They all seemed preoccupied and tongue-tied, till Sister Angélique said to Jacques, "The doctor's orders say the compresses for treating the patient should be soaked in the coldest water possible, to reduce the inflamation. If I could have water from the well, that'd be ideal."

"Jean," said the peasant, "go draw a bucket of water."

The farmhand went out; and Luizzi noticed that the plowboy Jacques had sent to the relay stop for news was no longer in the house. He was anticipating some new predicament, when Jacques, rising, said in a bad-tempered voice,

"Come! One last drink, to the wounded man's recovery, and then let those who have to sleep tonight go to bed!"

They'd all filled their glasses and were getting ready to end the meal by responding to Jacques's toast, when a man appeared in the doorway, which the farmhand had left open, and said jokingly, "I hope you're not going to drink without me!"

No sooner had he spoken than the whole company rose, and the old blind man grabbed a knife off the table and cried, "Bertrand! It's that villain Bertrand!"

Jacques stopped his father, while the other guests around the table seemed to be standing there petrified by intense fear. Marianne, Jacques's wife, had thrown herself in front of her husband, but he gently moved her aside and said coldly to the newcomer, "If you're thirsty, there's cider here for you."

"And some wine too, if I'm not mistaken," said Bertrand, stepping forward to take the bottle. He was a tall man, with long red hair, and a few locks of white, falling to his shoulders. He wore the goatskin coat typical of peasants in the lower Maine region and in Bretagne. He was armed with a double-barreled shotgun of some value and a highly ornamented hunting knife.

They all looked at each other, waiting with painful anxiety for what would happen, till Jacques, setting his hand on the bottle Bertrand was about to pick up, said firmly, "You can have what I'm offering, but you can't have what you want to take."

"As you wish," said Bertrand, unbothered by that refusal. He picked up a jug of cider and drained it in one draft. No sooner had he finished than there was a loud noise at the door.

"What is it?" asked Jacques.

"It's me," said Jean from outside.

"It's the cold water for the wounded man," said Sister Angélique. "Let the boy in."

"Ah!" said Bertrand gravely, "so that officer is here? Let the boy in, and guard the door carefully."

The farmhand came in and set his bucket of water down in the corner.

"Close the door," said his master.

The boy hesitated.

"Leave the door open," said Bertrand. "My men will at least be able to see the fire in the hearth, and that'll cheer them up."

Two men stepped into the doorway and flanked it, half in and half out of the house, with their guns in their hands.

"Is everyone in position?" asked Bertrand.

"Yes," replied one of the sentinels.

"Good," said the leader of the Chouans, going to the door and glancing outside the house.

Jacques's eye followed his movements attentively, and Marianne in turn anxiously watched her husband's slightest gestures. "And now," said Jacques, "are you going to tell me what you want?"

Bertrand sat down by the fire. Jacques motioned for his wife, his son, and his servants to go wait at the far end of the room; then he took a seat on the other side of the hearth, next to his father. Sister Angélique and Luizzi stepped forward between the Chouan and the master of the house, as if to position themselves as neutral intermediaries in the matter about to be discussed. Bertrand, with his head lowered, toyed awkwardly with the strap of his gun and seemed unable to speak. They could hear the storm beating down on the house from all sides.

"I'm waiting," said Jacques after a short silence.

"Did you give shelter to a wounded infantry officer?" asked Bertrand abruptly, as if he were relieved at finally being prompted.

"Yes."

"You have to turn that officer over to us."

"He's dying!" cried the nun. "And that would kill him."

"And even if he were as healthy as I am, I wouldn't give him up to you," added Jacques scornfully.

"Listen, Jacques," said Bertrand, "I came here as a friend, and I'm asking you nicely for what I could take by force."

"True," said Jacques. "You could have us all killed right here, me, my father, my wife, my children. You can murder us all if that's your good pleasure. You can..."

"You know perfectly well I won't do that, Jacques," replied the Chouan impatiently, "even though you refused to take up arms for the righteous cause."

"You'll have to do it," said Jacques, "because I'm not going to hand over the officer, and if you want to have him you'll have to step over my dead body to get to him."

"You've certainly changed, and you must like the new regime a lot," said Bertrand coldly, "for you to risk your life like that for a man you don't even know."

"I'm risking my life because that officer, whoever he is, is in my house, and I don't want anyone touching that man, any more than my wife, any more than my father..." Jacques's own thoughts suddenly seemed to make him grow angry. "I don't want anyone touching him, any more than a straw from my roof or a nail from my walls."

"Hey! No one's going to touch a nail or a straw of yours," said Bertrand. "But that officer is a stranger, and it can't matter much to you to hand him over. Besides, listen! This morning Georges was arrested by the police, and he's being taken to the prison at Angers. We need someone who'll answer for Georges's life. If you'll hand over that man..."

"You should've picked him up this morning," said Jacques, "when he was dying on the ground outside."

"You should've left him there, so we could've found him," replied Bertrand.

"You would've found him dead," said Sister Angélique.

"Possibly," said the Chouan. "In which case there'd have been one fewer of them. But since he's alive, he has to be of some use to us. We can exchange him for Georges. Come on, where is he?"

Bertrand stood up and headed toward the wounded man's room. Sister Angélique threw herself in front of the door. "Don't go in! The slightest commotion could kill him!" she cried in a tone of supplication.

"Bertrand!" cried the old blind man in a loud voice. "You asked me some time ago why my son didn't take up arms and why I didn't advise him to do so. It's because I didn't want him mixed up in a war with murderers and thieves."

"Are you saying this for my benefit?" asked Bertrand.

"Yes, for your benefit," said old Bruno, advancing toward him.

"I'll give you an answer in a little while," said Bertrand. "But first I have to see that officer. I beg your pardon, Sister," he added. "Don't make me use force. I'm going to get in, because I mean to get in."

"Just you dare try!" cried the nun, setting her back against the door and raising toward Bertrand the crucifix hanging from her rosary.

Bertrand took off his hat and crossed himself. He looked all around in annoyance, but he didn't dare lift his eyes to the girl; and he went back to his seat, grumbling like a mastiff looking for something to bite.

"Are you going to be done with all this nonsense soon?" asked Jacques.

"Right away, if you like!" cried Bertrand loudly, suddenly standing up and aiming his shotgun at Jacques.

But while the Chouan was moving toward the wounded man's door again, little Matthieu slipped behind his father and handed him his own gun, which had been hidden in a corner of the room. In an instant Jacques had his gun leveled in turn at his enemy, while the boy, rushing at Bertrand, pushed down the barrel of his gun. It all happened in a flash, and Jacques cried in a loud voice, "If anyone moves or takes one step into this room, Bertrand drops dead!"

There was a terrible moment of silence, during which they could hear the muffled gusts of wind and the rain lashing the flagstone threshold. Then a shot was fired, and Jacques's gun dropped from his shoulder, which had been shattered by a bullet. It was one of Bertrand's men hiding in the darkness in the courtyard who'd slipped the barrel of his gun between the two sentinels and easily taken aim at the peasant.

"Who fired?" cried old Bruno.

"A Chouan," said Jacques. And then Marianne's and little Matthieu's cries let the old blind man know it was his son who'd been hit.

What followed was a scene of indescribable chaos and peculiar terror. The blind man, armed with a big knife and crying, "Bertrand! Bertrand!" rushed at the spot where he thought the leader of the Chouans was standing. But he stepped aside, and Bruno began running around the room with his knife raised, shouting furiously, "Bertrand! Bertrand! Where are you? Killer! Murderer! Where are you? Oh, you want to try it again?" He ran back and forth across the large room that way, bumping into the furniture, waving his knife, and still shouting, "Bertrand, where are you?" while everybody who stood in his path moved aside in fear, telling him who they were. Finally he ran into his own son and grabbed him by the arm, saying hoarsely and furiously, "Who are you?"

"It's me, father. Calm down, you're going to kill us all."

"Did they hurt you?"

"They broke my arm! It's the one you're holding—you're hurting me."

Bruno dropped his son's arm and backed away with a cry, and the knife fell from his hands.

Bertrand kicked away the knife and said calmly, "You asked for it, Jacques."

"Murderer! Thief!" cried the old blind man.

"Neither one nor the other," said Bertrand. "But I want what I want, and I feel like you should know that. If Jacques hadn't picked up his gun, nothing would've happened to him. He wanted to have his say, and we answered him."

"Your time will come," said Bruno.

"When it's God's will."

"You dare invoke him after a crime like that?" said Sister Angélique.

"Yes, Sister," replied Bertrand. "I'm not like some of those among us: I don't do harm for the sake of doing harm, and I don't kill the people who attack me."

"But you rob the people you don't kill," said old Bruno, to whom robbery seemed if possible even worse than murder, because it lacked the political justification the Chouans gave their revolt.

"That reminds me," said Bertrand, pointing out Luizzi. "I assume this is the traveler who says he was waylaid. Well, I swear if it was any of our men who did it, they'll be severely punished, and this stranger won't be able to say we're just a bunch of highwaymen."

Meantime Marianne and the nun had cut away Jacques's vest and exposed his wound. While they were washing it, Bertrand returned to his seat. For lack of tending, the fire had almost gone out; and the lamp, whose flame was blown about by the wind that rushed into the room, threw a sad and dying light on that scene of desolation.

Bertrand spoke again, addressing Luizzi. "Whereabouts were you stopped?"

"I can't say exactly," said the baron, whose courage had fled in the face of all these new and unfamiliar dangers.

"Well, at least, how far were you from Vitré?" pursued the Chouan.

"I was asleep in my carriage, and I really don't know..."

"Don't shake like that. We've got no quarrel with you. Nobody here means you any harm. Tell me: what did they take?"

"Well," stammered the baron, "my papers, my money..."

"What were the papers?... How much money did you have?..."

"There was my passport... some letters."

"And how much money?"

"How much money... I don't know."

"What! You don't know?"

"About two thousand francs."

"In gold or in silver?"

"In gold," said Luizzi, answering quickly to hide his distress.

"And what carriage were you riding in?"

"A post chaise."

"There are lots of different kinds," said Bertrand, examining the baron with a look that added mightily to his distress.

"It was... It was... a caleche."

"Ah!... And I assume you had luggage, trunks?"

"Yes, yes."

"And what was in those trunks?"

"Well..." said Luizzi impatiently, "what people put in trunks... clothes, suits..."

"I just want everything to be returned perfectly to you, besides weapons, if you had any."

Since that wasn't a question, Luizzi was spared having to answer.

Bertrand went on, "And what's your name?"

"My name... I can't... I can't tell you..."

"We'll see it on your passport, if you really have a passport that can be seen."

"It seems to me," replied the baron, who'd finally understood into what trouble he'd put himself by his lies and hesitations, "it seems to me it can't matter much to you who I am. I'm not asking for my carriage or my money back; just let me go, that's all I want from you."

"Yes, indeed!" said the Chouan. "I can believe that. And I even think you don't have much reason to miss the money and the carriage you lost."

As he spoke, the plowboy Jacques had sent to the relay stop came running in.

"Well, Bonfils!" said Bertrand. "Did you accomplish your master's errand?"

The boy stopped, saw Jacques was wounded, and lowered his head.

"Will you answer, fool?" said Bertrand angrily. "I heard the story this man told old Bruno at the crossroads, and I know where they sent you, so talk: what did you find out?"

"Oh, hell," said Bonfils. "I'll tell you. There hasn't been a post chaise through Vitré for two days."

"I suspected as much," said Bertrand. "Hey, you there, men! Grab this rascal, string him up like a calf by all four feet, and toss him to the bottom of the big pond."

"Me?" cried Luizzi, backing away from the four or five armed peasants who'd come in together. "Why me?"

"Because that's what we do with spies."

"But I'm not a spy, I'm a stranger in these parts!"

"So who are you exactly?"

"I'm... I'm Baron de Luizzi."

"Baron de Luizzi!" echoed a woman's voice. Sister Angélique immediately stepped forward. Looking into his face, she said, "You're Baron de Luizzi?"

"Yes, Armand de Luizzi."

"Yes," she said, examining him. "Yes, it's true..."

"Who are you, Sister, since you seem to know me? Might you have paid a visit occasionally to the place I've just come from?"

"I don't know where you've come from," she replied. "But as for me... I'm... But perhaps you've forgotten me, since it's been ten years... I need to speak to you, Armand, though I've found you too late..."

While the baron, saved by that unexpected intervention, tried to put a name to this woman's face, which had made such a strong impression on him, Bertrand came forward and said to Sister Angélique, "So you know this man?"

"Yes."

"You're positive?"

"Yes."

"Then he can stay here. As for the rest of us," he added, raising his voice, "let's be off, because it's almost daylight."

"And the officer? What about the officer?" cried the Chouans standing by the door.

"Is the stretcher ready? Go get him, and don't hurt him."

Old Bruno rose from his chair. "You win today, Bertrand, but my turn will come."

"Be quiet," replied the Chouan. "Don't give them the idea to burn down your house and loot your barn. I did everything I could to save you from disaster."

Jacques, with his wife and his servants around him, said nothing. And while they all stayed at the far end of the room, Luizzi and the nun stood aside to make room for the stretcher carrying the wounded officer.

As the stretcher passed in front of Sister Angélique she looked at the wounded officer. Drawing back in horror, she cried, "Henri!..."

He turned, raised his head slightly, and cried out. Then he fell back, murmuring dully, "Caroline!... Caroline!"

The stretcher bearers had stopped. But at a gesture from Bertrand they moved on, while the Sister of Charity hid in Luizzi's arms and cried, "Oh, my brother! My brother!"

Chapter XLVII: A Convent Intrigue

"Caroline? Caroline?" said Luizzi in surprise, as if the name of the young woman before him evoked in his mind only a memory as vague as the one prompted by her face. "Caroline! Caroline!" he repeated, without attaching any more intimate sense to the word "brother" than he meant when he'd called the nun "Sister."

"What!" said the young woman sadly. "You don't remember anymore?" She stopped and glanced around her.

Jacques, noticing her look, hastened to say, "If you need to speak privately with this gentleman, Sister, go into the other room. You can be alone there, and I hope no one'll disturb you there now."

She thanked Jacques with an affection gesture, and led the way into the other room, murmuring quietly, "My God! My God! How strange!"

Luizzi followed her and closed the door. Then he approached her and said, "Caroline! Caroline! Yes, I know that name. But so much has happened to me since I last heard it..."

The nun moved aside the edges of the white wimple that hid her face, and went on, "Look at me, Armand, and look carefully. Don't you see anything familiar about my face?"

"Yes," said Luizzi, examining her beautiful saintly features. "But the memory it evokes is very odd, as if it's doubled. I feel like I knew you much younger, and at the same time much older."

"And you're right, Armand: you're remembering both the child you saw in Toulouse and the grown woman, the noble unfortunate sister who took the place of a mother to me, and whom I'm said to resemble so much."

"Oh, Caroline! My sister!"[15] cried Luizzi. "Caroline! Poor child! And this is how I was fated to find you again?"

"Alas," she went on, "ever since Sophie—Madame Dilois, you remember?—was forced to leave Toulouse..."

"By my own fault."

"Oh, how I've suffered since then, Armand!"

"And now that she's dead..."

"Dead!" exclaimed the nun.

"Yes, dead, under the name Laura de Farkley, and again by my fault. Because I've been fatal to all those I've loved or who've come close to me."

---

[15] As the Devil explained in Chapter XXII, Caroline Dilois is the illegitimate daughter of Madame de Crancé by Baron Hughes de Luizzi, Armand's father; she is therefore Armand's half-sister.

"My God! How is that possible?" she cried.

"I can't... I mustn't tell you... But you, Caroline—what's become of you for the last ten years? What has your life been like?"

"The sad, painful life of a poor child with no family."

"You have to tell me about your misfortunes, Caroline. I have to mend them..."

"I owe you that story, brother, and I'll tell it to you. I'll tell you everything. May God forgive me, and you too, for speaking still, as I wear this saintly habit, of sins that caused me such terrible punishment, of feelings that penitence couldn't extinguish, and that no doubt the Lord keeps alive in me so they can serve as my eternal torture!"

"Speak, Caroline, speak. I'll make allowances. Destiny, which has cursed everyone in our family, has weighed on you as it has on me, I fear. But you had neither wealth nor title nor anyone to protect you, and I can only pity you."

Luizzi brought his sister a chair and sat next to her, already saddened by the thought that he was about to hear the story of a guilty or ruined life. The girl paused for a moment to compose herself, then began like this:

"You know in what way Sophie was forced to leave Toulouse. Still, in her despair she didn't forget the poor child she'd adopted. She left a sum of sixty thousand francs in my name with Monsieur Barnet, her lawyer and yours too, I believe. According to Sophie's wishes, those funds will be turned over to me at my majority. Part of the income paid for my maintenance and my education, and part Monsieur Barnet reinvested and added to the capital. A few days ago I got a letter from that worthy man to tell me my fortune has now grown to almost eighty thousand francs, and that it's a substantial enough dowry for me to make a respectable match, if I choose to return to the world—because I haven't yet taken my vows."

"And I hope you'll never take them."

"I'll take them soon, brother. I know the world, and I know all it contains in the way of duplicity."

"Where have you lived, poor sister, to have formed such a bad opinion?"

"From the day Sophie left Toulouse to the hour at which I'm speaking to you, I've lived at the convent."

"And you claim to know the world?"

"Enough not to want to know it any better," replied Caroline with a deep sigh, and she let a few tears drop from the beautiful blue eyes she lifted toward heaven.

"By placing you in a convent, did Monsieur Barnet think he was carrying out poor Sophie's wishes?"

"The worthy lawyer acted for the best. Perhaps you remember Madame Barnet, and how harsh and bad-tempered she was? After two weeks in her house, I considered it a blessing when my guardian suggested putting me in a convent of the Sisters of Charity. One reason seemed to settle the question for

Monsieur Barnet, but he never explained it to me, though I never forgot his strange words on the subject: 'You're the daughter of a Luizzi,' he said, 'though you don't have the right to bear that name. The world has been the fatal ruin of every member of that family; some implacable doom seems to pursue them. Enter a convent, child, and may God give you the desire to stay there till he calls you to him! May you find shelter there from the fate that has struck down all those of your blood!'"

Caroline stopped, and Luizzi grew thoughtful. "That's what Barnet told you?" he asked after a brief silence.

"That's what he said, brother. And perhaps you can explain the doom he warned me of."

"I might know of it, but I can't explain it to you—it's forbidden. In any case, it must be both terrible and powerful, since it managed to reach you even in a house of God, and it made you guilty and miserable. But go on, sister, I'm listening."

"I was eleven when I joined the Sisters as a boarder. I lived a happy, carefree life till I was sixteen—a little spoiled by the goodness of the nuns, if my companions were to be believed. They said the nuns wanted me to take my vows so the convent could acquire my modest fortune, which seemed large in the eyes of women who'd taken a vow of poverty."

"That's not impossible."

"Don't believe that, Armand," said Caroline with a look of ingenuous faith. "No one ever said a word to me about my fortune. No one ever said anything to give me reason to think the little I possessed could be coveted by the Sisters."

Luizzi thought that might just be proof of their great skill. But he kept his reflections to himself, as much not to interrupt the girl's story as to spare her having her illusions shattered about the people among whom she seemed to have decided to live out her life.

Caroline went on:

My difficulties began when I'd turned sixteen. Till that age I'd lived with the young boarders who'd entered the convent like me. We'd grown up together: all of us the same age, all with similar tastes, all enjoying and seeking out the same pleasures, all devoted to the same interests, all sharing the same studies and the same work. Only one sorrow occasionally troubled my sweet carefree existence: on certain days my companions left the convent to spend time with their families, and they exchanged invitations to visit each others' families; and when they returned to the convent they shared reports on the fun they'd had. I never got an invitation like that, and I often asked the Mother Superior why not. She told me the other young ladies' families couldn't invite me because they didn't know me; then she dried my tears by giving me some trinket I wanted very much, or an exemption from work, and I was consoled for having neither family nor friends.

Once, when I was going to spend a few days in the country with Monsieur Barnet, I asked one of my good friends to come see me there; she agreed, but she didn't keep her promise. I reproached her for it when we got back to the convent, but she just answered, "Mother wouldn't let me." Humiliated, I ran to the Mother Superior; she tried to persuade me that, knowing that at Monsieur Barnet's I wasn't with my own family, my friend's mother had found my invitation inadequate. For the first time that explanation didn't satisfy me; for the first time the idea of my isolation in the world became clear to me, and provoked in me a sadness that the attentions of the nuns managed to dissipate at first, but that my new isolation at the convent soon brought vividly back to me.

One by one, day after day, all the companions with whom I'd spent my childhood left the convent to return to their families. Others took their places, but they weren't my age. I remained a child as long as I could so I wouldn't be lonely, but the other girls weren't growing up alongside me. As soon as the other boarders turned fifteen or sixteen they went home to their families, and at nineteen I was as alone as an old man who's lived too long and who's seen all his friends fall around him. As young as I still was, my childhood memories were mine alone, and I had no one to whom I could say the sweet words, "Do you remember...?"

That's when I asked for and was granted the favor of wearing the novice's habit. And that's also when Juliette entered the convent.

"Who's this Juliette?" asked Luizzi.

"Juliette was my only friend in the whole world, after Sophie," replied Caroline.

"Was she from Toulouse?"

"I don't know..."

Her mother, Madame Gelis, was a poor widow who kept a notions shop in Auterive and rented out books. But the income from her business was so small that, with no hope of saving up a decent dowry for her daughter, she planned for her to become a nun—for Madame Gelis and her daughter were women of good birth, and Juliette preferred the poverty of the cloister to a position in the world dependent on people whose coarse breeding might've shamed her. And yet it seemed as if that decision had cost her, because when she entered the convent she was sad and pale; and she seemed so miserable that I soon took a great interest in her. I was hoping for a friend.

There were certainly a few other novices my age. But I have to say, the ones going into the care of the sick were mostly ignorant, coarse, lower-class country girls; and those going into teaching the boarders already put on such pompous, crabby airs that I had no one with whom to share my careless laughter when I was happy, nor in whom to confide my tears when I was sad.

Juliette was the friend I wanted. She was only two years older than me, though when she arrived her pallor and her thinness made her seem older. At first I didn't like her—or rather I was afraid of her. She had small eyes, but her glance was so piercing it seemed to penetrate to the conscience of anyone she looked at. Her strawberry blonde hair gave her an extraordinary appearance. She was tall and slender, and she moved so slowly and so languidly that her entire life seemed to be concentrated in the fire of her eyes, the way all her elegance and energy were contained in her smile, which was full of fondness or sarcasm, depending on her mood—a mood I found strange at first.

The first few days we knew each other at the convent we were fairly cool toward one another. But soon we got along better, and when I'd heard her story and she'd heard mine, we swore true and eternal friendship. That friendship was a sweet hope for me and a consolation for her. I became as cheerful and confident as I'd been before, and she fully recovered her health. I liked her all the more because she was treated harshly by the Mother Superior and the older nuns—no doubt because she was poor—and I was often able to soften their severity toward her. Juliette was grateful; and whether I forgot some duty of my noviciate, or whether I broke the rules of the convent in some way, she carefully hid my mistakes, and thus spared me either painful punishment or the even more painful annoyance of having to go confess and ask the Mother Superior for forgiveness.

Ours was an innocent, genuine friendship; I had nothing I didn't share with her, I had no desire she didn't support eagerly. And yet a day came when I wondered whether she liked me as much as she said. She'd received a letter from her mother, and all day I could see she was in tears. I asked her why she was crying, but in vain: she stubbornly refused to tell me. That evening, as we were walking together in the garden, I begged her so insistently that she finally said, "Why do you want to hear about a misfortune neither you nor I can prevent? Because it's my poor mother who's been affected."

"What's wrong?"

"You wouldn't understand, because you've never lived outside this convent. My mother has been cheated by some merchant, and she's being held responsible in his place."

"Is this about a bill of exchange?"

Juliette looked at me in such surprise that I couldn't help laughing in spite of her sorrow. "Who taught you that term?" she asked.

"Have you forgotten that before I came here I lived at Monsieur Dilois's, and though I was just a child I already had my spot in the accounting office of the business my adoptive mother ran?"

"Yes, yes," said Luizzi, interrupting Caroline's story. "I can remember that sweet child seated at a big desk and impishly writing out the invoices Charles dictated to her."

67

"Poor Charles!" said Caroline. "He's dead too."

"Yes, yes, he is. My poor brother!" he replied,[16] overwhelmed by the painful memory, which—like all those he was summoning—evoked a calamity of his own making. But, as if to chase them away, he quickly added, "Go on, Caroline, go on."

She continued:

It was indeed a bill of exchange, which Madame Gelis couldn't settle, and for payment of which she was threatened with the seizure and sale of her business inventory. I believe the total came to about twelve hundred francs.

"What!" I cried. "And you didn't tell me? I can give it to you!"

"I'm not asking for charity, nor is my mother," said Juliette with a pride that wounded me, but that I quickly forgave.

"If you don't want me to give it to you, I can lend it to you."

"Oh, we'd be so grateful!" she cried. Then she stopped and reconsidered. "On the other hand, no… If that became known in the convent, God knows what people would say! They'd claim I pleaded for it, I begged you for it, I took unfair advantage of our friendship… No, no."

"And just because you're afraid of gossip, you refuse to help your mother?"

"My poor mother! My dear mother!" cried Juliette, bursting into tears. "How can it be that I have nothing, nothing set aside, not even a piece of jewelry, nothing I can send her!"

"But I have money."

"No. The Mother Superior would punish me severely for accepting that favor. She'd say I extorted it."

"She won't hear anything about it."

"That's impossible."

"I guarantee it."

"But how will you manage it?"

"That's up to me—as long as you accept."

For a long time Juliette hesitated. But eventually my pleas, and especially my promise that the Mother Superior would never know about it, overcame her pride and she agreed. I wrote right away to Monsieur Barnet, asking him to come see me.

My letter was so urgent he came immediately. As soon as we were alone in the parlor I said, "Monsieur Barnet, I need twelve hundred francs."

"Well, good God, what for?" he cried in astonishment.

"I need twelve hundred francs," I repeated. "My fortune is in your keeping, and I'm asking for that amount."

---

[16] Again, in Chapter XXII the Devil reveals that Charles was the illegitimate son of Hughes de Luizzi, and therefore Armand's half brother.

"I still need to know what it's for. Because if the Mother Superior has prompted you to make this request, I'm not going to be a party to that kind of extortion."

"On the contrary, the Mother Superior can't ever hear about this."

"Well, that's even more serious, and I certainly won't give you a sum like that without knowing what this is about."

"It's about saving a poor woman someone's trying to ruin." And I told him the story of Juliette's mother's predicament.

Monsieur Barnet thought for a long time before answering. "It's possible... I'm even willing to believe it's true, because you can't always think the worst about other people. Besides, child, this is the first time you've asked me for money, and it's for a good cause. It might bring you luck; it might even ward off the evil destiny that pursues you... I don't want to refuse you. I'll bring you the twelve hundred francs."

"Not here! And so you can be sure I'm not deceiving you, send the money directly to Madame Gelis, in Auterive."

"Caroline," said Monsieur Barnet affectionately, "not for a moment did I think you were deceiving me. I thought maybe someone was deceiving you."

"Oh, Monsieur Barnet!"

"But I don't think so anymore... I'll send the money tonight, and you'll be satisfied with me."

I thanked the worthy man as much as if I were the one he was saving, and I hurried to give Juliette the good news.

Her reply displayed perfectly the delicacy and pride of her spirit. "It makes you so happy," she said, hiding her tears, "to be able to help those you love."

I comforted her as much as I could for the favor she'd been forced to accept out of poverty, and we became closer than ever.

"Whatever it is you've done, Caroline," interrupted Luizzi, "that one action will counterbalance plenty of sins. A good deed is a fine way to start out in life."

"Alas, that good deed has been the root of all my misfortunes. The good deed Monsieur Barnet hoped might... That good deed doomed me."

"What! Always, everywhere, evil is the price or the consequence of good!" thought Luizzi... "But tell me, Caroline, how could that action have been the cause of your misfortunes?"

"Here's how..."

What I've just told you about happened in August. Toward the end of September Madame Gelis came to Toulouse and visited us in the convent. The way that worthy, unfortunate woman thanked me left me embarrassed. Her gratitude to the person who'd saved her honor and her life knew no bounds; and in her enthusiasm she said, "I'd resolved to die."

"And I wouldn't have outlived you, mother," cried Juliette, falling into Madame Gelis's arms.

The sight of their mutual affection gave me pain: I realized more than ever how alone I was in this world. It seemed to me I'd rather have been my unlucky impoverished friend, who at least had a mother, than be the lucky girl whose wealth had saved her.

Still, among the many testimonials of Madame Gelis's gratitude, she offered me one that gave me particular pleasure. "I've come to take my daughter away for a few days," she said. "Please agree to come back with her to the home I owe to your good deed. Come—you'll be welcomed like a rescuing angel. Don't say no; it would shame me, it would reproach me for the good you did me, by making me think it embarrasses you."

"And I don't want to do that, ma'am. I accept happily, as long as the Mother Superior gives me permission to go with you."

"All you have to do is ask her."

I ran to the Mother Superior, who at first refused me with a coldness I'd never seen from her. Her severity angered me, and I couldn't stop myself from saying that wasn't the way to make me tolerate life in a convent. She reacted so badly that I saw I'd been wrong to let myself get carried away.

Surprised by my own earlier boldness, I changed my tone and begged her to grant me my wish as a favor to me. "Alas, this is first time I, a poor orphan, have found someone willing to receive me, someone who doesn't spurn me— and you're denying me the first consolation that could help me forget I've been abandoned!"

My tears seemed to move the Mother Superior more than I expected, given the way she'd received me, and in the end she replied, "Go ahead, Angélique." (That was the name I'd taken when I entered the noviciate.) "Go ahead. I could've hoped for you to spent this week somewhere other than with Madame Gelis; but since you wish it so passionately I'll allow it. I want to show you that here you'll always find forgiveness for your mistakes and a willingness to satisfy your desires."

"That's a kindness," thought Luizzi, "that can only be explained by my sister's sixty thousand francs." But he kept his reflections to himself, so as not to interrupt Caroline's story.

She went on:

The next morning we set off for Auterive in an open carriage Madame Gelis had hired for the short trip. I can't even tell you, Armand, what sweet, vivid emotions I felt during that journey. You'd understand if you knew what it was like to have lived for years behind the walls of a convent, in a place where you know every hallway and every room by heart, where things are so continually the same that a stone working its way out of a wall or a broken flagstone in a corridor is a major event and the topic of conversation. You'd understand, brother, if you knew how sad it is to go for a stroll in a garden bounded by a wall within which you know every tree, along every pathway of which you've walked a thousand times, past flowers you've counted one by one, and into which you only go with any curiosity the morning after a storm, to see if there are branches broken or plants uprooted—some damage to mend that will give the lucky recluses a day or two of fresh and unaccustomed labor.

But that day I found myself within a horizon not limited by an ivy-covered wall, on a road that didn't end at a gate blocked by a grille that was never opened. I didn't see austere faces passing by in silence with their eyes lowered soberly. I didn't hear those eternal monotone voices, whose words I could predict even before they were uttered. All along the road there were sturdy travelers walking quickly and talking in loud voices about where they were going, bright girls laughing together and only muffling their loud laughter when they caught sight of our novice's habits, so they could greet us modestly, as if all joy must fall silent before us. And no sooner had we gone by than they went back to singing and talking loudly. On the other side there were carriages passing by, full of fashionable ladies; and since it was harvest time we saw large groups of men, women, and children carrying baskets, and mules and horses with their wicker saddle panniers full of grapes, going to pour them into the press and then heading back empty—or full of small children waving and singing as they greeted passersby from those high ambulatory seats.

In all directions I saw life and activity that both surprised and delighted me. I watched and listened. Everything was new to me: the red brick houses along the road, the long avenues leading to great chateaux, the distant steeples marking villages. I was fascinated by everything that went by; I admired the big wagons pulled by ten horses, and my eyes followed some beggar riding a mule. Everything astonished me—from the high white and blue Pyrenees I could see in the distance to the ditches by the side of the road, in which the water flowed through flowering reeds; from the immense elms growing free, in the shade of which stood shepherds' huts, to the blackberry bushes along the road, from which children were gathering the dark fruit.

In the evening we reached Madame Gelis's house in Auterive. It wasn't a fine, handsome house like Madame Dilois's, but neither was it a bleak, narrow cell with a locked door that let in the howling wind and the freezing cold. There was a big fire in the hearth; the servant brought us a well-made supper; and we could raise our voices and laugh and loosen our wimples without being scolded severely or threatened with having to kneel in the middle of the refectory. We were awfully happy that night. I shared Juliette's room, and we were free to talk together without being parted by the curfew bell that always announced at the same hour that it was time to sleep—as if sleep could be commanded at a certain hour.

That was when I made my first mistake. I was talking to Juliette about that day's journey so enthusiastically that she smiled as she listened.

"What would you say," she replied after letting me list everything I remembered, "if you could see the festival in Sainte Gabelle, which is tomorrow?"

"A festival?"

"Yes, the finest festival in the area."

"Can't we go?"

"In these novice's habits? It wouldn't be appropriate."

"You're right."

"It's not that there's any great harm in going to watch the games and the dances all the mothers take their daughters to. It's just that our novice's habits would get us noticed, and if we were noticed it wouldn't be to our advantage."

"Why not?"

"Because you can't look pretty in a wimple and coif. Take you, for example: if your hair were done nicely you'd be as pretty as a picture, the belle of the whole festival."

"Don't tease me, Juliette."

"I'm telling you the truth. Your skin is so white and your eyes are so sweet!"

Caroline paused for a moment and said to her brother, "I'm telling you all this nonsense because I want you to know the whole truth. Besides, Juliette spoke to me that way because she loved me so much that she was always boasting about me."

"I believe it," said Luizzi. "Go on, Caroline."

While Juliette was saying all that, she was taking off my wimple and my coif and untying my hair, which fell loose to my shoulders. She paused for a moment, examining me almost angrily, and said in a low voice, "Yes, you're really beautiful—perhaps too beautiful!" But almost immediately she drove away that unpleasant thought. "You'd be wonderfully pretty with your hair braided like this," she went on cheerfully, arranging the hair around my face. "And if you put on one of those shabby dresses I can't wear anymore, I'm sure it would give you a charming figure. You want to try?"

"First let me see in the mirror what I look like with my hair done this way."

"No, no. When you're completely dressed you can look at yourself. I think you won't even recognize yourself."

Without giving me time to respond, she took off all of my heavy clothes and helped me into a silk dress and an embroidered shawl. She did my hair and decked me out as well as she could, then led me to a tall mirror and said, "Now look!"

She was right: I didn't recognize myself, and I cried, "Is that really me?"

"I'm just saying, if you showed up at the festival like that, you'd make all the dancers stare."

"Just so long as I didn't dance," I said, laughing at her excitement.

"But you'd dance wonderfully with a figure as pretty as yours! And then it's so easy to dance the way people do now; all you have to do is keep in step with the beat."

And as she spoke she began to sing a tune and dance with exquisite grace, in spite of her novice's habit. She smiled in that charming, attractive way she had; and when she gently lowered her sparkling eyes, their sweet glance seemed to sway in time with her movements and her singing.

"You're the one who'd be pretty dressed like this!" I cried. "Here, put on your dress."

"Oh, I've got plenty of others. You'll see, it'll be like being at a ball, just with the two of us!"

With incredible speed she threw off her habit and put on a dress that revealed her neck and a hint of her shoulders. You can't imagine how fetching she looked like that, so lithe and slender, with her hair falling in ringlets along her cheeks! "Here," she said, arching her lovely back, "walk like this. Let's say a handsome young man passes by and bows to you. If you don't know him, you look away coldly; if he's just an acquaintance, you acknowledge him with a slight bow; if he's a friend, you nod your head and gesture like this with your hand." With an ease and an elegance that delighted me, Juliette acted out everything she described. Then she said, "Go on, try it."

And while I imitated her, she exclaimed over and over, "You're so charming! It's like you've been doing this all your life—really! If you wanted, I bet with a couple of lessons you'd dance as well as I do."

"Oh, no, not that!"

"We'll see. I'll begin, and you do what I do."

Next thing you know we were facing one another, and she began to sing and dance. Then it was my turn, and in spite of myself I really enjoyed it, because Juliette seemed so happy and proud at seeing me look so pretty. She said so again and again, adding, "If the Mother Superior and Monsieur Barnet ran into you at the festival they wouldn't recognize you."

"Nor you either!"

"And it's so much fun! Peddlers selling every possible thing, dancing under the trees, games, and such a crowd! All the fine ladies from nearby with their daughters and their husbands, the young men from the whole area who've come on horseback or by carriage, strolling through the crowd, paying compliments to the prettiest girls, asking them to dance, eyeing them amorously! If you could go, you'd be surrounded by so many admirers it would drive all those prissy girls crazy—the ones who didn't want to invite you to their houses."

"Yes, yes," I said sadly. "But that's a pleasure we can no longer allow ourselves."

"True. You're right. And it'd be better to go to sleep than to think about all that, now that all we can do is be sorry to miss it."

We took off our pretty dresses and went to bed; but for a long time I dreamt of dancing and music and handsome young men and celebration and pleasure. They told me I was pretty, that I was lovable, that they loved me. Never at the convent had I slept so restlessly, and it was very late before I calmed down from the excitement aroused in me by that sweet, innocent evening.

When I woke the next morning I was alone in the room. When I went to get dressed, I couldn't find my novice's habit; only the dress I'd tried on the night before lay on the chair. I called Juliette, but she was downstairs, in her mother's little shop, and she couldn't hear me. I dressed as well as I could and went down. I rushed headlong into the shop, and found myself face to face with a young man who was returning books to Madame Gelis. I was so embarrassed I fled into the back room of the shop. Juliette followed me; she was wearing her novice's habit.

"What did you do with my clothes?" I asked.

"They're in your room."

"I couldn't find them."

Juliette began laughing. "People always do a bad job of looking when they don't want to find something."

"I swear…"

"Do I look like the Mother Superior to you? Don't swear and don't lie. The advantage of being free is, it saves us from a terrible vice—hypocrisy. When you don't make a sin of the slightest little thing, you don't need to lie to hide it. You felt pretty dressed like that, and you wanted to go on being pretty; it's no great crime."

"You're wrong not to believe me, Juliette. Come upstairs yourself and you'll see."

"In a while. I have to go give Monsieur Henri the books he's asking for."

Juliette left me. I went back upstairs to my room. I looked everywhere, but I couldn't find my clothes. So then I waited for her to come explain their extraordinary disappearance. Having nothing else to do—I beg your pardon, brother, for sharing such trivialities—I began to look at myself in the mirror, and I imitated Juliette's poses and smiles and looks, and in my vanity I was lost in that game when Juliette came in.

"Very good," she said, "very good! If Monsieur Henri had seen you like this he'd have thought you were even prettier."

I was so upset I was about to cry.

"Come on, come on," laughed Juliette. "Let's find your clothes now; I want you to put them back on. It's wrong of me, isn't it? But I'd look so ugly next to you in my wimple and my big black robe, and I'd be jealous."

"You're crazy!" I said, and I hugged her.

We looked all over the room without finding anything. Just as Juliette was beginning to lose patience, Madame Gelis came in and explained what had happened. Apparently the servant had tipped over an oil lamp on my clothes while she was trying to clean them, and Madame Gelis had taken them to a dry cleaner. She was threatening to fire the servant, who refused to admit anything; but Juliette, who was always so kind and so tolerant, pleaded for the woman so well that her mother forgave her.

Juliette and I were left alone. "Well," she said with her usual sweet cheerfulness and easy good humor, "it's been decided that you'll be the only pretty one. We'll go out and walk around town a little. I'll look like a strict chaperone responsible for a pretty schoolgirl. They'll look at you, and I'll say solemnly, 'Lower your eyes, miss.'"

"But if I go out like this, can't you do the same?" I begged.

"Oh, no! If they heard about it at the convent I'd be punished severely. You're rich, and they'll forgive you, but as for me…"

"We're a long way from Toulouse. No one will know."

"I don't dare."

But I begged her so hard she gave in. I dressed her. She was so pretty like that; it showed off her lithe figure in all its grace. The sparkle in her eye and the warmth of her smile lit up her face in its frame of long curly hair with an expression I couldn't have imagined. The opening in her dress showed off the suppleness and whiteness of her neck, around which she'd put a narrow velvet ribbon. For all her praise of me, she was much the prettier of the two.

When we were ready we set off together. We met a lot of people, all heading toward Sainte Gabelle. Many of them spoke to us, and they always said to Juliette, "Aren't you coming to the festival with this pretty girl? We'll see you at Sainte Gabelle, won't we?" And Juliette answered in some embarrassment, "I don't know, I don't think so."

I asked her why she didn't tell them truthfully that we couldn't go.

"I don't dare,"

"Why not?"

"Oh, because out here people don't think the way they do in the convent. If I said seriously that holy women of God like us can't get mixed up in pleasures of that kind, they'd think we were pious fools. And besides, it would sound like we're criticizing all the girls who're going to the festival, and the mothers who're taking them there—because it's an innocent pleasure even though it's forbidden to us."

"Aren't all pleasures forbidden to us?" I asked with a sigh.

"Oh," said Juliette carelessly, "I don't care about events like this. I know what they're like. I'm only sorry to miss it for your sake, since you've never been to one before. Yes," she went on, smiling sweetly at me, "I can understand your curiosity: a village festival is so much fun! And really, if I dared…"

"You'd take me there?"

"By myself?" she cried. "Oh no, that wouldn't be right. But I'd ask my mother to go with us."

"Your mother? What could anyone say if your mother came with us?"

"Nothing, I'm sure. And yet... But I'd never dare mention it to her... And yet if you wanted to ask her..."

"I wouldn't dare either."

"Still, I'm sure it would give her the greatest pleasure."

"No, no. She'd feel obligated to say yes. Coming from me, a request like that might seem like a demand."

Juliette seemed a little hurt by that thought, but after a moment's hesitation she replied, "I can't blame you for that scruple, since you're so innocent about the world's ways that you can't think otherwise. But, believe me, it's a finer thing to give someone a chance to show their gratitude for your generosity than to keep them from mentioning it."

"Oh, in that case," I cried, "I'll ask her whatever you like; I'll ask her to take us to that festival."

"And I'll thank you on my mother's behalf," said Juliette, "because you'll be acting kindly both to her and to me."

As soon as we got back to Madame Gelis's house, Juliette went to tell her mother I wanted to speak with her. They stayed away together so long I was afraid Juliette had told her what I was going to ask her to do, and that she didn't want to agree to it. But when I mentioned it to Madame Gelis she agreed so quickly I knew I'd been mistaken. That excellent woman was so happy to be able to satisfy a wish of mine that I understood Juliette had been right to think it's a good deed, on top of a generous action, to invite an expression of gratitude for it.

Luizzi listened to his sister in astonishment. This girl—who claimed to have had some awful experience in the world—spoke of that world with such naive good faith that he couldn't help smiling at her latest insight. But he was determined not to let her see his reactions to her story, so he kept quiet.

Caroline had stopped, and in that moment of silence they could hear the dismal force of the storm whining around the house. The continuous gloomy murmur of the rain, cut by the long howls of the wind, seemed to throw a veil of sadness in advance over whatever the baron was about to learn. He urged her to go on.

We set off for the festival. Oh, what a sweet, lovely journey! You know, brother, it was one of those autumn days in the south of France that are almost as beautiful as a fine spring day. It's not the liveliness and effervescence of nature in springtime, bursting out of its shell and exploding in showers of green. It's languorous, worn-out nature, which seems to be undressing to go to sleep. It's not the sudden gusts of a warm May breeze, carrying the heavy fragrance of

76

lilac and honeysuckle; it's the mild, soft air of September, rich with the ethereal perfume of dried clover and yellow straw and ripe fruit and the fallen leaves that begin to carpet the ground. And inside you it's not the blood stirring, the chest heaving, and the heart wanting to cry out and weep for no reason; it's a weariness of soul, a regret for a past you never had, the memory of a dream that never ended, and tears that fill your eyes without sorrow.

I can't describe the sweet delight I felt at being part of that unknown life. If I'd been alone, I'd have sat at the foot of a tree to look and listen, because the closer I got to the festival the sadder I became. Everyone going by was so happy! They called to each other and hurried to get there, for it was last festival of the year, and winter was coming, and they wouldn't see each other again till spring. For me it was my first festival, and it would be the last in my life, because my winter would end only in the tomb, and only in heaven would I find spring.

Tears fell from Caroline's eyes, and Luizzi said, "Are you crying, sister? Come now, drive away these gloomy thoughts and take hope!"

That's what Juliette said when she saw me crying, for I was crying then just as I am now, and I can't describe the sudden vertigo that overcame me. I felt a terrible anger rising in me against my destiny. All those people going by— some in large groups where brothers, mothers, children called out to each other by name; others alone in couples, where you could read on their lips the words you couldn't hear—and the distant continuous sounds of the band, and the happy cries of the dancers... all that movement, that life, that commotion, it all dizzied and intoxicated me.

And I don't know what compulsion it was in me, who a moment earlier had been trudging so sadly and so pensively toward the festival, that made me now urge Juliette on, saying, "Come on, come on! Let's dance! Come on, just once... at least once!" It was the vertigo of a traveler standing on the bank of a rushing stream, who throws himself in to keep up with the water racing by, racing and racing by unceasingly.

We arrived. There were a thousand games I wanted to play and arrays of jewelry and other ornaments I imagined wearing—everything filled me with desire: I wanted to join the peasants arguing while passing around a ribbon or a piece of lacework, I wanted to sit down at the meal spread out on the grass at the foot of a sycamore tree, I wanted to dance in a circle with the little girls and sing those songs from the mountains about pretty shepherdesses and the hunters who meet them and fall in love at first sight. I was governed by some force inside me that drove me toward everything around me.

Then we went into the dance hall. We hadn't even sat down before we were invited to dance. I saw Henri again, the man I'd seen that morning in the shop; he was dancing with Juliette. Another young man took my hand and led me out. I didn't know how to dance, but it seemed as if, in the peculiar state I was in, I could easily and unconsciously imitate what I saw someone do. And soon people were looking at me more than at other girls, and people around me were whispering that I was pretty, and I found I was happy. It was a giddy joy that made me feel light and didn't surprise me. I'd already lost my mind: I—a daughter of God, sworn to poverty and seclusion—was already lifting my eyes at men's passionate glances, and already filling my heart with the triumph of vanity.

When the contradance was done, Henri came over and invited me to dance. When he came to get me I hadn't yet recovered from my emotions after that first attempt. The band began, but it was no longer the same kind of dance. Henri put his arm around my waist and led me out, making me spin rapidly as we went along. At first I was so surprised that I just closed my eyes and let it happen, but gradually I felt like my steps began to match the beat better, as if some music more subtle than that of the band were guiding my feet. I opened my eyes to see where I was. I can't describe the feeling: I was being whirled around a broad circle with frightening speed, a thousand faces raced by next to me, my lungs were burning, and I felt my clothes floating around me as if they were being whipped up by some wind at floor level, my hair lifted away from my temples as if to expose my face to eyes whose glances I saw only as flashes igniting and going out almost immediately. My hand was on Henri's shoulder, and all my weight was in his powerful arms. My heart leapt, my chest heaved, I felt my lips tremble and my eyes cloud over—till they met Henri's, and I saw his face close to mine, and his breath was hot on my brow, and he looked deep into my eyes. I was enthralled beyond words; it was as if his breath were lifting me off the ground, as if I were bound to him by some invincible force. I no longer felt the arm that held me, as if in my turning I were connected only to his eyes, and something within us would have to snap to separate us. I was afraid, I was cold, my heart stopped, my eyesight failed, and I fell into his arms.

When I came to, I was with Madam Gelis, who was saying, "It isn't right to make a girl waltz for so long when she isn't used to it."

Waltz! So I'd been waltzing! All I knew about that dance was that its very name was forbidden at the convent—it was a blasphemous word. I clung to Madame Gelis like a child who's done something wrong and who's looking for protection beside her mother. But she told me coldly to get hold of my emotions. I realized I wasn't protected, and I gave way to tears—but the attention and curiosity that drew to me made me ashamed. I got a grip on myself and looked around. I saw how casually people who were used to it reacted to the pleasure that had overwhelmed me, and that made me sad again. But that sadness soon faded into a soft melancholy that left me detached from myself, so to speak. I refused to dance, but I watched the dancing and the waltzing. That joyful sight made the pleasures I'd just experienced resonate more mildly in me, and I bathed my spirits in that resonance, and smiled.

But when I saw Juliette had taken my place in Henri's arms I felt a kind of anxious, almost jealous curiosity, I have to admit. She spun around so casually, so easily, with such freedom, that I began to doubt whether I could've looked that seductive in everyone's eyes, especially in Henri's shining eyes, which seemed lost in Juliette's lively glance. When she came back to me she radiated a joyful, triumphant scent that choked me. I became sad again. I forgot the festival and the dance, and I thought about you, brother.

"Me?" cried Luizzi.

"Yes, you, Armand. I wanted to talk to you, the way I'm talking to you now. I wanted to say, 'Save me from the convent, save me from the tomb, save from despair, so I can...' I couldn't have expressed it, but I understood I'd been exiled from a life whose quickening I'd just begun to feel; and though I hadn't yet experienced it, I felt close to hating the prison that would separate me from that life forever."

Night had fallen. Henri offered to escort us home; he gave his arm to Madame Gelis, and Juliette and I followed them. I couldn't help acting a little cold toward her. Whether because she intuited a feeling I myself didn't understand, or because in her devoted friendship she forgave me my unfair sulkiness, she was more affectionate than ever. "Well!" she said, "I told you so: you were a huge success!"

"I'd save that praise for those who deserved it all the way to the end."

"No, no," she laughed. "You were like those heroes in tales of chivalry, who enter the lists at the start to win the greatest prize, and then watch with scorn while all the other knights scramble for the leftovers."

"I didn't think I'd earned such a glorious victory."

"And yet your prize is in front of you."

"Who?"

"Poor Monsieur Henri Donezau, who'd give a lot for us to be walking in front of him, if only so he could catch a glimpse of the silhouette of the beautiful fairy who put him under a spell."

"Shush, Juliette," I cried, feeling my heart pound as if it would burst, as if it had been filled with more hope than it could contain. "Shush! You're mistaken."

"Child, are you forgetting I haven't lived my whole life in a convent, that I've seen love... that maybe I've been in love... and that I'm not mistaken? Henri's in love with you; it's one of those sudden passions that strikes like a flash of lightning."

"And that vanishes just as fast, right?"

"No. It strikes a heart the way lightning strikes harmless straw, and consumes it down to ashes."

Juliette's tone of voice and choice of words surprised and troubled me. "Have you experienced that, to speak of it the way you do?"

"There's more than one school for learning those secrets. Haven't I lived with my mother up to now? And don't you think boredom sometimes drove me to read a few of the books I heard people praising every day?"

"And those books taught you what love is?"

"No. None of them ever described truthfully what goes on in a heart that's falling in love: the emotions of love are too abundant, too varied! But those books sometimes shed light on what it feels like; they give a name to the suffering or the joy you live for, and that name is always the same: it's the start of a sketch that reminds you of a face you know, a syllable from which you can finish the whole word. Because, you see, love isn't born—it awakes; and God has placed it at the very bottom of our hearts, next to his own image, eternal and all-powerful just as he is."

Oh, brother, how sweetly those words rang in my ears! I'd already lost their meaning, but they went on vibrating in me like distant music whose melody you can't quite catch, but whose sweetness inspires you to dream. I didn't answer—I was afraid to answer. And when we reached home I wanted to be alone; I missed my nun's cell, where I could've stayed awake and dreamt without anyone noticing.

The next day I perused the shelves of Madame Gelis's little lending library, as if I were trying to guess which of those books could tell me what I was feeling. I didn't dare ask Juliette, who'd gone back to her usual indifference and resignation, nor Madame Gelis, for whom all those treasures of the mind and the heart were worth only what she could charge for them. Nor could I simply steal one at random: not even my great desire was enough to give me the strength to do it. But I found a book, forgotten in Juliette's room.

Luizzi trembled to think what book might've been left deliberately for Caroline to discover—because he assumed that, motivated by either facetiousness or corruption, that girl Juliette had done everything she could to lead an innocent heart astray.

But he was reassured, and even thought his assumptions might be unjust, when Caroline lowered her voice and said, "It was a book called *Paul and Virginia*."[17]

Luizzi breathed again, and said with a smile, "And did you read it?"

"Yes. And I saw the truth of everything Juliette had told me: that love doesn't always take the same form in every heart, but it causes all those varied

---

[17] *Paul et Virginie* (1788), a novel by Jacques-Henri Bernardin de Saint-Pierre. Very successful, widely known, and culturally influential, it presents an innocent, sentimental vision of romantic love, and extols modesty and virginity. From Luizzi's point of view, nothing could've been safer for Caroline to read.

emotions that have a single name. I understood that once love has been aroused it fills the soul—whether it has grown gradually over the years or has suddenly entered it. I read that book, and then others. I got up at night while Juliette was fast asleep, and I devoured those books by the dim light of a night lamp, my body frozen—but I couldn't tear myself away from those unknown emotions I thirsted for. I read a tragedy by Shakespeare, *Romeo and Juliet*, in which the lovers had fallen in love at first sight, just the way I'd loved Henri. I read *The New Héloïse*."[18]

"*The New Héloïse?*" said Luizzi.

"Yes," replied Caroline. "I read it starting with the first page, where it says it's the story of a fallen woman."

When Henri came in the evening—because he came every evening—I watched him whispering with Juliette, and I knew he was talking about me; and she'd tell me how he didn't dare confess to me the love that was driving him mad, how the sight of me left him speechless and trembling, how he didn't dare look at me or speak to me. And, knowing he was feeling everything I felt, I told myself he loved me the way I loved him.

But the day of our departure was drawing near. I can't say I was afraid to see it come; no, it represented hope for me. That emotion I couldn't share or keep to myself, that I couldn't speak about or find somewhere to dream about, that love whose confession rose to my lips but that I had to suppress, that presence of Henri's that filled my heart without letting it burst—all of that was an unbearable torment. A mute who can't cry out for help when he's in danger, or a swimmer whose strength fails him just as his hand touches the shore, must feel something like the torture I experienced every evening when Henri came near me and spoke to me with a constraint as painful as my own.

I looked forward to the solitude of the convent as an escape from that endless struggle; but the morning of my departure I found a letter addressed to me in a book I was reading. I didn't open it, because I guessed it came from him, and I meant to give it back to him. But he didn't show up, and Juliette didn't dare give it to her mother to return to Henri.

"You can reject him," she said to me, "but you can't make it as obvious to him as that. It would be cruel, it would drive him to some violent act, something a passion like his wouldn't hesitate at. It's enough for you not to answer him."

"So you didn't answer him?" asked Luizzi.

---

[18] *La Nouvelle Héloïse* (1761), by Jean-Jacques Rousseau, was probably the best-selling novel of the eighteenth century. In a love story that pits authentic emotion against conventional morality, and physical attraction against artificial notions of virtue, the fallen heroine has sex without marriage—though later she's redeemed as a faithful wife and mother.

"Alas," replied Caroline. "To keep from answering I would've had to keep from reading his letter."

I'm not sure how it happened, but that morning when I put my nun's habit back on, not knowing what else to do with it, I hid the letter under my wimple. I took it with me. Oh, the hair shirt our ascetic Sisters sometimes put on in their zeal for penitence couldn't itch and burn like that paper lying against my breast! To admit how I struggled during the whole journey, how many times I reached to remove the letter that was consuming me, how many times my hand dropped impotently as if I'd tried to tear out my own heart, would be to confess to you a madness that makes me blush and that still isn't cured.

I got to Toulouse, almost determined not to read the letter; but something strange happened that robbed me of my courage. When I returned to the convent everyone was so surprised by the change in my face, they all exclaimed with such pity at my pallor and my look of suffering, that I could no longer doubt the power of a love that had produced such sudden changes in my usual good health and serenity. How can I put it? It was precisely because everything suggested I was harboring some consuming wrong within me that it became impossible for me to resist the thought of scratching the sore that was both creating and destroying my life.

That night, alone in my cell, I read the letter.

"And you answered it?" asked Luizzi again.

"You'll read it, brother, the first one and all the others. And you'll read my replies."

"You have them with you?"

"Here they all are," said Caroline, handing him a parcel inside a small silk bag. "They'll explain what made me answer Henri, and how my own letters came back into my possession. I kept them, not out of hope, but out of remorse—for they remind me every day how guilty and wretched I was."

He took the letters and was about to begin reading when she stopped him, saying, "Wait a moment, till I've left. I'm going next door to the wounded farmer's bedside, to kneel and pray to God to forgive me for the love that burned in my heart, and which I discovered a little while ago still isn't extinguished."

Here was what Luizzi read:

Chapter XLVIII: A Correspondence

Henri Donezau to Caroline:

Forgive me for daring to write to you—I who never dared speak to you. Alas! When I was with you I felt so inhibited, I was trembling so badly, that I could never have found the strength to say anything to you that you might've rebuffed in your strictness. Even now, when I imagine this letter in your hands, and that you might reject it scornfully or read it indignantly, I hesitate; because I think I wouldn't be able to stand those proofs of your contempt or your anger. I hesitate, I tremble once more. And yet on the other hand I lack the courage to accept a life of despair without at least trying to dispel it.

I love you, Caroline. The word I shouldn't write to you, the word that must anger you, slips out like a cry of pain I can't control and you can't conceive.

Being bolder around your friend, I was able to speak to her of a love that might offend you. Alas, in trying to kill my hopes she only fed the passion that drives me mad. She told me how alone you are in the world, and with what saintly courage and noble resignation you bear that isolation. She told me of your goodness and generosity; and I—who already loved you for your celestial beauty and perfect grace—loved you for the noblest and purest virtue in you. So, having no hope for myself, I placed my hopes in you. The saintly pity that led you to rescue Madame Gelis might bend for a moment toward the cry of a pitiful wretch. Misfortune alone isn't the cause of all suffering, and you'd forgive the one who loves you, just as God forgives the one who suffers.

But if the goodness and nobility of your soul inspired you to forgive a fault that tormented only me, how would I know? Who would tell me I hadn't offended you? Oh, forgive me—but I need to know it, I need a word from you to tell me so, or I must die. Yes, I feel sure, if I'd had the strength to remain silent, all my life at the bottom of my heart I'd have retained the despair of a love not spoken. But now that I've spoken, I need to know how wrong I've been. Your silence alone will tell me. If within a week I've heard nothing to suggest I haven't provoked the scorn of the one I respect as a vision of angels on earth, you'll never hear of me again. For the tomb is mute, and despair can find refuge there against scorn.

—Henri Donezau

When Luizzi finished that letter he wanted to laugh. It seemed ridiculous, idiotic. That gentleman, who right from the start referred to the tomb as some refuge all prepared for him to enter, just the way he'd speak of opening his umbrella in case of rain—that gentleman struck him as an awfully feeble seducer, unless he was actually in love. Our baron knew that for mad fantasies and sen-

83

timental nonsense, there's nothing like true love. Then it occurred to him that if seduction had reached the point of mimicking the language of true love, even in its most exaggerated form, that only made it craftier. He also remembered the letter wasn't aimed at a woman of the world—for whom the continued good health of all the men who were going to die for her in the past guarantees the safety of all the men still threatening to kill themselves—no, it was addressed to a young recluse with no defense against a lie; and who, in the tale she'd just told him, had proved how easily her imagination could be aroused.

So he moved on to the second letter; but then he noticed he'd missed the postscript to Henri's letter, which read:

P.S. I've secured the allegiance of the convent gardener; whatever you give him he can easily convey to me.

That made Luizzi hum the tune to "Boy Beloved by the Ladies," from *The Sisters of the Visitation.*[19] Sighing at the thought of what he was about to learn, he went on reading the letters while humming in some alarm, "*Oh, be so good as to spare me the rest!*" also from *The Sisters of the Visitation.*[20]

Here was Caroline's answer:

Caroline to Henri:

Why would I scorn you, sir? I have no right to find fault with an emotion that, in the world, creates legitimate relationships. If the expression of that emotion slipped out, in spite of my position, it can only be because it wasn't made clear enough to you that I've renounced all other hope than that of devoting myself to the service of God. I therefore forgive you, and if that forgiveness isn't enough to give you the strength to go on living, you should know that not all suffering occurs out in the world, and the silence of the cloister hides many a cruel sorrow.

—Caroline

Henri to Caroline:

I received your letter, Caroline. Yes, you're a saint before God, you who took pity on a madman! And yet you suffer; do angels really weep? Oh, you who with a single word soothed and overcame the despair in my soul, perhaps you're without comfort! I don't know what your sorrows are, Caroline; but if it were in the power of anyone besides yourself to cure them, don't forget there's someone here on earth who lives only because of you and who will live only for you.

---

[19] "*Enfant chéri des dames.*" As noted earlier, the song was made popular by François Devienne in his 1792 opera *Les Visitandines*, whether or not he composed it himself. That opera presumably comes to Luizzi's mind because the plot concerns girls forced into a nunnery against their will.

[20] "*Ah! Daignez m'épargner le reste!*"

Forgive me for my foolish assumptions—but if I thought the vows you'll soon take had been dictated by the tyranny of your guardian or by that of the people around you, believe me, I'd find a way to save you. I might be mistaken, but I can't believe so much grace and so much beauty must be buried in a cloister. Those gloomy sanctuaries foster nothing but despair and remorse. Even virtue, when it takes refuge there, cannot shine its brightest; it cannot achieve its noblest goal, that of guiding the weak and retrieving the lost by its example.

And you, Caroline, you who could make a lovable virtue of the burning love your beauty inspires, you to whom heaven owes happiness in exchange for all the happiness you give, must you live unknown by anyone but me, unimportant to anyone but me? No, that's impossible. There is, there must be, some power you can't resist that's imposing this terrible sacrifice on you. Oh, if that's true, I'll find it out; and if I'm right, woe to those who dare do violence to you! I know the guardian who controls your destiny; I'll go to him and question him.

It's no longer just my sorrow that torments me, it's yours. You're suffering, you said so in your letter; so I have some right toward you... I have the right to protect you, perhaps even to rescue you... My life has a purpose. I'm happy, I'm proud... Count on me.
—Henri

"Hmm, hmm!" said Luizzi to himself when he'd finished that letter. "Here's a fellow who's moving awfully fast! I'm afraid to read my sister's answer. She must have one of those nun's hearts that, from constant steeping in God's love, catch fire at the first spark of human love that falls on them."

While he thought about that, he glanced at the postscript to Henri's second letter, which was inconsequential:

P.S. I enclose a letter from Madame Gelis to her daughter. I'm sending it through you so the Mother Superior can't examine it.

Luizzi moved on to Caroline's reply.

Caroline to Henri:
If I'm writing to you again, sir, if I'm committing a new wrong, it's to repair the wrong I did in replying to you the first time. I act freely, sir, and I will take the veil freely. Therefore give up any attempt to impose the belief that I'm not content with the destiny that awaits me. I've never hoped for any other, and I wish for no other.
—Sister Angélique
P.S. You'll find enclosed Juliette's reply to her mother.

"Well, that's certainly clear," thought Luizzi. "I'll be curious to see what Monsieur Henri found to say to such a categorical dismissal."

Henri to Caroline:

Miss,

Read this letter, which is no longer the work of a lunatic driven even more mad by a moment of joy and hope than he was by despair. This is the work of a man of honor who asserts the right to justify himself. Be so good as to listen to me. I know your life and your situation as well as you do. I know you have no family or friends, and that you can count on no one for advice or protection. If in those circumstances you had quit the world at an age when you could appreciate it, I'd believe you sought in the convent a refuge in solitude that you wished to make permanent.

But since, starting in childhood, you've been under the guidance of persons with a direct interest in pushing you to a resolution that will leave your fortune in their hands, I believe you've been led astray; I assume threats and even force have led you to a decision I know by now is voluntary. I can the more easily suspect that about you, who are alone in the world, when I see families whose full authority isn't enough to tear their child free from commitments made under the influence of skillfully implanted ideas; when I see a mother's tears powerless to overcome the ruthless greed of the women who control you, and who pit against that maternal despair a religious vocation prompted entirely by the fear they know how to inspire in the unfortunate girls they've captured.

If that's true about so many others, I can believe it's true about you; I have to believe it, when you tell me the silence of the cloister hides many cruel sorrows. I misunderstood what you meant—let that be my excuse. You're happy, and that's all I wanted. Forgive me for not being able to understand that happiness. The idea the world gives us about happiness is so far from the idea you've been given, that you wouldn't understand me either if I tried to explain the happiness you might find in the world. You have no mother, Caroline, you have no family; but when a woman has given the man she loves the sacred name of "husband," she finds a mother and a family all at once. The present is made sweet by the affection of the woman who adopts her as a daughter; the future is made beautiful, for someday young lives will come, demanding a mother's sacred love and giving her in return the respectful obedient love of children. She'll love, and be loved; whatever happiness God has allowed us on earth is contained in those words.

And I'm not talking about the love of the man you would've chosen; I'm not describing the constant adoration he'd give you in return for the happiness you'd give him. You wouldn't understand me, Caroline, if I told you how proudly he'd show you off, saying, "She's the most beautiful, she's the finest, she's the purest." You'd understand me even less if I described the intoxicating delight there is in that union of two beings joined in a single life, smiling at one another, living for one another, happy everywhere and with everything—whether the pleasure of a festival leads them out into the joys of the world together; whether in solitude they pause to dream together in the sweet sounds of the countryside;

whether they go out, carefree and happy, to a brilliant performance where their joy together will cause envy; whether they come home in the evening arm in arm, quietly confiding to each other their fondest hopes and their passing thoughts; whether they stay by the fireside amidst their family and their beloved friends, happy with a relaxed happiness, surrounded by genuine affection, at the center of which their avowed love still seems to be their secret, since only they know how vast it is.

Oh, in all those things there are inexpressible delights that the heart seeks without even knowing it. But to dream of those delights, to look to them in the hope of soothing the pain you feel, you have to be in love, you have to suffer. And you're not in love, and you're content. You have to be like a soul in hell that envies the happiness of the angels; and you're in heaven. You have to be me, and not you.

Therefore farewell, Caroline, farewell. You'll never hear from me again. Has God really sent his angels to earth to sow despair and death?
—Henri

Luizzi made a face. The love in Henri's letter struck him as ridiculous, but its reasoning seemed solid enough. All things considered, a girl who was pretty and witty and refined must have better things to do than be a nun. He hastened to open the next letter to read Caroline's reply, but instead he found another letter from Henri, dated more than a month after the previous letter.

Henri to Caroline:
Ten days ago the convent gardener brought me a sealed packet addressed to me. I opened it, trembling with giddy joy, full of insane hope. It contained Juliette's reply to the letter from her mother that I'd included in the last letter I wrote to you, in which I said farewell forever. I can't begin to describe the depth of my disappointment: it was like a bright sky suddenly closing and leaving me in darkness. Dying must entail suffering like that; but you don't always die when you suffer like that. When the delirium of my sorrow had abated, I sent Juliette's letter on to Madame Gelis, and I was left crushed. And then I thought, that letter had been mine—a letter you'd touched! And I wanted it back at any price. I realized it must mention you; and if I'd had it in my hands I don't know if I could've kept myself from breaking the seal. But it was gone; and though I wasn't able to retrieve it, I wanted to know what was in it.

I went to Auterive and saw Madame Gelis, and I asked her for news of her daughter. "She told me she's happy," she said. I didn't dare ask her about you. Finally, trembling, I mentioned your name. She only replied, "My daughter says Mademoiselle Caroline has changed a lot, and she spends her nights in tears and her days in prayer." I made her repeat that, and then I left like a madman.

I hurried to your convent, and it was only when I was about knock at the door of your prison that I remembered there were impassable walls between us.

Oh, those walls! I would've battered them down with my forehead if I could've rescued you that way. But some shred of reason told me to conceal from all eyes the madness you might be punished for. I wandered all night around that place—where you weep, where you suffer. I was driven mad with anger at my own powerlessness.

Oh, Caroline, listen to me. I know you suffer, you weep. Only the place you live in could make you despair like that. Take a chance: trust in the honor of a man who has never broken his word, and I'll rescue you—and then you'll never hear from me again.

Or am I mistaken? Might your despair arise from a sorrow like mine? Might you be in love, and separated from the one you love? Well, then, Caroline, if that's how it is, take a chance and tell me. Tell me, and the man you love will become my brother; I'll look for him, I'll find him, I'll overcome all obstacles, I'll reunite you, and then you'll never see me again. I won't be there when you're happy; I'll go far away from you, because I'd have too much hatred for the man who makes you happy.

One more thing—one more thing, I beg you! Oh, trust me, Caroline! Love is also a religion, and that religion has its martyrs who are willing to sacrifice themselves at the altar they've sworn to worship. I'm waiting. Remember, I'm waiting, and if I get no reply, I can't answer for what I might do. Have pity on me, and pity on yourself.
—Henri

When he was done reading that, Luizzi scratched his ear. "This love has a southern flavor to it, something of the hyperbolic style of Gascony, or I'm very much mistaken. Still, the newspapers are full of stories of suicide for love, of crimes of passion, of horrors done for love's sake. So you can't deny people like that exist. This Henri—who, if I understand correctly, is none other than the wounded officer who was just brought here—is, according to old Bruno, a valiant soldier. That doesn't usually suggest a dishonest man. So it's possible I don't understand this at all."

And he went on with his reading.

Caroline to Henri:
Why write to me again, sir? Why persecute me in my despair? Leave me to my misery. All of your suppositions are false. No, I'm not in love. My God, what would become of me if I were in love!
—Caroline

Henri to Caroline:
I was right, Caroline: you are in love. The last line of your letter proves it to me. Now allow the friend in whom you confided to reply calmly to your question. "What would become of me," you ask, "if I were in love?" Have you for-

gotten you're free, and your sad solitude in life at least has the advantage that it leaves you mistress of your own fate? At the age you've reached, Caroline, your guardian owes you an accounting of your fortune. Soon you'll be able to dispose of it, and of yourself, without needing anyone's consent. The women in charge of the convent know that, and they'll be sure you know it on the day they can turn your wishes to their profit.

You ask what would become of you, Caroline? You'd become the honored, beloved wife of the man you love, the sainted mother of a family, spreading her love around her like the gentle warmth that causes young virtue to bloom; you'd become the sovereign mistress of a heart that would be your slave; you'd become the joy and honor of a new family, the perfect model of grace, the object of everyone's admiration and respect; you'd become everything God wanted you to be. That's the destiny that terrifies you, the destiny that's yours if you dare to seize it.

But even as I reveal a glimpse of that happiness to you, I tremble to have to add a new despair to your suffering. For if you don't dare give yourself to the man you've chosen, could it be because he's unworthy of you? Could it be he doesn't love you? Both of those thoughts are equally absurd. Your heart makes me unable to believe the first, and my own heart tells me the second is impossible.

What is it then that makes you suffer so much? What secret are you keeping from me? Oh, Caroline, tell me. I love you enough to find out that you love someone else, and to give you to him and rescue you, even if it costs me my life!
—Henri

"My word," thought Luizzi. "This is either completely imbecilic or shockingly crafty. Either this gentleman has no idea what's going on, or he insists on her telling him everything. Let's see what my poor sister replied."

Caroline to Henri:
Come save me, Henri!

Henri to Caroline:
You love me! I'm the one! You love me, Caroline!... Oh, let me fall at your feet, let me thank you and worship you. Oh, I wish I could tell you the joy inflicted on me by your words, which burned and crushed me: I closed my eyes, I staggered, I thought I'd die... Then I fell to my knees and called your name at the top of my voice: Caroline! Caroline! Oh, you've put your trust in me, and you'll be happy, I swear... I'll live for your happiness, your bliss will be the soul of my life, it'll be the heart of my heart, which would stop beating at a single one of your tears.

I can tell you no more today... I'd go mad... Even now I'm weeping... I tremble... I have doubts... I'm afraid of going mad... Is it true that you love me?

Caroline to Henri:
Yes, Henri, I love you. I love you because you took pity on a poor girl who was sad and alone, I love you for the noble goodness of your soul, and no doubt I love you because it was God's will, since I loved you before all that.

After those two letters, it was nothing but a lovers' correspondence, in which Henri and Caroline poured out their hearts to each other: naive confidences from one, rhapsodic dreams from the other, cherished hopes, wild desires, everything necessary to the upkeep of a love affair—that gushing inexhaustible spring that begins to dry up the day you touch your lips to it!

Among all those celestial sentiments, however, a few earthly thoughts slipped in. First, Henri explained to Caroline what her legal rights were. Then came all the planning to abduct her and run away. On that subject there was a truly admirable letter from Henri, in which he confessed his poverty to Caroline, and a reply from Caroline that brought tears to Luizzi's eyes. She begged Henri's pardon for being richer than he was—so naively that the baron was on the verge of thinking the sentimental conventions of light comedy at the Gymnase were in fact realistic.[21] Then he had to admire the skill, once that point had been established, with which Caroline worked to eliminate that discrepancy. She boldly asked Monsieur Barnet for an accounting, and demanded that he remit to her, in care of Madame Gelis, all the income of her fortune from the time she'd reached the age of eighteen.

At last, letter by letter, note by note, Luizzi reached the moment when everything had been made ready for Caroline's escape. Henri was to come wait for her at a door the gardener had agreed to open for them. Luizzi thought he'd reached the finale at last; just one short note remained for him to read, and it contained only these few words:

Henri to Caroline:
You've deceived me disgracefully. I'm returning your letters. I want nothing of yours that would remind me how close I came to making a mistake.
—Henri

Luizzi was baffled, and for a long time he sat pondering that unexpected conclusion. Then he called his sister back from the next room; studying her with curiosity and pity, he asked, "And since the day you got this note, you've heard nothing?"

"Nothing."

"You haven't seen Henri again?"

"Today is the first time I saw him since the day I left Auterive."

---

[21] The Théâtre du Gymnase, founded in Paris in 1820.

90

"You don't know who could've slandered you to him?"

"I have no idea."

"What about that Juliette?"

"Her? Oh, no! It wasn't her. She hadn't seen him again any more than I had. She didn't even know my plans; for once I'd begun that guilty relationship I no longer dared to confide in her. I couldn't bear having to blush before such submission and virtue. I didn't want to make her an accomplice to my sin, because her friendship would've driven her to keep my secret, and her conscience would've reproached her bitterly for her weakness. Besides, you saw how much Henri insisted on secrecy."

"Then how do you come to be here?"

The night I was to escape with Henri, I left my cell. As I crossed the garden I was shaking and could barely stand up. It was a dark night, and the whole convent was fast asleep. Finally I reached the fateful door. "Well?" I asked the gardener.

"Monsieur Henri came," he said, "but he left almost immediately, after giving me this packet and this note."

I thought some unexpected obstacle had delayed carrying out our plan. I asked the gardener if Henri was going to return that night, but he'd told him nothing more. I wanted to read the note to find out what was going on, but there wouldn't be enough light in my cell. Then I thought of the chapel, which stood near that garden door. I went there furtively; and there, by the light of a votive candle burning before a relic of St. Anthony, I read those terrible words that broke my heart so badly that I fainted.

When I came to, I was lying on the flagstone floor of the chapel. I woke as if from a nightmare, not understanding why I was there, unable to recall what had happened to me. Finally, when I did remember, I felt such intense despair that if the sanctity of the place hadn't touched my soul I'd have smashed my skull against the flagstones, just the way my heart had been broken. I staggered back to my cell, and spent the rest of the night with my soul lost in deep despair, unable to decide whether to live or die.

By bringing me sunlight, in a sense morning showed me the path to follow. As soon as I could see the place where I'd loved so much, suffered so much, and hoped for so much, I knew I'd be unable to live there any longer. A few days later I persuaded the Mother Superior to send me to one of the other branches of the Sisters of Charity. I was supposed to finish my noviciate at Evron. I went there by myself, taking with me my secret and my despair. For the six months I've lived there, I've spent my time in the hardest labor, working at the hospital in Vitré, constantly at the bedside of the sick, hoping the sight of others' suffering would ease the consuming fire of my own. But in vain: I envy the bodily suffering that breaks so many men.

I came here to carry out the holy duty to which I've dedicated myself, before I saw once again the man who ended my life. For I no longer live, brother, I no longer have hope.

"You must have hope, Caroline," said Luizzi firmly. "There's some terrible plot behind all this, and I'm going to discover what it is."

"What are you going to do, brother?"

"I'll go see Henri, and question him."

"Alas! It might be too late."

"That's what I'll soon find out."

And Luizzi went out into the larger room, where old Bruno was still up.

Chapter XLIX

"Monsieur Bruno," said Luizzi, "is there someone here who could lead me to where Bertrand's gang is hiding?"

"Once I could've taken you there myself," replied old Bruno. "I know all of the Chouans' hideaways; there isn't one I couldn't have found with my eyes closed. But now that I'm blind, I can't be as sure I'm not making a mistake."

The baron couldn't help smiling at the old man's peculiar boast—and the contradiction he delivered in the same breath. "Besides you," he asked, "isn't there anyone who could guide me? I'd pay him for it."

"Hmm. That little fellow Matthieu knows all the paths like the back of his hand. If I told him where Bertrand's likely to be at this hour, he could take you straight there. But that would be exposing both of you to gunfire, unless you were with someone who could vouch for you."

"What if you came with me, Caroline?" asked Luizzi, turning toward his sister.

"Me?" she said, blushing. She hesitated for a moment, then stammered, "What influence would I have over those men? You saw I couldn't do anything for Henri, when I tried to save him before I knew who he was."

"Maybe so," said Bruno, "but you also saw how a word from you was enough to save this gentleman, whom you knew."

"It doesn't matter," said Caroline. "Give up this idea, brother. Don't expose yourself to some awful danger just to hear an explanation that might just cause me renewed pain."

"But don't forget," replied Luizzi, "your honor's at stake... and maybe your happiness too."

"Is that how it is?" said old Bruno, rising. "In that case, here I am. I'll go with you, and little Matthieu will guide us."

"But doesn't that mean exposing you to the same danger you warned us about earlier?" asked Luizzi.

"Oh, it's not the same. There are things between Bertrand and me that'll make him more careful."

"That didn't protect your son from attack," Caroline pointed out.

"It wasn't Bertrand who fired the shot, nor did he give the order for it. Let me just ask you one thing, Sister Angélique, since you've been so good and so charitable to us poor folks. Is it true your happiness depends on this gentleman finding Bertrand's gang and seeing the prisoner?"

Caroline hesitated again, then lowered her eyes as she answered, "I can't oppose my brother's wishes, and if he insists on seeing Monsieur Henri..."

"Yes, sister, I do. Besides, consider that Henri is defenseless in the hands of men who might make him pay with his life for the courage he showed against them. We have to save him too."

"Then save him, brother, and God protect you!"

"When we can start?" asked Luizzi.

"The sooner the better," replied Bruno. "Give me enough time to wake Matthieu and get him up."

"Listen," said a loud voice from the big bed that filled one corner of the large room. Luizzi and Caroline approached, and found Jacques sitting up. "Listen," he repeated. "I'm willing to let my father and my son go, since it's a question of Sister Angélique's honor. When my poor little girl asleep here almost died of smallpox, Sister Angélique came to us without fearing contagion. She spent days and nights by my daughter's bedside, and she saved her. For that life, which she saved, I can risk another life; so Matthieu can go with you. As for you, father, you know what you're doing, and I won't stand in your way." He turned to Luizzi. "But you have to give me your word of honor, sir, that you won't take any other advantage of what you'll see. You have to swear before God you'll never tell anyone about Bertrand's hiding place, and if the leaders of the troops stationed in this area were to find out you'd been to the place the Chouans are hiding, you won't give them any information that would lead them there."

"I give you my word," said the baron, "though I'm surprised at your asking for that, since those wretches shot you."

"That's a score to settle between Bertrand and me. That's blood he owes me, and I don't want him paying it to anyone else. Now go settle your business; I'll settle mine when the time comes."

A moment later little Matthieu was ready. It was agreed that Caroline would wait at the farmhouse for Luizzi's return. The baron set off, accompanied by the boy and the old blind man. Daybreak was coming, but as long as it was night they walked in silence. They followed rough and ruined paths, always along thick hedges. As soon as the sun began to rise they met peasants on their way to work the land. Then things picked up, and the roads were filled with the narrow carts typical of that region, pulled by great teams of at least three pairs of oxen and four horses, controlled by immensely long reins. On the one hand, the terrible state of the roads required the use of such vast forces to haul even small loads and to pull the carts out of the potholes they got stuck in; on the other hand, it was a matter of vanity for the peasants to harness as many horses and oxen to a single cart as they could, just to take a few sacks of wheat to market.

Luizzi, filled with the importance of the mission he'd volunteered for, saw all that without paying much attention to it. Nor did he notice the strange appearance of the peasants driving those carts: wrapped in goatskin cloaks, their long straight hair escaping from under the large red bonnets that covered their heads, with wooden clogs on their bare feet and their bare legs wrapped in ill-fitting leather gaiters, and wearing short trousers open on the outsides of the knees. The soft monotonous song almost all the peasants sang as they walked didn't distract him from his own thoughts; and yet he was struck by the way people spoke to Bruno whenever they met him.

"Hey, how's everybody at home? Will Jacques be down a long time with that shoulder? Is it serious?" they asked over and over. Events at the farmhouse only three or four hours earlier were already common knowledge. They all asked about it with interest, but no one made a single comment, whether in blame or in praise, about what either Jacques or the Chouans had done. Luizzi voiced his surprise to Bruno that the news of his son's injury had spread so fast.

"There's nothing extraordinary about it," replied the old man. "Half the men we've just met might be in the gang. Now that they've struck their blow, they've gone back to their farms, and the gendarmes can go look there without suspecting a thing."

"I can't understand that."

"It's simple enough. They know how many hats and bonnets—men and women—there are in each house. If the gendarmes show up at lunchtime, say, they ask for a head count, and you have to report who's out in the fields and who's at market, and if anybody's missing they make a note of it. But since the morning after an action the fellows are present, or out working, there's no way to know who's in a gang. In fact sometimes they ask for information about an attack from the very men who carried it out. To catch the villains involved in the Chouannerie, they'd have to drop in on houses without warning in the middle of the night; and it isn't healthy for gendarmes to be wandering on these roads at night."

"So that means we'll find Bertrand at his house?"

"No, no! They know about him! If he goes home occasionally, it's only after dark. We'll find him out on the Great Heath, with four or five others who have to hide for the same reason."

"So this morning we met some of the men who attacked your house last night?"

"Even better, I bet we spoke with the one who fired the shot… You remember the stocky fellow who said, 'Let's hope it's nothing'?"

"It wasn't him, grandpa," said little Matthieu. "I know who it was."

"Did you tell your father?" asked Bruno, not at all surprised at the secret the boy had kept.

"I'll say it first with my clog, when I kick that boy Louis, Petithomme's son, the first time I meet him out in the pastures."

"Oh, so it was Petithomme?" asked the old man calmly. "Jacques should've suspected him long ago. As for you, little one, look out for that boy Louis. He's two years older than you. Punch him in the eye, that's the place."

"Don't worry, grandpa, it won't be the first time I've left my mark on him."

Then, without any further concern about how his grandson's quarrel might turn out, Bruno stopped and sniffed the air around him. "We must be near the Great Heath."

"Yes, grandpa," replied Matthieu.

"All right. Look on the left for a little path through the broom. Bertrand must be in the den by the old bridge."

The boy soon found the path. Luizzi, seeing a heath more than a league across stretching before him, asked if they still had far to go.

"We're going more or less to the middle of the heath," replied Bruno.

"What?" exclaimed the baron. "The Chouans are hiding in such an exposed spot?"

"Look: ahead of you, a little to the left, you'll see a small rise. The old bridge is at the foot of that hill. A lookout on top of the rise, hidden in the broom, can easily survey the entire heath. At this very moment Bertrand already knows three people on foot are heading toward his hideaway. He's waiting, because there are only three of us; if they'd seen a whole company of soldiers, he'd already be making his escape the opposite direction."

"But what if they advanced from several directions at once?"

"They could come from ten directions and it wouldn't matter to him. There are twenty hidden paths out of the heath. The fellows would scatter and slip away between the soldiers like a hare between two hunters. There's only ever been one way to fight a war against the Chouans."

"And what's that?"

"To seize their wives and children and take them peacefully to town without hurting them. Oh, those poor devils would give up quick without a home and a bed! It wouldn't take a week. They'd hurry in to surrender their guns and ammunition so they could see their families; and once they were disarmed they'd have to keep the peace." Old Bruno suddenly paused, then said, "Listen! Did you hear that *hoo hoo*? They're sending someone out to have a look at us."

They went on walking, and Luizzi noticed that the heath, which at first had looked so uniform, was crisscrossed in all directions by deep gullies or ravines eroded by the rain, and was broken here and there by patches of broom at least five or six feet high.

As they were emerging from one of those thickets they found Bertrand standing before them. "Where do think you're going?" he cried.

"We're going exactly where we are," said Bruno. "Because you're the man we're looking for."

"Now that you've found me, what do you want?"

"This gentleman will explain, because it concerns him."

"Hell!" said Bertrand. "Wasn't it enough that you almost wound up at the bottom of the pond, which is what would've happened if Sister Angélique hadn't intervened?"

"It's on her behalf that I'm here now," said Luizzi.

"To save that lieutenant?" asked Bertrand with a glower.

"Yes, to save him."

"Sister Angélique should mind her own business!" said Bertrand angrily. "Anyway, too bad for you for getting involved in all this! And too bad for you too, Bruno, for getting involved as well. You did wrong: you showed a stranger the way to the old bridge. That's treason, and you know what the price is!"

"The reason that brings this gentleman here," replied Bruno calmly, "has nothing to do with the Chouannerie. It's just about Sister Angélique. Explain it to him, sir, and settle the matter."

Luizzi was about to speak, but Bertrand went on, "Since you wanted to see the den by the old bridge, now you have to go all the way. And since you're so curious, I'll show you a path none of you knows about."

He set off along a kind of ditch half full of water. Luizzi hesitated before following him, and Bruno said to him quietly, "This is no time to retreat. There must be men to our left and to our right, and maybe even behind us, who'd pepper our backs with bullets if you looked like shying away."

So Luizzi began walking, and after ten minutes they reached the bottom of a ravine whose banks had once been spanned by a double-arched bridge. One of the arches still stood, and beneath it nine or ten men were gathered around a fire they'd lit. They paid no attention to Bruno and his grandson, but they circled around Luizzi, muttering to each other, "It's the spy from last night."

That description struck Luizzi as a bad omen. But he hadn't chosen this mission without knowing it would involve some risks, so he pretended not to notice the Chouans' hostility toward him.

Meanwhile little Matthieu went over to one the Chouans who was standing apart, and said cheerfully, "Morning, father Petithomme! How's my buddy Louis?"

"All right, I guess," said the Chouan.

"Oh, are you here, Petithomme?" asked Bruno in a friendly tone of voice.

"Yes, father Bruno. And I hope all's well at home?"

"Not bad, not bad."

Neither the boy nor the old man betrayed the slightest emotion as they spoke to the man who'd shot the father of the one and the son of the other.

Meanwhile Luizzi could see nothing to suggest the lieutenant had been brought here, and he waited for Bertrand to question him. The latter took a seat on a big rock, propped his elbows on his knees, leaned close to the fire, and asked him, "What is it you want?"

"What I fear you can't give me: I'd like to see your prisoner."

"What do you want to say to him?"

"That's a secret between him and me."

Bertrand lifted his head and looked at Luizzi in surprise. Then he resumed his position and stretched his hands out to the fire, and called out to one of his men, "Go fetch the wounded man!"

97

A moment later Henri appeared, and Luizzi was able to look him over. He was a man of twenty-five at most, built like a Hercules, with a small head and a low forehead, and whose complexion under his black beard would've been ruddy if he'd been healthy.

"Go ahead and talk together," said Bertrand. "Don't mind us. We'll give you time."

"Have you come to negotiate my release, sir?" asked Henri.

"No," replied the baron, "I'm here on behalf of the person who recognized you at Jacques's house."

"Mademoiselle Caroline, whom they call Sister Angélique, and who has two first names for lack of a last name," said Henri brutally. "What does she want with me?"

"Nothing," said Luizzi, repelled by the man's coarseness. "But I have the right to demand an explanation."

The lieutenant looked around carelessly. "An explanation, here! It's not a convenient place, and my right arm's in a sling, but that doesn't matter. If these peasants can lend us two sharpened sticks, I'm your man."

"I hope you're not implying I'd have the poor taste to come ask you for that kind explanation here and in the state you're in."

"Well, I have no other explanation to give you," said Henri, turning his back to him.

Luizzi was shocked at the tone and the manners of this man, whose letters had led the baron to picture him as a handsome, melancholy sort. At first he could think of nothing to say to Henri's brutal response; and he might just have let him leave if the other man hadn't turned around and said offensively, "But it occurs to me, I'd certainly like to hear by what right you've come here to meddle in my business."

"By right that your business is my business, sir," said the baron haughtily. "By right that I'm Baron de Luizzi, and Caroline is my sister."

That revelation seemed to stun Henri; and when Luizzi added, "And I know everything, sir!" the lieutenant let himself get carried away in awful cursing.

"Well!" he cried. "How nice that you know everything! Go report me to my superiors, have me cashiered out of my regiment. After all, what do I care? Besides, these beggars here have been promising to finish me off since yesterday. Let them do it at their leisure—I'd just as soon get it over with."

Luizzi assumed some feverish delirium caused by his wound had turned the young man's head. In any case, he was flattered at the impression he'd made just by mentioning his own name, and he went on more gently, "Listen, sir, I doubt the military authorities have any interest in punishing a misdeed like yours, especially since it can be mended."

"Ha! How the devil do you expect me to mend it on a salary of twelve hundred francs?" replied Henri with a shrug.

Luizzi had come here with a chivalrous notion of his mission, and he hadn't given up on the goal he'd set himself. So he barely listened to that odd reply, still discounting it as the result of fever, and he answered firmly, "Your lack of fortune, sir, is no obstacle. My sister's personal fortune is nothing much, it's true, but I can augment it enough to satisfy all the needs of a respectable rank."

The lieutenant's sluggish intelligence seemed to be waking slowly; like a man trying to understand what was being said to him, he stared at Luizzi and stammered, "Caroline was already quite an eligible prospect... Good for her if you can make her even richer... I might've done better to have married her... If only I hadn't listened..."

"To outrageous slander."

"I'm not saying Mademoiselle Caroline ever did anything reprehensible," muttered Henri through clenched teeth.

"But maybe for a moment you thought she had, and that moment was enough to destroy her happiness forever, and I assume yours too. But there's still time, sir; she hasn't taken her vows, she still loves you, and if you've now seen through your error, prove it to me by accepting her hand."

To deliver that speech Luizzi had struck a heroic pose, with one hand on his hip and the other held out to Henri. He'd declaimed his lines so theatrically that all he lacked was a Spaniard's cape and a rapier to embody drama at its finest, and Henri's astonished reaction just made the baron keep going in the same vein. "I've come to you in genuine sincerity, sir. Answer me in the same way: are you a free man?"

"Free to get married? Yes, if I can be free to leave this place."

"In that case, what answer should I take to Caroline?"

"My word! That I'm quite ready to marry her," said Henri again, with a look of surprise and even confusion in his eyes.

"On her behalf, thank you, brother," said the baron, still riding his chivalrous hobbyhorse. Then he relaxed into a more paternal tone, and with a skillful transition he went on, "Who could possibly have misled you enough for you to send Caroline a note like this?"

Henri took the note and read it. He remained silent, as if deep in solemn reflection.

"I know," said Luizzi, still spinning out fine phrases. "I know love, which so often refuses to face facts, can also be convinced of wrongdoing on the slightest suspicion. But tell me who the source of these lies was."

"Oh," said Henri, still staring at the note, "I can't and shouldn't name anyone..."

"I understand," said Luizzi. "But I fear that girl Juliette..."

Henri started, but he replied immediately, "No, on my honor, Juliette never said a word to me to damage Caroline's reputation."

"So then it was...?"

"Don't ask, baron. You don't know the people who misled me."

"As you wish. I honor your scruples. But what we have to think about now is finding a way to get you free. Let me handle the negotiation," added Luizzi, delighted by his own preeminence. "I'll make these people see reason."

"You can try. But please let me keep these letters."

"You'll find your heart again in them," replied Luizzi warmly.

He handed the packet of letters to Henri, who began reading them with an absorption that made Luizzi smile as he went back to Bertrand.

"You're finally done," said the Chouan. "Bruno just explained the whole business to me. It seems the nun is your own sister. Good for you—she's a saint. Since you have nothing else to do here, you can go, and the sooner the better."

"The thing is, I can't leave here alone, because Bruno didn't tell you everything. Yes, Sister Angélique, as you call her, is my sister. But this lieutenant was engaged to her for a long time; misfortune separated them, and today they've found each other again. I want to secure their happiness by seeing them married."

"Marry a nun!" cried one of the Chouans.

"She hasn't taken vows yet," said Luizzi.

A murmur ran round the assembled men.

"Shut up!" cried Bertrand. "It's none of our business! And to prove it to you, sir," he said to Luizzi, "I'll tell you plainly that the lieutenant and the nun can get married as much as they want as soon as we've gotten Georges back in exchange for our prisoner."

"You mean you won't give him to me?"

Bertrand looked at Luizzi in astonishment. "Why would I give him to you?"

"A woman's honor is at stake, and the happiness of the one you call a saint."

"A fine saint," said Bertrand, "who has lovers in the army!"

"You forget to whom you're speaking!" said Luizzi.

"You forget as well!" cried Bertrand, advancing on Luizzi with the butt of his shotgun raised. "Do I even know you? I let you come in here when I could've sent you scampering with a couple of bullets. I let you talk to this lieutenant because old Bruno was with you and I'm responsible for injuring his son. But do I owe you anything? Take my advice, get out of here. Take yourself off while I'm still willing to let you go, and don't wear me out with your Parisian gentleman's airs, you hear?"

Luizzi was probably about to say something stupid, but Bruno spoke up. "Come on, Bertrand, don't be disagreeable. The gentleman's right."

"You keep out of it, Bruno," said Bertrand. "You've already stuck your nose in too far."

"And I'll stick my nose in as far as I want, you hear, Bertrand?" said the old blind man angrily. "You think you can scare me with your loud voice? I've heard you trembling and praying, Bertrand!"

"Shut up," said the Chouan, aiming his savage look at the blind man. "Shut up! You'll bring trouble down on yourself."

"And what if I won't shut up, and what if I want to say what you did! Bertrand, don't make me say it…"

"I'd certainly stop you," replied the Chouan, loading his gun.

"Don't hurt the old man!" cried the other Chouans. "Jacques was enough."

Their leader advanced with his gun raised, and Bruno called out in a tone of command, "Come over here, Bertrand, come over here!"

Bertrand obeyed, and followed the old man a little distance away from Luizzi. The other Chouans withdrew outside the arch of the bridge, but since the curve of the vault served to carry Bruno's words, the baron could hear what was said as well as if he'd been standing right next to the blind man.

Bruno was saying to Bertrand, "Have you forgotten the attack at Andouillé? Have you forgotten how our leader, Balatru, was killed by a bullet between his shoulder blades, even though he was walking ahead of the rest of us? I, who was next to you, am the only one who knows who fired that shot. You want me to say it out loud?"

"Balatru was betraying us," said Bertrand, lowering his head.

"You were Balatru's wife's lover, and you married her, that's all."

"Well? And?" said Bertrand, clenching his fists.

"And? And when I threatened to report you to our leaders, you got on your knees on the ground and you begged me, 'Don't betray me! If ever you ask me for the life or death of a man, I'll spare him or kill him, as you wish.'"

"Are you asking me to spare the life of this lieutenant?"

"That first, and then something else. It was Petithomme who shot Jacques."

"Who told you that?"

"Wasn't it him? Matthieu saw him."

"Yes, it was him."

"I don't want him to be able to try again. You know he almost married Marianne. Last night he tried to do what you did that other time, and…"

"All right. I'll take care of it. Anyway, he's no good, and I have my suspicions about him. It isn't much to ask… But as for the lieutenant, I can't do it."

"You can if you want…"

They were interrupted by a little sound from up on the edge of the ravine, and a Chouan came sliding down through the brambles, saying in a low voice, "Hey, boys! It's the Red Pants!"

"Where?" asked Bertrand.

"At the edge of the big woods."

"All right. Relax, and go back to your position." Then Bertrand turned to Bruno again. "How do you expect me to put that to the others?"

But he was interrupted by the appearance of a second man. "Hey, boys! Here come the Red Pants!"

"From which direction?"

"The big pond."

"Go back to your position, and everybody get ready," said Bertrand.

The news had prompted Henri to stand up and come toward Luizzi, but the latter motioned to him not to interrupt the conversation between the two peasants.

Just then Bruno was saying to Bertrand, "This is a good opportunity: send your men away, and leave the lieutenant here with us."

"I'll go see if that's possible," said Bertrand calmly. And he walked away, throwing menacing glances in the old man's direction.

Luizzi approached Henri, who said, "This seems like rescue just in time..."

"I doubt it," said Luizzi. Then he went over to Bruno and whispered, "Look out. I suspect some kind of treachery."

Just then Bertrand returned, looking intensely agitated. "We've been betrayed. There are more than three hundred of them, coming from all sides."

The Chouans gathered around Bertrand, and the word "Betrayed! Betrayed!" spread through the group of a dozen or more men.

"Betrayed and doomed!" said Bertrand. "They're advancing in a circle and searching the heath like they're beating for game."

"It's old Bruno who gave us away!" cried Petithomme, and Bertrand looked to see what effect that accusation would have.

"If I'd betrayed you," shrugged Bruno, "would I be standing here among you?"

"He's right! He's right!"

"And the rest of you seem awfully easily discouraged," Bruno went on. "Seriously, you can't escape and slip away between a few hundred soldiers? Don't you know about the path that..."

"I know all the paths," interrupted Bertrand. "But from the way they're going about it, we'd be lucky if three or four of us didn't get caught or killed. Still, there's a way we can all be saved, without any of us running any risk."

"Show us."

"Here he is," said Bertrand, turning to Henri. "You know the den you were kept in. We can all fit in there and hide. You'll let the soldiers come, and when they get here you'll tell them we left the heath at least two hours ago. They'll stop searching around here, and we'll be as comfy as fish in water."

"All right," said Bruno. "I promise."

"Me too," said Luizzi.

"But I can't agree to betray my side," said Henri.

"Oh, I'm not worried about you," said Bertrand. "I know you won't say anything."

"What are you going to do?" asked Bruno.

"He'll come willingly with us, and he won't make any noise while we hold him, or else he'll stay here and there'll be one more corpse on the heath."

"Are you forgetting I asked you for this officer's freedom?" asked Bruno.

"So he can betray us," replied Bertrand.

"Save your life, Henri," said Luizzi. "Swear on your honor not to reveal their hiding place."

"I can't do it," replied Henri.

"In that case," said Bertrand, drawing his hunting knife, "walk ahead of me and don't stop."

"Go ahead and kill me," said Henri. "I'm not taking a single step."

"You asked for it," said Bertrand, moving back as if to give himself more room to swing the knife at Henri.

"If you commit this crime," cried Luizzi, "I withdraw my promise!"

"Fine! You'll get the same as he does."

"They're drawing together and getting closer!" murmured a voice from up on the bridge.

"Come on, make up your mind!" cried Bertrand.

"Just a moment," said Luizzi. "You're forgetting one thing: if we're left here alone, the soldiers who show up, and who don't know us, won't believe what we say, and they'll still go on searching."

"He's right," said many voices.

"Whereas," went on Luizzi, "if one of their officers assures them you're long gone, they'll believe him."

"True again," said Bertrand. "But he has to agree to do it."

"Agree, Henri!" said the baron.

"Here they come!" cried a Chouan, running down from the hilltop where he'd been the lookout.

"Come on," said Bertrand, quickly slinging his gun over his shoulder to make it easier to use his hunting knife. "Going once, going twice, will you swear to tell them we've been gone since this morning?"

Henri still hesitated.

"My word, too bad for him!" shrugged Bruno.

"You won't do it?" said Bertrand. "In that case, goodbye." He raised his hunting knife.

Henri turned pale and shrank back. "I swear on my honor," he said, his voice straining, "to say nothing about where you are."

"That's not it," said Bertrand. "You have to say we left a long time ago. Come on, don't make such a fuss! Your skin has turned so ashen you must want to save it."

"Here they come!... Here they come!" murmured a voice from the bushes.

"All right, let's get this over with!" said Bertrand, raising his knife.

"Fine!" said Henri. "I give you my word as an officer to say whatever you want."

"Good," said Bertrand.

Luizzi was delighted at Henri's decision, thought it seemed a little tardy. He reflected that there are circumstances in which it's a blunder to let danger come so near that it's obvious you're afraid.

"Remember," said Bertrand, "the Bruno family will answer for what you do. Every one of them, men and women, will suffer death if we're betrayed."

"All right, all right!" said old Bruno. "Think about yourself, and let us worry about the rest."

Bertrand motioned to his men to follow him. For a while he led the way back along the ravine in the direction from which they'd brought Henri; then he and his men vanished into the bushes. But before they'd gone that far, Luizzi saw Bertrand point out Bruno to the man named Petithomme. He mentioned it to the old blind man, who pondered what he'd just learned for a moment. "Damn!... Damn!..." he said, shaking his head.

"It's your own fault, grandpa," said Matthieu angrily. "Why did you have to tell Bertrand we knew it was Petithomme who shot dad?"

"You're right, my boy, I made a mistake. But I didn't think Bertrand would dare try a trick like this."

"You accused him of something terrible," said Luizzi quietly, "and therefore..."

"You heard that?"

Luizzi nodded. Bruno hesitated for a moment; then in a louder voice he said, "There's a better way to save the men than just waiting here, and that's to go out and meet the soldiers and keep them from coming any closer, by telling them the whole gang is gone."

"You're right," said Henri. "Let's hurry, and take the shortest path out."

They immediately left the ravine and followed a path bordered on both sides by tall broom thickets. At first they moved quickly, but then Bruno stopped and listened. All they could hear was the distant calls of soldiers, letting each other know where they were. Bruno set off once more, but fifty paces later he stopped again. "We're being followed—I'm sure of it. Matthieu, didn't you hear anything?"

"It's true," said Matthieu. "To our left, in the broom. I'll go see."

"Stay here, youngster," said the old blind man.

But the boy didn't listen to him, and pushed his way boldly into the thickets. Luizzi and Henri followed his progress by the waving of the broom as he advanced. About thirty paces from where they stood waiting, that waving suddenly became more violent, as if a struggle were going on there. Then the waving began to move away again, as if Matthieu had resumed walking; and then it stopped.

"Youngster! Matthieu! Stay here, fool!" cried the old man in agitation.

No answer. Luizzi felt a strange fear, and he began moving toward the spot where the boy had vanished. Henri followed him and stopped him a dozen or so paces away from Bruno, who went on calling Matthieu.

"That boy's a goner," said the lieutenant. "You saw the broom waving in the direction he went."

Luizzi was about to share his fears with Henri, when they heard a muffled blow and an awful cry. They turned around. Old Bruno was still standing, on the balls of his feet, with his arms stretched out. His face was contorted by terrible convulsions. They ran to him, but before they reached him the old man fell on his face with his arms extended, and they saw that some horrendous blow from behind had crushed his skull.

Henri and Luizzi exchanged a look of horror, then stared wildly about them. All was calm, nothing moved, and they could hear only the repeated calls of the soldiers as they came closer. Luizzi might've been a coward, and Henri was considered a brave soldier, but the deathly pallor on their faces betrayed the great terror that filled them both. Luizzi tried to speak, but his lips moved in vain and his voice was stuck in his throat as if pressed down by some overpowering weight. They stood facing each other, stock still, frozen.

Hearing a slight sound, they spun around and stood back to back, the better to face whatever danger threatened them. They stood that way for almost a minute, and it was only then they realized the noise was Bruno's last convulsions as he thrashed in the throes of agony. An identical impulse of pity made them kneel down to try to help him; an identical impulse of fear made them get back up and look all around. Nothing moved, and they stood even closer together.

And yet, after having held them helpless in its grip, that terrible stillness was suddenly shattered, and they began to shout and move around confusedly. Luizzi took out his handkerchief and waved it above the broom thickets while he cried out in a piercing, terrified voice, "Over here! Over here! Over here!"

Soon Henri joined him in the same shouts. The frenzy provoked by their fear was even greater than the immobility it had caused before, and they were still shouting and waving their handkerchiefs when they were surrounded by soldiers. While Luizzi described to a captain the sad events he'd witnessed, soldiers brought in the body of little Matthieu. The deep impressions of fingers around the poor boy's neck proved he'd been grabbed by the throat and strangled by hands of frightful strength.

Luizzi's and Henri's shouts, by drawing a great many soldiers to the place where Bruno's body lay, had broken the circle that had been tightening slowly around the ruins of the old bridge; and the soldiers were forced to conclude that the Chouans had taken advantage of the confusion caused by the awful murder, and had slipped away and left the heath—for not a single man was found in the den or cave they'd chosen as their hiding place, and the beaters saw no sign of anyone.

Meanwhile Luizzi, who was to meet Caroline at Jacques's farmhouse, had been chosen to deliver the sad message of the death of that poor man's father and son. He barely thought of the happy news he expected to bring Caroline, so filled was his mind with the cruel task he had to carry out. He trembled as he set off on the path back to the house, while Henri, whom he'd arranged to meet in Vitré, went away with the soldiers.

The baron paused for a moment at the gate of the farmyard before going in. The house was shut up, and no one came out. He made up his mind to go inside. Everyone was gathered in the main room: Jacques seated by the fire, his wife kneeling on the floor and weeping in her husband's lap, the servants huddling in a corner staring at each other in fear, the little children pressed between Jacques's legs and their mother's arms, and Caroline standing next to them.

When Luizzi entered, Jacques rose. "We know everything, sir," he said.

"Who could've told you?" cried Luizzi.

"A friend who was passing by… Petithomme."

"Petithomme!" cried the baron. "He's the one who shot you yesterday, and he's the one I saw Bertrand giving the sign to today to attack your father!"

"Petithomme!" repeated Jacques, aiming a terrible glance at his wife; while she, flinging herself back, wilted under his glare. Neither one nor the other said a word. Jacques mopped his brow with the back of his hand, for he was drenched in sweat. Then he said calmly, "Sister Angélique, you've recovered your fiancé. Marry him, if he's the only man you ever loved. There's nothing left for you to do here. Farewell."

"I can't abandon you in the midst of this calamity," said Caroline.

Jacques said nothing, but he frowned slightly, and with a peremptory gesture he urged the nun toward the door. She left, accompanied by her brother.

Chapter L: Conclusion According to Luizzi

As soon as Luizzi and Caroline had left that scene of desolation, the baron told his sister about his conversation with Henri. But he told it like a man who wants to achieve a goal he's set for himself; in other words, he passed over in silence the lieutenant's strange answers when he'd first accosted him. Nor did he tell his sister about Henri's stunned and guarded reaction; instead he invented astonishment and joy that made Caroline blush delicately. Still, when she insisted on knowing what slander had prompted her fiancé to return her letters so abruptly, Luizzi, who didn't want to admit how superficial his explanation with Henri had been, could think of nothing better than to blame it all on someone who by nature was easy to hold responsible for any bad deed, and who was far enough away to keep Caroline from checking up on the truth herself. Madame Barnet, the lawyer's wife—with her shrewish temper and her harsh words, whose needle was never done darning holes in her husband's socks, and whose tongue was never done poking holes in other people's reputations—Madame Barnet became the source of all the calumnies that had provoked Henri's behavior.

Caroline was easily persuaded by her brother. Together they discussed what had to be done so she could leave the branch of the convent where she was now living. To avoid a possibly lengthy debate, Luizzi decided she wouldn't return at all, and they'd go directly to Laval. But one obstacle stood in their way: they had absolutely no money. Luizzi thought it would be easy for Henri to resolve that difficulty. So they walked to Vitré, where the baron found them lodging in the least shabby inn; and he left Caroline there while he went to call on Henri.

He found him sitting up, in spite of his wound, and writing. When Luizzi explained what he needed, Henri was quite embarrassed, and the excuses he stammered out were rather beside the point, though it was perfectly normal for a lieutenant to have saved nothing from his meager pay. To the baron, with his two hundred thousand livres a year, it seemed impossible for a man of standing to be unable to raise a few thousand francs on the spot, and he thought it natural to suggest that Henri borrow it from friends or from the regimental paymaster. But the lieutenant explained angrily that he couldn't draw on the funds of officers who were as poor as he was, and he ended by saying, "If we were in Paris I'd have no trouble finding you enough to get you out of this godforsaken region, even if I had to pawn my epaulettes; but in this hole there isn't even a pawnshop. It's no wonder people say Bretagne is a land of savages."

The baron found it odd that for Henri the measure of a decent civilization was a pawnshop; but that still left him worried about how to get out of his bind.

Henri had no suggestions, and Luizzi was left to assume that, if he was so reluctant to ask his peers or his commanding officers for money, it could only be because he'd already gone beyond discretion there. The conversation didn't leave the baron with a better impression of Henri. But Luizzi had thought up such a handsome plan of action, and had created for himself such a noble role as a protective, devoted, and generous brother, that he did all he could to erase his bad opinion of Henri. He reminded himself it was common for a lieutenant to spend his youth in debt, and that all those lieutenants in excellent plays and comic operas, who seduce the women so gallantly, always carry as many IOUs as love letters in their pockets.

Luizzi was on his way back to the inn where he'd left Caroline, when he was pulled out of his reflections by a cry of surprise and by hearing his name spoken in astonishment. He looked up and saw a traveler getting out of a stage-coach that had stopped at the relay station. The man was Monsieur Barnet, the lawyer.

"By God!" cried Luizzi. "You're heaven-sent!"

"And this is a heaven-sent meeting. Where the devil have you been for the last eighteen months? I wrote to you twenty times, and never got an answer."

"I've been abroad," said the baron, embarrassed. "But what about you? What brings you to this part of the country?"

"Very important business, and a no less important act of affection. The first is a law case on which the fortune of one of my clients depends—over a million and a half, my word! A serious business: nothing less than an alleged will that would deprive Monsieur de Bridely of sixty thousand livres a year."

"You mean Count de Bridely? I think I know him. Isn't he the third son of the old marquis... a rascal of some kind?"

"No, no..." said Barnet in low voice, as if he were sharing a secret. "The old marquis's dead. This is his son, whom he acknowledged and legitimized."

"Monsieur Gustave!" cried the baron. "But he's just another con man!"[22]

"Even so, his rights are indisputable. And you know, baron, indisputable rights are always respectable, even when the holder is a crook. Besides, the Marquis de Bridely behaved very well in the circumstances. I was the one who discovered the inheritance luck had sent him, and he put the case into my hands, and if he wins it'll mean a fee of a hundred thousand francs for me."

"Certainly worth traveling two hundred leagues for."

"Even so, the expectation of a fee like that might not have been enough to make me leave Toulouse, if I hadn't needed to see someone in this part of the country who's also of interest to you, baron."

"Caroline?"

---

[22] Count de Bridely was last mentioned in Chapter XLI, in connection with his having robbed Madame de Marignon. He is in fact Gustave Ganguernet, son of Ganguernet the practical joker.

"Have you seen her?"

"Yes, I saw her, and she's here."

"Come on, come on, all aboard!" cried the stagecoach driver.

"Aren't you getting off in Vitré?" Luizzi asked Barnet, who was heading back to the stagecoach.

"The Bridely case is being tried in Rennes tomorrow. I won't get there till this evening, and I'll have to stay up all night with the barrister who's representing our side, to make him familiar with the important evidence I've brought."

"But what about Caroline?"

"I was planning to write to her, and see her on my way back. The date of her majority is coming up, and I have to render her an accounting of her fortune, and I'd be delighted to have you there so you can judge how well I've invested it—though I'm sorry all that money is going to go to a convent."

"No, no," said Luizzi firmly. "Caroline's getting married."

"Bah!" said Barnet, getting down from the stagecoach step. "To whom?"

"An officer, a certain Henri Donezau."

Barney frowned. "I feel like I know that name…"

"All aboard!" cried the driver. "You're the only one left, sir! We're already two hours behind the Laffitte et Caillard coach,[23] and we won't make up that time."

"I guess it's goodbye!" said Barnet. "Give me your address here."

"I plan to leave tomorrow. I'm returning to Paris."

"All right then, in Paris! I'll come back by way of Paris and see you, because you and I have business—and serious business—to discuss."

"Wait a moment! It's too long a story to explain, but I was stopped by some Chouans and robbed, and now here I am…"

"With no money. Damn! That's awkward. I only brought what I needed for the journey, because I knew I'd be traveling through an area in the middle of a civil war. Here's all I can do for you: a letter of credit on a banker in Rennes. You should easily be able to get it discounted, unless you'd rather I send you the money. You'd have it by noon tomorrow at the latest."

"That sounds better," said Luizzi, who had good reason for not wanting to go to a bank, where he might be asked for a passport to confirm his identity.

Luizzi and Barnet parted, and the baron went to tell his sister about the encounter. Her own news wasn't as good: one of the nuns from the convent, having heard what had happened at Jacques's, and not seeing Caroline return, had come to ask her about it. Angry at her new decision, the nun threatened to report her to the authorities; and though she had no grounds for doing so, the threat still

---

[23] The Messageries Générales Laffitte et Caillard was a real-life stagecoach line that started in the 1820s, used here as a competitor to the unnamed line in the story. The first partner's name was variously spelled Lafitte, Laffite, and Laffitte.

terrified Caroline. That troubled Luizzi further, because if he had to appear before some magistrate he could prove neither who he was nor what legal standing he had toward the young nun. He resolved to leave Vitré as soon as possible.

No sooner had he reached that decision than he got a note from Henri, who wrote to say he'd had a recurrence of his fever and was unable to come to Caroline to ask her forgiveness. Luizzi hurried to the lieutenant, whom indeed he found bedridden. Together they agreed that Luizzi would set off for Paris immediately, and once there he'd secure the necessary permission from the ministry of war and have the banns published, and as soon as his wound was healed Henri would come join them.

All that worked perfectly, at least as far as it related to Luizzi's departure. The next day he got the money Barnet had promised him, and three days later he was in Paris. Once he was there his days were filled with teaching Caroline about the world she was about to enter. They made countless purchases of furniture, fabric, dresses, jewelry. They went to the theater, where the baron ran into lots of old friends, who welcomed him the way you would a man just returned from traveling in Italy or England, and didn't inquire into the real reason for his absence. He introduced some of them to his sister, and within a few days Luizzi's loge at the Opéra had become a rendezvous for fashionable gentlemen begging to be allowed to offer their compliments to the beautiful Caroline de Luizzi.

Everything was going just as he'd hoped. He'd forwarded to Henri his permission from the ministry of war, and the lieutenant had replied that his wound would soon be healed enough to allow him to travel. Then one morning, when the baron was alone with Caroline in her apartment, a servant came to announce that a lady was asking to see her. Caroline knew no women in Paris: Luizzi hadn't wanted to present her anywhere before she was married, since he was in some difficulty about what last name she should use in society. So they were both surprised by her having a visitor, and Caroline told the servant to go ask for her name.

The servant returned and announced, "Mademoiselle Juliette Gelis."

With an exclamation of surprise, Caroline ran to the anteroom and threw herself into Juliette's arms with all the joy of a trusting soul reunited with her dearest friend. Then she quickly led her back to the parlor and introduced her to her brother.

Luizzi examined the woman curiously while she greeted him with lowered eyes. He saw his sister's description hadn't overstated her beauty, but he also noticed what must've eluded Caroline in her unworldliness: a striking languidness expressed in Mademoiselle Gelis's somewhat tired features, a weary suppleness in her slender, shapely figure that suggested a serpent's power to strike at its desired prey or the sinuous seductiveness of an Indian dancer aiming to smother a lover in her caress. But rather than let that reaction make up his mind for him, he resolved to listen carefully to what Juliette said, so he could judge her on better grounds than her face and her figure.

After the first outpourings of their fond reunion, in which the two friends cried out and kissed and held hands, came the time for an explanation. Luizzi took on the task of describing his chance meeting with Caroline and her chance meeting with Henri Donezau. As he did so he watched the effect of his story on Juliette. She listened to him with a smile on her lips, nodding her head gently in a way that suggested her approval of the happiness her friend had found by good luck. She turned to Caroline and held out her hand, saying in a heartfelt way that seemed to echo Caroline's joy, "So you'll be happy! Yes, happy—because he loved you very much. And he's a fine young man." Then, turning to Luizzi, she went on with charming grace, "I thank you for her sake, sir. She's your sister, but you don't know as well as I do how much she deserves the happiness you've brought her. By making her happy, you've repaid the debt others owed her."

A tear shone in Juliette's eye, a gilded tear lit by the glow of a grateful heart—a heart that, though powerless to help the girl she loved, was thankful to the man who was able to help her. All of Luizzi's doubts and suspicions evaporated before such deep devotion and such genuine affection, and he waited with interest to hear the story Caroline was pressing Juliette to tell.

"Alas," replied Juliette, "nothing could be simpler than what happened to me. When you left our convent I found myself alone, because you were my only friend, and persecuted, because you were my only protector. My courage—or rather the friendship that had sustained me, the strength I thought was in me but was only in you—suddenly fled. I took fright at the future I'd made for myself, and the impossibility of escape only added to my despair. I didn't dare admit it to my mother; she might've been able to bear the cost of supporting me at home, but I didn't want to make her burden greater. But she'd guessed at my suffering, and she blamed herself. That's when she wrote to you to send you the money you'd been accumulating with her…"

Juliette stopped, and Caroline said, "My brother knows all about it…"

Juliette went on, "Her letters went unanswered, as did mine."

"The Mother Superior in Toulouse must've kept your letters, and the one in Evron must've done the same with those from Madame Gelis," said Luizzi.

Juliette lowered her eyes and said softly, "I'm not accusing anyone of such an outrage, though the treatment I had to put up with certainly leads me to believe pious women would've been capable of that."

"But tell me what brought you to Paris," said Caroline impatiently.

"A wicked deed, which I've come here to confess to you," replied Juliette. "But a wicked deed that isn't irreparable. Just when I'd finally lost all courage, an old friend of my mother's who lives in Paris wrote to her, suggesting she acquire a business here like the one in Toulouse, a lending library. It was a valuable property, and by paying cash she could get it at a fraction of its real worth. Caroline, you and this gentleman don't know what poverty is like, you don't know what it's like for a mother to be offered a chance to rescue her daughter from a life of misery, to be reunited with her, to make a future for her."

111

Juliette stopped again, as if she were choking on the confession she was about to make. Then she went on in a strained voice, "Don't blame my mother! My mother used the money you'd arranged to have deposited with her. She bought that business, and we came to Paris... But the money's ready," she went on firmly, after her voice had dropped to make that painful admission. "It's ready, and I've brought it with me. I've known for a week you were in Paris, and it's so I could bring you the money that I put off coming to see you. I found the means to get it all, and now I've come without fear or shame to tell you I love you and I'm happy to see you again."

As she spoke, Juliette made as if to find something in the pocket of her dress.

"What are you doing?" cried Caroline. "I don't want it. You might've had trouble raising it. No, Juliette, no. Shall we consider it my gift—not to you but to your mother—on the occasion of my wedding?..."

"Accept it, miss," said Luizzi, softened both by Juliette's honorable feelings and by Caroline's gracious generosity.

Juliette resisted for a long time before finally accepting. Luizzi thought it right to leave them alone together, since the hearts of those two girls must be full of innocent secrets they wouldn't dare share in front of him. Entirely reassured about his sister's future, by Juliette's words as well as by the interest she herself had inspired him to feel in her, he went away.

Chapter LI: Continuation

From that day on, Juliette became Caroline's constant companion; she went with her to the theater and out walking. Caroline took delight in dressing up her friend, and she did her the honors, so to speak, with an innocence that made Luizzi smile. With sweet joy she often said to Juliette, "Oh, I'll get you married. I'll find a good match for you."

But no matter how hard she tried, Caroline couldn't achieve for Juliette the success, in admiration and respectful compliments, she herself found without even looking for it; and Juliette replied with a smile whose bitterness Caroline couldn't fault, "What can you do, my dear, I'm poor!"

As for Luizzi, who was delighted at having found such a pleasing companion for his sister, he tried in a thousand little ways to make Juliette forget her supposed misdeed over the money. A month passed in that way; everything was ready for Caroline's wedding. Without noticing, Luizzi had gotten in the habit of seeing Juliette every evening, to the point of feeling upset at her absence if she was late. He encouraged Caroline's affectionate liberality toward her friend. It was he who gave, through his sister's hands; and Caroline innocently saw in it only a generosity that, having filled her to overflowing, now spread to those she loved. As for Juliette, she was—or affected to be—quite ignorant of his benevolence; for she maintained toward Luizzi a tone of trusting modesty that made it clear to him she was unaware of his attentions.

Without precisely being in love with her, he began to fall a little under her sway. She seemed to have two different natures, which acted on him equally. Her looks, her manner, her eyes, her smile, breathed a voluptuousness that affected him deeply; her words, her feelings, her behavior, had such a solemn purity that he didn't dare listen to the desires that rose within him. In any case, Luizzi had no opportunity to see Juliette alone; and he indulged himself in some kind of undefined feeling for the girl. It had never occurred to him that he could marry her, and he scorned the idea of making her his mistress, first out of respect for Caroline, whose friendship for Juliette he didn't want to dishonor, and then because he realized the circumstances gave him so many advantages in a seduction of that kind that it would be quite wrong.

And yet he couldn't see Juliette or be aware of her presence near him without feeling drunk, as it were, on the scent of love that seemed to float about her. He looked at her then, not with the sweet ecstasy of sacred love whose beams seem to dissolve the human form of the beloved to reach her soul and embrace it in an ineffable caress... but instead as if his eyes were undressing her to feast on the unpredictable supple curves of her soft shoulder or her delicate foot, to dream of her naked as a temple priestess with her long flaming hair spread out around her, returning his fierce kisses with lips forever moist whose touch would devour him, to hear that voice explode in delighted cries of pleasure and lust, to feel that slender body writhe feverishly in the heat of love like the strings of a harp as it melts and protests in the fire into which it's been thrown. Then Juliette would say something solemn and innocent, and immediately he'd reproach himself for his mad desires and the vivid dreams into which his imagination wandered.

Meanwhile all had been made ready: Luizzi had reserved the apartment upstairs from his own for Henri and Caroline, in which one room would be set aside for Juliette. The marriage contract had been drawn up, and Luizzi had made sure it conformed to his sister's wishes. Though in fact he was providing Caroline with a dowry of five hundred thousand francs, he bowed to her tactful sensitivity: she didn't want the witnesses or even the lawyer to think Henri owed his entire fortune to her, so it was stipulated that the groom was bringing to the union a fortune of two hundred and fifty thousand francs and the bride a dowry of the same amount.

Henri arrived the morning of the very day the contract was to be signed, and the wedding was due to be performed the next day. Luizzi and Juliette were both present with Caroline when Henri entered the parlor. The baron couldn't help but notice the lieutenant's awkwardness and unease as he approached his intended. Henri's past bad behavior was excuse enough for that embarrassment, and Luizzi thought his own and Juliette's presence could only make it worse; so he told her he needed to consult her about a purchase he'd just made that he wanted to show her in private, to keep it a surprise from the newlyweds.

Juliette seemed not to hear him; she remained seated next to Caroline, who, with her eyes lowered, stammered as she replied to Henri's almost incoherent remarks. The baron was surprised to see that Juliette was observing them both attentively; he assumed it was just an innocent maiden's curiosity about a conversation between lovers. Still, noticing Henri's and Caroline's increasing embarrassment, he repeated his invitation to Juliette.

This time she rose quickly and said with feeling, "Yes, you're right. I'll come see what you bought, but only to admire it, because I know your gifts are always in the best taste and of the highest quality; and should a woman wish for anything, you can and do satisfy that wish with charming eagerness. I'm saying this in front of your future brother-in-law, so he knows how spoiled Caroline has been in terms of care and attention."

Her words struck Luizzi as oddly didactic in tone; while he led Juliette away, Henri gave her a look that was close to anger, and Caroline, trembling and upset, seemed to be imploring her brother with her eyes not to leave her defenseless against Henri's displeasure.

No sooner had they withdrawn than Juliette said to Luizzi, "Well then, sir, let's see this secret present you mean to give Caroline."

"The fact is, the gift isn't much, just a silver service for the newlyweds' home; the real present I hope I've given them is the privacy we've just left them in. They'll finally be able to speak of their love from their hearts."

He'd led Juliette to a small boudoir in his own apartment, where he offered her a seat. But she declined, and absently repeated his last words, "To speak of their love from their hearts."

"Could there be any better way to pass the time for lovers who haven't seen each other for so long?"

At first she said nothing; she seemed preoccupied by some anxious thought. Finally she said, "The marriage contract is to be signed tonight, isn't it? And they're to be married tomorrow? We should leave them to their lovers' talk."

After that she seemed to regain her composure. She sat on the sofa at one end of the room; leaning back on the cushions, she positioned her head so she could look up at the ceiling. That posture showed off magnificently the curving line of her lithe, slender body; where it lay over her hips, her dress emphasized its noticeably prominent contour; and, being slightly hitched up by the pressure of her body, the dress revealed the beginnings of a bold, shapely, attractive leg. Never had Luizzi seen Juliette so carelessly displayed; the provocative charm she always emanated now joined with the particular allure of this voluptuous pose, and he was filled with a burning desire to possess her.

At that moment he remembered the adventure of the stagecoach and Madame Buré's undoing, and even more the moment of delirium in which the Marquise du Val had given herself to him; and he hoped to achieve a triumph no less speedy now.[24] He sat down beside Juliette and, picking up on her own last words, he said, "They're speaking of their love. They're happy."

Juliette responded with an almost scornful smile, and kept her eyes on the ceiling. "I hope they are."

"Don't you envy them that happiness?"

She sat up suddenly and looked at him in surprise. Her eyes met his, which gleamed with desire, and a fresh astonishment appeared on her face, and now she seemed to want to look past his eyes to the depths of his mind. Slowly, and still in some surprise, she said, "You're asking me if I envy them their happiness?"

"Yes," he said passionately. "Haven't you ever thought it would be sweet to hear someone say, 'I love you'?"

Juliette let out a long slow exclamation, like someone who's just found the answer to what was puzzling her, and who's made clear a secret thought that was long uncertain. All she said was, "Ah!"

---

[24] See Chapter V for Madame Buré's stagecoach seduction, and Chapter III for Luizzi's seduction of Lucy du Val in her boudoir.

That *ah!* seemed to mean, "Ah! You're in love with me! That's how things are!" And that *ah!* contained neither anger nor shame, for a slight smile of pleasure and triumph flashed across Juliette's lips. But then she suddenly lowered her eyes, and recovered her coldness and reserve.

Luizzi went on, "You haven't answered. Didn't you understand me?"

"Perhaps better than you think."

"So what's your answer?"

"Do I have to answer? Do I owe you the secrets of my heart?"

"You can share them with a friend."

"In matters of love, only men have friends. A woman can only speak of what she feels to herself, or to the one who makes her feel that way."

"Do you know much about the mysteries of love?"

"Perhaps more than you think."

"Ah!" he cried. "I'd be delighted to hear what you've learned."

"It might amuse you for a moment, baron," she said gravely. "But you wouldn't want to have that pleasure at the cost of forcing me to stir up memories, and I can only enjoy the happiness of friendship by leaving those memories asleep at the bottom of my soul."

"So you've been in love?"

"Yes," she said with difficulty.

"You've been loved?"

"I've been betrayed," she replied sadly.

Luizzi had long since gotten over the sensual impulse that had brought him to this point. But now he found himself involved in a conversation about emotions, and he thought his honor and his self-esteem required him to keep it going. He asked delicately, "Perhaps he was unfaithful?"

Juliette frowned slightly. "No, baron. Someone who's never loved can't be unfaithful in the usual sense of the word. And in the sense you're giving it, perhaps, a man to whom you've granted no favors can't be unfaithful either."

"I beg your pardon. You said you'd been betrayed."

"Oh! Betrayed as no other woman has ever been in her life! Imagine a poor girl whose friend—the only friend she trusts in the world—persuades her that a young man she met by chance is in love with her. Imagine that the young man agrees to keep up the illusion by every means possible, by the most dogged pursuit and the most passionate correspondence. Now imagine that, when he's gotten ten an avowal from the poor misled girl, he drops her for no reason... Because the trick's been played, because he no longer needs her as a disguise for his affair with the poor girl's friend."

"Oh, certainly, that sounds awful. But could such a crime really have taken place?"

"Yes, yes," replied Juliette, with a strange look on her face. "And the details of that betrayal would astonish you. But you must see how hard it is for me to speak of it..."

116

"I'm sure," said Luizzi, seeing a way to bring these sentimental confessions to an end. "And now I understand your painful surprise when I asked you if you envied those two happy lovers close by."

She smiled, and lay back, resuming her seductive pose with such careless abandon that he had to assume the girl was just unaware how provocative she looked. She fixed her piercing eyes on him, and a thousand varied expressions ran across her face in a few seconds. Then all her animation ebbed, giving way to a long, intense examination that troubled him and rekindled the disturbance in his senses he'd felt earlier.

He drew near her and pressed his body gently against hers. She stayed still and didn't look away.

"Juliette!" he murmured softly. "Oh, tell me: would one betrayal in love make you give up on all love?"

"And what good would it do me to be in love?" she asked, either feelingly or mockingly.

"You just don't know how intoxicating the pleasures of love can be. Of all the women I've ever met, there's none whose presence made me feel it as intensely as you do."

She didn't blush, but she seemed annoyed. Then she recovered and, gently biting her twitching lips to suppress a smile that irritated him, she said, "And those intoxicating pleasures, I assume you could teach them to me?"

That question would've been so blatantly flirtatious if it had been intentional, that it could only be so naive as to be ridiculous.

"Teach them to you, Juliette?" replied Luizzi, again drawing close enough to breathe the aroma of love this woman exuded. "Teach them to you? Oh, that would be inexpressible ecstasy!"

He took hold of her hand, and she didn't withdraw it.

"Maybe for you," said the former nun with despairing candor. "As for me, I believe only in the sorrows of love."

"It has its hours of delight, believe me," he said as he slid his arm around her waist. In her attempt to resist, she arched, like a bow under tension, and thereby caused her thigh to press against him, while throwing back her heaving breast and her straining face.

"Believe me, Juliette," he murmured again, his voice full of arousal, "that's the essence of life, and the way to forget all your sorrows."

"I don't understand," she said, her voice broken and trembling.

"Oh!" he said, pulling her entirely into his arms. "Can't you sense it's already unbelievably intoxicating just to feel our hearts beating, one against the other?"

And Luizzi, carried away by his burning desire, pressed his lips to Juliette's half-open, panting mouth. He felt her whole body vibrate, he saw her half-closed eyes grow veiled and hidden behind her eyelids, he took hold of that lithe, unguarded body. Determined to take advantage of one of those moments of mental confusion that cause even women with the most imperious natures to fall, he was already thrusting aside the last obstacles that her immobility put in his way—when suddenly, rising like a snake that's been stepped on, she stood up and pushed him away. Shaking all over, her teeth chattering, she cried out loudly in a strained voice, "No! No! No! No!"

She seemed to be addressing herself rather than him. Luizzi, confused, tried to find something to say. But giving him no time either to apologize or to pursue her, she said in the same troubled tone, "Let's go back to your sister."

She left the boudoir and burst back into the parlor where Henri and Caroline were. The lieutenant was sitting so close to his intended that he quickly drew back when he heard the door open. Caroline lowered her eyes; she was blushing, ashamed, upset. And Luizzi found the equivocal glance Juliette threw back at him to be at the very least extraordinary: coming from any other girl, it could've been intended to mean, "The same thing was going here as in the other room."

Chapter LII: The Consequences of a Joke

Just then several visitors arrived, and Luizzi was not a little amazed to hear announced, among the other names, the Marquis Gustave de Bridely. He was about to greet him with a coldness that should warn the ex-Elléviou how displeased his host was by this visit, when his manservant handed him an urgent letter, saying the messenger was waiting for an answer.

Luizzi took it, and at the same moment Gustave handed him a note, saying as he did so, and looking delighted by own witticism, "Here's another letter, sir, which between your hands I've been asked to place."[25]

Pursuing his wish to be rid of this man's company, Luizzi coolly accepted his letter and opened it first. When he'd read it he said aloud, "Oh, so Monsieur Barnet is here?"

If he hadn't been off on one side of the parlor with Gustave, he would've noticed the remarkable effect that news produced on those who heard it: Juliette and Henri exchanged a quick, fearful glance.

But Gustave explained, "We arrived an hour ago, and I hurried here. But Monsieur Barnet's note isn't the only one you've received... I'll leave you to your correspondence."

With that, the handsome marquis moved—with a poise that spoke of more than comic-opera conceit—toward the pair on the other side of the room. Now only Luizzi's absorption in reading the letter Pierre had brought him kept him from hearing Gustave's exclamation at the way Juliette and Henri looked at him. Caroline noticed; but Henri had quickly approached Gustave to lead him into a distant corner and speak to him.

Before Gustave had time to reply, Luizzi turned toward him and said, with considerable insolence, "This letter concerns you, sir."

"Me?" said Gustave in a tone of disrespect.

"You," repeated Luizzi with scornful anger. "And I need an explanation from you on this matter. Be so kind as to follow me."

"Here I come, here I come!" said Gustave, not at all troubled by the baron's lofty manner. They moved into the boudoir where the scene between Juliette and Luizzi had taken place earlier. Eying him up and down, Gustave asked, "Well, baron, what's the matter?"

---

[25] The quotation is from *Beverlei* (1768) a play by Bernard-Joseph Saurin. The awkward syntax in French is the source of the unintentional humor (the play is a tragedy), and the line was much quoted. The original reads, "*C'est une lettre / Qu'entre vos mains, monsieur, on m'a dit de remettre.*"

"The matter is, you are..." Luizzi paused, then went on, "I'm reluctant to use certain terms, but you'll find them written in this note, with which I'm in complete agreement."

Gustave took the note, and read the following:

Sir,

I unwittingly introduced a schemer and a man without honor into Madame de Marignon's circle. That man without honor, that schemer, was you. She has forgiven me for the mistake I made. You KNOWINGLY introduced to her another schemer of your type. That man is the so-called Marquis de Bridely; for that, I cannot forgive you. If, as rumor has it, you've gone insane, I'll send you my doctor. If you're in your right mind, I'll send you my witnesses in an hour.

—Cosmo de Mareuilles

The marquis was silent for a moment, while the baron eyed him angrily. Finally the young Elléviou handed the note back to Luizzi and chuckled, "You agree with everything in that note?"

"I do, sir!" he replied, carried away by his rage.

"With the part about you as well as the part about me?" asked Gustave, prancing about.

"Sir!" cried the baron, whose anger had led him to forget how insulting Mareuilles's letter was to himself. "Sir, such insolence calls for punishment."

"So you want to fight two duels instead of one?" asked Gustave calmly. "As you please. I'm not particular, and I'll go first or second, depending on what suits you."

"I don't fight people like you," said Luizzi contemptuously. "I throw them out!"

Gustave went pale with anger, but he contained himself and went on, "One moment, please! You'll fight me, baron, because since we're alone we can speak freely. You knew very well who I was when you gave me a letter of introduction to Madame de Marignon. For you, I was an instrument for a little revenge, an instrument that now you'd like to throw out of your parlor into the street; but that's not going to happen, sir. I bear a nobler title than you do. I'm almost as wealthy, because I won my suit as the legitimate heir to the late Marquis de Bridely. I am now, by irrevocable judgment, the Marquis de Bridely. And you can be sure I won't now tolerate treatment I wouldn't have tolerated when I was just the actor Gustave, bastard son of Aimé Zéphirin Ganguernet and Marianne Gargablou, née Libert." As he said those words quietly but firmly, Gustave stepped toward Luizzi with a menacing look.

"None of that," replied the baron coolly, "will make me forget you owe your title and your fortune to a low trick..."

"A low trick you found delightful while it was useful to you..."

"Well then, sir, what is it you want?"

"I'll tell you. Our interests are both involved in this matter; we can't separate them. Monsieur de Mareuilles cannot be allowed to make accusations like this against either you or me with impunity. Either I'll fight him—and I promise you I'll know how to force him into it—and you'll serve as my second; or you'll fight him, and I'll serve as yours."

"I refuse."

"Be careful!" said Gustave, with the composure of a man for whom a duel is a trivial enough thing that he can calculate the consequences exactly. "Be careful! If you reject me as your second, I'll let Monsieur de Mareuilles know, which'll mean you admit to the wrongdoing he accuses you of; whereas to accept me is to show you're convinced you were in the right, it's to have affirmed out of friendship then what is now an incontestable legal fact, it's to have believed me then to be what I am now, the Marquis de Bridely."

Luizzi considered, then replied, "You might be right, as long as you remember there was a fraud involved, which disgraces the legal Marquis de Bridely just as much as the actor Gustave."

"Oh, come now! I got out of that fraud charge without a verdict. Don't be so particular, you who got off a murder charge by reason of insanity!"

"What! You know about that?" cried Luizzi in horror.

"Monsieur Niquet was the lawyer for the family that sued me."

"And Monsieur Barnet?..."

"My dear sir, I learned what I know by a remarkable coincidence. It's an odd story, I promise!"

"As you might imagine, I'm not especially interested in hearing it."

"I do imagine that. You have a secret of mine; I wanted to have one of yours, and I've kept it."

Luizzi considered again, then said, "I accept your proposition, but on one condition: that I fight Monsieur de Mareuilles first."

"That's your prerogative."

"Now I need another witness."

"Why not Henri Donezau? I think that's who I saw in your parlor."

"You know him? Oh, I see. You must've met him in Toulouse when you were with Ganguernet."

"Exactly."

"I can't do it. He's marrying my sister tomorrow."

"Your sister!" cried the marquis.

Luizzi read his astonishment in a certain light, and responded to that. "My sister, sir. Yes, my sister. My father's daughter, just the way you're Ganguernet's son."

"And you're marrying her off to Henri?" asked Gustave in surprise. "Though in fact," he went on with a knowing air, "in her position, with no name, no family..."

"There happen to be no marquis fathers for sale!" said Luizzi, offended by his impertinent tone.

Gustave laughed, and said with exquisite conceit, "Don't I play my part well?"

"You can drop it with me. But we have other things to deal with. I'll go find a friend. My sister and Henri can't hear about what's going to happen. Please go back to the parlor for a while: since you know Henri, you'll have to give him some explanation for what's going on."

"Oh, I have an excellent story about a lost child for that."

"Good. Tell them Monsieur Barnet's letter requires me to leave immediately. You can receive Monsieur de Mareuilles's witnesses. Make the rencounter for tomorrow morning at seven. The wedding's at ten o'clock at the town hall, and at eleven at the church; everything as hush-hush as possible. If I prevail, we'll be back before ten. Otherwise, you can give my sister a letter accounting for my absence, and they can go through the ceremony without me."

"Understood."

Luizzi sent a short reply to Cosmo de Mareuilles, and then left. Gustave went back to the parlor. Henri latched onto him, on the pretext of showing him the apartment the baron had prepared for the newlyweds; and Caroline and Juliette were left alone together.

Everything took place as Luizzi had arranged: Mareuilles's witnesses came to set a time for the rencounter, and they agreed on the next morning.

When the baron got back, his lawyer had already come, and the time for the reading of the marriage contract had long since passed. Juliette, Gustave, and the couple to be wed were the only people present—Luizzi having wanted to spare his sister the anguish of having her painful words, "father and mother unknown," heard by anyone except those familiar with her situation. Henri, to whom Luizzi had already given the sum the contract stated he possessed, was now handed a portfolio containing Caroline's dowry, since as was customary the contract would serve as the receipt. Henri was surprised by such punctiliousness, and expressed his embarrassment to Luizzi.

"Business must be transacted in accordance with the rules," said the baron with a gracious smile. "I have reasons I'll explain tomorrow—at least I hope so—that force me to take such care over this."

Juliette, Henri, and Gustave exchanged a covert glance. It was already late, but for the remainder of the evening Luizzi, preoccupied by the duel that awaited him in the morning, was oblivious to the anxious but mute sadness that had come over Caroline.

The next morning his other witness arrived at six thirty. Luizzi handed Gustave the letter that would explain his absence to Henri in case it went badly for him, and the three of them set off for the Bois de Vincennes. When the parties are determined to fight, the preliminaries for a duel don't take long; but this case entailed explanations that dragged things out for a while.

With his usual smugness, Mareuilles said, "I expected Baron de Luizzi, who I assume is here to clear his honor, would be seconded by honorable witnesses… Of course I'm only referring to one of them," he added, bowing to Luizzi's second companion.

Gustave wanted to speak, but Luizzi stopped him and, with a loftiness that diminished Mareuilles's cockiness considerably, he replied, "For my choice of witnesses, whoever they might be, to seem remarkable to you, sir, would require first of all that I'd come here to clear my honor. But make no mistake about it, I've come here to punish a fool's conceit and a boor's insolence."

"And I'll carry on the punishment, sir!" added Gustave. "I, the Marquis de Bridely, will do you the honor of fighting you, Monsieur de Mareuilles, son-in-law to Madame Olivia de Marignon, daughter of that bawd Madame Béru, who kept a gambling house and a brothel!"

Mareuilles, who was more or less aware of Madame de Marignon's antecedents, turned pale at Gustave's words and cried angrily, "Scoundrel!"

"Come, come!" said Gustave. "Don't get all worked up like that, you little Monsieur de Mareuilles. I've just come from Bretagne, where I heard all about you."

Mareuilles, visibly troubled, turned to one of his witnesses, a young man with the charming looks of a sweet pale child, and said, "Come on, du Bergh, let's get this over with!"

"Oh!" laughed Luizzi. "Is that Monsieur du Bergh? I'm delighted to meet Monsieur du Bergh. This duel wouldn't have been the same without him!"[26]

"What do you mean by that?" asked the young man in a high voice like a flute.

"Come, gentlemen," said Mareuilles. "We aren't here to get acquainted. Where are the swords?"

"Here," said Luizzi's second witness.

The ground on which they stood not being judged suitable, they went deeper into the woods in search of another spot. After a long half hour of walking they found a flat open area. They handed the swords to the two enemies, who went at each other with a forthrightness that proved they both had the courage of their convictions, while also with enough skill and caution to show they both meant to defend themselves as much as they meant to harm the other. However, Mareuilles, fired up with anger provoked by what Luizzi and Gustave had said earlier, put more intensity into his attack, and soon Luizzi was forced to retreat.

After a few more sallies Mareuilles stopped. "Are you hurt?"

---

[26] This is Edgard du Bergh, mentioned in passing in Chapter XIX as the supposed son (of dubious parentage) of the Baron du Bergh who was poisoned on his wedding night.

"I can't feel it," said Luizzi, attacking again. But Mareuilles made him retreat again, till the baron had backed up so far he'd reached the edge of a small field of clover.[27]

Mareuilles stopped once more and said scornfully, "I'd be happy to kill you, but it wouldn't *suit* me to reap you! I don't want to have to hunt for you like a *diamond* in the rough!" he added with a laugh.

"Very funny," replied Luizzi in the same bantering tone. Then, with a lunge at Mareuilles, he added, "Come, let's see which of us will have to use a *spade* to bury the other!"

"Well punned!" said Mareuilles, parrying quickly and retreating in turn before the baron's heated attack. "But I wouldn't care to join your *club*!" he added, for once again he'd wounded the baron in the arm.

"I'll keep fighting till my *heart* fails me!" replied Luizzi; and as they fought, over the clash of their swords and their furious laughter, they exchanged puns that at any other time they'd have left to the lesser wits who make word-play their stock in trade.

"Very nice!" said Mareuilles. "You've got a good *hand*!"

But at that moment the baron thrust so hard that his sword pierced Mareuilles's shoulder.

"That's the *trick*!" cried Gustave, seeing Mareuilles fall. "And the *game* is ours!"

Almost immediately Luizzi, who'd lost a lot of blood from his two wounds and whom only anger had sustained, felt faint and dropped next to his adversary. Seeing the two men lying there unconscious, their witnesses thought only of reviving them. Luizzi was the first to come to; once he was sure Mareuilles was still breathing, he left the dueling ground and returned to his carriage.

"Would you like to go home?" asked Gustave.

"No, it would frighten my sister and cause a big scene. She'd want to postpone the ceremony, and I can tell you I have no desire to begin those tedious preparations all over again. These cuts are nothing, they just struck me in the flesh of the arm."

"True, but they're near the wrist, and in cases like this there's a risk of tetanus. You can't fool around with sword cuts."

"Can't I go to your place?"

"With pleasure, though I'm just living in furnished rooms. But we'll see Barnet there too; he's staying next door to me, and I can leave you in his care while I go warn your sister."

"That'd be perfect."

---

[27] The French word for clover, *trèfle*, is also the word for the card suit known in English as clubs, prompting the series of card game puns that follows.

An hour later they arrived at the rue du Helder. Barnet was out. They sent for a doctor, who bled the baron and prescribed complete bed rest. It was then almost ten o'clock.

"Hurry to my place," Luizzi said to Gustave, "and tell my sister my firm wish is that she get married even without me there, and that I'll be back around two. After that you can tell Henri, and I'll have myself taken home."

"That's not advisable," said the doctor.

"We'll see," replied Luizzi. "In any case, leave word here for Monsieur Barnet to come see me the moment he gets in."

Gustave did as the baron wished, and went away.

The loss of blood from his wounds, and the bloodletting the doctor had carried out, had left Luizzi extremely weak. As soon as he could stop worrying about everything that had to be done, he fell into a stupor very close to sleep. He couldn't tell how long it lasted, but he came out of it when he heard the sound of the door opening and the clock striking noon.

The person who entered was none other than Monsieur Barnet. Luizzi motioned to him to come closer, and the lawyer cried, "Well! What's this I hear? You've been wounded in a duel!"

"It's nothing, it's nothing," he replied, surprised at his own weakness and the intense pain caused by the two wounds he'd thought were so trivial.

"It's too much for a man with pressing business that requires his immediate presence. Are you aware you were almost ruined by an old scoundrel named Rigot?"

"Yes, yes, but he lost his suit."

"The first round, yes, but he appealed. In your absence I dragged the case out from one step to the next. But the final verdict will come next month, and we have to prepare every possible defense."

At that moment Luizzi remembered that the Devil had told him his fortune had been restored; and if he'd been alone now he would certainly have summoned him to pick a quarrel with him about it.

But Barnet went on, "Since this isn't the time to discuss highly entangled business with you, tell me why you weren't taken back to your place, where I was surprised not to find you."

"If you went to my place you must've have figured it out, because you saw Caroline, I assume?"

"Not at all," said Barnet sourly. "She sent out some impertinent maidservant to tell me she couldn't see me."

"You'll have to forgive her. A woman has so much to do on her wedding day."

"What!" exclaimed Barnet in a loud voice. "She's getting married?"

"By this time," said Luizzi with a glance at the clock, "it must be a done deal."

"And you married her off to that Henri Donezau?" cried Barnet again, articulating every syllable in shock and anger.

"In fact, yes."

"Oh my God! I've come too late."

"What is it?" cried Luizzi, sitting up. "Has Monsieur Donezau deceived me?... There might still be time..."

The door opened and Gustave came in, followed by Henri and Caroline; with a cry she ran to her brother's bedside.

"It's nothing, good sister, less than nothing... Calm yourself..."

"You promised me you'd be brave," said Gustave. "Don't take fright like this. Remember, the doctor said strong emotions would be dangerous for the baron, and that you could make him more ill than he is now."

"I'll be quiet, I'll be quiet," replied Caroline, drying her tears. "But he can't stay here, he should come back to his apartment..."

"You're right," said Luizzi. "Gustave, please arrange everything."

Gustave left the room, but Henri remained; and his presence, mute so far, reminded Luizzi of what Barnet had said. Though alarmed in spite of himself at the lawyer's words, he still managed to sound cordial as he asked the lieutenant, "So, should I call you brother, sir? Is the ceremony done?"

"Yes, my brother, my brother!" replied Henri, very moved, as he held out his hand to the baron.

Luizzi observed that Barnet was studying Henri, and that he gave a little nod of approval at Henri's words. Soon they began to make ready for Luizzi's departure; and while everyone was busy the baron motioned to Barnet and said to him quietly, "What did you mean when you said, 'I've come too late'?"

"Nothing, nothing... it was connected to another matter... I might've proposed a different match for her..."

"You think Henri isn't a man of integrity?"

"I'm not saying that; but he isn't rich, and perhaps..."

"Were you thinking of the Marquis de Bridely?"

"He has an income of a good sixty thousand livres," replied Barnet happily, as if he were delighted to have a chance to explain what he'd said.

"Why didn't you write to me?" asked Luizzi, who was still a little mistrustful.

"Oh, damn! Because... because..." Barnet hesitated. "Because the marquis hadn't yet won his case," he added quickly, as if he'd just thought of that explanation.

All was now ready for Luizzi to be moved. He walked downstairs with a fairly firm step; but once he was in the carriage its movement dizzied him so badly that more than once he almost passed out. Finally he reached his own apartment; and it wasn't without a certain sense of dread that he found himself once again lying sick in the same bed in which he'd nearly died at the hands of his servants.

Still, the care he got from his sister and Barnet comforted him; but in spite of himself, and to his surprise, he found he couldn't consider Henri's presence reassuring. That idea worried him so much over the course of the day that by evening he had a high fever; and when the doctor came he wasn't happy with the state of the wounds. "You must have absolute physical and mental rest, baron. Otherwise the consequences could be serious."

"I'll spend the night by my brother," said Caroline.

Gustave glanced at Henri and made a funny face, and Henri said, "I assume my brother-in-law thinks that's unnecessary?"

"Why would he?" asked Juliette sharply. "No one could take better or more attentive care of the baron. Nuns know how to treat wounds."

"But weren't you a nun too?" asked Gustave mockingly.

"Do you think it would be appropriate for me to stay in a man's room?" asked Juliette with injured dignity.

"It would at least be the generous thing to do," said Gustave, with a glance at Henri and Caroline.

Juliette bit her lip angrily and said nothing.

"I'll stay," said Caroline. "I want to stay. And since it's already late, you should all leave, I implore you."

"Come along, Henri," said Gustave. "Come along, my friend, and resign yourself…"

Henri left, looking disappointed, and Juliette watched him go with intense curiosity. No sooner had the others left the room than she approached Caroline and said, "I'll stay here in the building; I'll go to bed fully dressed, and if you need me, come upstairs and I'll be ready."

Then she turned to Luizzi; bending over him close enough for her warm breath to disconcert him, she said quietly, "Goodnight, baron! Goodnight, Armand!"

When Juliette was gone, Luizzi could still hear her resonant, passionate voice saying his name like an avowal. Left alone with Caroline, he thought over everything he'd seen and heard that day that struck him as ambiguous. But it was nothing but slight gestures, passing glances, fragments of words, which he tried in vain to reconstitute and which always fled from him. From time to time his reason prevailed enough for him to be aware that his imagination, heightened by fever, gave hidden meaning to countless little incidents that in fact had none.

But almost immediately his thoughts began to spin again. All of those trivial incidents crossed and recrossed his mind like the flotsam from a shipwreck drifting on the waves from side to side in the dark while a castaway standing on a rock tries in vain to seize hold of anything. The physical vertigo the castaway would eventually experience slowly gained on Luizzi's mind. He could feel it, and he wanted to snap out of it; but, unable to turn his attention away from the doubts that floated within him, he resolved to settle them: he picked up his little bell.

Then he glanced at Caroline sitting in an armchair at the foot of his bed; she'd gradually drifted off to sleep. In any case, the Devil's voice and presence were perceptible to no one but him. He shook the little talisman—but it made no sound, and at that moment his arm became totally rigid, his body bent backward like a bow no human strength could unstring, and his jaws clenched hard enough to shatter his teeth.

He realized he was suffering from that terrible disease called tetanus, a fairly common consequence of wounds that have penetrated the muscles. He couldn't move to ring his bell, nor cry out for help, and then he felt as if someone had struck him a terrible blow on the head. He closed his eyes, and he saw...

Chapter LIII: Tetanus

He saw a light brighter and more dazzling than his eyes had ever beheld. It was so intense, so piercing, that it passed through opaque objects the way ordinary light goes through crystal. It was so blinding that it cast the shadows of the candle flames on the walls. This wasn't the magical light that had overcome walls and darkness and distance and all intervening objects to show him Henriette Buré in her terrible dungeon; it was a transparency that allowed objects themselves to be seen, though he could also see beyond them, as if everything he saw were made of glass, which conceals nothing but is still visible; it was an astonishing, magnificent spectacle, in which everything was filled with light and everything radiated light.

He thought he could see past his room to the empty parlor, furnished just as it was; past that parlor to the dining room and all it contained; past that to the entry hall where Pierre was asleep on a bench. Above his own head he thought he could see through the ceiling to his sister's apartment; recognizing each piece of furniture, he carried out his strange inspection with delighted curiosity. He looked around carefully for any furniture he might've missed; he examined every piece of furniture, and found he could see the minutest objects inside each of them. He let his eyes, so to speak, wander from room to room, noting every detail of their decor, because they were unoccupied, and though he marveled at the sight, he could've wished for a little more life in them—till he recognized Juliette's room.

She was there, and Henri was pacing the floor, while she spoke to him animatedly. Luizzi listened, and found he could hear just as well as he could see. Sounds reached him clearly and directly, as if nothing stood in their way, as if they were crossing open space devoid of anything but the air that carried them. And this was what he heard:

"You can say what you like, Henri, but you're trying to deceive me. I know you, and I know you've got a crush on that little idiot Caroline."

"What the devil's got into you? I do have to sleep with my wife, after all."

"And what if I don't want you to?" she cried furiously.

"Then let's get out of here! I'd like nothing better. I've got the brother-in-law's five hundred thousand francs in my pocket. Let's take advantage of him being sick in bed. In two days we can be out of France."

"Yesterday we could've done it; but now that Barnet's in Paris it could be dangerous. He's the kind of man who'd run to the police to report us at the slightest suspicion, and the telegraph moves faster than a stagecoach."

"Does that old snake of a lawyer know everything?"

"He doesn't know the details. The old crook doesn't realize I was the one who threw Caroline's nun's habit onto the lamp so she'd have to wear other clothes and she'd feel obliged to go to the festival at Auterive. I assume nobody could've told him how I persuaded the little fool you were in love with her, and how the channel that worked so well for the letters we sent each other made her crazy for you."

"Does she really love me?" asked Henri, with the vanity of a bull.

"Go ahead and brag! Come on, darling, if I hadn't dictated your first letter, and if you hadn't had all the rest written by your sergeant major, that good-looking Fernand who writes pretty good comedies, I don't think she'd ever have lost her head for you."

"Those letters?" he said dismissively. "They weren't anything special. You can't imagine how much they bored me when the baron gave them back to me when we were with the Chouans and I finally read them."

"Didn't you read them when you wrote them?"

"I copied them, and devil take me if I understood them. But I've had to study them, and now I can say like anyone else, 'You'll be the soul of my life, the heart of my heart.' I can spout platonic love from the rooftops."

"That must be how you reduced Caroline to quite a state the first time you were alone with her, and if we hadn't shown up just then, I don't know..."

"You're one to talk! You were as red as a rooster when you came back in with the baron."

"Oh, that's different."

"How?" he asked bluntly.

"What can I say, darling? The baron's a handsome man, he's got an income of two hundred thousand livres, and since you're married..."

"Watch out!" he said, raising his fist.

"Oh, please! What are you going do anyway?"

"I'll break your arms, his and yours," he said with a fierce, vicious look.

"Blah, blah, blah! You've become a blowhard, that's all."

"Let's not go there. You've played enough tricks on me in my life, and this last one is the biggest of all."

"Thanks! I got you a wife worth five hundred thousand francs."

"I could easily have married her without your help."

"Really? You would've married her without my introducing you, your fine eyes would've made her burn without me to kindle the flame; and of course, you'd have gotten two hundred and fifty thousand francs as your part of the dowry without my getting her to point out that clause to her brother?"

"Oh, I know you can be clever when you get involved... But that poor woman—I swear, I pity her!"

"And I pity the baron too, darling: he wants me so bad, so bad..."

"This again!"

"I promise I behaved virtuously. And as recently as yesterday, in his boudoir, I wanted to toy with him... But my God, there was a point where I sensed my head wasn't in control anymore, and if he'd really, really wanted to..."

"Juliette!" murmured Henri furiously.

"Oh, go sleep with your wife and leave me alone!"

"By God, you're right," he said angrily. "Here I go!" He turned to the door.

"Henri!" cried Juliette, getting up. "If you leave here tonight, it's over between us!"

"Fine," he said, coming back. "Don't shove your baron in my face, and let's talk seriously. Going back to Barnet: what makes you think he suspects something?"

"Here it is, since I have to tell you everything. It's about the six thousand francs he'd given Caroline, which I'd deposited with my mother, and which were meant for your supposed elopement..."

"All right, we pocketed that six thousand, and you were able to find a nice place to come stay in Paris, thanks to the money you and the good Lord gave us."

"Well, Barnet began inquiring about that six thousand francs in Toulouse, while I was still there; the nuns told him they knew nothing about it, and that Caroline must've taken it with her to Evron. Since old Barnet knew the nuns let their favorite do more or less whatever she wanted, because they were hoping to get her fortune, he seemed satisfied with that explanation. But recently, on his way back from Rennes, he made a detour by way of Evron, and he asked the Mother Superior there whether Caroline had brought money with her, and she said no."

"But the way you explained it to Caroline settles it."

"For her, yes. But not for Barnet, who heard unflattering things about you in Vitré. With that, plus the missing six thousand..."

"But couldn't she have brought the money back to Paris with her?"

"Sure! And you think, if Caroline had six thousand francs on her, the baron would've been forced to borrow money from Barnet to get from Vitré to Paris? That's especially what made the old rascal suspicious. So then he remembered the first twelve hundred francs he'd deposited with my mother, and he thought the six thousand might've gone where that went."

"Where'd you hear all this?"

"Oh, from Gustave, who was with that old buzzard of a lawyer, and who—knowing nothing about anything—said he knew me, when Barnet mentioned my name one day."

"And what did Gustave tell him?"

"Not much, luckily! He said he'd known me when I was a bit player at the theater in Marseilles."

"Nowhere else, I hope?"

"Oh, no. Gustave never came to Aix when I was there with my mother."

"That whore!" cried Henri, as if the word Aix brought back vile memories.

"Oh, she was just... plying her trade."

"And she certainly gave you a fine one!"

"Hell! It was no worse than yours. And without the July Revolution, when you managed to shoot old Bequenel with the excuse that he was a spy, and steal all the fake letters of credit he was discounting for you, I'd like to know where you'd be now! It was worth at least a lieutenant's epaulet to you, thanks to the glowing recommendation I wrote for you—whereas there are plenty of others, who really did fight bravely against the Swiss guards and the Royal Guard, who've been cast aside or sent to Algeria as ordinary foot soldiers. So don't act all superior about what I was before you met me."

"Still, you kept it up..."

"And you had no objection, as long as it put food in your mouth," replied Juliette with a look of disgust. "But now that you've got a lot of money..."

"Well, now I don't want the baron sniffing around you."

"And I don't want your wife to be your wife."

"But what do you expect me to do?"

"Just do nothing. She's as innocent as a two-day-old baby, I guarantee."

"Sure, but someone might ask her questions: her brother... Barnet..."

"You think?" She gave a mocking laugh. "You think Barnet's going to walk up to Caroline and say, 'Ma'am, be so kind as to tell me whether your husband has...'? Give me a break! You see, darling, you'll never learn how to behave like respectable people."

"You're just the opposite: you put on the airs of a princess, the manners of a prude..."

"Oh!" she cried enthusiastically. "You see, that's because women have more in their heads and their hearts than you men do. If I'd been alive during the Revolution, I'd have been a field marshal... Or if I'd lived earlier, I'd have been du Barry...[28] But there's nothing I can do now, with men as stupid as they are greedy."

"Does that include me?"

"Oh, I like you, that's different. But you know, if you weren't such a jealous animal, I wouldn't leave that baron a single sou of his two hundred thousand francs a year..."

"I'm rich enough as it is."

"Come on. I'll let you have Caroline, I don't even care, and I'll take the baron."

---

[28] Madame du Barry was Louis XV's last official mistress. She was of humble birth, but worked her way up the ranks of high society as a notorious courtesan. (Her title of nobility was a face-saving device of the king's.) She was guillotined during the Revolution.

"All right," said Henri. Then he changed his mind and cried, "No, absolutely not!"

"You won't?"

"No! I loathe that baron, you know. I loathe him because you like him. He pleases you, with his fancy talk and his yellow kid gloves and his high and mighty airs... If he were an old man, that'd be different, I wouldn't care. But him? No, a thousand times no."

"Fine. But if you think about having Caroline, you'll just see!"

"All right, we'll see."

"Be careful! She tells me everything, and if something happens I'll know."

"And if something happens?"

"I've got your fake letters of credit, darling."

"You miserable whore! You kept them?"

"They're in a safe place. I've taken my precautions."

Henri slapped his brow angrily.

Juliette went on, "Oh, I know you, sweetheart. I told you, you'd like nothing better than to drop me now—thanks!... Anyway, if that's what you want, go to your wife... You're a free man..."

"The devil take my wife! I don't care about her."

"More than you'll admit you do."

"I give you my word of honor I don't. It was just for appearances' sake. Because, think about it, I'm spending quite a peculiar wedding night here."

"I can see the nuptial chamber would've pleased you better than my room."

"It'll remain inviolate, I promise you."

"For tonight, anyway, I'm sure."

Struck by a new thought, Henri suddenly stopped in front of Juliette. He studied his accomplice for a long time, as if to gauge by her looks what her capacity for lechery was. Then he said, "Maybe not..."

"But Caroline won't come upstairs."

"But you'll come."

"Me?..." And at that despicable suggestion she allowed herself a smile. Then she added, "In fact, that'd be funny... But no, I don't want to, I'm not in the mood."

"Come on!" he said, taking her by the hand and pulling her toward him. "Don't be so straitlaced! You'll get in the mood."

"Leave me alone. You're hurting me. You're always such a brute."

"You know you're the only girl in the world for me," he said, taking her in his arms.

"Oh, you're unbearable!" she said, surrendering. "It comes over you like vertigo."

"So come on, come on."

"No. That room is right over the baron's room."

"That's exactly what's funny about it."

Lifting Juliette in his massive arms, he began carrying her across the apartment, while she exclaimed, "Henri, this is a terrible idea!... You're possessed!... What a monster you are!" Then, changing her mind, she wrapped her arms around him and said, "But that's what I like about you, you rascal!"

Luizzi watched them go toward the nuptial chamber. They crossed the threshold. In his horror and outrage he wanted to cry out, and in fact he did utter a terrible cry. But the entire delirious vision disappeared; he was plunged into total darkness; he cried out over and over in vain. He could see nothing, hear nothing, feel nothing. Suddenly he opened his eyes, and he saw...

Chapter LIV: Encounters

He saw Juliette, Henri, and Caroline leaning over his bed, trying to keep him from breaking his arms and legs in the horrible convulsions tetanus had now provoked following his rigidity. In spite of the unspeakable agonies he was experiencing, he had—as is often the case with that mysterious disease—a perfect awareness of everything going on around him, and full command of his reason. Seeing Henri and Juliette caring for him so assiduously, Luizzi had to conclude that for several hours he'd been in the grip of a fantastical delirium; and at that moment he suddenly realized the danger he was in. He remembered that twice already he'd been taken for a madman; he understood that, since he was constantly obsessed with whatever the Devil revealed to him, everything certain had been cast into doubt, all appearances looked like lies, and he assumed anything he couldn't explain was corruption and crime.

The fear that his natural propensity would lead his mind to fasten onto one obsession and spiral down into madness gripped him so intensely that he resolved never again to probe life's mysteries, but to go forward like ordinary men, being guided no longer by the false light of hell that stained everything blood red, but by the simple light of his own judgment, and to see the best side of everything and everyone. Perhaps Luizzi's reaction toward the Devil was like Orgon's reaction to Tartuffe: when the hypocrite leaves that gullible gentleman's house, the latter cries, "That's it! I give up on all good men!"[29] Now that Luizzi wanted to renounce his mania for knowing the truth, he said to himself, "That's it! Now I'll believe all men are good!"

The rather difficult convalescence that followed an illness so resistant to healing dissipated all of Luizzi's fears, which the disease had magnified in that appalling vision. Henri was very attentive to his needs. As for Juliette, she faithfully kept him company, reading to him and engaging him in conversation with unfailing cheerfulness, grace, and modesty. He found her more attractive than ever, because to the pleasure of her sweet, relaxing company was added the intoxicating magnetism that still affected him in spite of himself. By the time he was able to get up and go out he was completely in love with Juliette—or rather, reverting to the peculiar passion she inspired in him, he lusted for her like a seminarian and dreaded her like a child.

Luizzi's circumstances had, however, changed in one significant respect. In the same way that he'd sent the Marquis de Bridely for news of Mareuilles, the latter had asked young du Bergh to inquire about Luizzi's health. Those vis-

---

[29] From the play *Tartuffe* (1664), by Molière. The line in French is *"C'en est fait, je renonce à tous les gens de bien..."*

its had been repeated daily in both directions. Gustave had managed to inform Madame de Marignon—with whom Mareuilles lived, since he was her son-in-law—that he, the Marquis de Bridely, now had an income of sixty thousand livres; and that seemed to excuse his past peccadilloes. His attempt to swindle her was recast as the folly of a young man, whose expectation of inheriting a great fortune gave him permission to behave less circumspectly than other poor rascals, given the certainty that he'd eventually be able to make full restitution for what he stole. They'd grown used to seeing him; and though he wasn't among the intimate friends of the family, they did allow themselves to mention the Marquis de Bridely casually among the distinguished names of the young men who frequented Madame de Marignon's salon. It was even whispered that the beautiful young Madame de Mareuilles was sorry to have lost out, if not on Gustave's looks and fortune, than at least on his title as a marquis.

Luizzi in turn had politely welcomed Edgard du Bergh, whose visits, though purely formal at first, had grown friendlier. That young man's delicacy and sweetness, and the way he lowered his eyes like a girl and spoke in a high, precious voice, had appealed to Luizzi. He'd invited him to visit on his own account, and Edgard had taken advantage of the invitation. The result had been a kind of reconciliation, by way of their intermediaries, between Luizzi and Mareuilles; and the baron—not meaning to take things further, but simply as a man of the world—had devoted his first outing to visiting his adversary, whose recovery was proceeding much more slowly than his own.

A reconciliation between those two men, who'd fought each other with enough courage to be able to toss off witty insults while they dueled—no matter how bad their puns were—was easy to bring about. Mareuilles held out his hand to Luizzi; they embraced and forgave each other, because they'd hated each other too openly to retain any hidden animosity now. Besides, all they'd wanted to do was kill each other, and people in society don't hold a grudge over a trivial thing like that. If Mareuilles and Luizzi had fallen out over some political issue, over a woman, over who had better horses or clothes, it would've meant hatred to the grave; but only a boor could refuse to forget a matter of spilled blood.

After he'd seen Mareuilles, Luizzi asked to see Madame de Marignon, who received him with the gracious sociability of a woman who knows when to forget and when to remember, as needed. He tried to see in this refined, poised, dignified old woman the wild Olivia, the libertine Olivia; and beneath her stiff exterior he recognized a fundamental easygoing tolerance that conformed to the prudishness around her while despising it.

Madame du Bergh, who was present, thanked Luizzi for his gracious reception of her son. And he met Madame de Fantan again, who told him her daughter was married, and the beautiful young Madame de Mareuilles. Luizzi left Madame de Marignon's completely reconciled with that circle, whose vileness the Devil had shown him. Indeed, since his first terrible illness the baron had spent so much time exposed to the vulgar, ridiculous vices of the middle class and the common people that he found the superficial, carefree atmosphere of a high-society salon refreshing. He listened with new pleasure to the gilded, flattering conversation of people with good manners, and he promised himself never to stray beyond that elevated sphere again.

Only a few days after that first outing, Luizzi received a letter from Monsieur Barnet, who'd left Paris shortly after the famous duel. In his letter the lawyer entreated the baron to come to Toulouse to put some order in his affairs there, and he told him about a plan that appealed to him. The Deputy for the arrondissement in which Luizzi's biggest properties were located had just died, and there was going to be a new election. Barnet, who controlled a substantial number of votes, wasn't inclined, out of principle, to give them either to the far-Left opposition candidate or to the Legitimist candidate; furthermore, out of personal hatred, he didn't want to give them to the government's candidate, who'd robbed him of a tax collector's position Barnet had wanted for his law practice. He therefore offered his votes to the baron, promising him success if he came to campaign in person.

Luizzi shared the letter with his family, of which Juliette was now practically a part; and with intense pleasure he saw her come alive for the first time as she wished for his success and got carried away in painting a brilliant picture of his future in politics. At first he was won over by that enthusiasm, but then he .remembered the minute examination to which every unfortunate candidate is subjected, and he began to fear his past wouldn't be easy to explain to unimaginative bourgeois voters. Still, a surprising discovery and an occurrence no less strange drove him to accept.

A few days later, at Madame de Marignon's, he casually mentioned the candidacy he'd been offered. Everyone congratulated him on his luck.

"You'll be elected, won't you?" asked an elderly aristocratic gentleman with a stoop. "It's about time France was represented by a few names that'll remind her that not all of her glory dates from the present. The Luizzis go back in history to the Albigensian wars; they stood side by side with Lévis and Turenne in those memorable events."[30]

"It's also about time, my dear Marquis d'Andeli," said young Madame de Mareuilles, "for Deputies who aren't all small-town lawyers or country doctors or iron and cloth dealers. Those gentlemen have invaded every salon with their brown suits and their dirty shirts and their ungloved hands. They're at the king's, they're at the ministers', they're everywhere, and a poor woman can't find anyone to talk to unless she wants to discuss the salt duty or customs tariffs. They don't dance, they don't listen, they don't laugh."

---

[30] The Albigensian Crusade in the early 1200s was a brutal military campaign launched by Pope Innocent III to eradicate the Catharist heresy in southern France. Lord Guy de Lévis and Viscount Raymond de Turenne were commanders on the Catholic side.

"True, but they vote," said a lady who was considered a wit. "That's their chief concern."

"And especially that of the ministers," added a gentleman known for his bold opinions.

"The thing is, Lydie," said a young woman whose face Luizzi couldn't quite make out, because she was leaning back by a window and almost hidden under her hat, but whose voice particularly struck him, "I don't agree with you. It'd be better not to deprive your salon of the last well-bred men we have left, rather than encourage the baron to disappear into that crowd of respectables—who are very respectable, I'm willing to believe, but who sweat enough politics and boringness to poison any salon the moment they walk in. It's an infectious evil, a smell that sticks to you. Take my husband, for example, who's barely old enough to take his seat in the Chamber of Peers, and who's already infected with that obsession. When he comes back from a session of the upper chamber, it's like when Monsieur de Mareuilles comes home from the jockey club: my husband reeks of politics and yours of tobacco. I'd almost prefer a captain in the National Guard."

Luizzi was trying to remember where he'd heard that voice before, when he was distracted by the bold, masculine voice of another woman, who was grandly beautiful in every sense of the word grand, and who replied with impetuous passion, "And what do you want men to do in our day and age, if they don't go into politics? Isn't it, always and everywhere, the goal of every man of intelligence and strong will to dominate his rivals, to make a name for himself, to gain preeminent power others are forced to acknowledge? Politics is the only career that can lead to that goal nowadays. So any man of virile ambition has to go into politics."

"By that reasoning," said the young woman sharply, "you'd have approved of a man of honor who sought that power and fame you speak of during the most horrifying days of the Revolution! You'd have approved of a true gentleman who, for example, entered Bonaparte's army to earn a general's epaulet or a field marshal's staff; or of a marquis from an ancient family who became a senator so he could be an Imperial count!"

"Most definitely, ma'am."

"I'm surprised to hear opinions like that from Countess Cerny, daughter of Viscount d'Assimbret, a woman who bears two of the finest names in France!"

"Opinions I'm not at all surprised to hear Countess Lémée doesn't share!" replied the grandly beautiful woman.

"Countess Lémée!" cried Luizzi, "... née Turniquel,"[31] he added to himself, as if to complete Countess Cerny's thought.

---

[31] Countess Ernestine Lémée, daughter of Eugénie Peyrol, née Turniquel, was last seen in Chapter XLI, regarding the rival suitors for the dowry at Monsieur Rigot's house. Ernestine was "née Turniquel" (not Peyrol), as Luizzi observes,

"The same, baron," said the young woman, bowing graciously to Luizzi. "And I was curious to see whether you'd recognize me."

"Oh, you know each other," said Madame de Marignon, who wanted to put an end to the increasingly sharp sparring between the two ladies.

"We spent a few days together at my uncle Monsieur Rigot's house," said Countess Lémée. "I hope you won't hold that nasty little lawsuit of his against me, baron. I was happy he lost. It was partly the fault of a certain Monsieur Bador, to whom he'd entrusted the case. But—though his incompetence cost me expectations of a fairly nice inheritance—I have to thank that dear man, since now there can't be any bad blood between us."

Listening, Luizzi admired the former Mademoiselle Ernestine Turniquel's imperturbable composure.

Then the woman who'd been addressed as Countess Cerny said to him, "Ah! So you knew Monsieur... de Rigot?"

"I had that honor," replied the baron fairly coolly—since he wanted to take Countess Lémée's side, so she'd do the same for him—while he searched his memory for where he'd last heard the name Cerny.

"My sincere congratulations, sir," replied Countess Cerny in a tone close to insolence, while she studied him carefully.

Madame de Marignon, again wanting to end the conversation, this time about Rigot, asked Luizzi, "And for what district are you hoping to be elected?"

"For Aude, in the town of N—."

"You'll have a terrible opponent there," said the old man who'd spoken first.

"Who's that, my dear d'Andeli?" asked Madame de Marignon.

Luizzi had already been surprised to hear that name, and seeing poor Laura de Farkley's father at Madame de Marignon's, and on such terms of intimacy, struck him unpleasantly.[32]

The old man went on, "Yes, baron, you'll have a terrible opponent, a man who can count on the support of all of our political friends."

"And he is?..."

"Monsieur de Carin," said the marquis.[33]

"Monsieur de Carin?..." echoed Luizzi.

"You know him too?" asked Countess Cerny, seeming very interested.

---

because as the offspring of Arthur Ludney's rape of Eugénie she was technically without a family name.

[32] In Chapter XXII Laura de Farkley (a.k.a. Sophie Dilois) revealed that she was the illegitimate daughter of the Marquis d'Andeli.

[33] Guillaume de Carin was last seen in Chapter XLV, in which his wife Louise thought he was trying to kill her father to inherit his title.

"Yes, very well… very well…" replied Luizzi slowly, rendered pensive by all those names brought up one by one, as if to stun him with a thousand terrible memories.

"Ah!" went on Countess Cerny. "Now he's what I call a warmhearted man of great ability. Without his firmness of character he'd have wasted his life. He was married to a fool who ended up going mad; he's endured suffering that would've broken another man."

"At least he didn't endure the suffering of being deceived by his wife," said Luizzi bitterly.

Everyone burst out laughing, and Countess Cerny blushed to the whites of her eyes.

"Come now," laughed Madame de Fantan. "Madness excuses everything; the poor woman didn't know what she was doing. On the other hand, Cerny led a dissolute life before marrying you, and it's not easy to break habits."

Luizzi now remembered that Count Cerny was the man who'd behaved less rudely than the other men around Madame de Carin.[34] While he gathered his recollections one by one, ambiguous glances ran around the room like flashes of lightning on the horizon.

But Countess Cerny put a stop to them with one imperious look, and went on, "No matter what he was, Monsieur de Carin has found distraction from his sorrows in a life of distinguished service, and he's made a success of it. Oh, baron, if Monsieur de Carin is the opponent you have to face, I despair of your chances."

"Well, I'll do my best," said Luizzi with a determination whose source the others couldn't know, but which arose from the indignation he felt at the countess's praise for Monsieur de Carin and everyone's badmouthing of poor Louise de Carin. "I'll do my best, and perhaps I won't lose as badly as you think."

"I honor your courage," replied Countess Cerny.

"Get ready to spend plenty of money," said the old Marquis d'Andeli. "Carin wrote to me that he already had a serious opponent, a rich foundry owner in those parts, a certain Captain Félix Ridaire."

"Félix Ridaire!" echoed Luizzi.[35]

"Yes, and Monsieur de Carin is all the more worried because—aside from his rather extreme opinions—this Monsieur Ridaire is said to be a man of indisputable ability and of integrity beyond all suspicion."

"Captain Félix Ridaire!" repeated Luizzi with a scornful smile.

"You know him too?" they all cried.

---

[34] Count Cerny was mentioned briefly in Chapter XLIV, as someone who supported Madame de Carin when the rest of the aristocracy abandoned her.
[35] Captain Félix Ridaire, last seen in Chapter VII, was Henriette Buré's cruel, domineering fiancé and imprisoner.

"Yes, yes," he said with the same determination. "I know him, and I'll take him on, just like the other one."

"You know everybody in the whole world!" laughed Countess Cerny.

When a few people rose, noisily breaking up the circle, Luizzi drew closer to the countess. "And I believe I have the honor of knowing you too," he said quietly.

His words were prompted by his great disgust with all the praise given so generously to people he knew were unworthy of it. In addition, if Countess Cerny's name had recalled Madame de Carin's story, the name d'Assimbret had triggered a memory of the libertine viscount who was a regular at mother Béru's brothel and who'd cheerfully robbed Libert of his nights with Olivia and roughly driven away that boor Bricoin.[36] Luizzi was motivated by a vague wish to upset this woman by showing her that in all our lives there are things that can be used against us.

So when she replied with a laugh, "I don't believe you do, baron," he continued, "And yet, countess, I could explain how a woman like you, charitably forgetting the consideration she owes to Count Cerny's name, could find herself at Madame de Marignon's, presumably acting out of deference to her own maiden name, Mademoiselle d'Assimbret."

"What? Sir!" said the countess quickly in alarm, with a meaningful glance toward Madame de Marignon. "You know…?"

"Many things," he said, encouraged by the reaction he'd produced. "And perhaps I can reassure you about Count Cerny's attentions to poor Madame de Carin."

Luizzi intended only an allusion to Louise's innocence in the matter, of which he felt confident. But Countess Cerny seemed baffled. She blushed, looked fearfully at Luizzi, and stammered, "That's impossible… sir… you don't know…"

"I know everything," replied Luizzi, delighted to press on with this mystery, since it was succeeding beyond expectation.

And, while Countess Cerny's eyes followed him in terror, he bowed and left, thinking to himself, "Is there no woman whose secret life can't be attacked, even at random, without awakening the memory of some shame or some remorse?" The idea saddened him, and came close to reviving all of his suspicions about Henri and Juliette. Still, he reflected that, as far as Louise de Carin was concerned, he knew nothing besides what he'd learned from the poor woman's manuscript. He remembered that the Devil had left him in doubt about the truth of her story, and that her tale had all the signs of a paranoid obsession. On the

---

[36] Viscount d'Assimbret, Countess Cerny's father, featured prominently (mostly just as "the viscount") in the auctioning off of young Olivia Béru to the twelve libertines in Chapter XXVII. Bricoin was Olivia's abusive lover. Olivia Béru is now Madame de Marignon.

other hand he considered that, even if her account wasn't the product of madness, it would be natural for Madame de Carin not to admit voluntarily to a misdeed that would only offer others a weapon to be used against her.

The result of all that careful reasoning was that the outrage Luizzi had felt on hearing Monsieur de Carin and Félix Ridaire praised was eased by the doubts that now filled him; and his momentary determination to use what he knew against them in the election campaign now struck him as unwise.

He'd reached that point in his thinking when he got home. He was regretting having let himself get carried away so far as to claim knowledge whose source he couldn't reveal—when another carriage than his own stopped at his door. The footman jumped down and opened the door, revealing a luxurious interior occupied by a woman. From back at the carriage gates where he'd stopped, Luizzi heard a lively voice say, "For Baron de Luizzi, right away... Then home!"

An elegant hand, sumptuous in shape and dazzling white, passed a note to the footman, who closed the carriage door, went over to the porter, and tossed him the note, repeating his mistress's orders: "For Baron de Luizzi, right away." Then he climbed back onto his place, calling out to the coachman, "Home!" The carriage vanished as fast as its two splendid horses could pull it.

Luizzi thought he'd recognized the woman's voice, and he wasn't mistaken. He read the note, which ran like this:

Sir,

What you said to me requires an explanation between us. Since I believe I'm addressing a man of honor, I have no hesitation in telling you I expect you this evening at ten. We'll be alone.

—Léonie de Cerny

At first the note delighted Luizzi, and he looked forward to replying to the invitation. But when he thought it over he concluded it would be difficult for him to satisfy Countess Cerny's curiosity; he realized the little he knew about the relationship between Count Cerny and Louise de Carin wouldn't be enough for a woman who was probably extremely jealous: after all, only a powerful emotion could've driven her to take the extraordinary step she'd just taken. And he reminded himself that, no matter what, he'd have to account for where he got his information—and Luizzi had no wish to explain how he'd happened to be staying at the madhouse where Madame de Carin was confined. He decided it would be easier and wiser to send her his regrets, and he went up to his apartment intending to think it over.

He found everyone gathered in Caroline's room. They were planning to go to a melodrama at the Porte Saint Martin, and they were all excited. Caroline seemed especially delighted, and both Juliette and Henri were in great spirits. Luizzi had noticed that the lieutenant's manners had become more polished by contact with well-bred people, and he shared in the collective pleasure. Young du Bergh and Gustave de Bridely were also going. Luizzi declined on the pretext of his health and because anyway, he said, he's seen the play. He wanted to keep his evening free, though he hadn't yet decided whether he'd go see Countess Cerny.

Still, over supper he mentioned his visit to Madame de Marignon's. He named the countess with some emphasis, to see if Edgard du Bergh could tell him anything about her. It worked, though not necessarily to satisfy his curiosity, because Edgard spoke of Countess Cerny with burning enthusiasm for her beauty and the deepest respect for her virtue. Once again Luizzi, as he listened to du Bergh, failed to observe the troubled look on Juliette's face at the name Cerny; but his thoughts were completely focused on the countess, and he replied to Edgard, "I know how beautiful she is, and I don't doubt she's irreproachable. But don't you think she's very jealous?"

"Her?" cried du Bergh. "Not at all, I swear. Though he gets along well with the countess, nobody could live more independently than her husband. I don't believe she has a jealous nature, and anyway the count gives her no occasion for it. Though he was once one of the most fashionable men in Paris, he's completely changed his way of life. He's become ambitious; and since his wife, I believe, has more ambition in her nature than other women, they get along wonderfully."

That news didn't square with the countess's shock at what Luizzi has said about the supposed intrigue between Count Cerny and Madame de Carin; so he remained baffled, and let the others prepare to enjoy the horrors of *The Tower of Nesle*, which had just recently opened.[37] When the others went away to get ready, Juliette stayed behind in the parlor with Luizzi, who was lost in thought. She interrupted his reverie by saying plainly, "I'm afraid we're not going to have much fun at the play, because you aren't willing to go with us and sit through a second performance."

"You're mistaken," he said casually. "On the contrary, I'm very interested in the play, and if I wasn't still so weak…"

"What's it about?"

"The story?" he said, giving her a look. "My word, it's fairly difficult to explain. I'll leave it up to the playwright to handle that…"

"It's about a queen of France who took lovers…"

"Whom she had thrown into the Seine after nights of drunken debauchery," he added.

Juliette's face lit up with a savage look and a lascivious smile, and Luizzi was suddenly struck by the idea that a nature like hers could understand the cruelty and lechery of the crimes attributed to Jeanne de Bourgogne. Prompted by the constant desire Juliette kindled in him, he drew closer to her and said, "The play paints a marvelous picture of the depraved pleasures, the savage embraces,

---

[37] *La Tour de Nesle* (1832), a play by Alexandre Dumas, premiered at the Théâtre de la Porte-Saint-Martin. The story concerns a real-life fourteenth-century royal scandal of adultery, debauchery, torture, and murder.

the delirious intoxication love can inspire; and you'll find that portrait surprising, I'm sure."

She raised her glistening eyes to him with a look that trembled like starlight through mist. Luizzi felt as if he were drenched in it. Without thinking, he took her in his arms, and—bolder than he'd been up to that point—pulled her onto his lap, sought her lips with his, and kissed her. She writhed under the kiss; then once again she tore herself away from him and fled, crying, "Oh, no! No! No! No!"

Luizzi might've decided to follow Juliette to the play, convinced that beneath her reserve the girl was hiding a love that consumed her and would make her yield to him that very night, if he could take advantage of her being aroused by a play like *The Tower of Nesle*. But as he was vacillating between his desire to possess Juliette and his duty to accept the countess's invitation, he received another note, which ran like this:

Baron de Luizzi has not informed me whether he will accept my invitation. I await his answer, and I especially await Baron de Luizzi.

—Léonie.

Once again the baron reminded himself that it would be wrong to take advantage of the weakness of his sister's friend; to escape from renewed temptation, he replied immediately that he would have the honor to call on Countess Cerny at ten. Meanwhile he'd heard Henri and Caroline talking and laughing in their room, where they'd gone earlier to dress. But Juliette returned before they did; as they heard the other two coming back, speaking to each other with the sweet intimacy of a happy couple, she approached Luizzi and said, "I absolutely must speak to you tonight."

"What time?"

"When we get back from the play."

"That'll be midnight," he said, calculating that he could be back from Countess Cerny's by then.

"At midnight then, or later if need be."

"Where will I find you?"

"In my room. If you're not afraid to go there, I'm not afraid to receive you there."

He nodded his agreement, and tried to take her hand, but she withdrew it, saying meaningfully and with a deep sigh, "We'll see... We'll see..."

Henri and Caroline came in, followed soon after by Gustave and Edgard, and they all left. Luizzi remained alone, reflecting on his two appointments, and here were his thoughts on the subject: "The more I observe the world, the more I see that the thing that matters most is love—or what passes for love, pleasure. Women think about almost nothing else, whether lawful or unlawful. Now, it would be difficult for them to dwell on it so much, if men didn't get involved at least a little. But men don't want to appear to care about it too much—not from discretion but from vanity, because they want to be seen as persons of poise and gravitas. So it seems like the part I'm playing, that of a curious bystander, is a little foolish. Here's my chance—twice over—to get out of it. Juliette will be mine whenever I want, tonight if that's what I want; but the woman whose surrender would please me much more is Countess Cerny. A virtuous woman, a woman of strong principle: that would be a real triumph and a delightful way to pass the time!"

To understand the baron's whim in deciding to drop Juliette to go to Countess Cerny, it should be repeated that the former affected him only physically, and as soon as they were apart he remembered nothing of the physical power she had over him. Countess Cerny, on the other hand, had all of the assets of rank, intelligence, and high repute that would tickle a man's desires when he thought about them; and Luizzi, still aroused by his encounter with Juliette, transferred to the chaste countess all the desire the passionate girl inspired in him.

Still, he was pursuing the hope of possessing Countess Cerny without seeing a way to bring it about. What would he say to her? After all his pretensions to subtlety, wouldn't he look like an idiot if he had nothing to tell her besides the meager fact of Louise de Carin's story? With that fear of looking ridiculous in mind, he reflected on the circumstance that up to that point the stories the Devil had told him had only shown him his past actions in a bad light, and never guided his future actions. He therefore decided to learn about Countess Cerny's life, to be prepared to take advantage of it when he visited her.

So, finding himself alone for the first time in a long while, he summoned the Devil; and when the Devil suddenly appeared he was dressed so strangely that at first Luizzi thought he was someone else.

Chapter LV: A Priest

He was wearing dull black stockings that revealed a slender ankle and a rounded calf—the kind of shapely leg in short trousers that our grandmothers admired so much and that is an awful deformity in nature. He had on black cassimere trousers that were very tight over his slender knees below his short powerful thighs; he had a bit of a belly and wide hips; he wore a black silk waistcoat and a little string necktie, on which rested a plump double chin; his face was rosy, sweet, and smiling, with a small mouth and lovely teeth, lying eyes, and slightly curly hair; his hands were white and scented; his linen was very fine and dazzlingly white, but unstarched—that terrible treatment that makes cloth look like cardboard—roomy, elegantly rumpled linen; and finally a small black coat with a single line of buttons. All in all, he was an adorable little priest, unless he was the Devil: it was hard to tell, since he'd hidden his cloven hooves in the prettiest little shoes in the world, shiny and slim and delightful.

Though he was eager to get information from him, Luizzi couldn't help expressing his surprise at the form Satan had assumed to come to him. "Where've you been, dressed like that?"

The Devil replied in a piping little falsetto, "I just made a German archbishop and a canon drunk."

"Fine work for a creature like you!"

"It's one of the more challenging things I've attempted. I thought I'd never push them to the sweet mortal sin you call gluttony, and which includes drunkenness."

"Men who'd drunk nothing but water their whole lives, I assume?"

"On the contrary, master, fellows who were so accustomed to the strongest wine that there was a point I thought I was going to slide under the table."

"Why would you care to get them drunk today, if that's what they do every day?"

"Because they don't get drunk, and that's how those raving Jesuits keep their consciences clear. God gave man food for nourishment and wine to quench his thirst, but he didn't tell men, 'Every day you'll eat a pound or two of food and you'll drink a bottle of wine.' He told them to partake according to their needs. So you see, that archbishop and his canon had gradually gotten their stomachs used to such enormous needs that it would make you tremble. Between the two of them they could make a wasteland of a table with twelve place settings—three courses—and a basket of fifty bottles of Bordeaux wouldn't trouble them at all."

"But that's appalling piggishness!"

"Piggishness, sure, but not gluttony, because it never resulted in either drunkenness or indigestion. And what is it that makes any action wrong? Excess. What constitutes sin? Excess. So, when the day came that I'd have to fight over the souls of those two prelates with a couple of puffed-up angels, I'd have had to work too hard, since I wouldn't be able to say they'd ever eaten or drunk beyond their natural needs. I foresaw the Jesuitical argument a clever adversary could pull from that fact, and I demolished it in advance. It's done; I've just left those two religious men dead drunk under the table, where I arranged them one lying on the other, crosswise, to the greater glory of God."

Luizzi noticed that as Satan talked he sounded a little tipsy and he stumbled over his words. This wasn't the somber, serious Devil who'd told him the story of Eugénie, nor the skeptical, mocking Devil who teased him with sarcasm; it was a happy Devil, sweet, perfumed, dolled up.

"To tell you the truth," Luizzi said, "I assumed you were busy with more important things than that."

"What could be more important to me than corrupting men? You think I've got a classification system for various vices that makes me impressed by some and dismissive of others, like you do among yourselves? You think I find the powerful man, drunk with conceit, who sacrifices the peace of a nation to his ambition, less guilty than the peasant who trades the tranquility of his home for a couple of liters of bad wine? You think I care about the difference between a high-born woman who sneaks her lover's children by adultery into her husband's family and the streetwalker who puts her clients' children into the foundling home? You can keep those pathetic distinctions; they belong to you."

"You think human morality doesn't judge those cases equally?"

"Do you live according to your moral principles, you poor wretches? You don't even live according to your passions: because the most natural in all animals is love, and you never stop lying about the passion you're designed to feel."

"I don't understand."

"Go out on the street, master, and find some pretty girl, remarkable for her beauty and her youth; you might even notice her hidden under her rags. But if one of those insipid creatures come to life from a fashion magazine goes by—hooded in silk, with hair so slick it could be a satin cap, her body cinched into a corset that gives her a figure like an hourglass, padded with muslin wads that give her impossible, immoral hips, holding up and balancing a shape that isn't hers and that she exaggerates immodestly beyond the ample proportions of the Venus Callipyge[38]—you'll instantly drop the pretty girl whose beauty is natural and real, and chase after that bundle of white linen and shiny silk."

"That's just a question of illusion. We're misled by appearances."

---

[38] The Venus Callipyge is a well-known and much-copied Classical marble statue in Naples. "Callipyge" comes from the Greek for "of the beautiful buttocks."

"You're lying! You know exactly what's going on. There are women of whom you know that at night nothing feminine remains except their sex, and who still dazzle you by day because they artfully supplement all the beauty they lack. You adore them for the corset that gives them a big bust, for the bustle—you call it sauciness—that gives them an Andalusian rump, you go mad for their waists laced up tight like sausages. You don't like women anymore, master, you like rubber and starch and cotton."

"Well! As long as we're talking about women, what do you think of Countess Cerny?"

"A tall robust blonde woman, very much a woman all over except her heart; because they say she's opinionated and bold and ambitious. She's a fine piece of sculpture made flesh. If she ever takes a lover she'll make him her servant—not out of love but out of ambition. At least that's how the world sees her."

"If she ever takes a lover, you say? So she's never had one?"

"Never."

"So what made her take such a fright when I threatened to tell her her secrets?"

"Well, master, you think women have no vices or misdeeds to hide other than those of love? Doesn't it occur to you they might dread ridicule more than shame?"

"What!" cried Luizzi, leaning toward the Devil, who was stretched in an armchair, unbuttoning his waistcoat and gasping like a man who was overfull. "Is the countess unable to have a lover?"

"I'm telling you, she's got a fine body, she's one of those women who preserve the original form of their primitive kind, one of those magnificent Norman creatures come from the Slavic lands to conquer France, naturally noble and fecund and lavish and hardy; in short, a woman, a complete woman."

"But her ambition has displaced her other emotions?"

"I wouldn't say displaced, but distracted."

"What do you mean?"

"She became ambitious, so as to stop being a slut."

"Fine. But she kept it secret, and it was easy enough to quit that she was able to give it up while she was still young."

"It wasn't easy for her, because it didn't stay secret."

"So the count is jealous?"

"Of his wife? No. Of what you call his honor? Yes."

"I assume he watches her as strictly as a Spanish duenna?"

"You'll visit her at ten, you'll find her alone, you'll leave when you please, without him caring at all—barring unusual circumstances."

"So my visit won't have the result I was hoping for?"

"You might obtain in one night what many others have been refused after years of genuine love and passionate devotion."

"You think?"

"I'm even sure that if you fail, it'll be your own fault."

"But can you give me a little advice?"

"Me?" sighed Satan. "No. In all eternity I only ever loved one woman, and I couldn't win her."

"And that was?"

"The Virgin Mary!" said the Devil with his cruellest smile. "And for that she was made mother of God."

"And all the rest?"

"All the rest? I left them to men, with the exception, as I told you, of Eve. Since there were only two of them in the world, I had to get involved so she'd deceive her husband. If there'd just been one single nasty stuttering one-eyed hunchbacked halfwit around, I'd have been spared the trouble. Since then I've kept out of it; so my advice wouldn't be that of an expert."

"But tell me, is she one of those women whose guard you can get past by a surprise attack?"

"I don't believe in surprises like that, unless the women they're aimed at are completely oblivious to what men want from them; and there's no one like that these days."

"Especially when they're married. But is she the kind whose imagination you can stir up with glances and words and dirty pictures?"

"I don't believe in the power of such quick arousal, if it isn't already a habit of thought and feeling. You can't easily make a sober man drunk; but a man who drinks himself silly every night is easy to make drunk."

"That's not what you just told me about that archbishop."

"On the contrary. The archbishop may have drunk, but he never got drunk. There are women who indulge in three lovers in one night, and who still aren't drunk with love. It's what Diderot rightly called the savage beast,[39] what Juvenal explains so well with his *Lassata viris et non satiata recessit*."[40]

"But if that's the case, what is Juliette, whose presence exerts such an immediate and powerful influence over me?"

The Devil seemed to be embarrassed. Then he went on, "Not everything that arouses you will satisfy you once you possess it. Some foods are appetizing only to look at."

"And yet, it seems to me that Juliette…"

---

[39] Denis Diderot (1713-84), a French philosopher and creator of the *Encyclopédie*. The reference is probably to one of his many maxims: "Only a single evil act separates a fanatic from a savage beast."

[40] Juvenal (55-128 AD), a Roman poet. The line is from his *Satires*: "And exhausted by men, but not yet satisfied, she came home."

"Probably won't profit by the desires she arouses," interrupted the Devil. "Monsieur de Mère, Olivia de Marignon's last lover,[41] quoted an atrocious witty remark one day when he was describing how a woman he'd loved had suddenly given herself to another man."

"And what was that witty remark?"

"He was trying to say you shouldn't rock a woman's high principles, or agitate her heart, or turn her head, or disturb her senses—and then fail to be there at the right time to take advantage of the exact moment she's chosen to give in, if she's strong, or is unable to resist, if she's weak."

"What's the remark?"

"It's by a woman."

"And the remark is?"

"It's by a woman of genius."

"The remark! The remark!"

"It's by Madame de Staël."[42]

"Satan, you're making fun of me!"

"My dear sir, I'm only the Devil: I don't have the right to be as explicit as a woman, especially a woman of genius."

"Is it your priest's getup that's made you such a prude?" laughed Luizzi.

"On the contrary, master, I kept this on because I have to tell you a witticism that's a little smutty, and it wouldn't go with any other kind of clothing."

"Well, the remark? The remark?"

"All right! The remark... it's that... *It's not always the man who stokes the fire who puts something in the oven.* Think it over, and you'll understand your relationship to Juliette and Countess Cerny."

Luizzi was delighted. "So you think I'll have the countess?"

"That'll depend on you."

"How should I go about it?"

"There's a schoolboy's question, my friend!"

"It's getting late, and you're not telling me anything."

"We've got time," laughed the Devil. "Countess Cerny's story isn't long, considering what you need it for, nor is her husband's. I'll tell it to you in the carriage while you take me to the faubourg Saint Germain, where I have to visit a devout young woman."

"I thought you traveled through the air."

"Sometimes, but those lunatics made me drink so much I'd get lost among the chimney pots."

---

[41] See Chapter XXIX for the long platonic affair between Madame de Marignon and Victor de Mère.

[42] Anne Louise Germaine de Staël (1766-1817), a prominent woman of letters and political theorist, famous for her novels and plays as well as her analytical and historical writings.

"Oh, by the way, that reminds me, I don't know where the countess lives."

"Rue de Grenelle, in Saint Germain, number —. I'm going near her house first, then to the Ministry of the Interior."

"You're involved in politics?"

"Yes, I have to deal with the election in N—."

"Where I'm a candidate."

"I thought you hadn't decided."

"I have, if you're willing to answer one question."

"Which is?"

"Is Madame de Carin's story true?"

"Perfectly true."

"So Count Cerny wasn't her lover?"

"Not at all."

"I can vouch for that to his wife?"

"She's as sure of it as you are."

"As sure as I am? So then what can she want from me?"

"I can tell you what she might want from you, to use your expression: she wants to hear from you how it is you know Count Cerny wasn't Madame de Carin's lover."

"And my assertion of it will convince her?"

"Probably, since she's already convinced of it," laughed the Devil. "But that won't explain to her how you come to be so certain yourself."

"Do I have to tell her I read Louise's manuscript?"

"That'd be the simplest, most logical way. But that would also be the way to have not the slightest chance of success with her."

"So there's another way?"

"It's half past nine. Let's get in your carriage."

"Are you trying to trick me again?" asked Luizzi as he rang for his berline, which he'd ordered long since.

"No, I swear sincerely that you'll learn everything that can be known, and everything you need to know, about Countess Cerny."

A moment later they were in the carriage and heading to the faubourg Saint Germain.

"Now," said Luizzi, "please tell me Countess Cerny's story."

"Here it is," replied the Devil. And he settled into a corner of the carriage and began.

Chapter LVI: Countess Cerny's Story

You should know that I'm going to visit a little woman who's definitely an exception in this day and age. She's pretty, elegant, shapely, with soft white skin, of a good family, and a lawyer's wife, no more and no less; and as a result a woman ripe for a compromising affair or a romantic adventure. Besides, she has a heart with a certain capacity for fanaticism and a large dose of whimsical willfulness in her nature, which—if she'd fallen into the right hands—would've led her into one of those mediocre lives that subsist on a multitude of secret little sins and private scandals; an existence, by the way, that provides happiness to wives and almost always to their husbands.

"Is this Countess Cerny's story you're telling me?"
"That'll come in good time," replied the Devil. Then he went on:

I didn't think for a second the little creature was worth my trouble, and I'd left her downfall to men and women. But then her mother had the notion of entrusting her to an old curate, who redirected toward religion the fanaticism I was counting on taking advantage of, and redirected toward pious devotion the willpower that would've made her persevere in evil as soon as she'd dipped a toe into it!

My little lady became observant. She loved and married an honorable man, and before you know it she was a settled, honest wife, and then the caring, attentive mother of two lovely children. That struck me as taking things a bit far, and I decided to turn all of those good qualities in my direction. "By God, ma'am!" I said to myself, "you're devout: I'll make you a fanatic. You're persevering: I'll make you stubborn. You're attentive: I'll make you suspicious. Your domestic life is a paradise: I'll make it a hell."

"You're absolutely pitiless!"
"Oh, come on!" said the Devil. "I'm a better Christian than all of you are: I treat my neighbor like myself."
"And by what delightful means did you achieve those lovely results?"
"I gave her all of those excellent faults the same way she'd acquired all of her good qualities."
"And how was that?"
"She'd become a good woman through the care of a saintly guide. I gave her an evil one."
"So he could undermine that woman's good principles and undo the worthy curate's work?"

"Not at all!" laughed the Devil, rocking back and forth on the silky cushions in the carriage. "I didn't undermine the edifice of her virtue, I overbuilt it. Cutting away at its base and making it top-heavy are both excellent ways of toppling a monument. I took advantage of one of the most original types of conscience ever invented."

"And what was that type of conscience?"

"First I have to tell you there's a certain religious morality that consists of calling a sin anything that's a pleasure. Fakirs and Trappist monks are the champions of that morality. For them, not only is eating more than you need a crime, but eating just what you need with pleasure is a sin. So, having gotten my curate promoted to vicar general—first of all to make him believe in his own merit, tripping up his virtue in passing—I had him replaced by a young priest of the fakir type, still hot from the seminary and theological debate, and I sent my little woman to him."

"And he fell in love with her?"

"Good God! How stupid you are sometimes!" said the Devil, sounding disappointed. "I really despair of you. I told you I took advantage of a certain extremely original type of conscience. That doesn't seem to me to have much to do with a commonplace cliché like a confessor in love."

"Look, can we get to the point?" asked Luizzi, wounded by the Devil's words. "What is this type of conscience?"

"It's the one I was talking about, the one that consists of seeing all pleasure as a sin. It's scruples taken to their limit. So, one day, when my charming fanatic was at confession…"

"So she'd already reached the point of sanctimony?"

"She'd reached the point of a hair shirt."

"What! A hair shirt?"

"Yes, a hair shirt."

"Where the devil would you even find one nowadays?" cried Luizzi.

"Where people like you can't see them, since the women who wear them aren't in the habit of letting them be looked at."

"Well, a devout woman sounds quite amusing!"

"Ha, ha!" said the Devil, licking his lips lasciviously. "It's a wonderful flavor, perfectly spiced, deliciously sweet! A devout woman in love, that's a ragout of honey and pepper, of jam and chile, that scorches and caresses the palate. But you need a stronger stomach than yours for a feast like that. To stomach that kind of love you need one like my archbishop has for gluttony; and both kinds are often found under the same robe. But coming back to my fanatic, the day she was at confession… Here's the conversation I had with her."

"So her confessor was you?"

"Everything evil is me. Father Molinet was speaking, but I was whispering the words to him. So I said softly and unctuously to my little sweetheart, 'Since the time I've had the guidance of your conscience, my daughter, I've noticed that as regards most worldly things you're on the true path to salvation. But one doubt torments me; for when I find a virtue as pure as yours, I want it to be perfect... if there can be anything perfect other than God.'"

"You said that? You, Satan?"

"Why not? God is perfect, since he made me. He's only perfect because of that; because if evil didn't come from me, it would have to come from him, and then to the devil with his perfection! But you're always interrupting me."

So I said that to my fanatic, and she replied, "I've searched my conscience carefully, and I can find no other sins than those I've already confessed to you."

"But there are some sins one can commit in ignorance."

"Tell me what they are, father."

"Enormous sins."

"Oh, I'll shun them. Speak, I'm listening."

"Then answer me honestly. How long has it been since you were in childbed?"

"Eighteen months."

"Have you lived in chastity and abstinence for eighteen months?"

"I'm married, father, and I don't think I'm failing my religious duty when I obey my husband's desires."

"And what is the result of those desires?"

"I'm not quite sure how to answer, father, and..."

"You've not had a child for eighteen months?"

"No, father. My last delivery was difficult, and my doctor warned me of serious consequences if I had another child."

"The villain!" I cried.

"My health is so fragile..."

"Oh, miserable creature!" I went on in a deep voice. "Your health is too fragile to bring forth the child who wants to be born, but it's strong enough to obey your husband's desires, as you put it in your atrocious expression! Your union is no longer a sacred bond, it's a squalid debauchery that defies the will of the Lord, who said, 'Be fruitful and multiply.'"

"But I thought..." she replied, trembling.

"You thought, you wretch!" I cried in fury. "You thought... and that was your downfall... that presumption, that vanity... You thought!"

I let out a few exclamations and mumbled a few fragments of Latin; because with a few "ums" and a few "uhs" and a few "ohs" nicely delivered through pursed lips you can make excellent sacristy Latin. I pretended to calm down, and I explained to my little penitent how our fathers with the greatest learning in theology had considered a mortal sin any pleasure that had no goal but pleasure, and I terrified her with the idea of the long trail of infanticides she'd made herself guilty of.

"She's an idiot!" cried Luizzi. "And she just happened to run into an imbecile!"

"Master, I know a woman like her who changed confessors nine times in search of absolution for that crime—or even just to find a priest who wouldn't ask her about it—without success. So she gave up."

"Gave what up? Sin?"

"Oh, no. Absolution! But that wasn't the case with this woman."

"So what happened with her?"

"What happened was, she told her husband to make his bed elsewhere, unless he wanted a third child. The husband protested at first, but she stood firm. He insisted, and she replied like a fanatical zealot. He called her crazy, she called him a vile libertine. They turned bitter, insulting, angry. They hate each other now, and—thanks to the way I managed things—the wife goes to confession every morning, and the husband sleeps around town every night."

"Oh, come on! You're lying!"

"If you don't believe me, I'll have you come up and see her. Because here we are at that Madame d'Arnetai's door."

"Thanks. Should I have the coachman stop?"

"No need," said the Devil.

"Go ahead and open the door."

"No need," said the Devil again.

"Put down the window."

"No need," repeated the Devil.

Indeed, Satan ran the tip of his pinky nail around the four sides of the window, and the glass came free as if it had been cut with the finest glazier's diamond; and he immediately slipped out through the opening he'd made. Just then Luizzi remembered it wasn't to hear Madame d'Arnetai's story he'd brought the Devil along in the carriage with him, and he grabbed hold of his leg; but he was left holding only the Devil's shoe.

He was about to get upset, but the Devil, who'd hung onto the door, poked his head back through the broken window. "Give me back my shoe."

"Tell me Countess Cerny's story."

"Count Cerny was one of the handsomest men of his day, and one of the greatest libertines. Give me back my shoe."

"Countess Cerny's story!"

"Count Cerny paid a visit to Aix, where he lived such a happy life it almost killed him, thanks to a pretty girl whose face was as fresh as a rose. Give me back my shoe!"

"Countess Cerny's story, or no shoe!"

"Count Cerny, home after the long illness provoked by the pretty girl, and cured of his libertine ways, reemerged in society and fell in love with Mademoiselle Léonie d'Assimbret."

"Finally we get there! And Mademoiselle d'Assimbret?..."

"Count Cerny pursued her with such assiduous attentions that in the end he compromised her."

"And Léonie?..."

"Count Cerny was ordered, by his family and by Mademoiselle d'Assimbret's family, to marry Léonie."

"But her... what about her?" cried Luizzi impatiently.

"Count Cerny refused with all his power."

"You're joking with me!"

"But, impressed by Mademoiselle d'Assimbret's vast fortune, Count Cerny ended up marrying her."

"Excellent! And since that time?"

"On their wedding night..."

"Look out, Satan! I have my little bell!" cried Luizzi.

"On their wedding night, Count Cerny approached his bride's bed with a solemn air..."

"Had she deceived him?"

"Count Cerny made a long speech, far too long a speech, and after a thousand circumlocutions he told her the whole truth."

"What truth?"

"He explained how the love sickness he'd caught in an instant and suffered from for six months had left him..."

"Impotent, maybe?"

"You're the one who said it! Count Cerny is impotent, and that's Countess Cerny's whole story!"

"Impotent!" repeated Luizzi, doubled over with laughter.

"My shoe, please!"

"Impotent!"

"My shoe! Quick, my shoe! Because you've now reached Countess Cerny's door!"

"Impotent!" cried Luizzi again, remembering what he'd said to Countess Cerny—*I can reassure you about Count Cerny's attentions to poor Madame de Carin*—and laughing at the way she would naturally have interpreted that.

"My shoe! My shoe!" repeated the Devil.

"Impotent! Impotent!" repeated Luizzi.

THE DEVIL'S SHOE

Chapter LVII: The Wife

The carriage had stopped, and Luizzi was laughing so hard he still hadn't complied with the Devil's request. He'd kept the shoe in his hand, and he got out still holding it and still laughing and mumbling the fatal word, "Impotent! Impotent!" He reached Countess Cerny's door that way, and asked the servant to announce him. Luizzi's laughing demeanor must've struck the footman as odd, because he examined the baron with surprise and glanced several times at what he was holding. Luizzi finally realized from the man's expression there must be something unusual about his own appearance, and only then did he notice he had the Devil's shoe in his hand. That just increased his hilarity, and he laughed even louder as he told the servant to announce Baron de Luizzi.

While the footman went away, the baron, left alone in the vestibule, looked around for the Devil to give him back his shoe. Not seeing him, he began to examine the shoe itself. It was a charming shoe: slender, graceful, arched, made of soft gleaming leather, lined in pink satin as shiny as enamel—the kind of shoe destined to be left by a woman's bed, and designed to show off the pretentious elegance of the man who wore it.

Luizzi was still admiring the pretty shoe, still laughing, and wondering whether the Devil had meant to forget it by the bed of the lovely fanatic he'd gone to visit, when he heard the servant coming back. Not knowing what to do with his friend Satan's shoe, he tucked it into the side pocket of his suit coat and proceeded to Countess Cerny's apartment. He was made to cross three vast rooms in different styles: a Roman dining room, a Gothic parlor, and a Renaissance library. Then he passed through a bedroom that was pure Louis XV, and at the furthest extremity of the house he entered an octagonal Chinese boudoir furnished with the most eccentric extravagance.

The walls were covered in black lacquer; the curtains and the upholstery were black satin with brightly colored silk embroidery. The sofas were low, and covered in similar fabric, which also lined the ceiling, so at first glance the boudoir resembled a fervent chapel. But when he discovered, by the light of the pale pink candle enclosed in a lamp of Bohemian crystal hung from the ceiling by delicate bronze chains, all the bizarre designs, all the fantastical birds with their bright plumage, all the grotesque figures whose yellow faces gleamed in the shiny black enamel of the lacquer, when he saw all the whimsical translucent porcelain and the heavy embroidery in glistening silk and the little tables heaped with a thousand nicknacks in wrought gold and chased silver and the wonderful flowers in vases of all kinds and the stunning perfumes wafting from astonishing incense burners, he realized he was in a temple of fashion in the most bizarre and outrageous form fashion can assume.

And then in the next moment, when he'd had time to take in the effect of that splendid room, he decided the dark radiance of this den and the refined ugliness of all the decor were perhaps not as unreasonable as they seemed at first. Indeed, tall blonde Countess Cerny was half lying across the black satin of those sofas; she was wearing a white muslin dress that set her off against the dark upholstery like the ghost of a fairy in the night; her head rested against a cushion whose down, swelling in its black cover, stood out around her dazzling face and framed it admirably, while the ample curls of her beautiful long blonde hair spread out in rich golden strands on that sober dark background.

Countess Cerny was beautiful; but as he looked at her Luizzi recognized how right the Devil had been when he spoke of the seductiveness of the borrowed graces with which a woman adorns herself. In fact, Countess Cerny's own beauty was now eclipsed by the magical attraction of that bold contrast, and the brilliant white of her dress and the honeyed blonde of her hair got all the credit for the first rush of admiration that filled the baron's heart. The surprise he felt put an end to the hilarious mood that had taken hold of him, and he could greet the countess without laughing in her face. He gravely took the seat she motioned him to—for she seemed too moved to speak.

"I've come at your summons," he said, "and I'm waiting to hear your explanation for the favor I've received."

"I'm not sure whether you can call a favor an explanation that may become very serious."

"You're right, countess, and nothing concerning you can be or should be less than serious."

"I'd like to understand you better, sir."

"I don't know how to explain it more clearly."

"And yet to make you explain yourself clearly is exactly what I want to do," she said with some effort. "What do you mean when you say nothing concerning me can be less than serious?"

"You insist on an explanation, and I obey," said Luizzi, who found that the refined atmosphere revived the social ease of his good breeding. "Yes, countess, everything concerning you must be serious. An affair of the mind would be serious with a woman whose intellectual superiority has allowed her to study and resolve the greatest social and political questions. Friendship would be serious with a woman who exercises in her choices all of the devotion and resolution that make her affection so sacred. And lastly, if one dared to be in love with Countess Cerny, that passion would be serious, because it would be founded on both the greatest esteem for the most noble character and the deepest adoration for the most perfect beauty."

The candid directness of that praise, and the sincere and respectful tone in which it was delivered, embarrassed Countess Cerny at first, but didn't seem to annoy her. Still, after a short pause she replied with a smile, "The truth is, I admire how much you gentlemen scorn us."

"Countess!" cried Luizzi. "How can you speak of scorn? Please believe that my respect for you is as real as…"

"Oh, don't justify yourself," she interrupted. "You didn't understand me. I admire how little you value us, if the word scorn frightens you. You can't spend a moment beside a woman without contorting the conversation so you can tell her she's beautiful and made to be loved."

"The thing is," he said with a smile, "it's difficult to admire and take in too much in a single glance. The mind's eye, like the body's, is caught involuntarily by whatever strikes it most. And—for those who don't have the honor to have been allowed to appreciate in an intimate setting the power of your abilities— it's quite natural for them to be distracted into admiring what you can't hide: your subtle wit, your exquisite refinement, and the purity of your beauty."

Without sitting up, she turned toward him, examined him carefully, and said with a frank smile, "You're skillful at coming back to your point, but I think it's false. It seems to me a man's admiration for a woman, if she deserves that admiration, should include everything that makes her deserving of it; and if you can forget so easily the high qualities you speak of, it can only be because you barely acknowledge them in her."

"Oh, countess, how mistaken you are!" he said firmly. "Please hear me without misconstruing my intentions, and perhaps you'll see how right I am."

"I'm listening," she said, clasping her hands above the black cushion behind her and resting her head gracefully on her joined hands.

"One thing you should believe in, countess, is the sincere, genuine respect you inspire, the pure profound esteem you deserve. Another thing you should believe is that it's easy—not so much to forget those two noble sentiments—but at least to let them be overshadowed by an adoration that's more intense and more passionate, though hopeless."

"I'll grant you that much, sir," she said with a smile. "I'm not hypocritical enough to deny it."

"Well then, countess, just as the purest love can prevail for a moment over the respect you deserve, so a passionate desire can prevail for a moment over that pure love. The man who sees you for your beauty, your refinement, your wit, can't help loving you. The man who could see you here—who could see your beautiful face resting so fetchingly on those lovely hands, as well as your gorgeous body arranged in all the grace and fullness of its perfection, your flowing hair unbound by the confinement of any cap and cascading onto those divine shoulders—the man who could breathe the intoxicating perfume that is the air of this oasis, the man who could see that light so veiled as to be a mystery—that man, countess, could forget for a moment, just a single moment perhaps, the respect due to your virtue, a respect more tender than sacred love, to feel instead that there's no woman in the world who exudes such a powerful intoxicant, and to dream of that most ineffable blessing—that of possessing such beauty."

While Luizzi was speaking, his voice hesitant and full of feeling, Countess Cerny had averted her eyes, slowly lifted her head, and sat up on the sofa where till then she'd been lying. A vivid blush spread across her cheeks, and her strained breathing showed she was reacting to his words with what he had to assume was embarrassment and shame at hearing such an avowal.

He hastened to cry, "I haven't offended you, countess. I replied to a general question with an honesty that perhaps I shouldn't have made so personal, but that ought not offend you. I spoke of the involuntary kindling of a flame any woman as beautiful as you can spark—but that only you can purify without extinguishing it."

Countess Cerny still didn't reply, but she seemed less embarrassed and less bothered. Not wanting to leave her with any negative impressions, Luizzi went on, "Must I attack you to defend myself? Must I anger you to calm you? Must I tell you it's your own fault for being both so saintly and so attractive?"

"No, no," she replied with a smile. "There's really no point in starting again. But you've taught me something I'm delighted to know: it's possible to remain polite while telling a woman the most impertinent things."

"Oh, countess!..."

"I don't hold it against you; on the contrary. It's a skill I'm delighted to find you have. After all, sir, we haven't yet touched on the subject that brought you here; we're still far from the explanation I asked you for."

"What explanation is that?" he asked, feigning surprise.

"'I can reassure you,' you said, 'about Count Cerny's attentions to poor Madame de Carin.' Kindly tell me how you could give me that reassurance, which you yourself volunteered."

"Forgive me for singing Madame de Carin's praises in your presence, countess," replied Luizzi, to whom it didn't occur to give her a truthful or offhand answer. "But I'd stake my honor on poor Louise's innocence."

"You have proof of that innocence?"

"I have my conviction of it."

"Nothing more?"

"Nothing more."

"That's not what your words seemed to imply, sir."

"I beg you," he said firmly, "not to give them a meaning they don't have."

"And what meaning could I have given them, sir, unless it's that you have some specific and certain knowledge that a liaison the whole world talked about didn't have the guilty consequences imputed to it?"

"Do you believe strongly in those guilty consequences?" he asked with a smile.

The deep blush that rose to her face and the questioning look she aimed at him showed him he'd gone too far. She continued, "And why shouldn't I believe in those consequences, sir?"

Trying to retreat, he stammered in embarrassment, "Count Cerny's opinions, his principles…"

"Are you aware that, as far as principles of fidelity go, Count Cerny doesn't set himself up for a model?"

"His rank…"

"His rank would certainly allow for a liaison with the Marquis de Vaucloix's daughter."

"His love for you…"

"We've never pretended to be a passionately attached couple."

"Madame de Carin's virtue, whose purity I can vouch for…"

"None of this is an answer, sir. Why do you think I'm wrong to believe Count Cerny was completely unfaithful?"

The words "completely unfaithful" made Luizzi laugh out loud. Then, finding himself under pressure from her persistent questions, and hitting upon a word that could serve as an ambiguous response, he replied, speaking as slowly as possible, "Complete infidelity, as you put it, is a crime of passion of which you… of which you cannot believe Count Cerny… is capable."

Though she seemed to be in agony, the countess seemed just as determined to drive him to a categorical reply, for she went on impatiently, "Well! And why I shouldn't I think Count Cerny capable of it? Come, sir, you who have the gift of expressing anything, can't you find a suitable circumlocution to explain what you're trying to reveal to me?"

"Is there really something I have to reveal to you? Then why force me to explain," he replied in a pleading tone, "since you've understood me so well?"

"I?" she said with admirable astonishment. "I understand nothing, unless it's that you have reasons I'm unaware of for hiding the basis of your conviction."

Luizzi found the countess's persistence so extraordinary that he wanted to bring the long equivocation to an end. Still, since he'd feel ashamed to wound in any way a woman who truly deserved great pity for her misfortune and great respect for her resignation, he replied gently, "If I'd done you the wrong of making you question Count Cerny's fidelity, as so many others have, wouldn't you forgive me? I'd simply ask you to forget a thoughtless remark that slipped out in the course of conversation. Why would you be less forgiving when I tried to make you believe your husband could not have been unfaithful to you?"

He'd said that in the most pleading, subdued, appropriate manner. But he was on such slippery ground that unwittingly the last phrase had still come across as a meanspirited joke.

Countess Cerny replied firmly and loftily, "Those, sir, are not the words of a man of honor. I'm asking you directly and openly, where do you get your conviction of Count Cerny's innocence? Answer me the way I've asked you, without ceremony. I can and I will hear your answer, whatever it may be, without you having to dress it up in seemly phrases. I'm listening, sir."

"Well, countess!" he said, feeling that the tone of her question dictated the tone of his reply. "I know everything you know..." Then he stopped, unable to commit himself to making a more explicit avowal to a woman whose distinguished elegance hampered him even more than her virtue did.

"Well! And what do you know, sir, that I know and that you don't dare say?" she replied loftily. "Wouldn't I already have heard the thing you can't repeat?"

"All right, since I have to say it. I know everything Count Cerny himself— with embarrassment that must've been even greater than mine—told you on your wedding night."

The countess hid her head in her hands and let out a cry. At that moment the door of the sumptuous boudoir opened, and Count Cerny appeared.

Chapter LVIII: The Husband

He held two pistols in his hands. He was pale and trembling. His staring eyes were fixed on the baron, to whom he said in a voice shaking with anger, "Who told you that, sir?"

It's fairly difficult to describe Luizzi's astonishment and the genuine alarm he felt on seeing Count Cerny come in armed like that. Certainly if he'd been in the house of a man of low character whose guilt of some terrible crime he'd discovered, he wouldn't have dreaded the even more terrible measures the man would take to escape the scaffold than he now dreaded what this high-born nobleman would do to escape ridicule. Not knowing what to reply to the count's question, Luizzi—whose vanity kept him from showing the slightest fear in the presence of a man of his own rank—turned coolly to Countess Cerny and asked, "So, countess, this was an ambush?..."

But the surprise and terror visible on her face showed better than any answer that she was as astonished as he was by the count's entrance. "You! You— here!" she cried to her husband.

"Yes, I. I, who heard at Madame de Marignon's about the zeal with which this gentleman took up Madame de Carin's defense. I, who was told about his eagerness to reassure you. I, who knew you'd be curious, and who shared that curiosity."

"Well, sir?" asked Luizzi.

"Well, sir," replied Count Cerny. "That curiosity isn't satisfied."

"And I'm unable to satisfy it."

"So it will be the countess who does it for you, sir."

"I?" she said.

"You, ma'am," he replied, locking both doors of the boudoir.

"You heard how upset I was; you heard my questions, sir," she said.

"I heard Baron de Luizzi's answer. He said he knows what I told you myself on the night of... of... anyway, on our wedding night. It's possible for a secret like mine to be guessed at; but circumstances like those Baron de Luizzi mentioned must've been revealed to him. We were alone, ma'am, and it wasn't I who turned that conversation into an amusing anecdote."

"But sir," she said, "the way I interrogated Baron de Luizzi must've shown you..."

"That he wasn't the one to whom you told the story. I don't doubt it; but you certainly told someone. And if you'll tell me to whom you told it, and this gentleman will say from whom he heard it, it's possible I can trace the path by which the story traveled."

163

"On my soul, sir, I swear to you," she cried, "I never uttered a word that could lead anyone to suspect…"

"Don't lie in the teeth of the evidence, ma'am!" replied Count Cerny, his barely suppressed fury suddenly exploding. "Since this gentleman knows everything that was said between you and me, it can only be because either you or I spoke of it."

"Come now," said Luizzi. "What do you mean to do? What do you want?"

"So you still haven't understood me? Impotent, you said! I may be impotent to create life, but I certainly have the power to bring death."

"Murder!" cried the countess, leaping up in terror.

"No, ma'am," replied the count bitterly. "Vengeance—vengeance the law allows for, and the law permits since it excuses it! I find my wife's lover in my wife's room, and I kill him."

"Sir!" she cried. "Those are two despicable crimes: you kill a man and you dishonor your wife… And you'll have to kill me too, because I in turn will avenge the murder you'll have committed."

"So it'll have to be both of you," he said bitterly.

"That's impossible!" she cried, distraught, while Luizzi remained devastated and silent. "That's impossible! People will hear our cries… they'll come… You can't kill both of us so fast that one of us won't have time to call for help."

"Before I came in here I sent all the servants away. I anticipated your resistance, and nothing can save you now." As he spoke the count took a step backward and leaned against the door, as if to cut off any escape and to give him room to aim his shots. He cocked his pistols.

"Sir!" she cried. "This is an abominable crime, a crime for which there's neither excuse nor forgiveness."

"It's a crime that your betrayal alone has provoked."

"What betrayal? I'm innocent, I swear, innocent of any betrayal. I've respected the name you gave me."

"Yes," laughed the count, "in all the ways that no longer mattered to me."

"Oh!" she cried in disgust. "Don't remind me of what you dared to tell me. That was your first crime, and from the day you dared speak that way to your wife I should've expected to see you crown such despicable behavior with murder."

The count shrugged and gave a scornful laugh, then went on in a faintly mocking tone, "Come now, ma'am! Don't parade irrelevant virtue. I told you—and I'm happy to repeat it in front of this gentleman, since he must know it too—I told you I wanted to be generous to you, that I didn't want to chain your existence to a cadaver, that I'd be able to bear, without seeking revenge, what the world calls an affront and I called consolation. I told you that—apart from scandal, which I would never tolerate—I was ready to permit you anything, resigning myself in advance to a fate so many other men accept only after the fact.

I told you that; it might've been a folly inspired by love, the only folly allowed to me, but it wasn't despicable."

"It was despicable, sir," cried the countess in exasperation, "despicable! Because you anticipated that my adultery could extinguish whatever suspicions arose from my childlessness, and that an heir with your name, if not with your blood, would be the best rebuttal to those conjectures."

"That's true, ma'am," said the count with the awful brazenness of a man who, having been driven to crime, can afford to be openly cynical.

Luizzi stood up and said coolly, "Let's finish this, sir. A while ago I hoped that at the point of committing it, a double murder would repel a man I thought was just temporarily deranged by uncontrollable anger. But now I have to acknowledge that a man who made a proposition like that to his wife is capable of the lowest, most despicable crimes."

That remark only made the count respond again with the cruel laugh that revealed the fury unleashed in his soul. He was silent for a moment, then went on, "Well, sir, I made that proposition and I'll renew it now."

"What are you saying?" asked the countess.

"Come, Baron de Luizzi," cried the count bitterly, "my fine Baron de Luizzi, who speaks so sweetly to women and who teases them so wittily on the misfortunes of their husbands: here's one I'm giving you to console... She's pretty, she's young, she has every attraction—even the one you rarely find in a married woman... Well then, I give you this woman. Become her lover right now, on the spot, in front of me, and I'll forgive you both: you, because I believe you're quite capable of perpetuating the name that will otherwise die with me; the countess, because she'll have to keep secret a sin that would dishonor her."

Countess Cerny fell into a chair and hid her face in her hands.

Luizzi replied, "The fact is, sir, I didn't think it was possible to add anything further to your vileness... and yet this disgusting joke..."

"A joke, baron?" laughed the count. "Not at all, I assure you. I'm speaking seriously. What? This charming boudoir, this beautiful woman, this romantic incense, all of that doesn't carry you away, doesn't excite you?... Come now! I believe fear has reduced you to a more pitiful condition than mine! Show a little courage, a little presence of mind. On my honor I swear to you, if you're able to do what I'm asking, you'll walk out of here after having possessed the most beautiful, the noblest, the most seductive woman in the world. All your powers of wit and seduction will never get you as delightful a mistress... Well, look here, sir! It's in critical circumstances that great character is revealed!"

"Ah!" cried Luizzi. "You're a villain!"

"All right!" cried the countess, getting up with a wild look. "I accept. It was out of curiosity that I led Baron de Luizzi into this trap where he'll die. If it takes my honor to save him, let him have it! I give myself to him... I'll save him!"

That answer made Count Cerny livid, but he suppressed his newly kindled rage, while Luizzi cried, "Oh, countess, countess! Your suffering is keeping you from thinking clearly!..."

"That's not very gallant, baron!" laughed the count. "Look, the countess is bravely playing along with the joke; is it harder for you than it is for her, my dear sir? What more do you need to obtain supreme pleasure?"

No words could describe Luizzi's anger as he trembled at pistol-point on such a subject. What was happening to him was so far outside a man's normal experience that he was more dumbfounded than frightened. Not knowing what else to say, he cried, "All right, sir, fire here, at my heart. Put an end to this—kill me. It's in your interest not to miss."

As he spoke, Luizzi violently pulled open his coat, the better to expose his chest to Count Cerny's bullet, and the Devil's shoe, which he'd put in his pocket, escaped and fell to the floor. The count automatically followed it with his eyes; whether in fact the shoe surprised him, or whether he wasn't sorry to find a pretext for retreating before a crime that appalled him in spite of himself, he said in his mocking way, "Good God! That's an odd kind of purse!"

Luizzi meanwhile thought the occurrence might be an unhoped-for rescue by the Devil. Regaining a little confidence, he replied just as mockingly, "A purse that holds terrible secrets, and that might someday tell the secret of the murder that's going to take place here."

"Might it hold the secret you told the countess?" answered the count in the same bitter tone.

"Yes indeed, because it belongs to the person who told me the secret, and who left it in my carriage earlier."

The count angrily picked up the shoe and examined it with grave attention. "It's unusually elegant, and there aren't many men who could fit into it."

"I'd say you're right!" said Luizzi, recovering his capacity for wit.

The count glanced at the baron's feet, as if to compare them to the shoe in his hand. Realizing it couldn't be Luizzi's, he murmured slowly, in the low voice of someone who's just had an idea that's growing clearer, "Few men indeed could fit into such a shoe. But there's one man who's famous for the elegance of his adorable feet, and for the care with which he shows them off. And that man... that man is perhaps the only one in whom a woman might confide a secret like that, without thinking she's failing her obligations. That man might also be more treacherous than other men, if he thought he'd been betrayed. That man..."

As he spoke the count was turning the shoe over in his hand, when suddenly he moved closer to the candle, for he'd found a name written in the usual way inside the lining. He cried out, "It's him!... It's Father Molinet!... It's your confessor, ma'am!"

"Father Molinet!" cried Countess Cerny. "Never, I swear it!..."

"Oh, don't lie!" said the count in a new, harsh tone. "Don't spoil with pointless oaths your only chance of my forgiving you. A priest! A priest! Betraying the secrets of the confessional! But that man's capable of anything. The mess he made of Monsieur d'Arnetai's marriage is proof enough of how far he can carry his vile meddling. But, to tell you the truth, ma'am, I thought only a woman as foolish as Madame d'Arnetai could let herself be influenced by the indecent counsel of a shameless priest."

The countess stared at Luizzi with a puzzlement he could easily understand, but that he neither could nor would resolve. He glimpsed the possibility that the count would turn his rage against someone other than himself; and in his present urgent peril he didn't feel generous enough to sacrifice himself to protect an innocent man—whom the Devil, after all, could defend, since it was he who'd compromised the priest.

The count too kept terribly silent, and looked back and forth from Luizzi to the countess. Finally he said, "So, you are the three who know that awful secret? Then it's still the same number of victims—because you, ma'am, I forgive. You're devout; I haven't been able to keep you from that passion, so I can't hold it against you. As for you, baron, you'll have to die."

In demolishing Luizzi's hopes, those words restored his courage as a man of honor, and he replied coolly, "In that case, spare yourself a pointless crime. I don't know Father Molinet, and he wasn't the one who told me your secret."

"A pathetic and tardy admission! Your answer was too explicit. He was in your carriage earlier; I assume he was going to Madame d'Arnetai's, since she lives near here. Anyway, I'll soon find out if it was him."

"Go ask him, count!"

"No, sir, I won't ask him. I'll be cleverer than that; I'd have made an excellent prosecutor, I swear, and I'll prove it to you. Nobody leaves his shoe in a carriage, unless for a reason that perfectly matches Father Molinet's provincial habits. Since our priest isn't a wealthy man, he's forced to make even his most exalted calls on foot. His vanity makes him face the mud in the streets in shoes that don't matter, which he quickly swaps for these charming shoes just before going into a house. I'll go to the d'Arnetais'; the priest should still be there; if he isn't, I'll go to his house and return his shoe on your behalf. If he's embarrassed I'll know I'm right. I'll find a way to make him talk after that; and if what you've admitted to me is true, his fate will be sealed just as irrevocably as yours, baron."

"You forgot about mine," said the countess. "Think about what I said, count. If you commit this crime, I'll accuse you in public, everywhere, I swear to God!"

"Well then, you'll get what's coming to the other two."

"Fine, sir," she said. "Shoot. But I don't want to leave you with a mistaken notion that could lull you to sleep. After these murders you'll have to keep going. I don't know who told Baron de Luizzi the secret, but it wasn't Father Molinet, because he wasn't the one I told."

"He's not the one you told!" cried Count Cerny furiously. "Who was it then, you wretch?"

"It was a man I love, a man who'll guess why you killed me, and who'll avenge me, sir."

"A lover of yours, perhaps?" asked the count, laughing coldly again.

"Yes, sir."

"That's a stupid trick, ma'am, which doesn't fool me," he replied, recovering his composure. "No, ma'am, the thing is all too clear. From you to the priest, from the priest to this gentleman: those are the intermediaries, and those are the voices that must be silenced."

The discussion had gone on so long that all three actors in that peculiar scene had grown weary of their own emotions, and all of them had come a long way down from their initial excitement. Luizzi was no longer in the fine state of bravado in which he invited the count to kill him. Countess Cerny, overwhelmed by the feelings she'd experienced, had dropped onto the sofa where she'd looked so beautiful earlier. And the count, who'd withdrawn to the door of the boudoir, no longer felt the transports of fury that could've made it possible, at several points in the conversation, for him to carry out his awful intention.

But while his courage failed him, his thoughts returned to torment him. It was no longer a matter of avoiding ridicule, the fear of which had driven him to those terrible threats; it was those threats themselves whose memory he now wanted to blot out. The countess and Luizzi couldn't be allowed to leave that boudoir after what he'd said to them. For a long time that idea oppressed him, but without restoring the furious resolve he'd exhausted over the course of that long argument. He was reduced to the terrible state of having to commit murder out of necessity rather than out of anger.

Abruptly getting impatient with himself, he spoke again, like a man trying to whip himself up by his own shouting, and lashed out wildly, "Come, baron, come, ma'am, you asked for it—let your will be done!"

So saying, he aimed the barrel of one of his pistols at Luizzi, who drew back with a cry.

"Oh, so you're afraid?" said Count Cerny, who, in spite of himself, no longer able to rise to the mad exaltation needed for such a crime, seized on any excuse to avoid it.

"Afraid!" said Luizzi, mastering his first weak impulse. "No, sir. But there are some dangers no man is ready for, and one of them is treacherously premeditated murder."

"Well then! You can both save yourselves. What I told you to do earlier you can still do, in such a way as to satisfy me. Here's how: the countess will write you a few letters, of the kind you send to a lover; letters with different dates, of course. You'll write replies to those letters, so as to prove the countess has been your mistress. I want a proper romantic correspondence between happy lovers. And finally you'll each write a letter addressed to me, in which you'll say you're handing over the correspondence to me in recognition of my having spared both your lives: one as a coward, the other as a fallen woman. Once I have those proofs in hand, I'll let you live, and I'll allow you to leave this place freely, if that's what you want."

"Never!" cried Luizzi.

"I'm not going to argue," said the count firmly. "I'll give you an hour to think it over and agree to what I'm asking. If you haven't done everything I require within that time, it's because you'd rather die. As for Father Molinet," he added, tossing the shoe onto the floor, "I know a way guaranteed to silence him."

The count went away, leaving the countess and Luizzi alone together.

Chapter LIX: A Love Story in an Hour

No sooner were they alone than Countess Cerny rose and bolted the door from the inside. Then she turned to Luizzi. With an expression of terrible mad resolve she stood face to face with him and said, "Well, baron, what are you planning to do?"

"Nothing for myself, countess, and everything for you."

"That's not an answer, sir. We can only save each other by ruining each other's honor. We can't leave here, you with a reputation as a coward, I with the notoriety of a fallen woman. Are you willing to sacrifice your honor?"

"Would you dare sacrifice yours for me?"

"It's not a question of me, sir. Our positions aren't the same. My husband can only carry out these crimes with impunity by accusing me of an adultery he'll have punished by a murder tolerated under law. You have a better chance... Your death won't dishonor you... To have been my lover won't disgrace you."

At first Luizzi didn't answer; so many ideas prompted by his situation collided chaotically in his mind.

"You don't answer, sir? Do you want to write those letters?"

"No. I won't buy my life at the cost of your honor."

"Say rather your own honor," she replied, watching him intently.

"As you please, countess. I won't buy my life at the cost of my honor."

"Then we'll have to die," she said, lowered her head. "To die innocent... innocent and dishonored?..."

She'd thrown herself into a chair with an expression of despair. He looked at her; never had she seemed more beautiful. He moved closer to her. "Life and death have the same price... It's up to you to choose between them."

She looked at him for a long time, as if trying to discover what was genuine in his heart. Then she stood up and replied slowly, as if she wanted to make sure he understood every word, "Will you obey that choice, no matter what it is, sir?"

He hesitated, but in the end replied firmly, "I'll obey."

"Then let's write the letters, sir."

"Let's write," said Luizzi with a deep sigh, and in such turmoil that he truly didn't know whether it was for his own sake or for the countess's he was making that cowardly decision.

"Come," she said, opening a small desk. "Write, sir. Because I don't believe it's usually the woman who initiates a romantic correspondence."

He sat at the little velvet-lined desk and picked up a pen. But instead of writing he began to daydream.

"Well, sir? Do you refuse to save me?"

"No. It was my reckless words that doomed you, my infernal curiosity that led to this catastrophe... I have to save you, since you want to live—save you at the cost of my own honor. That's a consequence of the fatal destiny I've chosen; let it be carried out, I'm ready..."

He picked up the pen again, and quickly wrote the word *Countess*; but after that effort of imagination he could go no further. None of the sweet expressions he'd so often deployed in the past would come to him, and he went back to day-dreaming while he gazed at Countess Cerny. She was seated beside the desk, facing him; the horror of her situation had added to the beauty of her features a look of exaltation that riveted him. He studied her for a while, admiring that no-ble, ethereal face—so gracious and smiling earlier, so pale and frightened now. It occurred to him that the sad change he noticed could soon grow even worse, and if he hesitated any longer this beautiful young woman would soon be a cold, bleeding corpse; and he was filled with a noble resolve to save her. For it must be said that at that moment he completely forgot about himself; constructing in his mind the story of a man who's seen a woman, who's surrounded her with admiration, and who's now decided to speak up, he immediately wrote the fol-lowing letter:

Countess,

There are some dangers from which not even the purest virtue can protect a woman, for there are flights of passion all of her modesty can't prevent. When she inspires love, even unintentionally, she must resign herself to hearing its avowal. If that avowal offends her and her pride suffers, she must take pity on another's even more cruel suffering, and she must be forgiving. You'll therefore forgive me, ma'am. In any case, what I'm presuming to write to you isn't news. Love, even when it's unspoken, carries conviction enough to persuade a woman; she's aware of being loved long before the words are spoken to her—the lan-guage of one heart addressing another is unmistakable. A woman who, out of vanity, listens to the world's flattery can be deceived; but a woman who, like you, has preserved the innocence of her emotions amid the most serious con-cerns of the mind cannot be mistaken about the feelings she inspires. The soul has an ear that hears only the voice of another soul, and can hear it no matter what.

I'm not saying a woman is obliged to be pleased or flattered by the confes-sion of a love so strongly felt; but I do assert that she can't deny its sincerity, and that's the only comfort to which I aspire. The fact is, ma'am, you wouldn't withhold your good esteem from a man who devoted himself passionately to the noblest and most beautiful image of God, who knelt before God's holiest, most perfect creation; then must I be in the wrong because you are that celestial im-age and that perfect creation, and I kneel before you? That wouldn't be just, and

justice belongs to you the way beauty does—for like beauty, justice comes from
heaven. You must therefore have forgiven me.
—Armand de Luizzi

When he'd finished the letter he handed it to the countess, whose eyes had been fixed on him while he wrote, as if pitying this man whom she'd placed in the terrible position of having to choose between death and dishonor. She took the letter and read it once through quickly. Then she reread it. A sad, gentle smile crossed her lips, and she said, "How painful this is, sir, and how many illusions it destroys."

"How so, countess?"

"It forces me to acknowledge, sir, that a man can speak to a woman of a love he doesn't feel, with all the conviction of true love. It forces me to realize that what for you right now is an awful necessity can become a game in some idle moment."

"Don't think that, countess. As I wrote those words, I can't say I was feeling the love I spoke of, but I asked myself how I would love you if I ever dared love you."

"Is that true?" she asked, looking at him closely.

"Yes, countess. And if that letter doesn't contain a full enough or respectful enough description of the passion you ought to inspire, you can forgive it on account of the understandable mental stress under which it was written."

"Yes, yes," she replied with a sigh. "You're noble and good to me, sir: you're sacrificing your honor for the weakness of a woman who's afraid. Believe me, I thank you from the bottom of my heart." She paused to wipe away a tear that trembled at the tips of her long eyelashes; then with an effort she went on, "Now it's my turn, baron. I have to reply to this letter."

She read it through once more and began to write, while Luizzi considered her with the same melancholy feeling she'd had, reminding himself that his own recklessness had doomed this woman and blaming himself for the tears she couldn't always wipe away fast enough before they dropped, bitter and genuine, onto the sheet of paper on which was playing at happiness and love. Here was what she wrote:

You love me, sir; you tell me so too well for me not to believe it, and I believe it too firmly not to admit it to you. That admission of your love is a fault, I know, I feel it. To admit the love I inspire is to admit it neither surprises nor offends me, it's to accept it even when I can't return it, it's to think myself worthy of it when I ought to reject it, it's to demand the worship when I cannot grant the prayer—in short, it's to be unjust, and I don't want to be unjust to you. Therefore forget me, sir, forget me forever; and then I can remember proudly that you loved me, I can remember gratefully that you weren't willing to be loved.
—Léonie de Cerny

She handed him that letter, saying, with the sweet sad smile that lent her face such touching melancholy, "I'm moving awfully fast in that letter. I'm saying much more than a woman should say, even with genuine feelings in her heart. But we're in no position to spar at length over our emotions. Read it."

He read the letter, and reread it, as she'd done with his. Then with mocking melancholy he said, "What were you complaining about, countess, when you said men might make a game of expressing the tenderest feelings? You think that, knowing what desperation drove you to write this letter, it isn't awful to imagine some flirt writing it to a man who truly loved her?"

"I don't think a flirt could've done it," she said with innocent candor, "because I enlisted my heart to answer you, just as you did to write to me. I asked myself what I would've felt if I'd ever been loved with the love you expressed, and that's what I concluded."

"Oh, so that's how you would've replied if your love had been genuine?" he asked, looking into the charming face that was so beautiful in its sadness, so resigned in its suffering.

"Yes, truly, I think so. But what does it matter? We have to hurry, we have to finish this terrible love story. Your turn, sir, your turn..."

He picked up the pen, but this time he didn't pause before beginning his letter; he wrote quickly, almost like a man who's listening to his heart and letting it speak. And she watched the expressions flitting across his face as it reflected all the different feelings he was putting down on paper. There was such candid truthfulness in that involuntary expression of what he was pretending to feel, that anyone could've believed he was really feeling it.

So the countess, who'd been watching him closely, didn't wait for him to hand her the letter. As soon as he'd finished it she said, "Let's see, let's see." She took the letter and read:

Countess,

What can it be that you're asking of the one who loves you, when just your appearance, just your manner, delights and troubles him? When the grace and beauty you show anyone, when the little of your soul you expose to all the world, is enough to fill his soul with the most holy and devoted love? With what kind of love are you asking him to love you, when just for him you lift a corner of the impenetrable veil that conceals the chaste and innocent beauties of such a pure soul? When, putting aside for a moment the dazzling attractions that adorn you everywhere and belong to everyone, you give him a glimpse of the mysterious unknown delights that surpass all his dreams? Oh, countess, is the man for whom you deign to unveil yourself like that worthy of it?

The neophyte dazzled and thrilled by the light that fills the forecourt of the temple fears he won't be able to bear the radiance of the celestial beams escaping through the barely open door to the sanctuary; and I stand before you, as trembling and uncertain as he is, fearing I'll be unable to love you any more than I do, since I barely loved you enough for what I already knew of you. Yes, countess, when I loved you with all the power of my soul, I assumed you could ask no more of me; and now I find I've given my whole heart to what was only a part of you.

You've been both too good and too cruel to me. You've been like an angel of beauty passing veiled before a miserable mortal. At the majesty of her bearing, at the grace of her appearance, at the fluidity of her walk, the fool gives her all the admiration he possesses; then, in passing, the angel lifts the hem of her robe, raises one corner of her veil, and the poor wretch wonders what praise he can offer to that celestial beauty he didn't even dream of. So he bows low and asks for mercy. And that's what I too must do; for the letter you wrote me is the partly open door to the sanctuary, it's the robe slightly lifted, it's the raised veil—it's your heart, whose light and beauty I've glimpsed.

Oh, forgive me for not loving you more than I already did, but no man can give more than his heart and his life. You can only die once for the one you love, and you can't give her more love than your heart is capable of holding.

—Armand de Luizzi

When the countess had finished reading that letter she put her hand over her heart as if to contain its beating. Then, forcing herself to smile at his emotions, she said, "This letter is very silly, sir. No one in the world writes like that, and you're not lending much realism to the love story we're writing."

"Perhaps, countess, I was no longer writing to an imaginary woman about my imaginary passion; perhaps it was truly to you I spoke. Because what I said in that letter is true: I know about you what the world doesn't know, I know the strength and nobility of your soul, I know no woman has ever been more worthy of men's respect and adoration than you, and no man could ever have enough for you. The expression of that feeling might sound silly, countess, but the feeling itself is rooted sincerely in my heart, I swear, and that's what you have to believe."

"I'd like to thank you for your high opinion of me, baron," she replied, giving him a look the way you hold out your hand to a friend. "But we don't have the time. I have to write back," she added, her voice choked with tears. She picked up the pen and wrote:

I thank you for your love, sir. I thank you even for the fervency that goes beyond your love—not that I think I deserve it in the way you say, but because I'm happy to have inspired it in a man like you, even when he's mistaken. I'm not the veiled angel of beauty; because you know everything about me, except perhaps for the painful wounds I don't dare show. The sanctuary of my soul doesn't give off the blinding light you imagine; and you might be surprised, if you entered it, to find it's a sanctuary of mourning and a refuge of despair. So you'll understand why I thank you for your love. Keep it just the way it is, kind and forbearing toward me, and as honorable and devoted as you yourself are.

As she wrote that, Countess Cerny shed abundant tears, which from time to time she brushed away, before taking up the pen again and going on. "Look," she said to Luizzi, her voice breaking, "look at what I've replied. Oh, I don't feel brave enough to continue this awful game."

"Don't forget, your life depends on it."

"What point is there in saving it now? A life that'll be without honor, and will have been without love!"

She hid her face and her tears while he read her letter. When he was done reading he looked at her. But she'd given way entirely to despair; and Luizzi, turning resolutely to face the desk, began to write quickly.

Can I have misunderstood you, countess? Could the life all the world considers so tranquil and so happy be one long series of sufferings bravely endured? Might the serenity of your soul, which people take for coldness, merely be a laughing mask concealing regret and despair? Could it be true that the love I feel for you—a love stronger and more genuine than I've told you—could it be true that my love was a comfort to you? Oh, if only I could hope so, countess! If I could believe that, then I could spare you the suffering you endure, the risks you run! Oh, say the word, Léonie, just say the word, and I'll save you. Understand what I'm saying, I beg you. Whatever misfortune hangs over you, I can free you from it by calling it down on me.

Oh, if it costs me my honor, it's yours, you know that... If it costs me my life, it's yours, and it won't be lost if it's given to protect you! So take it, countess—because it will amply be repaid if you tell me, before I undertake a struggle to the death, "Armand, I will love your memory!"

She was still crying when he'd finished his letter. "Here," he said in a pleading tone, "Read this... Read it carefully."

At first she looked at the letter without being able to read it. Then she firmly wiped her eyes and reread it slowly, with her full attention. When she was done she gave him an eager, questioning look, and there was joy mixed with her tears as she said, "To whom should I reply, Armand?"

"To me, Léonie!" he cried, falling to his knees before her.

"To you, Armand, isn't that right? To you, here in this place, at this moment?"

"To me, here, to the me who'd die to save you."

"Well then, Armand!" she cried. "I'll reply to you: no, I won't love your memory... because I love you!"

"Ah!" he cried, picking up all the letters they'd written and tearing them to pieces in a fit of heroic pride. "Let the count come in now! He'll have to kill me ten times over before he touches you, Léonie!"

"No, Armand, no! If you die, I'll die!" she replied, her face lit up with mad exhilaration. "I'd die a fallen woman in the eyes of all others, an innocent woman for you alone!..." She stopped. Giving him a look of smoldering pride, she went on, "A guilty woman for you alone, if you like!"

"Léonie!" he cried, taking her in his arms. "Is that true?"

"Yes, yes!..." she cried, her voice fading. "I'm yours! Yours!... Because I love you!"

As she spoke she hid her face in her hands, while he carried her, in her mad despair, toward the sofa where only an hour earlier she'd looked so beautiful and so calm. She dropped onto the sofa, still covering her eyes with her hands, and murmured in a muffled voice, "Oh! That light!"

Luizzi wanted to blow out the candle burning in the crystal lamp, but he couldn't reach it. While the countess buried her face in the cushions to hide her sin even from herself, the baron caught sight of the Devil's shoe. He quickly picked it up and set it on the candle in lieu of a candle snuffer.

Suddenly the room turned black as hell, and the Devil's shoe danced on top of the candle.

EXPLANATIONS

Chapter LX: A Chapter from a Novel

While all that was going on in the boudoir, Count Cerny had gone back to his apartment, and for a long time he'd mulled over the terrible plan to which he'd been driven by the fear of looking ridiculous—a more powerful motive than you can imagine, for there are men who've preferred to avoid it by suicide than to face it. But once he was alone he considered more calmly the deed he'd thought himself brave enough to commit, and he realized he'd expected too much of himself.

Still, the drama needed a conclusion. He couldn't just go open the door and let his two prisoners walk free without their having written the letters he'd demanded; and he no longer had the resolve needed to secure by murder the only kind of silence that's guaranteed. So he began to look for a way out for himself, in case Luizzi and the countess had refused to write the supposed lovers' correspondence. By dint of searching, he finally saw a fairly simple solution: if the two of them were capable of preferring death to a cowardly act that would dishonor them both, they must have within them some honorable principle to which he could appeal with complete trust. The only remaining difficulty was how to take advantage of that fact. He outdid himself dreaming up such extravagant schemes that finally he came back to the simplest of all to carry out, just as he'd fallen back on the simplest of ideas for how to get out of the hole he'd put himself in. That idea was to acknowledge frankly the steadfastness of the baron's and the countess's behavior, and to congratulate them for it, with the pretense that he'd thought them capable of it all along and had only been trying to test them to make sure. Then he'd add that, now that he knew they were honorable persons, he could trust them and would require no other guarantee than their word.

The count had prepared a pretty little speech to that effect, and he waited impatiently for the hour to be up. But he didn't cut short the deadline he himself had set, first because he wanted to maintain in the prisoners' minds the air of implacable resolve he'd shown at the start, and then because in his inmost self he continued to hope they'd written the compromising letters that would serve as a better guarantee than any other.

Finally, when the hour rang, the count, carrying his pistols, returned—rather embarrassed, in spite of himself, by the figure he would cut. He was armed because he anticipated the possibility that all of his schemes might fail, and there might be a fight, and he was still willing to accept murder as his ultimate resource against his wife and the baron.

The whole house had long been asleep when the count passed through the suite of rooms leading to his wife's boudoir. At the door he listened, and heard nothing; he assumed the baron and the countess, sunk in despair, were waiting in terrified silence. That made him rely even more on the effect of his entrance, pistols in hand, to get what he wanted from them. He turned the knob, but the door didn't open, which surprised him. Among all the simple notions that had passed through Count Cerny's mind, the idea that the prisoners might've locked themselves in for protection hadn't occurred to him. In his first flush of anger at that unexpected obstacle, he called out, "Open up!"

There was no answer. He immediately gave the door a vicious kick to force it open; but it seemed to have been solidly secured on the inside. That resistance fed his anger, and he began hammering at the door like a madman, sometimes with his feet, sometimes with the butt of his pistols.

There are lots of houses in Paris in which the servants, far away in the kitchen or the vestibule, can easily hear doors slamming in the private apartments, voices making threats, furniture sliding from one end of the parlor to the other, mirrors shattering, windows breaking, porcelain dishes flying out the windows, and not pay any attention besides saying to each other, "Monsieur and madame are having an explanation." Then, wrapping themselves in the wise discretion of well-trained servants, they let the storm rage and the lightning strike the furniture undisturbed. The next morning they pick up the pieces—taking care to make some pretty little precious nicknack, supposedly a casualty of the fight, disappear into the bottom of their own trunk or into the possession of the secondhand dealers.

But it must be said that Count Cerny's household didn't have those excellent habits. Dignity and tranquility had always prevailed there. So when the servants heard someone pounding repeatedly on a door, they assumed some accident had happened to the count or the countess—a fire, burglars, who could say? Some of them ran up, half dressed, just as the count, after an extraordinary effort, had broken down the door, knocking over the furniture piled against it, and entered the room. Finding himself in pitch darkness, the count called out angrily, "Where are you two? Where are you?"

Just then he glimpsed a silhouette in the doorway, and quick as a flash he jumped to one side and fired a pistol. He heard a body fall, then a terrible cry; and a voice that was neither the baron's nor the countess's cried out, "Help! Help!"

It was the voice of Count Cerny's valet. In his transports of rage, the count was still looking for his prisoners in the darkness, determined to make them pay for the blood he'd just shed. He stumbled around, bumping into the walls, colliding with the furniture, till he reached the window, whose drapes were drawn. He assumed the two wretches were hiding there, and he violently flung back the curtains. The window was open.

Of all simple ideas, the simplest hadn't occurred to him: that windows are exits just like doors, a little more dangerous perhaps, but in any case preferable to a pistol shot and pointless dishonor. The count stood stock still at the sight, while the servants ran in and the valet he'd shot at felt himself all over to make sure nothing was broken. The count's astonishment turned to raging fury as he found himself surrounded, and he ordered the servants to light a candle and withdraw.

One of them, the kind of manservant who's learned his job in a certain way and who won't carry it out in any other way even in the midst of the most awful catastrophe, had been in the habit of illuminating the boudoir by lighting the crystal lamp that hung in the middle of the room. So when the count called for light, that clever servant, instead of putting the first candle he could find on the mantelpiece, set about lighting the lamp. He climbed on a chair, and the first thing he found was the Devil's shoe, which he dropped on the floor as if he'd touched a snake, crying, "Say! What's that?"

The reappearance of the shoe, and the use to which it had been put, struck the count as a bad joke, and he kicked it aside angrily, reflecting that now he was at the mercy, not only of the baron and the countess, but of the owner of that shoe. Still, it was thanks to his intemperate rage that he discovered something that might otherwise have escaped his attention. On the floor he saw some torn-up sheets of paper; they were the fragments of the letters Luizzi and the countess had written. He picked them up carefully and put them in enough order to be able to read them. He dismissed all the servants and read that peculiar correspondence. And then he realized that in their carelessness the fugitives had left terrible weapons in his hands.

Presumably letters of that kind wouldn't have been enough by themselves to convict a woman of adultery; but those letters—whose authenticity nothing other than the assertions of the accused could call into question—could doom them both, reinforced as the letters were by the couple's escape together out a window in the middle of the night; and especially when the husband's straightforward behavior, and even his violence, to which there were witnesses, would add to the belief that he'd tried to catch them in *criminal conversation* and they'd fled at the risk of their lives.

All of those circumstances, as we've said, seemed to come together wonderfully and back each other up; so at a glance the count could see his way to the basis for a charge of adultery against his wife. Besides, the truth would've sounded too much like a fantastical tale, even if Luizzi and the countess had dared to tell it. Still, they could do it, either by going directly to a magistrate or by going straight to old Viscount d'Assimbret, the countess's father; and before he set any plan in motion Count Cerny wanted to be clear about what might've happened.

Not wanting to let any of his servants into his confidence about what he was going to do, after having unintentionally let them in on the secret of his wife's flight, the count collected money and a sword cane, and set off on foot. He got into the first carriage for hire he saw, and had himself driven to his father-in-law's. It was a little after one in the morning when he left home. He didn't enter the viscount's house, but only had the doorman summoned, to make sure no one had called since eleven, which was when he'd locked the couple in his wife's boudoir.

From there he went to the police station in his neighborhood, and—without filing any complaint—told the magistrate of his wife's disappearance, and made sure she herself hadn't shown up before him. Now confident he was in a position to file a charge rather than face one himself, he had himself driven to Luizzi's house, where people were still up. The count knocked quietly and asked for Baron de Luizzi. The doorman told him he wasn't back yet. Count Cerny insisted, saying it was on a matter of the utmost concern to the baron.

"I'm not surprised," replied the doorman, "because less than half an hour ago a messenger handed me a letter for Monsieur Donezau, who'd just come home with his wife and Mademoiselle Gelis. The letter was from the baron, and was to be given instantly to Monsieur Donezau. The messenger was in such a hurry that I carried it up to Monsieur Donezau myself. All of his servants had gone to bed. I found him still up, along with madame, and no sooner had he read the letter than he said to his wife, 'I have to go out right away...' and the next moment I pulled the bell cord. He hasn't come home yet either."

"But I assume the baron will be back," said Count Cerny, "and this business is so urgent I'll have to wait here for him, or for his brother-in-law, Monsieur Donezau."

"That's easy," said the doorman. "Just go upstairs to the baron's apartment, and his valet will let you in, and you can wait for him as long as you like."

"Very good. Here's two louis for you. There's no need to tell Baron de Luizzi someone's waiting for him; besides his own valet, no one should hear about it."

Count Cerny went upstairs to the baron's apartment. He rang quietly, not wanting it to be heard in Caroline's apartment, since perhaps she'd learned, from the letter brought to her husband, what had happened to her brother, and she might try to warn Luizzi someone was waiting for him. The count told the valet a different story, a story backed by a large tip. In any case Pierre, as the master's valet in a good house, knew all the names of any weight and almost all the faces of the aristocracy; so when he saw Count Cerny he let him in to his master's apartment and made him comfortable there.

In spite of Caroline's astonishment at seeing her husband leave her so suddenly, in spite of the worry she felt, there was one ear even more alert than hers in that house: it was Juliette's, because she was waiting for Luizzi. When she heard someone ring downstairs, and then enter the baron's apartment, she as-

180

sumed he was back, and she expected him to come upstairs to her; but a half hour passed, and all was silent. Pierre was asleep, stretched out in the Voltaire-style wing chair that often served as his bed in the antechamber; and downstairs the doorman remained on guard alone—if you could call "guarding" the kind of sleeping on your feet that's the exclusive property of Paris doormen.

Juliette was greatly disappointed; but presumably the passion that drove her was even greater, because she decided to go find Luizzi, thinking he was in his apartment. The baron had had a small interior staircase built to get directly from a room next to his dining room up to his sister's apartment. Juliette used that staircase, moving quietly, and approached Luizzi's own room. She could hear someone pacing in that room, and assumed the baron was going through one of those inner struggles that precede the moment at which you surrender to a desire you could consider guilty. No doubt she feared his uncertainty might be resolved to her disadvantage, and she pushed open the door.

Entering, she found herself face to face with Count Cerny: having heard the sound of the door, he'd come forward quickly to meet whoever was coming in. They stared at each other in great surprise, then both...

Chapter LXI: Commentary on the Previous Chapter

"That's enough for now," said Luizzi, interrupting the Devil.

And in fact it was the Devil who'd been telling him that story in the parlor of a suite in a small hotel, while he listened with more attention than he'd ever paid to the wicked old storyteller. He didn't interrupt, and he made no remarks about the style or the form of a narrative he found extraordinary: it had the feeling of a chapter excerpted from a novel, describing events long since past. Luizzi's restraint came from knowing that the Devil took advantage of the slightest interruption to draw out endlessly—more than any novelist or writer for the daily serials—whatever story he was telling, and to wander off into digressions, whether moralizing or licentious.

"That's enough for now," said Luizzi. "I know everything I need to know to make a firm decision."

"You're mistaken. Listen at least to the scene between Juliette and Count Cerny. It'll only take half an hour, though the scene itself lasted more than three hours."

"I know everything I wanted to know, since it proves either the count didn't pursue us or he's on the wrong track."

"So much so, that he went back home and hasn't come out again."

"Everything's going wonderfully in my favor. We can leave without fear."

"Have you taken your precautions?"

"Let's see," said Luizzi, as if to review all he'd done and make an exact accounting of it. "As soon as I'd dropped Léonie off at this hotel, I wrote to Henri; he came, and brought me enough money to leave Paris and prepare for a journey."

"Did you tell him why you were leaving?"

"No, of course not."

"Where you were going?"

"Even less."

"You're making progress, baron; you're keeping your secrets to yourself. Then what?"

"Then I went out myself to hire a berline, whose coachman, thanks to my liberality, valiantly promised to drive his master's horses to death and get me to Fontainebleau in five hours."

"I like that coachman. And is that coach going to come pick you up here?"

"No, he'll wait for us at the corner of the rue de Richelieu and the boulevard." The Devil began to laugh, and Luizzi looked at him in surprise. "What's so funny about that?"

"It's the place you're starting from that strikes me as odd. You could've chosen better than in front of a brothel and a gambling den."

"It was the coachman who suggested that rendezvous point, saying he'd be less conspicuous than if he parked in front of a house that was closed up and quiet."

"That coachman's a gallant fellow. It shows he has a certain understanding of devious business. The lad will go far... Anyway, where were you?"

"I've reached the point where I'm waiting for nothing more than for you to be gone before I leave myself, and get to Fontainebleau, and from there find transportation from one village to the next all the way to Orléans, without anyone suspecting which direction we've gone."

"Don't forget, I'm at your disposal to tell you anything you want to know."

"You're becoming too obliging, Satan."

"I want to make things right with you, master. I don't want you to be able to say, as you have up to now, that if you've done a lot of stupid things, it's because I didn't give you good enough information. So, come on, think carefully: is there anything else you want to ask me?"

"Nothing at the moment," said Luizzi, getting up to go to the room where the countess sat writing to her father.

"Baron," said the Devil, stopping him. "You know my opinions haven't always been conveyed to you in my stories, that I've often thrown people and events in your way that spoke in my name. Remember everything you've seen since you got out of the prison madhouse, and ask yourself whether, at the moment you're about to commit yourself to an act of this importance, there's anything in all that which deserves some explanation."

Luizzi thought it over, but, recalling everything the Devil had said about his adventure with Countess Cerny, he found nothing that didn't seem perfectly clear. In any case, Satan's insistence on offering his help struck the baron as decidedly self-serving, and he assumed the Devil wanted to deflect him from the course he'd chosen. On the other hand, his thoughts were entirely with Countess Cerny, and he was eager to hear what she'd written to her father. Dawn was coming, and it was time to flee.

He went to the countess's room, where she was seated at a table on which lay her letter, finished and sealed long since. "Léonie," he said, "it's time to leave Paris. Give me the letter, and I'll put it in the mail. That way no one will be able to intercept and question either someone from the hotel staff or an outside messenger. Come, Léonie."

The countess, who was resting her elbows on the table and her face in her hands, lifted her head slowly. A cold pallor had spread across the beautiful features that had glowed with such health the night before. The blank whiteness was animated only by the blueish red around her eyes, revealing an inner weariness that only the fire of a high fever allowed her to overcome. Her eyes shone with anxious excitement beneath heavy, listless eyelids. Her hair fell in disorder around a face that only the night before had been so charmingly framed by her beautiful blond curls. Her whole body gave off the despondency of a woman who's used to the serenity of a tranquil life, and the weariness of a soul that's just gone through its first struggle with suffering.

She looked at him at length and said, "Armand, there's still time. Think about yourself before we leave Paris. Consider that it's my life you're ruining, and that I think you're too honorable not to know it's also yours you're ruining."

"Léonie, why are you asking me to reconsider what I'm about to do? Are you already dreading your future?"

"Today like yesterday—guilty today, as I was innocent yesterday—all honor and respect are finished for me. I'll never return to my husband's house, because if I returned I'd tell him I'd done wrong, and he'd have the right to punish me. I'm resigned to eternal exile in this world. But you, Armand: can't you see what kind of future existence you're preparing? Marriage forbidden to you!... No family, or a family bowed beneath the word adultery, which I've earned! No society, because people will use every insult to try to make you pay for the wrong I'll have done in society's eyes. Think it over, Armand. I can leave alone... I'll have fled my husband, but you won't be my accomplice, and I alone will be compromised."

"Léonie, you granted me permission to die for you; have I not earned the right to live for you?"

"Is that what you want, Armand?" she asked, holding out her hands. "Well then, I'll accept your life the way I'd accepted your death, and I'll repay it with my whole life."

"Let's go, then! Let's go!" said Luizzi, who'd prepared in advance for their departure from that hotel.

Chapter LXII: Flight

They left the hotel together in what they were wearing, he in evening clothes, she in a muslin dress; because at the late-night hour they'd escaped from her boudoir, at the moment they'd decided to run away together, neither of them had thought about the wretched necessities of material life that add small miseries to the greatest grief. In any case, the shops where Luizzi could've procured the usual supplies for a journey weren't open. They went slowly to meet their carriage, passing a few workmen setting off by night on the long walk to their day's labor—who were surprised to see this woman in her uncovered hair and muslin dress and this man in yellow kid gloves and polished boots, on foot in the mud.

But they soon reached Frascati's,[43] and the baron, hearing the laughing voices of men and women in the courtyard as they left that establishment, quickly opened the carriage door and handed Countess Cerny inside before anyone could see her. Then, while the coachman was getting down from his seat, Luizzi followed the countess into the carriage just as a noisy group was passing the door to the restaurant. He could hear a woman's voice crying, "Say, who's that going off in the berline?"

"Ha!" said another. "It's Palmyre, I'm sure of it, trying to pull a fast one on his broker!"

The countess sank quickly back into a corner of the carriage, while outside another voice, in the shrill, singsong tone so typical of lowlife girls, called, "Hey, Gustave, since you found Juliette again, tell her to come see her old friends sometime! She's one who could cut the ground out from under even the cleverest fellow!"

The names Gustave and Juliette presumably wouldn't have been remarkable enough to alarm Luizzi, except that he thought he recognized the voice that answered her in the distance as that of Gustave de Bridely himself, saying, "Juliette's got other fish to fry now…"

That strange coincidence so astonished Luizzi that he couldn't help sticking his head out of the carriage window to see if he'd been mistaken or if it really was the marquis. But the countess's "Be careful!" drew him back into the carriage, and the poor woman's wretched state occupied his attention so completely that he soon forgot the odd occurrence that had struck him as a fresh warning.

---

[43] As noted earlier, the Maison Frascati was a popular café and pastry shop, with gardens and ballrooms and gaming tables. Presumably the Devil was referring to Frascati's when he made his remark about a "gambling den" near their coachman's chosen rendezvous.

The countess, sunk in one corner of the carriage, shook both from the cool of the morning and from the chill of the fever she was running. She was no longer the proud, magnificent woman whose commanding beauty and great stature suggested the kind of masculine courage normally associated with large, powerful physiques. She was now a weak, wretched woman: fearful, desperate, weeping, trembling, in pain, plucked abruptly out of a life of resignation, of routines untouched by physical suffering, and thrown suddenly into an adventure that lacked nothing, not even the stripping away of the barest necessities.

Luizzi drew closer to her and spoke to her gently, begging her to have courage.

"I do. I do." But her words were uttered through chattering teeth, and her voice shook as much as her body.

"Oh, Léonie! What are you afraid of? Your life belongs to me now, and I'll protect it."

"Don't worry," she replied, in a tone more despairing than courageous. "I'm not afraid of dying."

"I'll defend your life against slander too; and if I'm not strong enough to defy the whole world we'll flee to some foreign country, we'll seek refuge together under an assumed name."

"Yes, we will, Armand! As soon as you can do it we'll flee France, we'll go hide someplace where no one but us will know my sin!"

"Your sin, Léonie? Is it a sin not to want to sacrifice your life to a man who'd sentenced it to being no more than one of resignation?"

"It's a sin, Armand. But I don't repent committing it, if you love me."

"Oh, Léonie! What a word!"

She fell confusedly to her knees in the carriage, and with her hands raised to him in supplication she cried, "Oh, Armand! Love me now! Love me! You will love me, won't you?... You'll always love me?... Oh, if you didn't love me... what would become of me... my God!"

He took her in his arms and reassured her, with the most sacred oaths, of the constancy and devotion of the love she was asking from him. She was cold, and she shivered in his arms.

"You're in pain," he said, "and I made no preparations!... I didn't even protect you against the cold."

"It's nothing," she said, forcing her teeth to stop chattering. "Don't worry about that."

"No, I'll have him stop before we leave Paris, I'll have some shop opened, I'll get everything you need..."

"No, no," she said, appalled. "Let's just get away quickly."

But he could see her suffering increasing by the minute. She'd pressed herself into the corner of the carriage; there, overcome by weariness, cold, and fever, she remained unmoving, shivering, mumbling inarticulate cries, and replying to everything he said with a curt, distracted, "I'm fine! I'm fine!"

Finally, through the closed windows of the carriage, he saw the multitude of carts that reach the edges of Paris at the break of day. The men who drove the carts were all muffled in the kind of short coat of heavy striped cloth called a roulière. In spite of the countess's words, Luizzi made the carriage stop, got out, and called to one of the carters going by, "My good man, would you be willing to sell me your coat?"

"My coat!" said the carter with a look of astonishment. "Uh," he went on, waving his pipe, "what would you be wanting with my coat, baron?"

Hearing himself addressed so correctly, Luizzi looked at the man. He thought he recognized him, but he couldn't exactly recall him. Not wanting to be drawn into conversation with him, no matter who he was, he said, "I forgot to bring mine, and I'm freezing. I'll pay you enough for you to buy ten, if you need."

"Well, well," said the carter. "So you've become rich again, Monsieur de Luizzi? All the better," he went on, unfastening his roulière. "Ah, it's not like back home: old Rigot's ruined, old Mother Turniquel's dead, and Madame Peyrol, who wanted to give her whole fortune to her daughter, the peer's wife, lives with old Rigot in a shabby little house next to her uncle's old chateau. They both live off the miserable stipend they get from Count Lémée, Madame Peyrol's son-in-law."[44]

"Ah!" cried Luizzi, illuminated by all those details. "Is that you, Little Pierre?... So you left the stagecoach job?"

"Yes, indeed. I had quit that to become old Rigot's coachman, because he made me some big promises. But he had to give all that up... It was an awful business, baron, but not as awful as what happened to old Mother Turniquel... Didn't you know? Turns out Madame Peyrol wasn't Mother Turniquel's daughter."

"What! Eugénie?..."

"It seems she was the daughter of some great lady whose child was stolen long ago. The old woman kept it secret till her last days, since she was afraid she'd be abandoned by the girl who was taking care of her. But when the last rites were read, the fear of the Devil was stronger than the other fear, and she confessed everything."

"Did she say the great lady's name?"

"Wait a moment, wait a moment!" said the former postilion. "It was a certain Madame de... Cliny... Cany... Cauny... That's it, Cauny.[45] But who the devil knows what's become of her in the last thirty-five years! Ah, baron, none of this would've happened if you'd been willing to marry that poor woman."

---

[44] As a group, this cast of characters was last seen in Chapter XLI, though some have been mentioned more recently.

[45] Madame de Cauny appeared in Chapter XXIX, where she spoke bitterly about men who seduce women for sport.

"Cauny!" repeated Luizzi. "I know that name. I've heard it mentioned somewhere."

He might've questioned Little Pierre further, but the carter, who as he'd been speaking had approached the berline, now drew back hastily and cried, "Oh, my God! There's a sick woman in there!"

"It's all right! It's all right!" cried Luizzi, tossing Little Pierre half a dozen louis and quickly getting back into his carriage. He found the countess completely prostrate, slumped on the seat. He picked her up and positioned her so that she huddled crossways on the seat with her upper body resting on the baron's lap and her head in the corner of the compartment. He supported her in his arms and protected her head against the shaking and bumping of the carriage. He wrapped her in the roulière and considered her as she lay there, pale, cold, almost dying. "Léonie! Léonie!" he whispered, pressing her to him. "Be brave! Be brave!"

"Thank you!... Thank you!" she said, as if she were half asleep. "Oh, that feels good... It's warm."

A tear came to his eye at those words from a woman so well-born, so comfortably settled in life, so dazzling, and who was thanking him for protecting her for a moment from the cold. He pressed her closer against his own heart, he wrapped her in his arms, as if they could cover her whole body. Leaning close to her, he kissed her icy brow.

She gently freed her arms from the roulière wrapped around her; putting them around his neck, she hung there, and without opening her eyes she murmured, "You love me, don't you? You love me?"

"Yes, Léonie, yes, I love you!... And as God is my witness I'd die before it occurred to me not to love you as the most honorable, most saintly of women!"

"Thank you!... Thank you!... You won't abandon me, will you?"

"Oh, hush, Léonie, hush!... Me, abandon you!... Oh, never... never!"

She opened her eyes, whose glassy shine betrayed her burning fever, and gave him a drooping look as she repeated, "Yes, you love me!... Oh, yes, you love me, don't you?... And if I die you won't despise me!"

"Léonie!" he cried, letting his flowing tears fall onto her face. "How can you speak of dying?... Oh, you're suffering, you're suffering!..."

"No... You love me!... Talk to me, talk to me like this... You do me good!"

She lifted her arms from around his neck, took one of his hands, and pressed it to her heart as she said softly, in a voice that faded gradually in the sleepy prostration produced by weariness and fever, "Love me... Love me very much... You won't have long to love me... No, not long... And yet I'm happy... very happy... Armand... I love you!"

As she spoke she was pressing his hand to her heart; and as her voice faded that pressure lessened. Then she let her arms drop, and her head fell back, and she seemed to have fainted away completely. Luizzi looked at her. For the first time in his life he felt something like the love that belongs to the last years of a man's youth, the love that makes him fully a man, the love that's protective and devoted, that's founded on self-confidence, and that doesn't worry about the future because it's based on feelings of honor no man believes he'll ever abandon; a pure, sacred love that has none of the blindness of the dreamy, confident love of adolescence, nor the impetuous passion of youth at its peak, but one that foresees the struggle ahead, and has counted all the sacrifices it'll have to make, all the constancy it'll have to show, and accepts the struggle bravely, bearing the sacrifices joyfully, glorying in the happiness it has and even more in the happiness it gives.

Never had Luizzi's heart been so full of such a noble sentiment, and for the first time as well he felt almost proud of himself; for he could see a kind of nobility entering his existence, and he sensed he had the courage not to fail it. At that same moment, seeing Countess Cerny so prostrate she wasn't even surprised by his silence, he thought about the best means to help her elude all pursuit. For that he needed to be sure what was going on in Paris; so he summoned Satan, knowing the Devil's voice would be audible only to him, and promising himself to speak such that the countess couldn't hear him and wouldn't wonder at a conversation that, for her, would be nothing but a meaningless monologue.

Chapter LXIII: A Contrast

Satan appeared. He'd discarded his priest's clothing, and was very correctly dressed in black, with a ribbon in his boutonnière made up of all the colors of the rainbow, presumably representing a dozen different medals and decorations. If, along with those clothes, he'd had clean hands and white linen, he could've passed for a diplomat from one of the smaller German states, who spend their time soliciting all the important ribbons from all the little courts of the German Confederation. But apart from his black suit Satan's shabby appearance gave him a look of grimy poverty that could easily have belonged to one of those bottom-drawer con men who invent medals for themselves to cadge dinner from gullible innkeepers or to sell ointment to the deputy mayors of villages.

Luizzi's situation didn't give him time to inquire into the Devil's reasons for choosing that dubious look; as soon as the latter had settled onto the seat facing him in the carriage, the baron said quietly, "Tell me what the count's up to right now in Paris."

"To inform you properly, I'll pick up the story at the point where I stopped. Before I begin, however, I want to remind you, master, it was you who refused to hear me out to the end."

"I know. But hurry; I won't interrupt, just as I didn't when you started."

"Then gather your courage, because before I begin I have to tell you you're going to hear some peculiar things. But then, since you want to know human life or human actions at their most hidden, you have to dare to look them in the face. They're often hideous: just as the anatomy of the human body deals with every kind of filth, that of the human life would be incomplete if it didn't go beyond the clean, white surface."

"Will you hurry up! You always excite my curiosity and you never satisfy it completely."

"Then listen." And the Devil resumed his story.

As I told you, Juliette, thinking you'd come home, and annoyed that you hadn't come to the rendezvous she'd given you, decided to go downstairs to your apartment; and she entered your room just as Count Cerny was advancing to meet her. At the sight of a stranger, Juliette stepped back in confusion; at the sight of a woman, the count stopped and bowed deeply.

"I beg your pardon," she said. "I thought Baron de Luizzi was at home."

"He's not back yet," he said. "I'm waiting to see him."

They both bowed, he meaning to remain in the room, she meaning to withdraw, but both of them with a look of surprise at the other. Presumably Juliette was the first to recall the circumstances in which she'd seen the man she found here so unexpectedly, because almost immediately she was filled with a kind of horror. She turned away quickly, as if to elude his inquiring eye, and moved rapidly to the door. And presumably also, the horror the sight of him had inspired in her, and her hasty retreat, gave Count Cerny's memory the certainty it had lacked till then; for he moved even faster to get between the young lady and the door, and stopped her just as she was about to leave. "Are you Juliette Gelis?"

"You're mistaken, sir," she replied boldly. "I don't know you."

"You shameless little minx!" he cried, seizing her violently by the arm and dragging her back to the middle of the room. "Don't act like you don't know me, because I certainly recognize you."

At first she lowered her head and bit her lip in anger; but after a moment's silence she began to eye him with contemptuous insolence; and she answered in a tone of coarse bravado, "All right, yes, I'm Juliette Gelis, and what have you got to say about that?"

"What have I got to say?" asked the count, approaching her with his fists clenched, like a man who can barely restrain himself from extreme violence. "What have I got to say to you, wretch? Don't you remember what happened between us in Aix?"

"In Aix!" cried Luizzi, interrupting the Devil, and connecting that fact to the tale he'd heard the night before.

The Devil gave him a scornful smile. "You promised not to interrupt me."

"You're right, Satan. But since you're my slave, be careful I don't bind you to me so tightly that I rob you of the joy of making others miserable!"

"As you please! But don't make so much noise, or you'll wake up that woman who's sleeping."

"Well, speak then—speak!"

The Devil pushed back from his brow the long, greasy, dirty hair that covered his face, and picked up his story, always with the limp, pendulous smile typical of a mouth withered by shameful debauchery.

"You remember what happened between us in Aix?" Count Cerny asked Juliette.

"Well, it seems to me you enjoyed it at least as much as I did! I did everything you wanted, you paid me, we're even."

As she spoke Juliette moved to the door, but the count stopped her and said, even more angrily than before, "Not yet! Because I paid more for that night of fun than the money I gave you! You must know that, wretch!"

"My word! That's a risk you take when you go where you went. Besides, it hasn't killed me, nor you either. And in this fallen world I think the best thing to do is not to worry about what's done and gone."

Juliette's first words had exasperated the count, but the last thing she said caused him to contain his rage. He reasoned, rightly, that his continued anger would be an admission of the dire consequences of his first encounter with Juliette; and he replied more calmly, "You're right, let's drop it... And you especially, don't speak of it any further," he added, dropping into an armchair and motioning to her to come closer. Then he went on, "Since I find you here at Baron de Luizzi's, I assume you must have a greater interest in my silence than I do in yours. So be honest with me, and I'll be discreet on your behalf. You're now Luizzi's mistress, aren't you?"

"No, count, I'm not."

"Considering the morals I know you have, and the hour of night I find you here, however, that's the most respectable explanation I can think of for your being here."

She gave a scornful little shrug. "It's possible what you're suggesting could've happened, if I'd found him here, though the fact is nothing like that has happened between us."

"The baron doesn't find you to his taste?" he asked, looking her up and down.

"He'd have to have no taste for that! Anyway, don't act so superior," she added, sitting down next to him. "You loved me for more than one night, and if I wanted, you'd still come back to me occasionally."

The count made a face, but since her words proved to him she was quite unaware of his misfortune, he contained himself. "I'm not saying no, though it seems to me you've put on prudish airs that must make you less entertaining than you used to be."

"That's for the baron's benefit, but I won't play straitlaced with you. Besides, you know, you're still handsome—even handsomer than you were before. Ah, I've got to admit, my dear, good behavior pays off," she added, leaning amorously toward the count. Under her infatuated and lascivious eye, he turned pale and drew back.

Juliette noticed. Straightening up, she went on, "Don't be afraid! I'm not going to rape you. Anyway, I know you're not physically capable of being unfaithful to your wife."

"Who told you that?" he cried, full of rage. "Baron de Luizzi, perhaps?"

"No, no. It was that little du Bergh, who was saying at dinner tonight that you think about nothing besides ambition and politics these days. Besides, I know perfectly well that when you love someone you don't want to cheat on them. Take me, for example: I swear, if Henri weren't sleeping with his wife now, I'd never have thought of being unfaithful to him with the baron."

"Oh!" cried Luizzi, suddenly enlightened by a terrible flash, "so that awful vision I had when I was ill was true?"

"Didn't you summon me to learn about the relations between Juliette and Henri?" asked the Devil. "I obeyed, and I showed them to you by the only means I was allowed to use then."

"Then why didn't you show up to tell me that what I was about to see was the truth?"

"You asked for the truth. You were in the throes of tetanus, so you couldn't hear me. I showed it to you—what more could I have done? Anyway, didn't I tell you this morning to think back and recollect whether you had anything to ask me?"

Luizzi's mind was reeling under those awful revelations, whose blows came one after another. He forgot the woman stretched out in the carriage in fitful feverish sleep. Borne along by all the fears that assailed him, he cried out loudly, without controlling his voice, "Finish the story, Satan, tell me everything. I'm listening, I'm listening."

With his cold, mocking impassivity the Devil continued:

When Juliette told him it would hardly have occurred to her to cheat on Henri with the baron, Count Cerny replied to that whore, "You'd have been all the more mistaken, because right now Henri isn't with his wife. He's gone out."

"To go see another woman, I assume?"

"No. It's not a matter of a woman for Henri, though a woman is very much involved in the reason he's gone out."

"Well! Could it be about some mistress of that nincompoop Armand?"

"No," said the count, getting worked up. "No. The woman in question has never been and never will be Baron de Luizzi's mistress."

Satan stopped there. Half-closing his eyes and laughing his wickedest laugh, he looked at Countess Cerny, who was tossing and turning in her sleep, and said to the baron, "What do you think of that, master? What a thing for a husband to say!"

"You rascal!" muttered Luizzi. "I'm not interrupting you, so don't interrupt yourself. Keep going."

The Devil assumed a malevolent expression the baron had never seen on his face before. Without responding to Luizzi's name-calling, he went on with his story.

"She has never been and never will be his mistress," said the count.

"Neither she, nor any other woman," replied Juliette, "unless I feel like allowing it. The poor boy is a fool in love with me."

"Me, in love with that whore!" cried Luizzi loudly. "Oh! I loathe her! I despise her! Wretched fallen woman, foul creature!"

At that moment Countess Cerny woke up with a cry and threw herself back into a corner of the carriage.

Chapter LXIV: A Dream

"Armand! Who are you talking about?" she cried in confusion. "Who did you call a foul creature? Who did you call a wretched fallen woman?"

"Oh, not you, you poor unlucky woman!" cried Luizzi, falling to his knees before her. "Not you, who are bound to me more than ever by the bonds of misery! Because the suffering you've been through and the suffering I foresee undoubtedly stem from the same source."

"Now you foresee more suffering? Armand, you've waited too late to think it over."

"No, Léonie. You won't be the cause of my sufferings."

While he spoke he could hear the Devil's harsh, spasmodic laugh as he crouched there on the front seat of the berline with his savage eye devouring the honorable, beautiful woman he'd finally succeeded in pushing into sin.

"No, it won't come from you," went on Luizzi, raising his voice as if in response to the Devil's mockery. "You won't be the cause of my sufferings, and if any consolation remains in my life, it's from you that I look for it, from you alone, you understand?"

Satan's laugh rang even more harshly in his ear. Annoyed by his infernal slave's insolent mockery, he cried out in fury, "Scram! Scram!"

As the Devil vanished he whispered in Luizzi's ear, "Don't forget, master, you're the one who's sending me away!"

Astonished by his cries, which seemed to be addressed to no one, Countess Cerny gave him a worried look.

"Forgive my incoherent words, Léonie," said Luizzi. "But while you were sleeping I followed a train of thought so sad, with such foreboding premonitions, that for a moment they drew my mind far away from you."

"Me too! During the awful sleep that overcame me, I received sinister warnings—if it's true that God sometimes gives a dream the power to show us a future our reason or rather our hearts can't predict."

"And what was that dream?" asked Luizzi, whose imagination, accustomed to supernatural revelations, was always looking for illumination beyond the things that regulate other men's behavior.

"It seemed to me," she said, in the low voice of someone searching for a memory and with the expression of one who dives into the past so as not to leave out any detail, "it seemed to me I was in a shabby little room at an inn in some wretched village. As shabby as it was, it was the one I'd been given at that inn, because long ago, they told me, some important person had stayed there... Wait... That important person was the pope."

"A room the pope had stayed in? That's surprising."

"No, that room really exists in Boismandé.[46] And as I've thought more than once since yesterday of going to seek shelter near that village, at the home of my aunt, Madame de Paradèze, it's no surprise if that detail, which I've often heard about, got mixed up in my dream; I understand that now. So I was in that shabby little room. I was ill, in the middle of a cold night that froze both my body and my heart…"

"Yes," said Luizzi sadly, "it was the actual cold that troubled your sleep and got mixed up in your dream. Your genuine illness prompted your imaginary feeling that you were ill."

"Maybe so. But what has no connection to what I've felt and suffered for the past few hours is what came to me in that room; it's what so strangely coincided with the words I heard in my dream… and that you actually spoke here next to me," she added, drawing closer to him.

"Go on, go on," said the baron, using the informal *tu* with her, as she'd just done with him. Both of them moved into and out of that more intimate form of address: dropping it when they touched on a subject that didn't involve their shared destiny, picking it up again as soon as they needed to remind each other that from now on they were everything to each other.

The countess went on in the same sad, frightened tone in which she'd begun her story. "Yes, I was alone and ill in that shabby little room. I said I was alone, Armand, because you weren't there. But there was a person sitting next to that terrible bed and another person sitting at the foot: a man and a woman. I feel like I'd recognize the man again if I saw him. His face was pale, and bore the marks of a debased and debauched life. He had long black hair that hung over his face; and the dirtiness of his linen and his body would've made me take him for some low traveler who'd come to look at me out of curiosity, if I hadn't noticed in his boutonniere a multicolored ribbon that suggested he'd been awarded a number of important decorations."

That description, which bore a strange resemblance to the form the Devil had assumed to visit him, filled Luizzi with icy terror. Drawing close to the countess, he asked quietly, in a voice whose shaking didn't seem warranted by his simple words, "Oh, so he had a ribbon in his boutonniere?…"

"Yes," she went on, without noticing his agitation. "As for the woman at the foot of my bed, she was young, and she might've seemed pretty without the wild glint in her eyes as she looked at me with a stare that pierced my heart like hot steel."

"You didn't notice her face?"

"No, not exactly. Sometimes she looked as young as a girl of sixteen, pure and innocent in spite of the fiery gleam in her eyes. Sometimes she looked older, and then she had a bold, lascivious expression that horrified me. Meanwhile there they sat, the man next to me, the woman at the foot of the bed. It was the

_____

[46] See Chapter XI for that story.

195

woman who spoke first. She said to the man, 'Well, master, are you satisfied?' He turned to me with a look in his eyes even more horrible than hers and answered, 'This one's all set...'" The countess paused; after a little thought she went on, "He called the woman Jeanette or Juliette... I can't remember which... It doesn't matter. 'This one's all set,' he said. 'She's been contemptible, adulterous. She's mine. But has the other one denied God, and has the incest taken place?' 'Not yet,' said the girl. 'In that case, go,' said the man, 'and don't delay. Time's passing, and the fatal deadline will soon expire.' 'I'm off, master!' she replied. Then, turning to me, she added with a cruel smile, 'You can die now. Because, thanks to me, your lover has abandoned you, and you'll never see him again.' No sooner had she spoken those words than she vanished, and the man laid a hand of iron on my heart and cried, 'Come now, fallen woman, foul creature, you're mine!' At that moment I woke up, and it seemed as if the words you were speaking rang out over my sickbed like the echo of the words I was hearing in my dream."

"Or rather, it was in fact my own words, which found a meaning in that half-waking dream in which reality mingled with your own imagination."

Luizzi had listened to the countess's story with great attention. In a way he'd shared in its terrors—up to the point where the man in the dream had spoken of incest and a soul that denied God. Still affected by the horror of what he'd heard from the Devil earlier, he thought he glimpsed in Countess Cerny's dream another terrible warning from that terrible secret-sharing source, and he'd attached a name to every actor in the scene. To him, the woman was Juliette and the man was Satan. But the detail about incest suggested how far he'd gone astray, because nothing in his life corresponded to that word. So he used all the arguments available to what we call reason to drive from the countess's heart the chimerical fears that troubled her; and in seeking to persuade her he persuaded himself first.

Meanwhile their coachman had kept his word, and they'd reached Fontainebleau. They ordered the carriage to stop at the entrance to the town—because, just as they hadn't wanted the coachman to be able to say where he'd picked them up, they didn't want him to be able to say where he'd left them.

Luizzi quickly took care of all the precautions necessary for Countess Cerny to be able to enter the town without being noticed. He left her alone in the berline for a moment while he went to get the things a woman needs for going on foot. The handsome, elegant baron wandered through the streets of Fontainebleau, entering shops to buy a shawl, a hat, and a veil for the countess. When he came back to her—the sight of a man carrying in his hands all the purchases he'd just made causing great surprise in passersby—they entered Fontainebleau together and went to hide at the Cadran Bleu Hotel, which is right near the stagecoach stop and on the main road.[47] That would enable them to take either a private carriage or a public stagecoach to get away, without risking being recognized as they walked through town again, in a place that's a year-round destination for idle Parisians.

The first thing Luizzi did when they reached the hotel was to secure a bed for the countess. She lay down, and resting her body soon eased her spirits; she was able to consider her situation less fearfully, from every angle, and to think rationally so as not to make that situation worse by taking rash steps. On his side, the baron found the time necessary to take care of the logistical details of the journey that lay ahead of them, and to summon to the hotel all the tradesmen who would furnish both of them with clothes more appropriate than the ones they were wearing.

Money is a power whose potential has yet to be calculated fully, just as the potential of steam power has yet to be calculated fully. Indeed, thanks to money, in Fontainebleau—in Fontainebleau!—Luizzi managed to find a tailor, a seamstress, and a dressmaker who in twelve hours produced everything he could possibly need. After having taken care of all those details—which the countess noticed with the tender gratitude of a heart that's in love and that pays attention to everything, even a pin, if that pin means "I'm thinking of you"—after having taken care, as we were saying, of all those details, Luizzi, though he was with the woman he was ruining, felt he had time to think about the woman he was abandoning; and the memory of his sister, left in Juliette's and Henri's clutches, made him despair. He wanted to know the outcome of Juliette's conversation with Count Cerny; but he didn't dare leave the countess, who said over and over, sadly and feebly, "Stay, Armand. I'm frightened when I'm alone. I feel like I'll never see you again."

On the other hand, even if she'd been asleep he wouldn't have dared to summon the Devil in her presence, out of fear of the transports of anger Satan's long stories could drive him into. After long consideration, however, he decided he knew enough about Juliette and Henri to want to rescue Caroline from their clutches. Not sure whom he could call on to protect her, he resolved to communicate directly with her. He wrote:

Caroline,
As soon as you receive this letter, leave your husband's house without him seeing you. Don't tell him I've written to you. Set off immediately for Orléans. I'll be waiting for you at the post coach hotel, where you'll ask to be dropped. Don't worry about the journey, and don't be alarmed at what I'm asking you to do. If anything in the world is a danger to your life, it's staying in Paris. Con-

---

[47] The Grand Hôtel du Cadran-Bleu (the Blue Dial) was a historic hotel in Soulié's time, and still survives in some form today.

sider that my own life might depend on your following my advice without delay, and that I'm counting on you to save me.

—Armand de Luizzi

He added that last sentence to his letter to help make up Caroline's mind, knowing she'd do for his sake what she might not do for her own, since hers was one of those souls for whom, in a manner of speaking, devotion is life, and whom God has consecrated to the happiness of others.

When that letter was done, Luizzi, who'd been led by a sin into a path of kindness and benevolence, wanted to come to the aid of all the lives he felt he'd compromised, and he thought of the unfortunate Eugénie. The challenge was to find someone to whom he could entrust the task of doing what he wanted to do for Madame Peyrol; in his current position he could think of no one better to ask than Gustave de Bridely. In reproducing the letter he wrote to him, we'll make sufficiently clear the reasons that led the baron to a choice that, at first glance, must seem fairly peculiar.

My dear Marquis de Bridely,

I'm sure you remember Monsieur Rigot and the odd condition he imposed on the marriages of his niece and his grandniece. You must also recall how, by a whim whose secret you know as well as I do, I decided to visit that house in your place.[48] Here's what's going on now: Monsieur Rigot is ruined, and young Countess Lémée is brazenly abandoning in poverty both the old man who gave her her fortune and the mother who made sure she got it.

In the few days I spent at Monsieur Rigot's, if I didn't gain much respect for him, I did at least learn that Madame Peyrol was the most honorable and perhaps the unhappiest woman I'd ever met. Seeing that noble, distinguished woman in the midst of a family as coarse as hers, it occurred to me repeatedly that she was the child of an aristocratic family who'd been stolen from her mother. Now that groundless suspicion has become a reality, and I have reason to believe Madame Peyrol was the daughter of a certain Madame de Cauny.

I can't promise that's the real name of Madame Peyrol's mother; but you'll find out from her for yourself when you see her, because I want you to see her as soon as possible. She lives in a little house below the chateau in Taillis, a few leagues outside Caen. Please go see her in person, and give her, on my behalf, the money you'll draw with the letter of credit on my bank that I'm enclosing. You'll make clear to her that this isn't charity, it's a loan, and I'll expect reimbursement when she finds her family and the fortune to which I believe she has a right.

The hardest part of your interview with Madame Peyrol, my dear Gustave, will be to persuade her to accept this money; but there's one argument that will probably be more effective than any other. That argument is the hope you'll give

---

[48] See Chapter XXVIII.

her of finding her family and, as a result, of being able to repay me fully. I be-
lieve you'll be able to give her that hope more surely than I could; and, if I re-
call correctly, now that I'm thinking more clearly, the name Madame de Cauny
is connected in my memory with that of Madame de Marignon, whose story you
know as well as I do. So question her on that subject, question her with the care
and discretion her past calls for, though the name de Cauny doesn't strike me as
one whose recollection would make Madame de Marignon blush.

That's what I expect of you, my dear Gustave, as a friend from whom I
have the right to ask for a favor. In carrying it out you'll be repaying me for
everything in the past, and you'll be guaranteeing my deepest gratitude for the
future. I'm entrusting you with a mission of honor; "the name you bear" is my
infallible surety that you'll carry it out honorably.

—Armand de Luizzi

When the baron took something on, he knew how to take precautions just
as well as anyone else. Indeed, he'd lived an ordinary life for a long time before
the fantastical life into which the inheritance from his father had thrown him;
and—as long as he didn't consult the Devil—he was neither more wicked nor
more foolish than the next man; all in all, he was perhaps better and cleverer
than average. The letter he'd just written, and the care he'd taken to make sure it
accomplished what he wanted, are proofs we're all the more pleased to present
because, if that poor young man hadn't lacked for misfortunes, neither had he
been spared slander.

Rather than having those letters receive the tell-tale postmark they'd get if
he dropped them into the mail in Fontainebleau, he gave them to a stagecoach
driver to put them in the public mailbox in Paris; and once again the power of
money prevailed over the regulation that explicitly forbids stagecoach employees from accepting sealed letters. But Luizzi couldn't deploy the power of money so often without being reminded that the power would end when the money
did; when he'd bought the forgetfulness of all the tradesmen he'd summoned, he
realized the sum Henri had procured for him would still be enough for a fairly
long journey in ordinary circumstances—but if something unexpected forced
him to leave France sooner than he wanted to, he'd find himself in some difficulties. And of all the miseries that could discourage him, the most painful
would've been that of seeing Countess Cerny reduced once more to the material
miseries of poverty and the shameful little privations she'd gone through, because they were the ones he could most easily prevent.

However, not wanting to let anyone in Paris know where he was hiding, he
decided to write to Monsieur Barnet to ask him for all the money he'd need to
last him several months at least. The only difficulty was where to have the lawyer's reply to him delivered. With all the precautions he was taking, he didn't
want to risk being spotted in any large town; so he wrote to Barnet to gather all
the cash he could, to lock it in a well-sealed strongbox, to send that through the
mail with a declaration of its contents, and to send him the key by a different

route in a letter addressed to… And here the destination was still blank, because he hadn't yet decided on one.

That decision was the great question of the moment, and Luizzi consulted the countess. By his calculations Caroline should reach Orléans almost as soon as they did, and a day's wait should be enough to reunite them all. But Orléans, like Fontainebleau, was too close to Paris for them to be able to stay there long without danger. So he shared his plans with the countess, so that together they could decide on what direction they should go and where they should stop.

When he'd described to Countess Cerny all the measures he'd taken, she replied gently, "I in turn have to share with you, I won't say a decision I've made, but an idea that came to me. As you know, it's impossible for us to leave France together without your having arranged your affairs such that we don't need to return. Based on a few things I overheard at Madame de Marignon's, things said by a certain Gustave de Bridely, it seems we urgently have to go to Toulouse to make sure of your absolute right to a fortune that's been unjustly challenged."

"It appears there are no secrets in society," said Luizzi with a smile.

"You're the last one who should be surprised at that. In any case, I do know it. Well, my dear, the wisest and most prudent course would be for you to go directly to Toulouse. You'll make your arrangements for the future more effectively in person than by a correspondence that the slightest mischance could obstruct."

"You might be right, but would you dare go with me to a city that's home to all of the noblest names in France?"

"I wouldn't do anything so foolish. Though I know no one in Toulouse, having never been there, there are lots of people from Toulouse I know from having often seen them in Paris. But I can wait safely for you someplace where you'll come find me after you've settled all of the business necessary for our flight."

"No, Léonie, I'm not going to leave you all alone in some wretched village, exposed to pursuit by your husband, who, in spite of all our precautions, might still find out where you're hiding, especially if I'm away long enough to go to Toulouse and settle my affairs and come back to get you."

"If bad luck allowed the count to find me, believe me, your presence would be a greater misfortune than your absence. I don't want to predict the consequences of that encounter; they could be terrible. If he found me alone, on the other hand, it would mean I might've fled alone. And even if he used the authority he has by law to force me to go home with him, believe me, Armand," she added, holding out her hand to him, "I'd figure out a way to escape from him and come back to you wherever you tell me to meet you."

"I believe you. But, Léonie, you don't know what life would be like in a wretched village where you'd be alone, without support, with no one to turn to for help in case anything happened to you, even if it was just getting sick."

200

"That's why the refuge I've chosen has none of those drawbacks."

"So you've already chosen a place?"

"I think I spoke to you about an aunt of mine, Madame de Paradèze. Her estate is a few leagues from Boismandé, so the road we'd take to get there would also lead us in the direction we want to go. I plan to stay with her while you're away."

"How will you explain your reason for being there?"

"I'll tell her as much of the truth as I have to. I'm Madame de Paradèze's sole heiress, and she loves me like a mother, and I'm sure her affection for me will easily embrace the condition I'll impose: that of not telling my husband I've sought protection from her against his awful persecution."

"Are you quite sure of her discretion?"

"I'm as sure of her friendship as I am of your love, Armand. Hers is a soul that has suffered much, a heart that has shed many tears, an existence that has never had anything in the world besides my love, and who's mine as I am yours."

"But," he insisted once more, "will she be the only one who's in on the secret of your visit to her?"

"I wouldn't be able to hide my presence from Monsieur de Paradèze, her husband. But he's an old man, past eighty, crippled by age and infirmity, and who in any case wants whatever my aunt wants, because he owes her his fortune and even the name he bears."

They went on discussing the matter at length: he appalled at the idea of abandoning her even for a moment, she persevering in her generous decision and trying to make him understand that the best way to guarantee their future was to give it a solid foundation in the present. In the end the countess's plan was so sensible and could be carried out so quickly that Luizzi finally gave in and said, "You have every great quality, Léonie, even that of reason; and you have no quality to which I wouldn't want to be a slave."

"You call reason what's only love, my dear. Believe me, when you love your happiness you can find within yourself all the wisdom and the strength needed to protect it. Now think about when we can leave for Orléans. It's still a good idea for us to go by public stagecoach, because, for people who arrived on foot, hiring a post chaise would probably attract more attention than we want."

"You're right about everything."

He went out immediately and returned in a few minutes to inform her they'd only be able to leave Fontainebleau at five in the morning, and even then they were unlikely to find seats in the stagecoach. He also told her that, in case they couldn't, he'd found out about a carriage for hire—at a price that would shock no one and that wouldn't draw too much attention to people who wanted to remain unseen—which would take them to Orléans.

Chapter LXV: Love

Meanwhile the rest of that day had passed in preparations. After serving them a very late dinner, a maidservant from the inn had lit two candles and had gone out, saying, "Monsieur and madame will be woken at four o'clock tomorrow morning."

Luizzi and Countess Cerny remained alone. Nothing in this world should be spoken ill of unconditionally; nothing, not even the miseries of life that had seemed so hateful to Luizzi earlier that day. Everything has a purpose that redeems it from complete censure; and poverty itself—that misfortune so despised it seems no exaggeration to call it a vice—poverty itself retains, among its rags, its sufferings, and the tatters it drags behind it, some glimmers of joy, some moments of pleasure that become the sweetest recollections of life. The truest word that might ever have been uttered by lips that often spoke of love was that of the courtesan who achieved fame and fortune and who, with the sad lightheartedness of a great lady, cried, "Whatever became of the good old days when I was so miserable?"[49]

But the hour had come when, having thought of all the possible contingencies of their situation, the baron and the countess had nothing left to think of but themselves. She lay on her bed, looking at Luizzi, who was seated by her side with his head bowed as he pondered whether there was anything left to do. It pleased her to see how concerned he was for her, sitting next to her, without addressing her. Then he gently looked up at her, and her eyes boldly met his. They were both struck deeply by the same feeling: they both understood that at that moment the seriousness of their situation had vanished, that the fallen woman and her accomplice were gone, that nothing remained but two lovers in a small room at an inn, a room with only one bed. The countess lowered her eyes and blushed.

Luizzi, who could tell from her blush that she'd had the same thought he'd had, was grateful to her for it from the bottom of his heart. But the flush of modesty in this strong-willed woman, who'd given herself to him so bravely, inspired in him a childlike shyness he hadn't thought he was still capable of. As a result, he felt what any fearful lover feels who has no claim other than that of knowing he's loved, and who's afraid of offending his beloved by taking her

---

[49] Soulié gives a slight paraphrase of a saying ascribed to Sophie Arnould (1740-1802), an actress and opera diva well known for her succession of famous lovers, women as well as men. The saying is usually quoted as, "*Ah! c'était le bon temps, j'étais bien malheureuse!*" ("Ah, those were the good old days, I was so miserable!").

avowal as granting him a right. Though skilled at speaking of love when that love is only the expression of a heartfelt wish, he's reluctant to speak of it when it'll come across as the expression of a desire. Then he looks for ways to conceal his own embarrassment, because that embarrassment is itself already an admission of what he feels; and he suddenly begins to talk about something as far removed as possible from his thoughts, and from the thoughts of the woman he's addressing.

Luizzi probably wouldn't have felt that embarrassment so intensely, except that he understood nothing could be more hurtful to a woman like the countess, in the situation she was in, than the eager urgency with which he'd press her for a favor which, at least for her, had been up to that point only a sacrifice made to misery. That fear of hurting her was strong enough for him to look for something other than a reference to their being alone together to put an end to the awkwardness that kept them apart. So he said gently, with feeling, "Do you still feel ill, Léonie?"

She lifted her beautiful large eyes, which had grown so tender, and with a slight shake of her head she replied, "No, Armand, I feel better now. These hours of rest have allowed me to recover completely."

"That's good news, Léonie, because you'll need all your strength to face the destiny I've prepared for you."

"I'll be strong, Armand, I'm sure I will. I promise I'll be strong."

She stopped, and he lowered his head, feeling in his heart the unfamiliar stirring of a love he'd never suspected. The fact is, you don't desire a woman you love with a sacred love the way you desire a woman you love with a burning passion. The joys you dream of finding with the former aren't the same as the joys that are called the amorous pleasures. Those joys include hours of ecstasy in which life dissolves in delight from no other cause than two people whose eyes meet and mingle and lose themselves at length in each other. There are tranquil, serene intoxications that have no need of the fervent embraces of physical love, but that move from one soul to another through a hand lying in another hand that burns with the fire it receives in exchange for the fire it gives. But that joy is so rare, that happiness is so divine, that it can't be sought, it can only be found. You find it some evening as you sit together under some majestic oak, looking out at a vast landscape whose immensity creates solitude; you find it in some mysterious hidden corner of a theater, where all eyes are directed at the stage, leaving to those in love the freedom to look at each other.

So Luizzi was sad, since he had none of those joys and didn't dare ask for the other kind. His head was down, and his heart felt oppressed, almost sad. The countess was watching him, because he wasn't looking at her; and perhaps she understood him, as he'd understood her, because she in turn tried to help him by drawing him out of the painful embarrassment in which he found himself. So as not to pull him abruptly from his thoughts with a start, she said quietly, "And you, Armand? Do you feel all right?..."

He raised his head and looked at her. She lifted her arm slowly from the bed and reached out her hand to him. He took it passionately, and replied, his voice filled with happiness, "Thank you!... No, no, I feel fine..." Turning fully toward her to see her better, he added, "I'm content just like this..."

"Yes... That's right... And I'm content too, Armand... I no longer feel what's happened to me... I'm content..."

As she spoke her eyes closed: she seemed to be pressing to her heart the tender look he gave her. For a long time they remained gazing at each other like that, tasting in its fulness one of the joys we spoke of earlier, whose secret is known to few hearts. Then a time came when the weariness of the previous night and of that day, devoted to active concerns and lacking even a moment of rest, finally crept up on him. His head dropped slowly to his chest, though his eyes never left hers.

With a quick involuntary gesture she squeezed the hand she held and drew it to her. "You're suffering, Armand," she said in alarm so tender it went straight to his heart.

"No," he replied sadly, as if he were sorry she'd noticed his weariness. "No, I feel strong. How can I not be as strong as you?"

"You've had no rest, Armand, and you must need some. Remember," she added with timid emotion, "remember we're leaving tomorrow... and you need to rest too."

"Yes," he said, giving an almost melancholy look around, "I'll rest somewhere... over there..."

"Armand," she said, squeezing his hand and shedding a single happy tear. "Armand, you're good and you're honorable. I thank you."

"Léonie!"

"Yes, I thank you. You've tried to forget I belong to you... Yes, Armand, I understood... And you love me... You love me very much..."

"It's you, Léonie, you who are good and honorable, you who gave yourself to me."

"And I'll be yours forever, Armand," she said, reaching out to him. "Oh, yes!" she cried. "Yes, come here near me. I'm proud to be yours."

And soon they were in each other's arms, happy with a joy that can't be described, because it's a joy that can only belong to a few, whereas the language that speaks of love belongs to all of us and can only have the coarse meaning we give it.

When that night was over—when in the long conversations of those short hours all had been said of those joys that so dazzle a life that everything else seems drab by comparison, when the first barriers to a long-lasting intimacy had gently fallen—the morning arrived, and with it the cares of departure.

Two people of their age and temperament couldn't experience the transporting joys of very young lovers delighted by the personal attentions to which they devote themselves so happily; instead they took a quiet joy in paying each other those attentions and in knowing they were one another's completely. Luizzi was happy as he watched the proud, beautiful Countess Cerny, accustomed to being cared for by other hands, loosening and brushing her long hair before the small mirror in that room at the inn, and arranging it almost awkwardly around her face—still beautiful, though a little less perfectly groomed.

She too was happy when, as she glanced around in search of one of the thousand fripperies so necessary to a woman, she saw Luizzi unwrap some large parcel or open some vast pasteboard box and find what she was looking for, proving he'd forgotten nothing she wanted. That mutual joy was pure and without second thoughts in both their hearts, because it meant a day, an hour spent together; they had no need to tell each other bravely it would always be a joy. In a few days they'd resume the abundant luxury of their lives, and this time would become a memory free of regret, after having been a joy free of fear.

Ah, love! Love is a supreme force that weakens and bends the proudest spirits and makes them taste the joy within the smallest things. And that was so true for Countess Cerny and for Luizzi that, when the time came for the final preparations for their departure, she shared the tasks with him and insisted on doing them herself, with such sweet ease, with such a light heart—both of them forgetting they'd just gambled and lost their lives—that they found a moment of joyful happiness in their flight, the way a married couple might whom chance, some accident, had thrown into a difficult situation in which they lacked nothing but the material comforts of life.

Finally the hour came. Together the baron, giving orders for loading up the parcels he'd bought, and the countess, carrying in her hands the things she had to have with her, climbed aboard the stagecoach, into a compartment that was empty because he'd reserved all the seats.

A NEW STORY (That Will Be Found To Be Old)

Chapter LXVI: Recognition

As they rode along in the stagecoach they pressed close to one another, still under the spell of that night of love; for the heart is like an instrument that, having been played intensely by a strong hand, goes on resonating long after the bow that touched it has been lifted. Then, when full daylight arrived, the mysterious thoughts that had been flowing around them slowly faded like beloved ghosts vanishing in the sunlight. Little by little the reality of their situation came back to them with the reality of the natural world as it awoke gradually with the day.

That was when Luizzi said to Countess Cerny, "I've wanted whatever you wanted, Léonie. But are you quite sure of Madame de Paradèze's protection?"

"As sure as you can be of a kind, tolerant heart in this world."

"Sometimes that's a sign of weakness, Léonie."

"Of course, and I'm not holding up my aunt as a model of the kind of heroic courage that performs legendary feats of devotion. But if she has a weakness, it's only for kindness; because she's well able to resist any pressure that would push her toward a mean action."

"I believe you, but someone might persuade her that it would be good for you to return to your husband."

"That could only happen in one of two ways: either if someone who's close to her had an interest in persuading her of that, which isn't likely; or if that person, even if they existed, had an influence over my aunt that equaled my own."

"I don't doubt your influence over anyone," he said with a smile. "But forgive me for trying to foresee every future danger to my happiness, even if it's illusory... What makes you so confident of your influence over her?"

"Her affection for me, as well as her heart. Come, Armand," she added, smiling. "Aren't you reassured? Don't you think that's a good enough guarantee?"

"It's just that not everyone in the world loves you the way I do. I begin to think there are only two equally powerful kinds of love in the world: the one I have for you... and a mother's love for her child."

"Well then! Madame de Paradèze is like a mother to me... Or rather I'm like a daughter to her, because she had the misfortune to lose her own."

"Oh, did her daughter die?"

"I don't know, for I used the word 'lose' in its literal sense: that daughter was truly lost, or stolen from her mother."

"Oh!" said Luizzi in great astonishment, prompted by the coincidence between that story and Eugénie's story, which he'd heard the day before. "So Madame de Paradèze's daughter was kidnapped?"

But the baron hadn't even finished asking the question before he realized he was mistaken, since the names Paradèze and Cauny were so dissimilar that Little Pierre wouldn't have confused them. Besides, it was such an unlikely coincidence that he dismissed the idea and merely replied, "She's not the only mother who's suffered that sad fate. I recently heard of a similar case: a woman who just found out she wasn't the daughter of the coarse, brutal, low-born woman she'd always known as her mother, but was the child of a noble family from whom she'd been stolen."

"And did she find her real family?"

"I don't believe so."

"Alas! Perhaps it'll be a blessing for her never to find them. A poor girl, raised among the common people, learning their low, coarse manners, who's suddenly thrown into a world that's all new to her, a world that, having sympathized with her for a couple of days, comes to look at her with curiosity, then with contempt and ridicule, and doesn't spare her the cruellest, most humiliating mockery... I think that would be a sad destiny!"

"No doubt that would be true of a poor girl like the one you describe; but there are few women who could hold their own, in no matter how elevated a world, as well as Madame Peyrol."

"Madame Peyrol!" echoed the countess in surprise. "I feel like I've heard that name. Isn't she Countess Lémée's mother?"

"Exactly right. She's the niece, or rather the supposed niece, of that famous uncle, Rigot."

"That surprises me! Countess Lémée is awfully pushy for someone of good lineage."

"Her mother would make you feel differently about her; and certainly she more than anyone is living proof of the hereditary power of noble blood."

"But is she really of high rank and family?"

"I couldn't say. Have you ever heard of a certain Madame de Cauny?"

"Madame de Cauny!" cried the countess, stunned. "That's my aunt!"

"Another of your aunts..."

"The aunt whose house we're going to, Madame de Paradèze, formerly Madame de Cauny."

"That's odd," said Luizzi, who was even more stunned than she was. "And yet... Hold on while I try to remember... So her daughter disappeared a few days after she was born?"

"The very day."

"And she lost her in Paris?"

"In Paris."

"Around 1797?"

"In 1797 exactly."

"Then it's her!"

"Are you sure?" she asked, very moved.

"As sure as you can be about anything, based on the coincidence of the dates and the similarity of the circumstances."

"That would bring such great joy to my poor aunt!... Oh, Armand, you have to find out."

"I'll do it, I'll do it."

"Still, you'll have to be absolutely sure it's true before saying a word about it to my aunt. I don't know whether the poor woman will be strong enough to withstand the joy of finding her daughter—but I know she'd die if she gained that hope for a moment and then lost it again forever."

"Trust me, Léonie! I'll take every precaution; and if I can make it possible for you to return a daughter to her mother, you'll have amply repaid the hospitality you're going to ask her for."

"That's right, Armand, and I swear I'd be delighted to repay her that way. My poor aunt! She's been so unhappy, she's suffered so much, that heaven owes her that consolation in her old age."

"Tell me everything you know about the circumstances, so I can direct my investigation in the surest way."

"I'd be happy to. It's a fairly bizarre story, and I've got plenty of time to tell it to you; and you need to have heard every detail for the ending not to amaze you."

Luizzi drew closer to Countess Cerny to listen with all his heart to a story he'd already been told would be interesting, recounted by a voice whose every word was sweet to his ears.

May we be forgiven if curious readers, to whom we serve as the faithful secretary passing on the tale our unfortunate friend the baron heard, don't read it with the same delight he felt as he listened to it; for we aren't in a position as favorable as the countess was toward her audience for receiving the attention and indulgence of those who wish to learn the secret of poor Eugénie's birth. However, this was how Countess Cerny told it:

Chapter LXVII: The First Relay Stage

"I have to tell you first, my darling Armand, unless you already know it, for you know so many things, that my father, Viscount d'Assimbret, and his sister, Mademoiselle Valentine d'Assimbret, were left orphans in childhood. They were entrusted to the guardianship of Monsieur de Cauny, the father of my aunt's first husband, who died at the beginning of the Revolution. That Monsieur de Cauny was a widower; since his sister, who hadn't married, still lived in Bretagne, he found his female ward a burden and put her in a convent a few leagues outside Paris. As for the boy, Viscount d'Assimbret, my father, he was brought up with Monsieur de Cauny's son. They were educated together, entered service in the king's household together, and remained friends, though their personalities were very different. The glance you shot at Madame de Marignon when you first mentioned my father's name to me shows you know enough that I don't have to tell you what his youth was like."

"Yes, he was a dashing fellow."

"That's a polite term for a young man who's been more than wild. I thank you for choosing it."

Anyway, the fact is, while my father spent his life alternately in the most distinguished salons of the court and in the loosest boudoirs in town, young Monsieur de Cauny was unsparing in his pursuit of serious, weighty studies, and took part passionately in the debate and practice of the new ideas that were emerging on all sides. In truth, he and my father were perfect representatives of the two worlds of that era.

My father—carefree, superficial, bold, reckless, despising the bourgeoisie without knowing them and not even acknowledging their ability to think, mocking what he called the grievances of the peasants and treating the phrase "the people" like empty sounds devoid of meaning—was the perfect example of the society that idled away its time in the little salons of the Trianon and took the previous fourteen centuries of the monarchy as the guarantee of its future. Like so many others, he had no inkling—till they burst forth in fury—of the internal workings of the society that was remaking itself beneath the shreds of royal authority and the authority of the clergy and the nobles, and which suddenly cast them aside like worn-out rags as it stood forth in all of its power. When the first independent actions of the Constituent Assembly[50] showed him that a genuine

---

[50] The declaration of the Estates General in June 1789 that they now formed a National Constituent Assembly, with authority equal to the king's, was an important early step toward the Revolution.

national effort to change the structure of government was underway, he treated those first signs as impertinent jokes, and to him the rising of the people was a pitiful riot. He was present at the famous banquet of the Versailles palace guard, and was prominent there for his vehemence.[51]

Monsieur de Cauny, by contrast, was a friend of most of the men gaining renown and the attention of the nation at that time. With great enthusiasm he'd embraced the ideas of social reform—possibly, like so many people, without seeing that those reforms could only be carried out by starting with the destruction of the country's political framework. Or possibly he saw all of the likely consequences of his ideas; and his actions would seem to suggest that. While my father spent his nights at parties at La Muette[52] or at Lucienne's or at the Opéra, Monsieur de Cauny spent his nights at meetings planning the spread of ideas about liberty, helping to prepare the immense movement that would sweep away those who'd given birth to it.

While Viscount d'Assimbret sought the votes of the loveliest women, Monsieur de Cauny canvassed those of serious men; and he turned his back on the court forever the same day my father drew the admiration of the courtesans by the graciousness with which he picked up the queen's fan and gave it back to her, while delivering a quatrain that's always been attributed to the Count de Provence, later Louis XVIII, but which was certainly my father's. Only the context of the circumstances could've excused the boldness of those lines, not merely from my father's lips but from those of the highest-ranking prince, considering the quatrain was addressed to Marie Antoinette; but the standards for both poetry and etiquette are lower for improvised wit, and that example was considered delightful:

"Anticipating whatever desire you please
Amid the sweltering heat,
I bring you the zephyr breeze;
the lovers will follow en suite."

Well, as I was saying, the very day my father earned the envy of the court by a lucky turn of wit, Monsieur de Cauny was named to the meeting of the Estates General as a Deputy of the Third Estate for the seneschalty of Rennes.[53] And not long after, while my father was drawing attention at Versailles for the

---

[51] In October 1789 the officers of the palace guard held a lavish banquet whose reactionary anti-reformist toasts, along with the extravagance of the menu at a time of general scarcity, made it into a notorious act of royalist provocation.

[52] The Château de la Muette, on the edge of Paris, was a favorite residence of Louis XVI and Marie Antoinette.

[53] The 1789 meeting of the Estates General was mentioned above. The three constitutional Estates were the clergy, the nobility, and the commoners; Monsieur de Cauny is therefore standing as a commoner, a democrat. A seneschalty or stewardship was a medieval administrative unit.

fervor of his devotion to Louis XVI's interests, Monsieur de Cauny resigned from the position he held in the king's troops. His resignation was considered an act of treachery, and all the officers of the company to which he belonged vowed to punish him for it. As you know, Armand, the more you've loved a man, the more you hate and despise him when you think he's failed in his duty.

My father, driven by that feeling and outraged by Monsieur de Cauny's treason, volunteered to carry out the officers' retribution, and issued a challenge to the man who'd been his friend for so long. At first Monsieur de Cauny refused to fight: his philosophical principles made him consider dueling barbaric. His position in the National Constituent Assembly led him to believe political quarrels couldn't be settled by single combat. But the reasons he articulated, as well as a much stronger reason he didn't mention, couldn't withstand the provocation of Viscount d'Assimbret's insults. A rencounter took place, and my father was badly wounded. It caused a great scandal, and people took sides against my father, saying he'd given offense in ways he hadn't. The rumor went around that the court, unable to stand up to the Assembly as a body, wanted to do away with it one man at a time. The word "murder" was bandied about, for a proper duel with half a dozen witnesses.

As you can imagine, everyone who knew my father to be among the bravest and most upright officers in the royal guard was incensed by those accusations. The rumors even reached the royal family, which felt it necessary to express their support for my father; that was interpreted the way everything was in those days. People said Louis XVI had praised my father for his actions and had held him up as an example to all the king's officers; as a result, the name d'Assimbret gained a fame that later led to its being one of the first on the list of those to be banished.

I haven't told you the secret reason Monsieur de Cauny declined for so long to give my father the satisfaction he demanded, but you've probably guessed it. Monsieur de Cauny was in love—truly in love—with my father's sister, Valentine, though at that time she was barely fourteen. But apparently even at that age she was already mature in mind and in beauty.

"Ah!" said Luizzi with a bitter sigh, "I can see that, just like nowadays, convents were no defense against seduction."

"There was no seduction, I assure you, my dear Armand. Their mutual passion took root and grew as they grew up..."

Every time the elder Monsieur de Cauny sent the young viscount to visit his sister, he—bored to death by a journey of several hours that ended in a convent parlor—made his friend come along. Eventually my father, finding that those visits interrupted his life of pleasure, asked his friend—who, he claimed, had lots of time to spare for boredom—to go visit the girl alone and bring back news from the convent that he could pass on to his guardian as if he'd been there himself.

Monsieur de Cauny, though he was young, first loved Valentine as a charming child who had no protector besides himself; for the elder Monsieur de Cauny, constantly sickly and an invalid, almost never left home. Then, when she grew up and became beautiful, he loved her as a woman. They were used to seeing Monsieur de Cauny at the convent, where in fact for a long time he presented himself as coming on behalf of his father, Valentine's guardian. No one suspected his visits no longer had so respectable a motive; and when the quarrel broke out between Viscount d'Assimbret and Monsieur de Cauny, since no one told the Mother Superior there'd been a breach between the two families, Monsieur de Cauny went on seeing Valentine right up to that regrettable duel.

Chapter LXVIII: The Second Relay Stage

At that point in Countess Cerny's story they reached a relay stop, and the stagecoach pulled up. The countess paused, because it would've been hard for her to talk over the shouting of orders and the swearing of the postilions harnessing the horses. Meantime Luizzi had a look at the travelers in the other compartments, both inside and on the roof of the stagecoach, most of whom had gotten out. He was happy to observe that he recognized no one, either from a distance or up close—for he was beginning to doubt his memory for faces, and hardly ever recognized people at first glance.

As he was finishing his inspection, with his head still out the window, he heard Countess Cerny calling to him with a laugh, "Armand, I have to beg you for alms."

Turning around, he saw at the opposite window a weak, sickly, pale girl of about fourteen who spoke in a plaintive whine. He took a hundred-sou coin from his pocket and handed it to the beggar, who looked at it for a moment with joyful astonishment, then resumed her sad manner.

"That's a lot," she said. "Thank you, ma'am." She stopped; but as she turned to go away she added in a low voice, as if talking to herself, "It's a lot, and yet it's not enough!"

"What's that you say?" asked the countess quickly, calling her back, for she'd been struck by the girl's charming face. "Why isn't that enough, child?"

"Oh, I'm not asking for more, ma'am. It's more than I've ever gotten since my elderly father and I have been living on public charity. But we have to get to Orléans as fast as we can; and I was saying to myself it wasn't quite enough to pay for my seat and my father's up there on the roof."

"Armand..." said the countess, giving Luizzi a pleading look.

He called over the driver and said, "Let that child and her father ride up in the roof section; I'll pay whatever it costs."

"Thank you, ma'am! Thank you!" cried the delighted beggar, still addressing the countess, as if she understood instinctively that the generosity she'd received came from her rather than from the man who was carrying it out. "Thank you!... Here's your money back, since you're paying for our seats."

"Keep it, child," said the countess. "And when we get to Orléans, come see me before you leave town."

"Yes, ma'am!" said the girl, curtseying and running to an old man who was sitting on a stone by the inn door. The way he listened to the girl, without lifting his head, showed he was blind, and all he knew of his surroundings came to him through his ears.

213

Turning to Luizzi, Countess Cerny said with a smile, "You see, Armand! I'm already spending your fortune."

"It's frightening!" he replied in the same tone, and they exchanged one of those smiles and glances that convey more love than the sweetest words.

Then the stagecoach set off once more, and the countess said, "Now it's time for me to pick up my story again." She continued as follows:

As I said, Monsieur de Cauny had gone on seeing Valentine right up till his duel with my father. At that point delicacy of feeling imposed a sacrifice he hadn't thought necessary on account of mere differences of opinion, but that couldn't be refused on account of the blood he'd shed so unwillingly. He stopped visiting the convent and—resolved to see Mademoiselle d'Assimbret no more—he wrote to her for the first time and explained the reason for their separation. After having lamented the outcome of that rencounter, he ended his letter by promising Valentine he'd never forget the love he'd confessed to her, and saying that, if a happier day came when he could recover the brother's friendship, he hoped he could recover the sister's love as well. But he added that to him that hope seemed remote, that he expected the march of events would lead to terrible misfortunes, and that he wasn't afraid to admit to her he was anxious enough about the future of France to regret the part he'd played in the revolutionary movement.

If I'm right, he added, *and if ever you and your brother need a protector—I no longer dare say a friend—don't forget I'm yours now, as I was before, tomorrow as I am today; and I won't draw back from the path I've chosen, since I can perceive the distant chance of being able to protect those I love."*

"The story I'm telling you," observed Countess Cerny, "contains every ingredient of a novel. I'm even including love letters and quoting them word for word. The thing is, that letter of Monsieur de Cauny's led to terrible consequences for him, and the sentence I quoted was the very one cited at his trial."

"So Monsieur de Cauny perished in the Revolution?"

"He and so many others who wanted to muzzle the lion after unleashing it. But that's not what's important for you to know. I'm getting to the circumstances that led to the loss of my aunt's baby daughter, my cousin."

"No, no, tell me everything, because in uncovering the truth sometimes the most trivial details are more illuminating than the weightiest events."

"Then here's the next part of the story…"

Having recovered from his wounds, my father remained in France till the Tenth of August,[54] always hoping order would be restored, unable to believe a

---

[54] On August 10, 1792, armed insurrectionists stormed the Tuileries Palace, killing hundreds of the king's Swiss Guards; the abolition of the monarchy soon

revolution could topple the throne, and especially not conceiving that subjects could ever go so far as to try their king and sentence him to death and execute him. When Louis XVI was taken prisoner, the viscount, who'd been among the bravest of those who'd defended the Tuileries, had to go into hiding; and soon he left to join the princes in exile. Presumably as he fled he remembered he was leaving his sister behind in France without a protector, for by then the elder Monsieur de Cauny was dead. But, for one thing, the danger he himself was in made it impossible to bring along Valentine and make her share the same dangers; for another thing, he believed, as so many did, the exile would last no more than a few months, and soon he'd be back in Paris, and one military campaign would be enough to make the entire rebellious population see reason. Like so many others, he was wrong.

That was the period in which all the monasteries and religious orders were broken up and scattered; and a day came when municipal officers, backed by a platoon of soldiers, forced their way into the convent where my aunt still lived, and on the spot, without giving the poor nuns time to make any preparations, drove them out, leaving them on the street without money or resources or even a guide. Each of them had enough to do to take care of herself without worrying about the others; but most of them at least knew where they could go, since all those whose families had fled France had long since departed from the convent. That left only Valentine truly abandoned on the street, knowing neither what to do nor what would become of her.

"Yesterday, Armand, you pitied me—a grown woman in the prime of life, riding in a carriage with a man sworn to protect her—you pitied me because I was suffering a little from cold and fever. Now imagine what must've been the sufferings of a poor girl of fifteen suddenly thrown out onto the street, dressed in a nun's habit that drew the coarsest insults from passersby, and even abuse by children in the villages she passed through! For those children pelted her white robe with mud as they chased after her and shouted terrible insults. My poor aunt went two days without eating and spent two nights in the ditch along the road. That's a form of suffering it's taken for granted people of our kind have never had to endure; and certainly if you met Madame de Paradèze now in her magnificent chateau you'd consider it a tall tale if you heard that a woman of her title and rank could ever have been more miserable than that beggar girl to whom we just gave charity."

"That surprises me less than you might think," said Luizzi. "I myself have been spared a night outdoors thanks to a peasant's hospitality; and only a chance encounter saved me from being arrested as a beggar and a vagrant. But please go on."

---

followed. "The Tenth of August" became shorthand for what historians consider "the Second Revolution."

The countess continued:

That misery lasted a long time, almost two weeks, till Valentine managed to reach Paris. The only thing she'd kept from her past life was Monsieur de Cauny's letter. A woman never loses and never throws away her first love letter. She'd kept it without any hope for their love; and when she was driven out of the only shelter she knew, she dismissed the idea of going to ask for protection from the very Monsieur de Cauny who'd shed her brother's blood. But misery is powerful; and after having wandered the streets of Paris for two whole days, living off the alms hunger had taught her to beg for, she decided to appeal to the man she loved.

She went to his address and didn't find him there; for he, having learned of the brutal dispersal of her convent, had set off immediately to offer her his protection, and he was looking for her in all directions, following the trail of all the nuns along all the roads they'd been seen on, one going this way, another that way. He caught up with several of them, but not with Valentine; and he returned to Paris in despair—only to be told that a girl, a nun, had come and asked for him; and when she heard he wasn't there she'd gone away after saying her name was Mademoiselle d'Assimbret. He was angry that she hadn't been received in spite of his absence, and he took it out on the doorman whose callous insolence he assumed had led the man to drive her away.

That small incident, which would've been of no significance between Monsieur de Cauny and one of his servants, became a very serious matter between Citizen Cauny and Citizen Follard. The next day Valentine came back to the house again just as the fired doorman was about to leave it; and Follard shook his fist at her and cried, "Those going out will get their revenge on those coming in!" That wretch belonged to a committee whose chairman had once been music teacher to Monsieur de Cauny, who'd always treated him well, and to whom he even owed his present position. Out of gratitude, that man came to warn him he'd been reported by his doorman for giving shelter to nuns, and that in spite of all of his efforts the committee had decided to summon Citizen Cauny to account for his aristocratic compassion.

Monsieur de Cauny, who already knew where a denunciation like that could lead, thought the best way to reply was to inform the committee that he, Citizen Cauny, couldn't have committed a crime against the public safety by receiving Citizeness Cauny, his wife. So he completed the marriage formalities— very expeditious in those days—and married my aunt, Mademoiselle d'Assimbret. Her own need for safety might've driven Valentine's decision more than love would have. The days she'd spent in misery, with no one to turn to for help, had made a vivid impression on the mind of a girl who was still practically a child. She often spoke of the misfortune of being left alone and friendless in the world. Her fear of that kind of abandonment has lasted her

216

whole life, and no doubt contributed to her choosing a course I've always considered unfortunate, and that my father still calls despicable.

"Despicable!" cried Luizzi, interrupting Countess Cerny.

"Let me finish the story, and then you'll understand how I could be right according to my way of thinking, and how my father could speak that way according to his. For several years their marriage brought nothing but happiness to Monsieur de Cauny and my aunt. But eventually it resulted in persecution for both of them, which they certainly hadn't anticipated. A chance visit brought the old music teacher I mentioned earlier to call on Monsieur de Cauny, and he met his wife. The way he looked at her led her to ask why he was examining her like that, and Monsieur Bricoin replied…"

"Bricoin!" cried Luizzi, interrupting the countess once again.

"You know him too?"

"No. But unless I'm mistaken, that's the name of the man who had the good luck to be Madame de Marignon's first lover."[55]

Since you know that, no doubt you already know he was the man my father drove out of that woman's house by beating him with a walking stick. That man hadn't forgotten him; and he answered my aunt's question by telling her he was only staring at her because he was struck by her strange resemblance to a certain Viscount d'Assimbret he'd known. When my aunt explained the resemblance by telling him she was the viscount's sister, she had no way of knowing how that left her exposed, and she couldn't have guessed at the plans for terrible vengeance concealed in the man's peculiar parting words: "Farewell, ma'am. We'll see each other again! We'll see each other again!"

As you can imagine, Madame de Cauny quickly forgot the trivial incident I've just described, and it didn't occur to her to connect it to the persecution that struck a few weeks later, when her husband was arrested on one of the thousand pretexts that could so easily get a man imprisoned and killed in those times. Since he'd written to my father, he was accused of corresponding with the exiles; as a result, they searched his papers. The letter I mentioned, in which he predicted the excesses of the Revolution, became the basis for a charge of treason. Meanwhile my aunt found herself once again alone with her weakness and her fears.

Even a woman who knew more of the past, or who knew more about the perfidious deeds the wicked passions can lead to, would've been fooled by the way in which Monsieur Bricoin came to offer her his assistance when, as he claimed, he heard Citizen Cauny had been incarcerated. The tale of how that man, through the hope he constantly offered the unfortunate Valentine, wormed

---

[55] Bricoin was last seen briefly in Chapter XXVII, where the music teacher was the abusive, tyrannical lover of Olivia Béru, later Madame de Marignon.

his way into her confidence and learned all her secrets, is the tale of a poor abandoned woman, alone in the world, for whom that isolation was her greatest fear. Presumably Bricoin learned everything he wanted to find out; for it was based on his advice that Monsieur de Cauny, anticipating his fate, drew up a will giving his wife full possession of his entire estate if he died childless, and guaranteeing her half if he didn't. That clause was appended to the will, because at the time Madame de Cauny was pregnant.

Meanwhile the Reign of Terror, which had bowed down France for eighteen months, had begun to weary of its bloody work; and a few months after making that will Monsieur de Cauny had begun to hope, with some cause, he'd be set free in time to see the birth of the child his wife was carrying in her womb. But on the very day Madame de Cauny delivered he was taken from his prison and perished on the scaffold.

It isn't hard to see how a woman like my aunt could easily be upset by imaginary fears under any circumstances; it's even less surprising that such a terrible occurrence as that could've driven her to fear the impossible. Bricoin persuaded her that the fury of the executioners would stretch as far as the newborn child; thanks to the despair of a woman who was ill, weak, alone, ready to die of sorrow and sickness, he managed to persuade her to let her infant go, saying he knew a way of entrusting the child to safe hands...

Chapter LXIX: The Third Relay Stage

The stagecoach stopped again, and Countess Cerny paused her story once more. Just then the little beggar girl came up to the carriage door, showed her pretty face in the window, and said in a charming way, "My father's here, ma'am, and he wants to thank you personally for what you'd done for us."

An old man came forward; he was blind, just as the countess had assumed, but his austere features, beneath the long white hair that hung over his face, retained a look of pride and determination. "You've done a good deed, ma'am," he said, "and God would be unjust not to reward you for it. You didn't just give this child alms, you might've given her a family by making it possible for her to reach the town where she can find information about the parents who abandoned her."

Without replying to the old beggar, the countess turned quickly to the baron, saying, "This is so strange, Armand! Another lost, abandoned girl! How many of the poor things can there be who've been thrown out into the world, for there to be two, in a manner of speaking, just in this small stagecoach?"

"Strange indeed," said Luizzi, sounding more concerned than surprised. "Strange indeed," he repeated to himself, wondering whether it was his slave whose infernal power was placing all of these extraordinary encounters in his way and thereby alerting him to his presence, as he'd threatened to do.

Meanwhile the countess had responded to the old beggar with great interest and with the courtesy of a woman who has respect for misfortune. "I've asked the girl not to leave Orléans without coming to see me again, sir; now I'll ask you to come with her, because if I can be of use to you, I'd do it with great pleasure."

"For whom should I ask?" said the old blind man.

"Ask for... ask for..."

"Be careful!" said Luizzi, quickly stopping her. "Don't forget, saying your name out loud could be risky..."

"You're right." Turning to the blind man, she replied, "There'll be no need: I'll have you put up at the place we'll be staying."

The stagecoach was ready to set off again. The passengers all returned to their seats, but this time Countess Cerny didn't pick up her interrupted story right away. Her conversation with Luizzi focused on what had just happened, and they both promised—each of them for private reasons—to pursue that new mystery to its resolution.

That prompted him to say to her, "Let's not forget, we've got more than one mission of that type to carry out. Please tell me what became of the unfortunate Madame de Cauny in the clutches of that villain Bricoin."

"Alas! She married him."

"What!" he cried. "So Monsieur de Paradèze…"

"Is none other than Bricoin, who, when that marriage had made him rich, concealed his low birth under a name borrowed from the landed gentry. But—so you don't condemn my aunt for having acted carelessly and thoughtlessly, and lose respect for her—I have to explain the underhanded trick Monsieur Bricoin used to achieve what he'd been hoping for from the first moment he met Madame de Cauny."

Though her fears for her safety and that of her child, which he knew how to play on, had delivered her helpless into that man's hands, her lack of attraction for his coarse appearance, in addition to his advanced age—for Monsieur Bricoin was already over forty at that time—defended her against all of the thinly veiled proposals he heaped on her.

At that point she experienced a misfortune, which I can confide in you, Armand, and which perhaps can excuse her error in marrying Monsieur Bricoin—though that misfortune itself could be considered an error on her part. Valentine, who was young, pretty, charming, and alone, met—among the men drawn to her by her name—an eminent man, uncommonly skilled at convincing a woman of feelings he didn't have, and ruthlessly cynical in his pride at having played on those feelings, who dedicated all of his infernal powers of seduction to adding Madame de Cauny to the list of his victims. That man, whose name my aunt has never been willing to tell me…

"That man," interrupted Luizzi, "was named Monsieur de Mère."

"You know him?" asked the countess, astonished once again.

"Don't you realize I know everything about Madame de Marignon's past?"[56]

"So Monsieur de Mère had some connection to Madame de Marignon?"

"He was her last lover, as Bricoin had been her first."

That revelation made Countess Cerny pensive; she too began to wonder at how those different destinies acted on one another without ever seeming to intersect. She replied, "So it was Madame de Marignon's last lover who delivered Valentine into the hands of her first!" She paused, then went on, "I assume you know the cowardly, insulting rejection with which that Monsieur de Mère repaid the love of a woman who'd honorably trusted him, and toward whom his behavior was all the more villainous since she had no one in the world to defend her."

"Still," said Luizzi, "she got revenge, to the extent a woman can, by dragging him brazenly through the mud of his own infamy, before a large company,

---

[56] See Chapter XXIX, not only for Madame de Marignon's platonic affair with Monsieur de Mère, but for Madame de Cauny's bitter denunciation of de Mère as a deceitful lover.

and in the presence of Madame de Marignon, who at that earlier time was only beautiful Olivia Béru."

"Yes, replied the countess, "thanks to the connection beautiful Olivia—since that's what you call her—had kept up with the viscount, whom she'd located in England, she felt justified in bringing Madame de Cauny into her circle, in spite of the shameful position she was living in then."

Luizzi couldn't help noticing the expression the countess had used, "shameful position"; and he admired the powerful influence of worldly proprieties on even the strongest and fairest minds—since she now considered it perfectly respectable to go visit a woman whose life of thirty years earlier she characterized with such contempt.

Meanwhile Countess Cerny continued:

What I didn't know, because she never told me, was that my aunt had found Monsieur de Mère again, and she'd delivered the outburst you describe. In any case, heartbroken by the terrible experience she'd just had of the perfidy of some men, she gave up hoping for love and felt the agony of her isolation more than ever. Circumstances now favored Bricoin: always assiduous toward the young widow, sparing her the headaches of dealing with practical matters, protecting her from the rapacity of schemers and the general perfidy of the world, he seemed to be the only protector she could ever expect to find. Besides, he spoke constantly of marriage; and that sacred bond, whose holiness Madame de Cauny had valued during the two years she'd spent with her husband, was the only one that could secure the presence in her life of a man who'd make her life his life, her happiness his happiness.

Another reason, which I've waited to tell you about because I can't see it the way my father sees it, also must've helped poor Valentine to her decision. She hadn't seen her daughter since the day she was born. Bricoin, whether he was lying or telling the truth, always told her the people to whom he'd entrusted the baby had left Paris but were about to come back. My father might be right: that man might've given a mother the hope of being reunited with her child as the price of the sacrifice he was asking for; Bricoin might even have promised Madame de Cauny to give her back her daughter the day she agreed to marry him. Whatever the reasons were, the wedding took place, and a few days later Monsieur de Paradèze—for he adopted that name when he married my aunt—announced to his new wife that he was almost positive her daughter had died.

"Do you think him of capable of such a crime?" asked Luizzi.

"What you've told me about Madame Peyrol," replied Countess Cerny, "proves—assuming she is that poor lost child—that Bricoin didn't take his villainy that far. In any case, he never produced legal proof of the child's death; and for more than thirty years my aunt has lived with the awful uncertainty of not knowing whether she does or doesn't have a daughter. All of my father's investigations have come to nothing; for I have to tell you it was my father who, out of hatred for Monsieur de Paradèze, worked the hardest to find Monsieur de Cauny's child and heir. 'He made the child disappear to get the whole inheritance for himself,' my father said. 'I'll make her reappear again, to drive that villain back into the poverty he should never have escaped.' That was the way my father always talked about his sister's husband."

"But aren't you afraid that, considering the hatred there is between those two men, it's risky for you to go stay with Monsieur de Paradèze?"

"As I told you, Monsieur de Paradèze is now an infirm old man crippled by illness, who no longer has the strength to carry out any intention, since he barely remembers what he once was."

As the countess spoke, they reached Orléans.

ANOTHER NEW STORY (That's Old)

Chapter LXX: The Last of the Old Guard

In accordance with what he'd written to Caroline, Luizzi checked into the post coach hotel without giving his name. They didn't press him for it, especially in light of his generosity to the first servant who took charge of his luggage. In spite of what the police claim, money is a passport every bit as good as the one marked *Travel Permit*, which the friendly worthy officer hands over so politely.

Once Countess Cerny and Luizzi had settled into their rooms and been served a meal, it occurred to them to send for the old blind man and the beggar girl who, on their instructions, had followed them to their hotel. They sent them word to come upstairs to their rooms, and urged them to tell their story.

This was what the old man told them:

"You see before you a man who's past his eightieth year. I was born in 1752, and in 1770 I joined the French Guards.[57] Don't be surprised by what I tell you; at the age of eighty, and in the state I've sunk to, I've earned the right to say anything. So, I was eighteen and I was one of the handsomest men in the company; I have to admit I hadn't noticed it, till a beautiful woman of those times let me know through her chambermaid. Apparently that beautiful woman had a husband who didn't satisfy her; he was named Béru, and he played the violin wonderfully, but that's all."

At the name Béru, Countess Cerny and Luizzi looked at each in such astonishment—for the countess knew about Olivia de Marignon's past—that neither of them really took note of the old soldier's odd way of speaking as he continued:

"It seems Madame Béru was bored of her husband, and he didn't care for her much either; and one time when she came to see us on parade, where I was turned out magnificently, I thought I noticed her picking me out from the whole line. I didn't say anything, but I thought to myself she could be a mistress who'd suit me fine: well dressed, prosperous-looking—she must keep an excellent cook. I looked her in the eye, and it didn't annoy her; and I heard her ask one of the officers, 'Who's that handsome man, the third one in the front row?' The of-

---

[57] The French Guards, an elite infantry regiment, were part of the royal Household Troops.

ficer must've told her my name and address at the barracks of the French Guards, because that night I received a little love note, which I had the corporal read to me, inviting me to call on the beautiful lady, with the pretext of her asking me for news from home, since I'm from around Orléans and so was she. I accepted the invitation. I'll say no more, out of respect for the lady here, and for the child who's listening, but nine months later to the day Madame Béru delivered a pretty little girl they named Olivia. I've got a good memory for names, and with reason," added the old soldier in a tone full of meaning.

Countess Cerny and Luizzi exchanged another glance, both of them increasingly confounded by the strange accumulation of all these circumstances; and the baron was growing truly alarmed as he recalled the Devil's threats.

The soldier went on:

Now, I have to tell you that—besides the nice little presents my sweetheart gave me, which allowed me to dress in fabric good enough for an officer and white linen I changed twice a week—she'd also promised me her patronage; but that patronage was so long in coming that in 1789 I was still just a soldier in the French Guards. Meanwhile my girl had made her fortune; but since she wasn't my girl before the law, I couldn't make any claim on her; and by 1793, when she'd gone to England, I was a soldier of the Republic. Since then I can't say I've had news of her; you might think I went to Italy to get some, but Italy's not exactly on the way to London.[58] When I got back to Paris I heard she'd been seen around. I was still a soldier of the Republic; but I was so well supplied with money—my word!—that I didn't think too much about going to look for my girl. The money came to me from an odd business I have to tell you about.

One night, as I was passing by a mansion on the rue de Varennes, I was jostled by a man who had a package under his arm that was crying. It was a dark night. I looked at the man, who seemed frightened.

"Where are you going in such a hurry," I said, stopping him, "that you've stepped on the toes of a grenadier from the Italian war as if he were nothing more than a cobblestone?"

"I'm going somewhere you could go for me, if you'd like to earn a good reward."

"Could be," says I.

"In that case," says he, "take these twenty-five louis and this child, and deliver them to the foundling home."

I took the twenty-five louis and I looked at the mansion the man had come out of. It was a handsome building, with a tall carriage entrance with two fine columns: a real faubourg Saint Germain mansion. Since I'd grown up under the Old Regime, I said to myself, "All right, clear enough! A great lady who's

---

[58] The soldier is referring to Napoleon's campaigns in Italy in 1796-97.

cheated on her husband while he's away, or a young lady about to get married, that's all!"

I took the child from the hands of the doctor—because he must've been the doctor: doctors have never been good for anything else—and I carried it away as nicely and gently as I could. They'd fastened a piece of paper around the baby's neck that I was discreet enough not to read, considering I don't know how to read, which doesn't matter at all now that I'm blind. And by the light of the street lamps I was having fun looking at the fine cloth swaddling they'd wrapped around the child—when I in turn bumped into a man who was as surprised as I was at seeing me in dress uniform with an infant under my arm. The fact is, it didn't look natural, and I had no cause to get angry when the man confronted me, saying, "Hey, soldier, where the devil did you find that child?"

"By God!" I said, picking up on his idea, "I found it over there, by the rue du Gros Caillou, howling like a poor thing."

"What do you plan to do with it?"

"I'm going to take it where it belongs, to the foundling home."

So then he stopped and thought for a long time. Then he said, "Will you give me the baby?"

"Hold on, friend," says I, "you don't just hand over a poor little creature to the first fellow who comes along like that without finding out what he's going to do with it."

"I'm going to raise it," says the man, "and feed it. I have no children; it'll become mine. Anyway, I need it."

"You need a child!" says I. "Maybe when you're old, but you look to me like a young whippersnapper." Indeed, I could see by the light of the street lamps how young he was.

"Though you're a soldier, I guess I can tell you. My wife, who wasn't my wife at the time, meaning to save me from the draft, declared I'd made her pregnant; so I was forced to marry her. But she wasn't pregnant, and she didn't get pregnant. The due date's coming up, our trick's going to be found out, my wife's false declaration is going to make her, as well as me, liable to serious punishment."

"That isn't exactly a tale of bravery," says I, "but anyway, what's done is done. Besides, you can't make good soldiers out of good husbands. Take the child, and give me your address so I can go thank you on its behalf."

I had an idea of my own when I asked him for that. Two days later I went in search of information, and I found out Jérôme Turniquel was an upstanding fellow, worthy in every way of the trust I'd put in him.[59]

Sometime later, when all I had left of my twenty-five louis was the debts it had allowed me to incur on credit, I thought again about finding my girl; but I

---

[59] See Chapter XXXV for this story told from Jérôme Turniquel's and Jeanne Rigot's point of view.

had to leave Paris right away to take care of some business for France, seeing as how I was still a soldier of the Republic. I went to Egypt,[60] where all I got was the plague, which I got over, because I was a good-looking fellow and an oda-lisque from the seraglio nursed me out of love. I was away in foreign parts for several years.

I came back around 1803, hoping to find my family; but apparently my girl had turned into a great lady, and I couldn't get any news of her. By then I was a soldier in the Consular Guards.[61] I spent my time in the various capitals of Europe, right up to the campaign of 1814;[62] by then I was a soldier in the Imperial Guards. The emperor's fall robbed me of any hope of promotion; but I still didn't quit the military life, and I was still a handsome man, still well turned out, when in 1830 a gunshot—which went and killed an old Chinaman who didn't say boo—passed so close to my eyes it left me blind.[63] By that point I was a soldier in the Royal Guards.

The old soldier stopped. Striking a pose that showed more pride than seemed justified by his story, he added, "Believe me, everything I've just told you wasn't for the sake of talking about myself; it was just to tell you that after sixty years of active service I was refused admission to the Invalides,[64] with the excuse that my wound wasn't a wound and that anyway I'd gotten it while firing on civilians; all of which is to say I was dismissed with a miserable pension of a hundred and twenty-five francs, out of which they told me to put food on the table every day; all of which is to tell you how an old soldier, which it was my honor to be, has been reduced to begging. That's my whole story.

"Now the little one will tell you hers, which I don't understand a word of, maybe because I can't see anymore, but which you can believe, because, since the day she found me on the road half dead of hunger and gave me half of her bread, I've known she was an honest girl. She's always told me exactly what people give her, and I've always divided it exactly with her. Isn't that right, my girl?... Because, you know, between us it's a matter of honor! She's the one who asks, I'm the one they give to. Old age always provokes sympathy; and

---

[60] The reference is to Napoleon's campaign in Egypt and Syria from 1798 to 1801.

[61] The Consular Guard was created in 1799 to defend the Republic, but it didn't oppose Napoleon's coup of that same year, and it became the emperor's personal elite corps under his direct command. In 1804 it was renamed the Imperial Guard.

[62] The 1814 defensive campaign in northeastern France led to Napoleon's defeat and overthrow and exile to Elba.

[63] In the 1830s France was involved in the Opium Wars in China.

[64] Les Invalides was the national institution for the care and housing of disabled veterans.

though I shouldn't say so, I'd like to see myself: I must make a handsome blind man."

Chapter LXXI: A Good Resolution

If during that account we didn't sufficiently describe the baron's and the countess's exclamations of surprise, if we didn't explain that the story made such a strong impression on them that they didn't notice the speaker's quaint turns of phrase, it's because we've assumed the reader could imagine those exclamations and that impression, and also because we'll see the results below.

No sooner had the old soldier finished speaking than Countess Cerny, who'd been the most eager to hear the beggar girl's story, stopped her just as she was about to begin and said to her gently, "I thought I was stronger than I am. The journey was so tiring that my eyes are closing against my will; let's put off till tomorrow the story of your misfortunes; I'll be better able to listen to them."

Luizzi understood her intentions, and he had the old man and the girl taken back to the room that had been prepared for them. The countess's expression betrayed a preoccupation that wavered between vague fears and equally vague hopes; while the baron's face seemed frozen in a look of uncontrollable terror.

Finally she chose between the warring emotions she felt, and with bold excitement she said, "It's the voice of God speaking in all of this. It's his wise care that has put all these extraordinary things in our path, as if to give us the opportunity to do a good deed that someday, when we stand before his justice, can counterbalance the sin we're committing."

Luizzi didn't answer aloud, but he thought to himself, "It's more like the voice of hell giving me these warnings. It's the power of Satan opening before me all these tangled paths on which I'm supposed to get lost."

"Don't you agree?" she asked, surprised by his somber thoughtfulness, since for the first time he'd been deaf to something she'd said. "Do you think, on the contrary, it's a threat of some kind? Because it's all too extraordinary for there not to be a lesson hidden within these events."

"I don't know," he said in a tone of deep discouragement. "Everything that arises out of me frightens me; my life is a mystery that appalls me; and, I'll admit, right now I have faith only in the protection God must grant you—you who are so saintly and so pure before him, you whom he must've set beside me to keep me from getting lost entirely on the path down which I'll perish."

"Armand! Armand!" she cried. "Why this weakness, this terror? Nothing that could alarm us about our own destinies is implied by these strange encounters!"

"The thing is, for me they might have a hidden meaning they don't have for you."

As he spoke, his expression was filled with the somber resignation to some invincible fate that comes over a man whose plans for doing good have all led him to do evil.

The countess was deeply astonished, and she too said in discouragement, "You might be right. God places the punishment next to the sin."

"What do you mean?"

"That, barely on the threshold of the fallen life to which we've condemned each other, you might already be regretting it…"

"Léonie!" he cried. "Do you know what you're saying to me? Am I such a wretch that you could even think it?" He came closer to her and went on, "Oh, if that's how it is, then you're right: the punishment lies next to the sin, because I've already earned your contempt by my weakness."

"No, no, Armand," she said, drawing closer to him in turn, and raising her hands to lift his long hair away from his worried face, as if she meant her hands to drive away the thoughts that darkened his brow. "No, I haven't thought that about you, my own Armand. I was afraid, that's all! But it wasn't of you, I swear! Not of you, whom I trust. Not of you, who I know has lived a life marked by strange misfortunes, and who, I believe, needed to be loved to be happy. And I—I love you so much I'll turn away the fate that's made you suffer so much."

"Yes, yes," he replied, pressing her to his heart. "You're the angel of my life, you're the hand God's holding out to me to save me in the storm, you're the light by which he'll guide me through the night. Speak! What you tell me to do, I'll do. What you want, I'll want."

"Well then, believe me, Armand, let's accept as a sign of God's protection everything that has astonished me and terrified you. Let's finish by our own efforts the work he seems to have placed in our hands. Let's reunite a mother and a daughter. God, who counts good deeds among the virtues, will accept that one as the greatest and holiest that can be accomplished on this earth."

"You're right. It would be a good deed on your part and an expiation on mine. And now I can tell you I'd already thought of that."

He told her about the letter he'd written to Gustave de Bridely, and the way in which he'd referred Gustave to Madame Peyrol. She listened to him with a sweet smile, and when he was done she kissed his brow. As if she understood all the accusations he bore against himself, she said, "Armand, you can see you're an honorable and good person when you want to be, and it's only false lights that lead you astray…" Then she went on, "We have to find out whether the Marquis de Bridely carried out his mission. You mailed your letter last night from Fontainebleau; he must've received it this morning; and by this time, for it's already night, if he's capable of understanding you he must've have left Paris. You should write to Madame Peyrol to make sure; and if he's not with her yet, then we'll go ourselves to tell her the secret, which can't be entrusted to a letter; or rather we'll give her a rendezvous here, where we're expecting your sister, and where there'll be three of us who owe their happiness to you."

"I'll do as you say," said Luizzi thoughtfully. "You should rest. I'll write while you sleep, because I also have to write a long letter to my lawyer to explain my plans to him, so that a twenty-four-hour visit to Toulouse will be enough to wrap up my affairs there."

The countess withdrew into the bedroom of the small suite they occupied, and Luizzi remained alone.

Chapter LXXII: The Slave

No doubt Luizzi was right when he'd told Léonie she was the angel of his life, for in leaving him she seemed to take with her all the hope, the faith, and the charity she gave him: hope in his future, faith in God's mercy, charity for those around him who were suffering. As soon as he was alone all of his doubts returned: once more he began to reckon up his life, weighing all the good and bad outcomes he though he had the power to find his way through and overcome. He reminded himself that waiting long enough to get an answer from Madame Peyrol—or waiting for her to arrive—exposed both him and the countess to the risk of being recognized in a town where half the major roads in France intersect. He argued to himself that after all he couldn't sacrifice his safety or the countess's for the sake of a woman whose fate wasn't his responsibility, and who'd find her mother sooner or later anyway without him needing to compromise himself for her. Gustave de Bridely's mission would do enough for now to rescue Madame Peyrol from a poverty that shouldn't be so terrible a misery for a woman who'd been raised to be used to the rough ways of the common people.

The one question that troubled the baron in all that benevolent self-congratulation was whether or not Gustave had carried out his mission; and he had a way of finding out that was too simple for him not to make use of it. Besides, he was aware of the ease with which he'd previously let himself be cowed by the presence of the creature he called his slave, and he resolved to assume the authority over him that at times had allowed him to fight back against that spirit of evil.

He therefore summoned Satan, and Satan appeared in a form still more extraordinary than any he'd adopted before: he'd assumed the face and figure of Akabila, dressed in his jockey's uniform.[65] He had the Malay slave's look of fearful, cowering servility—a servility that always seemed on the brink of rebellion and vengeance. Luizzi didn't think Satan had actually prompted all of his own recent reflections, but he assumed the Devil had guessed at his resolution and had shown up in the shape of that slave to let him know in advance he was submitting.

Luizzi surveyed him up and down with a confident look that made Satan lower his eyes. Then he asked in a peremptory tone, "Did Gustave set off for Taillis?"

"Yes, master, he did."

---

[65] Akabila, Monsieur Rigot's mysterious sidekick or jester, last appeared in Chapter XL.

"Will he carry out my mission?"

"That's the future, master, and I can't tell you that."

"Fine, but what were his intentions when he left?"

Satan tossed a sheet of parchment onto the table. "That'll explain better than a long story you might not have time to listen to."

Luizzi opened the parchment. It was a family tree. Here it is:

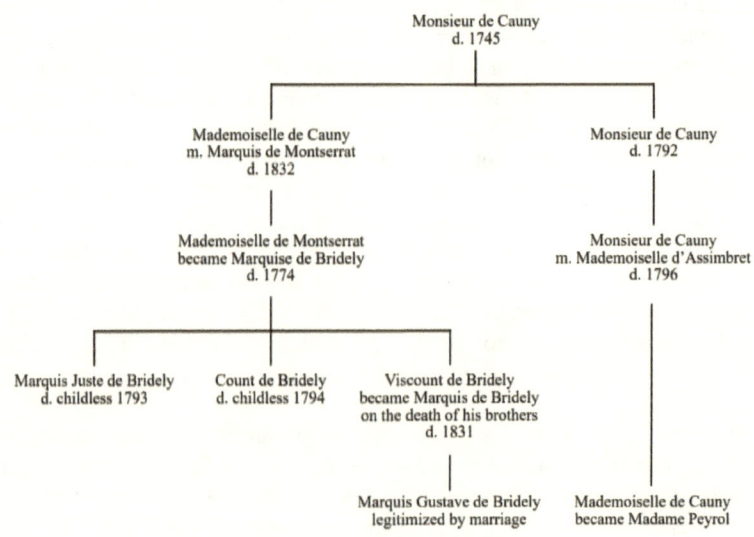

"What's the meaning of this?" cried Luizzi.

"Look at it carefully and read it carefully. You're of too good a family not to understand a family tree, and you've been too well educated not to understand the laws of inheritance; so you must see that the Marquis de Bridely and Madame Peyrol descend from the same ancestor, and that the Marquis de Bridely received, through his father and his grandmother, his great-grandmother's inheritance, which otherwise would've gone to the last surviving heir of the de Cauny line, if the de Bridely line had died out."

"And is Gustave, that alleged heir—legitimized by fraud—aware of that fact?"

"He's so well aware of it, that it was the substance of the lawsuit he won in Rennes, thanks to the work of your lawyer Barnet."

"Poor Eugénie! Whose clutches have I delivered you into!" cried Luizzi, giving Satan a horrified and pleading look.

But standing before him he no longer found the cringing, grotesque slave he'd seen earlier. The Malay had cast off his ridiculous shameful livery and now stood there naked, with the hideous smile and the savage expression of a cannibal eyeing the victim he's about to devour. At the sight of him Luizzi was moved to indescribable terror, his head spun, he felt his knees giving way before the king of evil, he let out an awful cry, and he was about to beg him for mercy when the door opened.

Chapter LXXIII: Continuation of the Previous Chapter

The door opened, and Countess Cerny came in. As he'd done once before—and contrary to his usual practice with Luizzi—Satan remained in a corner of the room. The baron, who'd been ready to bend the knee before his slave, stood up and ran to the countess like a frightened child to its mother. If his terror hadn't somehow choked him, he would presumably have cried out in horror and begged her to save him; but he couldn't utter a word, and his eyes were fixed on the corner of the parlor, where the Devil, still in his savage form, stood unmoving.

"Armand! Armand!" cried the countess. "I heard you speaking, I heard you moving around, you seemed not to be alone... and yet there's no one here," she said, giving a worried look all around.

Luizzi had recovered a little from his extreme emotion. "No one indeed, except the remorse that eats at me, the infernal demon that possesses me."

At that reply, delivered haltingly in a tone of profound despair, she gave him a sad look; then she placed her hand gently on his brow and said quietly, "If it's so awful for you to contemplate the past, have the strength to look away from it toward the future."

The Devil began to laugh, and Luizzi started.

"Alas," she said, seeing his reaction, "I fear the future terrifies you as much as the past. Was it foreseeing the future that threw you into such terrible despair?"

He was about to make some reply to reassure her, when suddenly he heard a man outside the door shouting, "They're in there! I recognize the countess's voice!"

The door of their suite was flung open, and Count Cerny appeared, followed by a police officer and two gendarmes. "That's the guilty woman, and that's her accomplice," said the count, pointing to his wife and Luizzi.

The gendarmes came toward Countess Cerny. Showing more dignity than fear, she said, "No need to touch me. I'll go with you."

"Then seize that gentleman!" said the officer, pointing to the baron.

Luizzi, confused by the rapid succession of emotions and events, looked around wildly, as if searching for some weapon with which to defend himself and the countess; but he found only Satan, with his savage expression, pointing slowly toward the open door to the countess's bedroom. It wasn't cowardice or calculation that urged Luizzi toward that way out; he hadn't decided basely to abandon the countess, and he didn't calculate that he could help her more effectively if he were free than if he were caught. It was an irrational and involuntary act, one of those irresistible impulses toward safety that come over a man in danger, a purely physical movement that made him rush out of the parlor. In her bedroom he saw another open door, ran through it, saw a small staircase, ran down it, found himself in the courtyard, crossed it, reached the street, and—as if driven on by some irresistible force—ran straight ahead till he'd crossed the whole town and found himself out on the high road.

It was a dark night and the streets were deserted. That was why he'd been able to escape; for though by the time he'd run twenty paces from the hotel he was already safe from pursuit by the gendarmes, anyone in town who'd seen a man fleeing bare-headed with a crazed look in his eye would probably have taken him for a madman or a robber. When fatigue finally forced him to stop, he sat down by the side of the road on one of those piles of paving stones that tell travelers the government is always thinking about repairing the roads, though the potholes always tell them they'll never do it.

Luizzi sat there on that strange chair for quite a while before he could calm the excited beating of his heart after that long run. He couldn't think yet: he was still too out of breath to have any ideas. It was only when he could finally draw air freely into his lungs that a few thoughts made their way into his head again— but once the passage was open they flooded in. Seeing himself there, out on the high road in the middle of the night, he thought of the countess, whom he'd just left defenseless in the hands of her husband; and he felt both disgust and shame for himself.

For a moment he was filled with a worthy resolve, and he stood up to go back to Orléans; but no sooner had he taken the first step than he heard a voice in the dark saying, "Fool!"

Turning around, he saw Satan, who'd given up Akabila's form and assumed a less extraordinary shape. He was dressed like a traveler—if you could call travel dress the normal shabby clothes we all wear every day. But his tailcoat was buttoned up to his chin; he had on tall fur-lined boots that came up almost to his thighs; a heavy roulière overcoat was draped over his shoulders; and a cap whose edges were pulled down over his ears served in place of the shapeless black felt thing known as a hat.

Luizzi was too unhappy with himself not to blame someone else for his undignified behavior; so as soon as he recognized Satan by the light in his eyes that cast a livid green glow all around him he cried, "Who summoned you, slave?"

"You did."

"You're lying."

The Devil turned his back on him and said coldly, "You've lost your mind, baron."

"Yes… yes," said Luizzi. "It's true, I did summon you—but it wasn't here, and I didn't tell you to follow me."

"Did you order me to leave you?"

That reply filled Luizzi with one of those uncontrollable rages that have to be expressed through some act of violence. He would've given a great deal for the impassive figure before him to be an ordinary man with whom he could fight, to kill or be killed. But he knew he was powerless compared to his terrible slave, and that feeling of impotence just fed his fury, which, having no outlet, he began to take out on himself. Striking his chest, he cried, "Ah, I'm a wretch!"

"A fool!" said the Devil, not at all surprised.

"I'm a wretch!"

"A fool!"

"I'm a madman, truly a madman!"

"A fool, truly a fool!"

"Look out, Satan! I'll bind you so tight by my side I'll make you sorry you're investing all your time in my doom, while a thousand other victims escape you."

"So be it. Where are we going?"

"Back to Orléans."

"Let's go."

And they began to walk.

"Who are we going to see?" asked Satan. He flicked one of his front teeth with his thumbnail, causing a dazzling spark to leap forth, which he used to light a pipe of a very odd design: the bowl was immense, and it was attached to one of those long, flexible tubes you wind around yourself. Noticing that Luizzi couldn't help staring at it, the Devil said, "You like my pipe? It's worth taking a good look at. Ever since Gothic architecture went out of style, I've wanted to make use of the little details in the way it depicted me; so I made myself a pipe out of my tail and my horns."

There are some wild ideas nothing can resist; they arouse the soul by what might be called mental tickling—so abrupt and unexpected that it summons forth a spasmodic laugh, the same way tickling works on the body even in the midst of the most terrible suffering. Luizzi therefore couldn't help laughing, and the Devil, still smoking calmly through his tail, went on, "Where are we really going? Orléans?"

"Yes, to find Léonie."

"In that case we'd have done better to take that side road, which leads to the place where they lock up madwomen and women of ill repute."

"Léonie, imprisoned with women of ill repute!" cried Luizzi.

"Since her husband had her arrested, it was presumably to throw her in prison; and since they were throwing her in prison, they could hardly put her in with thieves and murderers."

"Oh, Léonie! Léonie! What should I do?" cried the baron, stopping, overwhelmed by despair and not knowing where to turn.

The Devil sat down on one of those piles of paving stones, crossed his legs, and—while he went on smoking out of one side of his mouth—out of the other side he began to whistle:

Boy beloved by the ladies,
In every place I've been
A favorite with the wives,
Not so much with their men."[66]

"Satan, shut up!" cried Luizzi, goaded to fury again by the Devil's lack of decency and thinking he was mocking him for his good luck with women.

"It's a little old-fashioned and comic-opera style, I know. But if that bores you, here's something brand new:

Gold is an illusion,
Make sure you know how to use it."[67]

Luizzi had become quite accustomed to the Devil, so it wasn't surprising that he read a particular meaning into those words, however strange they seemed in the present circumstances. So no sooner had Satan sung the refrain we've just quoted than the baron began to hunt through his pockets. He didn't have so much as a single hundred-sou piece on him. That unpleasant discovery, coming in the midst of the whole cruel adventure, only stoked his anger, which built once again into rage when he heard Satan, who seemed to be well up on comic opera, go on with great composure:

"I've lost everything, there's nothing I fear.
Can I really consider life to be dear?"[68]

Luizzi fell into a frenzy; if he'd been holding a pistol just then, he would certainly have blown his own brains out, but he was unarmed. So he began to examine the pile of paving stones, looking for one with which he could smash his skull—when he felt a hand take hold of him and tug gently, and then a child's voice said, "At last, it's you!"

He turned and—in spite of the darkness of the night—recognized the little beggar girl. "You, child?" he cried. "Who sent you?"

"The lady."

"How were you able to see her?"

---

[66] "*Enfant chéri des dames*," from François Devienne's 1792 opera *Les Visitandines* ("The Sisters of the Visitation"); this is the third time Soulié has referred to or quoted it.

[67] "*L'or est une chimère*," from *Robert le Diable*, an 1831 opera with libretto by Eugène Scribe and music by Giacomo Meyerbeer. The next couplet runs, "Isn't the real wealth on earth finding our own amusement?"

[68] "*J'ai tout perdu, je ne crains rien: Pour moi, la vie est-elle un bien?*" This quotation, presumably from another operetta or comic opera of the period, has not been traced.

"I was at the foot of the stairs when she came down, because the whole hotel had been awakened and stirred up by what had happened. The lady was accompanied by a man with an officer's sash. When she saw me, she said to him, 'This is a poor beggar child I brought here and whom I meant to help and protect. Allow me to give her a present that will at least provide her with shelter from misery for a little while.' The man with the sash was nodding his agreement when the gendarmes came back, saying they didn't know where you'd escaped to. 'I'll recognize him,' I said to the lady quietly. 'Thank God!' she replied. 'Then try to find him, and give him this, and tell him I've been arrested and he shouldn't come back to Orléans, he should go to Toulouse as we'd planned. I'll find some way to get word to him there.'"

As she spoke, the girl handed Luizzi a purse containing what little remained of the money Henri Donezau had brought him.

"But what about her?"

"Her? She went on to say, 'Tell him that tomorrow I'll write to my father, and I'll have nothing to fear. Tell him you and the old blind soldier will wait here for his sister, Madame Donezau, and you'll secretly have her go on to Toulouse.' Just then the man with the sash came over to tell her to hurry up, and she went away. So then I left and I followed the road, always going straight ahead, thinking that, in the state you were in when you passed me, you wouldn't have thought about turning."

"And now you've found me!"

"And if I understood the last look the lady gave me, she expects me to bring her an answer. What should I tell her?"

"That I'll do what she suggests and I'll soon be back and in a position to save her. You understand?"

"I understand, and I'll tell her what you just told me."

"Tell her also it took only a moment of madness to drive me to..."

The Devil began to laugh, and Luizzi—realizing he was acting petty in sending protestations and explanations of that kind to a woman who'd so plainly and nobly demonstrated her bravery on his behalf—broke off and began again, "Tell her I'll save her, even at the cost of my life."

"I'll tell her," said the little beggar girl.

"But it just occurred to me: how will you find a way to get into her prison?"

"Oh, that's easily done," said the girl as she began walking away.

"You know someone there?"

"No, but I'm sure I can get in."

"That's impossible: you don't know how well guarded those places are."

"Oh, I thought about it while I was running after you," said the girl, who was already some distance from Luizzi, "and I found a way."

"What way?"

"I'll steal."

She vanished; and while Luizzi stood there, stunned by her naive answer, the Devil, releasing an immense cloud of pipe smoke, said, "So, twelve men will gather. One will be a butcher whose entire moral theory is that passersby shouldn't take the sausages hanging from his door without paying for them. One will be a horse dealer who knows from experience that the way to control vicious animals is by beating them with a whip. One will be a phrenologist who'll see in that child's actions material for a whole chapter on the innate predilection for theft. One will be a sugared-almonds peddler who, when he goes home, will be delighted to tell his daughter, who's four and who steals his candies, 'If you aren't good, I'll send you to prison like that little beggar girl.' One will be a lawyer who wants to find out whether the way the court administers the law looks like justice to him. A couple of them will be idiots who think in good conscience they should just decide yes or no on the facts of the case, without worrying about the consequences of their decision. Round out the total with four or five merchants and shop owners in a hurry to wrap up the court's business so they can get back to their own. Tell all those men they're called jurors and it's their job to uphold the interests of society. Assume that with a word or two you can give them a reasonable idea of justice and injustice. And that child will be sentenced to prison, which is to say to a life of crime, for the noblest action ever inspired by gratitude."

"But can't that girl find a lawyer to defend her?"

"No money, no lawyer, master."

"The law provides one for every person who's accused."

"A public defender, a beginner with no experience, and the least experienced of all of them. Because if it was for a murderer who'd poisoned three or four people, a mother who'd killed her own children, a son who'd cut his father's throat, if it was a question of some horrifying crime, there's be a line at the prison gate for the chance to represent the defense in such a splendid case. But a child who's going to steal a loaf of bread or a pair of wooden shoes? Who do you think is going to care about that? Since there's no fee, what glory will that bring? What crowd of beautiful women and curiosity seekers is that going to attract to the assizes? No one's going to pay any attention, master, not even you—the one who's going to benefit from the crime!"

"You never stop mocking! You think you're so great, because you criticize a few scattered failings in organized society. That's a job twenty little liberal speechifiers have already beaten you at!"

"And it's a job twenty mediocre speechifiers for the other side have already killed with a single word."

"The principles you're defending must've been pretty feeble if they were killed by a single word!"

"Oh, but it's an all-powerful word in your clever country, baron!"

"What word is it?"

"It's the word OLD. Tell the most progressive man of his century, 'Hey, you've been saying the same thing for twenty years, it's tired, it's boring, you're repeating yourself'—and with that argument a man the most skillful debaters couldn't have beaten is reduced to silence by a popinjay. It's the *ultima ratio* of idiots. Your arts, your politics, your philosophy, are all subject to it. A run of twenty or thirty years for each school of thought, that's the limit; then a new one comes along, usually an old one made to look new, which will suffer the same insulting banishment. For an eternal spectator of the periodic rise and fall of the same ideas like me, don't you think I must be bored stiff by it all?"

"That's the work of a society trying to break out of its old shell and looking for a way to take off, freely, on new wings, into a vaster space."

"You're mistaken. It's the desperate last effort of a doddering old man trying to cling to life. You're an old, worn-out nation. You no longer have a single one of the primitive instincts that lead to great discoveries and reveal to the intelligence new worlds of genius. You're obsessed with an endless desire for change, which just shows the sickness you've brought on society: you rebuild your lives from the ruins of everything you've knocked down; you remake religion with the same Christ the Supreme Being already abolished, you remake spiritualist philosophy with the same Malebranche Voltaire already debunked,[69] you remake your aristocracy from the same nobility obliterated in '93, you remake painting in the same Rococo style already shamed into exile by the classicist David;[70] in short, you—the kings of fashion!—borrow your architecture, your furniture, your fashions, from the architecture, furniture, and fashions of centuries that were repudiated twenty years ago. If you actually let some powerful new idea sprout and grow, it's only so you can pluck its flower and then say 'you're old and worn out' when it's barely reached maturity. And in the midst of all that poorly repainted, poorly chewed-over senility, you think you're in your prime! You're an exhausted people, an obsolete old dotard who needs either children, with their virginity cut short, or superannuated courtesans, with their kisses coated in gypsum and cochineal. Blech!"

With that final exclamation the Devil threw around himself such an astounding cloud of flaming reddish smoke that Luizzi drew back in fear. The next day the newspapers in the Loiret region reported that a great brightness on the horizon had caused concern that some farm was on fire, but the local astronomers had quickly realized the light was produced by an aurora borealis whose description they'd forwarded to the Academy of Sciences to be added to the list of all the auroras observed up till that time.

---

[69] Nicolas Malebranche (1638-1715), a Catholic priest and rationalist philosopher who tried to synthesize the ideas of St. Augustine and Descartes with a theory that God plays an active role in every aspect of the world.

[70] Jacques-Louis David (1748-1825), a preeminent Neoclassical and Historicist painter who led the turn away from the Rococo style.

The Devil's diatribe had fortunately distracted Luizzi from thinking about the danger the beggar girl was exposing herself to; and he was trying to figure out a way to keep the promise he'd made to Countess Cerny, which the girl was carrying to her, when in the distance he heard the hoof beats of the horses pulling a stagecoach coming from Orléans. When the coach drew within hailing range he called out to ask if there was room on board.

Against all likelihood, the stagecoach stopped, and the driver climbed down and said, "Come on, let's go, up top in the roof compartment!"

As Luizzi quickly climbed aboard he noticed the Devil had preceded him. He was presumably about to send Satan away, when the third person in the compartment spoke up:

Chapter LXXIV: An Artistic, Colorful, Modern Poet

"Would you like a scarf to cover your head, Monsieur de Luizzi? Because I see you forgot your hat back in Orléans."

The baron was astonished to hear himself addressed by name. He tried to see who was speaking. By the pre-dawn light that was starting to invade the darkness he saw a young man of twenty-nine or thirty, gaunt and bony, with a pointed beard, whose long ill-combed hair rather showily framed the noble but emaciated contours of a handsome face.

Noticing Luizzi's examination, the young man went on in a rather declamatory style, "You don't recognize me, baron? Yet it hasn't been that long since we met. But that interval, which perhaps only amounted to a few years in your life, has brought me practically to old age. Thinking—even more than passion or misfortune—quickly breaks a man down. It's the burning mirror that gathers all the sensory rays of human existence to produce by reflection the consuming fire known as genius. That's why in my books I've always spelled the word *reflexive* with a c and a t, *reflective*, so everyone understands that the moral process of the fires of creation is exactly analogous to the physical process of the fires of destruction."

"This is great stuff!" said the Devil quietly, giving the young man a protective look and nodding his head approvingly.

"Oh," said Luizzi, "so you're a writer?"

"I'm a poet."

"You write verse?"

"I'm a poet."

"And you know me?"

"Yes, I know you," declaimed the young man, "and it seems some strange destiny has driven us toward one another in circumstances in which you alone could understand me and I alone could understand you."

"Excellent, excellent!" said the Devil, while Luizzi still wondered who this man who knew him could be.

"Forgive me," he said, "for not having a clear recollection of where and under what circumstances we met before. Please tell me where I had the honor of knowing you."

"All I can tell you," replied the stranger in an odd kind of singsong, "is that I was in danger when we met the first time, and you're in danger as we meet again now. That's what I said to myself then: that man came to your rescue, and you'll rescue him someday. I gave my word, and I've kept it. As I was passing through Orléans I overheard a muttered conversation about a man who'd run off with a woman, and how the woman had been arrested, and the man had fled. A

242

premonition drove me to ask the man's name, and the answer was your name. So I said to myself, the time has come and the opportunity will soon arise, because events involving people don't happen without a reason, and they all have their inevitable consequences, and I couldn't hear your name like that without knowing I was bound to see you again soon. It was destiny's wake-up call alerting me to some upcoming event. So I kept an eye out all around from up here on the roof of this stagecoach, and when I spotted a man by the side of the road, bareheaded on a cold night, first I said to myself, 'There he is!' and then I called out to the driver, 'Pull up, that's a man toward whom I have a debt to discharge!' And he stopped, as you can see. And now we're even, baron."

Luizzi had listened to that monologue with his mouth hanging open and his eyes wide, while the Devil followed every turn of the speech with a slight nod, and ended it with a swoon of admiration. It took the baron some time to extract the little bit of sense from that flood of words; he was doing work similar to that of Musard, for example, when he hunts for a melodic motif in the complex cacophony of an opera by Monsieur Meyerbeer.[71] Somehow Luizzi managed to figure out more or less what the poet was trying to say; but—like a chemist for whom the difficulty of a discovery makes the result even more precious to him—thanks to the challenge it had been for him to understand the poet, he became even more curious to know to whom he owed the favor the man had done him. So he said, "I'm grateful to you for your kindness and for your intercession just now. But may I be informed to whom I owe my thanks and what the circumstances were that led to my owing them to you?"

"Ha, ha!" chuckled the Devil at that convoluted syntax. "Not bad, not bad!"

Before Luizzi could express his surprise at Satan's reaction, the poet went on, still in that nasal singsong, "You shall hear. Both the time and the place for you to find out are approaching. There is a place in which I'll tell you the secret of our first meeting. That place will serve as a commentary on my words, and being there will shed the necessary light on those words, and then you'll know me perfectly."

That made more sense, and Luizzi tried to recall who this man could be whom the Devil had placed on his path to get him out of trouble. Indeed it was quite possible that without his intercession the driver wouldn't have agreed to pick up an individual out on the high road without a passport—and even more importantly without a hat: for the lack of a hat is inarguable proof of running away from some shady business. A man can have no shirt, no stockings, no shoes, without arousing suspicion; but there isn't a single officer charged with the public safety who wouldn't feel justified in arresting a man without a hat. A

---

[71] Philippe Musard (1792-1859) was a composer of light-classical "promenade" music: popular dances, like waltzes and the can-can, and other dinner-concert music. In his pieces he often borrowed themes and tunes from other composers.

hat is the greatest guarantee of individual liberty: I recommend that aphorism to hatmakers.

Luizzi's memory was doing him no favors. Noticing how hard he was pondering, the poet said, "Don't hunt for it, baron, because you might find it, and if you found it I'd have nothing to reveal to you."

"Excellent, excellent!" muttered the Devil.

"No," went on the poet, "I'd have nothing more to say to you, because from then on you wouldn't be able to understand me."

"On the contrary," said Luizzi, "it seems to me remembering could only help in that kind of revelation."

"You're mistaken, because then you'd be seeing the man you once knew—or rather whom you thought you knew—and then you'd judge him by your own character and not by his. And then when he finally said, 'Here's who I am,' your thoughts would hover for a moment, suspended in the space between the illusion of your opinions and the reality of his life, before falling into doubt—the great abyss at the bottom of which our century thrashes."

Satan seemed to be delighted, but it all went over Luizzi's head; and he did what the audience sometimes does at a play: having struggled to understand the opening scenes, it gives up and just lets it all flow by, waiting for some favorable moment to guess, if it can, at the meaning of what's going on.

Meanwhile morning had come and the sun was visible on a horizon heavy with mist. The poet pulled out his watch and looked at it, then cried out in triumph, "I knew it!"

"Knew what?" asked Luizzi.

"I knew the utter vanity of the thing called science."

"And what makes you say that?"

"Well, not much in point of fact, but a secret instinct I had, a mental revelation that the men who want to substitute experience for ideas, logic for original thinking, are just coddling popular ignorance with false, absurd tales on which they've built a reputation that it's now time to undermine, to restore the preeminence of men of imagination."

"And how," said Luizzi, dumbfounded, "does the sunrise seem to you to prove the absurdity and the falsity of science?"

"How? Well, by a paltry fact, the most commonplace of all, a fact about which the experience of the ages should leave us in no doubt."

"What fact?"

"The fact of the exact time of sunrise. Look here," said the poet, showing Luizzi the time on his watch and the time listed in an almanac. "They differ by almost ten minutes."

All of Luizzi's gratitude for the favor the man had done him couldn't stand up to that reply, and he burst out laughing; whereas the Devil bowed deeply to the poet.

"You're laughing, baron?" said the poet. "You're so intimidated by the sterile faith this age has in physical science that you refuse to acknowledge its error even on such a trivial point?"

"Forgive me, but setting error against error, I'd rather put my trust in astronomers."

"This is a first-rate chronometer, which is off by less than a second a year."

"Your faith in your watch is a great tribute to science," said Luizzi politely.

"That's because I draw an important distinction, sir, between science based on numbers and science based on physical facts."

"But..." objected Luizzi with the diffidence of a man who's absolutely in the right and who hesitates to show another man how stupid he's being. "But... sunrise is a physical fact."

"Of course!" cried the poet. "But it's a physical fact that's been very poorly observed; because, after all, this watch is right. How can science reconcile the discrepancy?"

"Let's assume your watch, which I imagine was synchronized in Paris, shows the exact time a few leagues outside Orléans, which isn't actually true. Still, there'd be an even simpler explanation for the discrepancy you observe, namely that the sun hasn't yet risen."

"What!" said the poet, sounding like a man who's just been insulted. "That's a joke in poor taste, baron. It seems to me I can see the sun."

"Yes, sir, you see it, and yet it's still below the horizon."

The poet began to snicker with a superior air. "And no doubt science can explain that?"

"Perfectly. It's a result of refraction."

"You mean reflection?"

"No, sir, refraction."

"Don't know what that is," said the poet, putting his pince-nez back on so he could study the sun. "I see it or I don't see it, that's all. Still, it amazes me that science, that fraud of every age, can deny the simplest miracles of the Middle Ages while claiming to prove I don't see what I see... But come, baron, enough about all this. My mind's made up—I'm utterly convinced—for me it's a matter of conscience—I can't be converted."

"Who is this person?" Luizzi whispered to the Devil.

"He's a literary and artistic eminence, a man of art and the imagination."

"But I've never met anyone more ignorant."

"That's how it is," said Satan. "Surely you must know that nowadays the fashion is that genius is an eagle and science is a cage."

The conversation came to an end for a moment; Luizzi felt no desire to pick it up, and it was the poet, who'd been absorbed in a vague observation of the sun through his pince-nez, who cried, "Well! Here's something new and strange!"

"What's that?"

"Till now no one has understood the sunrise poetically—not just its gentle smile and its flowing locks of cloud, but the great thoughts it transmits to the soul in the golden rays along which it glides as swiftly as a railroad car along the tracks."

"You're right, sir!" cried the Devil. "And that's what prompted Shakespeare to say, in that sublime couplet:

When you've always been virtuous,
You love to watch the sunrise."

Luizzi—who remembered those lines very well from the comic opera *Montano and Stephanie*[72]—turned aside so as not to laugh in the poet's face.

Meanwhile with deep admiration the poet said to Satan, who looked exactly like an ordinary man, "That's very true, sir! Oh, that Shakespeare certainly had ideas, thoughts like red-hot iron tempered in a maiden's tears. Are you translating Shakespeare?"

"No, but I adore Shakespeare."

"And you're quite right to, because he's the greatest of all poets, and those few words you've just quoted have that bittersweet flavor of the English bard that can be recognized everywhere, by everyone. But he was born in a time when poetry was possible, in a century of iron and silk, of steel and velvet, of great battles and carefree gallantry. And he was great and fecund, because he had enough space to send out into the world the giants born in his imagination."

"But it strikes me," said Satan, "isn't the world just as big now as it used to be, with plenty of space for giants?"

"How do you expect poetry to find its footing in an age of petty egotistical things? What even slightly serious oeuvre is possible in the presence of people who've devoted their lives to the material interests of existence?"

"But I wonder," said the Devil, "haven't material interests always played an important part in human existence?"

"That could be, but men in ages past also had passions as great as they themselves were. Everything nowadays has shrunk to fit the little men of our times. Society is just a vast comic-opera show, with a chorus from the Théâtre du Gymnase."

"In that case, take the past ages as your audience and write a tragedy."

"A Roman tragedy?" asked the poet scornfully.

"No, a French tragedy."

"Tragedy is impossible without religion and destiny."

"Don't you have a religion and a destiny?"

"A religion and a destiny the public doesn't believe in anymore."

---

[72] *Montano et Stephanie* (1799), a comic opera composed by Henri-Montan Berton from a libretto by Jean-Élie Bédéno Dejaure.

"Then follow Horace's lead, and depict the events of your own life—*domestica facta*."[73]

"Sir, Horace was a very fine fellow, for whom I have great respect, but I can't listen to him. He's like one of those uncles in a comedy, who's always handing out advice and never handing out money to his rascal nephew; he's useless and passé, and I don't need him. The only things that might still have theatrical power are the dramatic scenes tucked away inside our old chronicles and legends."

It struck Luizzi that Horace's *domestica facta* meant exactly what this man claimed to want, but he knew him well enough by now to see he scorned Horace on the same basis that he admired Shakespeare. He also noticed that the poet had a certain collection of words he used to dress everything up, as if words changed their meanings when he applied them to something else. So for him the most gripping event was old and boring if it came from history, but the latest foolishness was of enormous interest as long as it was presented as coming from a "chronicle."

So he was still just listening as the man went on, "I should tell you that the real purpose of my journey is nothing less than to study our national history on the actual sites and in the popular memory of every region, where it's been correctly recorded in all of its color and truth."

"What an admirable project!" said the Devil. "So you must already have begun your observations?"

"Yes," said the poet carelessly, "I've collected a few."

"The seat you've chosen, up here on the roof of the stagecoach, is ideal for that," said the Devil.

The sarcasm was so blatant that even the great man was taken aback; but after a careful look at the speaker he thought he looked so sincere that he decided to let it go.

Satan went on, "You can see a long way from here."

"And from a great height," replied the poet, sublimely unafraid of banality.

"My word! I'm delighted by your way of thinking about art," said the Devil. "And since chance has allowed me to meet a man of such intelligence and insight, I'd be more than happy to help you in this glorious enterprise and share with you a few of the most peculiar old stories from these parts, because I'm from around here."

"They must be fascinating," said the poet scornfully.

"I don't know if the story itself is worth much, but it's of interest to some people at least."

The Devil was looking straight at Luizzi when he said that, so the baron quickly replied, "So it's a modern-day story?"

---

[73] The Roman lyric poet Horace (65-27 BCE) often used his own private life and his inner life as his subject.

247

"Not exactly, but there are some people whose families go way back, and as a result they listen to certain old stories with great interest."

"Is it a legend or a chronicle?" asked the poet carelessly.

"It's a chronicle, in the sense that it has to do with events in the visible natural world. But it's also a legend, since the Devil plays a part in it."

"Really?" said the poet with a smile. "That can be amusing."

"I'd spare you the trouble of telling it to us, sir," said Luizzi, who feared whatever the Devil might reveal, no matter from how long ago.

"No, please, I insist," said the poet.

Luizzi was on the brink of exploding in anger at the Devil; but, hoping to avoid listening to his story, and determined to dismiss him at the first opportunity when they were alone again, he flung himself into a corner of the compartment so as not to hear it.

But the storyteller still hadn't begun.

"Well, sir?" cried the poet. "Have you forgotten your story?"

"No, I'm ready. I was waiting to start it till we'd come around the next corner, so as to be able to show you the scene of the adventure I'm going to tell—which I believe a man of your genius could fashion into a reasonably dark tragedy."

"Do you mean a history play, sir? But where is this place, the setting of the history you think is suitable for the stage?"

The Devil pointed toward a low hill that rose fairly near the road. "Do you see a few large stones set in a circle at the summit of that rocky height, looking like they once formed the base of a great tower?"

"I see them very clearly," said the poet.

"Well, that's all that's left of the ancient castle of Roquemure."

"Roquemure!" cried Luizzi, starting up in his seat.

"Have you heard of it, sir?" asked the Devil, like any honest ordinary man about to tell an anecdote in a social setting.

"Yes, and I'll be curious to hear what story you have to tell about it."

"The story of its destruction."

Luizzi eyed him warily; but Satan, wrapping his greatcoat around him, seemed not to notice his questioning look, and began thus:

TRAGEDY OR HISTORY PLAY

Chapter LXXV: Act One

One day in May of the year 1179, about an hour before nightfall, two women sat in the great hall of Roquemure Castle. One was about forty; she was tall, and the thinness and pallor of her face attested to a troubled soul and broken health; there was a passionate sadness in her eyes, and a weary lethargy in her slightest movements. She must once have been very beautiful. Behind the physical and moral prostration that bowed her down could still be glimpsed the remnants of an uncommon vitality and a very strong will. Anyone looking at her could see her heart must be burdened with a great sorrow or a great remorse.

Next to her sat a tall, slender young woman, blonde with a rosy complexion; her gray-blue eyes sparkled with bold, willful desire whenever they weren't veiled beneath her eyelids; her long hair grew out in the tight curls that some say are a sign of hot blood and voluptuous appetite. The older woman was Ermessinde de Roquemure, wed at sixteen to old Sir Hugues de Roquemure, who was already over sixty when she married him. The younger woman was Alix de Roquemure, married barely a year to Gérard de Roquemure, the son of Hugues and his first wife, Blanche de Virelei.

A few steps from the two women stood a man at a lectern on which a book lay open. From time to time he read a few lines aloud and then explained and commented on them to a couple of dozen men and women seated around the great hall on bales of straw—for the only movable seats in the room were those occupied by Ermessinde and Alix; and if the listeners had chosen to sit on the benches built into the wood paneling along the walls, they wouldn't have been able to hear venerable Father Audoin, whose voice, weakened by age, couldn't have filled that immense space. They were all listening with pious reverence to the priest's paraphrase of certain Bible verses, for he was explaining one of the most interesting passages: he was classifying all the demons and describing their various attributes.

Everyone was listening, except Ermessinde and Alix, whose eyes kept straying elsewhere, suggesting their thoughts were focused on something beyond that room. They were clearly waiting for someone to arrive, because they both turned their heads at the slightest noise from the far side of the inner courtyard that occupied the space between the great hall and the tower containing the main entrance to Roquemure Castle.

The priest's remarks, the audience's attention, and the two ladies' distraction had all been going on for two hours. The commentator's loquacity ran out before his listeners' attention—a quality typical of that long-ago time, and which gives it a picturesque touch! Soon a deep silence fell over the hall. None of the lower-ranking people gathered around their lady dared either comment on the commentator or make fun of him—another unusual and very characteristic detail! The only behavior that seemed universally human was the poorly disguised impatience of the two ladies: they constantly tangled the red wool they were both winding—but while Ermessinde patiently tried to untangle hers and then stopped in complete distraction after failing to pay much attention to what she was doing, Alix abruptly snapped her yarn and tied it together at random without worrying about the knots she was scattering through her work. The women's characters were fully expressed in those small behaviors: weary resignation on the one hand, thoughtless hasty anger on the other.

Noticing that the sun was almost touching the top of the entry tower, which stood on the west side of the castle, and was about to leave the highest crenelations in shadow, Ermessinde said quietly to Alix, "It's getting late, my child, and your husband hasn't returned."

"Neither mine nor yours. Did you expect them so soon?"

"No, they said they wouldn't be back till two hours after sunset."

"That's right, I'd forgotten."

So it wasn't their husbands those two women were waiting for.

"Excellent!" said the poet. "I can see how that would make a very nice opening scene."

"Wouldn't it?" said the Devil. Then he went on, "No sooner had the women spoken than a great noise was heard at the gate, and the chains of the portcullis and the drawbridge began to squeak in their iron pulleys."

"Very good," said the poet. "That could become a few lines of verse for one of the women:

I hear the grinding of the chain upon its iron ring,
Drawbridge falling and portcullis rising...

That would make for a picturesque contrast: falling versus rising—not bad, not bad. Go on," he said, licking his lips as if to savor the poetic honey that had just flowed from them.

The Devil continued:

Neither of the women said what you said. But Ermessinde suddenly stood up and cried aloud, "It's him!" and Alix shot a quick glance toward the gate and gave a deep sigh. Clearly Ermessinde had the right to express openly her pleasure at the newcomer's arrival, whereas Alix couldn't, in spite of the concern and distress she felt. But her feelings must've been powerful, because now she too rose and said to Ermessinde, "I'll retire, ma'am. I don't wish by my presence to intrude on the reunion of a mother and a son after an absence of four years. Please make my excuses to Sir Lionel de Roquemure, my brother-in-law."

"You may go," said Ermessinde. And as she watched Alix leave she thought to herself...

The poet interrupted:
"Does she so hate my son, that she must flee his coming?
Perhaps she loves him, and within her troubled heart
Concealèd love takes on the shape of hate?
That would certainly set up the plot nicely."

"No doubt," said the Devil. "But that's not what Ermessinde said to herself, since her son had been away from Roquemure Castle for four years and Alix had only been there a year, and she had no reason to think they'd known each other before then and could either love or hate each other."

Instead, as she watched Alix leave she thought, "She's unhappy too; she cares too much for my happiness for that. Happy people are the most selfish."

A moment later Lionel entered the great hall. Kneeling before his mother, he said in the customary way, "Bless me."

Ermessinde placed her hands on her son's head and looked at him, but she couldn't speak. She motioned for everyone to withdraw. No sooner was she alone with Lionel than she raised him to his feet and embraced him, noticing how handsome he was and how much he'd grown, and feeling alarmed at his pallor—all of that in the space of a moment. Then her words flowed along with her tears, and she cried out, "Ah, here you are at last!"

For his part, her son had looked at his mother with sad, affectionate attention; and instead of responding to her joy he said, "So it's always the same thing here, always tears, and you always the one weeping?"

"I'm weeping for joy at seeing you again."

"No, mother, you weep every day. Tears of joy don't leave your eyes sunken, and don't fade so quickly."

"Let's not speak of me, Lionel, but of you. Won't you tell me everything you've done in the four years you've been gone?"

"I will tell you, and I'll tell my father too."

"Yes, but first, sit here and listen to me, because now you're a man, for you're twenty-two. If my husband... if your father doesn't embrace you with as much fondness as I do, don't show any anger at the coldness of his welcome. You've lived at the courts of princes, among men of all kinds, and you know you often have to conceal at the bottom of your heart the discontent you feel."

"Yes, mother, I've lived in many lands since I left you; but everywhere I saw fathers love their sons if they hadn't betrayed their blood."

"Yes, Lionel, you're right," she said sadly. "And yet, I beg you, be meek with him and endure his words, however harsh they may be."

"Has he then summoned me back to him to make me suffer, as I did before, all of the same mistreatment and humiliation?"

"He called you home because he needs you. The Lords of Malize, that turbulent, vindictive family, let no season go by without giving him serious cause for complaint."

"And does my father complain?" asked Lionel bitterly.

"Your father is eighty-four years old, and a suit of armor is heavy at that age."

"Well! Doesn't he have his eldest son, my noble half-brother Gérard, his favorite son, to defend him?"

"Why do you mock him like that, Lionel? Your brother Gérard was born weak, puny, sickly, crippled…"

"And above all, mother, he was born a coward, a scoundrel, and a liar… Ah, I don't understand how he and I could be of the same blood."

Ermessinde blushed at her son's words…

"That could be replaced by an aside," interrupted the poet, "because I'm beginning to understand…"

"What do you mean, an aside?" asked Luizzi, who'd completely forgotten the Devil's original point in telling this story to the poet.

"The gentleman is writing a play," said Satan.

"Oh, I see. In that case, go on with the story."

"He, he, he!" laughed the Devil, giving him a mocking look. "So it interests you?"

"Yes, I'm curious to see how it ends."

"Whoa, whoa! We're only in the second scene of Act One!"

"Then get on with it!"

The Devil continued:

Lionel failed to notice his mother's embarrassment. She, now hearing a great noise at the entrance gate, clapped her hands. Everyone returned, and Ermessinde whispered to Lionel, "There's no need for Sir Hugues to know I spoke to you in private. Above all, stay calm."

Lionel, who'd been seated at his mother feet, quickly stood up and gave his long brown hair a shake with a firm flick of his head. His height and his slenderness, his soft pallor, and the elegance of his almost diminutive hands and feet wouldn't have suggested a soldier's power, without the nimble ease with which he walked and stood; for a man's grace is his strength.

"Grace and strength imply a contradiction," said the poet. "But that's all right, keep going. You said the father, Sir Hugues, was arriving?"

"Yes," said the Devil.

He was an old man with a mass of tangled white hair, a pendulous lip, and rheumy eyes; he stooped and walked with difficulty, leaning on a tall staff. As he entered the great hall he glanced quickly around at everyone present and shouted, "What's all this straw doing here?"

"It was to provide seats for all the pages and the servant girls around Father Audoin," said Ermessinde.

"Couldn't they listen to him standing up? They can talk about love and dancing all day long without thinking about sitting down; but when it's a question of listening to an old man, they've got to be comfortable—is that it, ma'am? Because listening to an old man talk is awfully tiring."

Ermessinde wanted to answer, but old Hugues shouted, "Take that straw back to the sheds! The day might soon come when you're trapped here by the lances of the Lords of Malize, and you'll be more than happy to have that straw to ease your hunger!"

The servants obeyed in silence, while the old man muttered furiously, "Look at the defenders of Roquemure Castle—men who sit listening to a priest talk! And no one's in charge!"

"Here I am, father!" said Lionel, stepping forward.

The old man looked at him for a long time without a word. He eyed him up and down, barely containing the agitation that filled him. After that examination he turned away and went to sit on one of the long benches on either side of the immense fireplace at one end of the hall, which was blazing in spite of the season. He motioned for Lionel to approach. The boy's mother, who stood facing him, beside the old man, gave him a look pleading with him to contain himself, for the young man's expression showed how angry he was at the welcome he'd been given.

"You're awfully late getting here!" said old Hugues.

"I got here before the danger," said Lionel, crossing his arms.

"Perhaps the threat of danger wouldn't have come if you'd returned earlier, as I ordered."

"I doubt my presence would've kept my brother Gérard from roaming the lands of the Lords of Malize by night and stealing their vassals' daughters and livestock; that's what provoked the threat."

"Where did you hear those lies?" cried the old man angrily.

"The complaints of the Lords of Malize have reached all the way to King Philippe Auguste."[74]

"And you defend the merits of the complaints of your enemies?"

---

[74] Philippe II, known as Philippe Auguste, was King of France from 1180 to 1223, though Soulié seems to think he was already king in May 1179. He was the first French monarch to style himself "King of France."

"Before the king I told them they were lying; but before you, father, I have to admit I think they're in the right."

"So it was to stick up for them that you came home?"

"I came home to fight them, and they won't touch a single stone of this castle while I'm standing between them and its ramparts."

"Isn't that nice!" said Hugues with a bitter smile. Then, watching carefully for the effect of his words, he went on, "But in the four years you've been away from this castle, how could it be you never found time to come home?"

"I went to Aquitaine and I fought on the side of the Gascon nobles against Richard the Lionhearted. I met him three times in battle, and three times we broke our lances, each against the other, without him giving an inch, without me retreating a foot."

"I know that; but you didn't stay in Aquitaine."

"The next year I was before Rouen with King Henri VII, and twice I scaled the ramparts armed with nothing more than my sword."

"I know that; but then where did you go?"

"I went to the Berri region when Henry II, King of England, had seized it by treachery, and I fought against him."

"I know that; and you carried your banner forward further than any other into the ranks of the enemy. But after you left Berri, what did you do?"

Lionel blushed and stood there in embarrassment. Surprised by his silence, his mother gestured to him to answer. So, controlling his distress, he said hesitatingly, "Six months ago I went to Arles, to see the coronation of the Emperor Frederick Barbarossa."[75]

"Six months ago!" said Hugues. "But where were you eighteen months ago?"

"Perhaps I lost track of the duty of a warrior for a while. I followed Henri Court-Mantel[76] to the tourneys and jousts he held in Paris and throughout the Gallic regions."

"Oh," said Hugues, eyeing Lionel even more attentively, "so you followed him to the jousts beautiful women are so fond of?" He voice shook with suppressed anger as he went on, "Did you have no adventures in Paris worth reporting to your father?"

"None!" said Lionel, looking at his mother.

"None?" said the old man, rising. Lionel lowered his eyes. "That'll do!" said Hugues, as he limped away. Such was the first interview between father and son after an absence of four years. Lionel and his mother remained alone...

---

[75] Frederick Barbarossa (1122-90), king of Germany and later Holy Roman Emperor. Again, Soulié's chronology is a little off, since Frederick became emperor in 1155.

[76] Henri Court-Mantel was the French form of an English epithet for King Henry II of England, "Henry Curtmantle," after the short coat he wore.

Interrupting his story, the Devil said to the poet, "Of course you understand I'm just sketching out the main points of the scene. For the most impact on stage in a really well-crafted play, it'd be better to handle it like this:

THE FATHER: Where were you eighteen months ago?

THE SON: Four years ago I was in Aquitaine, where I did thus and such, etcetera—a long speech about that, describing battles and so forth, then:

THE FATHER: Where were you eighteen months ago?

THE SON: Three years ago I was in Normandy, where I did thus and such, etcetera—another fine speech with period details about siege warfare, then:

THE FATHER: Where were you eighteen months ago?

THE SON: Two years ago I was in Provence, where I did thus and such, etcetera—another big speech about equestrian contests and courtly love, with all the medieval color you can manage, and then:

THE FATHER: Where were you eighteen months ago?

THE SON: A year ago I was in Picardie, where I did... And here, you understand, the father interrupts him and says, I've heard enough! So then the audience also understands something important happened eighteen months ago."

"You're involved in the theater?" asked the poet in the sympathetic tone of a fellow-artist.

"I've made a careful study of the modern drama."

"It's just that the bit you did just now is really good! The son who talks about everything he hasn't been asked about, and the father who keeps stubbornly asking—it gives the scene a certain mystery."

"A mystery that will probably be resolved in the next scene," said Luizzi impatiently.

"Well," said Satan, "we're just lifting a corner of the veil, a tiny corner, and here's how..."

Ermessinde, left alone with her son, immediately said, "Tell me, what did you do eighteen months ago? Why didn't you answer your father when he asked you what you were doing then?"

"It's just that I was in love, and that love must remain a mystery. I met a woman with whom I fell in love with all the passion of a heart that's never been in love."

"And was that woman beautiful?"

"Oh, mother! How could she not have seemed beautiful to me, who loved her, since she seemed beautiful even to those who told me to flee from her, for she was frivolous and flirtatious? She was so beautiful, mother, so seductive, that those who hated her didn't dare look at her or listen to her, for fear of falling in love with her!"

"And did she deceive you, Lionel?"

"She deceived me, mother. She gave herself to another man."

"And do you regret her?"

"I hate her, mother!"

"And have you forgotten her?"

"I curse her every day."

"Oh, my child, you still love her!"

"No, mother, no, I no longer love her," he said with an effort. "I would happily see her die."

"That's because you still love her."

"Me? Oh, mother!" said the young man angrily. "I could kill her!"

"So you're still madly in love with her."

Lionel was silent. His mother, taking him in her arms, said, "And what is that woman's name?"

"A year ago I swore that name would never cross my lips again."

"Keep your secret, my son, and above all keep your hatred."

"Act One could end right there," said the poet.

"To hell with your drama or your tragedy!" cried Luizzi angrily. "I'm trying to listen to the story, and you're ruining it for me!"

"Well, come on, the gentleman is a poet," said the Devil.

"Baron de Luizzi," said the pale, gaunt writer, "you're a wealthy man and a great lord, I believe. On both counts I'll forgive you for your bad temper, because we're not hearing this story with the same ears."

The baron didn't feel obliged to reply to that feeble attempt at an insult; and he said to the Devil, "Well, sir, are you going to finish the story?"

"I beg you pardon," said Satan. "I don't see what you find so interesting in it."

Luizzi was furious, and he wanted to pinch the Devil's arm till it bled. But he knew he'd only burn his fingers, so he sank back into his corner.

The Devil went on:

Chapter LXXVI: Act Two

Just as Lionel and his mother came to the end of that explanation, old Hugues entered the great hall of the castle once again. The tables were being set for supper, and all the inhabitants of the castle arrived one by one. Night had fallen. Now they were waiting only for Gérard, and Gérard didn't appear. All of them were surprised, except the old man. When his wife expressed concern at Gérard's absence, he replied sharply, "Those who go riding across country often meet obstacles that delay them; but it's surprising that those who have only a door to pass through can't show up to meals on time. Where's Alix?"

"Someone go remind her," said Ermessinde.

The old man lowered his head; but his savage eye beneath his long over-hanging eyebrows was fixed on Lionel. Alix entered. Lionel sat impassive and unmoving.

In a sickly sweet tone the old man said, "Well, my child, so you don't want our company? When Gérard's away there's no one here who pleases you? And yet I can introduce you to a brave, handsome knight, my son Lionel."

Alix and the young man bowed coldly to each other. Hugues watched them carefully.

Ermessinde, who was seated by her son, said to him quietly, "Don't be surprised by the cold welcome you got from your brother's wife. She's still rather shy."

With a bitter smile Lionel replied, "Nothing surprises me, mother."

As you can see, it was a strange return, and a strange welcome, and—between a sister-in-law and a brother-in-law who'd supposedly never met be-fore—a strange greeting. And though it was getting late, all of them sat silent: the old man seemed neither angry nor alarmed by the prolonged absence of his eldest son; Alix didn't ask about him; Lionel, lost in thought, watched the flames dancing in the fireplace; Ermessinde watched her husband anxiously, as if she dreaded what would follow that silence.

At that moment they heard a noise at the castle gate, and soon Gérard en-tered. Alix rose and ran to him with an urgency that seemed peculiar after her earlier indifference. But at the sight of him she quickly backed away, blushing and lowering her eyes with a look of anger and distaste. Gérard was so drunk he could barely stand up; he stumbled as he moved toward his wife. Hunchbacked, lame, short, ugly, red-faced, and stained with wine and mud—for he'd fallen off his horse—Gérard would've turned a peasant girl's stomach. Alix could there-fore say nothing, in spite of her wish to give her husband a gracious welcome.

As for Hugues, no matter how angry he felt at seeing his dear son degrade himself in front of so many people, he wanted none of them to express their disgust, and he glared at them all with a look that said, "Which of you will dare criticize my favorite?" Ermessinde kept her eyes lowered, Alix had turned her face away, and Lionel was watching her with a scornful smile. All the rest acted like they hadn't even noticed Gérard's entrance, and they all kept to themselves.

"Hey, what did I hear at the gate?" cried Gérard. "My brother Lionel is back?... Hic!... Hey, hello!... Hic!... Hello, Lionel... Hic!... Give me a hug!"

Lionel sat with his arms folded.

"You won't give your brother a hug?" cried the old man angrily.

After his mother gave him a beseeching look, Lionel obeyed. But as they hugged, the mud and wine on Gérard's clothes touched the young knight's suit of chain mail; turning to a page, Lionel said disdainfully, "Wipe off that mud and wine. The finest steel can be tarnished and rusted if you don't act quickly to clean off that kind of stain; and someday noble armor that's been eaten away like that will be unable to protect its wearer."

There couldn't be much objection to the care Lionel had taken; but Hugues felt quite clearly that the suit of mail was a symbol of the reputation of the Lords of Roquemure, and Lionel's words were a bitter warning of the danger Gérard's disorderly behavior represented for that reputation. Hugues gave his younger son a look of hatred, while Ermessinde had the food served to distract everyone's attention, and Alix wiped away a bitter tear.

Meanwhile Gérard wandered around, addressing loud bawdy comments to the pretty girls who served that noble house. Hugues said nothing, and patiently put up with all those insults, not wanting to criticize his favorite in front of Ermessinde and Lionel. When supper was finally served, they all sat down; Gérard took his seat, though he certainly needed nothing more, and after a few minutes he fell asleep with his head on the table. During the whole meal Lionel kept his attention on his mother, while Alix, blushing with shame and outrage, silently drank her own tears.

When it was time to withdraw, Hugues rose and gestured in a way understood by three or four valets, for whom no doubt that silent order was nothing new: they took hold of Gérard and began to carry him out of the great hall. Hugues pointed to a door, the door leading to Alix's room. She, absorbed in her feelings of humiliation, hadn't seen what happened; but when the valets were about to go through the door leading to her apartment, she cried out vehemently, "Not in my room! Not in my room! Take him to the stables!"

Old Hugues glared at her. "Your own husband! Your own husband!"

"A drunken man!" she replied with a look of supreme disgust. And she rose to go.

Ermessinde and Lionel happened to be in her path. Ermessinde tried to talk to her to calm her down; but Alix, pushing her away, said angrily, "Leave me alone, leave me alone, you and your son!"

Alix was probably referring to Lionel; but he, who hadn't moved, thought she meant Gérard, and he replied, "He's no son of hers, ma'am."

At those words—as if the sound of Lionel's voice, addressing her for the first time, had caused some kind of unexpected reversal in her—Alix turned to the valets and said, "My father-in-law is right. He's my husband, and love must excuse such a minor lapse. This way."

The valets obeyed her; she let them go out ahead of her, then she left, after giving Lionel a glance of insulting bravado.

Lionel stood with his eyes fixed on the door through which Alix had left, while Sir Hugues observed his son's deathly pallor and the compression of his lips. The old man didn't get up; he made no sign or movement, but someone sitting close to him would've heard him mutter to himself, "Oh, so it's true."

A moment later, as if in answer to the thought he'd just expressed, he ordered all the servants to withdraw. Lionel and Ermessinde remained alone with Hugues. The old man said, "Leave us, Lionel. Your mother will have something to say to you later."

Lionel exited, and Ermessinde found herself alone with her husband. That must've been an uncommon and dreadful occurrence for her, for she seemed both surprised and shaken. Barely waiting for the footsteps of the departing servants to fade away, Hugues pointed to where Lionel had gone and cried angrily, "He must leave the castle tomorrow."

"Who?... Lionel?"

"Tomorrow, before sunrise."

"Lionel!" repeated Ermessinde in horror.

"And cursed be the day he came here, just as cursed as the day he was born!" exploded Hugues.

She bowed her head, while the old man shook with anger and stamped his foot. She seemed crushed. Finally she made a timid effort to say, "What has he done to be treated so harshly?"

He didn't answer, and his silence emboldened her; she went on more confidently, "Is it his fault he witnessed a scene that's all too common in this house?"

"No," said the old man bitterly, "but I don't want this house to witness a repetition of an even more shameful scene."

"I don't understand."

"You're Lionel's mother!" he cried in a ringing voice. "And you don't understand?"

She bowed her head again, and stammered, "I haven't forgotten the past, my lord, but I don't know what you see in the future."

"Listen to me, Ermessinde," said the old man more gently. "You sullied my old age, and you filled my heart with despair for an injury I can't avenge; but I've made you unhappy too. You've been weeping for twenty-two years; I'm tired of my misery and of yours, so listen to me: Lionel is in love with Alix."

"He doesn't know her. Tonight is the first time he ever saw her."

"He's known her for a long time. Eighteen months ago..."

"Ah, here come those famous eighteen months!" cried the poet, interrupting the Devil in the full flow of his narrative, which Luizzi was following with the closest attention.

The baron could barely contain his impatience, and he replied to the interrupter with such marked politeness it could only come across as impolite. "You know, you'd be the finest man in the world if you could just let me listen to this story from beginning to end without constantly interrupting."

"I'm sorry," said the man of genius, "but I believe this gentleman is telling the story for my benefit."

"Look," said Satan, "I think I'm beginning to bore you both, so I'll stop there."

"No, no!" cried Luizzi vehemently. "Keep going, I want to hear how it ends."

"Are you a playwright too?" asked the Devil.

"I have no pretensions that way, but I'm just as interested as this gentleman in that kind of diabolical ballad."

"Say!" said the Devil in surprise. "You must know this one, since you know it's going to involve the Devil!"

"I feel like you told us that beforehand. In any case, please... I'd be very grateful if you finished it."

"I'd be happy to." And Satan went on:

While Ermessinde listened in astonishment, Hugues continued, "Eighteen months ago Alix was in Paris, and eighteen months ago she met Lionel there, at the great tourneys where he made such a name for himself. I didn't know about that when she came to Orléans to visit the only close relative she had left, the Lord of Péruse. It was at his house I saw her, and it was to him I addressed myself to obtain her. She was an orphan; she had nothing but a wretched estate she couldn't protect against either rebellion by her vassals or incursions by her neighbors. Her mother's sins had left a stain on her name that made any honorable marriage unlikely. But she was young, beautiful, and seductive, and I hoped the love she'd inspire in Gérard would cure of him of his shameful life of debauchery.

"When the Lord of Péruse gave me Alix's answer, I was surprised to hear him say she'd accepted with delight the offer to make her the daughter-in-law of the Lord of Roquemure. I assumed either she understood the desperation of her own situation, or she was ambitious, and the hope of marrying a rich heir hid Gérard's faults from her—for I swear, I hadn't misled the Lord of Péruse. I was to leave Orléans the next day; we talked it over, and agreed that Péruse and his niece would visit this castle a few days later."

"Which indeed they did."

"Yes. Alix came, and she married Gérard without betraying either loathing or disgust. It was only later I learned—from the Lord of Péruse himself, who'd found out about it on a visit to Paris—that Alix had known Lionel there, and your son's love for that queen of beauty had been proclaimed by the most resounding deeds."

"So it was her!" murmured Ermessinde.

Hugues didn't hear her, and went on, "I'm not being unfair to Lionel; I know his worth. I was surprised Alix preferred Gérard to him, but Gérard will inherit this castle and all of its vast estates, and her ambition fully accounted for it. I felt secure in that—till our quarrel with the Lords of Malize led me to summon a man capable of avenging the offenses against me; for I have a son who's no son, not even a man, but he's my own son, and the shame he causes me is magnified by the pride you take in Lionel. So I agreed to let him come to the castle.

"You know what conditions I attached to that, Ermessinde. I told you, 'I'm summoning Lionel, and I'll treat him as if he weren't the child of adultery; he doesn't know it, and he'll never know it. I'll agree that I owe him a favor, but I want you to pledge to make him leave again, even the very day he gets here, if I order it.' I don't hold it against him that he knows he's handsome, brave, and strong. I don't hold it against him that he resents the favoritism of the man he thinks is his father. It isn't because he has contempt for Gérard that I want him to leave; I want him to leave because he's in love with Alix and she's still in love with him."

"That's impossible!" cried Ermessinde, desperate for some response to his decision to separate her from her son once again.

"Impossible, Ermessinde?" said Hugues bitterly. "Impossible, you say? But when I married you, you were in love with one your father's pages, a fellow with no name and no wealth; you brought him into this castle as your brother, and he left you as your lover!"

"It's true!" said Ermessinde, lowering her eyes. "But Alix won't forget the duty she owes her husband."

"You certainly forgot! And yet I was neither a shameful libertine nor a wretched shapeless cripple. I was an old man, but an old man with a name distinguished by several victories and several honorable battles."

"It's true!" she said again, bowed down by those unfortunate memories.

"And do you remember the night I caught you, naked and mad with love, in your seducer's arms, in the arms of that vile Genoese, that Zi...? But I've sworn never utter that despicable name. Do you remember that, as weak and ill as I was, Ermessinde, I meant to kill you both, and I was knocked down by a single blow from..." Once again the name stuck in the old man's throat.

He went on, "I was knocked down like a child, onto the very bed where you'd just wronged me. And I was about to die there, with a knife to my throat, when Father Audoin entered. It was he who, unable to free me from the villain's iron grip, persuaded me to swear, on the life he was sparing, that I'd never betray the secret of your crime and I'd forgive you. I agreed to that cowardly condition. I agreed, Ermessinde, because I still loved you, as my child and my hope, because I was afraid to see my white hair ridiculed by those who'd mocked me the day I chose you as my wife. I gave my word. An hour later I would've bought it back at the price of my soul; and for the last twenty-two years that memory has weighed on me and eaten away at me... Well, I don't want my son to inherit that misery. I don't want to hear him crying out for mercy some night under your son's knife, and for me to run in, weak and shaking, to tell him, as the priest told me, 'Swear to forget, swear to forgive, and your wife's lover will let you live!' No, no, I don't want that... I don't want that!"

Ermessinde was silent, while the old man spoke with such angry intensity that it gave his body the appearance of strength. A mother's heart is capable of great resignation; and that mother, hoping to avoid being separated from her son, humiliated herself enough to say, "Not all wives have lost their sense of duty, as I did; and Alix..."

Hugues gave her a pitying look. "You committed a great crime, Ermessinde; and yet I'd trust you, who were guilty, more than I'd trust Alix, who I think is still innocent. Lionel must go; I demand it. You know what you have to do. It's you who'll make him leave the castle. I don't want to have to justify to him a decision he might want me to explain, because I might just tell him."

"Oh, no!" she cried. "Don't make me blush before my son! I'll send him away!"

"I'm counting on it. He'll leave tomorrow."

"At daybreak."

"So have him sent for."

"I'll go to him."

Ermessinde left the great hall, and Hugues summoned two servants, who took him to his apartment, holding him up by his arms; for it had been a hard day for the old man, whose only remaining strength was that of his iron will.

"Blah, blah, blah!" said the poet, interrupting the tale once again. "This is so clumsy. The story's over: we know the mystery of Hugues's hatred, we know about Lionel and Alix being in love, our curiosity is satisfied, and the audience is either leaving or booing. The play's a failure."

"But it strikes me," replied the Devil, "there still remains the working out of those passions."

"The working out of those passions? You mean like in *Zaïre* or *Phèdre*?[77] It's been a long time since the seventeenth and eighteenth century platted out their surveyor's map of the human heart. Besides, my dear collaborator—

---

[77] *Zaïre* (1732), a tragedy by Voltaire, and *Phèdre* (1677), a tragedy by Racine, are two pillars of French dramaturgy.

because if I write this play you'll be my co-writer; I'll put my name on it but you'll get a quarter of the profits—what historical flavor, I ask you, can the working out of a passion have?"

"Historical flavor doesn't seem like the highest priority in a play," said Luizzi.

"Oh," said the poet, "then we're going to fall back on the tragedy of admiration or weeping, which is to say boredom in verse."

"I beg your pardon, gentlemen," said the storyteller, "but I think you're both wrong. Passions can have a historical flavor, because the passions unfold according to the customs of their time and are marked by them. It's a long way from a crude Norman of the Middle Ages, whose answer to everything is the sword, to a sophisticate of Louis XIII's time stuffed full of Spanish gallantry and madrigals; it's a long way from a Regency libertine, wallowing in debauchery while dressed in lace, to an Imperial hussar doing his wooing with his riding crop in his hand."

"Maybe so," said Luizzi. "But besides the working out of the passions and historical flavor, this story has a resolution, and that's mostly what I want to hear."

"Let's see!" said the poet. "If it doesn't work as a play, maybe it could be a novel."

"I'll continue," said the storyteller, "and I hope the resolution will prove to you that the passions have a historical flavor and they unfold according to their century and the customs of their time." He went on, "Ermessinde was alone. Her husband's demand, to which she'd agreed so readily while he held her in the grip of cruel memories, seemed appalling to her as soon as she had to inflict it on her son. What could she say to Lionel for that exile from his father's house not to strike the young man as the vile whim of an unbearable tyrant?"

"She could tell him the truth," said the poet.

"No, sir, no!" cried the storyteller. "There exists a maternal reticence much greater than maiden prudishness. To tell a son—who's always respected you as the purest and saintliest of women—'I'm just an adulteress'; to tell a child who's proud of the name he bears with distinction, 'Your name isn't yours'; to add to the admission of the sin the admission of a lie that's lasted for twenty-two years—no, it isn't possible, no mother could do it, at least not without a terrible struggle, without..."

"Without a beautiful soliloquy," said the poet. "In fact, that was the beautiful soliloquy. So, once the soliloquy was over, what did the mother do?"

"Here's what she did..."

She went to her son, who, after what Hugues had said, was waiting for his mother. Summoning all of her courage, she said, "Lionel, you must leave this house at daybreak."

"I was expecting that, mother."

263

That reply stunned Ermessinde. After looking at her son for a long time to try to discover what could've given it away to him, she went on fearfully, "And why were you expecting it?"

"You can see I was right to expect it."

"But you had a reason to fear this misfortune?"

"Yes, mother."

"And what was it?"

"Can you give me the reason you came to tell me I have to leave?"

The poor mother was silent. She thought she'd been found out, and she hid her face in her hands and wept.

Lionel came to her and said tenderly, "Wasn't his welcome enough to warn me? But don't cry, mother, for all this will come to an end. My father hates me. Why does he hate me? I'm going to find out."

Ermessinde saw she'd been mistaken. Retreating from the idea of humiliating herself before her son, she replied, "He knows about your love for Alix."

"And that's why he's sending me away?" he asked with an incredulous smile.

"That's why, Lionel, I swear."

"Yes," he went on bitterly, "that might be true. But that's not why he sent me away four years ago, that's not why he's hated me since the day I was born. Never mind. I'll go, I'll leave this castle, never to return. Just one more night, and my father will never hear tell of me again."

"You've made up your mind awfully quickly, Lionel."

"I wanted to spare you the trouble of pleading with me, mother. And now that you've found me as submissive and obedient as you could wish, good night. You can rest till morning."

"Won't I see you before you go?"

"Oh, of course you'll see me; we're not going to part like this."

"You're not planning some act of violence, are you, Lionel? Your resignation frightens me."

"I'm imitating your own resignation, mother."

"Oh, mine's very different! But forgive me for not trusting your apparent calm; it's not in character for you."

"Time changes everything, and eats away the hardest marble."

"Humiliation endured with such patience sometimes harbors dreams of vengeance."

"Are you dreaming of vengeance?"

"This—this stubborn silence—is how misery leads to crime, Lionel."

"Did your misery lead to crime?"

"No, but perhaps it began with one."

"Mother!" he cried, taking a step back. "Mother!" he repeated in a terrible voice. But he quickly composed himself. Falling to his knees before her, he said, "Oh no! You're the purest and saintliest of women. Forgive me for having forgotten that you're resigned enough to blame yourself, so I don't blame the husband who makes you suffer, the father who's throwing me out. No, mother, no, you're not guilty—you whom I've seen, ever since I came into the world, serving this household as a model of the most steadfast virtue... No!... But you're unhappy, and that unhappiness must come to an end, for you and for me."

"What are you going to do?"

"I can't tell you till tomorrow, mother."

"And till then?"

"Till then I swear I won't fail in the respect a son owes his father."

Ermessinde left her son, dreading what would happen, but not strong enough either to predict it or to prevent it. A spirit cannot spend twenty years in habitual submissive obedience with impunity: the crease relentlessly imposed on a firm character ends up being permanent. The finest tempered steel no longer straightens when it's been bent too long. Ermessinde had reached that point: everything in her was broken, even maternal love—which, having readily bent beneath every humiliation to protect and shelter her son when he was small and weak, could no longer straighten up against him now that he was big and strong.

No sooner was she gone than Lionel himself left his room and went to the great hall of the castle. A woman was waiting in one corner, with a lamp next to her. At the sound of Lionel's footsteps she turned suddenly and cried out. Lionel ran to her, and saw it was Alix. She was weeping, and tried to hide her tears, but she couldn't: the tap was open and couldn't be shut off at will. So, unable to hide her suffering, she gave it free rein: ashamed of having been found weeping, she wept even more.

Lionel's heart was doubly defended—by the despair of his betrayed love and by the rejection of his filial affection—and he was miserable enough to be pitiless. He said coldly, "Has your husband thrown you out of his bed, that I find you here in this icy room in the middle of the night?"

An hour earlier Alix would've replied with some insulting quip; but now she was entirely beaten, and she wrung her hands and said, "Yes, he threw me out."

When Lionel had asked her that harsh question, he'd expected its humiliating assumption to wound her. Now that the assumption had been proven true, he realized his words hadn't been sarcastic, but a crude insult. "He threw you out!" he cried.

"Yes, he threw me out, with scorn and insults and blows, because..." She stopped and began to cry again.

Pity, resentment, and love competed in Lionel's heart, but anger won out. He'd loved this woman so much, he blamed her so much for having sunk so low after he'd raised her so high in his own heart, the misery she'd brought on herself reminded him so cruelly of the happiness he could've given her, that he couldn't offer her a single word of comfort. He replied bitterly, "Our fates haven't been joined, Alix, but they're similar. The man who should love you mistreats you, just as the man who should bless me curses me. You've been thrown out of your bedroom, and I've been thrown out of the castle."

"You?" she cried in horror. "You're leaving?"

"Tomorrow morning."

"Then who'll protect me here?" she asked in despair.

Lionel felt his heart opening, ready to forgive. That appeal, made in all the abandonment of misery, would no doubt have touched him coming from any other woman. But Alix had done him too much wrong, and he only said, "Haven't you chosen a protector who won't leave the castle?"

That cold reply caused Alix to recover all of her pride. "Sir, forget you found me here, weeping and moaning, and I'll forget I found you brutal and disrespectful to a woman in tears."

That reproach struck Lionel directly in his pride. The feeling that had made him so implacable was the same feeling that now made him suddenly change his tone. He didn't want anyone to be able to say a woman in tears, no matter who she was, had pleaded with him and he'd rebuffed her. So after a short silence he said, "I'll forget everything, ma'am, except what you tell me to forget. I'll forget the past, for which I have so many reasons to curse you, but I'll remember the present, for which you have the right to despise me. I'll remember I found you sad and weeping, and I didn't offer you my help and my support. I'll beg your forgiveness for that unworthy conduct by asking you to accept that help and support now."

"I thank you. I've lived this way for a year, and I can go on doing so."

"What!" he said in genuine surprise. "This isn't the first time Gérard has dared to treat you this way?"

"And I assume it won't be the last."

"Have drunkenness and debauchery made him lose his mind?"

"You're mistaken, Lionel. He was fully in his right mind when he did it."

"Then why did he throw you out?"

"Because I refused him, because he knows I don't love him. He's not as unjust as your father is to you: what reason does he have to throw you out?"

"Because he knows I love you!" Lionel replied, crossing his arms and standing before her as if to say to her, "Look how weak and cowardly I am!"

"Oh!" Ermessinde cried with a joy she couldn't contain. "So you love me?"

"Yes, I'm mad enough for that!" he said, ashamed to admit it.

"You still love me, Lionel, you just told me so," she said, trembling with intense emotion.

"I told you so?..."

"Yes, Lionel, you love me, and..." She stopped, glanced around furtively, then drew closer to him and said, "And I love you."

"You do?"

266

"You know I do, Lionel. You whose heart is full of pride, you know very well why I married your brother. You know very well you told me once your father would never accept as his daughter-in-law the daughter of woman who'd lost her reputation. You insulted me by insulting my mother, Lionel. You were pitiless toward her."

"That's because your mother passed on to you her frivolous nature and easy virtue."

"Oh, you wouldn't say that if you knew who the man was who seduced my mother and to whom I owe my birth. He was like you, Lionel. He was passionate, ruthless, handsome, and brave, like you are. She loved him the way I love you, and she threw herself away for him the way I'm throwing myself away for you."

"So who was he?" asked Lionel arrogantly.

"A Genoese nobleman who had every kind of beauty and charm and wealth and seductiveness, even that of being fatal to all the women he loved."

"And his name?"

"His name... I can tell it to you now: a strange, unknown name. They called him handsome Zizuli, and he vanished from France the way he'd come, abandoning my mother, who'd left her husband and her family for him."

"Everyone who knew you in Paris knew about it."

"But not even my bitterest enemy ever held it against me; and you threw it harshly in my face."

"I said it while offering you my hand and my name, Alix."

"Yes, but to live outside France, to bear that name like a stolen name. Well, I wanted to show you I'd have that name in all its splendor. I wanted it, and I got it."

"And does it weigh on you?"

"Enough to make me want to throw it on the ground. You're leaving the castle tomorrow, Lionel; if you want, tomorrow I'll leave too."

"You!" he said, feeling a stirring of all his desires with the intensity of ardent love in a vigorous body—a blind, willful love rooted in the senses as well as the mind. And added to it was the idea of payback, by taking Alix away from the brother who'd taken her away from him, and who left him no place by the paternal hearth. "Is that what you want? Is that what you want? Well then, so be it! But then it isn't tomorrow we should flee, it's tonight, it's in an hour."

"In an hour!" she said, now frightened at seeing the moment of action so close.

"Yes, in an hour. But are you deceiving me again? Will you come?"

"Do you doubt me, Lionel?"

"You've already deceived me once, Alix."

She hesitated, looking around wildly.

"You won't dare do it," he said.

Alix turned toward her nuptial chamber as if to listen for her husband's snoring. She glanced at Lionel, who smiled scornfully and repeated, "You won't dare do it."

Suddenly, as if struck by vertigo, she threw aside her lamp, which went out, and she cried, "Well then, come on, Lionel! Let's flee!"

It was a dark night; thick clouds, gathering slowly, intensified the darkness. Wanting to interpose a sinful act between Alix and her vacillation, Lionel took her in his arms...

"I understand completely," said the poet. "Here we'll obviously have to drop the curtain."

"It certainly seems unavoidable," laughed Luizzi.

"Who knows?" said the Devil. "Theater doesn't balk at trifles like that."

"Are you joking, sir?" said the great literary man playfully.

"Not at all. There've been precedents that make me very hopeful in that direction. The only thing that would make the scene difficult would be having an actor ready to perform on cue..."

"Especially if the play ran for a hundred performances," said Luizzi, getting carried away far enough to join in a joke in rather poor taste, especially considering his circumstances.

Chapter LXXVII: Act Three

"So," said the poet, "that'll be the end of Act Two."

"All right," said the Devil. "Let's begin Act Three in the middle of the night, at the moment when Lionel—having taken the necessary measures to make Alix leave with him—went to see old Hugues."

In the time that had passed, an awful storm had arisen in that infernal darkness, and it was raging outside and in, with terrible flashes of lightning and peals of thunder. Meanwhile Ermessinde had gone to her husband and told him of her conversation with her son. However, she mentioned only the young man's submission: she hoped to soften Hugues by saying Lionel's love for Alix must be weak, since he'd put up so little resistance to his father's wishes, and there was little risk in letting him stay around Alix, especially at a time when he'd be out on the battlefield, lance in hand, more than he'd be at the castle.

"Oh, that's the danger, Ermessinde," sad the old man. "For women are made such that they fall for a man who spends all his days and all his hours at their feet, ready to obey their least desire, a slave to their every passing whim or their most extravagant wish, an assiduous servant whom they repay in love since they can't pay him in gold... Or else they fall for a man who barely looks at them, a man who places his ambition ahead of them; and one night he comes back to the castle covered in blood and dust, his eyes shining with victory, borne along by the triumphant shouts of his soldiers, and the women are intoxicated by the sight of him and open their arms so he can rest from his noble labors on their bosoms. And that's what'll happen to Alix one night, when her husband is passed out drunk on his bed and her lover walks by her open bedroom door with his head held high. Isn't that more or less how it happened, Ermessinde?"

Ermessinde was silent a while, then answered, "As you wish, milord. He'll obey."

Just then the door opened and Lionel entered. The sight of his mother made him stop, since he hadn't expected to find her with the old man.

"Who rang for you?" asked Hugues harshly, turning toward him.

"What are you doing here?" cried his mother, hurrying to him.

Lionel paused; he had the distracted look of a man who's just committed his first crime. Then he composed himself and, gently fending off his mother, he said, "Since fate has ordained it thus, you can be a witness, mother, to what I've come to say to my father."

"You swore to leave, Lionel."

"And I will leave."

"You swore you wouldn't try to see our lord and master."

"I swore I wouldn't fail in the respect a son owes his father. So it's with respect I've come to question him."

"Be still!" cried Ermessinde. "What could you have to ask him?"

"I have to ask him, mother, why you're always weeping, and why I'm always banished."

"You want to know?" cried Hugues, rising quickly.

"Oh, be quiet, be quiet, both of you!" said Ermessinde, turning from her son to run to her husband.

Hugues looked at her, and felt pity for both mother and son. "Get out!" he said to Lionel. "Don't ask me about what I've kept locked in my heart for twenty-two years."

Those words dazzled Lionel like a beam of fatal light. "For twenty-two years!" he repeated slowly, turning to give his mother a look that held all of the suspicions that had arisen in him on hearing that interval of time.

The mother couldn't withstand her son's terrible gaze. Her shame, always falling back on her head like the eternal boulder of Sisyphus, drove her to her knees as she cried out to her husband and her son, "Have mercy! Have mercy!"

Lionel stood still with his eyes closed; then with an effort he drew his hand across his brow to wipe away the cold sweat that drenched it—for his thoughts had covered a long sad distance in that short moment. He'd reviewed his entire past, and all of his past had been explained. Coming back to the present, he opened his eyes to make sure he wasn't dreaming, and saw Hugues looking at him with savage joy and his mother on her knees not daring to meet his glance.

Lionel wasn't one of those relaxed, humane people whose hearts can be filled with sudden noble pity. He didn't forgive his mother, though he knew how long she'd suffered for her sin. But between Ermessinde's sorrow and Hugues's joy, he didn't hesitate. Bending toward his mother, he said, "Rise, ma'am, and don't cry. Lionel de Roquemure will protect you now."

"Since you wanted to know why I hate you," said the old man, "there is no Lionel de Roquemure here anymore."

"You're right, old man! Keep your name—I blush at having borne it."

The old man smiled contemptuously.

"Oh, don't laugh, Sir Hugues de Roquemure," went on Lionel. "Let each of us have what belongs to him. Earlier there was a young man here who held out his sword over the Roquemure family, and the spark that leapt from that sword was so bright no one thought to look beyond it, no one knew that name had fallen into the hands of a feeble old man and a cowardly idiot. Now that the name is no longer his, the bastard will withdraw his sword to help him walk, for he has nothing left but his sword to lean on, and he'll let men's gaze reach all the way to you. Let it be as you've said, Sir Hugues de Roquemure! You take back your name, and I'll take back my glory. I'm satisfied with that division."

"And what name will you attach to that high glory to claim it?"

"The name I'll make for myself."

"Why don't you take your father's name? You can sustain its renown."

"Whatever it was, it must've been carried nobly, since the man who couldn't pass it on to me was able to touch my mother's heart."

"He was indeed a rich and noble adventurer, that magnificent Genoese, who pleased women by his beauty and left them nothing but dishonor in farewell."

"A Genoese! A Genoese!..." repeated Lionel with a terrible premonition. He went on haltingly, "And his name?... His name?..."

"You can use it, Lionel. It's notorious for villainy and crime and beauty. Use it, and plenty more women will give themselves to the handsome Zizuli."

"Zizuli!" cried Lionel so loudly that it echoed through the castle.

Hugues was stunned, and Ermessinde stood up, as if she'd heard the roar of a wild animal.

"Zizuli! Zizuli!" repeated Lionel, staring at his mother and the old man in turn.

Hugues was delighted by Lionel's horror and despair, though without understanding the reason for it. He turned to Ermessinde and said with a cruel laugh, "Look where adultery leads, Ermessinde!"

"You don't know, Hugues?" said Lionel, drawing closer to him. "You don't know, you feeble old man who failed to kill his wife's lover, that your daughter-in-law is my father's daughter, and my father's daughter gave herself to me?"

"Alix!" cried Hugues and Ermessinde together. "Alix!"

Ermessinde fainted and dropped to the floor. But old Hugues, finding some strength in his anger, threw himself at Lionel and seized him, shouting, "Help!... Help! Soldiers, help! Death to Lionel! Death to the villain! Death to the incestuous villain!"

Lionel, his mind reeling under the shock of that terrible revelation, pushed the old man roughly away, so that he fell next to Ermessinde. Out of his wits, Lionel fled from the room and ran through the long corridors that had led him to his father's apartment. Pale, icy, shivering, he reached the great hall, where he was to meet Alix.

"You took your time!" cried a voice nearby. Lionel turned, and by the light of one flash of lightning after another, he saw his sister Alix before him. "What crime have you just committed?" she cried, seeing him shiver and tremble.

"Adultery and incest!" replied Lionel, pushing her away, while the storm broke in all its fury.

"What did you say? Have you forgotten I was waiting for you?"

"Then come with me if you dare, Gérard's wife!"

"I'm no longer that," she said, pushing open the bedroom door with her foot to reveal the wretch lying in his own bed with his throat cut.

"Ah!" cried Lionel, drawing back. "Murder too!"

"He was beginning to wake up, and I was waiting for you!"

"Then come with me if you dare," repeated Lionel, who'd lost his mind. "Zizuli's daughter, Gérard de Roquemure's adulterous widow—you're the incestuous fiancée of Zizuli's son!"

And—whether it was the two of them loudly repeating those terrible words or whether some infernal voice was uttering the words beside them—it seemed for a moment as if all the echoes of Roquemure Castle rang with the words *adultery, murder, incest.*

Then Lionel fled. Crossing the vast courtyard that separated the great hall from the castle gate, he heard the horses whinny at the sound of his armor. Though he was in a hurry to get away, and get away fast, he passed them by. But at the castle gate he saw a quick saddle horse held by a page, a superb mount Alix had ordered to be made ready for their escape. Instinctively he seized the bridle and leapt onto the horse. The portcullis rose and he left the castle, with no aim but to get away, giving no guidance to his horse, who galloped down the hill with the speed of a stag.

While all that was happening on one side of the castle, a no less horrible scene was unfolding in Sir Hugues's room. The old man and Ermessinde had risen from the floor.

"Lionel! Lionel!" she called, dragging herself toward the door by which her son had left.

"Don't worry," said the old man furiously. "You'll see him again."

Hugues wanted to go after Lionel, but Ermessinde threw herself in his way. His anger redoubled; drawing his dagger, he stabbed the poor woman. He thought he was free, but with the last of her strength she clung to him, holding him back. In the delirium of his rage he struck at her hands with his dagger to make her let go. The struggle lasted long enough for Lionel to get away. Finally Ermessinde collapsed, and Hughes was able to leave his room.

His cries, and hers, had long since roused everyone in the castle. They ran into the great hall Lionel had just left, where they found the old man furiously questioning Alix. "Where is he? Where's your lover? Where is the villain?"

She made no answer. The old man ran to his son's room, calling, "Gérard! Gérard!"

He was in there a long time without making a sound, and without anyone else daring to cross the threshold. When he came back out of the room, it was if some superhuman power were animating that feeble, aged body. The pallor of his face was frightening, and his white hair stood up on his head. Not only had he seen his son's corpse in that room, but outside, lit by flashes of lightning, he'd seen the man he believed had killed him, passing by beneath the castle wall as he fled. No doubt some demon had inspired Hugues, no doubt some awful idea had taken hold of him—one of those ideas that fall upon a man with the speed of an eagle and clutch him in talons of steel—for he uttered neither cries nor curses; but in a clipped, forceful voice unrecognizable as his, he gave a few orders.

Obedience was normal for the servants at Roquemure Castle, and yet never had orders been carried out as quickly as they were now, so appalled and surprised had all the staff been by the firmness of Hugues's voice and the self-assurance of his manner. Ermessinde, Alix, and Gérard's corpse were taken out to the castle courtyard, where three superb stallions had already been led, rearing and whinnying. The ropes were ready, and in a moment Gérard's corpse, and the dying Ermessinde, and Alix, who struggled with all her might, were bound to the three chargers.

No sooner were the knots tight than Hugues cried out in a voice of thunder, "And now let the judgment of hell be carried out!"

The portcullis opened, and the stallions, their steaming nostrils flaring at the hot scent of the other horse ahead carried in by the gusts of the storm, rushed out the gate.

Meanwhile other servants had gathered immense piles of wood and straw in the great hall of the castle. As Hughes strode firmly back into the hall he met the old priest, Father Audoin, whose age and frailty had caused him to rise late from his bed, and who had therefore witnessed only the punishment of the guilty. "What's this I hear? Gérard is dead?"

"Yes, and you can pray for the salvation of his soul."

"Ah! I've just seen the terrible vengeance you've taken for it, and it's above all for your soul I must pray."

"Don't waste your prayers, priest! At the sight of my dead son I asked heaven to grant me vengeance, but it was hell that answered me. The price of that vengeance is my soul, which I'll be sending there."

Then the old man shut the door of the great hall, and a moment later they could hear the crackle of the flames and the roar of the bonfire. Soon Hugues appeared before them all: he'd climbed to the top of the highest tower, and there, between the fire in the sky and the fire on earth, he stood as motionless as a white statue. From the summit of his blazing castle, by the light of the flames that seemed powerless to consume him, because he was to be their eternal and imperishable fuel, he witnessed the fulfillment of the vengeance hell had promised him.

The racing stallions had galloped down the hill, chasing each other, rearing up one against the next, while Gérard's corpse swung from side to side, striking the flanks and the rump and the neck of his horse, while the dying Ermessinde clung by one desperate hand to her horse's mane, while Alix fought to untie the knots that bound her to hers. As for Lionel, he'd let his noble steed run free; and, accustomed to a firmer hand, it had taken the path back to the castle. He noticed only when he saw the light of the fire ahead of him. Without understanding it, he was staring at the red glow of the flames mingled with the white fire of the lightning, when suddenly the first stallion passed next to him; and as his own proud beast reared to come to a stop he saw his brother's bleeding corpse tossing about. He cried out, and his cry was answered by another. He turned to see Alix passing on the other side, pale, disheveled, haggard, and then she too vanished ahead.

Just as when he'd learned the secret of his birth, he didn't believe it now, and he closed his eyes and wanted to run away. Then he heard a voice calling him. He opened his eyes again, and saw Ermessinde reaching out to him with bleeding hands and crying, "It's me, Lionel! It's your mother!"

At that new sight, fear, icy fear, sank into Lionel's blood and bones, and he felt he was about to lose his grip on both his mind and his body. He clung to his horse, looking around in horror to see if all those phantoms, which had rushed past him in a flash, had vanished completely. But there they were again, all three of them riding back to him, their horses rearing and bounding and running into each other, throwing their riders around on their backs: one a corpse, one a woman bleeding to death, and the last another woman—but that one twisting and turning with shouts of rage. And voices he knew all too well cried out, "Lionel, Lionel, it's me!... It's your mother... It's your sister!"

Terrible words to the poor man's ears, that made other terrible words ring over and over in his soul: *murder, adultery, incest*! Horrified, distraught, he pressed his heels into his fiery horse's flanks, and it fled with astonishing speed. Its light, slender legs skimmed the ground, while its mouth played with the bit of the bridle, which Lionel's faltering hand had dropped. Now the mighty chargers began their furious chase again, and their heavy hooves struck the path like the hammers of a hundred blacksmiths. Lionel's horse whinnied at the sound of their hoof beats, fleeing from them and returning to them, then whinnying in answer and slowing down to let one of the stallions catch up.

Lionel turned and saw Alix, panting and distraught, reaching out to him and vanishing once again as her horse carried her away. Lionel's horse stopped. A second stallion brushed past it. Lionel covered his eyes so as not to see, but he felt his brother's corpse lurch against him as it swung from side to side, striking the flanks of the horse that bore it away. Again Lionel wanted to flee; he shook and cried out—but then he felt two hands hot with blood fasten themselves around his throat. It was his mother, and she cried, "Save me, Lionel! Save me!"

He pushed her away and struck his horse furiously, and it ran, it ran wildly, with its nostrils smoking. But the stallion that carried Ermessinde rode even more furiously, biting at its muzzle, pressing against its flank, running just as fast, and the bloody hands of the adulterous mother never left the neck of the incestuous son. Then, in a burst of wild rage, Lionel drove his horse again, tearing into its sides with his spurs, driving it on with his shouts, overtaking all the stallions that pursued it, till he finally broke free of the phantom's convulsive grip. But still he could hear Ermessinde cry out, "Oh! A curse upon you!"

At that cry, the miserable wretch, whose mind was going, stopped and turned back to the phantom that had cursed him in his mother's voice. But now it was Gérard and Alix who circled him, their stallions rearing and threatening each other with their hooves. He rode off again, lying down against his horse's neck and closing his eyes. Now Alix caught up with him; leaning toward him, she grabbed hold of him, shouting to him in a voice that used no breath, a deep, broken voice that seemed to want to tell him something no one but he should hear, "Lionel, it's me... Lionel, it's me... It's your Alix, whom you love!" As he struggled to shake off that horrible grasp, she added despairingly, as if to soften his heart, "It's me... it's your sister..."

For Lionel it was as if incest, murder, and adultery had been fastened to his sides by hell itself. Distraught, enthralled by fear, he fled, he fled, he fled. But the fiery stallions pursued him and pursued him still. His maddened horse, no longer knowing which way to go, ran in endless circles around the hill at the summit of which the castle burned; and at the top of the highest tower Lionel could see the tall figure of Hugues, turning slowly like a marble statue on a pivot to follow them all with his eyes as they rode.

For an hour the terrible stampede went on like that, circling the fire amid the howling wind and the flashes of lightning whose white fire split the clouds reddened by the blaze, amid the claps of thunder mixed with the wild whinnying of the horses and the loud cracking of the structure as the castle collapsed. The furious terrible chase never slackened—till Lionel, with horrifying oaths, called on all the powers of this world for help, and since no help came, he called on all the powers of hell, and they responded. At that moment, in the delirium of his fear, Lionel gave himself and all his posterity to Satan, till there should come a descendant virtuous enough to break the infernal pact.

They say a supernatural creature, mounted on a steed of fire and leading Lionel's horse in its wild gallop, spoke quietly to the miserable man as it bore him away across country. Then, when the pact was settled and Lionel had ratified it—by throwing his spurs off into the mud and spitting on a cross they passed and staining his sword in his mother's blood—his horse stopped, dropping with fatigue; and the stallions that still pursued it fell to the ground around it.

When Lionel recovered consciousness, his mother was dead but Alix still lived.

Chapter LXXVIII: Transformations

Luizzi had listened to that horrifying tale with an ashen face and a chill in his heart.

The poet himself had been borne along by the storyteller's sinister voice. But now he recovered his imperturbable self-assurance and said to the Devil, "What, sir? Alix still lived?"

"Yes. Didn't she have to give birth to the first son of that line sprung from adultery and incest, to Lionel's son, to the grandson of Zizuli the Genoese?"

"Ah, very good. You're quite right, the ballad needs an ending. I say the ballad, because you realize an ending like that is impossible on stage, unless it's in a play by Franconi.[78] Do local legends still speak of that Roquemure family?"

"No, the name died out with Hugues and Gérard."

"But aren't there any stories about that Lionel or his son?"

"They say in the course of that astonishing ride he'd been carried in less than an hour deep into Languedoc."

"So there are Roquemures in Languedoc?"

"I don't believe so, because, according to the pact, Lionel's son had to take his grandfather's peculiar name and make his own name by rearranging its letters."

"And what name did he make?"

"Well, think about how those letters can be rearranged."

Luizzi, almost as terrified by the story he'd just heard as his ancestor Lionel must've been by that awful struggle, cried out impulsively, "No, no, there's no name in all of Languedoc that resembles that one."

"I beg your pardon," said the storyteller. "There is one. And if the gentleman, who's so interested in quaint tales, is going all the way to Toulouse, I suggest he have a look in the public library. In one corner, to the left as you go in, forgotten at the back of a bookcase, he'll find a little manuscript written in Occitan that tells the life of Lionel's son, who played a part in the Albigensian wars.[79] His name was..."

---

[78] This—a joke about the horse-stampede grand finale of the Devil's story— could refer to several generations of the Franconi family, who were playwrights and impresarios and whose specialty was a blend of theater and equestrian circus: Antonio Franconi (1737-1836), his son Henri Franconi (1779-1849), and the latter's son Adolphe Franconi (1801-55).

[79] As mentioned earlier, the Albigensian Crusade of the early 1200s was a bloody religious war in the south of France, pitting Catholics against the Catharists they considered heretics.

"What does his name matter?" said Luizzi, quickly interrupting the Devil. "What happened to Lionel's supposed son?"

"According to the terms of the pact with the Devil, he had ten years to choose the thing that would make him happy and would save him from damnation."

"And what did he choose?"

"Nothing. Surrendering to the whims of his wealthy, adventurous, carefree life, he realized only when the time was up that he'd let the ten years slip by."

Luizzi started. Carried away by his fears, he cried out like a man who's just awakening, "What's today's date?"

"The first of September, 183—..."

"Three months! I have only three months left," muttered Luizzi to himself. He fell into deep thought. Three months remained for him to make his choice. But wasn't that enough, if he knew how to use the time to understand the world, if not by direct experience than at least by having Satan tell him about it?

Meanwhile the poet had been chatting with the other passenger, both of them discussing ways of extracting a play or a dramatic piece of some other kind from that tale, like two fashionable men of letters. Just as Luizzi began to listen to them again, the stagecoach stopped. The storyteller got out, bowing to his two companions and saying, "I beg your pardon for having babbled on like that. I'm sure I must've bored you. But what can you do on a stagecoach ride except tell stories?"

Delighted at the chance to have a private conversation with him, Luizzi let him get out and then followed him. When they'd gone a short distance from the stagecoach he motioned imperiously for Satan to follow him.

The traveler obeyed, saying, "I understand you, baron. You were offended by the story I told, and I assume you want to call me out for it. But I'm in neither the right mood nor the right profession to agree to a duel, least of all with you."

"You villain!" cried Luizzi threateningly, fully convinced it was the Devil who stood before him mocking him.

"Your threats are pointless, sir. I'm a priest; and though my behavior in the past gave rise to scandal, I believe I've atoned for it by the austerity of a life of seclusion, devoted to study and meditation."

"What's the meaning of this joke?" replied Luizzi furiously.

"Here it is. On my way back from Paris to the village where I'm the parish priest, I met a young fool who knows you. I took advantage of my secular clothes, which concealed from him what I was, to show him to what sadly insane extreme you could push a literary mania that feeds on nothing but incest, murder, and bloodshed. I told him that legend, which I'd read when I was in seminary at Toulouse and I was researching old local traditions in the library."

"But that story?" said Luizzi, stunned by the other's man calm. "What about that story?"

"They say it's the story of your family, because you can spell Luizzi with the letters in Zizuli. I have to admit, I was astonished not only that you'd never heard it but that it had such an effect on you."

The baron had one of those moments in which we doubt our own sanity. He cried, "So you know me too?"

"I've known you for years, baron, and we're connected by a tragedy that must induce eternal remorse in both of us."

"Who are you?" cried Luizzi, more and more appalled.

"I'd hoped not to tell you my name. But I haven't devoted myself to a life of self-mortification only to flee, like you, from eternal shame. I'm Father Sérac!"[80]

With those words, which seemed to petrify Luizzi, the traveler bowed and went away. No sooner had he gone than the baron, thinking the Devil was playing games with him, called out, "Satan! Satan! Come back!"

Since that had no result, he rang his little bell, and Satan appeared. The form he'd adopted this time frightened Luizzi even more than when he'd shown up as Akabila: the baron seemed to see Count Cerny before him—it was him in all of his looks, his bearing, his mannerisms.

In his initial surprise Luizzi couldn't tell if he was dreaming, whether this was the Devil or the count himself. Finally he resolved to speak to this person, whoever he might be. "So you're here?"

"Here I am."

"What do you want with me?"

The Devil smiled. "Weren't you expecting me, baron?"

"Yes, I summoned you, slave," said Luizzi, finally recognizing Satan by his savage smile.

"And I came, master."

"Why did you show up in that form?"

"Because it might come in handy."

"Oh, like the form you just cast off a little while ago?"

"A little while ago? I haven't seen you since last night."

"So who was the man who just left me?"

"What! You didn't recognize Father Sérac, the Marquise du Val's former lover?"

"But wasn't that you, appearing in his form?"

"Oh, yes, on the road from Orléans, last night. It's true, I put on his clothes, because the worthy priest was well wrapped up against the cold, and I hate being cold."

"So it wasn't you who boarded the stagecoach?"

---

[80] Father Sérac's story—including the account of what he did that led him to repent and take holy vows—appears in Chapters XII-XIV.

"I couldn't: the priest was there before you, with the poet, and there was only enough room for three."

"So it wasn't you who told me that horrifying story?"

"I never talk about my business."

"But is the story true?"

"It's written down."

"Will you give me a straight answer for once in your life?"

"I don't know what you mean by a straight answer."

"Is that story true? Answer yes or no."

"What do you mean by true?"

"Did everything that man told us actually happen?"

"Yes and no! Yes for you, since you're naive enough to believe in it; no for those who'll stupidly think it's a tall tale."

"But come now, independently of what I think and what others think, what's the truth?"

"In those days they said the sun moved around the earth, and it was true. Now they say the earth moves around the sun, and now that's true."

"But surely, of those two possibilities, one of them is true!"

"Perhaps, unless the truth lies between the two."

Luizzi realized he'd never get Satan to say what he didn't want to say; and he began to think about both the Devil's stubbornness in not answering in this instance, and the fate that, during the course of this odd journey, had brought him face to face with most of the people whose lives had been mixed up with his. He detected a struggle going on around him between Satan, who was pushing him toward his doom, and some unknown force that was trying to save him. That priest who'd been placed on his path—and who'd warned him the fatal hour in which he'd have to make his choice was fast approaching—wasn't he the unwitting mouthpiece of that protecting power? And the man himself, who after a life of terrible dissolution had repented and begun a life of steady decency, wasn't he an example being offered and held up to him?

The baron's train of thought was interrupted when he had to get back on the stagecoach. But this time he was determined to think things over carefully without being swayed by any outside influence, and as he turned away he said to Satan, "Leave me alone."

"I can't do that right now."

"What do you mean, you can't? What if I don't want to hear you?"

"Then block your ears."

"But don't I already know your voice can pass through the strongest obstacles?"

"That won't be the case this time, because it isn't for your benefit I'll be talking."

"For whose then?"

"For your traveling companion."

279

"That poet?"

"For him."

"And what do you have to tell him?"

"Two anecdotes: one so he turns it into an awful novel, the other so he commits a bad deed. And yet he could turn the first anecdote into a good deed, and turn the second one into a fine comedy."

"How do you know he'll choose wrong?"

"Because I know the man, and I know all men; and because your century loves hideous paintings and scorns realistic portraits."

"And what are your anecdotes?"

"You can listen to them."

As they were talking they reached the stagecoach, and they got the last two remaining seats.

"Well!" said the poet when he saw Luizzi, "what did you do with our storyteller?"

"I let him go back to his parish."

"What! He was a priest?"

"The priest of this village."

"My word! For a priest, he certainly tells some peculiar stories, and he knows some very edifying ballads!"

"Wasn't that Father Sérac?" asked the Devil, joining the conversation. "If so, I know the ballad he told you. It's the only one he knows, and he tells it to everyone who comes along—just like an opposition politician who's always making the same speech, and a government minister who's always giving the same response to it."

"It wasn't without certain possibilities out of which you could make a good play, except for that stampede of corpses," said the poet. "I'll consider it."

"Oh, you're a playwright, sir?" asked the Devil. "What a fine thing it must be to control a whole audience by the power of your thoughts, to keep it breathless in your grip, to make it tremble and weep at will!"

"Well, yes," said the poet as smugly as possible. "That's one of the pleasures I've experienced from time to time."

"What surprises me," said Luizzi, who found himself extremely irritated by this literary gentleman who'd done him a favor, "is that people don't write comedies. There are certainly plenty of inspirations from life to draw on."

"Comedies!" cried the poet. "Where would you find one?"

"You can find them out on the high road just as easily as in a salon."

"You should ask instead how you'd write it," said the Devil.

"Well, they way they used to in the old days," said Luizzi.

"In the old days, sir, they dared to mock and condemn," replied the Devil. "Nowadays you can't do that anymore."

"You think people are more constrained and inhibited now, more enslaved in our age of liberty?"

With a scornful smirk the Devil replied, "In an age when vice is universal in society, there's no audience to laugh at vice. It's not a good idea to make fun of thieves in a prison; they won't forgive you for retelling their crimes, unless it's to learn how to imitate them."

"Still," said Luizzi, "these days, now that social distinctions are getting blurred, you can say what you want, without worrying about a reaction that used to be monolithic from a whole class sticking together."

"Come on!" said the Devil. "Who would dare depict an independent Deputy who wants to sell out, an embezzling banker, an incompetent attorney, a blowhard general, a corrupt judge, a dishonest barrister? The Chamber of Deputies, the banking industry, the legal profession, the army, the magistracy, the bar would rise up! They'd cry insolence, the undermining of morals, the collapse of the social order, the fires of revolution. In Louis XIV's time people made fun of the marquises who attended the king's levée; I defy you to put on stage the valet who dresses your own sovereign. They used to depict idiotic bailiffs; no ministerial power now would dare allow you to show an imbecile police chief. If you want to depict a brutal insolent workman, you'll find a thousand brutal insolent workmen—not counting the good ones and the fools—who feel entitled to object, and who'll boo your play while saying you're slandering the common people. If you invent a squalid, merciless rich man, you'll be thrown out of the salons for being envious and for being driven out of your mind by poverty. If you invent a careerist scholar puffed up with false learning, all of the learned bodies will rise up against the ignoramus who's trying to tear them down. If you invent a literary popinjay who ruins the jokes he steals by passing them through his pen, the gutter press will tell you you're an idiot. You're reduced to making fun of hunchbacks and of Englishmen who speak French badly: that's the sum total of your comedy. The kingdom of laughter belongs to clowns, as long as they go all the way to absurdity; because if they go only as far as realism, people will recognize some citizen belonging to some class that doesn't want to be made fun of. Equality before the law has killed satire against persons; equality before vice has killed comedy. When an old house is crumbling, it's dangerous to stick a hammer into the cracks; when a whole society feels itself teetering, it doesn't want anyone to point out the crevices in its walls. It slathers itself in laws, it whitewashes itself with respect for human rights, it props itself up with moral codes, because it's afraid of the slightest push. It's no longer just one social class that stands united against all realistic depiction, it's society as a whole—and what man is strong enough to fight that?"

"Plus which," said the poet, "all that vice lacks depth and energy. These days it's hard to find even a little bland folly…"

"I assure you, sir," said the Devil, "there are still some enormous follies…"

"Or a little listless passion…"

"I promise you, there are still some grotesque passions…"

"Our lives are ordered and supervised by regulations and travel permits and gendarmes and passports…"

"I can attest there are people who evade all those controls…"

"For a little while, maybe, till they end on the scaffold…"

"Permanently, and while keeping their reputations…"

"Here's an example," said the poet. "Leaving aside the diabolical element in the priest's story, a thing like that would be impossible in our times."

"In what way? Is it incest it would lack? That's just a matter of chance—and you, Baron de Luizzi, have run across a case of the most horrifying, the most complicated, the most hideous incest…"

"Me?" said Luizzi.

"There are more cases than you think, sir," replied the Devil, "and you've bumped into more than one in the salons of Paris. But most particularly, baron, you've shaken hands with a judge who, being caught in an intimate encounter by the girl's brother, was forced by that brother—on pain of his slitting both their throats—to marry the girl. And do you know who that poor girl was? She was the daughter of that very judge, who'd been her mother's lover! And do you know why the brother was so insistent on reparation for an offense that hadn't really taken place? It's because his sister was pregnant, and he wanted to hide his own act of incest by making his sister commit two of them!"

Oh, come on!" cried Luizzi in disgust. "That's not possible!"

"I'm not saying it's possible, I'm saying it's true. And what if I told you the story of the father who carefully raised his daughters according to strictly materialistic principles, in total moral corruption, so nothing would stand in the way of his villainous intentions?"

"And did he carry out the crime?" asked Luizzi.

"The funny thing is—if you can find anything funny in the whole business—it was precisely the father's teachings that prevented the crime."

"That strikes me as unlikely," said the poet.

"Here's how it happened…"

The day the philosophical father decided it was time to ask his daughter for that criminal love, she answered, "No, I don't want to."

"Do you have prejudices against it, my girl?"

"Of course not. But you're old and ugly."

"Well then, if you won't consent willingly, I'll take what I want by force."

Upon which the girl picked up a knife and cried, "Stay away, or I'll kill you!"

"You'd kill your own father, you wretch?"

"Well, didn't you teach me a father's just a man like any other?"

And no matter what he tried, the moral corrupter was unable to overcome his daughter's terrible logic: "If the only thing keeping me from giving myself to you is a moral prejudice, then the only thing keeping me from killing you is also just a moral prejudice. And I'm without prejudices, thanks to you."

"Stories like that aren't fables invented for fun," said the Devil. "They're true, the people in them are real, you know them all, and you bow to them respectfully. So don't be surprised any more by Father Sérac's fantastical tale."

"So it's true?" asked Luizzi.

"Based on what I've just told you, there doesn't seem to be anything implausible about it. It isn't the crime itself that would be implausible, since as you can see our own century offers even more horrifying examples. It's not the mystery of Lionel and Alix being related to each other that's implausible, since the fact of their being brother and sister was concealed beneath two adulteries, and there are completely legitimate confraternities that remain undiscovered."

"This all seems to me rather extraordinary," said the poet. "Civil law has certainly hampered comedy by killing off the premise of long-lost unexpected recognition."

"I could prove the contrary on the spot," said the Devil.

"My word," said the man of letters, "go ahead. I'd be delighted to have an opportunity to find out that our century lacks nothing that made earlier ages so fertile in great works!"

"I assure you, it lacks nothing," said Satan. "Neither vices nor follies nor passions nor strange occurrences nor odd characters... except..."

"Except what?" asked the poet.

"Except a man of genius to turn it all into art," said Luizzi.

"So says the millionaire baron!" scoffed the poet. "What's lacking is an audience that can appreciate it."

"So says the writer who's been booed!" said the baron.

"It lacks both one and the other, gentlemen," said the Devil with a bow for each of them. "And now that we're all in agreement, I'll begin."

COMEDY

Chapter LXXIX: The Banker

It was early in the spring of 1830. In a luxurious office on the second floor of a large building on the rue de Provence, a man sat carefully reading the newspapers his servant had just brought him. That man was the banker Matthieu Durand.

"The banker Matthieu Durand!" cried the poet. "I know him well. He has an estate a few leagues outside Boismandé, where I'm actually supposed to visit him on my way back from Toulouse."

"Ah!" said the Devil. "That's an odd coincidence, and I'm not sure I should keep going."

"On the contrary, the story's much more interesting when you know the people involved. I won't be sorry to hear a full account."

"As you wish. In any case, apart from a few details this story could be that of lots of people."

And Satan resumed:

At that time Matthieu Durand was only fifty-five, though he looked older. The deep lines that crisscrossed his broad, open, thoughtful brow were a testament to the constant stresses of an active, hardworking life. However, when he wasn't busy—a rare occurrence—his face expressed a marked benevolence for everything around him; and the sound of his voice, encouraging rather than patronizing, seemed to convey to everyone, "I'm happy, and I want you to be happy too." Still, one might've noticed that his good fortune seemed to fill him with pride rather than happiness, and that he was eager to show it off and let it be pondered, as if he enjoyed it best for its effect on others. It wasn't a matter of humiliating people who came to him, it was more to show them by his personal example what any man can achieve by patient labor and honorable behavior.

Furthermore, the overall impression left by Durand's appearance was one of strong, quick intelligence. When he listened to someone discussing business, his slight frown gave him a look of absorption, of missing not a single word or gesture or movement; that capacity for taking everything in was so lively and so complete that when he replied his habit was to give a rapid summary of everything he'd been told, with remarkable clarity and precision. After that came his observations, either accepting or refusing or modifying the propositions he'd just heard. That's when Durand's most important and at the same time most hidden quality became manifest: a cold, calm, polite stubbornness in his ideas, a stubbornness that led him never to change his mind no matter what argument was advanced.

I say deliberately that he was oddly stubborn in his thinking, because he changed his mind more easily than anyone. So, after rejecting some deal and loftily refuting its reasoning, he might suddenly offer his name and his capital to support that same deal. At other times he might extend a large line of credit to a businessman just when all the other bankers were beginning to doubt his solvency, and when he himself knew better than anyone the troubled state of the man's affairs. Furthermore, no one had ever been able to deduce his reasons for reaching decisions so contrary to his own interests; some said it was whim, others that it was generosity—but it was difficult to attribute fantastical whims to a man of such great probity in the general conduct of his business.

Generosity might've been a better explanation for his behavior, because Durand had a reputation for being generous, though sometimes he'd been known to be adamant in refusing certain requests for help. Only one man thought the real explanation was sheer calculation. That man was Monsieur Séjan, the chief clerk at Durand's bank. But he couldn't explain what the aim of that calculation was. Once when someone asked him what branch of arithmetic it was that led Durand to lend a hundred thousand francs to a bankrupt debtor, old Séjan merely replied, "It's indirect arithmetic." What could "indirect arithmetic" even mean? Monsieur Séjan didn't explain, and retreated into stubborn silence, which he made look profoundly subtle by a slight smile and a slight wink. Those departures from the narrow path of sound business practice, though they were fairly frequent, didn't cause any alarm; for Durand's reputation for probity and competence was beyond suspicion, and he was rich enough to risk ruin without anyone noticing...

"But I see no point in drawing out the portrait of Matthieu Durand any further," said the Devil, interrupting himself, "and I think his own actions and words will do a better job of depicting him than I could." And he went on thus:

So Matthieu Durand was in his luxurious office, a fine room decorated with magnificent paintings, hung in sober green wallpaper with a wide border of black velvet, and furnished with the supreme extravagance that can pay top price for what's handsome and good. When he'd read all the newspapers with great attention, the banker opened one of the drawers of the massive desk at which he was seated and pulled out a sheet of paper, which he read with even greater attention. He crossed out a few lines, added a few more, and began rereading the contents from start to finish, half muttering the words aloud, while with the pen in his hand he gave the text a final polish by fastidiously adding commas and other punctuation. Then he tugged on one of three bell ropes whose cords, each of a different color, hung above his desk. Still, he didn't ring till he'd looked the paper over once again—like a mother who's finished dressing her child and who, after having inspected his clothes fold by fold, pin by pin, and his hair curl by curl, places the child a few steps away so she can better review the whole ensemble and make sure nothing's missing.

A moment later his servant appeared, and Durand said, "Send in Monsieur Léopold." As the man was about to go the banker added, "Take the little staircase that leads from here down to the mezzanine, where Monsieur Léopold must be waiting. Bring him back the same way; there's no need for the people in the anteroom to see I have a visitor."

The servant left; and the banker, remaining alone, opened the correspondence that had been set down next to him. He mostly just glanced at the letters and sorted them into small pasteboard file boxes. He added annotations to a few, and two or three whose contents seemed to upset him he put away in his desk.

Finally the servant returned with a young man of about twenty, who came to a stop before the banker as if struck by respect and admiration.

"Let them know I'll be receiving visitors in a moment," said Durand to his servant, who withdrew. Then he turned to Léopold and said gently and benevolently, "Monsieur Léopold, I have a favor to ask of you."

"A favor! From me?" cried the young man intently. "What must I do, sir? You know my life is yours, and if I have to sacrifice it…"

"No, my boy," replied the banker, damping his enthusiasm with a gracious smile. "The favor I have to request won't require your life, but it does call for promptness and discretion."

"Oh, if it's a secret, believe me, I'd die rather than give away a word."

"You're exaggerating the importance of what I need you to do, Léopold."

"That's too bad, because I'd like to find some way of finally proving my gratitude. All of your employees think of you as a father, sir, but to me you were a god of salvation."

"Your mother was left penniless, and though your father died of his wounds in 1815, he was denied a veteran's pension. That's a serious injustice."

"And you nobly repaired it, sir. You came to my mother's rescue."

"Could I leave a brave soldier's widow destitute?"

"You took care of me, and it's to your generosity I owe the education I received. That was a good deed…"

"Yes, Léopold, I think it was a good deed, and I believe I have the right to say so myself. The thing is, you see, I left my village barely knowing how to read. The little I know now I had to learn by stealing hours from the work that kept me alive. I learned to read without a teacher, I gradually got rid of my peasant's dialect without a teacher; and then when I finally got a starting position I didn't want to seem more ignorant than my young friends who'd graduated from the lycées, and I tried a little Latin."

286

"By yourself?"

"By myself, in my garret room. I wanted to learn a little history, a little math. I enjoyed chemistry, I studied physics. Well, if I were to admit everything, I learned to play the violin, and decently. By dint of hard work and frugality, I was able to undertake a couple of small business deals, then some larger ones, always acting alone, but always persevering, and in the end I made myself what I am now."

"You've made yourself into one of the most important men in France."

"At least one of the most respected, I hope. But let's get back to the favor I have to ask of you. Here's a memo, a letter, anyway a document I need four or five copies of. Take it home, and make the copies this evening. Your time at the office isn't mine to dispose of, and Monsieur Séjan would object if I took you away from your work. So I'm counting on your kindness for this."

"Oh, sir!" said Léopold in embarrassment. "Don't speak of my kindness. Every hour of my life belongs to you."

"Above all, don't show this to anyone, not even your mother."

"I promise, sir."

"By the way, how is she?"

"Very well, and she'll be delighted to hear…"

"That I asked about her health," said the banker with a smile. "And no doubt she'll go around singing the praises of Monsieur Matthieu Durand, who asked about Madame Baron."

"Don't hold her gratitude against her!"

"I was joking, my boy. Your mother is an honest, worthy woman. She exaggerates a little what I've done for her, but that feeling arises from a virtue so uncommon that I'd commend it, if her gratitude were addressed to someone other than me. Anyway, give her my best."

"I thank you on her behalf, sir. But when will you need the copies?"

"Tomorrow morning."

"Then I'll bring them first thing, since you're not leaving for The Pond till tomorrow morning."

"You're right, tomorrow's Sunday, and I'm going this evening. My daughter would scold me if I didn't get there till tomorrow; she's going to a dance at a neighbor's place in the country, and I'm taking down who knows how many little trinkets for her."

"I could spend today making these copies."

"No, we'd have to get permission from Monsieur Séjan to release you. Better would be for you to come out to The Pond tomorrow and spend the day with us. You can come to the dance in the evening. Men who dance are always welcome."

That suggestion made Léopold blush; he lowered his eyes in embarrassment and hesitated.

Durand frowned slightly. "Can't you do me that pleasure, sir?" he asked a little curtly.

"It's just that an invitation like that overwhelms me, because I know it's the most flattering possible reward for those of your employees to whom you extend it. My mother will be so happy, so proud!..."

Durand's face cleared, and he replied with charming benevolence, "Well, if you find you're not too bored at The Pond, someday you can ask her to come along with you."

"Oh, sir!" said Léopold with tears in his eyes, and choking with gratitude.

"That's all right, my boy!" said Durand, holding out his hand.

Léopold was so overjoyed, his heart was so full, that he seized the banker's hand and kissed it, like the hand of a king who's just granted one of his subjects some major pardon.

Durand watched him go, and the intense self-satisfaction he'd kept inside till then spread across his face. He lifted his head proudly and let out a muffled exclamation of triumph. Then he paced around his office two or three times to give that emotion time to dissipate. When he was fully composed he sat back down at his desk and rang the bell. The servant reappeared.

"My word," said the poet, "you seem to know that excellent Matthieu Durand very well. He's what I call a really good-hearted man. He has only one fault I know of."

"And what's that?" asked the Devil.

"Do I have the honor to be addressing one of his friends?"

"I'm Count Cerny," said the Devil, "and I'm only telling you something I learned by a very odd chance. You can say anything."

"Well, mixed in with all of his fine qualities and his financial acumen, Monsieur Durand has a fault that lowers him to the level of the shabbiest peddler of cotton bonnets."

"And that fault is?"

"It's a classic, but a classic taken to extremes. And his Monsieur Séjan jokes about it whenever he buys a new book. The first thing he does is count the lines on the page. If there aren't as many as in a compact edition of Voltaire, he says the author and the publisher are robbing the readers."

"I can't agree," said the Devil. "It seems to me, as far as modern literature goes, the more lines there are on the page, the more they're robbing the readers."

"What?" said the man of letters.

"But let's get back to Matthieu Durand," said Satan. "His servant had just entered..."

Chapter LXXX: The Builder

"Who's waiting to see me?" asked Durand.

"Here are the names," said his servant, handing him several small pieces of paper.

The banker looked them over, pausing at one of them. "Who's this Monsieur Félix from Marseilles?"

"A very elderly gentleman, who looks at least seventy-five. He was the last to arrive."

"So he'll be last."

"The first was the Marquis de Berizy."

"Send in Monsieur Daneau, and beg Monsieur de Berizy's pardon; it was an appointment made in advance."

Monsieur Daneau entered a moment later. He greeted the banker with noticeable awkwardness, no doubt arising from his diffidence at finding himself in the presence of one of the wealthiest financiers in Europe.

Durand didn't seem to notice Daneau's embarrassment, and as he motioned him to a chair with a welcoming gesture he said, "I'm seeing you first, sir, because I know there's never enough time to get all your business done, and time's a resource that can't be wasted without serious consequences. So, please tell me how I can be of use to you."

Daneau was a tall, broad man with a red face and large feet and hands; everything about him suggested a robust development of the physical powers fueled by red meat and Burgundy. Yet beneath that rough surface a quick, subtle intelligence was visible, and he expressed himself easily and correctly. While Durand considered him with the clear direct gaze by which he seemed to untangle the most obtuse locutions and the most involved business matters, Daneau coughed and lowered his eyes and began thus: "Sir, the errand I've come on today is rather bold; but you'll forgive it in a man who stands on the brink of ruin and dishonor on the very eve of seeing his fortune made. I'm a building contractor."

"I know that, sir."

"I currently have six houses under construction. I was expecting to put them on the rental market in April of this year, by finishing the interior work over the winter. But the weather's been so severe it's been impossible to get as much as an inch of ceiling or a yard of painting done, so I'm no further along than I was six months ago. However, not anticipating a winter as hard as the one we've just had, I'd made a number of commitments for this month and the months to come. I could easily have fulfilled those commitments if my plans hadn't been thwarted by weather that doesn't come along as often as once in ten years; I'd have found the money, either by mortgaging those houses or by selling them. But as easy as it is to raise money on a house that's finished and bringing in rent, it's correspondingly impossible to do so when there's a lot of work still to do. Only we builders have a clear enough sense of their future worth, and of the expenses that remain, to see the undoubted outcome of the business and have confidence in it."

"I understand you perfectly, sir," said Durand, observing the man even more carefully. "But those houses, even unfinished, still have a tangible value, on which it shouldn't be difficult to raise funds."

"I can't hide from you, sir, that the present value of those houses is already committed, for the most part. I estimated the six houses I was building would be worth three million, and I had barely three hundred thousand francs to start the work. So once I'd paid for part of the land, I mortgaged it to begin building. Once I had the ground floors done, I borrowed on them to build the second floors, and so on. Today I'm about a million two hundred thousand francs in debt in mortgages on those houses, plus four hundred thousand francs in commitments on orders whose payments I'd spaced out across April, May, and June, figuring by then my cash flow would be assured by the ease with which I could borrow on houses worth a total of three million. But now they won't be worth that till July, and even then maybe not."

"How so?" asked Durand, who seemed to be questioning the man more to find out how he thought about business than to understand the business himself.

"Here's how. After I'd paid all my contractors in installments, thanks to the money I borrowed, I had to settle up my accounts with them at the start of winter. That already began to make them nervous; so when it came time to finish the work, they asked for half in cash, half in installments. Today's the end of the first fortnightly pay period after work began again, and I have to pay out thirty thousand francs, including fifteen thousand in cash for the workmen; and in three days it'll be the end of the month, and I'll need sixty-two thousand francs for the partial loan repayment that's due. So here's where I stand, sir: if I can't get those fifteen thousand francs this morning, the workmen won't be paid this afternoon, the work will stop, my houses will sit unfinished, and my credit will be ruined; and if it comes to bankruptcy and seizure of assets, houses that in three months, with a hundred thousand écus of work, would be worth three million, might sell, maybe a year from now, by authority of the court, for twelve or fifteen thousand francs, because between now and then they'll deteriorate since they won't have been sealed and secured against the weather. I'll be ruined by a deal that should've made me rich, and that would've made me rich if the winter hadn't been so awful."

For a long time the banker thought over what he'd heard, while the builder anxiously studied his face for any sign of his decision. Finally Durand turned to Daneau and said, "How many contractors are you dealing with?"

"A lot, sir, because I had to divide up the work to get it done faster. So for those six houses I have that many different contractors for framing and metal-work and carpentry, plus six chimney builders, six painters—all of them honest men, sir, who've gotten where they have by hard work, for they all started with nothing."

"Fine, fine! So that comes to about thirty or so contractors, honorable men, according to you?"

"Yes, sir, all of them with excellent reputations."

"And men who have the vote, no doubt.[81] And what about the masonry contractors?"

"I'm doing the bricklaying myself, because I'm a master mason."

"Doesn't matter, since you had to subcontract with suppliers for brick and stone and plaster and lime and sand. And you had to pay a lot of laborers."

"Two hundred laborers, and more than twenty suppliers."

"Oh, very good, very good! And they've put a great deal of trust in you?"

"Nothing I've done up to now would've jeopardized that trust."

The banker looked at him candidly and said with great benevolence, "You won't jeopardize it now."

"How's that possible?"

"Listen, Monsieur Daneau, I'm not involved in your line of business; but based on what you've just told me, you must be dealing with men who got where they are by hard work."

"That's true for all of us, Monsieur Durand. I learned my trade as a ma-son's apprentice. It's the same story for all my contractors."

"And that's my story too, Monsieur Daneau. I came to Paris forty years ago with a hundred sous and a wish to make my own way. I'm a man of the people, just like you, just like your contractors, just like your workmen; and I won't fail men who haven't been as lucky as I was."

"Oh, sir!" cried the builder. "That's an act of generosity!"

"Only of justice, Monsieur Daneau, that's all. I'm not some great lord, I'm a peasant's son, a laborer's son, and I haven't forgotten what I was."

"Oh, sir!" cried Daneau again, unable to put his gratitude into words.

"I'm doing it for you, for them, for the workmen who would've suffered from your ruin as well."

"Oh, if only I could tell them!"

"There's no need. The pleasure of being of use is already reward enough. But I should tell you how I intend to handle this business. You'll give me a gen-eral mortgage on your houses."

"That's only fair."

"And I'll open a line of credit for you of four hundred thousand francs."

---

[81] In 1830, the date of this episode, the right to vote belonged to men at least thirty years old who paid 300 francs or more in direct taxes.

"A line of credit!"

"Yes, Monsieur Daneau, that's the only way I operate. Every time you have to pay a bill, you'll do it by means of a note drawn on my bank—a note that'll be made good within twenty-four hours."

"But that's worth a hundred times more than cash, sir, and I won't need cash the moment it's known I'm backed by the firm of Matthieu Durand."

The banker didn't seem to hear him, and went on, "As for the fifteen thousand francs you need today, draw them on me, and give your contractors the money orders, to be remitted to my cashier. Furthermore, Monsieur Daneau, now that I've become your backer, I'd like all the bills you sign to be payable here; that's part of the accounting system I've instituted in my firm."

"But that's overflowing my cup, sir: that's giving my note of hand the value of ready cash."

"I'm delighted that suits you. Beyond that, Monday morning I'll meet here with my lawyer and with yours. I'll give the order to be passed on to the mortgage department, and we'll get it all settled in two days. Tomorrow, if you can, come out and spend an hour or two at The Pond; we'll be able to talk more freely..."

"I'll be there, sir, I'll be there. But... but... allow me to say... to thank you... to...," the builder stammered with tears in his eyes.

"Forgive me, Monsieur Daneau. I've got people waiting to see me, and I have to send you away."

"Yes, sir, of course..."

"Goodbye, and see you tomorrow."

And he had the builder shown out before the latter had a chance to unburden his heart of all the gratitude that filled him, so that no sooner had he reached the office door than he began looking for someone to tell about the banker's goodness and generosity. So badly did Daneau need to share the feelings oppressing him that he began to praise Durand to the servant who was waiting for him at the bank door with his cabriolet. He stopped two or three of his friends to tell them he'd opened an account with the banker Matthieu Durand, the most benevolent man in the world—so straightforward and so good and with so little pride that he, Daneau, had the most complete admiration for the man.

"Well, I think he deserved it," said Luizzi, who was listening out of sheer idleness.

"What!" said the Devil. "Lending on the security of a mortgage—what could be more generous! Demanding enormous guarantees—what could be more benevolent!"

"You're a gentleman, Count Cerny," said the poet, "and you don't like finance. All of your little witticisms won't change the fact that your portrait of Matthieu Durand makes him look admirable."

"Admirable, that's the word," said Satan. "And you'll understand that when you see the reverse of the medal. But to show it to you, I have to go on with my story, and we have to return to the banker's office."

Chapter LXXXI: A Gentleman and a Pauper

The Marquis de Berizy had just been shown in. The greeting Matthieu Durand gave him was perfectly polite, but marked by the modest reserve that showed he understood the difference between himself and the man he addressed. If you'd seen them standing there together—the Marquis de Berizy, a rather carelessly dressed man of fifty with a tanned complexion and rough hands, and the banker Matthieu Durand, meticulously combed and shaved and dressed, with white hands and pink nails—you'd certainly have taken the nobleman for the bourgeois and the bourgeois for the nobleman. The banker's soft, melodious voice also sounded more aristocratic than the marquis's loud, almost hoarse speech. But closer examination would've revealed that the care with which the banker spoke and in what he said proved he wanted his fine manners to leave a good impression; whereas the casualness of the marquis revealed a man used to being unapologetically at his ease.

"To what do I owe the honor of a visit from the Marquis de Berizy?" asked Durand.

"Here it is, sir. Are you aware that by order of King Charles X I've just been named a peer of France?"

"I know it, as does everyone."

"And like everyone else, do you perhaps wonder how I reached the peerage?"

"You bear a great name, marquis."

"And you bear the name of an honest man, Monsieur Durand—which these days is worth just as much. But the truth is, it's not entirely because of the great name you speak of that I reached the peerage; it's because I'm one of the richest landowners in France. The king believes men of large fortune have a greater interest in maintaining the civil order than those whose aspirations to fortune are based on future revolutions. So you see, I'm a peer of France for the same reason that would make you one tomorrow, if you wanted."

The banker smiled disdainfully.

The marquis went on, "But that isn't the point. Let me return to the business that brought me here. I got news of my promotion to the peerage after I'd spent twenty years accustomed to being nothing more than a bumpkin who's useful to my country—for part of my fortune is based on agriculture. We neglect the land in France, Monsieur Durand; we forget agriculture is an industry... But listen to me yapping away as if I'd already begun serving as a Deputy! Anyway, I'd been living quietly on my land when it pleased the king to make me a peer of France. I'll therefore do my best to be a good peer of France. But in addition to the political duties I'll have to carry out, there's one I mean to impose on myself, and that I assume you won't disapprove of; for the splendor of your establishment here proves you don't agree with the economists who claim all money spent on luxury is a theft from the public prosperity. I haven't come to Paris to be ruined; but since the king has raised me to a prominent position, I mean to sustain it by a suitable outlay."

"I understand perfectly," said the banker, choosing his words carefully, like a man who means to show he can be patient.

The marquis noticed, and went on, "I beg your pardon for telling you all that; but that preamble will make clear to you why I have a service to ask of you and what that service is. As I said, I've decided to relocate to Paris. So I sold a forest whose management I can no longer oversee, and I intend first of all to buy a mansion in Paris, and then to invest part of the capital I've realized, either in the public funds or in a banking firm, so as to use the interest on my active capital to offset the dormant capital I'll sink into a mansion."

"And you've chosen my bank?" asked Durand, betraying a slight emotion.

"Yes, Monsieur Durand, I've chosen your bank, because your reputation for probity and honor is acclaimed throughout France."

"We have to have that, we men of the common people," replied the banker, once more assuming his air of modesty.

"Plus which," laughed the Marquis de Berizy, "you're worth twenty-some million, which is no trivial accessory."

"My supposed net worth is much exaggerated, sir," said the banker with one of those looks that confirms what the words deny. "But whatever my fortune is, it was honestly gained; it's the fruit of patient labor, for I started with nothing. I'm the son of a poor man, a laborer who left me nothing but an honorable name, a love for hard work, and some honest principles."

"And as you see, Monsieur Durand, in spite of what people say, that was a rich enough inheritance, an inheritance that has multiplied splendidly in your hands."

"I'm honored by it."

"And with good reason... But tell me what I should expect from you. Will you take on the investment of my capital?"

"I'm at your orders, marquis, and it's a done deal if my bank's usual terms are agreeable to you—for my firm doesn't grant privileges, and I can do more for the Marquis de Berizy than I'd do for the least of my depositors."

"And I ask for no more than that. Can you tell me the terms?"

"Forgive me, marquis, but I'm obliged to see other clients, whose business is more urgent than yours, for they've come to ask for money instead of offering it. If you'd be so good as to step into the office of the head of my accounts department, Monsieur Séjan, you can arrange matters with him; everything he does will be done well."

The marquis bowed in assent, and Durand rang the bell. His servant appeared. "Who's waiting?" asked the banker.

"That old Monsieur Félix."

"Oh," said the Marquis de Berizy, "an old man who's almost eighty. Now I blame myself for having kept you so long."

"Some unfortunate fellow who needs my help," said the banker to the marquis while he wrote out a note.

"I know you welcome them with a kindness that must bring a lot of them here."

"Not everyone thrives, marquis, and I never forget where I came from," said Durand sentimentally. Then he handed the servant the note he'd written, and said, "Show the marquis to Monsieur Séjan's."

The marquis and the banker bowed to each other politely, and for a moment Durand was left alone. "Ah," he muttered to himself through clenched teeth, "those great lords need the man from nowhere. They reach that point, they all reach that point."

"Is this the reverse of the medal you were promising us?" interrupted the poet.

"It's about to begin," said the Devil, "for a moment later Monsieur Félix was announced."

The man's appearance had the dignity inherent in robust old age. He dressed simply, without looking neglected. Matthieu Durand examined him with a quick once-over that didn't seem to disconcert the old man, and he in turn studied the banker with a close attention that only the authority of great age could excuse.

Durand was all the more offended by it because he felt the man was imposing on him. So, without offering him a seat, he said, "Who are you and what can I do for you?"

"This letter will explain, sir," replied Monsieur Félix, and without waiting for Durand's reply he pulled up a chair and sat down.

The banker found that implied rebuke rather bold, and he gave the old man a look to warn him he was being impertinent, but his glare was quelled by the other's tranquil, serene countenance. Durand opened the letter and read it; it contained only a few lines, written in haste:

Sir—and friend,

Monsieur Félix, the bearer of this letter, is a retired businessman who's suffered terrible misfortunes. I'd be grateful to you for anything you can do for him.

"This letter is from Monsieur Dumont, of Marseilles?" asked Durand.

"Yes, sir."

"Of course I'll help a man recommended to me by Monsieur Dumont," said the banker haughtily. "Here's what I can do for you, sir," he added, taking a stack of coins out of his desk drawer and offering them to the old man.

"That's not enough," said Monsieur Félix.

"What's the meaning of that tone?" cried Durand.

"Please listen to me, sir."

"All right, but make it fast; I have business waiting."

"I'll try to be brief. I come from a prominent family in trade. My father provided me with an excellent education."

"That's a benefit I myself didn't enjoy, sir."

"You?..." said the old man with a frown. Then he went on, "It's true, I've heard that. I was luckier. I was twenty when my father died and left me an immense fortune. But his investments in India and China, which had prospered in his hands, collapsed in mine."

"You hadn't been raised in the hard school of poverty, sir. You only know the value of money when you've accumulated it by your own labor."

"I'm sure you're right, sir. In any case, by the time the Revolution broke out my business had begun to totter, and the war with England robbed me of several valuable cargo shipments; and I was ruined and forced to declare..."

"Bankruptcy," interrupted Durand, as the old man hesitated to say the word.

"I declared bankruptcy," said Monsieur Félix firmly. "I fled France with a few of my assets, and I was convicted..."

"As a bankrupt?" asked Durand with a start. Then he recovered and went on, "Well sir, what can I do about all that?"

"Here's what. I left France more than thirty years ago. I spent that time, not in rebuilding the fortune I'd lost, but in making enough to pay back my creditors or their heirs, so as to rehabilitate my name. I just about managed that, sir: I gave them everything I brought back from the United States; I have nothing left, but I'm still short fifty thousand francs."

"And I assume you've come to ask me for it?"

"I've come to ask you for it, sir."

"Forgive me, sir, but the truth is, I don't understand you. I want to believe your story, and I don't mean to say anything unkind. But I can't play treasurer for every bankrupt in France."

"Don't forget, an old man of eighty is asking you for the means to retrieve his honor."

"I'm not the one who made you lose it."

"Of course fifty thousand francs is a huge sum, but you've occasionally spent that much to buy a painting."

"I think I've got the right to do whatever I want with my fortune," said the banker bluntly. "Because I earned that fortune sou by sou, I wasn't somebody's rich heir. My father..."

"Your father!" interjected the old man with intense feeling.

"My father didn't leave me millions to throw away. He was a laborer, sir, truly an honest laborer. I was born in poverty, I grew up in poverty, and that, sir, is why I don't feel obligated to mend the follies and blunders of people who were rich and didn't know how to stay that way."

"If you knew what feeling drove me to this drastic action, you'd have pity on me."

"Go ask Monsieur Dumont, sir."

"I'm sorry," said the old man solemnly as he rose to go. "I thought you'd understand me better than he would." He bowed to the banker and left.

"Well then!" said the Devil, interrupting his own story. "What do you think of your benevolent millionaire now?"

"My word," said Luizzi, "he had good reason. To shovel fifty thousand francs at the first fellow who comes along would strike me as a little foolish."

"I know people who aren't that rich who've handed two hundred and fifty thousand over to some rascal because it pleases their vanity," said the Devil.

That reminded the baron of his foolishness in the whole business with Henri Donezau,[82] and he fell silent, not wanting to give Satan a chance to say anything offensive to him that he couldn't ask satisfaction for, since the Devil and priests declined to duel.

"You really just resent bourgeois finance," said the poet, "and your depiction of the gentleman proves it."

"You'll see," said Satan. "But before we introduce new characters, let me wrap up with Matthieu Durand."

After Monsieur Félix left, the banker paced angrily around his office for a while. After a few minutes he rang violently and said to his servant, "If the gentleman who just left ever comes back, you will not receive him."

"Very good, sir."

"Who's still there?"

"A dozen people who told me they've come in reference to Monsieur Daneau."

"Excellent, excellent!" said the banker, with all his good cheer returning. "Send them in."

The first one was a metalwork contractor.

"What's this about, sir?" asked Durand, as if he didn't know why the man had come.

"I just want to ask you for a simple explanation. Monsieur Daneau gave us vouchers payable by your cashier and promissory notes redeemable here. The vouchers weren't paid, and we're afraid the notes won't be either."

"They will be, and the vouchers too, sir."

---

[82] See Chapter LI, in which Luizzi gives Henri Donezau that amount so he can appear to have his own fortune when he marries Caroline Dilois.

"Ah!... So what he told us was true? Monsieur Daneau has a line of credit with you of four hundred thousand francs?"

"That's right, sir."

"You've saved him, sir."

"I didn't do it just for him. I know what his commitments were to you and to lots of others. And as long as I'm able to, I'll back a man on whom the fortunes of so many honest men depend, and the fortunes of so many laborers in turn."

"Oh, Monsieur Durand, that's the act of a good heart! No other banker in Paris would've done that."

"It's not just the banker who did it, sir, it's the man who remembers what he once was; a man who, like you, started out as a laborer; in short, a man of the common people."

"Oh, we know you're a friend to the working man and to honest men."

"I do what I can for them, and I'm sorry I can't do more."

"And, in your position, is there anything you want, Monsieur Durand?"

"Nothing for myself... But I sometimes wonder whether, if the rights of the common people were better represented in government..."

"I'm a voter, Monsieur Durand; and if you ever stood for election..."

"I've never thought about it... But you must be in a hurry. I'll initial your vouchers and they'll be paid."

And the metalwork contractor went away delighted.

Then came the other contractors sent by Daneau: ten, twelve, fifteen of them... and it was ten, twelve, fifteen repetitions of the same scene, with minor variations, till the moment Monsieur Séjan appeared in his boss's office.

"Well, Séjan, where do we stand?" asked the banker.

"It's always the same thing, sir. I'm afraid the end of the month will be difficult. I almost don't dare to press our mortgage clients out in the provinces any further, because so many of my demands for payment just come back."

"They're not for significant amounts."

"Sure, but they add up to a lot. Ten, twenty, thirty thousand francs of open credit aren't much; but we have over six hundred lines of credit like that on the books. We have over six million francs committed that way. We have almost double that out in small business loans in Paris, for which our security amounts to nothing more than paper whose worth I'm dubious of: the volume of transactions in signed notes of hand is frightening."

"I agree. But my signature is enough for the Bank of France to accept all the notes I send it. So there's no problem for now. Still, it'll take prudence for us to avoid a catastrophe, so we'll gradually retrench that kind of business. Have you seen the Marquis de Berizy?"

"Yes, of course."

"And how much does he want to deposit?"

"Two million, and I came to ask you what you want to use that money for."

"Put it in the three-percent funds."

"They're at eighty-two francs and twenty-five centimes."

"So?"

"The smallest thing could cause a drop... We have over thirty million in customer deposits committed in those funds... The slightest panic would make the three percents fall. The Algerian expedition might fail;[83] the new elections might go badly."

"They'll turn out fine, Séjan."

"In what sense?"

"In the sense that we'll force those in power to come to us."

"And if they don't come? If there are shocks that unsettle the government funds?"

"Then we'll wait for the funds to rise again."

"But what if your depositors get alarmed and want to withdraw all their money, some of which is committed in stocks and the rest in the government funds? Consider that a drop of ten francs—which wouldn't be extraordinary in a revolution—would mean a loss of over four million for us, just to reimburse the capital placed in the three percents."

The banker listened to Séjan with a smile of condescension, and replied cheerfully, "My poor Séjan, you're always reasoning as if you were still working for L— or for O—. All the calamities you speak of could happen—except the one in which anyone, even for a moment, doubts the solvency of the firm of Matthieu Durand."

"No one will have doubts, sir. And I know the bank is rich enough to weather any catastrophe. But your personal fortune might be lost."

"I'd rather have my fortune than that of the King of France, Séjan!" cried the banker enthusiastically. "Mine's more secure than his, which is based on popularity. The House of Bourbon may fall, but the house of Matthieu Durand will stand!"[84]

Séjan raised his eyes to heaven; and the banker, having supplied the signatures the bank's principal manager had come to him for, called for his carriage and left for The Pond.

Neither Luizzi nor the poet made any remark. So the Devil continued thus:

---

[83] In July 1830 a French expeditionary force conquered the city of Algiers—the first step toward what eventually grew into the French colony of Algeria.

[84] Soulié's original readers, in the late 1830s, would've known in hindsight that indeed the Bourbons would fall within months, in the July Revolution of 1830, and all of Séjan's fears of public unrest and financial instability would come true. The Devil's listeners, Luizzi and the poet, likewise know what's coming.

Chapter LXXXII: Another Kind of Gentleman

The same day those various events were taking place at Matthieu Durand's bank on the rue de Provence, another scene was being performed, by a very different character, on the rue de Varennes in the faubourg Saint Germain. The lead actor was Count de Lozeraie. He was past fifty: a tall man with an aquiline profile and a cold haughty manner, who went about with his nose in the air, and spoke through pursed lips, and dressed with a care that knew how to borrow from the fashions of the very young what might be appropriate for someone his age, without falling for what was ridiculous in them. At that moment he was in his study, a luxurious room glistening with brocade and gilt furniture and pricy curios and valuable porcelain. Still, he seemed to be about to leave, because a valet had just handed him his hat, his gloves, and his riding crop, telling him his horses were ready.

Just then a young man of twenty-four opened the door to the study and greeted the count.

"Oh, are you finally here, Arthur?"

"They told me you were asking for me, father, so I hurried to come down."

"You could've hurried a little faster."

"I'm sorry, father, I was finishing a letter to a friend, to Monsieur..."

"Stop right there. I'm not asking you to tell me what you were doing. Your name and your rank should protect you from connections unworthy of you."

Arthur lowered his eyes and didn't answer.

His father went on, "I sent for you to ask you not to make any commitments for this Sunday."

"I wish I'd known earlier, father, because I've practically promised."

"It's enough that you know it now," said his father curtly. "You've been invited for tomorrow to the Marquis de Favieri's; he's giving a ball at his country house in Lorges, and I insist on your going."

"I'll go, father, I'll be happy to go," said Arthur eagerly.

"I thank you for your obedience," said his father less harshly. "But take care not to set limits on it, please; and if you can, get rid of that mopey, melancholy air you drag around everywhere. Tomorrow you'll meet Mademoiselle Flora de Favieri. She's a very attractive girl, and her father's immensely rich; do your best to please each other. You understand?..."

At first Arthur reacted to his father's words with great surprise, but then he seemed content. Still, he hesitated a moment to express the thoughts inspired in him by the last thing his father had said. But as the latter was looking at him with a severe, questioning eye, he made up his mind to speak. "Of course, father, I think I understand you; and I have to believe, based on what you've just

301

said, you wouldn't disdain an alliance with a man who works as a banker, just as the Marquis de Favieri does."

"The marquis is a member of one of the noblest families in Florence," said Count de Lozeraie sternly. "Commerce and banking, which in France have always been considered beneath the nobility, don't carry the same stigma in Italy. Monsieur de Favieri didn't become a banker, he remained a banker just like his ancestors. That's very different from men in finance in this country, who are mostly petty bourgeois upstarts."

The happiness on Arthur's face suddenly drained away, and he replied tentatively, "Still, there are some very respectable men among all those bourgeois."

"That wouldn't matter to you, I assume. What do you have to do with those people?"

"Nothing, father," said Arthur, clearly distressed.

The count considered his son, as if he doubted the truth of what he'd said; then he went on sternly, "You're Viscount de Lozeraie, don't forget that in future—if by chance you might've forgotten it before."

"Never, father... I've done nothing..."

"I'm not asking you to defend yourself. A gentleman trusts his son's honor. Just remember you're going to Monsieur de Favieri's with me tomorrow."

"I'll go with you, father."

Arthur was about to withdraw, and the count was getting ready to go out, when Monsieur de Poissy was announced. Count de Lozeraie motioned to his son to leave them alone.

"This is good timing," said the count to Monsieur de Poissy. "I was about to come see you on my way to Saint Cloud."[85]

"I've been out all morning, because business won't take care of itself."

"And where do we stand?"

"The Algerian expedition is going to happen. It's been settled."

"And what do you hear from our people at the ministry of war?"

"I hardly dare to tell you."

"What! Is a sacrifice like that going to be wasted?"

"Not if you raise the amount."

"Again!" cried the count impatiently. "I thought the four hundred thousand I already gave was enough."

"There are so many people to satisfy."

"But if I decide to make another sacrifice, can I be sure this time I can count on that provisioning contract?"

"There's no doubt about it."

"And what are they asking?"

---

[85] The Palace of Saint Cloud, a few miles outside Paris, was the country residence of King Charles X.

"The thing is, it's a deal worth three or four million in profit," said Monsieur de Poissy.

"I know that. But what price will I have to pay?"

"It'll take another hundred thousand écus."

"A hundred thousand écus! That's outrageous!"

"For a profit of four million?"

"Ah!" said Count de Lozeraie, "what times we live in! In the past the king would've granted the gift of a deal like that to one of the lords at court, and that would've been enough to make his protégé's fortune. But it's no longer the king who rules, it's partly the Chambers of Deputies, that rabble of hairsplitters and moneygrubbers, and partly the ministries, full of clerks come out from behind all the shop counters in France, where they learned how sell everything including their honor."

"That's a good thing when you've got the wherewithal to buy."

"It's a bad thing when you have to pay ten times what it's worth."

"Is that hundred thousand écus going to be a problem for you?" asked Monsieur de Poissy, carefully examining Count de Lozeraie.

"Me?" said the count haughtily. "I'm ready to pay it; but I don't want to be cheated. I need guarantees."

"Can you have guarantees in a negotiation like that? It's a matter of good faith."

"Are you aware I'm advancing more than six hundred thousand francs?"

"I'm sure you are. But can you doubt that, when a man with your name is mentioned, he'll easily win out over all his competitors? The minister himself will have no other choice."

"You think so?" said Count de Lozeraie knowingly. "Well, we'll see! I'm going to the king; I'll find the minister there, I'll survey the terrain, and I'll give you an answer tomorrow."

"Should I come here to get it?"

"Surely you have an invitation to Monsieur de Favieri's. I'll see you there."

"Fine. But they're waiting for an answer; what should I tell them?"

"That I'm thinking it over."

"There are offers higher than yours, which might be accepted between now and tomorrow."

"I still can't pay an amount like that without thinking it over, without taking some steps."

"An explicit promise will be enough. From a man like you, his word is a sacred commitment."

"I know that," said the count with a conceited smile. "That's why I don't give my word lightly... Let them wait."

"That's good enough," said Monsieur de Poissy. "I'll arrange it so nothing's settled till the day after tomorrow."

"I'm counting on you. You've got as much stake in it as I do... I'm off to Saint Cloud; goodbye."

Just as the count was about to leave, his servant entered once again and announced Monsieur Félix from Marseilles.

"I don't know him," replied the count. "What kind of man is he?"

"An old man, almost eighty. He says he has a letter of recommendation to you."

"Ah, some beggar, I assume... I'm not here."

Without thinking about what he'd just said, Count de Lozeraie left his study, crossed the parlor, and entered the vestibule before the servant had a chance to tell Monsieur Félix that Count de Lozeraie was out.

Seeing him, the old man rose and greeted him respectfully, holding out a letter to him as he said, "From Viscount de Couchy of Lyons."

Without returning the old man's greeting, the count stopped and took the letter, which ran like this:

My dear count,

The bearer of this letter is a worthy elderly man who lost everything in the Revolution. He'll tell you his story, and I'd be very grateful for anything you can do for him.

The count tossed the letter onto a side table and said to the servant, who'd followed him, "Give this man two louis and have my horses brought around."

"Sir," said Monsieur Félix, placing himself between the count and the door, "I didn't come here to beg for alms."

"Then for what, if you please?"

"It's about a restitution, sir."

"A restitution! I never borrow money, sir, and if I did it wouldn't be from someone like you."

"Indeed, sir," said the old man loftily, "I wasn't referring to any personal debt you might have with respect to me."

"That would be unlikely."

"Perhaps. But I'm speaking of the debts of Monsieur de Loré, your father-in-law. He borrowed a great deal of money from me abroad, before the exile, and I've come to ask you for repayment."

"Me?... I'm not the guarantor of Monsieur de Loré's debts, if in fact he ever owed you anything."

"Still, sir, his daughter, who was your wife, inherited from him."

"In that case, at the very most it would concern my son, who received his mother's inheritance. But where are your deeds for the loan?"

"When I've explained the circumstances in which I helped Monsieur de Loré, you'll realize the truth of what I'm telling you, though I can't say I have the specific deeds."

"Oh, I understand!" said the count angrily and scornfully. "Some story you made up based on circumstantial details you learned by chance... You've come too late, sir. I know that trade, and I advise you to go practice it elsewhere."

"And I also understand," said the old man sternly, "that Count de Lozeraie knows better than anyone how to make up a story based on circumstantial details you learned by chance."

"What's this wretch talking about?" cried the count.

"Me? Nothing," said the old man meekly. "But you told me my claim concerned your son. I'll address myself to him."

"Throw this man out!" cried the count violently.

"Consider," said the old man, "that the honor of Monsieur de Loré's name is at stake."

"Monsieur de Loré's name, like mine, is above this kind of low intrigue."

"Your son might not agree."

"I forbid you to see my son, sir. I know young people are easily swayed, and I warn you, at the slightest attempt on your part I'll know how to put a stop to it. The law punishes that kind of confidence game."

"It also punishes the counterfeiting of titles of nobility."

At that word the count was stunned at first, then flew into a violent rage. But old Monsieur Félix had already withdrawn by the time he erupted; and Count de Lozeraie, turning to Monsieur de Poissy, said vehemently, "This is what we members of the ancient nobility are exposed to: schemers use our names to extort us by threatening us with scandal."

"And what do they hope to gain by it?"

"My God, to give a laugh at our expense to that whole world of little liberals who like nothing better than a chance to slander us, and who think the magistrates are just doing our bidding when they punish those schemers. Till we can throw rascals like that to the bottom of some dungeon, so they'll never be heard from again, we'll be the target of the vilest intrigues. But we can only hope that day is coming."

Count de Lozeraie mounted his horse and rode away at a fast trot.

"Well!" said the Devil. "How does my gentleman strike you?"

"He strikes me as being like lots of other people," said the poet. "When you've got a big name, you get infatuated with it. But the part that strikes me as curious is that Monsieur Félix. He's the mysterious *gray man* of your story. What kind of man is he?"

"What I don't see," said Luizzi, "is what connection there can be between Matthieu Durand and Count de Lozeraie."

"All will be revealed in its time," said the Devil, "and if you listen you'll find out. I write neither tragedies nor comedies, but I know how to build suspense by pacing my effects, as they say in the theater."

And Satan went on:

Chapter LXXXIII: A Campaign Circular

The next day, Matthieu Durand was strolling along one of the paths on the grounds of The Pond, rereading once again the document he'd read over so carefully the day before, of which Léopold had brought the copies he'd asked him to make. It was about midday, and Durand seemed to be awaiting something impatiently; he kept looking back as if to see if someone was coming. Finally he spotted a man at the far end of the alleyway, whose arrival pleased him. That man was Monsieur Daneau. Still, in spite of his pleasure at seeing him, the banker didn't advance to meet him: he kept on walking as if he hadn't noticed him, but slowly enough for the other man to catch up, and he went back to his reading as if he were completely absorbed in it.

Daneau soon drew near. He greeted Durand, who gave him a friendly nod and said, "I beg your pardon. I'm all yours in a moment. If you're not tired, let's take a stroll together."

"I'd be honored."

The banker didn't answer, and went on reading while the builder walked next to him. Now and again Durand shrugged at something he read, then let out a little laugh and a few expressions of well-meaning pity, like, "Poor man!... He's mad!..."

Finally what he read seemed to move him, and he said to himself, "There's real feeling here... I can't blame him for his enthusiasm. The truth is," he said, turning to Daneau, "there's more gratitude among the poor than there is in high society."

"I'm sure of it."

"Look, here's something that struck me as ridiculous at first, and that ended up touching me, because I believe in the good feeling that prompted it."

"What's it about?" asked Daneau, obligingly letting himself be drawn into the banker's confidence.

"A worthy poor man, whom I pulled out of trouble, and whose idea of how to thank me is to solicit the support of the voters in his arrondissement on my behalf."

"Why, that strikes me as a very natural idea. And has he already carried it out?"

"No, thank goodness. He sent me a draft of the circular he plans to write, and here it is."

"You don't approve of it?"

"See for yourself whether I can," said Durand, handing him the paper.

While Daneau read it carefully, the banker, with ill-disguised anxiety, followed the effect the text had on him. Finally the builder said, "This letter doesn't say anything besides the exact truth. In describing you as both the ablest banker in France and the most upright, and by enumerating all the services you've rendered to commerce and industry, he says no more than what the world already knows."

"I might've done a good deed or two, but it's a far cry from that to what he wrote."

"My word!" said Daneau with the generous impulse of an honest man. "If I had to write a letter like that I'd have said a great deal more."

"There's quite enough here as it is," said the banker with a smile.

"Forgive me, Monsieur Durand, but can I ask you, is it your intention to run for election?"

"To run for election! No, certainly not."

"But would you be willing to be a candidate if you were asked?"

"It's a big question... Being a Deputy is a heavy responsibility, especially for a man like me. Consider that if I were in the Chamber I'd see myself as the representative of the people, the manufacturers, the businessmen; and it would be a great challenge to try to champion their rights, which the powers that be stubbornly dismiss."

"Those rights could have no finer representative or better defender."

"I'd support them heart and mind, I assure you, because I myself am a man of the people, and I strongly resent the constant affront they face."

"Well then, sir, allow me to join with the voter who wrote that circular."

"No, no! If I let anything like that go forward, I wouldn't want his name to appear on it. He's a worthy fellow who was more imprudent than ill-intentioned, but who doesn't have as clean a reputation in business circles as, say, yours would be."

"Mine, Monsieur Durand! I owe it to you to have preserved my good name! And if you'd allow me, I'd add it to the bottom of this letter."

"Yes," said the banker with affected indifference. "I understand your name would attract plenty of others."

"It's yours that would do that, Monsieur Durand, and if I showed this letter to all my associates they wouldn't hesitate to sign it."

"Certainly, if a letter like that were signed by a great many voters, I might decide to put my name forward. It would encourage me, it would..."

"I can promise you two hundred signatures in the next two days!" cried the builder, carried away by his wish to express his gratitude to Monsieur Durand.

"That would be a great many names..."

"Will you allow me to try?"

"It might be a pointless effort..."

"That's my kind of work, Monsieur Durand; that's my kind of work," said Daneau, proud of having prevailed over the banker's modesty.

"Then do your work," said Durand with a smile. "But since you force me to it, I want to make one thing clear: that it's the common people I'm addressing, that I'm a child of the common people, that it's from the common people I want to receive a mandate, that it's for the common people I want to carry it out."

"Yes, sir, yes. And you'll see, the common people will be grateful."

"Very good, Monsieur Daneau. Let's hide that paper, and not mention it again today. But you're not familiar with The Pond—I'll show you around. You'll be able to appreciate construction on this scale, since that too is your kind of work."

For the next hour the banker and the brick mason wandered through the magnificent grounds, with its rare trees planted here and there and its flowing water courses and its perfectly maintained flowerbeds. Their progress brought them to the banker's palatial dwelling, an old chateau that had belonged to one of the greatest families in France and that still preserved its moats and feudal drawbridges, which were now lowered only to receive the man of the people, Matthieu Durand.

"And it was the work of that same Matthieu Durand," said the poet, "that the same Matthieu Durand so skillfully got Daneau to sign. That strikes me as a pretty good trick."

"It's not a particularly literary trick," said the Devil. "Usually, in serious literature, you're more likely to put your name to what you haven't written than to let other people sign what you wrote."

"What a slander against literature, sir!" said the poet.

"Just as my portrait of Matthieu Durand will be taken as a slander against finance," said Satan. "If you shout 'Stop, thief!' in the street, plenty of people turn around."

Luizzi would've been interested to see an argument break out between the Devil and the poet, but the latter fell silent, and Satan went on:

308

Chapter LXXXIV

That night everyone mentioned so far in the story showed up at Monsieur de Favieri's ball; and among the beautiful women in the rooms could be seen Mademoiselle Delphine Durand, seated next to Mademoiselle Flora de Favieri. The latter was a tall, dark, serious girl who hid her naturally passionate expression beneath an icy, proud demeanor. The former was petite, blonde, and graceful, and affected a kind of disdain that only managed to achieve impertinence. Delphine gave the impression that she depended on her own strong will; Flora, that she owed her imperious air only to the deference that had always surrounded her. Flora's character seemed to be the one given to her by nature; Delphine's the character her position had given her.

In any case, in spite of their contrasting personalities, they'd begun the same conversation in the same tone. They'd both exclaimed at how beautifully the other was dressed; they'd discussed the fashion designers most in vogue at the moment; and they'd agreed that the queen of hairdressers was Mademoiselle Alexandrine on the rue de Richelieu. That subject naturally led to the one that's listed in the manual for how to run a ball: the young ladies entertained themselves by making fun of most the women in the rooms, and laughing over the men who came parading by the two of them.

They were interrupted by Monsieur de Favieri, who came up to his daughter and said—in that mocking, caressing Italian way that makes you doubt the sincerity of the words—"Flora, I came in person to present Monsieur Arthur de Lozeraie, whom I've mentioned to you."

Flora de Favieri responded to Arthur's bow with a slight nod and an imperceptible smile. Arthur then greeted Delphine Durand like someone who knew her, but still with a bit of reserve.

No sooner had he moved away than Delphine said to Flora, "So you're receiving Monsieur Arthur de Lozeraie?"

"Yes," said Flora, with mocking self-pity.

"Oh... And have you known him a long time?"

"This is the first time I've met him."

"And... what do you think of him?"

"Um..." replied Flora, turning to Delphine. "I didn't look at him."

"I've heard he's a remarkable young man, very distinguished, with a very great name."

"And very handsome, isn't he?"

"Yes," said Delphine.

"Well, my dear, you must've been taught the same lesson I was, and presumably the same lesson as lots of other girls. Monsieur Arthur de Lozeraie has friends who introduce him like that in every house where there's a rich heiress to marry."

"You think?" cried Delphine quickly.

"My father warned me about it."

"And is that why your father's receiving him?"

"I doubt it," replied Flora scornfully. "A rather disorderly fortune, a great name whose origins are a little murky—that's not what would appeal to either Favieri the banker or Favieri the marquis."

"But in spite of all that, he might appeal to you personally, mightn't he?"

"To me? A young man who's a little nobody, who trembles before his father like a child of twelve, who affects to lower his eyes in the presence of a woman as if every girl were threatening to devour him with love!"

"I can assure you," replied Delphine dryly, "he dares meet their eyes when he finds them attractive."

"You're right, because he was gazing at you in ecstatic silence."

"You're mistaken. It must've been you."

"You'll see proof it isn't me: if you'll allow me, I'll leave you to go give a few orders."

Flora rose and went away. Just then Arthur approached and asked Mademoiselle Durand for the honor of a dance.

Delphine replied curtly, in a low voice, "You came too late."

"Are you already committed for the entire evening?"

"I mean Mademoiselle de Favieri has gone away."

"You know very well it wasn't for her sake I came."

"There's no reason for us to talk so long together."

"If you're concerned people will notice, I'll withdraw."

"Oh, it's not for my sake. I'm worried your father will scold you."

That whole exchange had taken place quickly, in low voices; and those few words were enough to show you Delphine was one of those spoiled, rebellious, strong-willed children in whom every impertinence has been indulged by others and allowed to themselves. The conversation also showed this wasn't the first time Delphine and Arthur had met, and there was a little young people's secret between them.

Still, Arthur had no sooner heard the last thing Delphine said than, girding himself with superhuman courage, he sat down on the chair vacated by Mademoiselle de Favieri, thereby going beyond the strict bounds of propriety, which he normally respected more than anyone else. Delphine couldn't help smiling at the victory she'd just won, but that wasn't enough to satisfy her: she blamed Arthur for not having pleased Flora—though she'd probably also have blamed him if Flora had found him charming. Some women are so happy to pick a quarrel with a man they love that anything can serve as a pretext, especially when that love is in fact no more than a feeling of despotic vanity.

"Even so," said the poet, interrupting the narrative, "Mademoiselle Durand is a delectable person."

"Enormously wealthy, and who—if she met a man capable of mastering her—would become the sweetest, most charming woman in the world," replied the Devil.

"That's what I always thought," said the poet.

"A woman her father should marry off to a man like himself: distinguished, but a man of the common people."

"Be careful," said Luizzi. "This gentleman has said he'd marry her."

"I'm a man of the people too, gentlemen," said the poet, drawing himself up.

"And between men of the people, like you and Matthieu Durand, no one would try to make invidious comparisons," said the Devil with a smile. "But if you'll allow me to continue, you'll see your chances are perhaps not as good as you imagine."

Arthur, seated next to Delphine, was saying to her, "So, you won't dance with me?"

"No."

"But you'll dance with other men?"

"Yes."

"We'll see about that."

"You'll see."

At that moment Léopold approached Mademoiselle Durand to ask her to dance, but she replied, "I'm sorry! I gave my promise to Viscount de Lozeraie."

"Ah!" said the latter quietly. "You're an angel!"

"I didn't refuse that gentleman for your sake, I can tell you."

Arthur was delighted, thinking her answer was just prompted by residual temper. He was wrong; it was a true reflection of her thoughts. If instead of Léopold, who was her father's clerk, some other young man of good name had approached her, she would've accepted. But her vanity couldn't resist the pleasure of making the lowly clerk aware his presumption had been misplaced and he was just a little boy compared to Viscount de Lozeraie.

"So you'll dance with me?" asked Arthur again.

"Neither with you nor with anyone. Leave me alone, and go ask Mademoiselle de Favieri."

"I promise you, I have no interest in dancing with Mademoiselle de Favieri."

"Maybe not; but if your papa wants you to, you'll have to."

Stung to the core, Arthur said nothing. The contradance was about to start when he noticed his father motioning to him. In spite of everything, in spite of his unhappiness at displaying his obedience like that, he went to the count, who said curtly, "Have you asked Mademoiselle de Favieri to dance?"

"She wasn't there anymore," said Arthur, blushing, "and…"

"Who's that girl you were talking to? You seem to know her."

"Her father's Matthieu Durand, the banker who's so rich, so…"

"All right, all right! I know who Matthieu Durand is: some kind of upstart laborer."

"They say he's very respected, very upright."

"You expected him to be a scoundrel? What the hell would he be if he weren't an honest man? In any case, stop being so attentive to his daughter."

Arthur didn't know what to say. Luckily for him, his father was approached by the Marquis de Berizy and Matthieu Durand himself. The marquis told Count de Lozeraie he'd like to speak with him a moment, and the latter was about to follow him, when Delphine, coming up to her father, said, "Are we going to stay much longer?"

"But, Delphine, the ball just started."

"I don't care," said the spoiled child. "I'm bored and I want to leave."

"As soon as you like. Or rather, as soon as I've discussed business with these gentlemen for a moment."

"My God! You bring your business all the way to a ball, papa? You surprise me!"

"It's even more surprising, miss," laughed the Marquis de Berizy, "that at your age and with your looks you bring your boredom to a ball!"

Something in the marquis's words conveyed the lofty tone of a very worldly man and made Delphine feel flattered by his paternal scolding. "My God!" she answered, "if I'm bored it's because I have nothing to do."

"Well, they're about to start dancing, and here's a young man," said the marquis, turning to Arthur, who was still standing with them, "who'd be delighted to entertain you."

"Only too happy!" said Arthur eagerly.

But a glance from his father stopped him, while Durand was saying to his daughter, "Come on, Delphine, dance at least once. That's almost nothing for a whole ball."

Putting on a little schoolgirl air, Delphine replied in an affected voice, "Whatever you say, papa."

Then, as de Lozeraie went away with de Berizy and Durand, she turned to Arthur and said, "You see, I'm copying you, and I'm a very obedient girl!"

Chapter LXXXV: A Business Transaction

While Arthur and Delphine went off to dance together, both of them delighted that circumstances had forced them into it—he in spite of his father's wishes, she in spite of her whims—Count de Lozeraie, the Marquis de Berizy, and Matthieu Durand withdrew into a small parlor, where they found a whist table occupied by four silent players. The newcomers sat down at some distance from them.

The Marquis de Berizy spoke first; after introducing de Lozeraie and Durand to each other, he said, "I beg your pardon, gentlemen, for bothering you with business in the middle of a ball, but the opportunity is too good for me not to seize it. I spoke to you, Monsieur Durand, about a forest I'd sold. Count de Lozeraie here is the buyer. According to the contract, he has to pay over the entire purchase price in three months. That payment must be made into my hands. Would it suit you, count, to make that payment to Monsieur Durand, since he's agreed to handle my funds? And you, Monsieur Durand, would it suit you to receive that money directly from Count de Lozeraie?"

"If that's what you'd like, sir," said Durand, "I'm happy to do it."

"Assuming a receipt from Monsieur Durand will settle my account with you, marquis," replied the count disdainfully, "I don't see any difficulty."

"It's for your sake I'm agreeing to this arrangement, marquis," said Durand loftily. "I urge you to believe that."

"The fact is," added the count with even greater disdain, "if I didn't want to accommodate you, marquis, I'd stick to the original terms of the contract."

"And I'd stick to our arrangement," said Durand.

"I thank you both for your great kindness," replied the Marquis de Berizy with a smile, "and I'll take advantage of it. I have to go back to the country on business, and I'm delighted the matter can be settled this way."

The count and the banker nodded in agreement.

"Tomorrow my lawyer will draw up a document to guarantee the validity of your payment into the hands of a third party, and everything will be perfectly in order," said de Berizy to de Lozeraie.

"Might Count de Lozeraie have any comments he'd like to add, any steps he'd like to take?" asked the banker.

"My man of business will come see you, sir," said the count.

"My head of accounting will receive him," replied Durand, "and he'll receive the money if someone brings it."

They bowed to each other, and were about to leave the small parlor, when there was movement at the whist table, and play came to an end. Just then the

Marquis de Favieri came in. "Have you had any luck, Monsieur Félix?" he asked one of the players.

The count and the banker spun around at that name, each of them privately recognizing the old man they'd each given such a poor welcome to the day before. Both were equally astonished to see him at the Marquis de Favieri's, but their surprise grew when they heard him reply carelessly to de Favieri, "No, in fact, I lost twenty-four tricks in three rubbers. Luckily," he added, pulling a billfold from his pocket and tossing a wad of banknotes on the table, "we were only playing for five hundred francs a trick."

"Ha! Ha! Ha!" laughed the poet. "That Monsieur Félix is a gem of an invention! Who the devil is he? He bears an odd resemblance to the *gray man*, the mysterious stranger in all those old plays by Alexandre Duval![86] Brrr! It's all very Théâtre Français!"

"And that Count de Lozeraie seems like a shady character to me," said Luizzi. "And yet it's a distinguished name."

"No," went on the poet, "it's that Monsieur Félix I want to meet. I tell you, he's my hero! I can see him now, opening his frock coat and unbuttoning his shirt and crying, 'Do you recognize this scar?' But all joking aside, who is this Monsieur Félix? I feel like I might've met him at the banker's."

"It seems like the trick with mysterious strangers works just as well to arouse curiosity in life as in the theater," laughed the Devil.

Matthieu Durand and Count de Lozeraie struggled to understand who this man could be who'd come to them as a penniless supplicant and whom they now found at the home of one the richest financiers in Europe, among a group of card players famous for the enormous stakes they played for, and indifferent to losing a sum anyone would consider large.

Now Monsieur Félix in turn noticed the two of them. As he passed solemnly by in front of them, he spoke in a lowered voice, but so they could both hear him. Eyeing first the banker and then the count, he said, "Pride and vanity."

Neither Durand nor de Lozeraie was a man who'd put up with an insult like that. But the man who'd delivered it was eighty years old. Both of them also remembered the way they'd received him, and the mysterious and almost menacing things the old man had said; and, no doubt held back by some fear known only to themselves, they let him walk away without answering him. But they looked at each other; and the certainty each had, that the other had heard the insulting word addressed to each of them, magnified in their hearts the instinctive hatred that divided them.

---

[86] Alexandre-Vincent Pineux Duval (1767-1842): playwright, actor, theater manager, and member of the French Academy.

The explanations that followed that ball gave the great lord and the banker even more reasons to hate each other. The first explanation took place between Arthur and Delphine. The young lover, the more awkward the more in love he was, thought he was making a great show of his passion by swearing to Delphine he was capable of defying his father's unfair prejudices. The girl asked him what those prejudices were, and Arthur was foolish enough to repeat them. The heiress could think of no better reply than to pass on to Arthur Mademoiselle de Favieri's contempt for him, while attributing her opinions to Monsieur Durand, so that on this occasion Arthur wouldn't come out ahead in terms of impertinence. It's easy to see how Delphine, whose character had been formed by her father's indulgent hand, could pass Count de Lozeraie's insults on to him; but it took special circumstances to drive Arthur to tell his own father what Delphine had passed on to him. Here's what had happened:

Monsieur Félix, having gotten himself introduced to Arthur during the ball, took him aside and told him he needed to see him about a money matter in which his mother's name might be compromised. Arthur replied that he was just as anxious to protect the honor of his mother's name, though he didn't bear it, as to protect the honor of his father's name, which he did.

Monsieur Félix seemed to find that answer charming, but he replied gravely, "If only God in his mercy had made the name you bear worth the one you don't!"

"Sir!" cried Arthur.

"We'll see each other again, young man," said the old man softly, "and then you'll understand I have a right to say that."

The result was that when Count de Lozeraie—who'd noticed his son's emotion when he took Delphine's hand to dance—felt he needed to repeat to Arthur his order to stop seeing that girl, he found his son's obedience less prompt and less absolute than usual. Arthur thought he should tell his father that marriages between the nobility and high finance were no longer such an unheard-of thing that he should reject the idea so contemptuously. The count, annoyed at that sign of resistance, felt he couldn't make clear enough to his son the unworthiness of his opinions, and he wrapped up a fine tirade on the respect one owes to one's name with these words: "I understand how men with names that have just sprung up, or members of the old nobility who've compromised theirs in risky speculations, might try to get rich or restore their fortunes by an alliance like that. But when your name is de Lozeraie, and you're as rich as you are, you can be more scrupulous in such matters. Yes, Arthur, it's now the duty of men like us to uphold the rigorous principles of honor and dignity that will soon restore to the nobility the prestige and the status it has partly lost."

"But father," replied Arthur, "how does it happen that that name and that fortune were both the subject of unfavorable comment tonight?"

It took no more than that for Count de Lozeraie to demand an exact account of everything he'd heard; and Arthur, beset by his questions, was driven to repeat to his father what both Delphine Durand and Monsieur Félix had said. All of the count's anger—or at least all of it that he allowed to show—exploded against Durand, and he warned Arthur that nothing in the world would make him agree to a marriage between the heir to his name and the daughter of an upstart peasant like Durand. Arthur had to consider that decision irrevocable, because the next day his father ordered him to go to London. He left Paris convinced he was being separated from Delphine, and not suspecting that perhaps, above all, his father was trying to keep him from meeting Monsieur Félix again.

On his part, Matthieu Durand, normally so weak toward Delphine, was now adamant. In vain she'd told him she'd die of despair if she couldn't marry Arthur, in vain she'd had hysterics: nothing had moved the banker. Still, Delphine had fired her two chambermaids, dismissed her drawing master, thrown her sheet music in her piano tutor's face, sent three hats back to Alexandrine, torn up a dozen dresses, and smashed a whole pile of lovely delicate furniture: all those displays of her deep distress had left her father implacable.

"Is it his title that interests you?" he asked her. "If you want, I can make you the wife of a marquis or a duke."

"I want to be Arthur's wife."

"But that Count de Lozeraie is a scheming upstart," went on Durand, the man of the people, "the son of some provincial bailiff who stole the title he wraps himself in."

"But aren't you the son of a laborer, father? That's what you tell anyone who'll listen."

"Oh, with me it's a different matter," said the banker with poorly suppressed anger. "I don't deny my origin, I boast about it, I honor myself for it, I take pride in it."

Delphine couldn't possibly have understood the reasoning from arrogance that drove Durand to say constantly he was a man of the people and yet to have that same quality offend him when someone else laid claim to it. So Delphine paid no attention to the difference as her father defined it; and, digging in her heels on the expression of her capricious will, she went back to crying that if she couldn't marry Arthur she'd die.

That went on for a week, at the end of which Delphine found out Arthur had gone to London. She felt humiliated by the news. Indeed, for a week she'd been surprised not to see Arthur climbing the walls of the estate, bribing a gardener or at least a chambermaid to get near her, offering to elope with her in a post chaise, and threatening to kill himself at her feet if she wouldn't give in to his desires. Since the blindness of her own vanity attributed to love all of her foolish carrying on about Arthur, she couldn't imagine that a man's passion wouldn't have gone even further, especially a passion she inspired. Arthur's departure therefore led Delphine to a cruel disenchantment—not in fact on her own account, but on his. She didn't think herself any less capable of inspiring the most extravagant passion, but she judged Arthur incapable of feeling it.

Her anger and disappointment should've put an end to her playacting of a nonexistent suffering; but admitting to her father she no longer cared about Arthur de Lozeraie would be admitting she could be wrong, so she went right on insisting, "I want Arthur, or death." As a result she refused to see anyone. She shut herself in her room and made her suffering her full-time occupation—which led her to produce a witticism I consider worth sharing: one day, when her father was reproaching her gently for neglecting her musical talent, she replied bitterly, "I'm already good enough at the piano that I can die."

Still, there's no doubt she would've been cruelly punished for her theatrics if her father had let her have what she wanted; but in the end she'd understood she wasn't going to succeed, and in the meantime she was having success of a very different kind, which gave her more pleasure than any other. She made her father anxious, and she kept the whole house in a state of alarm: the servants observed everything she did and watched over her at night and followed her when she went for a walk; they trembled when she looked at a knife or stood near a high window. All that served to distract Delphine from her disappointment; she noticed their concern and took pleasure in provoking it.

That was the state of things three months after this story began; and Durand, genuinely alarmed by Delphine's persistence, was beginning to feel his antipathy for Count de Lozeraie crumble before the suffering his daughter was causing him—till the following scene occurred...

"You keep talking about the hatred between Count de Lozeraie and Matthieu Durand," said the poet. "I think every hatred must have a motive."

"A motive?" said the Devil. "Does love have a motive? Why would hate need one? You hate each other because you hate each other, just as you love each other because you love each other. Still, the antipathy between the banker and the count didn't arise from one of those instinctive divisions that irreparably separates certain natures; I think they hated each other for a reason, but without knowing what that reason was. So their hatred had a motive. But there's no use looking for it in the past relations between the two men; it didn't arise from any wrong or injury either one had done to the other in society. They'd never been rivals, either romantic or political—those two fertile sources of quarrels, crimes, folly, and ruin. Their encounter at the Marquis de Favieri's was the first time they'd ever met, though they'd long known of each other by name. Their hatred sprang simply from their both having the same vice, which took a different form in each of them.

"If it were possible to explain one hatred in terms of another, I'd invoke one whose reality is uncontested, because it's seen so often in the world. The hatred between de Lozeraie and Durand was the same as the hatred between two women of loose morals, one of whom hides her sins hypocritically and wears her dress long enough to cover the tips of her shoes, while the other displays her shame boldly across her forehead and lets passersby catch a glimpse of her garter. The first woman, who thinks she can conceal her vices better by criticizing women who let theirs be seen openly, loathes the candid hussy who forces her constantly to proclaim her contempt for the life she herself leads in secret; while the second woman can't forgive the first for hanging onto a little bit of respectability, though she's just as unworthy of any esteem at all, and she hates her for using that to secure a better position in society. If you place an honest woman between those two, she'll feel contempt for both of them. But she'll have no reason to hate them, because they don't harm her own reputation. As for the two women, presumably they'll both hate her—but not as much as they hate each other."

"That seems like an awfully subtle distinction," said Luizzi, "and it doesn't explain the relationship between the banker and the count."

"Come on!" said the Devil. "That same hatred, slightly modified, can be found between two men, one of them a brazen crook and the other a hypocritical crook. It's almost always thieving creditors who drive crooked debtors into bankruptcy; honest men don't get involved. It's always the husband's mistress who tells him his wife is cuckolding him; an honest woman wouldn't do it. Vice has no more implacable enemy than vice. Change that feeling in a purely superficial way, call ridicule what I'm calling vice, and you'll find that same principle of hatred between those two upstarts, Matthieu Durand and Count de Lozeraie."

"Two upstarts!" cried the poet. "What! Count de Lozeraie was…"

"Was what?" said the Devil.

"An upstart?"

"Yes."

"Oh, so that's why you made him ridiculous?"

"No, that's why he was ridiculous, just like Durand," replied the Devil. "And that's why they hated each other. In a sense, both of them were ashamed of where they'd started; but one made a big show of it and arrogantly imposed the fact of it on society, the way fallen women try to impose the fact of their vices; while the other carefully hid it, since he craved a respectability he knew he didn't deserve, like a hypocritical woman. Durand was the arrogant man who thought he was strong enough to fight social prejudice singlehanded and defeat it, for his own gain; de Lozeraie was the vain man who submitted to that prejudice, also for his own gain. Durand hated de Lozeraie because he lied to maintain a position in life that he had no right to; de Lozeraie hated Durand because his affectation in boasting of his humble origins was a constant mockery of the care he himself took to hide his own origins. Both of them hated men who were genuinely of the high aristocracy—but they hated them less than they hated each other.

"From another point of view, you could say of those two men that one represented certain old-fashioned ideas, the other certain modern ideas. De Lozeraie was the traditional upstart, the one who conforms to stereotypes about the advantages of noble birth and does everything possible to make people believe he has those advantages. Durand was the modern upstart, the one who appeals to the principles of absolute social equality and individual merit, repudiating all family connections and all respect for heredity and imposing the *self* as a force relying on no outside help and almost equal to God. To tell you the truth, I think old Monsieur Félix summed up those two characters perfectly when he applied the word *pride* to Matthieu Durand and the word *vanity* to Count de Lozeraie."

"He must be some old friend of yours," said the poet, "some elderly gentleman of high and ancient lineage… You speak too well of him."

Without responding, the Devil went on, "Now that I feel I've explained more or less the relationship between those two men, and between them and the world, I'll go on with my story. I'll describe for you the various scenes that took place between them, and that were the consequence of what I've already told you."

Luizzi, who was familiar with the way the Devil told a story, reflected that he must have a good reason for stretching this one out; and he paid attention to see whether the tale would have the effect on the poet that Satan had predicted.

Chapter LXXXVI

It was now the beginning of July in the year 1830. Matthieu Durand had just returned from The Pond, where he'd left Delphine in such a state of agony that she'd come close to striking her father. He was once again seated in the office in which we found him at the start of this story. But the banker's face no longer shone with the serene happiness and utter self-satisfaction of a few months earlier. He seemed both more positively happy and more fretful: sudden waves of delight and anxious depression passed across his face. Those contrasting emotions reflected the variety of subjects passing through his mind. When he remembered he'd just been named a Deputy by three different local arrondissements and one regional department, an arrogant glow rose to his head and his eye shone with an imperious sparkle; when he considered how he'd arrived at that triumph, and realized he'd had to sacrifice the solidity of his business to his ambition, cold fear made him go pale.

Durand had the fever of great political gamblers: sometimes its burning transports make the patient delirious and lend him unnatural energy, sometimes its icy shivers make him tremble and knock him down like a man drained of all strength. Still, it was only when he was alone that he allowed the symptoms of his troubled condition to show; in public he got back in character and played his part with the composure of an actor who from long practice on stage can perform the gestures and the expression appropriate to his lines even though his mind is far away.

Since Durand knew a great many people were waiting in the antechamber to see him, he called for the list, and was not a little surprised to see, among thirty unremarkable names, that of Count de Lozeraie; and the name next to it was that of Monsieur Daneau. The banker considered for a moment what he should do about the count; then he said to his servant, "Make my apologies to Count de Lozeraie. Tell him my entire morning is taken up with business and I wouldn't want to make him wait too long. But if he wants to come back tomorrow or the day after, I'm at his disposal. As for Daneau, tell him to wait, because I absolutely have to speak to him. Then send in the others."

Once he'd given those orders, the banker got up from his armchair to receive his various callers while standing, and thereby force them to curtail their visit. That slight difference from the welcome he'd once extended to his petitioners, to whom he used to offer a seat with such graciousness—that slight difference showed that Matthieu Durand already felt it was a waste of his time to listen to petitions he would've spent long hours on a few months earlier. He expedited half a dozen voters who'd come to ask for his signature on some document, which he had to refuse, given that he'd committed himself to defending the rights of the people on the hustings, not in the offices of bureaucrats—which is to say in theory and not at all in practice.

"Ah, you see, theory is the finest thing the Devil ever invented to trouble the world! Take the philanthropist with the greatest love for mankind, give him power for twenty-four hours, and I can turn him into the vilest monster. Robespierre was a theoretician who wanted the best for France, and who, like all theoreticians, thought the end justified the means."

"Oh, Count Cerny!" cried the poet. "What an awful epigram for a supporter of the Bourbons! You make Robespierre sound like a Jesuit!"

"That might be my intention," replied the Devil, while Luizzi said to him quietly, "Satan, you're forgetting yourself."

"In any case," continued the Devil:

Matthieu Durand received and dismissed those voters with the superiority of a man who's utterly bored by their business. He didn't want to make compromises with those in government, he said. The same answer served for all, and each visitor went away delighted by the new Deputy's firm independence. It took no more than half an hour for the banker to deal with all the voters. However, one former purveyor to the Imperial army came in with a petition to the Chambers in which he demanded payment of a fairly large sum, accusing the government of having ignored his indisputable rights and claiming evidence of clear fraud; the banker read his petition from start to finish and said, "Sir, I'll do everything I can to support this request. I must and will draw attention to such a shameful theft. Your claims have been rejected because they date from a period whose glory and whose commitments the present government takes pleasure in repudiating. But the day of justice will come, sir, and it won't be on account of me or my friends if you don't get complete satisfaction."

"Do you really expect so, sir?" asked the former purveyor.

"The opposition's majority is indisputable, sir, its majority is all-powerful, sir, and the government will have to give us what we want—assuming the government remains much longer in the hands of men who abuse their power so perversely and so arbitrarily against anything popular and patriotic."

"Ah, sir," cried the petitioner, "you've restored me to life! Because I have to tell you, even though I hold these rights, which you yourself consider valid, I've been reduced to desperation: desperation such that if I could raise a little money in anticipation of the settlement of these claims—till the day they're finally recognized, thanks to your eloquent intervention—I'd consider myself happy."

"I'm sure you'll have no trouble doing that," said Durand, heading toward the door of his office as if to show his new protégé the way out, with an ease that suggested the banker had the capacity to become a cabinet minister.

"If you think so," said the purveyor, following him, "might it be possible for you, Monsieur Durand...?"

"For me, sir!" said the new Deputy. "Alas, no. My bank absolutely will not undertake that kind of business. I'd like to, but I can't. Still, I'm entirely dedicated to your cause, sir, and when your petition reaches the Chamber you can count absolutely on what you call my eloquent intervention." So saying, the banker opened his office door himself and bowed to the petitioner with an exquisite politeness that admirably masked his inner thought: "Do me the favor of going to hell!"

After that petitioner came another, who wanted to propose to Durand a plan for financial reform that would do no less than eliminate direct taxes, and the taxes on alcohol and salt, and the government tobacco monopoly; and make up the resulting budget deficit by cutting the salaries of all public servants in half. The banker, without conceding the radical implications of the reformer's ideas, enthusiastically approved of the principle and declared the time had come to carry out severe cuts in public spending and to put an end to the brazen waste of the people's wealth, adding that only then would it be possible to carry out the petitioner's ideas—ideas which in any case he undertook to present to the Chamber, so as to accustom the Deputies to hearing about cost savings and reform.

"That doesn't sound like the Matthieu Durand I know," said the poet, "the sincere, candid patriot all his friends admire."

"Perhaps not," said the Devil. "I'm not describing the one you know, but the one I know."

"I've never seen you at his place."

"And yet I'm often there," said Satan, and he resumed:

When Matthieu Durand had seen the great economist out with the same ceremony he'd used with the former purveyor, he told his servant to send in Monsieur Daneau; and he was very angry to learn that the builder hadn't been willing to wait, and had said he'd come again in the afternoon. On top of that, Durand was even more surprised to hear that Count de Lozeraie had said he'd wait till Monsieur Durand was through with business. The sight of the count sitting in Durand's antechamber filled the banker with such a gust of self-satisfied pride that for a moment he forgot Daneau's cavalier treatment, and called out loudly for his servant to send in all the other people who were waiting.

They were businessmen who, knowing Durand's great reputation for benevolence, had come—as Daneau had once—to explain their difficulties to him and ask for the generous assistance the builder had received. For these commercial petitioners, as for the earlier political petitioners, Durand had a ready-made answer: his new responsibilities as a Deputy took up all his time, and he'd handed the whole management of the bank over to Monsieur Séjan, who, he said, would do everything that could be done, and to whom he sent each one of them with perfect graciousness. The head of accounting received them with the impassive expression of a financier who turns the key to unlock his lips only to let slip out the words, "Sir, that's quite impossible." As result, Monsieur Séjan assumed the burden of the banker's callousness, while the latter preserved his reputation for benevolence and generosity.

When all the visitors had been seen, Durand was informed that Daneau had returned; the banker, wanting to savor to the last drop the pleasure of making Count de Lozeraie cool his heels in the antechamber, had his servant invite the builder into his office.

"You asked to see me next, sir?" said Daneau with a smile as he came in.

"Yes, sir," replied the banker rather curtly, "and I would've liked to see you earlier, considering the importance of the conversation we have to have."

"It's your own fault, Monsieur Durand," said the builder with obsequious politeness.

Durand frowned.

"It's your own fault," repeated the builder. "Didn't you tell me, the first time I had the honor of meeting you, time was a resource that shouldn't be wasted? So I took advantage of the many callers you had to receive, to go get some other business done."

A smile of bitter scorn appeared on the banker's lips, and he replied, "What we need to discuss was perhaps the most important business of all."

"What's it about?"

"I think I should warn you that the line of credit you opened with me will come to an end as of the fifteenth of this month."

"You're shutting off my credit!" cried the builder, stunned.

"And I expect," continued the banker without any sign of having noticed his exclamation, "within a month from now you'll have repaid the four hundred thousand francs I advanced you."

"Within a month!" cried Daneau, astonished once again.

"It seems to me you should be in a position to do so. I supplied you, as requested, the funds needed to complete construction. The houses are finished, and it's now July—when, according to you, they should be ready to bring in some return. It seems like time to wrap up your work, put the houses on the market, clear your debts, and realize your profits."

"Possibly so, sir. But if I suddenly put three million francs' worth of finished houses on the market, that'll depreciate their value far enough to cause me a loss that'll eat up not only all of my profit but even the money I put into them."

"That can't be, Monsieur Durand," replied the banker with imperturbable composure. "You put three hundred thousand francs into the work; when you came to me, you were mortgaged for one million two hundred thousand francs. I lent you four hundred thousand francs, also on those mortgages, which comes to a total of one million nine hundred thousand francs. There's quite a difference between that and three million, the value you yourself set on your properties; quite a difference, with plenty of margin for your profit."

"No doubt, sir. But the four hundred thousand francs you lent me was used to settle prior commitments. As I told you, I had to make new commitments, and—even now when the work is done—I still have over two hundred thousand francs in upcoming payments."

"Well then, Monsieur Daneau, that comes to two million one hundred thousand francs, and you'll still make nine hundred thousand francs, if your calculations are accurate and honest."

"They are honest, sir," replied the builder with some energy. "And they'll be accurate, if you give me the time I need to carry out the sale of my houses."

The banker opened a file and took out a document; and after reading a few excerpts from it to Daneau, he said, "As you can see, the terms of our contract are perfectly clear. I lent you four hundred thousand francs for four months against your mortgages. The four months expire tomorrow, and I'd be within my rights to demand immediate and full repayment. I'm not doing so; I'm giving you another month, and I'd consider that going a great deal beyond what's in my interest, if I weren't already accustomed to sacrificing my interests for the sake of other people's."

"The truth is, Monsieur Durand," said the builder in a pleading tone, "it'll be impossible for me to satisfy your request."

"In that case, you won't be surprised if I immediately take the necessary steps to secure the payment I have a right to demand of you."

"What!" cried the builder. "A seizure of my property!"

"It's up to you to forestall it by reimbursing me immediately."

"But you're treating me so harshly…"

"I thank you," said the banker bitterly. "Luckily I'm used to ingratitude. Any man who's dedicated his life to helping others has to expect this kind of thing. I wasn't treating you harshly when I opened my till for you; but now that I want my money back, I'm a harsh man. That's fine, I know what I have to do."

"Please forgive me for my hasty words, sir—I disavow them from the bottom of my heart. But I promise you, to press me like this is to ruin me. You understand business too well not to know that you only find buyers by not looking for them. You have to let them come to you, and I can't expect to pull off such an enormous sale within a month. In any case, they'd ask to pay in installments, and if I can't secure installments myself I couldn't grant that, and the sale would fall through."

"Take out a new mortgage to pay off my mortgage, and I'll agree."

"But it'll lower the value of my security if I'm forced to say it doesn't seem sufficient to a banking house like yours. Because everyone will assume that if you demand payment like that, it's because you think your investment is at risk; no one could put a different interpretation on your… I don't want to say your harshness... but your..." The builder couldn't find a polite word, and fell silent.

"Never mind that, go on."

"Yes, Monsieur Durand," went on Daneau emotionally. "No one will believe a man like you—who succors the poor, who's a pillar of industry, who's spent his fortune to help out honest men—could be so strict with me, unless I'd deserved it by not keeping my word, by some dishonest action. And yet, Monsieur Durand, I'm an honest man; I'm like you, as you've often said: a child of the common people who made my fortune by hard work and integrity. And you can't mean to take away not just my fortune but my reputation. You're not capable of that."

The banker appeared to be moved, and he replied, "Believe me, if I didn't have urgent need of my capital, I wouldn't be so strict. But even at the time I lent you those funds they were intended for something else. I made a commitment, and I can't do anything."

"In that case, sir," said Daneau in despair, "let me see... Let me see."

He was about to leave when the banker called him back. "Listen, Monsieur Daneau, I don't want people to be able to say I ever failed to help out an honest man, a man from humble beginnings like myself."

The builder returned with eager delight and waited anxiously for him to go on; but the banker seemed to find what he was going to say next somewhat awkward. Finally he made up his mind and continued, "Based on your calculations, you have a total of two million one hundred thousand francs sunk in those properties?"

"Yes, sir."

"Sell them to me for two million two hundred thousand francs, and you're completely free and clear."

"But, sir!" replied Daneau angrily, taken aback by the banker's proposal and forgetting that this same man who was offering him two million two hundred thousand francs had just said he had some other urgent need for his capital. "That would be depriving me of any profit for my work!"

"What! How much did you invest in it? To start with, three hundred thousand francs, a year ago, to buy the land. Everything else came from a succession of loans. That means your three hundred thousand francs will have brought you a return of a hundred thousand francs in the space of a year. That's a thirty-three percent profit. I don't know of any business that gives that kind of outrageous return; and the central bank, which people are always complaining about, falls so far short of a quarter of that on the capital it invests that it often doesn't commit as much as it should."

"That may be so, sir, but you're forgetting that in the transaction that concerns me, I've had to pay interest on all the capital I borrowed, as well as the broker's fees."

"Quite right, and I'll cover that."

"So I'll have run all the risks on this project, I'll have worked for a year..."

"To gain a hundred thousand francs: that strikes me as pretty fine, especially considering where you started from!"

"Well," said the builder proudly, "from the same place you did."

"Sorry," said the banker loftily, "I wasn't referring to the man, but to the capital invested. I haven't forgotten where I started, which was perhaps even lower than you."

"Here, sir," said Daneau with same impulsive resolve as a wounded man who, knowing he's in danger, holds out his arm or his leg to the surgeon to cut off. "Here, give me two million four hundred thousand francs and it's a done deal."

The banker put the loan contract back in its folder and replied coldly, "I did everything I could to help you. It makes me cross to find you so unreasonable. Farewell, sir; this business no longer concerns me. You can see Monsieur Séjan to settle your account."

"But, sir..."

"Excuse me. Count de Lozeraie has been waiting for me for two hours now; and—in spite of my wish to devote all my time to men who, like me, are nothing more than businessmen and industrialists—to make a great lord who's been so patient wait longer would be beyond impolite."

"I'll go see Monsieur Séjan," said Daneau, who was confounded.

Durand bowed; and while he was giving the order to bring in Count de Lozeraie, and the latter was entering, the banker scribbled a few lines, which he sealed and handed to his servant, saying, "To Monsieur Séjan, right away."

Here was what he'd written:

Be firm over the Daneau business, and for two million one hundred thousand francs we'll acquire properties that, if we take advantage of the right opportunity, will be worth more than three million.

As soon as the servant had left, the banker beckoned to Count de Lozeraie, and the two upstarts faced each alone.

"Matthieu Durand really did that?" asked the man of letters, looking at Count Cerny so seriously that Luizzi realized the Devil was beginning to gain the kind of attention he wanted.

"Yes."

"Are you sure?"

"I've named the people, I've given you the exact figures."

"But how the devil could you have learned all that?"

"I'll tell you when I'm done."

"Do you realize that, with a secret like that in your possession, you could gain quite a hold over a man like Matthieu Durand?" said the poet.

"Oh, I promise you," replied the Devil, "if his daughter appealed to me the way she appeals to you, she'd soon be mine... especially with what I still haven't told you."

At those words Luizzi began to guess Satan's intentions; and he listened as the latter went on.

Chapter LXXXVII

Now Count de Lozeraie, once he was alone with Matthieu Durand, seemed embarrassed by what he'd come to say; and to that awkwardness was added his resentment at being made to wait so long, a wait he was well aware the banker had prolonged as insultingly as he could. But the count's resentment was visible only in the compression of his lips, and he hid his anger under an air of polite ease. Still, Durand was too good a judge of men not to know he'd wounded the vain man before him to the quick, and he concluded that only some imperative need could've made him accept the insult he'd been offered. That realization led the banker to promise himself to treat the count in such a way as to make him feel he'd overplayed his hand when he'd acted so disdainfully toward him at the Marquis de Favieri's. To start with, Durand was careful not to save Count de Lozeraie from his embarrassment by opening the conversation with the kind of polite small talk that would've given the count time to recover his composure. Instead he offered him a seat, sat down himself, and leaned forward slightly in the way that expresses, "I'm listening"—all without saying a word.

The count made up his mind to speak; in his wish to control the feeling of humiliation that was still uppermost in him, he made such a violent effort to seem calm that he went all the way to the other extreme—angry impertinence—without being able to stop at the midpoint of firm, cool politeness. "I've been patient, sir," he said in a mocking tone he meant to sound gracious, but which contained a hint of stiffness. "I've waited on your pleasure. I've been made aware that wealth is sovereign. I can only hope I won't find it too despotic. The all-powerful usually show their benevolence to those who submit openly."

Rather than let the conversation proceed on that light footing, Durand replied with cold gravity, "I have much to do and little time, count. That must be a sufficient excuse for a wait that seemed long to you."

"Luckily I have lots of time and little to do," replied the count. "That'll explain to you why I was willing to waste so much of my time in your waiting room."

"Well then, count, if you wish to avoid us both wasting our time now, be so kind as to explain what brings you to see me."

That reference to the real purpose of his visit cut short the count's flow of empty banter. His embarrassment returned, and Durand understood even better than before that he held his enemy's most vital interests in his hands.

Still, after a short pause the count went on, "No doubt you remember, sir, the deal proposed to both of us by the Marquis de Berizy, by which I consented to make payment to you for a forest I'd just bought from him?"

"I remember very well that I consented to receive that payment toward the Marquis de Berizy's account."

Count de Lozeraie bit his lip in resentment at that cold, blunt repetition of the word "consented." In fact he'd let it slip without meaning to offend; but old habit had prevailed over his wish to be direct and polite, and he realized he was dealing with a man who was inclined to ignore nothing that carried even the least hint of superiority. The riposte hit the count hard, but it passed by fast enough that he went on right away, "Of the two million francs you agreed to receive, one million two hundred thousand have been deposited with you."

"Yes, sir, and you must complete payment within the current month."

"It's for that balance, sir, that I wish to ask you for an extension of several months."

"Ask me, sir?" replied the banker with an air of genuine surprise. "I must point out, sir, in this matter I am in truth merely the Marquis de Berizy's cashier, and only he can grant you that extension."

"I expected you to say that, Monsieur Durand, and in response I believe I should explain the circumstances that keep me from meeting the deadline."

The banker bowed; and the count went on, "When I made that purchase, sir, I'd hoped to secure the contracts to provision the Algiers expedition."

"I understand, sir," said the banker disdainfully. "And you counted on the enormous profits from that honorable speculation for the sum needed to pay for your purchase."

"No sir. At that time I had the full price of my purchase. But I was led into taking a chance on what you call a speculation by a vile schemer who, under the pretext of bribing the people who could grant me the provisioning contracts, stole an enormous sum from me."

At that news Durand couldn't suppress his joy, and he replied, "That, sir, is exactly what you can explain to the Marquis de Berizy, who'll understand perfectly."

"Not as well as you do, I imagine. The marquis is an old country gentleman who's lived entirely removed from the world of business affairs; whereas you, Monsieur Durand, know how things are done…"

"I have absolutely no knowledge of the kind of deal you've just described," replied the banker scornfully. "Those of us who've come up from nothing are familiar only with business that is… legal."

It's hard to say whether Durand's hesitation before using the word "legal"—rather than the word he'd initially meant to use, "honest"—arose from a residual politeness that kept him from insulting the count so directly to his face, or from his recollection of the previous scene, between him and Daneau, in which he'd taken such dishonest advantage of legality.

Still, the fact was that Count de Lozeraie noticed the banker's hesitation, and guessed the word he'd meant to use before substituting the other. But he was careful not to show it; resuming his grand airs, he added with uncharacteristic thoughtlessness, "No doubt the whole business wasn't exactly legal, and as a result it would be a strange thing to confess to one of those who make the laws, a member of the Upper Chamber, a peer of France."

"You find it easier to confess to a Deputy?..." replied Durand solemnly. "To a member of the Lower Chamber?"

The count realized the clumsiness of what he'd just said; hoping to pass it off with a tone of apparent cordiality, he cried, "Come now, Monsieur Durand, let's not playact pointlessly: you know as well as I do how these things are done, you're a man of the world!"

"I'm a man of the people, count," replied the banker with his insulting humility.

"Well then," said the count, whose own words seemed to scorch the roof of his mouth, "aren't we all men of the people, some more and some less, some a little higher or a little lower? Let's keep up with the times, and not burden the commonplace things of life with pointless gravity. In short, Monsieur Durand, yes or no, will you agree to grant me the favor I've come to ask you for?"

"And what exactly would that consist of?"

"To fulfill the contract I made with the Marquis de Berizy, by taking over onto your accounts the eight hundred thousand francs I still owe him. And of course I'd make all the necessary guarantees, and I'd give you a mortgage on the forest I've acquired. So really I'm asking for nothing more than a loan for a few months."

"Just for a few months?" asked the banker, who, though privately he still intended to refuse, was delighted to find out so much about Count de Lozeraie's affairs. "So you're sure you can repay it by then?"

"Absolutely sure. I'm marrying off my son."

Like a thunderclap, that news rekindled in Durand's mind the memory of the count's very first impertinence; and he replied with a smile, "Oh, you're marrying off your son? And I assume you're allying yourself to some family of the high nobility?"

"No, Arthur is marrying a merchant's daughter."

"Oh, a merchant's daughter?"

"But an English merchant, a man of substance in the City. You know, in England those alliances are quite common; and anyway the English bourgeoisie isn't, like ours, devoid of ancestors, devoid of antecedents. In that country they have what I might call a kind of bourgeois aristocracy."

"You mean to say an aristocratic bourgeoisie?"

"That's it, Monsieur Durand. I'm supposed to invest my daughter-in-law's dowry in one of my properties; by using the dowry to pay off the price of the Marquis de Berizy's forest, I'll fulfill that clause of the marriage contract and I'll clear my debt to you."

Durand made no answer.

The count waited for a moment, then said, "Well, what do you think of my proposition?"

The banker suddenly stood up. Putting as much loftiness as possible into the tone of his voice and the whole of his manner, he replied, "I think, sir, your proposition should more appropriately have been addressed first to the Marquis de Berizy; for it's easy to come to an understanding between gentlemen of a rank I assume to be equal. And if it happens that the gentleman at court is afraid to admit certain things to the country gentleman, given the great difference between them in their... views, I think, sir, the proposition would've been even more appropriately addressed to the English merchant than to the French banker—to the bourgeois aristocrat rather than to the bourgeois commoner. That's what I think, sir."

At those words Count de Lozeraie turned pale. A gleam of hatred shone in his eyes. But he contained himself, and replied with scornful insolence, "You're Matthieu Durand, and I'm Count de Lozeraie; the distance that separates us keeps me from perceiving an insult in what you've just said to me."

"I'm willing to offer you a telescope so you can perceive it."

"If the telescope is as long as a sword, it'll do."

"It'll be that long, if that's what you'd like."

"Then it'll do," replied Count de Lozeraie, and he withdrew.

The next day, the Marquis de Favieri and the Marquis de Berizy went to see the banker on behalf of the count, trying to intervene between two men whose age and standing made it impossible for them to risk their lives so thoughtlessly. But for the two or three days the negotiations lasted they found both men equally intransigent. Astonished by that stubbornness, they declared they couldn't serve as witnesses in a duel whose cause they didn't fully understand. The banker was the first to whom they made that objection; but he said he was unable to reveal the cause, whose secret belonged to Count de Lozeraie.

When they repeated their objection to the count and passed on the banker's reply, the count decided to admit to the two marquis the reason for his visit to Durand and the turn it had taken; and he hastened to add that Durand had behaved honorably in keeping his secret safe. On his side, the banker could only approve of Count de Lozeraie's behavior in sacrificing his vanity for the sake of smoothing away the obstacles that stood in the way of an armed rencounter.

"And did they fight?" asked the poet. "High finance fought a duel?"

"That wasn't the most remarkable thing about the whole matter," said the Devil.

Once the two adversaries had been brought to that position relative to each other, it was easy to get them to admit there was no serious reason for them to fight. Both of them, in fact, had been motivated much more by a feeling of personal instinctive hatred than by any customary sensitivity on a point of honor;

and, once the circumstances of their quarrel were known, no doubt they were afraid to give away the secret of their mutual hatred, and they both declared themselves satisfied.

In any event, the whole business turned out very well for Count de Lozeraie. The Marquis de Berizy offered to void their contract, since he'd found a new buyer for his forest; and that new buyer was Monsieur Félix from Marseilles, who'd interceded with the marquis with uncommon insistence to keep the quarrel between the banker and the count from leading to unpleasant consequences.

"Again that Monsieur Félix shows up just in the nick of time!" cried the poet. "Come on! He must be some hero invented by Monsieur Scribe,[87] one of those gallant fellows who always have a couple of million francs tucked away in their trouser pockets!"

"Oh, it's not without its cleverness," said the Devil. "The ancients used a god to wrap up their dramas: *et Deus intersit!*, as Horace says.[88] Monsieur Scribe invented the millionaire to achieve the same end; and if I myself had any faith, I'd prefer, in literature as elsewhere, the god Millions to Jupiter or Apollo."

And with that reply to the poet, the Devil went on:

However, Count de Lozeraie, having agreed to the Marquis de Berizy's proposition, was left having deposited one million two hundred thousand francs, intended for the marquis, with Matthieu Duran, who hastened to offer him immediate reimbursement once he learned of the marquis's new arrangements, when the latter entrusted his new funds to him. The count felt his dignity required him to ask the banker to keep the money, not wanting to give his adversary any hint that he mistrusted him, since it couldn't hurt him now that his fortune was secure.

Meanwhile Monsieur Daneau agreed to the sale the banker had proposed to him. Durand acquired the properties and took over the builder's commitments to his creditors; and as a result he owed them one million two hundred thousand francs, and he owed Daneau six hundred thousand—which, with the four hundred thousand he'd advanced to him, came to two million two hundred thousand francs, which was the price of Daneau's properties.

---

[87] Eugène Scribe (1791-1861): a dramatist and librettist known for writing "well-made plays." He wrote the libretto for Meyerbeer's 1831 opera *Robert le Diable*, referred to indirectly earlier.

[88] *Et Deus intersit!* ("And God intervenes") is a slight misquotation. In the *Ars Poetica* Horace actually cautions, *"Nec deus intersit"* ("Don't let a god intervene"), meaning the writer should avoid resorting to a (literal) deus ex machina if possible.

At that point came the July Revolution.

"A great revolution!" cried the poet.
"I'm very proud of it," said the Devil.
"Which launched France on the road to social progress."
"And overturned the divorce laws."[89]
"And overthrew the aristocracy!"
"And instituted the officer class in the National Guard."
"And reformed the people!"
"And created the Bal Musard!"[90]
"You hold a grudge against the Revolution, Count Cerny."
"For what? For having done nothing good? I wasn't expecting anything good. I'm not like Matthieu Durand, who expected great things from it, and who found only ruin."
"What! Ruin?"
"Yes. Listen."

---

[89] The 1792 Revolution had brought unprecedented access to divorce. Those laws were reversed after the Bourbon Restoration.
[90] Philippe Musard's light-classical "promenade" dinner-concert music of the period was referred to earlier.

Chapter LXXXVIII

If I explained matters clearly at the start of this story, using the example of how the Marquis de Berizy's assets were invested in the government funds and available for some attractive opportunity; if you can appreciate the banker's equivalent position toward a large number of his clients; then you can understand the enormous losses he suffered when, being forced to reimburse quickly all the cash deposits he held, he had to sell shares in the five-percent funds at eighty-seven that he'd bought at a hundred and ten, and shares in the three-percent funds at sixty-two that he'd bought at eighty-two. Nothing less than the great upheaval in commercial affairs caused by the Revolution could've brought about such a depreciation in the public funds and undermined the wealth of people who held shares in those funds as security against their own debts.

In addition, that depreciation overtook all assets and especially real estate located in Paris, which was rapidly being abandoned at that period. As a result, the deal with Daneau, which would've been so profitable at any other time, necessarily ended in a loss when Durand had to sell everything to repay the backers who were demanding their investments. He barely managed to sell, for a million eight hundred thousand francs, the properties that had cost him two million two hundred thousand, and which could've been worth three million, as he'd hoped.

Of course, two transactions as small as those of the Marquis de Berizy and Daneau couldn't have done serious damage to a bank like Durand's; but in explaining the unpleasant consequences of those two, I've tried to make you see the effect of lots of other transactions based on the same principles and overturned by the same event. In any case, two months after the July Revolution, the banker Matthieu Durand, seeking to satisfy the demands of his creditors without delay, found himself more or less ruined, with barely enough cash held in debts still outstanding, but not yet receivable, to cover what he still owed.

"Ruined!" cried the poet. "But he's been throwing more extravagant balls than ever!"

"You know very well that the ancients adorned the victim before immolating him," said the Devil. "A bank is even more poetic: it crowns itself in roses before going to lay down its balance sheet..."

However, Matthieu Durand hadn't reached that point yet, for he had only three creditors whose claims could be consequential. The most important of them was the Marquis de Berizy, who, as I've said, had invested with Durand the money from his recent sale of property to Monsieur Félix; the least significant of the three was Monsieur Daneau, who'd left in the banker's hands the six hundred thousand francs he'd made on the sale of his houses; the third was Count de Lozeraie, who'd left for England a few days before the July Revolution to settle his son's marriage. But the count's son, a gentleman of the royal bedchamber with the prospect of every good thing under the reign of Charles X, no longer seemed to the merchant in the City a suitable match under the reign of Louis Philippe, and Count de Lozeraie was forced to come back to France after two months without having secured the brilliant fortune he'd hoped for.

That was where the various characters in this story stood relative to each other on the first of September 1830. That day—to return to our starting point—Matthieu Durand was again in his office. But he no longer exhibited either the extreme happiness of the first time we saw him there, nor the anxious joy of the second time: he now seemed sad, though still arrogant, beaten down though still resolute—a man who wouldn't bend under his misfortunes, though he recognized their magnitude. That day the same two men we met earlier in the banker's office were there again. One was Monsieur Daneau, the other was the Marquis de Berizy: the genuine man of the people and the genuine great lord. Just like the first time, the banker was carefully reading a document that seemed to absorb his full attention—an attention so great that, though the builder and the marquis were there with him, the banker couldn't lift his eyes from the words, which seemed to cause him great suffering.

"What is it, sir?" asked the marquis after a while. "Bad news?"

Durand immediately pulled himself together and replied with an emotion in his voice that he tried in vain to control. "No, nothing but a lampoon, a vile lampoon attacking me."

"And it's affected you so much?" asked Daneau.

"The hand that wrote it, gentlemen, hurts me more than the blows it strikes. It's by a mere child, a young man I brought up, young Léopold Baron, who's used the education I gave him, and the secrets he learned through the intimate access I granted him, to shower me with slander and ridicule."

"What!" cried Daneau. "That little Monsieur Léopold, who never used to speak of you except to call you his father and his savior?"

"The same."

"Well! I can tell you now," went on Daneau, "his extreme enthusiasm never struck me as sincere; he was a wicked flatterer."

"And every flatterer becomes a critic," said the marquis. "That's the rule, and there's nothing surprising about it."

"A rather stale old moral," said the man of letters.

"A very fresh new moral," said the Devil. "Because it's eternal, and what's eternal is always fresh." Then he went on:

"Never mind all that," said the banker. "Gentlemen, I can guess the purpose of your visit. I assume you've come to demand the funds that..."

The marquis and the builder interrupted him at the same time, and they were both beginning to speak when each stopped to yield the floor to the other.

"Go ahead, sir," said the marquis.

"After you, sir," said the builder. "And if there's anything you need to say that I shouldn't hear, I'll withdraw."

"Stay," said Durand, "because I imagine whatever explanations I have to give to one will serve for the other too."

"As you wish," said the marquis. "I'll speak in this gentleman's presence, because, if I understand right, we're here for the same reason."

"I can believe it," said the banker bitterly.

"Monsieur Durand," went on the marquis, "you're an honest man. You owe me two million francs, and I've come to ask you to keep it."

"What!" cried the banker.

"They tried to ruin you, sir, by forcing you into premature repayment. I won't be an accomplice to a panic that has already led to so many disasters. You're my political enemy, but there's integrity between us. I believe in your probity, and I'm leaving you my funds, and I'll only ask for them back the day you feel you don't need them."

It would be hard to say which feeling was stronger in the banker: his happiness at the trust he inspired as an honest man, or his humiliation at receiving a favor from one of those great lords he'd wanted for so long to crush beneath the weight of his wealth. But after a moment's hesitation the better feeling prevailed; he held out his hand to the marquis and said warmly, "I thank you and I accept, marquis."

"Ah, there's the moral of your comedy!" cried the man of letters. "Hurrah for the gentleman! Isn't that right, Count Cerny?"

"No, sir," replied Satan, "because I should add that..."

Just then Daneau came forward, looking awkward and moved; and with admirable clumsiness he said from his heart, "You only owe me six hundred thousand francs; but if it would be helpful for you not to repay it, I haven't forgotten that you rescued me, and however little it might be..."

A tear came to the banker's eye, and he cried, "Ah, this makes up for everything! Thank you, Monsieur Daneau! But I can't accept. That's all you have in the world, and you need your capital to be able to work."

"Interest at five percent would be enough. I'm rich enough. Don't say no, I'd feel humiliated."

"That's a fine thing you're doing there, sir," said de Berizy to Daneau.

"And what about you, milord!" cried Daneau, carried away by his enthusiasm into addressing someone with a title whose abolition had seemed to him one of the most precious achievements of the July Revolution. "You, milord, have

336

acted even more nobly! Because, you know, I'm not accustomed to being rich, and if I lost all my money I wouldn't notice it as much as you would."

"But you won't lose it, my dear Monsieur Daneau," said the banker. "And I hope it'll increase in my hands just like the Marquis de Berizy's money."

A few minutes later the builder and the marquis left together; and at the moment of parting they shook hands on the steps of the bank—the former laborer and the great lord, the man who'd been decorated in the July Revolution and the former peer under Charles X—two honest men. That's my moral, gentlemen, not counting the one that comes all the way at the end of this story.

Meanwhile that two-fold act of selflessness had restored Matthieu Durand's confidence; he saw a new path to fortune opening before him. The two million six hundred thousand francs de Berizy and Daneau had left with him, as well as the one million two hundred thousand francs he owed Count de Lozeraie, were, as I've explained, covered by the cash held in debts still outstanding and that would be receivable within no more than a year. Durand therefore envisioned himself at the end of a year with available capital amounting to almost four million, after he'd cleared all of his commitments on time. As a result, his credit, which had tottered for a moment, would rise again even stronger, since he would've survived a catastrophe that had carried away more powerful men than he.

He needed only a year, during which he could also pull back, as much as possible, money he'd committed in a number of small investments; from that he expected to be able to count on more than another million francs, even allowing for a sixty percent failure rate from those investments. With his future brightening like that after having been so dark, Durand allowed himself strong hopes—but at that very moment he saw a new cloud growing on the horizon that opened before him.

Less than two hours after the Marquis de Berizy and Monsieur Daneau had left him, the banker received a letter from Count de Lozeraie, informing him of his return from England and asking him to make available to him the million two hundred thousand francs he'd deposited at the bank. That demand was significant enough to throw Durand's affairs into fresh turmoil. To meet it he'd have to compel payment on, or abandon, some fraction of the debts he was counting on collecting, and a result he'd suffer a new loss on those debts; for that wasn't a period in which such loans or sales could take place in the usual way. It would put Durand once again under water, when only an hour earlier his assets had finally exceeded his liabilities. It would force him to reveal, by negotiations of that kind, that he was driven to his last resources; it eroded and destroyed his credit—the financier's great asset—credit against which in fact no one till then could've pointed to a single delay in payment or a single action betraying any financial embarrassment.

Durand thought over his new position for a long time, considering it in its most unpleasant light. He reflected that he was about to risk his entire financial

337

and political life on a single throw; he thought about his daughter's future; he imagined the joy of all his old enemies. Finally recognizing that only a decisive stroke could save him, he went immediately to see Count de Lozeraie.

When the visitor was announced, the count remembered the long wait in his antechamber the banker had subjected him to. For a moment he had the impulse to pay Durand back with the same torture; but then, since what he'd heard about the banker's position made the count genuinely concerned about the funds he'd deposited with him, his financial interests prevailed over his pride and he had Duran shown in directly.

For the second time the two social upstarts faced each other. The two men's characters differed in this way: Matthieu Durand retained all the firm, quick decisiveness of a pride that takes a kind of satisfaction even in an act of self-imposed humbling; whereas Count de Lozeraie's vanity retained all the vacillation of a nature that seeks, through a thousand excuses, to escape from an unavoidable act of submission. As a result, Durand felt no embarrassment, no awkwardness in the count's presence, and he addressed him with the solid self-assurance of a man who's chosen his course without misgivings. He opened the conversation with, "Sir, I've come to deliver myself into your hands."

"What do you mean by that, sir?" asked the count, more alarmed by those words than flattered to be proclaimed the master of the destiny of the man he hated most in the world.

"I'll explain, sir." And the banker described to the count the state of his affairs, the way I've tried to explain them to you; and he ended his confession by saying, "As you can see, sir, the funds you deposited with me are perfectly safe; and if you still doubt the word of an honest man, my account books will convince you..."

Count de Lozeraie had listened carefully to Durand, and he'd realized, with well-disguised delight, that his money was intact. Once he was sure his debtor was solvent, he thought only of taking cruel revenge for the insult he'd suffered before. Interrupting Durand in the middle of the speech I've just reported, he said, "Bankers' account books will say whatever they're asked to say. They use a hieroglyphic language, or rather an elastic language, that proves either wealth or poverty, as needed. I'll admit, sir, I have no faith in such evidence."

The banker bit his lip; but he was determined to save both his fortune and his reputation. For the sake of pride in his future, he bravely sacrificed his pride in the present. So he replied, "It doesn't surprise me, sir, to find you share the world's prejudices about banking houses' accounting principles and the state of their books. All of the many procedures we've introduced to prevent the slightest appearance of fraud, by the careful check of one procedure against another, seem, to those who don't understand them, no more than an inescapable labyrinth in which we hope to trap any investigation by concerned parties. So I can't take offense at what you've just said. But we have between us something much simpler and much easier to understand; that is, the word of a man of honor, and that must suffice."

"And if it doesn't suffice, sir?"

"Do you doubt my word?" cried Durand.

"Even assuming I don't doubt your good faith, sir, don't I have the right to doubt your foresight? A fortune like that of Matthieu Durand, overturned in a matter of months—does that suggest much prudence or skill?"

"Have you forgotten that it took a revolution to overturn it?"

"Have you forgotten that you were one of those who brought on that revolution?"

"I don't see that I need to account to you for my opinions."

"But you do have to account to me for my money, sir."

"I've done so."

"I don't take payment in words, sir. And when I tell you I want my money, and I want it tomorrow, I'm speaking of hard cash."

"I've already explained to you," said the banker, clenching his teeth as if to hold back the anger that stirred in him, "I've already explained to you, that's not possible."

"A court of law will prove to you that nothing is more possible."

"Me, dragged before a court of law!" cried Durand.

"That's where men of bad faith go who won't pay their debts."

"There's another place, sir," replied the banker loftily, "where honest men go who've paid their debts."

"When that's happened to you, sir, I'll see whether a man like me should follow a man like you there."

"That's a decision you'll have to make sooner than you think."

"Not as soon as I'd like, because it'll be preceded by the return of my capital to my hands."

"You won't have to wait long."

"I'm still waiting for my money."

"Till tomorrow, sir."

"I'll have your receipt ready."

"Have your weapons ready too."

"Don't make me waste paper and ink, please."

"You'll waste nothing, I promise."

The banker left. He went straight back to his office and wrote to Daneau and to the Marquis de Berizy. Then he went to see the Marquis de Favieri, explained his position candidly to him, and asked him for the credit necessary to reimburse Count de Lozeraie immediately.

The Genoese banker listened to the French banker without letting his face betray whether or not he was inclined to do what he was asked. When Durand was done he replied calmly, "Leave me the list of your debtors and the total debt outstanding against which you wish to borrow. You'll have my answer in two hours, and I'll tell you under what conditions I'll undertake this business, if in fact I can do it."

Two hours later Durand received a note from the Marquis de Favieri, asking him to send him Monsieur Daneau and the Marquis de Berizy, and adding that probably everything would work out. Durand's wait was excruciating; but his joy was correspondingly great when his two witnesses came back to tell him he didn't need the million two hundred thousand francs, since Monsieur Félix had offered his guarantee to Count de Lozeraie, and the count had accepted, and had given his receipt for the sum Durand owed him, by making over to Monsieur Félix his claim on Durand.

"Monsieur Félix!" cried the banker, dumbfounded at finding that name once again mixed up in a matter of such importance.

"It's about time he was dumbfounded," laughed the poet. "As for me, I'll admit I'm only listening to your hundreds of millions and your three percents and five percents so I can find out in the end who this Monsieur Félix is."

"You can see I had my reasons for not satisfying your curiosity right away," said the Devil. "But now we've reached the climax—a fine theatrical scene, I assure you!"

To the banker's exclamation of surprise the Marquis de Berizy replied, "Yes, the same Monsieur Félix who stood in for Count de Lozeraie in the purchase of my forest, and who's now generously standing in for you."

"Who is this man?"

"I swear I don't know."

"I'll go see him," said Durand, who'd been made thoughtful by the strange news. "I'll go see him when this whole business is settled. Because I assume you haven't forgotten, gentlemen, that I have matters other than money to sort out with Count de Lozeraie."

"No, certainly not," replied the Marquis de Berizy. "And the general gathering is set for tomorrow at nine at the Marquis de Favieri's. We'll all proceed to the rencounter from there."

"Nine o'clock seems rather late," said the banker.

"We chose the time that Monsieur..." began Daneau.

"That time seemed agreeable to everyone," said the marquis, interrupting the builder. "Till tomorrow, Monsieur Durand!"

When he was alone, Durand felt a kind of cruel delight at the thought that he was finally going to be able to get revenge on the man who'd treated him so insultingly. In his first wave of anger he forgot everything other than the satisfaction of his pride. But when he remembered that the duel might have fatal results, and he ought to put his most urgent affairs in order, he thought of his daughter, whom he would leave in the midst of the maze of a liquidation of assets from which only he himself would understand how to emerge with a few scraps of his fortune.

When he was gone, what would become of that girl, brought up to have her every whim satisfied, and who'd learned not the slightest sense of financial order or economy from him? He came back in sorrow to the false education he'd let the child be given—a girl who could've been raised good and down-to-earth if he'd wanted—and he reproached himself bitterly for his carelessness. But no matter how much he suffered at the thought of the unhappy future he might leave his child, not for a moment did it occur to him to make the slightest concession to avoid the coming duel. His pride won out over every other feeling; and he turned his face away, so to speak, from all those painful reflections to keep them from weakening his resolve.

The next morning Matthieu Durand and his witnesses, and Count de Lozeraie and his witnesses, all met at nine o'clock sharp at the Marquis de Favieri's. The carriages awaited, the rules of combat were settled, and they were about to leave the parlor... when suddenly in came old Monsieur Félix. The two adversaries stopped at the sight of the old man, who said solemnly, "Gentlemen, I wish to speak to you in private before the rencounter that's about to take place."

"Sir," said Durand with a bow, "Count de Lozeraie and I both know what rationality would suggest to you to say to mediate a matter like this. But things have reached a point where neither of us could wait any longer without dishonor to us both."

"The gentleman is right," added Count de Lozeraie, "and for once I agree with him."

"Count de Lozeraie," said Monsieur Félix gently, "I believe I rendered you a great service in freeing you from your debt to the Marquis de Berizy. Monsieur Durand, I was no less useful to you in making it possible for you to repay Count de Lozeraie. It's in the name of what I've done for you both that I beg you to listen to me."

The two enemies both turned to their witnesses as if to consult them; and those men having said enough to show it was appropriate to give way to Monsieur Félix's request, the witnesses withdrew, and Durand and de Lozeraie remained alone with the old man. When everyone else was gone, Monsieur Félix sat down and gestured first to the banker and then to the count to have a seat, one on each side of him. The old man's venerable countenance, at once serene and strong, contrasted with the anxious impatience on the faces of his listeners, who exchanged a glance from time to time as if to promise each other they wouldn't give in to the old man's pleas.

Monsieur Félix considered them for a moment with a kind of fierce, stern attention. Then he began, "Six months ago, gentlemen, I came to call on each of you... You first, Monsieur Durand. I told you about how I'd been condemned

341

for bankruptcy, and I asked you for the means to restore my good name completely. You refused me."

The banker said nothing.

Monsieur Félix went on, "Then I called on you, Count de Lozeraie, and I spoke to you about my claim for restitution against your wife's fortune. You dismissed my claims with threats."

The count also said nothing.

Monsieur Félix continued, "If I understood what each of you said to refuse my claims, it amounts to this: One of you, Monsieur Durand, a laborer's son, who owes his wealth to his own self and his own hard work, didn't want to help a thoughtless man who'd foolishly squandered the enormous inheritance he got from his father; the other of you, Count de Lozeraie, the scion of a great family, counted on the power of the great name he bears to silence the complaints of a man he called a schemer…"

"What's your point, sir?" asked the banker and count together.

"This, gentlemen: to observe that I, an impoverished old man of eighty, found support and justice neither from the man of the people nor from the great lord."

The two antagonists were silent, for there was nothing they could say to that.

"You're the man of the people, Monsieur Durand?"

"I'm proud to say so," replied the banker.

"You're the great lord descended from an ancient line, Count de Lozeraie?"

"I'm not vain about it," said the count with a great deal of vanity.

"Well, then!" said the old man, raising his voice. "You, Matthieu Durand, and you, Count de Lozeraie, you've both lied shamelessly."

"Sir!" cried the two enemies, rising to their feet at the same time. "Such an insult…"

"Sit down, gentlemen, I beg you. If necessary, I order you. And if my eighty years are not enough to make you listen to me respectfully, I'll invoke a title that could make you both listen to me on your knees."

"On their knees!" cried the poet, who'd begun to pay close attention to the story.

"On their knees," replied the Devil. "The word was spoken, the action was taken. Listen."

The solemn voice in which old Monsieur Félix now spoke stunned the count and the banker. The same thought, the same suspicion, seemed to enter both men's minds at the same time; and, now observing the old man with a kind of fearful respect, they sat back down and bowed their heads to him. The old man studied them in silence, with an air of triumph mixed with a certain look of bitter pain. With an effort he mastered that emotion and went on more calmly, "I know both of your life histories, gentlemen, but I'm not going to repeat them here. It's my story I'll tell you, and it'll serve as a preamble to your own, which you can tell after that, in the way you're used to telling it."

He paused a moment, as if to collect his memories, then went on in a strong, firm voice, "In 1789 I was a merchant in Marseilles. My business had been very successful up till then. I was married to a wife who'd given me two sons. One was fourteen, the other thirteen at that time."

Matthieu Durand and Count de Lozeraie started.

"Don't interrupt me, gentlemen," went on Monsieur Félix peremptorily. "This story is so old I might get lost in it if I don't tell it in my own way. The elder boy had been in England for four years, getting an education. I planned for him to go into business, and I wanted him to be familiar from an early age with a country which, especially at that time, was our model for commerce. The younger boy was starting his studies at a secondary school in Paris. Like lots of other people, I wasn't alarmed by the beginnings of revolution in '89. But as events grew more urgent and my fortune seemed to be at risk in the great catastrophe, I sent almost a hundred thousand francs to England by making them over to my elder son, and I brought the younger son back from Paris, because the future looked blacker every day.

"You're aware, gentlemen, of the extremes to which revolutionary passions led at that time. I learned I'd been marked out as an aristocrat, because—then as now—wealth constitutes an aristocracy. Perhaps I might've taken my chances in a trial on my own; but I trembled at the idea of those terrible riots Marseilles had already seen, and which could burst into my house and cut my wife's and my son's throats in front of me. So I took steps: I transferred all the money I could make liquid to the Marquis de Favieri—the father of the one you know, who at that time was a very young man and who wasn't living in Genoa.

"Then, one day in February 1793, I secretly set sail with my wife and son and took them to Genoa. I'd planned on only a short absence, but I was gone long enough for my enemies to notice, and I was immediately added to the list of exiles. My assets were seized, and I was sentenced to death. That judgment meant little to a man who was out of reach of the scaffold. They went further: they called for the liquidation of my business, and since everything I owned had been sequestered, it was easy to prove my bankruptcy; and that bankruptcy, added to my having gone away, led easily to my being convicted for absconding.

"I wanted to return to France to contest that shameful judgment, at the risk of seeing the sentence against my life carried out. My wife's tears and the Marquis de Favieri's advice changed my mind; and I decided to leave for New Orleans, planning to get there ahead of the news of my conviction and to keep out of the hands of the people who'd robbed and disgraced me the considerable sums owed to me by the leading merchants of that town, who knew me personally, for that was my third trip to America.

343

"However, during my brief stay in Genoa I met Monsieur de Loré, and I lent him money.[91] He was a gentleman from Aix who, like so many others, had fled a death sentence, taking along his daughter, who was about fifteen at that time, and a young man of good family, an orphan, the last of his line, who was a ward of his. That young man's name was Henri de Lozeraie… Don't interrupt me, sir," said Monsieur Félix to the count, who'd made a sudden gesture. "So I set off, leaving my wife and my younger son, who was then seventeen, in Genoa, under the protection of the elder Marquis de Favieri and of Monsieur de Loré; I'd also notified my elder son to expect new instructions from me…"

"I have to tell you," said the Devil, breaking into his own narrative, "since the beginning of that story Matthieu Durand and Count de Lozeraie had made several attempts to interrupt, looking beseechingly at Monsieur Félix. But the old man had squelched them, either by ordering them to be silent, as I've mentioned, or just by the authority of his manner. The two listeners sat there pale and trembling, their heads bowed, not even daring to look at each other."

The Devil had a motive for that interruption, which Luizzi suspected. He waited for the man of letters to make some remark; but the latter, so quick to interrupt at the beginning of the story, now seemed to care only about finding out how it ended.

Satan resumed his account, continuing in Monsieur Félix's words:

"Lots of circumstances it would be pointless for me to share with you, including the challenges of communicating during a time of widespread war, kept me from winding up my affairs as fast as I'd hoped. I could neither send word to my family nor get news of them, and it was only four years later I was able to return to Europe. I was about to sail when I got a letter from the younger Monsieur de Favieri, the one you know, informing me of surprising developments. An epidemic had struck Genoa. Monsieur de Loré was dead, as was young Henri de Lozeraie, as was my wife. My son, after withdrawing in his own name all the funds I'd deposited with the elder Marquis de Favieri, had run off with Mademoiselle de Loré. All those events had taken place before the younger Monsieur de Favieri had returned to see his father, who himself, he said, had just died from the same illness that had carried off my wife.

"Struck to the core by the terrible news, I sailed for England, hoping at least to be reunited with my elder son. But there I learned he too had withdrawn the entire capital deposited there in his name, and had left England saying he was going to rejoin me in America. I went back, and from there I sought information, from every part of the world within my reach, about Léonard Matthieu, my elder son, and Lucien Matthieu, my younger son—for my name is Félix

---

[91] Monsieur de Loré was mentioned in Chapter LXXXII as Count de Lozeraie's father-in-law, whose debts to Monsieur Félix the count repudiates.

Matthieu; but no one knew a thing about anyone with either of those names...
And now, Monsieur Matthieu Durand and Count Lucien de Lozeraie, can you
give me any news of my two sons?"

"Father! Father!" cried the two brothers, falling to their knees before the
old man, who drew back from them.

"Really? On their knees?" cried the poet. "They both got on their knees?"

"Yes, really," said the Devil, "just the way you'd write it in a dramatic
recognition scene, just like you'd see it done at the Porte Saint Martin or the
Gaîté."[92]

"And what moral do you draw from this tale, Count Cerny?" asked the poet.

"No other moral than the one drawn by Monsieur Félix himself as he
backed away from them, crying out in anger..."

"On your knees, pride and vanity! That's where you belong!

"On your knees!—you who, consumed by a thirst for wealth, envious of
the men you'd seen prosper around you by hard work and scrimping, wanted to
rise higher than any of them; you who, craving a name whose fame would be
yours alone, denied your father's name, leaving him stained with an infamy you
could easily have washed away!

"On your knees as well!—you who, drunk with the vanity of having a great
name, and unable to make one for yourself, stole another man's name and
dressed yourself in it; you who also denied your father's name—your father
who'd only compromised that name to save you!

"On your knees, both of you! That's where you belong. And the only thing
missing, fine brothers that you are, is for you to rise up and cut each other's
throats. Go ahead now, I won't stop you!"

The poet had nothing more to say.

The Devil added, "If you wrote modern comedy, sir, I'd tell you the scene
that followed that recognition scene: the fury of the two men who'd each been
humiliated in front of the other, and their embarrassment and still greater fury at
having to embrace by order of their father."

"And did their father forgive them?" asked Luizzi.

"More than you can imagine," said the Devil. "He concealed his sons'
wrongdoing by his silence; he told the truth about that strange history only to the
Marquis de Favieri, from whom I heard it. And if I've repeated it to you, I have
to admit it was mostly to prove my argument and to show you that neither char-

---

[92] The Porte Saint Martin theater has been mentioned previously. The Théâtre de
la Gaîté had been prominent since the 1750s.

acters nor events nor morals would be lacking from a comedy, if you knew how to write one."

"And as is usual in any proper comedy, I assume everything was wrapped up with the marriage of young Arthur de Lozeraie and Mademoiselle Delphine Durand?" said Luizzi.

"Oh, no!" replied the Devil. "The reconciliation couldn't go that far. Thanks to the secrecy promised by their father, Matthieu Durand remains Matthieu Durand. He still talks about his humble origins, and the fortune he was forced to amass sou by sou and then later rebuild without any help from anyone, and his love for the common people from whom he sprang, and the education he gave himself at great pains. And I'm sure that, to keep up his act to the very end, he'll end up marrying his daughter, with a magnificent dowry, to some man who, like him, made his name by the power of his own fists."

The poet said nothing, but Luizzi cried, "What exactly do you mean by the power of his own fists?"

"Oh," laughed the Devil, "I mean any fortune you owe to no one but yourself."

"Even a literary fortune?" asked the baron, looking sidelong at the poet.

"Well, why not?" said Satan. "It seems to me that, considering the literature that's constantly pouring down on us so copiously, the power of his own fists must be one of the chief qualities of a man of letters."

But the poet was no longer listening, and the Devil went on pleasantly, "As for Count de Lozeraie, he's still Count de Lozeraie, more puffed up than ever with the antiquity of his own lineage, even more arrogant about it now that he knows it's in doubt; and, in spite of his loathing for the July Revolution, he's completely behind the new dynasty, which, being a little thin in great names, has just elevated him to the Chamber of Peers."

Chapter LXXXIX: Plain Events and a Plain Moral

As the Devil was finishing his story, the stagecoach stopped. Luizzi had listened willingly to the tale: it seemed so far removed from his own concerns that he'd felt none of the anxiety Satan's revelations normally triggered in him. Considering all the inane remarks and ridiculous asides the man of letters had interjected in the story, Luizzi had expected him to follow up the extraordinary conclusion of the tale with reflections in the same vein, and even with some novel literary theory to match; so he was surprised to see the poet remain perfectly silent about what he'd just heard. But he asked the driver the name of the village they'd stopped in, and when the driver told him it was Sar—, he ordered his luggage taken off.

The driver was surprised, and before obeying his instructions he checked his list and said, "But monsieur has paid for his seat all the way to Toulouse."

"Which means I've paid for it this far, it seems to me! And now I want to get off here."

"We're three leagues from Matthieu Durand's chateau," said the Devil quietly to Luizzi as they walked on ahead of the stagecoach.

"So? What's he going to do there?"

"Take advantage of the secret he's learned to force the banker to give him his daughter in marriage, along with a few of the millions he's regained."

"Oh! That's shameful!"

"You forget, master, as a man of letters that gentleman has the right to steal other people's ideas."

"He certainly chooses them badly!"

"You're too modest."

"Me?"

"You. After all, he's only doing what you wanted to do earlier to Gustave and to Ganguernet. That's the only reason you told them about Madame de Marignon's adventures. Look how glorious you are! To do evil, the Devil is reduced to copying you."

The shot was well aimed, and Luizzi didn't bother replying. Still, Madame de Marignon's name reminded him of his encounter with the old blind man, and therefore of everything that had preceded his flight from Orléans, right up to the moment when he was about to question the Devil about Madame Peyrol. So as he walked along next to Satan he thought seriously about how to thwart the schemes by which Gustave de Bridely could prevent Madame Peyrol's acknowledgment as Madame de Cauny's daughter.[93]

He was still undecided whether he should depend on his own resources or ask his slave for information, when suddenly the poet called out to him from a distance, crying, "Hey, baron! Baron de Luizzi!"

Luizzi stopped. The poet approached him and said, "Baron, I promised to remind you of the circumstances of our first meeting, and I was supposed to tell you the tale at Boismandé. You'll find it describes a life story perhaps even more mysterious than that of Count de Lozeraie and Matthieu Durand. If you're interested, I'll send it to you in Toulouse."

"I'll receive it with pleasure," said the baron rather coldly.

The poet went away, and the baron walked on with the Devil. "Just who is that man?" he asked.

"What! You didn't recognize an old acquaintance?"

"That man?"

"The one and only Fernand, hero of the pope's bed, seducer of Jeannette, for whom you served as a witness in a duel..."[94]

"Oh, yes! Now I remember. And that must be what he wanted to tell me at Boismandé."

"He would probably have gone on to tell you about his subsequent adventures with Jeannette; and since you've got more free time now than you will once you reach Toulouse, I can tell you about it."

"I'm really not interested. And I assume you're about to leave me now. I guess there's no one else you have to teach a lesson to while I listen?"

"I've done everything I wanted to do. But I feel like you could treat me a little more politely, baron; because, seeing how reluctant you were to hear anything that concerned you, I was careful to choose a story that didn't involve you at all."

"So was that the first time your words weren't harmful to me?"

"Who can say?" laughed the Devil.

"Get out of here!" cried Luizzi. "I don't want to listen to you anymore."

The Devil vanished, and Luizzi went on his way alone, now at leisure to think over everything he might have to do. He brought all of his obligations to mind. Right now there were three women whom he had to save from the difficult positions he'd put them in: Countess Cerny, Eugénie Peyrol, and his sister Caroline. Luizzi was sorry he hadn't been able to stop at Boismandé and go to Madame de Paradèze's chateau to inform her that the daughter she'd mourned for so long had finally been found, and to let her know about the misfortune that

---

[93] See Chapter LXXII for the family history that makes Gustave de Bridely and Eugénie Peyrol rivals to inherit from Madame de Cauny.

[94] See Chapters XI through XV for those various episodes and more.

had befallen her niece.[95] But he absolutely had to get to Toulouse. He found himself cornered, constricted in such a way that he couldn't act promptly or adequately. Still, he thought he ought to write to Madame de Paradèze to let her know of the lucky turn of events by which he'd discovered that Jérôme Turniquel's supposed daughter was in fact Mademoiselle de Cauny; but the time he lacked to stop at Boismandé was also the time he lacked to write that letter, and he decided to put off sending it till he reached Toulouse.

While he was thinking things over like that and making his plans, he noticed the day was growing late, and he'd now gone far ahead of the stagecoach, which hadn't shown up yet. He was walking close by a thick hedge, and he'd already seen several suspicious-looking characters pass him in both directions; it wasn't robbers he feared, but the police. It especially alarmed him that the face of one of the men who'd brushed by him seemed familiar. So he turned back toward the village of Sar—.

Soon he heard the noise of a vehicle approaching quickly; assuming it was the stagecoach, he stepped out into the middle of the road. But it was a post chaise, up behind which sat a little boy, who jumped down as soon as he saw the baron and said, "The driver sent me to run after you and the other gentleman to tell you the draft beam of the stagecoach broke as it was leaving the village, and it'll be the middle of the night before it's ready to go on."

That setback, though it would delay his reaching Toulouse, gave Luizzi a few hours to write to Madame de Paradèze. So he set off on foot back toward the village he'd just left, while the little boy looked all around and said, "Where'd the other passenger go?"

"Oh, he went to the devil, and you'll have to be awfully quick to catch up with him."

"That's all right, I'll keep on running after him."

"You'll have to run a long time."

"No, no, I'll catch up with the post chaise and tell the postilion to let him know. They're climbing a hill now, so they can't go very fast."

Without waiting for an answer, the little fellow ran off as fast as his legs could carry him. Meanwhile Luizzi headed calmly back to the village, composing his letter to Madame de Paradèze in his head as he went. When he reached the inn where all the passengers had gotten off, he called for a room and for writing materials, and closed the door.

After about an hour there was a knock at his door, and the innkeeper appeared, cap in hand. "Beg pardon for disturbing you, sir, but how far from here did you meet the little scamp who was sent to tell you to come back?"

"Something over half a league from here, more or less, next to a dark hedge sheltering some undesirables, I believe."

---

[95] Meaning Léonie de Cerny.

"The thing is, he's my son, and he hasn't come back, and neither has the other passenger."

"I told him the man had too big a head start on him, but he insisted on catching up with the post chaise and telling the postilion to look for him."

"Oh, is that what happened? The little joker must've caught up with them, and the postilion must've let him hop up on the spare horse, and he's liable to have gone on as far as Boismandé. And maybe whoever was in the post chaise gave the gentleman a ride to the relay stop as well; because I believe there was only a lady inside."

"Most likely," said Luizzi, who was eager to be rid of the innkeeper.

"Sorry to have disturbed you," said the latter as he withdrew.

Luizzi went on writing his letters. It was about midnight when the stagecoach set off again. Four hours later they reached Boismandé. Luizzi got down to find someone to deliver his letter to Madame de Paradèze. The first postilion he asked said, "I'll do it—give me your letter. In the morning I'm driving the post chaise that arrived tonight to Madame de Paradèze's."

"Oh!" cried Luizzi in surprise. "And who's in that post chaise?"

"A lady all by herself; an odd kind of lady, in fact, whom I recognized right away in spite of her hat and veil, a lady who used to be a servant at this inn."

"Who, Jeannette?"

"Say! You know her?"

"Yes, I met her a few years ago when I passed through here. But what business does she have with Madame de Paradèze?"

"Oh, I don't know, there's a whole stack of stories behind it. It was the old gentleman who got her a job here at the inn."

While Luizzi was still absorbing that surprising new encounter, he over-heard the stagecoach driver saying to another passenger, "Well, too bad for that gentleman! He must've stopped at some peasant's house when we didn't show up, and we passed him without his noticing."

"But you can't just leave the poor man somewhere along the way!" protested the officious traveler.

"All right, all right! He likes walking, so he can walk till he catches the next stagecoach. Besides, he might've caught the Laffitte and Caillard coach that passed us while I was having the draft beam fixed—since after all I'm four hours late. Come on, all aboard! Postilion, saddle up and let's be off!" Then, turning to another postilion, he said, "Since you were driving that post chaise, did you see that gentleman?"

"No, I told you: little Jacob, who was up behind, got down to talk to the first gentleman, while I went on. When I got to the foot of the hill I stepped into Mother Filon's roadhouse for a moment while my horses were walking up slowly. That's when Jacob ran up after me, caught up with the berline, and told the lady inside to let the postilion know. Then he came back to Mother Filon's, where there was party going on and where he must've spent the night."

"And you didn't see anyone on the road?"

"Nobody."

"Then to hell with that traveler!" said the driver. "All aboard! Let's go! Postilion, saddle up!"

Feeling confident they wouldn't ask him about the vanished passenger, Luizzi gave his letter to the other postilion, along with a generous tip, and hastened to get back on board. They set off, and reached Toulouse without further incident. As soon as he arrived he went to a small furnished hotel that enjoyed a fairly bad reputation, but whose landlady also had a name for complete discretion. When he'd secured a room he wrote a letter and then summoned Madame Périne, the landlady.

She came straightaway, and after curtseying to him she said, "What would monsieur like?"

"Someone reliable to deliver a letter."

"My son is as silent as a wall."

"And then I'd like you to find me clothes besides these."

It should be remembered that Luizzi had left Paris in evening dress. At Fontainebleau he'd had barely enough time to get a frock coat and a long overcoat. He'd left both of those at Orléans, and when Count Cerny caught him he'd fled still wearing the same clothes.

"What tailor shall I send for?" asked Madame Périne. "If monsieur doesn't know the town, I can choose from the best for him."

"I want ready-made clothes; I don't want to see anyone."

"Anyone except your lawyer, Monsieur Barnet, I assume!" said Madame Périne, who'd read the address on the letter Luizzi had given her.

"What makes you think he's my lawyer?"

"Oh, nothing, nothing... But usually when you write to a lawyer, he's your lawyer."

"Couldn't Monsieur Barnet just be a friend of mine?"

"If he is, then it's my mistake," said Madame Périne, starting to withdraw.

"Come now," said Luizzi, stopping her. "Do you think you recognize me?"

"Me? Not at all. I can see perfectly well the baron doesn't want to be recognized."

"What!" he cried. "You old witch, you haven't forgotten me?"

"Oh, what can you do, Monsieur Armand, having a good memory is one of the requirements of the job. You have to be able to tell the regulars from the birds of passage. Anyway I'd know your face because of your father's. The old baron spent many a good night here."

"My father?"

"Oh, sure! I can tell you that, now that he's dead and you won't go tell him to his face, 'I guess I can go to Périne's, since you certainly did.' Those were the good old days. I'm the one who set him up with that girl Mariette, with whom he had a daughter who didn't hide her parentage. You know Mariette, who left me to set herself up in exclusive business, out of love for Ganguernet, that practical joker who was involved in that whole story about Father Sérac."[96]

"Oh, yes. I feel like I met her once, at the Marquise du Val's."[97]

"That's right, the priest got her a position there."

"And what became of her?"

"Nobody knows. They say she's in Paris, where she moved after the illness that left her ugly and unrecognizable, which must be three or four years ago."

"Fine," said Luizzi, who knew enough about his father's lapses not to want to hear about any more of them. "Send that letter to Barnet and send me up some supper."

"Will you be having supper alone?"

He gave her a suspicious look; but then he remembered where he was, and understood he had no right to take offense. "On second thought, I won't have supper. I need sleep more than anything else."

"All right. You must be tired. You certainly look it."

Madame Périne left, and Luizzi, who was truly exhausted, went to bed and slept the sleep of the righteous in that respectable house. He didn't wake till four the next afternoon, and was sorry he'd lost so much time. He rang, and a pretty girl, as young and fresh and graceful as a rose, came in and sat down familiarly on his bed, saying in a Gascon accent, "What would you like, sir?"

He considered her carefully. She was charming, and he could see her teeth were pure white. That made him sad: he trembled to think what this child with the ingenuous face and the rosy complexion and the naive manner must really be; and he replied, "I want nothing from you."

She seemed offended by his answer, and drew back to the edge of the bed, saying, "I'm not the only girl here."

"I want to see Madame Périne," he said angrily.

"I'll go let madame know," she replied, and withdrew.

A moment late Mother Périne came in. "Well, by God, Monsieur Armand, Paris has made you awfully particular, and I don't know whether…"

"Listen, Périne," he said curtly. "I came to stay at your place because I don't want anyone to know I'm in Toulouse. Otherwise I'd have gone to some hotel or other. But since they report the list of travelers staying there to the police every day, I didn't do that."

"Oh, so you don't want the police to know?"

---

[96] See Chapters XII-XIV.

[97] Mariette appears as the Marquise du Val's chambermaid in Chapter III, and again in the chapters concerning Father Sérac—in which Luizzi had a great deal more interaction with her than he had at Lucy du Val's.

"No. And since I know you do your best not to let the police know the names of your guests, I chose your house."

"That's fine, and you should've told me that right away. Coming here is like being buried a hundred feet underground: no one'll know a thing."

"Ten louis for you if you're discreet."

"It's as if I already had 'em."

"Now tell me, has Monsieur Barnet come?"

"Him!" cried Mother Périne, taken by surprise. Then she recovered and went on, "Oh, my sweet Jesus, he wouldn't even know the way to this house, the poor man!"

"He'll find out."

"At his age? That'd be a sin! Besides, his wife would put his eyes out with her knitting needles if she found out he'd come here."

"Did he at least answer? Did he say something to your son?"

"Oh, say, that's true, you're right, he said, 'Tell the one who sent you I'll do what he wants.'"

"I told him to come here today."

"Did you say what time?"

"No, I just said today."

"Well, today doesn't end till midnight, so there's still a chance he'll show up."

"Fine. I'll wait for him. Have dinner sent up, and some paper and something to write with."

"Well then, since you don't want to be recognized, I'll have the same girl from earlier wait on you. That way no one else will see you. And old Marthe—you know!—old Marthe might well recognize you. The girl, on the other hand, doesn't know who you are. Besides, she's a good girl, surprisingly innocent. When you need her, ring twice. Her name is Lili. I'll go get your dinner ready; don't get impatient."

"Do what you need to, but hurry: I'm starving. And anyway, send me writing materials."

"Everything you need is in the desk."

Mother Périne left, and Luizzi wrote a long letter to Eugénie Peyrol, telling her her mother was alive and where she lived and who she was. Two hours went by. Then Lili arrived with everything necessary to set the table. She was skillful enough, but in a bad mood. Luizzi followed her with his eyes. When she'd finished setting the table he sat down. Lili casually took a seat by the fireplace. She seemed cross and put out.

"Does it bother you to wait on me?"

"Well now!" she said sourly in her strong Gascon accent. "Well now! I'm not here to be a servant. If I'd wanted to stay in service, I'd have chosen a better-off house than this."

"Oh, you were in service before you came here?"

"Yes, and in a pretty grand house too."

"Whose house?"

"Oh, I was at the Marquis du Val's."

"At the marquis's? And what did you do there? Because he's a widower, I believe."

"Well now! That's why I was there."

"Oh. And why did you leave?"

"You know, he bored me, he bored me to death. Did you know he's a Deputy? Under the pretext of giving me an education, he made me learn his speeches by heart. And when I couldn't recite them perfectly he threatened to have me arrested, because he's a magistrate of the king's court too."

Luizzi couldn't help laughing. The girl went on, "And then he had such odd habits, too! He wore fake calf muscles and false teeth, and I was the one who had to fasten them on for him."

"Where did he get you?"

"Well now! He got me from where I was before."

"And where were you?"

"Well, at another master's, where I had to work ten hours a day without a break. And you know, I don't really care for work, that's just how I am. I'd rather laugh and have a good time and do nothing, that's my nature. Anyway, that one was no better than the other one: and when he was supposedly working in his study he came to find me in my room at night and preached deadly boring morals at me."

"Nothing but morals?"

"My God, the other part didn't amuse me, though he was my first. I don't know if you know him, but he isn't good-looking, that Monsieur..."

Just as she was about to say the name, there was a knock at the door.

"See who that can be," said Luizzi.

Lili went to the door and opened it, and cried out in delighted surprise, "Well now! When you speak of the Devil you see his tail! It's him—it's Monsieur Barnet—the one I was just telling you about!"

Barnet came in sheepishly and said to Lili, "What! You here, in this house, you little wretch!"

"You're here too."

"I told you you'd wind up here, you nasty little slut!"

"My word, Monsieur Barnet, I have to admit," replied Lili boldly, "I'd rather have started here."

"To have reached this level of corruption, at your age! I beg your pardon, baron," said Barnet, bowing to Luizzi, "but you can't conceive the debauchery of the young. A child who hasn't yet turned seventeen, already settled in a life of vice!"

"My dear Barnet, I believe you had something to do with showing her the way, so spare the girl your lectures and let's talk seriously. Lili, leave us."

On her way out she laughed and made cuckold's horns at Barnet, who cried out furiously, "Oh, that's not true!"

"Well," said Lili, "junior clerks aren't particular. And your wife might be ugly, but she softens them up with good soup and good goose thighs and bottles of good wine she sends up to their rooms."

"Will you shut up, you little tramp!"

"Well now, maybe I wouldn't know, except we ate them with the clerks."

Barnet was scarlet with rage, and Luizzi would've been entertained if he hadn't really had some important business to talk over with him. He motioned to Lili to leave, and she went away, making the staircase echo with her Gascon voice as she sang a popular song:

"A la fount men soun anada,
Lou miou galant my a rancountrada," etc.[98]

And she sang it with a joyful, carefree lightness of spirit the most innocent girl couldn't have matched. Luizzi was revolted: vice in some hideous form is less painful to see than vice young and rosy and fresh and carefree. The latter is incurable, because it has no regrets, and no sense of the evil it does.

The lawyer lifted his hands to heaven, saying, "Young people these days!" Then, when they could no longer hear Lili, he turned to Luizzi and said, "You've really played a nasty trick on me, baron. What! To make me come to a house of this kind! A man like me! You're making me risk my reputation."

"I had no choice about where to meet."

"You could've come and stayed at my place."

"So Madame Barnet, the biggest gossip in Toulouse, could go announce on every street corner that Baron de Luizzi was back in town?"

"That's true. I forgot you wanted no one to know you were here. It's that girl who's upset me. But say, if I understood your letter correctly, you need a lot of money immediately?"

"Lots. I'm leaving France for a few years."

"You? And here I thought you'd come back for the elections!"

"I've given up on being a Deputy. I'm leaving. I'm going to Italy."

"Well, how about that! Is this about some business matter gone wrong?"

"No, it's just a whim: I want to see Rome. But in the meantime, let's have a look at the accounts."

"Right away, baron. And then, if you'll be so kind, you'll give me the signatures I asked for to wrap up your suit against that rascal Rigot."

"I'll give you all the signatures you want. But let's have a look at how much you might be able to get me in cash."

---

[98] "I went to the well, my lover met me there…" (This is Soulié's own footnote, since the text in thick Gascon dialect would be barely comprehensible even to a French reader.)

355

Together they sat down before a pile of folders and account books, and for an hour they calculated figures and sums. Luizzi was no businessman, but neither was he a complete fool; he knew how to make sense of the accounts he was shown. He examined them all the more carefully because the encounter between Barnet and Lili hadn't raised his opinion of the lawyer. But he was forced to acknowledge the latter's scrupulous integrity; and he couldn't help reflecting that this man—whose seduction had driven into a life of vice a child who otherwise might not have become what she was now—would've had qualms about robbing his client of a single sou.

But Luizzi had neither the time nor the inclination to dwell on such thoughts, and when the accounts had been made to balance he said to Barnet, "So, you deposited three hundred and forty-two thousand francs in ready money with the receiver general?"

"Exactly."

"Well, I need that money."

"How soon?"

"Immediately."

"Three hundred and forty thousand francs?"

"Yes."

"But you'll have to be able to carry it."

"My word, give it to me in banknotes."

"Drawn on what bank?"

"You're right—I keep thinking I'm in Paris. So get me as much in gold as you can between now and tomorrow."

"How much? A million écus?"

"Well, at least a hundred thousand francs' worth."

"I'd need two weeks to scrape together a hundred thousand francs in gold in Toulouse, if there's even that much here."

"Come now: what can you get me between now and tomorrow?"

"With a lot of work, and by going to the dealers who do business at high interest, in three days I could get you between twenty-five and thirty thousand francs."

"All right, thirty thousand francs will be enough at first. So I'll need letters of credit to get the rest of it from abroad."

"If you were going to Spain it'd be easy, because we have lots of correspondent banks in Spain, but since you want to go to Italy..."

"My God! I don't care—I'll go to Spain!"

"Oh!" said Barnet in surprise. "So you're not traveling for pleasure?"

"I believe I can go wherever I like," said Luizzi haughtily, "and I'm not making any unreasonable demands when I say I want my money."

"Fine, fine! I'll get you letters of credit for everywhere in Spain. I only need three or four days to do that. Should they be made out in your name?"

"No, please, in yours, and left blank. There's no need for anyone to know those letters are meant for me personally."

"By God! I'll answer for your money as long as I have it in my hands and I can pay it out in cash in a safe place. But to endorse a letter of credit, exchanging that money for paper—that I can't do."

"You know me well enough to know I won't have recourse to any action against you."

"You, baron, possibly not. But the third parties to whom you might pass those letters…"

"On the contrary, am I not obligated to repay before you are?"

"Yes, but you won't be in France when those bills come due."

"So you don't trust me for the value of what you're issuing me?"

"It's not that. I'll take every possible precaution, but you can only be sure of what you have in hand."

"Surely there must be some way?"

"I'm not suggesting you issue an endorsement without guarantee of payment: that would devalue a letter of credit you might need at any moment. But all you have to do is issue your guarantee of payment, by giving me authorization to mortgage one of your properties to make payment in your name; and I'll do whatever you want."

Luizzi did all the lawyer asked, because at every turn he could see blocking his way the obstacles that arise when you start from a false position; like a man who wants to survive no matter what the cost, he threw everything into the sea in the hope of escaping the storm.

Chapter XC: The Benevolent Officers of the Law

As Barnet had predicted, it took him almost four days to pull together the total in gold Luizzi had asked for. Meanwhile he was getting ready to return to Orléans. More than once he'd sent someone to the post office to see if any letters had arrived for him, and Barnet had also checked for him. Nothing had come. He was surprised to have had no news from Léonie, contrary to the promise she'd sent to him by way of the little beggar girl. Not knowing what to think of that silence, he'd decided to leave Toulouse, as we've said. The lawyer had booked him a seat on a stagecoach, which he would catch a few leagues out of town to avoid examination by the police inspectors who kept on eye on departing coaches.

All was ready, and he was about to leave Mother Périne's house, when Barnet—to whom he'd already said his farewells—came running up. "I've just been told a letter arrived for you, addressed to you at my house. But the odd thing is, they refused to deliver it to me."

"Where's it from?"

"Orléans."

"That's the one I've been waiting for, and I've got to have it, no matter what."

"Impossible. Apparently the letter is endorsed as deliverable only to you personally. 'If Baron de Luizzi were in Toulouse,' they said, 'we'd give it to him on the spot. All he has to do is come claim it in person.'"

"That'd be admitting I was in town, and I don't want to do that. But I can authorize you to receive any letter that comes for me, and I'll give you that authorization."

"That'll give away your presence in Toulouse just as much as showing up in person would, and it still might not be enough, since I presented them the authorization you gave me before, and it did no good. Forget about that letter, or better yet go get it yourself. What does it matter if anyone knows you were here, since you'll be gone in an hour?"

Countess Cerny's letter was all the more important for Luizzi because it probably contained instructions about what he should do; and it might render moot the entire business of keeping his arrival and departure secret. So he decided to go get it. He asked Barnet to have his luggage taken a couple of leagues out of town along the Paris road; then he went to the post office.

As soon as he'd stepped inside and explained why he'd come, the clerk gave him a look of surprise and said, "Oh, so you're Baron de Luizzi? Please wait just a moment while I go get the letter you want."

The clerk left the building; and Luizzi was growing impatient at not seeing him return—when the door opened and a police captain and two gendarmes came in. Ever since his adventure in Orléans, the police had become for Luizzi what they are for so many people: something repellent and frightening, the very sight of which upsets you, like the odious touch of some enormous spider or toad or snake. Luizzi hastened to turn away, but just then two large hands took hold of each of his shoulders, and the foreboding voice of the captain announced, "I arrest you, sir, on suspicion of the murder of Count Cerny."

The mere fact of his arrest had appalled Luizzi, because he understood right away it made it impossible for him to help Léonie or Caroline or Eugénie; but what should've horrified him more than anything else instead gave him a glimmer of hope. The absurdity of the charge reassured him; seeing it had nothing to do with abducting Countess Cerny, he replied, "Be careful what you're doing, officer! Count Cerny is as hale and hearty as you or me, and I don't wish to be the victim of a judicial error, or rather of a criminal plot and wrongful complacency."

"Tie up the gentleman!" said the captain.

"You're forgetting who you're dealing with!" cried Luizzi.

"Handcuff him!"

"I protest against this illegal arrest!"

"Make the gentleman march!" said the representative of the French state.

Once the gendarmes had begun pressing the butts of their muskets against the accused's kidneys, the baron had little choice but to decide to march toward the jail they were taking him to. Still, just as they set off he stopped again, and said to the captain, "I demand to be taken immediately before a magistrate!"

"I'm having lunch in town," said the captain to one of the gendarmes. "Here's his order for delivery to the jailer. Don't let him forget to put this gentleman in complete isolation!"

With that, the captain, taking off his tricolor sash of office, immediately reentered civilian life and went off to eat duck liver preserves with a pretty young woman who sold stockings and whose husband was a friend of his.

The captain's indifference had greatly deflated Luizzi's confidence in his name and in himself. He remembered the Devil often telling him there was one power that almost never lost its effect on men. So, turning to one of the gendarmes in whose hands he'd been left, he said, "How'd you like to earn ten louis? Take me to the magistrate."

"Isn't he cute with his ten louis!" said the first gendarme to the second. "He probably expects to find them in some crack in the floor in his future bedroom!"

"Shut up," said the other gendarme, who was from the area, and he led his companion over to a corner of the room. "He's one of the nobility in town. They say he's got enough money to buy the Place du Capitole.[99] If you're willing to take him to the magistrate, it isn't ten louis he'll give you, it's twenty-five."

"Twenty-five louis!" said the first representative of public order, his eyes shiner brighter than the brass badge on his shoulder strap.

"So that'll make fifty for the two of us," said the other.

"All right. How about if you suggest it, since you know him?"

"Thanks, but I'm not the one he made the offer to. It's up to you."

"No, no! He could claim it was my idea. I'd just as soon take him straight to jail." Turning to Luizzi, he said, "All right, fifty-louis man, pick up your feet!"

"Say!" said the other gendarme to Luizzi. " He must've heard you say fifty louis, that dope, as if anybody'd pay fifty louis for a silly thing like that! Just to go see the magistrate!"

"I'll give them to you right now," said Luizzi, "before we even leave this room."

"Well now!" said the first gendarme. "Might you by chance be innocent? You seem so sure of yourself, I'm beginning to wonder... You're beginning to wonder too, aren't you?"

"My word, yes, we're both beginning to wonder..." said the other gendarme.

"In fact, you might even be innocent."

"It's happened before."

"And since you've been so kind, we're going to take you to the magistrate."

"All right," said the other. "And as long as we're being nice, let's do it all the way. Take off his handcuffs so he can move his arms around."

"That's right, so he won't look too much like a convict."

"So he can take off his hat if he meets someone he knows."

"And reach into his pocket for his handkerchief."

Luizzi understood, and reached into his pocket for the fifty louis, with which he paid for the indulgence of the local constabulary. Once the transaction had been carried out, they were as gracious as could be. Since they couldn't call a cab—cabs being unknown in Toulouse—they led Luizzi along several shortcuts and finally brought him to the magistrate.

The baron was quite surprised to find himself entering the du Val mansion by the same little door that, ten years earlier, had led him to the unfortunate Lucy. He was even more surprised when the gendarmes led him to the very pavilion in which he'd met the marquise for the last time. He felt as if some strange predestination had marked that visit, when they took him to the boudoir in which she'd surrendered herself to him so madly.

---

[99] The Place du Capitole was, and still is, the elegant central square of Toulouse.

He'd waited there only a few moments before the marquis himself appeared, wearing a long dressing gown. The Marquis du Val was then a man of about fifty. He was an aging libertine worn out by debauchery; he'd retained all the vanity of youth, and he spent more time on his appearance than on his judicial hearings. It was only since his wife's death that he'd entered the magistracy and taken up what is called a position. As we know from the previous chapter, Luizzi was aware of that fact; but it had meant so little to him when Lili mentioned it that not for a moment had he expected to be brought before the Marquis du Val.

As soon as the marquis entered the room he motioned to the gendarmes to withdraw and said to Luizzi, "It's only because it was you, baron, that I received you, since I have to dress to go have dinner with our chief magistrate, and I've got barely half an hour. But with old friends and relatives you don't put on airs, and you'll allow me to go on with my dressing."

He rang, and a valet brought in everything the magistrate needed to dress up as a dandy. "So," he said to Luizzi, "you're here on account of that business with Count Cerny? Really! First you run away with the wife, then you murder the husband? That seems like taking things a little far."

"See here, marquis, is this charge of murder really well founded?"

"Not only well founded," said the magistrate, putting on silk stockings, "but pretty well proved."

"What do you mean, proved? So Count Cerny is really dead?"

"So dead," said the magistrate, putting on his trousers, "that he was found, with two bullets in him, in a small thicket next to the high road about half a league from Sar—, near Boismandé."

That news stunned the baron, for he remembered the form Satan had assumed to accompany him to exactly that spot; and he trembled to think it might've been one of the Devil's tricks to doom him altogether. He stood there, silent and overwhelmed.

The magistrate, who was stretching his suspenders and fastening on his trousers with particular joy, said carelessly, "Well, don't you just have the most excellent trousers! Trousers fit for an angel! Who's your tailor in Paris?"

Luizzi, who hadn't heard him, looked up with the air of a defeated man and said, "What! The count was found dead near the high road?"

"Yes, yes," replied the magistrate; and turning to his valet he said, "I've never been able to find trousers like that. Who did you say your tailor was, Luizzi?"

"I don't know," he answered, not at all in the mood for that kind of conversation.

"I'm sorry to hear it. I'd give a lot to have that tailor's name and address."

Not for nothing had Luizzi seen the world through the Devil's eyes. Counting more on that happenstance than on his innocence, he replied, "Wait a second... My tailor's name is Humann, I think..."

"Remember that name," said the magistrate to his valet while his put on his cravat.

Luizzi continued, "But still, even assuming the count really was murdered, why am I the one suspected?"

"Because the wife's lover is always the one with the best motive for getting rid of the husband."

"You think I'm capable of a crime like that?"

"That's what I said. I brought up the idea of a duel, with no witnesses, which would fit the circumstances; but that remains to be proved. Besides, there's the troubling fact that two swords were found next to the count, but he was killed by firearm; which would strongly suggest that, if he'd arranged a duel with you on the stagecoach, the duel was preempted by murder."

"And was Count Cerny really seen on the road to Boismandé?" cried Luizzi, rising.

"What do you mean, was he seen? You spent almost half a day traveling with him!"

Now the baron understood the Devil had dragged him into a fatal trap. He turned away to hide the pallor he felt spreading across his face, which could've been interpreted as evidence of his supposed guilt.

The abruptness of his reaction drew the magistrate's attention; pausing as he dressed, he cried, "What a fine jacket! Does that Humann make your jackets too?" Luizzi made no answer. Still full of admiration, the magistrate pointed the baron out to his valet, saying, "Just look at the cut of that! No creasing, and no bunching up, like the jackets I get made here in Toulouse. I absolutely have to have that tailor."

Luizzi had overheard; turning indignantly to the marquis, he said, "Is that what you received me for, marquis? Is that all I can expect from you?"

Summoned back to his duty, though he still kept an eye on the suspect's perfect jacket, the magistrate replied curtly, "Listen, baron, I've been assigned to investigate your case. I'm sorry to say, all appearances are against you—even the conversation we've just been having; because it had a purpose, believe it or not. Certainly if you weren't guilty you'd have shown a little more presence of mind in answering my questions, however devious they were."

Luizzi understood that the magistrate now wished to throw a veil, however clumsy, over the foolish frivolity of his words. Knowing he had no hope with this man unless he flattered his ridiculous obsession, he replied, "Oh, my dear du Val, I think you've mistaken an innocent man's natural anger for a criminal's distress. I'm quite ready to prove to you I'm not so filled with remorse as to neglect something as important as my appearance. As I mentioned, Humann makes all my clothes, and he's certainly the best there is in Paris. If you like I can give you a letter of recommendation to him. I'm one of his regular customers; he respects me, and he takes good care of the people I send him."

"Bring writing materials," said the magistrate to his valet. "And don't forget to address the letter, baron."

"No," said Luizzi, folding the letter and handing it to the marquis, who read the address: *Monsieur Humann, rue de Richelieu.*

The marquis was now fully dressed. He'd given his hair a suitably rakish angle, opened his waistcoat just so, and positioned the armholes of his frock coat; and he was drawing on his gloves when Luizzi said, "Well, my friend, one good turn deserves another! I hope you'll sign the order for my immediate release."

"Me?" cried the magistrate. "How could I do that? My dear fellow, you're under a capital charge."

"Then why did you agree to see me?"

"It's my duty to listen to the accused. It seems to me I carried out that duty more than adequately, since I'm only required to interrogate you within twenty-four hours of your arrest. Besides, my dear fellow, you didn't bring forward a single exonerating fact. All I can do is make sure they have the greatest possible consideration for your rank... Call in the gendarmes," he added, addressing his valet.

"This is an outrage!" cried Luizzi.

The marquis's gloves were on and he was holding his hat. He drew himself up and said sternly, "Don't make your position worse by misbehavior I'd be forced to punish."

"You?" cried the baron angrily, remembering just then what the Marquis du Val had been and what he still was, and also remembering Madame de Crancé[100] and Lucy and the girl at Mother Périne's. "You!" he cried. "You vile wretch! You, who've practiced every vice!"

The gendarmes entered.

"Gendarmes!" cried the marquis furiously. "Remove the accused! And see that he's treated with the utmost severity!"

Upon which he left. The two gendarmes took Luizzi away in such distress that he was escorted halfway across Toulouse without noticing the curious stares of all those who saw him and recognized him.

---

[100] See Chapter XIII for Madame de Crancé's involvement with the Marquis du Val.

Chapter XCI

If we recall the apparent circumstances of Luizzi's encounter with the Devil in the form of Count Cerny, it'll be easy to understand the horror that overcame the miserable baron when he found himself all alone in a dungeon, thanks to the kind attention of his cousin, the Marquis du Val. The way it looked to everyone was that he'd walked on ahead of the stagecoach with a traveler who'd then vanished. That traveler was thought by all to have been Count Cerny; certainly that's who he was to the poet, who'd asked him his name, and to whom Satan had given the count's name.

Luizzi had been locked up for a week; for a week he'd been removed from the lives of other men; and for that whole time every hour, every minute, every second had lasted its full duration. In the thirty-five years he'd been alive, he'd never known such a long span of time for reflection. For the first time in the ten years since he'd accepted his father's infernal legacy, he was able to ask himself at length why his life had been so unusual, so utterly swept along by a whirlpool of events over which he'd had no control; and how it was that the supernatural power granted to him had done nothing but plunge him into a series of misfortunes which that very power ought to have protected him against. And then he wondered whether that story in Genesis—which sentences man to misery the moment he touches the tree of the knowledge of good and evil—wasn't in fact the most sublime of all truths; and whether he himself wasn't the living proof of it, he who'd tried to see further than any other man into that terrible knowledge.

In the midst of those reflections he was sometimes seized by a wish to know what was going on outside his cell. In fact his eyesight and his hearing could've penetrated the places where his fate and that of all those whom he still loved was being decided. But he hesitated to use that power, so well aware was he that Satan's revelations had provided no more than the dire illumination that had constantly made him lose his way; and in spite of his fear of losing his honor and even his life, in spite of his fears for his sister Caroline, for Eugénie Peyrol, and for Countess Cerny, now exposed to urgent dangers, he resisted the temptation and didn't ring the little bell—neither during that week of waiting nor during the days in which he was made to appear repeatedly before the magistrates.

That good resolve would probably have held firm, even against the despair that haunted him, if two letters hadn't reached him from outside, bringing word of new miseries and new crimes. The first letter he received was the one that had led to his arrest, which the Marquis du Val agreed to let him see as part of the evidence, once the investigation was complete. The second letter contained the story the poet in the stagecoach had promised to send him, and which had also been entered into evidence, because it began with words that looked damning against Luizzi: *When I left you alone with Count Cerny at Boismandé, on the road to Sar—...*

Once he was back in his cell, Luizzi set aside that second letter, thinking it was bound to hold very little interest, and read the one from Countess Cerny.

ENDINGS

Chapter XCII: The Madhouse

It's only now, after five days of captivity, that I've managed to write to you, Armand. And though my heart is still stirred and broken by that terrible scene, I'll begin my account of what's happened to me since our misfortune—a misfortune I don't dare complain of, compared to the one I've just witnessed, which I'll also tell you about, since in your position you might be able to help.

That last phrase was the first blow that made Luizzi's resolution totter, so to speak. That appeal for his protection made him feel his helplessness—which he could bring to an end, since he had in his possession an extraordinary talisman that would enable him to escape from his imprisonment... or so he still assumed. However, that thought did no more than cross his mind like a small shadow, apparently leaving no trace behind. He went on reading:

So as not to mix up my own sufferings with the misfortunes I witnessed, I'll tell you what happened to me day by day, starting from when we were separated.

After you fled, I remained alone with Count Cerny. He told me, with the cynicism of a man who's already decided to commit a dishonorable act, that he would make me pay by the loss of my honor for your discovery of the secret that brought us together, which I still don't know how you learned. Count Cerny found our letters in my boudoir; he took them away, and in those letters, along with our departure from Paris, he saw evidence for a charge of adultery that would avenge him. What's infamous in Count Cerny's behavior is that, when he was laying out his hideous plans before me with such cold cruelty, it wasn't vengeance for his dishonor he was after, it was vengeance for the betrayal of his vile secret, the shameful condition to which his own debauchery had reduced him. When he was speaking to me he still thought I was innocent, he assumed I'd merely fled from his persecution, and you were no more to me than a protector, a devoted friend.

Armand, I wanted to pay him back for the wrong he was doing me, I wanted to wound the vanity that made him so vicious and so cruel, and I told him the truth... I told him you were my lover. I certainly succeeded. It was an agonizing torture to him, and I salted the wound with everything I could think of that was most moving in my love for you. It meant nothing to that man to hear I loved

366

you, that I loved you from the bottom of my heart—because I do love you, Armand, I love you because I've made you both happy and unhappy; because, if I've weighed down your life with a burden that may long encumber it, I've also seen that, for a few hours in the few days that were granted to us, my words soothed your spirit and my eyes made your heart forget its despair.

But he wouldn't have understood if I'd told him all that; and I found Count Cerny's shameful behavior so outrageous that I wounded him and humiliated him in the place where the wretch had hidden away his pride. Yes, I told him you were my lover and I loved you. But I also told him I'd given myself to you, and I told him how, I told him about that day I spent at your feet, that night I spent in your arms—I told him everything, the fire of our lovemaking, the number of our kisses. I sank that low, because I could see how every word I said irked him, how every confession of mine ate at him and wracked him in his impotence; and no woman in the whole world has ever felt so proud of being beautiful and so happy to have fallen.

Perhaps if we'd been alone together in some empty house I wouldn't have dared pay Count Cerny back for all the wrong he'd done me; but by having me arrested he'd also put me under the protection of the law, and he couldn't forget that a magistrate was waiting outside the door to take me into custody. So when he lost the battle he fled, leaving me in the hands of those who'd arrested me. That's when I met the little beggar girl and sent her to you. Right after that I was taken to the city jail.

The magistrate in charge of my case was a chivalrous enough man to understand that my preventive detention shouldn't be a punishment more awful than what I was likely to be sentenced to; though unable to prevent my confinement in the quarters for the accused, he asked me if I wouldn't prefer to have a private room in the part of the facility reserved for women who were insane, but mildly enough that they weren't considered dangerous. Between madness and criminality, between women who've lost their reason and women who've lost all self-control, between the nonsensical stories of the one kind and the foul language of the other, I didn't hesitate for even a moment, and I took the magistrate's advice. I was given a decent room, and I was able to reflect on my situation and write to my father to let him know of it.

The day after my imprisonment I didn't want to go outside: through the window I could see madwomen drifting around like ghosts, shuffling along with an imbecilic gait, their eyes staring or wandering, and singing, talking, gesticulating. One made herself a tiara of withered grass, as if she were going to a ball; one fastened a bride's bouquet to her dress as if she were walking to the altar; yet another cradled a piece of wood in her arms and offered it her nipple to suck and called it her baby. That one made me weep.

Still, I realized I could hardly find out how the little beggar girl would make contact with me unless I mingled, not necessarily with the poor madwomen themselves, but with the women guarding them, who came and went freely in all parts of that vast prison. So I went down into the yard and approached one of the guards and, with a little money, got her to go find out whether some child I'd promised to help and protect had come to see me. That woman knew what I'd been arrested for, she knew my name, and she knew someday I could repay her handsomely for any kindness she showed me; and when she went away she told me to wait for her to come back.

I'd found a seat in a corner of the large yard reserved for the madwomen's exercise, where I tried to avoid seeing them and being seen by them—when suddenly I noticed two women a short distance away staring at me with uncommon curiosity. Both of them must once have been beautiful, but age and suffering had already withered one of them entirely, whereas the other retained a vestige of good health amid her sorrows. The second woman's appearance struck me all the more because her face seemed familiar, and I felt that at the same time she too was trying to place me.

That mutual observation went on for a few minutes; and, out of some obscure impulse of pity, I might've been about to approach the two women, when the guard returned and told me the little beggar girl had indeed come to ask after me; but, in accordance with my husband's order to let me communicate with no one, the child had been sent away. That misfortune—because it certainly was one in my circumstances—led me to forget about the two women who were still watching me, and I went back to my miserable room, giving up all hope of learning what had become of you.

No sooner was I back in my room when through the window I saw one of the two women, the one I thought I'd recognized, closely questioning the guard I'd just left. In the midst of my despair, her curiosity aroused my own, but not enough for me to want to satisfy it immediately. Besides, I needed to think about you, Armand, and our lucky meeting, our astonishing love, our brief happiness, our misery come so quickly. Will I ever see you again, Armand? Does the fate that seems to pursue you extend to everything you come close to? I fear it's so, and yet I can say I'm not afraid; some secret voice tells me I love you the way you needed to be loved, and that if we were together you'd have been happy.

What a lot of vanity, right, Armand? But I feel I'm absolutely yours, though I was only yours for a moment: though hunted and locked up like a fallen woman, I feel so ready to sacrifice my life, my reputation, my freedom for you that I can't help believing that my destiny, which bound itself to yours so quickly and so tightly, was created to be its sister, its companion, its support. The old blind man found the little beggar girl by the side of the road to guide him; wasn't I also set on your path to take your hand, and isn't it too bad I found you so late?

Forgive me, Armand, for talking to you constantly about myself; but you need to know I didn't give myself to you the way I'd have given myself to just anyone else. I can tell you now that the first word you ever spoke in my presence dropped into my placid resigned life like a stone into calm clear water.

That trivial word unsettled me, and some voice in my heart said, look out! Why? I didn't know you. I've met plenty of men with greater names, and better looks, and more fame than you, but they all left untroubled that tranquility of mind and heart that constituted my happiness. Only you touched me, almost without having spoken to me. I resisted that sense of dread; and you must remember, Armand, the praise I heaped on a man whom I now consider contemptible. I wanted to punish you for making me question my own self-control when you spoke those fatal words about Madame de Carin, and I don't know what drove me to demand that you explain them.[101] It was a new experience for me to feel driven to do something my reason condemned. I wrote to you, and you came; was it heaven or was it hell that willed all the rest? As guilty as I am, I still want to hope it wasn't to doom you that I doomed myself.

I'm telling you all this, Armand, because that's what I was thinking about during the whole of that long day, because—having been whirled in just a few days through enough events to fill a lifetime—that was the first moment of stillness I'd had to pause and consider myself carefully and ask if I wasn't both the most foolish and the guiltiest of women. Minute by minute, word by word, I reviewed those brief, ardent, rapid pages of my life, asking myself if it wasn't just some delirium, some vertigo I'd let myself fall into; and in my heart I couldn't find a single moment of regret for having given myself to you; I felt there'd never be such a moment.

If only you knew, Armand—you who no doubt are in the midst of one of those times when you devour the hours with impatience, forced as you are to endure the sluggishness of the affairs that hold you back—if only you knew how the hours fly by when you're absorbed by a single thought! They flew so fast that night had already fallen without my having done anything but think over and over, since I couldn't say it to you, "Oh, I love you, Armand! I love you! I love you!"

The night would probably have passed just like that day, if the guard hadn't suddenly come into my room and interrupted my heart's soliloquy. Seeing her reminded me of the curiosity I'd provoked in those women; not knowing how to respond to her offers to help me, nor how to reward her when she didn't dare ask to be paid without doing me some service, I asked her who those two women were whom I'd seen together among all those madwomen wandering around alone—for one appalling thing I've learned here about madness is that it has the strange effect of keeping the madwomen from talking to each other, or loving each other, or helping each other. Is the heart lost when the mind is lost?

The guard replied to my question with another: "So you didn't recognize the younger one? But she recognized you."

"Who is she?"

---

[101] See Chapter LVII for that conversation.

"I'll tell you," she said, lowering her voice, "though out of consideration for her family we're forbidden to say her name to strangers. She's Madame de Carin."

I cried out in surprise... Madame de Carin, Armand! The woman about whom you spoke the fatal words that brought us together! Madame de Carin, whom I allowed to be slandered in my hearing, when I knew she was innocent, to protect the contemptible vanity of the man whose name I bore! Madame de Carin the madwoman, now locked up with Countess Cerny the adulteress! I can't even tell you, Armand, what passed through my mind: I envisioned the punishment standing beside the crime, and then I understood that all the empty, spiteful words we let slip so carelessly into the world can shatter the strongest lives. Alas! If I hadn't allowed Madame de Carin to be slandered, you wouldn't have spoken up, Armand, and I wouldn't have known you, and I wouldn't now be locked up in the same prison with her.

All those thoughts ran through my mind while the guard tried to explain why Madame de Carin was obsessed by the notion that Monsieur de Carin had tried to murder the Marquis de Vaucloix.[102] Her story was of little interest compared to my own train of thought, and I barely heard her when she told me the other madwoman was someone from your part of the country, named Henriette Buré, who believed she'd been locked up for years in an underground prison where she'd had a baby, and from which she'd been released only to be put into a madhouse and have her child taken away from her.[103]

The time had come for the doors to be closed. I was locked in, and I slept. For the first time in my life I learned that physical fatigue is a refuge from mental exhaustion; after all those nights spent in cruel unrest, I didn't wake till the day was already far advanced. My first thought was for you, and I hurried down to the yard. I could tell the guard had news for me, because as soon as she saw me she came quickly across the yard to meet me.

"Has someone come to inquire after me?" I asked.

"The little beggar girl is here."

"So she was allowed in?"

"It would've been hard to keep her out, since she was sent here under a charge of robbery."

"That child?" I cried. "That child? Impossible!"

"By God, she brags about it to anyone who'll listen, and if you could see her she'd tell you all about it."

I remembered the purse I'd given the girl. I assumed she'd kept it, and though that idea deprived me of the hope of finding out what had become of you, I blamed myself for having put temptation in the poor girl's way. I didn't want my meeting her to have brought about her doom, and I asked to see her.

---

[102] See Chapters XLIV and XLV.

[103] Chapters VII and VIII cover Henriette's story and its outcome.

"I can bring her to your room tonight, before lockdown," said the guard. "Her absence will only be noticed in the common dormitory, and I'll say she went to bed early. But you'll have to keep her here all night, since I won't be able to take her back to the jailhouse till tomorrow."

"That's fine. I'll be expecting her."

Just then I noticed Madame de Carin once again, and that Henriette Buré, the other madwoman, who never leaves her. It seemed they were avoiding me; I wondered if they'd been told the reason for my imprisonment; I forgot they were mad, and I felt humiliated and resented them for it. They passed by, and I couldn't help watching them as they went on. That's when I noticed that, out of all the women in that place, only they walked together and talked together; the guard told me they even shared the same cell. I can't express the feeling that drew me to them but also repelled me; I wanted to speak to them, and I was afraid to. I was afraid my interest in them would evaporate when they answered me with the same insane babbling that disgusted me in the other madwomen. I wanted to preserve my pity for them; being unable to comfort them, I wanted to be able to go on pitying them.

I'd reached that point in my thoughts when another madwoman wandering in the yard approached me, shouting with laughter and telling me she'd been Napoleon's mistress and had been crowned Empress of France. I turned away and wanted to go back to my room; but, as if she'd inspired others by her example, more women followed me with their shouts, their pleas, their curses. One took me for the rival who'd stolen her lover, another for the wretch who'd handed her over to her torturers, another for the witch who'd drunk her child's blood. I was alone in the midst of all those madwomen. I can't describe the horror I felt: that circle of confused faces, that symphony of nonsensical speech, terrified me. I felt my own reason going, I felt faint and near to collapsing, and I would've fallen down right there, since I couldn't get away from them—but then Madame de Carin and her friend hurried up and pulled me away from the angry circle of madwomen. They escorted me all the way to the door leading back to my room; and the one named Henriette Buré said, with a gentleness that struck me deeply, "Return to your room, ma'am, and if you have to stay in this part of the prison for a long time, try to avoid being exposed to that spectacle, because it could make you lose your mind."

"Yes," agreed Madame de Carin, "stay in your room. If Henriette hadn't saved me, I might've gone mad too."

So Madame de Carin didn't think she was mad. And was I myself in my right mind? I would've said exactly what she said. The calm helpfulness of those two women terrified me even more than the ravings of the others; disoriented and confused, I went back to my room, crushed and lost and doubting myself. I awaited the coming of the little beggar girl with terrible anxiety: it seemed to me that the child, in speaking of what had happened to me, would bolster my reason: I'd reached the point where I needed a witness other than myself. What an awful day that was! I plugged my ears to keep from hearing the cries of the unfortunate women wandering around the yard; I hid so as not to see the faces pressing against my window. Night finally came, without easing my fears.

I can't even tell you all I did, Armand. In trying to reassure myself I hadn't gone mad, I almost went mad. I sifted through my memories of childhood to convince myself they were still there. I recited lines by our great poets out loud to make sure I hadn't lost my memory. I tried to recall precisely all the names of all the people I'd met on such and such a day. In short, I was going mad out of fear of being mad... when I saw the little beggar girl come in. I ran to her, I sought the protection of the child I'd picked up on the high road.

Her first words did more to help me than all of my own efforts; she spoke of you. "I saw him," she said. She told me what you'd said to her.

You'll save me, Armand, won't you? You'll save me! Oh, you've already saved me: I was able to think about you, I turned to you, I put my hope in you, I felt my reason returning, and I was happy.

So far we've neglected to describe the emotions that letter inspired in Luizzi. We'd have had to interrupt his reading after every sentence. But now he himself stopped reading: that appeal to his protection broke his heart. That woman, locked up among madwomen, turning trustfully to him, who was locked up among criminals! He looked around in despair: he was alone... alone! He wept. He wept at being alone, he dared to weep because he was alone. Weak, proud man!

When his sorrow had eased, he went on with the letter.

However, Armand, the little beggar girl told me something that alarmed me terribly and surprised me just as much. Count Cerny had arrived by post chaise with a woman, and the next day he'd gone on by post chaise with that woman, and he was heading for Toulouse. Was he pursuing you? If so, he'd chosen a strange traveling companion. That fact reassured me a little.

That part of Countess Cerny's letter surprised Luizzi. He wondered whether the letter he'd written to Caroline had been intercepted by her husband Henri or by Juliette, and whether Juliette had tipped off Count Cerny and sent him in pursuit of his wife. Indeed, Countess Cerny made no mention of any reply from Eugénie Peyrol that might've reached her in Orléans, nor from Caroline, which ought to have reached her. The strange suspicion arose in his mind that it was in fact Juliette herself who was traveling with Count Cerny; but when he thought it over he found so little reason to believe it that he gave up the idea and went on reading the letter.

Alas, Armand, there was so little I could find out about you that an hour after the little beggar girl arrived I was able to turn my thoughts to her. She'd told me she'd given you the purse I'd sent you. I'd let that pass, thinking it was a lie, but now I said, "Listen, child, I'm too grateful for what you've done not to forgive you for a wrongdoing that your poverty can excuse to a certain extent. You were put in prison here after being arrested for robbery. If it was because of the money I gave you, because you kept it, I promise to tell the magistrates I gave it to you, so you'll go free…"

Armand, you can't conceive the hurt, the indignation, the shock that suddenly spread across the child's face. "Yes," she cried out through her tears, "yes, ma'am, I did steal, but it wasn't your money. I stole, because the only way I could get in here was by being arrested. I told the gentleman I'd do it, out on the high road. He can tell you. I didn't steal for me, I stole for you, ma'am, for you!"

Oh, my darling, how small I felt before that child! I would've begged her pardon on my knees for my suspicions. I took her into my arms and did all I could to soothe her weeping. She was so miserable, and I'd been so ungrateful to her! You can understand, can't you, that after that I was able to set aside my situation and yours and inquire about hers. I asked her who she was, what she was; I wanted to hear the life story she'd been going to tell us both but that I alone heard. Her story is both astonishing and simple.

She said she'd spent the first years of her life, when she was very small, locked away alone with her mother in a room only one man ever entered. Had she been born in prison? Was that man the jailer who came every day to deliver the pitiful prison rations? But in the poor girl's confused recollections it seemed to me the place she lived in couldn't be a real prison, and the conversations she remembered weren't those between a jailer and a convict. Still, she could remember neither the names her mother had carefully taught her nor the events she said had led to her imprisonment.

One day they took her mother away, and she herself wound up in the foundlings' home in Orléans. Her new life—for it seemed like a new life to her—soon erased her memories of her early years. Before then she'd never seen the sky or daylight or a flower or a tree: nothing that lived, besides her mother and the man who kept the two of them. That's rather surprising, Armand, because no prison in France is as harsh as the one that poor girl's mother was locked up in. Still, not daring to believe in such a despicable crime, I blamed the unreliability of her recollections—which would soon be explained to me in a shocking way.

We spent half the night talking. She told me how, driven by the idea of finding her mother, she'd escaped from the foundlings' home. I decided to ask the prison director to let me have her as my servant, explaining to him why she'd committed her crime and asking him on my behalf to dissuade whoever it was whose accusation would force her to go to trial. That was why I didn't hand her over to the guard when she came in the morning; and the woman was willing to deliver the letter I'd written to the director.

Because of what I've told you about the horrors I'd experienced the day before, I didn't want to go down to the yard. The little beggar girl, sitting around idly in my room, looked out through the window with her face pressed to the glass. Suddenly an indescribable cry rang out in the yard, and the girl turned to me in great distress and cried, "Oh, my God! My God! My God!"

She fell to her knees still repeating those words. I was hurrying to her, when my door was flung open, and there stood the madwoman named Henriette Buré. Instinctively I placed myself between her and the little beggar girl, for I sensed it was the sight of her that had provoked the madwoman's fit, and I wanted to protect the girl from her sudden fury—for indeed the woman seemed enraged. She paused for a moment on the threshold, her arms outspread as if to prevent any escape; she gave a glance around the room as quick and bright as a flash of lightning; and she noticed the child behind me. Before I knew she'd seen her, Henriette had rushed at me, and with a strength I couldn't resist she pushed me aside, practically throwing me to the far corner of the room. She picked up the girl and stared at her; then, without a word, without a cry, she squeezed her in her arms with shocking force.

I came forward again, meaning to tear the girl away from the madwoman. She saw me coming and, carrying the girl with a strength only delirium could've lent that fragile body, she rushed out of the room with her. I ran after them, shouting for help; but she was running so fast I was afraid she'd fall at any moment and injure the poor beggar girl in doing so. My cries brought two guards running, and they joined me in the pursuit.

When the madwoman saw she was about to be caught, she began to call out, "Louise! Louise!"

I assume that's Madame de Carin's name, for she came running, and placed herself so resolutely between us and her friend that we were forced to stop, while Henriette, exhausted, held the little beggar girl to her breast and stared at us with her eyes shining.

"Why are you chasing Henriette?" Madame de Carin asked the guards. "You know perfectly well she isn't mad."

Since the two guards didn't seem prepared to give up at those words spoken with every appearance of sanity, Madame de Carin turned to me and cried, "Keep them from hurting Henriette, ma'am!"

"I don't want them to hurt her," I said. "I just want her to give me back that child…"

Now for the first time Madame de Carin turned toward Henriette, and saw she was clasping the girl in her arms. She stepped toward her friend, who picked up a rock and brandished it at Madame de Carin, crying out, "Félix! Félix! If you come any closer I'll kill you!"

At those words Madame de Carin drew back with a cry. "Oh, it's not possible!… Henriette! Henriette!" she added, going closer again. "Don't you recognize me? It's me, it's Louise, it's your friend!"

374

Her voice seemed to calm the madwoman temporarily, for she replied less angrily, "Go away, Hortense, go away! You too have abandoned me, you've handed me over to your brother. You, with children of your own, have helped him steal my child from me!"

Madame de Carin stared at her in unspeakable horror. I tried to come forward as well, but Henriette turned to me and said with savage violence, "What do you want, ma'am? What do you want with me, mother? You've locked me away and cursed me. I accept your curse, I want my prison, I'm happy here, I'm here with my child, I never want to leave."

Madame de Carin watched with increasing horror as Henriette spoke to me that way, and she herself began to shake with fear and distress. Slapping her forehead, she wept bitterly and cried out, "Ah! Ah! Ah! They've succeeded! My God, she's gone mad... And I... And I..."

Stammering those words, she fainted and fell at my feet. Henriette looked at her: Henriette, who only the night before seemed to love her so, now coldly watched her writhing on the ground in terrible convulsions. Other guards, who'd come running while all that was going on, took Madame de Carin away, then tried to remove the little beggar girl from the madwoman who still held her in her arms; but the child, appealing to me, cried, "Protect me, ma'am, protect me! She's my mother! I recognized her!"

I was devastated. I didn't know what to say. But the guards paid attention neither to the child's pleas nor to the mother's fury. Luckily the prison doctor ran up just then and ordered that they not be separated; then he told Henriette she'd be allowed to keep her child, and even led her back to her room himself. I'd told him why I was interested in the child, and I asked him to keep me informed about what she and the madwoman would say to each other.

"I might be about to solve a mystery I've been studying for several years, ma'am," he replied. "And I'd welcome having a witness like you to what's about to happen."

We followed the madwoman, who'd already gone into her room. She held her daughter on her knees as if she were a much younger child; she rocked her and sang to her gently as if she were trying to put her to sleep. Then she broke off and said, "You hear me, child, you hear me clearly? If you ever get out of this tomb, you won't forget to say you're Henriette Buré's daughter, and your father's name is..."

"Léon Lannois," replied the child.

The doctor started at those words, and gripped my arm as if to alert me to listen carefully. "Léon Lannois!" he repeated. "Remember that name!"

The mother went on, "Will you remember the name of our persecutor?"

The child searched her memory before replying, "Yes, yes, it's Captain Félix Ridaire."

The doctor let out a muffled cry of surprise, while I just listened without understanding.

375

"You know your aunt's name too, don't you? The aunt I was counting on so much."

"Yes, mother: Hortense Buré, my uncle Louis Buré's wife." And then she added slowly, as if her memories were returning one by one, "And I'll also remember Jean-Pierre, whom you went to see when he was ill, the day you met my father for the first time. I remember everything, mother."

"And so it was all true," murmured the doctor.

The madwoman went on, "Very good, child. Look carefully at Félix—look at your torturer when he comes in. Look at him carefully so you'll recognize him if you ever see him again. I'll put you in your crib so he won't notice you watching him."

For the first time, the child seemed surprised by the madwoman's words. The doctor approached her and said quietly, "Do everything she asks, child. I'll be back soon, and so will your protector."

Then, without letting the madwoman notice, he picked up a notebook hidden in a corner of the room and handed it to me, saying, "Read that, ma'am, and since I can see you're an intelligent woman, I'll ask you afterwards what I should think about this strange reunion."

I read that manuscript, and I'm sending it to you, so that since you're at liberty you can consult a few legal experts about this case.

That manuscript was more or less a copy of the one included in the first volume of these memoirs, and consisted of an account of Henriette Buré's sufferings. The letter went on:

When I'd finished reading, I compared the little beggar girl's confused memories and poor Henriette's account; in my mind I reviewed word for word the scene in which the child, in her mother's presence, had retrieved all the names she'd told me she'd forgotten, and which I'd found in Henriette's manuscript. I was appalled by what I thought I'd discovered.

At that point the doctor returned, saying, "Well! You read it, didn't you?"

"Yes. The woman who wrote that wasn't mad."

"She is now. In suffering and in hope, she exhausted all the courage God gave her, and she had none left for the joy and the fulfillment of the hope that sustained her."

"What!" I cried. "Mad when she should be happy, mad when it was about to be proved she'd never been so!"

"It's a surfeit of misfortune, isn't it?" said the doctor, who seemed even more upset than I was by that discovery.

Suddenly remembering another unfortunate person, I said, "And what about Madame de Carin?"

"Oh, with her it's an absolute mania, quite incurable. She too has written down her story, and I'll pass it on to you if you're interested. It's remarkable for its specificity, its skill, and a kind of hypocrisy ordinary people wouldn't think a madwoman capable of. She's careful to conceal the misbehavior that forced her husband to treat her so harshly, and she barely mentions the name of the man who was quite notoriously her lover."

"And that name," I cried, as if struck with a sudden illumination, "that name is Count Cerny, isn't it?"

The doctor lowered his eyes, and replied like a man who feels he's gone too far in sharing confidential information. "I thought I should warn you you'd find his name there."

"But he wasn't her lover, sir!" I cried immediately.

He stared at me in surprised.

"I'm not mad," I went on. "I'm in my right mind. I'm here under a charge of adultery, brought by Count Cerny, and I can vouch for the fact that Count Cerny was not Madame de Carin's lover, that it wasn't possible, and here's why."

And then I told the doctor everything, Armand. If you could've seen the man's astonishment and shock, you might've thought that day was destined to make all of us doubt our own sanity. In great distress he replied, "Then if I can't believe in her madness, I have to believe in a whole series of crimes!"

I don't know where all those revelations might've led, but my conversation with the doctor was interrupted by a guard, who came to tell me my father had just arrived. The doctor withdrew, and Viscount d'Assimbret came in almost immediately.

You know my father, Armand, and you know he's always been a man of the world, who's lived his whole life as frivolously as he began it. I was afraid of how he'd react; in spite of myself I felt he had none of a father's usual majestic authority with me; and above all I dreaded the facetiousness with which he was likely to address me. But I was wrong: he was kind and good to me, and even while blaming me he made excuses for me—perhaps not quite along the lines I would've liked, but because, according to him, by taking a lover I'd done nothing worse than all the women he knew. What he couldn't forgive was my having run away; and what made him angrier than anything else was Count Cerny's behavior.

"A gentleman confronting another gentleman!" he cried. "A Cerny face to face with a Luizzi! And instead of coming into your room with a police officer, he didn't come in with a pair of swords? Wouldn't it have been better if he'd killed you both?"

That noble anger—or rather that nobleman's anger—did me good. I loved my father for preferring to see me dead rather than shamefully convicted of a crime. I clasped his hands gratefully as he went on, "He behaved like some peasant, like a City tradesman, or a lawyer without a brief who finds one at the cost of his own honor."

"He behaved the only way he knew how."

That surprised my father, and so I told him everything, Armand. I have to admit, his kindness to me, the seriousness with which he took on his role as my father, the anger he felt at Count Cerny's behavior—none of it could stand up to my story. When I told him Count Cerny's deep secret, he began to laugh so hard he couldn't stop; he rolled around in his chair, repeating over and over, "Impotent! Impotent!"

Then in the midst of his laughter he said, "Oh, what's happened to the Parliaments of the good old days? What a fantastic trial this would've made! I'd have had him examined by all the medical faculties in Paris, he wouldn't have dared to show his face outside for fear of children throwing stones at him in the street, and I have to admit I've never before despised or hated the Philosophes and the Revolution as much as I do now for having abolished all that."

With considerable difficulty I finally managed to make him more reasonable. He agreed to the several steps necessary to have me set free, and said he'd come back the next day with B—, our principal lawyer, whom he'd brought with him from Paris. While I've been waiting for them I've written you this letter, which my father will send—because without him I'd have been unable to do so. Send your reply care of him, at the post office, and tell me when you'll come back, because I need to see you. Send me back Henriette Buré's manuscript, after making note of all the necessary facts. Don't forget, we still have a daughter to reunite with her mother; and I've just shown you an example of the misfortune that can result from an unexpected recognition.

Just as I was finishing this letter, Armand, the doctor came back to tell me Madame de Carin's condition is worsening. Meanwhile Henriette has completely lost her mind; she rocks her child, she sings to her, she tells her the same thing over and over, and she now believes herself to be imprisoned in the horrible dungeon in which she gave birth to her child.

I'll close this letter now, for night is falling, and in spite of the consideration with which I'm treated here, I'm not allowed to have a light. I'll think about you; I have to, after all the terrible shocks I've experienced in just a few days. Do you remember that carriage ride on which, dying of cold and fear, I asked you to love me and be mine? Don't forget what you said to me. The more I write to you about the things I've witnessed here, the more I feel doubt entering my heart. My God! What is there in this world that's true? Of all the women around me, am I the maddest of all—I who believe I couldn't go on living if I didn't have as much faith in you as I have in God?

I'll see you soon, Armand. Come quickly. I can't describe the growing fear I feel, the rising despair. I feel like at the very moment I write to you some disaster is about to happen, either to me or to you. I can't conquer that feeling of weakness; only you can conquer it. Come, come!

— Léonie

Chapter XCIII: The Start of an Explanation

As he read that letter, Luizzi's thoughts and feelings were quite diverse—but he didn't react as another person might have; it just made him terribly sad. All those people who'd turned up again on his path, from the time he'd left Paris till now: Little Pierre, the old blind man, the little beggar girl, Father Sérac, Jeannette, even that Fernand who'd sent him a tale he dreaded reading, plus now Henriette Buré and Madame de Carin: all of them showed up again like actors in a play that's nearing its end. And he, the lead actor in that play, wasn't he also coming to the end of his life? And, with a charge of murder hanging over him, would that end take place on the scaffold?

That idea preoccupied him so deeply and at such length that he didn't hear his jailer come in to tell him his time in solitary confinement was over and he was now free to go down to the yard and mingle with the other prisoners. Surprised at Luizzi's apparent indifference to news that usually delighted its recipients, the jailer repeated it, saying only, "Did you hear? I said you're free."

The word struck Luizzi, and he cried, "Free! Free!"

He rushed out of his cell, imagining he'd been released from prison. But no sooner had he gone down the stairs leading to the yard than he stopped suddenly and turned back toward the jailer, who'd followed him laughing—as if to prove a jailer is capable of laughter.

"The fact is, I'm crazy," said Luizzi. "I forgot I don't even know how to find the way out of this prison."

"Out of prison!" said the jailer. "I said you were allowed to leave your cell. Have you forgotten you're to appear before the next session of the court of assize? Till then the only freedom you've been granted is to walk in the yard with your fellow prisoners."

Luizzi didn't answer; before the jailer had finished speaking he'd already remembered everything about his situation. The freedom he'd been granted was just to walk, and it was limited to four walls enclosing a hundred and twenty square feet of space. He cast a quick glance around the yard, in which he saw hideous men: young men and old, almost all sunk to a state of moral decay, almost all reduced to idiocy by vice that leads to crime or crime that leads to vice.

He was about to withdraw when he noticed a man watching him attentively. Luizzi was afraid he'd recognize in some wretched fellow prisoner still another person whose life had been mixed up with his own, and he was about to withdraw, but the man didn't give him time to do so. Coming quickly toward the baron, he said loudly, "Aren't you the brother of that nun they call Sister Angélique?"

"I am."

"So you're the man responsible for the death of both my father and my son?"

"Me?"

"My name is Jacques Bruno."[104]

Then Luizzi recognized him. "You, here? You, in this prison?"

"Well, you're here yourself."

"I'm here for a crime I didn't commit."

No words could describe the hatred and malevolence that rose to the peasant's face. "That'll be for the jury to decide."

"But how about you? What brought you here?"

"A good deed I did: Petithomme murdered my father and my son, so I murdered Petithomme."

"But how is it I find you in prison in Toulouse for a crime committed near Vitré?"

"I was only arrested yesterday, and I'd been away from home for a long time, even before I was arrested."

Luizzi looked at Bruno more carefully; for a moment it seemed to him he'd seen that man sometime since the day he left his farm—but where? He couldn't remember. The train of thought that had preoccupied him before the jailer came to tell him he was free to go outside came back stronger than ever; but this time instead of pushing it away in horror, he welcomed it and gave himself over to it enthusiastically. Whether the end that loomed before him would prove fatal or not, he was filled with a desire to clear up the mystery that surrounded him and in the midst of which he walked like a blind man, tripping over the slightest events in his life, getting lost on roads that seemed straightforward to everyone but himself.

Driven by that idea, he returned to his cell and resolved to read the letter the poet had sent him, and which he'd tossed aside scornfully. We reproduce it here word for word, but we decline to take any responsibility for it:

My dear sir,

When I left you alone with Count Cerny at Boismandé, on the road to Sar—, I promised, if not to tell you my whole history, at least to remind you of our first meeting and tell you what happened after that. Remember Boismandé; remember the pope's bed; remember the girl who gave herself to a traveler from the stagecoach you were in; remember that the traveler killed the man who tried to punish him for it; and remember that he ran away with the girl who'd slept with him. That traveler was me.

---

[104] See chapter XLIX for the murders of Grandpa Bruno and Matthieu Bruno by the Chouan Petithomme.

"I was right," said Luizzi to himself, forgetting in his preoccupation that the Devil had already told him about all of this. "The hour has come. Here's another illumination Fate is sending me. Let not the curse that follows me have led me to commit yet another rash act! Didn't I give my letter for Madame de Cauny to the postilion who was driving that same Jeannette, whom Fate might've caused me to meet again at Boismandé?"

Filled with that fear, he went on with Fernand's letter.

Remember also that I told you that young woman seemed to contain something extraordinary within her.

Luizzi remembered Fernand having said that, and he also recalled that the driver, speaking of Jeannette, had led him to understand her background wasn't that of an ordinary servant girl at an inn, and that she hadn't been destined for the position she occupied. As he recalled those circumstances, his curiosity grew; that made him advance even more resolutely along the path to discovery he seemed to be following, and he read on:

It's no surprise that girl had something extraordinary about her, for her situation itself was extraordinary; she was the granddaughter of a nobody, who'd become a great lord. That man's story is unbelievable: Long before the Revolution, his name was Bricoin, and he was a dancing master. He was already married before '89; but in '93 or '94 it occurred to him to seize the fortune and the hand of a certain Madame de Cauny, whose husband he'd had condemned to death. He succeeded so well that he married her, abandoning his first wife and a daughter named Mariette he'd had by her.[105] At that time, to elude the laws of bigamy, he changed his name and began calling himself Monsieur de Paradèze. By the kind of luck that normally belongs only to the lowest criminals, his wife died before finding out what had become of him, and left her daughter in the most wretched poverty—a poverty from which she escaped only by entering a life of debauchery.

The name Mariette, the word debauchery, the girl being abandoned in Toulouse—all of it came together to recall to Luizzi's mind what Mother Périne had told him about a girl named Mariette, whom she'd offered up to Luizzi's father. Might Jeannette be his own sister? And might he himself have helped rescue the man who would cause her downfall, the way he'd delivered his other sister Caroline to the wretch who now had her in his clutches? He didn't dare pause at that fantastical conjecture, and he went on reading the letter with an anxiety that grew ever sharper.

---

[105] See Chapter LXIX for some of this story, from another source.

Unlike her mother, the girl discovered the name her father had assumed and where he was living, and about twenty-two years ago she went to Boismandé, to the home of Monsieur de Paradèze, bringing with her the child she'd given birth to while working in Mother Périne's brothel.

That detail startled the baron. Indeed, the further along in the letter he read, the more he found it confirmed his own foreboding, warning him that it contained strange disclosures. For any other man than Luizzi, in anyone else's life, it would've required much more convincing evidence to arouse even the suspicion that Jeanette might be his sister; but after all that had happened to him in the form of surprising encounters, he had no hesitation in taking Fernand's partial revelation as a warning from Fate—though he still didn't realize the secret he'd just uncovered was nothing compared to the terrible secret he had yet to learn.

Meanwhile he went on reading Fernand's letter.

When Mariette reached Boismandé, armed with her mother's marriage license and with the birth certificate proving she herself was Bricoin's daughter, she frightened the old man enough to make him take responsibility for her life and that of her daughter. Monsieur de Paradèze kept the child with him, and sent Mariette back to Toulouse with a paltry enough stipend that she was forced to take a job as a servant in town. With a skill worthy of her, she'd carefully concealed Madame Bricoin's death from her father, so as to guarantee his cooperation out of fear of a charge of bigamy; but barely a year later he learned of his first wife's death. Now feeling safe from any risk, but unable to cut off the stipend he'd acknowledged legally as owed to his legitimate daughter, he kicked his granddaughter out of his house; and by means of a little money he found her a job at the inn where I met her, and where she'd been raised till the day I ran off with her.

You must also recall, my dear baron, that you were traveling from Toulouse along with a woman named Mariette; she was Jeannette's mother—a fine mother, worthy of the father who'd sired her! You must remember the care with which she kept her face veiled. Here's why: all the affection she'd felt for her child, as long as she hoped to interest Bricoin in her fate, had vanished the day that child was thrown out of Bricoin's house; and though she knew her daughter—a pretty, sweet, innocent girl—lived in Boismandé, she wanted to pass through without being recognized, fearing the inn servant girl might ask for some help from her mother, who was a servant in a wealthy house.

But what she hadn't hoped for from her peasant daughter, who lacked elegance and seductiveness, she did hope for from Jeannette, once she was in my keeping and had become elegant, but had remained, thanks to her nature, the slyest little minx in the world. Mariette tracked us down in Paris and took her daughter away—for Mariette had found a buyer for the girl, and she knew how

382

girls get sold. They left Paris together; and it was only by extraordinary luck that I found her again in Toulouse about a year ago.

In my lover's despair, I'd joined the army. I dreamt of military glory at the start of a revolution I believed would prove strong enough to pick up the fallen glory of the Empire. I'd become a company sergeant-major; my lieutenant was a certain Henri Donezau. He'd been Jeannette's lover, and had brought her back from Aix, where her mother had taught her the vile trade she'd once practiced herself. I wrote letters for that villain Donezau in an affair he said he was having with a nun in Toulouse; but one day when he was drunk he admitted that correspondence existed only to conceal one he was having with a novice named Jeannette. At that same dinner an actor named Gustave told me Jeannette was none other than Mariette's daughter, and Mariette was in hiding in Auterive under the name Madame Gelis, while Jeannette had adopted the name Juliette.[106]

At that revelation, which went so far beyond all the others, at the discovery of that horrible secret, which for Luizzi threw such frightening light on everything that had passed between himself and that woman, Fernand's letter dropped from his hands. He looked around in terror, like a man who feels he's been trapped in the inescapable coils of a destiny more powerful than he is. All the courage he'd had before, to advance down the path toward terrible revelations, fell suddenly away from him; it would be close to impossible to put into words all the new fears that entered his mind. Juliette was his sister,[107] and he'd left Caroline at her mercy; Juliette was the granddaughter of Monsieur de Paradèze, husband of that unfortunate Madame de Cauny, whose daughter he'd stolen from her; Juliette had presumably seen Luizzi at Boismandé and could've purloined the letter he'd written to Madame de Paradèze to tell her her daughter had been found; Juliette had probably also intercepted the letter he'd written to Madame Donezau from Fontainebleau, and, learning from that letter of his rendezvous with Caroline, had told Count Cerny which direction he and Léonie had fled, and had put the count on their track; Juliette was Gustave de Bridely's former mistress, and could've learned from him of Eugénie Peyrol's existence, and had presumably gone to Boismandé only to bring about that poor woman's ruin...

All those plausible occurrences, all of that complex web of incredible circumstances, made the baron's head spin and gave him the kind of vertigo his ancestor Lionel must've felt when he found himself pursued by those living

---

[106] See Chapter XLVIII for Caroline's account, in her letters, of her acquaintance with Madame Gelis and Juliette in Auterive.

[107] Like Caroline, Juliette is Luizzi's half-sister (and also Caroline's half-sister). See the Appendix for a family tree diagraming the baron's relations to Juliette and Caroline and other characters. At this point in the novel all of those hidden familial ties have been revealed, so the family tree contains no further spoilers.

ghosts who galloped after him through darkness lit by fire and storm! And presumably the delirium was the same too, for it led to the same result: Luizzi—who for the past month had resisted the temptation of isolation and the temptation of knowing the fate of all those whom he loved—couldn't resist the terrible confusion in his head, and he summoned Satan. Satan appeared.

Chapter XCIV

"You were right, master. It's all true. For once in your life you've understood how much evil a mere mortal can cause."

"So, Juliette...?" cried Luizzi.

"Juliette doomed your sister Caroline by making her marry Juliette's own lover. Juliette utterly doomed Countess Cerny by intercepting the letter you wrote to your sister, and handing it over to the count. Juliette, alerted by Gustave de Bridely to Eugénie Peyrol's parentage, went to Boismandé to keep the mother from acknowledging her own daughter. You've loved three women in your life, with the three different feelings that alone bring happiness to a man's heart: Eugénie as a friend, Caroline as a sister, Léonie as a lover. Juliette doomed all three of them. Wasn't I right, master, when I told you I needed that girl, and she'd serve me wonderfully as my tool to carry out villainous actions?"

Luizzi was stunned by the Devil's spiteful words. He was no longer the insolent dandy, nor the high-society priest, nor the Malayan slave, nor the ridiculous lawyer, nor the ugly peasant; he was no longer any of the people in whose shape Satan had appeared before him so many times; he was no longer even the fallen angel Luizzi had glimpsed at their very first meeting at Ronquerolles Castle—so proud in his defeat, so beautiful in his degradation. He was the god of evil, hideous in form, hideous in the expression on his face, with all the vileness, all the meanness, all the savagery, and all the cynicism of vice. Luizzi looked at him and trembled; for the second time he was filled with the terror and despair that had already nearly driven him to grovel at Satan's feet.

While Luizzi still struggled, the Devil went on, "Yes, it was Juliette who doomed everything you loved in this world; as the worthy descendant of a family born of incest and adultery, she was given every vice I promised your ancestors. She belongs to me the way all those with the blood of Zizuli in their veins belong to me."

"Not yet, Satan, not yet!" cried Luizzi. "One of them will escape you, I swear it."

"I wish him luck. Besides, does he need to give himself to me voluntarily? Do I need to sign a contract for him to belong to me? Don't I have my Juliette to doom him? Isn't it she who, though she could save him from the charge that hangs over him, leaves him sitting in prison, destined to die on the scaffold?"

"Who, Juliette?" cried Luizzi. "She could save me?"

"She could, master. When you'd long since returned, she was still with Count Cerny. She didn't leave him at Boismandé, for it was she who was traveling with him. Count Cerny was in that post chaise you met a little ways outside Boismandé; he was hiding inside it when I left you. The boy who'd let you know about the stagecoach delay caught up with the post chaise while the postilion had stopped for a drink, as you've already learned. All the vices, you see, conspire together wonderfully to bring about evil. The boy saw only Juliette, and he asked her to pass on the news to the first traveler she came across, and told her he'd already let you know. When she asked him—prompted by the evil genius who presides over all of that woman's actions—who the traveler was whom she'd seen on the road, little Jacob innocently replied, 'I heard him addressed as Baron de Luizzi.'

"You can understand, master, how welcome that news was to Count Cerny, who was pursuing you, and who, not realizing you were as penniless as you are now, assumed you were speeding toward Toulouse by post chaise. At his request, Juliette called back the boy, who was already heading home, and found out how long you'd be at the inn before starting off again. He told her you couldn't possibly set off again before morning. That was more time than Count Cerny needed to catch up with you; and it was only after night had fallen completely, and when they were about to reach Juliette's destination, that he got surreptitiously out of the post chaise and retraced his steps, carrying two swords.

"They were used neither against you nor against his murderer; for, at the very spot where I'd left you, a bullet fired from the hedge that borders the road dropped him dead. That was when the murderer dragged him into the thicket; that was when, presumably surprised by the arrival of a couple of straggling woodcutters, he had to abandon the body without robbing it—which set up the circumstance that's been so detrimental to your case, that the count wasn't killed by robbers but by some personal enemy, whose motive for killing him was above mere robbery. And who else, master, could've had a greater interest in Count Cerny's death than you?"

"And Juliette knows all that?"

"She knows that at exactly nine o'clock that night Count Cerny was just leaving her, and that at exactly nine o'clock you were six leagues away, writing your letter to Madame de Cauny; and she made sure to get hold of that letter."

"So I assume she knows who the real murderer was?" asked Luizzi in a tone of strained sarcasm that only betrayed his helplessness at struggling with as terrible an enemy as Satan.

"She hasn't the least idea."

"Well, I know who it was!" cried Luizzi.

"And his name would be…?"

"Jacques Bruno."

"Well!" said the Devil, quite astonished. "So it was Jacques Bruno. Well, well! Here you are, saved! You can tell that to the jury, and they'll believe you on the spot."

Satan's cold mockery disconcerted Luizzi, and he understood the impossibility of making such an accusation in court, with no evidence besides his own assertion and his sudden realization that the man he'd thought he recognized that night on to the road to Boismandé was none other than Jacques Bruno. So, like a drowning man who clutches at anything within reach, whether it's a glowing poker or a razorblade, he went on, "But I have Juliette's deposition."

"Another ingenious idea!" said the Devil, "and which can't fail either to save you or to doom you completely! It'll all depend on your sister Juliette."

"And what interest would she have in dooming me?"

"What interest would she have in saving you? Oh, if you'd only given her a fortune of five hundred thousand francs or so, like you did to your good sister Caroline, if only you hadn't robbed her of her lover, or if only you'd become her lover yourself…"

"What a horror!"

"You weren't the one who prevented it, master—you were pretty interested. But what can you do? The shame of the scaffold will have to make up for the incest you missed out on."

"Oh, no, Satan, no! Try as you might, I'm not going to die on the scaffold, and it'll be Juliette—the one you counted on to doom me—who'll save me. I'll pay her more to tell the truth than anyone's ever paid for a lie."

"What a good idea. You'll make Juliette richer than Caroline; you'll cover vice in gold and raise it higher than virtue. You really do make progress every day."

"All right, so be it. Since everybody in the world is crooked, I'll be crooked. Since everything here on earth is for sale, I'll buy everything."

"And you'll still be a sucker, baron, because usually you don't pay for what's yours by right: only crooks have to buy a good reputation, only the guilty go bankrupt to buy an acquittal. But you'll buy your acquittal for a crime you didn't commit. You fool, you poor fool!"

"Again, so be it. I'd be an even bigger fool if I let myself be condemned to death… Tell me where Juliette is, tell me where I can write to her, and I'll take care of saving myself."

"At this very moment, she's with Monsieur de Paradèze, her grandfather; and—though I've always refused to say a word about your future—I'd like to lend a hand in your attempt to save yourself; so I can promise you a letter will find her still at her grandfather's."

"That's good enough," said Luizzi, and he motioned for Satan to withdraw.

Chapter XCV: The Triumph of Fraternal Love

The decision Luizzi had made in a moment of despair wasn't as easy to put into action as he'd imagined: writing that letter to Juliette was not only a shameful deed, it was hard to do. How could he tell that woman he knew who she was? How could he avoid heaping well-earned reproaches on her? How could he say he knew she'd been traveling with Count Cerny, and not complain that she'd revealed to the count the direction he himself had gone with the countess? Still, he didn't flinch from the job ahead of him. The baron was one of those people who have a deplorable ability to find plausible reasons for everything they do; he was the kind of man who can put to profitable practice the theory once advanced by one of our greatest authors of patriotic light comedy: that only a fool or a rascal never changes his mind.[108] Now, Luizzi's motive for changing his mind about Juliette was certainly of a different order than merely to be awarded the Legion of Honor or a pension of twelve hundred francs—the motives that inspired our great playwright to frame the axiom we've just cited. For the baron it was a matter of life and death, of honor or disgrace—of his mortal life and honor, to speak the truth: for as to the destiny of his soul or the testimony of his conscience, he was happy to negotiate, like more than three quarters of humankind.

So he set himself to work. He wrote a letter, he wrote another, he wrote ten, twenty; but in the first letter his resentment at all the evil Juliette had done shone through in every line: he tried to make her ashamed of her behavior and appealed to her better nature. He set that letter aside for a few hours; but he re-read it just before giving it to Monsieur Barnet, whom he'd asked to send it on its way; and that second reading easily persuaded him that a woman like Juliette would be indifferent to reproach and untouched by an appeal to her feelings.

The second letter was less bitter, and focused more on her return to good behavior, and even began to touch lightly on the question of her venal interests. But that letter was still far from what Luizzi knew would be required to get Juliette to tell the truth sincerely. Finally, letter by letter—always unsatisfied at being unable to debase himself far enough or make himself forget enough of the wrong she'd done him—he let almost a week go by; and during that week nothing happened to change his mind about his fateful decision.

He wrote to Countess Cerny, and Countess Cerny didn't write back. He wrote to Madame Peyrol, and Madame Peyrol didn't write back. After two

---

[108] The thought itself is proverbial; but the reference might be to lyrics vaguely like it in the work of Marc-Antoine Désaugiers (1772-1827), a composer of comic operas.

388

weeks he'd reached the worst crisis his heart had ever known: he doubted all three of those women. That's when he wrote Juliette the letter that appears below.

No matter what, Luizzi is our hero; he's been our friend; and if we've specified how much time had passed before he wrote this letter, it's because we want the reader to understand that he proceeded gradually, almost imperceptibly, one step at a time, down the road to base cowardice; and he had to discard everything he loved to get all the way there.

Here was his letter:

Mademoiselle,

I learned by chance of the family ties that connect us. The news made me very happy; it seemed to me your tender affection for Caroline was prompted by some kind of intuition in your heart, and the affection I felt for you was a presentiment in my own heart. My happiness is made all the greater because what I've already done for one beloved sister, I could do for the other; and I hope, now that I know who you are, to be able to carry out my fondest wish very soon.

The ridiculous charge that keeps me in prison will drop easily before the proofs I can offer, and especially before the testimony I would already have summoned through the legal system—if I didn't prefer to owe it to a spontaneous offer prompted by the friendship with which I hope you'll now favor me. I await you here in Toulouse; you'll come, won't you? I have so much to tell you.

—Your brother and your friend, Armand, Baron de Luizzi

When Luizzi had written that letter, he sealed it without rereading it. He hadn't sent the others because they didn't accomplish the goal; he might not have sent this one because it overshot the goal.

Meanwhile his trial date was approaching. He'd sent his letter more than a week earlier, and no answer had come. What he'd been unable to achieve by debasing himself, he now hoped to extract by order of the court. He listed Juliette as a witness; the fateful day arrived without him knowing whether or not she'd appear.

What a grand, dignified day it was! All the great ladies of Toulouse were there in their finest clothes. The most illustrious of the nobility, the most distinguished of the bourgeoisie, the leading men of the law, were gathered together in that courtroom. The court sat, the jury was sworn in, and among them the accused recognized the honorable Monsieur Félix Ridaire, one of the wealthiest men of property in all of Haute Garonne; and solemn Monsieur Ganguernet, who sat there with a smile on his lips.

The facts in the case were clear, precise, and undeniable. Count Cerny, having set off by post chaise from Orléans, had switched from his carriage to the stagecoach in which the baron was riding. That was established by the driver's passenger list and by the testimony of several travelers, especially that of Monsieur Fernand, who'd been in conversation with the accused and with Count Cerny as far as the village of Sar—, where both men had gone on ahead of the stagecoach. Monsieur Fernand had left them together. When little Jacob, sent after them, had caught up with Luizzi, the count had vanished; the boy remembered clearly, and his testimony was quite definite, that the baron had dissuaded him from running after Count Cerny, saying he must've gone to the devil. The boy's deposition was corroborated by that of his father, to whom Luizzi had said the boy tried in vain to keep up the pursuit.

In other evidence, the two swords found beside Count Cerny appeared to prove that the husband and the lover had agreed to a duel; whereas the body, struck from behind by two bullets, showed without a doubt that the baron had turned a rencounter of honor into a murder. The body hadn't been robbed, which suggested clearly that Count Cerny hadn't been attacked by highwaymen. Then came Luizzi's clandestine arrival in Toulouse, the place he'd chosen to stay, the precautions he'd taken over money—everything including his being indifferent as to what country he wanted to go to, as long as he got out of France. In short, it was a prosecutorial masterpiece, that could easily have led to two innocent men being hanged instead of one.

Luizzi's entire defense was to object that no one had seen either him or Count Cerny wearing a sword; and therefore circumstance proved the real murderers must've left those swords next to Count Cerny after shooting him. Everyone was waiting anxiously when—the witnesses being summoned and Juliette not appearing—Luizzi's lawyer rose to ask for a postponement of the case till a later session, given the importance of that witness. But just then the bailiff announced that Mademoiselle Juliette had arrived at that very moment, and she was ready to appear before the court. Then a discussion broke out, and the charge against the accused was read out again, which prompted feelings of scorn and outrage toward Luizzi.

It is not the intention of this account to produce a dramatic article worthy of the *Court Gazette*, or to put excellent speeches in the mouths of certain witnesses and make others speak in incomprehensible gibberish, or to have the jury told idiotic nonsense, or to describe the great effort the judge of the assizes invested in finding the accused guilty, or to show the king's counsel enveloping the witnesses in specious questions designed to teach them what they didn't already know in such a way that they seemed to be admitting it; but we do have to report one of the most remarkable incidents of the entire trial, and what consequences it led to.

Attention was flagging, and the depositions of the witnesses—who kept on describing Count Cerny's disappearance after he'd been left alone with Luizzi, or the care the baron had taken to conceal his presence in Toulouse—no longer aroused the least interest. Everybody's mind was made up, when finally Juliette was summoned. All eyes turned to the door by which she entered. People whispered, finding her beautiful, charming, elegant. She inspired so much interest that some of it spilled over onto the accused himself, since several people knew she was his sister.

Finally she began to speak; lowering her eyes modestly, she replied, "I left Orléans with Count Cerny. He was in my carriage. We didn't catch up to the stagecoach till the village of Sar—, where it had broken down. It was about seven in the evening when we met the baron on foot on the road. Count Cerny was still in my carriage then, and nine o'clock had rung in Boismandé when he left me to walk back and rejoin Baron de Luizzi, whom he'd asked for satisfaction for some injury I was unaware of."

Juliette's deposition made Luizzi's heart swell; he felt like his salvation had suddenly arrived. But he was brought back to the reality of his situation when he heard the disapproving murmur that followed Juliette's words. Félix Ridaire said, "I beg Your Honor to ask the witness why Count Cerny was riding in her carriage."

"He had business in Toulouse, so we were traveling together. Once we reached Boismandé he was to go on alone."

Suddenly the king's counsel rose and put on his tasseled bonnet. "Before we go any further with these questions," he said, "I beg the court to allow me to state my reservations about this witness. According to the testimony of the driver, the postilion, and Monsieur Fernand, according to the statement of the accused himself, Count Cerny was in the stagecoach for several hours before it reached the village of Sar—. And now the witness has just told you she and Count Cerny didn't catch up with the stagecoach till they got to Sar—. There's obviously false testimony here. And when I've revealed the ties that connect this witness to the accused, you'll understand that the sentiment that misled her might've been admirable, but it shouldn't have gone so far as to lead her to commit perjury within these august precincts."

"I swear," cried Juliette, who genuinely didn't understand the king's counsel's objection, "I swear what I said is the truth!"

"Miss," said the judge, interrupting her in a fatherly way, "the court wishes to be indulgent with you. In strict justice it should ignore the family bonds you share with the accused, and, considering only the quality of your testimony, it should punish harshly a deposition that runs so contrary to all the other testimony we've heard up to now. But the court wishes to recognize that the strength of family bonds doesn't always depend on their legitimacy, and that your devotion to a beloved brother might've inspired you to tell a lie, which of course is wrong, but to which the court chooses to close its eyes."

"But..."

"Don't insist on it any further. Perhaps I've already overstepped my duty. In your own interest, in the interest of the accused himself—for whom testimony so false can only work against him, since it shows the nullity of his defense—don't add another word. Bailiff, remove the witness."

Juliette left, surrounded by affection; and as she passed by, everybody said, "Isn't that just a model of fraternal love! She didn't pull it off, but still, what she did was honorable and deserves the respect and admiration of all honest souls."

She left, as we said, and her triumph kept her from hearing the magnificent peroration by the king's counsel, who delivered a fulminating summing up against a man who, after having stolen from Count Cerny a wife whom he adored and whose happiness he'd assured, had basely murdered the man he'd already dishonored; a man who, though born into the highest ranks of society, had embraced a life of crime; a man who'd dragged through the mud the illustrious name of the virtuous Luizzi family; a man who... a man about whom... etcetera, etcetera.

The king's counsel's oratorical snoring lasted fifty-five minutes. The defense was no less fine, and lasted fifty-six minutes. The judge's horribly impartial summing up took twenty-one minutes. The jury deliberated for thirteen minutes, that unlucky number. And after two hours and twenty-five minutes, Baron de Luizzi was unanimously sentenced to death.

After Juliette's deposition Luizzi had stopped listening or even hearing. What could be said against him and what could be said for him had become equally indifferent to him. An inexpressible fury had come over him: he recognized Satan's hand in this latest blow struck against him; and Juliette, admired by all, walking nobly out of the same courtroom he himself would leave condemned and dishonored, seemed the perfect proof that evil alone was destined to triumph in this world. He returned to his cell firmly resolved to ask evil for his salvation, at no matter what price, if salvation was still possible for him. He summoned Satan.

"Well, master!" laughed the Devil. "The people have been wiser than you: they remembered the story of that man in ancient times who, having wished for happiness for his children, watched them die in their sleep.[109] The people have sentenced you to happiness; and the choice you'd soon have had to make, according to the terms of our contract, and which probably seemed difficult to you, has been made for you by the people."

"And you think I'm going to accept it?"

"I don't know how you can avoid it."

"Come on, Satan," said Luizzi, who'd recovered all of his animation. "Don't waste your time offering me bad choices I've already made. Twice before you saved me on condition that I surrender some agreed-upon span of my life to you. How much time do you need to get me out of here the way I got out of prison in Caen—healthy, wealthy, and exonerated?"[110]

"I'd need more time than you have left to give, master. It's now the first of December, 183*, and by a month from today you'll have to have chosen the thing that makes you happy and removes you from my power. You realize that, if you haven't chosen, you belong to me as of that last day?"

---

[109] The idea that there could be no greater happiness than to die in one's sleep is contained in an anecdote attributed to the Greek Cynic philosopher Diogenes.

[110] See the end of Chapter XLV and the beginning of Chapter XLVI.

"And you realize that if I die before having chosen, I escape you?—or at least I go back to facing the same odds as all those souls whose fate rests in God's hands. So your best interest is to save me, if you still hope to take possession of me."

The Devil laughed, then replied calmly, "Oh, master, you really think you don't belong to me already?"

"I don't want to discuss it. I've offered you a deal; will you take it, yes or no?"

"Listen, we're probably destined to live together for all eternity; and I don't want to have some damned soul hanging around me who tells everybody I failed to deal fairly with him. You're also distantly related to me, baron, since you're a descendant of that fine son of Eve who committed the first murder. I want to be a good Devil to my cousins, no matter how far removed. You've got thirty-one days before the choice you have to make; give me thirty of them, and you'll walk out of here not only healthy, wealthy, and exonerated, but admired by all as a victim of odious persecution and shocking judicial error. Among all the marks of favor men have granted you, you're missing one: celebrity; and I'll give it to you."

"And if I give you those thirty days, what'll that leave me?"

"Twenty-four hours to make a choice that only takes a moment. If you've seen all you've seen without understanding where happiness lies, you'll never know. If you choose well, I lose the game. If you choose badly, I win. It's a roll of the dice we were bound to end up at, you and I, and it's really just a roll of the dice. Pascal tossed a coin to decide on the immortality of the soul, and Jean-Jacques Rousseau threw a rock at a tree, having decided not to believe in God if he didn't hit the tree. You have an advantage over those two great geniuses, since you can doubt neither the existence of God nor the immortality of the soul—you who've seen the Devil in person and have bargained with him for your soul. And I didn't neglect the rest of your education either: I showed you fashionable salons, I showed you middle-class bedrooms, I showed you cottages and garrets; in the course of your life you've met men who practice law, magistrates, merchants, financiers, doctors, actors, streetwalkers; you've had dealings with pretty much every element that makes up society, and you must know where you yourself stand."

"Not yet," said Luizzi, "for I still have to find out what's happened to the only three kind, devoted women I met in my life."

"You want to hear their story? I'll tell it to you—I'll indulge you right to the end. Which one do you want me to start with? But listen to the clock chiming the hour: I want exactly thirty days of the thirty-one you've got left to live, and I'll subtract the time it takes me to tell the story from the twenty-four hours I'm leaving you. You can choose to hear the story before or after; I won't begin my tale without that condition, and you can interrupt the telling whenever you like."

393

Luizzi didn't hesitate. The choice he intended to make had been settled since he walked out of the courtroom, and—once he was free of the sentence hanging over him—it didn't matter to him whether he had a month or an hour to state it. So he said, "You can begin. I'm listening."

And Satan began to speak.

Chapter XCVI: An Honorable Woman

"Here's what happened to your sister Caroline, if she's the one you want me to start with."

Luizzi nodded his assent, and the Devil began.

You don't know your sister, baron. You've never been able to see her as anything besides a naive, pious girl who stupidly fell for a boor and was the victim of her own ignorance. You were mistaken, master. Caroline is a special soul, helpless before the prayers and sufferings of others, but strong against vice and calamity. You'll see whether I'm right about her!

As I told you, she didn't get the letter you sent her from Fontainebleau; that letter was delivered to her husband, and her husband passed it on to Juliette, and Juliette gave it to Count Cerny. You also know that Gustave de Bridely received your letter, which he passed on to Juliette, that virtuoso of the art of making the best of a bad position. Gustave, Count Cerny, Juliette, and Henri Donezau all left Paris that very night—following a conference to which your sister wasn't invited, on a subject I'll tell you about when I get to the people most directly concerned.

The Devil paused from time to time in his story, as if to leave room for Luizzi to interrupt; but the baron knew all too well he didn't have a minute to lose by taking advantage of Satan's civility. And so the latter was obliged to go on:

You must remember, master, that among the people you received regularly at home one of the most assiduous was young Edgard du Bergh. He was too sophisticated to want to come to a house where he'd be forced to endure the company of Henri Donezau; at the same time he was too unsophisticated to want to come there for the sake of a girl of Juliette's type. There are a hundred girls for sale in Paris who've got better style and better taste and are in better health; but between the yokel named Donezau and the minx named Juliette, there was your sister Caroline, and that's what drew du Bergh to your house.

As long as you were around he was careful to hide an attraction you'd be smart enough to spot, and skillful enough to keep an eye on, and decisive enough to thwart if you needed to. He didn't consider the husband an obstacle; he was more astute than you, and he'd figured out that a man as coarse and lecherous as Henri Donezau would prefer Juliette's passionate, lascivious nature. He suspected that your brother-in-law cared little for his wife, but he had no idea that when Donezau abandoned her she was still as virginal and pure as when she'd come to him.

It was the morning after Henri and Juliette both left that du Bergh really began to get his hopes up. That day he paid his usual call, and that day he found Caroline alone and sunk in the depths of despair. Indeed, in the space of twenty-four hours she'd learned of your running away with Countess Cerny, and of Juliette's departure, followed a few hours later by that of Henri.

"What!" said Luizzi in surprise. "They didn't leave together?"

"Listen, master, if you make me mix up all these stories, one inside the other, not only will we understand nothing but we'll never get to the end…"

So, du Bergh found Caroline in tears. "What's wrong?" he said.

Caroline thought du Bergh was a friend; you'd treated him as such. That's usually the first degree lovers are awarded in the best houses; and it's always the brother or the husband who signs their diploma—sometimes both at once. So she told him about the misfortune that had befallen her. Unhappiness blurs the mind's powers of perception, the way tears blur the eye's powers of vision. Caroline didn't notice the wicked joy the news brought to du Bergh's face. He promised not to abandon her, and to find out exactly what had happened to her husband, to you, and to Juliette.

You should understand that, given du Bergh's intentions, he was careful not to make slightest move in that direction: he began by letting the deepest despair run on for a few days; then, being a skillful seducer, he managed to inject into Caroline's mind the suspicion he was surprised hadn't dawned there on its own. One evening, sitting next to her, he said, "I'm ashamed to say it, ma'am; but your husband—the man who possessed your love, the man whom marriage had made the owner of that pure, charming beauty—your husband preferred over you a woman beneath you in every respect."

"You mean Juliette, don't you? You're mistaken, sir. She was more beautiful and more elegant than I was. I noticed his preference for her a long time ago; and though it made me sad, in fairness I couldn't blame my husband."

Du Bergh must've been astonished at that strange self-abnegation. He took for stupidity what was in fact just ignorance, and he replied, "The truth is, ma'am, you're too modest. You don't know your own worth. Besides, even if Monsieur Donezau had been led astray by an attraction I find hard to understand, his sense of honor should've kept him from bringing his mistress into his wife's home."

I should tell you, master, your sister had certainly heard the words 'wife' and 'mistress' used in society; but you have to understand it was hard for her to grasp what it could mean to be a man's mistress, since, for her, being a wife meant nothing more than taking his name. So she replied, "But in what way was she his mistress?"

The question was so odd that du Bergh didn't understand it. He assumed Caroline simply doubted the fact, the reality of it. Not realizing he should go easy on the complete innocence of a woman who seemed so hard to convince, he said frankly, "I can't conceal from you, ma'am, that I have absolute proof." Since that just made Caroline look at him in even greater surprise, he went on, "Forgive me for the confession I have to make to you, but I caught them alone together."

"What of it? My God, I've left them alone together twenty times myself!"

"I'm sorry," said du Bergh a little impatiently. "I blush at the word I find I have to use, but I saw them kissing."

"But he often kissed her the way my brother kisses me."

"He called her by her first name."

"Of course, just as my brother calls me by my first name."

That went well beyond the bounds of what du Bergh could conceive a woman's naivety to be. So, thinking there was no reason to spare a woman whose silliness was beginning to wear on him a little, he said to your sister fairly bluntly, "Well, since I have to tell you everything, I caught your husband in Juliette's bed."

"In her bed?..." cried Caroline. "Lying next to her?"

"Yes."

She blushed to the whites of her eyes, and went on quietly, "Without his clothes on?"

Driven beyond his limits, du Bergh laughed. "Both of them without their clothes on."

At that revelation Caroline hid her face in her hands. A strange confusion of ideas, suspicions, and doubts spun through her mind.

Meanwhile du Bergh, thinking only to add a turn of phrase for good effect, went on, "And so, ma'am, he left your bed only to go to that of your rival."

"My bed!" cried Caroline. "He was never in it, I swear to you!"

All suddenly became clear to du Bergh. That a woman like Juliette would make the demands she did of her lover was nothing surprising; demands like that are more common than you'd think. But it was Henri's acquiescence he had trouble crediting—till the conversation he'd just had with Caroline showed him that acquiescence had been absolute.

"Now you can get a sense, master, what splendid prey your sister would make for a man like du Bergh. A beautiful girl who's still a virgin is something rare enough to arouse the lust of any libertine; but a woman who's married and still a virgin—that's enticing enough to turn the heads of men much less dissolute than the handsome du Bergh."

"That's shameful! Despicable!" cried Luizzi.

"Oh, come now, master!" said the Devil, with his head on one side. "Come now! You know that's a tasty morsel, and Countess Cerny proved it to you. You

397

think you'd have committed the folly of running away with her if she'd really been her husband's wife, and the devoted mother of a family, with squalling children all around her and with her beauty worn down by lawful spousal possession and childbearing? No, master, you wouldn't have done it. You were seduced just as much by the spiciness of the adventure as by your mistress's true worth; and it doesn't become you to disapprove of something you did so eagerly."

"That was different!"

"Oh, that's the word everybody uses: 'With me, it was different!' They all have some reason to excuse in themselves what they condemn in others, and they're all acting in good faith. As for you, master, there isn't one bad thing you've done—and you've done plenty—that I didn't see you spit on when it passed by next to you wearing a different face from yours. Anyway, how do you know Edgar du Bergh didn't have perfectly good reasons to want your sister? How do you know that, if I wanted to turn this story into a sentimental novel for a literary review, I couldn't find ways to get you interested in that man's foul seduction, by describing him as being consumed by a love he couldn't fight—and it would be true! Or resolved to protect that young woman against her brother's impulsive abandonment and her husband's despicable rejection?—and that too would be true! But just because I dressed up my story in uplifting, moving language, the facts of the action wouldn't be any less vile and guilty, and that man's intentions wouldn't be any less those of a shameless libertine."

For, once he was quite sure of Caroline's ignorance, it took a lot of skill for du Bergh to get her to understand what he wanted from her. It's easy to ask a woman for the same favors she grants her husband; she knows what that's about. It's easy to ask a virgin girl for the favors she has yet to grant to anyone; she suspects they must consist of something different from whatever makes her a virgin. But to ask a woman who thinks she's already given everything there is for a favor she doesn't understand at all—that's hard work, master; and to pull it off it took a virtuoso of corruption.

So the struggle was long, and at first du Bergh was careful not to pursue any further the explanation Caroline had blurted out. He quickly withdrew to the role of friend and protector. That way he made sure of free access to Caroline's house. Your sister—left alone, without permanent resources, without the slightest idea how to administer a fortune—asked him to take over the management of her business affairs; that would require him to come see her frequently. Du Bergh accepted. He surrounded her with his attention, he was her eager and obedient slave, not a single tear fell from her eyes that he wasn't ready to wipe away, not a wish did she utter that he wasn't ready to carry out. He was sad with her, hopeful with her; and when he'd shown her clearly how a whole life could be connected to another life at every point, could dissolve constantly in the same emotions, in the same needs, in the same desires, he told her that's what was called love.

And then Caroline understood she'd never been loved like that; and here's what she said to him the day he made that confession to her: "So is that what you call love, Monsieur du Berg? That generous kindness, that devoted protection, that care to place yourself between me and any approaching sorrow, that touching concern for my pain, which makes you prefer my sad company to all the brilliant pleasures you're used to? Oh, how fortunate men are to be able to love like that! And what can women offer in exchange for such an emotion?"

"What they can offer, ma'am, is what I'd like to have from you: your unlimited confidence in that protection, your sincere trust in that devotion, and your sweet joy in being the object of it."

"I wouldn't call that love, sir. I thought that was gratitude."

"The fact is, though it's love, that's not all love consists of." As Caroline looked at him in gentle surprise, he went on, "You observed just now that I prefer your company to all the frivolous pleasures of the world, and you practically thanked me for it. I don't deserve those thanks, ma'am: when I come to you, it's because nothing could keep me away, it's because seeing you gives me joy, it's because hearing your voice delights me, it's because watching you listen to me is glorious to me, it's because my whole life is contained in you, it's because you're not only the mistress of my fate but also of my soul, it's because I'll live through you however you please, it's because I'll feel through you however you please."

Caroline listened eagerly to his words, searching her own heart, happy and proud of her influence over him; and she murmured softly, "And how—my God!—can so much love be repaid?"

"How can it be repaid!" cried du Bergh. "By being happy to be loved that way because you're loved that way by the one who loves you; by being proud he's your slave because it's he who's your slave; by accepting his protection only because it's his protection; in short, by feeling that only from him could you possibly receive everything—happiness, joy, sadness—and that he holds your soul within his, as you hold his in yours. That, ma'am, is how you repay that kind of love."

"Oh," she cried, "in that case, sir, I'm not ungrateful."

"Do you love me, Caroline?" he cried, moving closer.

"Monsieur du Bergh, what are you doing?" she said, drawing back in alarm. After a moment of silence she added, "You accused my husband and Juliette of addressing each other by their first names; if it was wrong for them, it must be wrong for us too. But it happened, and I feel I'm to blame, because you thought you had the right to address me that way."

Du Bergh was a little confused by the idea; but, thinking to take advantage of the ground he'd gained, he went on with well-feigned sadness, "You're mistaken, ma'am. That manner of speaking, which for me was just a momentary lapse, was their everyday habit. I addressed you that way when I had no right to, but both of them had the right to address each other that way."

"I don't understand."

"It's that the love I've been describing to you isn't all there is to love. It's that, in addition to that pure, saintly union of souls, there's another kind of love that's feverish and intoxicating. It's that when I'm near you, ma'am," he said, drawing closer to her again, "I feel my vision blurring, my heart pounding, my body trembling. Here," he said, taking her hand, "can't you feel how I'm burning? Look at me: can't you see my vision is cloudy?"

Caroline listened with a dread made even greater because she felt within herself the first stirrings of the sensations he was describing to her so passionately. "Leave me, sir!" she cried in fear. "Leave me!"

"Oh, that's because you don't know the ecstasies you feel when your eyes get lost in the eyes of the one you love!" And as he said that, his eyes, locked on hers, shone into hers with the burning rays of his love. "That's because you don't know the inexpressible delight there is in feeling the hand of the one you love trembling in your hand, feeling his heart beating against yours, his lips touching your mouth, his whole body surrendering to you."

And as he spoke he gently took her hands, he put his arms around her, he pressed himself against her, and fixed his lips to hers.

"So I assume she yielded?" cried Luizzi in anger and despair.

"You think she was capable of doing so?" replied Satan mockingly.

"What woman as ignorant as Caroline, as isolated as Caroline, as unhappy as Caroline, wouldn't have yielded in her position?" said Luizzi sadly.

"All of them might've yielded, but your sister withstood it."

"Caroline!" cried Luizzi joyfully.

"Caroline, whom you didn't trust, because you were on the verge of not believing in the virtue of even one single woman. Caroline, who, tearing herself from du Bergh's arms, cried out as if she'd suddenly been lit by a light from on high—for I have to admit, baron, God got involved..."

...Caroline, as I was saying, who cried, "Ah! That's what the crime is! Never! Never!"

At that point, with a single word, du Bergh lost all the ground he'd gained. He had in his hands a woman he could've persuaded that, no, it wasn't a crime; but he was clumsy enough to say, "It may be a crime for other women, but is it therefore one for you—you poor unhappy abandoned woman? For you, handed over by a thoughtless brother to a dishonorable husband? For you, disinherited of your family name? For you, who owe nothing to society, which has done nothing for you?"

The Devil fell silent; and Luizzi, watching him carefully, said, "And what did she say to those accusations against us all, which are so true?"

"Pointing up to heaven, she replied simply, 'Society is not my judge, sir.'" Satan observed Luizzi to see what effect those words would have on him.

"And you dare repeat that to me, of all people? Aren't you afraid I'll take advantage of it?"

"When you hear the end of your sister's story, you can take advantage of it if you like." Then the Devil went on:

After such an honorable answer, it was only right, wasn't it, master, that heaven sent to poor Caroline's defense a protector who saved her, a circumstance that snatched her from du Bergh's renewed efforts to seduce her? For that scene was repeated more than once, and yet Caroline still resisted, finding within herself more strength than other people get from all the bonds of family. She withstood the call not only of her abandonment and her isolation, but even of her love—for she loved du Bergh. And after the harm you'd done her, she had to withstand the harm du Bergh was doing her, for—determined to possess her—he spared nothing that might overcome her resistance. He let her sense the gradual approach of poverty; he exposed her to the insults of her creditors, to petty snubs by her servants, to everything that makes a soul despair to the point of blushing; and over and over, when he found her desperate and weeping, he said, "Be mine, and I'll restore your riches, your happiness, your dignity."

But every time she replied, "My riches are not of this world; my happiness comes from beyond; and I carry my dignity within me."

"Noble sister!" cried Luizzi with tears in his eyes.

"Noble sister, indeed," said the Devil, "because that's when news of the accusation against you finally reached her. And it arrived at a point when her misery had reached its peak, at a time when she had barely enough strength left to carry on her struggle alone. But when she heard you were in trouble she found enough strength to come to your rescue."

Countess Cerny had run away with you, with the lover who was saving her. Caroline ran away to escape from the man she loved and to rescue the brother who'd abandoned her. Léonie had run off with a wealthy man, and you shed tears over the few hours of hardship she endured with you, asleep in your lap; Caroline ran off all alone, on foot, begging for alms, to go bring the comfort of her words to one who'd lost that comfort—for it's you who lost it, master! And her journey was long, and she was spared nothing: not the profanities of innkeepers, nor the indecent remarks of passersby, nor hunger, nor thirst, nor the exhaustion that led her to fall sleep by the side of the road. And that was how, dragging herself along day after day, minute by minute, dying of fatigue, she reached that same inn at Boismandé from which Juliette had set off to pursue a life of vice, and in which you'd met her again as she pulled up in a splendid carriage.

Luizzi bowed his head at that cruel comment, and the Devil went on, "At that wretched inn, where the innkeeper granted Caroline a makeshift cot, there were two other women who were also in pain: Eugénie Peyrol and Léonie de Cerny."

"What! They were both there?" cried the baron.

"Both, master."

"How had they gotten there?"

"That's what I'll tell you about—if you think you still have enough to time hear it, because it's ringing four o'clock right now."

Luizzi calculated that he still had twenty hours to make his choice, and he asked the Devil to keep going. "But condense the telling, and skip the commentary, which you enjoy drawing out and which I can do without."

"What's this, master? You're treating me like some writer who gets paid by the line! But I'm putting a lot of care into this, and there's not a single decent novelist who wouldn't have filled at least a volume out of what I've told you in the last few hours."

Chapter XCVII: Grandfather and Granddaughter

"Plus, you'll be missing out, master," went on the Devil, "because I had a good scene to narrate for you: the conference between Juliette, Count Cerny, and Gustave de Bridely. You'd have seen the great lord's furious frustration at being brought down to the level of a streetwalker and a confidence man; you'd have seen vice, wickedness, and greed for money moving forward step by step, feeling each other out, then recognizing each other as kindred souls, boldly pulling off their disguises, and shaking each other by the hand. So, Juliette sold Count Cerny the secret of your flight with Léonie, in exchange for his help in finally getting Monsieur de Paradèze, Count Cerny's uncle by marriage, first, to acknowledge Juliette as his granddaughter, and second, to do everything in his power to keep Madame de Cauny—now Madame de Paradèze—from acknowledging Eugénie Peyrol as the daughter who was stolen from her."

"And with what money did the Marquis de Bridely pay for that favor?" interrupted Luizzi.

"He paid using the name and the fortune he'd stolen. At this moment, as I speak to you, a promise of marriage exists between the Marquis Gustave de Bridely and your sister Juliette."

"But I thought she loved Henri Donezau!"

"That just means it was better to be the mistress of Henri Donezau, to whom a fool had given an income of twenty-five thousand livres, than to be a streetwalker or a nun; but it was better to be the Marquis de Bridely's legal wife than to be Henri Donezau's mistress. Your sister didn't hesitate for a second."

"So I assume she's pulled off every scheme she was planning; and, because I didn't figure out what kind of woman she was till too late, I wasn't able to stop her."

"That's right! My word, it wouldn't have taken much for everything that's happened not to have happened."

"How so?"

"Let's imagine that my story about the banker Matthieu Durand hadn't produced the effect I expected; Fernand wouldn't have gone off and left us alone together."

"Sure, sure," said Luizzi bitterly. "I realize you tricked me by telling me that story was irrelevant to me. Never mind, let's get back to Juliette."

"All right. And in coming back to her, I have to say that if Fernand hadn't left us, he'd have told you Juliette's story, and once you knew she was your sister you'd have found a way to prevent the harm she did."

"So she succeeded?"

"You decide…"

A while ago I told you about Bricoin; you don't know Bricoin, master, and therefore you don't know he's a wicked creature come to extreme old age. The man who got Madame de Cauny's husband killed so he could marry her and get her fortune, the man who stole her child so he could marry her off and get her fortune, must carry within him an extraordinary passion for money.[111]

It could be you've never seen that passion when it reaches its final stage of madness; when—old age having relieved the victim of all self-constraint toward the world and all power to fight it within himself—he surrenders to it completely. It's no longer the madness of the miser who accumulates his wealth and squirrels it away, proud of the power it gives him and telling himself and others he'll be able to spend it someday when he feels like it: a sad comfort, a feeble pride, with which avarice tries to gild the hardships it imposes!

No, it's the decrepitude of that same vice: it's the old man, surrounded by riches, his money chests full, his granaries full, his wine cellars full, who's afraid of dying of hunger and thirst. It's that vice in senility, the old man dragging himself around the courtyards of his chateau, through the kitchens and the pantries, fighting with the chickens in the poultry yard for possession of a single grain of wheat, picking up a piece of bread crust to hide it somewhere secret in his bedroom, stealing a liard coin forgotten by a servant and adding it to the sack of écus a tenant farmer brought him the day before. It's something contemptible, idiotic, cruel, and weak, all at the same time; a passion that can't inspire hatred because it seems so much like a disability; something that can't inspire pity because there's so much slyness and meanness in the methods it thinks up to satisfy its needs. That was Bricoin, now become Monsieur de Paradèze.

Now, for many long years a woman of noble character and gentle, superior feelings, being powerless to escape it, had submitted to the life imposed on her by such a master. And she was weak too, for everything within her was broken: beautiful young Valentine d'Assimbret had become a trembling old woman, exhausted by hardship, hiding herself away to hide her rags, sunk to the point where she too stole a log from the fire to warm herself, stole bread to eat and wine to get drunk and to forget for a moment that she was cold and hungry.

That's the woman from whom Countess Cerny was going to ask for protection, that's the woman from whom Madame Peyrol was going to demand acknowledgment that she was Eugénie's mother. But as I've told you, Juliette got there first. The day she arrived, Madame de Paradèze was ill, stretched out on a pallet, with an old woman as her only sick-nurse, a woman no more impoverished than she was. Juliette rang at the gate of that chateau, which had once been so splendid—for back when she'd been thrown out of there as a child, the master's miserliness was still rational enough to understand that by spending only a tiny fraction of his wife's immense income he'd still keep enough to be rich.

---

[111] See Chapters LXVIII and LXIX.

And also, at that time, Madame de Cauny was in her prime, and her willpower, weak as it was, fought back against her husband's shameful parsimony.

For his part, he wasn't free of the fear of seeing his first marriage exposed; and since he knew Viscount d'Assimbret would welcome any excuse to punish him for having married his sister, he didn't dare hand his wife any reason for complaint that might've reached the viscount's ears. But once he was sure his first wife was dead, once Jeannette had been driven out of the chateau, he felt safe from any criticism and imposed his will as master. Still, it had taken at least twenty years to reduce Monsieur and Madame de Paradèze, and the chateau they lived in, to the state of degradation that greeted Juliette.

As I said, she rang at the gate of the chateau, and for a great while there was no answer. Finally, after a long wait, the one and only old servant, the one I mentioned, came to open the door and asked her what she wanted. She said she wanted to see Monsieur de Paradèze on urgent business concerning his fortune. The old woman let her in and, leading her to one small wing facing the grand courtyard of that immense chateau, she pointed to a long line of rooms and said, "You'll find Monsieur de Paradèze in his room, all the way at the end."

Juliette passed through several abandoned parlors; the wallpaper was coming off in sheets, and the paneling was rotting from the damp that came in through the broken windows. Going through room after room, she finally reached a closed door, which she opened without knocking. Inside a cramped room she found an old man sitting on a wretched stool whose legs had been sawed short, holding on his lap a portable stove on which a pot with a few sparse vegetables floating in water was warming without boiling. An old horse blanket covered his shoulders, and his feet and legs were wrapped in straw to keep them a little warm.

When he heard the door open he turned around and stood up. His hair hung down to his cheeks, his eyebrows hung down over his eyes, his cheeks hung down to his neck, his lip hung down over his chin: he embodied decrepitude in its filthiest, ugliest form. Seeing Juliette, he grabbed hold of the wretched stool he'd been sitting on and cried. "What do you want from me? I've got nothing, I'm a poor ruined man."

Juliette had been old enough when she left to know of her grandfather's vice, though she'd never been back to the chateau since she'd been thrown out. So she wasn't surprised by her welcome, and she replied boldly, "I don't want anything from you, and it's to keep you from being ruined that I came here."

The old man set down his stool and sat between Juliette and his stove, as if he were afraid she'd try to steal some morsel of his heat. "Well! Who are you? And what do you want?"

"I already told you, I've come to keep you from being ruined."

"Who could possibly want to rob me of the pitiful piece of bread I've got? Everybody knows I don't have a sou, and if I don't go out begging it's only out of respect for the name I bear."

"In that case," said Juliette, pretending to get up and leave, "I have nothing to tell you."

"Stay!" cried the old man, hurrying toward her to hold her back. "Stay. I recognize you now. You're Mariette's daughter, you're Jeanette, the inn servant girl."

"I'm you're granddaughter, and that's why I've come to save you."

"I have no granddaughter. I have no child."

"You have a granddaughter, me, and a daughter, Mariette. And if, in payment for what I've come here to tell you, you don't make me your heiress, there's someone who's going to take away everything you own, someone who can send you off to die in prison."

That threat horrified Bricoin. Hiding his head in his lap, he complained like a whiny child, "My wife is dead, there's no evidence against me, I'm innocent."

"No doubt the evidence would be hard to gather, but Madame de Cauny's daughter is still alive, and I know where she is."

"My wife's daughter!" cried the old man, standing up and racked by a terrible trembling. "She's coming to steal everything I own, isn't she? She wants everything that belonged to her mother! She wants to strip me naked, she wants to drive me to my death of hunger!"

"She's certainly capable of that," said the excellent granddaughter of that honorable old man.

"Oh, I'll stop her!" said Bricoin furiously.

"It won't be easy. She's a great lady, very powerful, very well connected in the world. I might be the only person who can stop her from doing you wrong."

"How can you do that?" asked the old man, drawing closer to her.

"And how can you reward me for that service if I do it?"

The old man lowered his head and said in a hurried, mysterious manner, "Well, over there in the corner I've got a fine piece of jewelry my wife wore when she was young. I'll give it to you."

Juliette wanted to test the limits of Bricoin's cunning and avarice, and she asked to see the jewel. The old man went to a corner of the room, lifted aside a shred of carpet, and pulled out a necklace, which he handed to Juliette.

She could easily tell it was gilt copper. She tossed it far away from her and turned to the door, saying, "I'm off to tell Madame de Paradèze her daughter's still alive."

The old man summoned enough strength to get between Juliette and the door, saying, "I won't let you leave, I won't let you leave!"

But she pushed him aside roughly, and he went on in a low, pleading tone, with a forced smile, "I was mistaken, Jeannette; you see, I put that necklace there to fool thieves if any happened to come. But I have some jewelry of real gold, and some diamonds too! Well! I'll... I'll... I'll let you see them!"

"Oh, hell! You don't understand. Listen to me: if your wife's daughter gets herself acknowledged, not only will she inherit all of your wife's property, but she'll leave you destitute."

The old man broke in dejectedly, "And that'll be my reward for the thirty years of happiness I gave my wife!"

Without responding to his exclamation, Juliette went on, "Not only will that woman leave you destitute if you outlive your wife, but she'll have the law on you for making her disappear years ago. The least bad thing that'll happen to you is, you'll be placed under interdiction and have control of your wife's property taken away from you while she's still alive."

"That's not possible, that's not possible!" repeated the old man, furious once again at the thought of being stripped bare.

Paying no attention to his interruption, and wanting to get straight to the point, Juliette said, "But there's still a way to prevent all that. It's to persuade your wife she saw her child dead, and therefore anyone claiming to be her lost daughter is a scheming con artist capable of the most despicable imposture."

"That's an idea. But how can we manage that?"

"That's your problem. I did my part by warning you."

"But wait," said Luizzi, interrupting the awful tale for the first time. "What motive that was so important did Juliette have to make Eugénie Peyrol fail?"

"My God, master," said the Devil, "you've got a poor memory and a feeble understanding of the laws that govern us. As you could see from the family tree I showed you,[112] Gustave de Bridely has already inherited a fortune that should've gone to Madame de Cauny, and therefore to Eugénie Peyrol."

"I can understand Gustave's interest in not bringing that whole business back to life."

"But can't you also see—since, by her marriage contract, Madame de Cauny willed all of her property, if she had no child, to her husband if he survived her—it would make Bricoin immensely rich? Mariette would inherit that fortune, and Juliette would inherit it from Mariette. She was marrying Gustave de Bridely. So a rascal worthy of penal servitude on the galleys and a whore who ought to have been branded on the shoulder[113] would turn out to be the sole heirs of one of France's richest and most eminent families."

"True enough, but for that plan to succeed, Madame de Paradèze would have to die before her husband."

"Yes, that was the hurdle, and they didn't talk about that hurdle, each of them feeling sure it was perfectly understood between them. The most urgent

---

[112] That family tree appears in Chapter LXXII.

[113] Till 1832 various crimes carried the added punishment of branding with a fleur de lis (the symbol of the French monarchy), usually on the shoulder.

thing was to prevent the acknowledgment of Eugénie Peyrol, then or in the future."

"And, based on what you've told me, I assume those two rascals have succeeded?"

"And it didn't even cost them much: a little bit of bread, a little meat, a little wine, that's all!"

"What do you mean?"

"Oh, master, what a dreadful scene it was!—the old man and the girl sitting by the old woman's sickbed, and she dying, almost an imbecile, and they telling her some con artist was brazen enough to try to pass herself off as her daughter. And when a few sparks of maternal love escaped from those ashes that were already almost cold, they fanned the ashes with wine and made them into mud. And with every glass of wine they handed the poor woman, they made her add another phrase of explanation to the statement they demanded from her. And that was how she wrote, as dictated by them, that having learned of a woman named Eugénie Turniquel, married name Peyrol, who claimed to be her daughter, she felt it necessary to state on her deathbed, being of sound mind and unconstrained in body, that the child she'd given birth to had died; and that it was with the intention of adopting her husband's daughter that she'd pretended to look for her, but that the difference in age between the two children would fortunately not have allowed her to carry out that illegal action."

"And they got a statement like that out of her?" cried the baron.

"Yes, master. And since the old woman could've rescinded that statement if she came to her senses, they did their best to keep her out of her senses. After being deprived of everything, she was given a surfeit of everything; and death, which neither hunger nor misery had achieved, came quickly through excess and overindulgence."

"Madame de Cauny's dead?" cried Luizzi.

"Dead, a few days before Juliette left to come give her deposition against you—for surely you realize her testimony contributed significantly to convict you, by showing that a deposition you counted on so much could only be false witness."

"But how did Eugénie reach Madame de Cauny too late to prevent that calamity?"

"Because, thanks to your kind forethought, she was attended by the Marquis Gustave de Bridely, who, while he waited for Juliette's scheme to succeed, took great care to make Eugénie travel from one province to another and another, so she'd never be reunited with her mother, Madame de Paradèze."

It was only when—worn out by all that pointless travel and having used up all the money she had left—she went back to her uncle Rigot's that she found the letter you wrote her when you got here, and which inspired her to make one last effort. She too set out on foot, like your sister Caroline; for she'd been harshly informed, more than once, that she could expect no help from her daughter, Countess Lémée; and she didn't want to tell her she was trying to secure her another fortune, for fear of having to endure sufferings even viler than those her daughter's ingratitude had already made her bear.

She left, she made her way courageously along her route, and she reached the door of that chateau only to learn her mother was dead, and to find herself threatened with arrest when she went before a justice of the peace and announced in what capacity she was there. For of course the others had taken care to put Madame de Paradèze's deathbed statement into the magistrate's hands, and he challenged Madame Peyrol with it at the first words she spoke to justify her claim. At that point, overwhelmed by fatigue and misery, she went to the inn at Boismandé, where she found Countess Cerny bedridden.

As Satan spoke those words the clock rang eight. Luizzi, aware that the time remaining to him was passing quickly, was about to put a stop to his conversation with the Devil. But then he calculated that he still had sixteen hours left, and he said, "Come on, hurry up. Tell me how I ruined the countess too, how I drove her—that happy, beautiful, noble creature—to suffer on a cot in a wretched inn. Show me I've got only one hope left in this world. Confirm the choice I've already made. I'm listening, Satan."

And Satan went on:

409

Chapter XCVIII: A Murderer

I'll pick up where Countess Cerny's letter left off.[114] Henriette, whose sanity had held up against misfortune, went mad in her joy. Madame de Carin, who'd been protected from madness—a sickness as contagious as the plague—by Henriette's friendship, lost her mind at the sight of her friend losing hers. Countess Cerny was left all alone, waiting for her lawyer's advice. A few days after she'd written to you she had a visit from a judge who was part of an investigative commission appointed to question her about what part she herself might've played in Count Cerny's death, through hints or suggestions you might've followed up on. You can't prove hints or suggestions; but proper justice requires keeping the accused from colluding in their line of defense; and Countess Cerny was temporarily placed in the strictest solitary confinement. Here I'd have a long story to tell you, master—not about what happened to Léonie but about her thoughts, her conflicting reflections, her inner struggle, in which you finally emerged victorious. Yes, master, she refused to believe in your guilt.

"Oh, thank you, Léonie! Thank you!" cried Luizzi.

"She refused to believe in the clear evidence against you; she refused to listen to her reason, which couldn't help but acknowledge the strength of that evidence; she refused to believe what her father told her, and she defied his authority. And when on the one hand the charge of adultery brought by Count Cerny was dropped thanks to his death, and on the other hand—the investigation into your case being now complete—Léonie was cleared of any charge related to it, she left Orléans to come to you in Toulouse."

"Oh, thank you, thank you, Léonie!" cried the baron once more. "Noble, generous heart, that should've been the sanctuary for my own heart!"

"A noble heart, indeed, for in her resolve she forgot no one; and as she passed through Boismandé she stopped to see Madame de Paradèze, her aunt, to find out what she'd learned about her daughter being alive. She arrived the very day Madame de Paradèze had just died. As she knocked at the gates of the chateau, her aunt's body was being carried out. And at the same moment Countess Cerny was being denied entry, Juliette was brazenly throwing her ex-lover, your brother-in-law Henri Donezau, out of the chateau."

"Him!" cried Luizzi. "It's true, I'd forgotten all about him. What had he been up to all that time?"

---

[114] See Chapter XCII for the countess's letter to Luizzi from the madhouse.

"That's another long story, which I'll summarize in a word or two: he'd gone after Juliette, thinking she'd run off with Count Cerny. You want to hear about it?"

"Skip it, skip it."

"Fine. Anyway, time's flying, and, though I don't have much more to tell you, I don't want to rob you of the little time you have."

"Listen, I've decided to give you twelve hours of my last day. Work it out so that, at the moment those twelve hours are gone, I know what kept Countess Cerny bedridden at that inn and prevented her from coming to me. Then you can take the thirty days of my life that belong to you; then you can set me free, as you promised."

"It's a deal." And Satan continued:

So Henri Donezau and Countess Cerny found themselves face to face at the gates of the chateau: one who'd just been thrown out, the other who'd just been denied entry. They didn't know each other, but they were both angry enough at the impudence of the new mistress of the house for Donezau to be emboldened to address Countess Cerny and share his complaints, and for the countess to ask him who the woman was who'd sent such a coarse, insulting refusal out to her.

"She's the lowest of tramps!" he cried. "She ran off from Paris with a certain Count Cerny, who in any case has been paid back in full for stealing that whore away from me!"

As you know, master, Countess Cerny wasn't the kind of woman to continue a conversation begun on that tone and in such terms; but the chance to find out who the woman was who'd been traveling with her husband made her willing to endure that man's company. She'd come from Boismandé to the chateau by carriage, and she offered to take him back with her. He accepted, and here was what they said to each other on the way:

"Well, sir, so you know the person who's living at Monsieur de Paradèze's chateau? And I assume you also know Count Cerny, who was traveling with her?"

"That's to say, I know him from having seen him a couple of times in Paris, because he had some run-ins with my brother-in-law."

"Ah! So your brother-in-law knew Count Cerny?"

"I believe it was especially Countess Cerny he knew."

"I doubt it," said the countess, who couldn't imagine any man of her acquaintance having a brother-in-law of her fellow traveler's type.

"I can assure you it was so: she knew him so well she ran off with him."

Countess Cerny managed to hide her surprise, thanks to her plan to let that man see nothing of her reasons for questioning him. "Oh, so this Countess Cerny ran off with your brother-in-law?"

"Yup, with Baron de Luizzi, as all France knows by now."

411

"Yes, yes, that's right, he's the one who murdered Count Cerny."

At that word Henri turned pale, and he stammered, "Whether he killed him or not isn't the issue; that's for the jury to decide."

Your brother-in-law's distress struck Léonie, and she looked straight at him as she said, "Surely only the lover who ran away with the wife could've murdered the husband."

"Possibly so, though I don't really understand killing your wife's lover. Now, killing your mistress's lover, that's another matter!" he added angrily.

The way Henri had spoken those last words made Countess Cerny in turn go pale. But she was afraid to betray the suspicion that had just occurred to her, and she replied calmly, "So I assume it's to go see your brother-in-law in Toulouse that you've come to these parts?"

"Me? That's none of my business, that's his lookout. Let him get out of it any way he can! I came about something else."

"And I assume your journey's been a success?"

"Halfway. You see, I know how to get revenge when someone insults me. I already taught one of them a lesson, and I'll soon teach the other one—that tramp who just threw me out of her grandfather's chateau!..."

"What!" cried Luizzi. "He told Léonie that? And Léonie didn't come here and reveal the name of the real murderer? Because it was him, wasn't it?"

"Time's flying, master, and if you interrupt we won't get to the end of the story." And Satan continued:

Yes, Henri said that; Henri gave himself away. What can you do, my friend? Crime would have it all too easy if it didn't have its indiscretions; God designed it that way. The corpse buried a couple of feet underground releases gases that give away its presence, the same water into which the drowned have been consigned makes the victims float back to the surface, fire consumes bodies without erasing the holes from their wounds, the intestines retain the traces of poison. The soul of man is no stronger: remorse sweats out at every pore, and the crime rises and trembles at the edge of the lips.

Yes, Henri Donezau said that. And because this time Countess Cerny couldn't suppress the horror that overcame her, Henri realized the mistake he'd just made. He probably would've snuffed out the suspicion he'd just sparked, by killing Léonie on the spot; but it was broad daylight, there was a postilion on the horse ahead, and he reasoned that this woman was a stranger with no motive for either dooming him or saving Baron de Luizzi. Still, he wanted to make sure of her; so, pretending he'd noticed neither her distress nor his own indiscretion, he said politely, "All that aside, ma'am, may I be permitted to know whom I should thank for the favor you've just done me?"

"My God, sir, my name will no doubt mean nothing to you. I'm Madame d'Assimbret."[115]

That didn't give Henri much; but her hesitation in saying it convinced him she wanted to hide her real name. At that point they reached Boismandé. Henri's first move was to ask the postilion the name of the person with whom he'd caught a ride back from Monsieur de Paradèze's place. You can imagine his horror when he heard the man say, "Countess Cerny"! And you should also understand why his horror increased when he saw Countess Cerny giving orders for her immediate departure for Toulouse, and when he heard she'd just sent word to the mayor of Boismandé to come meet with her.

It was nothing but a crime to Henri Donezau. And if you remember what he'd once said to Juliette, you know—assuming it was he who killed Count Cerny, thinking the count was his mistress's lover—he was no beginner. He even blamed Juliette for it: she'd pushed him from debauchery to cheating, from cheating to forgery, from forgery to murder. He didn't hold back from the career she'd laid out for him. So he didn't take long to decide to get rid of the countess. But the means were difficult, and the danger was urgent. One denunciation could get him arrested; and once he was arrested he was doomed, for there was no shortage of witnesses to Count Cerny's murder.

"I don't remember you telling me that!" cried Luizzi.

"That's because you never asked, master," replied Satan.

"Fine! So what did he do?" asked the baron, in a hurry to reach the end of the story.

"He counted on the special good luck reserved for criminals, and he counted on the brazen effrontery with which he would commit the crime to keep anyone from suspecting him. He went straight into Countess Cerny's room at the inn—but he was too late: he'd only had time to stab her once, not enough to kill her, when the mayor she'd asked to come see her entered her room."

"And the villain was arrested, wasn't he?"

"He's in prison, but not for trying to murder Countess Cerny, because he wasn't arrested then. He wasn't seen, and he was able to follow Juliette to Toulouse. But now he's in prison for murdering the count; and it's in Toulouse, to which he'd pursued Juliette, that he was arrested."

"So Léonie reported him?"

Without answering that question the Devil went on, "When Eugénie Peyrol reached Boismandé, she found Countess Cerny lying in bed, dying, unable to speak a word. Eugénie had been there with her for two days when Caroline got to Boismandé and found them both ill."

"But once all three of them were together, what happened to them?"

---

[115] Léonie d'Assimbret was Countess Cerny's maiden name.

At that moment midnight chimed. The Devil placed his finger on Luizzi's forehead and said, "And now I'm taking the thirty days you gave me."

A veil dropped over Luizzi's eyes, but slowly enough that he thought he saw the door of his prison cell opening, and Caroline coming in hand in hand with Léonie and Eugénie.

Chapter XCIX: Ronquerolles Castle

When the baron came to, he found himself back at Ronquerolles Castle, in the same room in which he'd signed his contract with the Devil ten years earlier. He was alone. This time he didn't have to rack his brains to remember the past; it came back to mind vividly, intensely, as if the thirty days just elapsed hadn't lasted a minute. Though he had twelve hours ahead of him, he quickly summoned Satan, and said, "It's you against me now! My choice is made."

"I'm waiting to hear it. And the moment you tell me what you want, you'll have it. Then it'll be up to you to be happy, if you can."

"I'll tell you. But first, you have to tell me how I was found innocent, so I don't go through life with the kind of ignorance that's nearly been fatal to me before."

"You spent ten of the thirty days in prison; you were brought here twenty days ago. That whole time you were in a state of imbecility, such that no one'll be surprised if you can't recall everything that happened during those days— because you can't remember if you can't think."

"But why was I released from prison?"

"Because Henri Donezau was fingered for Count Cerny's murder. He was held on the evidence of Jacques Bruno, who, though he was wanted for the murder of Petithomme, had escaped punishment for it up to that point. He'd been arrested for a robbery he'd committed on the high road, and he'd concealed his name so no one would connect him with the killing of the Chouan Petithomme. Donezau made the mistake of recognizing him as Jacques Bruno, and the latter got his revenge by identifying him as Count Cerny's murderer, whom he'd spotted shooting at the count from the thicket he was hiding in."

"So—finally!" cried Luizzi. "Crime has met its just punishment, and vice has found its just reward!"

"You think?" said the Devil with an inscrutable expression. "If that belief has determined your choice, look!"

Chapter C: The Devil's Magic Lantern

Immediately, one wall of the room seemed to change into a vast theater, on the stage of which a play was being performed, with Luizzi as its audience. At first he saw a large group of men: some were seated at a table, while others tossed small pieces of paper with writing on them into an urn. It was an election for the Chamber of Deputies. An eager crowd had gathered outside the door to that room, and they were talking, gesticulating, calling out. The outcome of the election appeared to be of great interest to the whole town: it was nothing less than a choice between the region's two most eminent men. Finally the voting was closed, and no one left while the votes were being tallied, so curious were they all to know who the winner would be. After a few hours it was announced that the new Deputy for that arrondissement was Baron Guillaume de Carin,[116] who'd come out a few votes ahead of his honorable opponent, Monsieur Félix Ridaire.

"Outrageous!" murmured Luizzi.

As if that word were the signal given by the stage manager at the Opéra, the scene changed. Now Luizzi saw a prison cell, in which a woman squatting on the floor held in her arms a child near death, and he recognized Henriette Buré; meanwhile another woman, clinging to the bars of that vile room, hurled insults at poor Henriette—and he recognized Madame de Carin.

"Horrors!" he cried.

Just as before, the scene changed again, and now it represented a magnificently ornamented church. Two chapels were draped in white; one of them shone with candles, wall tapestries, and splendid decorations, while the other was emblazoned with the coat of arms of a marquis. Two processions entered the church at almost the same time. The one moving toward the richly decorated chapel was that of Fernand and Mademoiselle Delphine Durand, Matthieu Durand's daughter. The one moving toward the chapel with the coat of arms was that of the Marquis de Bridely and Mademoiselle Juliette Bricoin, who wore mourning in honor of her grandfather over her wedding dress, and whose mother Mariette had just come into an enormous inheritance. Delphine Durand's witness was Count de Lozeraie, and Juliette was being given away by Edgar du Bergh.

"Enough! Enough!" cried Luizzi, and, just as before, his words caused the scene to change, and now:

---

[116] See Chapters XLIV and XLV, in which Monsieur de Carin may or may not have been trying to hasten the death of his father-in-law, the Marquis de Vaucloix.

In a room in a middle-class home, a small gourmet supper had been served. Around the table sat Ganguernet, old Rigot, and Barnet, and they were being waited on by Lili, who'd returned to the lawyer.

"Shameful! Disgraceful!" cried Luizzi.

The scene immediately changed again, to represent a vast gallery, through which a crowd of people were running:

First Monsieur Furnichon, now become a stockbroker on the exchange;

Monsieur Marcoine, now become a lawyer;

Monsieur Bador, now mayor of the city of Caen;

Count Lémée, a peer of France, now named budget rapporteur;

the Marquis du Val, in the room of some dancing girl from the Opéra, trying on a suit tailored by Humann;

Little Pierre, now promoted to stagecoach driver;

Madame du Bergh, offering herbal tea to her father confessor;

Madame de Marignon, heading a charitable committee for the education of girls;

Madame de Crancé,[117] whose daughter had recently given birth, sitting at the foot of her daughter's bed and instructing her on the duty of mothers toward their children;

Doctor Crostencoupe, elevated by acclamation to be a member of the Academy of Sciences;

Pierre, once the baron's valet, now married to Madame Humbert, the sick-nurse, and running a splendid furnished hotel—in which Luizzi recognized his own furniture;

Louis, now personal coachman to the Tsar of Russia;

Akabila, who'd returned to his own country and resumed his father's throne;

and Hortense Buré,[118] dismissing a maidservant who'd gotten pregnant.

All those people passed by, and passed again, smiles on their lips, joy in their eyes, their faces serene. Then it suddenly seemed to Luizzi that music— music so extraordinary he couldn't have conceived of it even at the bacchanals of the Bal Musard—had started up, and it was some kind of round dance, an incredible galop. All of the figures began to dance, to run, to fly; they came and went. Pleasure shone in their eyes, their voices rang with happiness; it was a delight to see them all so carefree, so giddy, so nonchalant. They came and went before Luizzi, smiling at him, calling to him. Then, mixing with the sound of the music and the heat of the dance, there arose intoxicating fragrances, creating a delightful delirium in which they all swam in ecstasy.

---

[117] Mother (out of wedlock) to both Caroline Dilois and the late Lucy du Val.

[118] See Chapters V and VI for the story of Madame Buré, Henriette's aunt, and herself a hypocrite and a murderer.

Now Luizzi felt all that frenzied movement jostling his body, and all of the feverish accents of the music agitating his heart, and the intoxication of the perfumes flooding over him and penetrating him; and just as he was about to call out to Satan to make the hellish scene vanish, suddenly he noticed Juliette: Juliette dancing, Juliette in the arms of a man whose face Luizzi could never quite see... Oh, how right Caroline had been when she'd said nothing could quite capture the gracefulness of that lithe figure, the wild abandon of that slender body! She spun, she spun, and her dress, tossed around by the breeze, revealed the supple, fluid shape of her body; her hair floated about her head; her half-closed eyes almost seemed to vibrate and pant, as it were, as they threw out all around her a glance drenched in voluptuousness; her trembling, parted lips revealed the white of her teeth; her whole body seemed to be tensed in a frenetic paroxysm of love; and Luizzi felt stirring within him all the burning desire that girl had never ceased to inspire in him; when suddenly she slumped and swooned in her partner's arms; she broke away from his grasp, and just as she fell she reached out to Luizzi, who, carried away by mad desire, flung himself toward her...

But just as his hand was about to touch Juliette's, another hand stopped his. Everything vanished, and he found Caroline kneeling before him, pale, exhausted, dying. "Armand!" she said. "You're saved!"

The baron lifted his sister to her feet; and after considering her for a long time, then pressing her to his heart, he said, "Oh, it was you, wasn't it, Caroline, it was you... It was you who saved me?"

"Yes, it was she," said another familiar voice, and when Luizzi turned he saw Léonie.

"Yes," added another voice, "it was she who saved you." And now Luizzi saw Eugénie.

At the sight of those three women, all the vivid terror he'd felt, all the awful heartbreak he'd endured, all the frantic desire consuming him only a moment before, was wiped clean from his soul. A gentle, serene, benevolent tranquility took its place; he felt only a vague sadness, a melancholy that seemed no more than the bitter aftertaste of a vanishing sorrow; and he said, "Oh, come, my angels! Come, you who ran to me and didn't abandon me!"

"No, Armand," said Léonie, "don't call us that. There's only one angel before you, and that angel is Caroline. It was she who, finding us ill at that wretched inn in Boismandé, restored our courage. It was she who healed us and saved us both. It was she who, when that difficult task was done—knowing the danger that threatened you and having learned how you could be saved—didn't hesitate between justice and the world's contempt. For I myself, Armand, worn down by misfortune, had come to doubt whether I should defy public opinion to the point of accusing my attacker of the murder of my husband, to save my lover. But Caroline didn't hesitate to accuse the guilty to save the innocent, and she did it with virtuous courage; for she had to endure the sarcasm of the judges themselves, who said it was to get revenge for his having left her that she was accusing her husband; and the world repeated that slander, and mocked her. She had to get Jacques Bruno to testify to the truth. She had to have the courage to save a man who seemed like he might never be able to thank her, because you'd lost your mind, Armand. But she wanted justice, even for a madman. And having saved you from dishonor, it was she who saved you from death. It was she who spent all those nights by you, and all those days, watching over your gestures, your words, your breathing."

"And you were both by my side," said Caroline, "and you sustained me through that hard task, and God put out his hand to guide me to the end and save you."

"Me!" cried Luizzi, remembering the choice he still had to make. "Me? It's too late—I'm doomed!"

"No, brother," replied Caroline. "And if it's true, as I've sometimes been told, that our family is sworn to evil and crime; if it's true, as Léonie says, that a terrible fate pursues you…"

"Yes!" cried Luizzi. "It's true! And it has hounded me everywhere. I wanted to put my trust in the things of this world, and they've all broken in my hands, so rotten and corrupted by vice they were. I wanted to learn the truth, and for me the truth has been nothing but a hideous, repellent tableau. I held out my hand to all those I met, and the hands of the lucky ones tore the hand I held out, and the hand I held out crushed all the unlucky ones I tried to help. Sister, sister—I'm cursed!"

"Armand," said Caroline, "have you never lifted your hands toward God?"

"Toward God?" asked Luizzi.

And just as his knees were bending, just as his hands were joining in prayer, a clock chimed, and a resounding voice cried, "The hour of your choice has passed, baron! Follow me!"

Instantly, as if the fires of a volcano had consumed it in less than a second, Ronquerolles Castle vanished, and nothing was left in its place but a deep chasm the local peasants call the Pit of Hell. They also say at that moment you could see three white figures rising from the rim of that abyss, rising toward heaven; and one of them, taking the lead and going to the foot of the throne of God, prayed for the two who'd hung back; and when the Lord had shown them they could enter, the pure virgin, the sinning girl, and the adulterous woman all fell to their knees and prayed for the soul of BARON FRANÇOIS ARMAND DE LUIZZI.

Appendix
Luizzi and his "Sisters" Family Tree

- Only one union, that of Armand de Luizzi's parents, is within wedlock; it is marked with a solid line. The unions out of wedlock are shown with dashed lines.

- Armand is related by blood only to Jeannette/Juliette and Caroline and Charles, who are his half siblings through their common father, Hughes de Luizzi. Lucy du Val and Sophie Dilois are Caroline's half-sisters through their common mother, Madame de Crancé. Armand is therefore related to Lucy and Sophie only nominally, through their mutual half-sister Caroline, and not at all by blood.

Stuart Gelzer

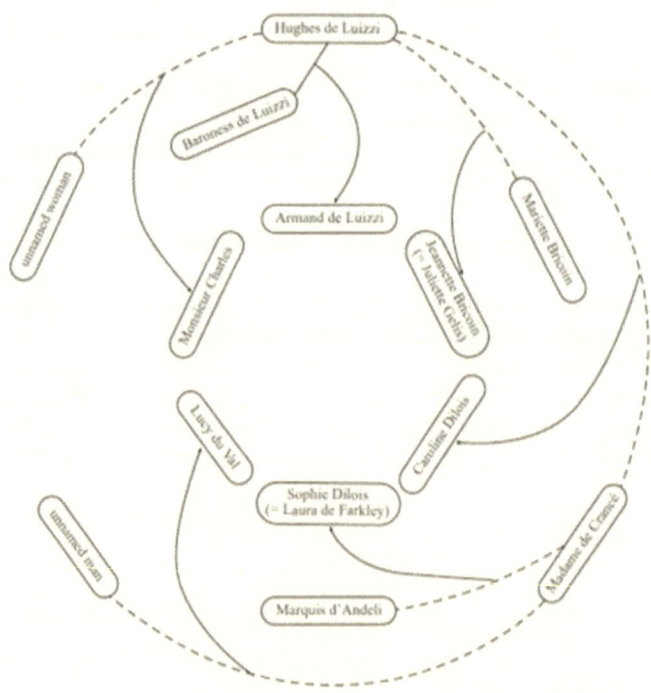

www.ingramcontent.com/pod-product-compliance
Lightning Source LLC
Chambersburg PA
CBHW020251030726
47499CB00001B/157